# ALSO AVAILABLE
# FROM ELLE KENNEDY

## Briar U Series:

The Chase

The Risk

The Play

The Dare

## Off-Campus Series:

The Deal

The Mistake

The Score

The Goal

The Legacy

A full list of Elle's contemporary and suspense print
titles is available on her website, ellekennedy.com

# THE PLAY

## BRIAR U

# ELLE KENNEDY

Bloom books

Sourcebooks and the colophon are registered trademarks of
Sourcebooks. Bloom Books is a trademark of Sourcebooks.

Published by Bloom Books, an imprint of Sourcebooks
P.O. Box 4410, Naperville, Illinois 60567-4410
(630) 961-3900
sourcebooks.com

Originally published in 2019 by Elle Kennedy Inc.

Cataloging-in-Publication Data is on file with the Library of Congress.

Printed and bound in Canada.
MBP 10 9 8 7 6

*To Sarah J. Maas, for your support and enthusiasm.*
*And for reminding me why I write.*

# 1
# HUNTER

THIS PARTY BLOWS.

I probably should have stayed at home, but these days "home" is like living on the set of a Kardashian reality show. Thanks to my three female roommates, it's estrogen overload over there.

Granted, there's a helluva lot of estrogen here at the Theta Beta Nu house, but it's the kind I'm allowed to be attracted to. My roommates are all in relationships, so I'm not allowed to touch them.

*You're not allowed to touch any of these women either...*

True. Because of my self-imposed abstinence, I'm not allowed to touch anyone, period.

Which raises the question—if a tree falls in the forest and you can't fuck anyone at the sorority-house party, is it still considered a party?

I curl my fingers around the red Solo cup that my friend and teammate Matt Anderson just planted in my hand. "Thanks," I mutter.

I take a sip and make a face. The beer tastes like water, although maybe that's a good thing. A nice incentive to not consume more than one. Morning skate isn't until ten a.m. tomorrow, but I was planning on showing up at the arena a couple hours early to work on my slapshot.

After last season's disastrous end, I vowed to make hockey my top priority. The new semester starts Monday, our first game is next week, and I'm feeling motivated. Briar didn't make it to the national championship last year and that's on me. This season will be different.

"What do you think about her?" Matt discreetly nods toward a cute girl in tiny boxer shorts and a pale pink camisole. She's not wearing a bra, and the outlines of her beaded nipples are visible beneath the silky material.

My mouth actually waters.

Did I mention this is a PJ party? Yup yup, I haven't had sex in nearly five months and I'm kicking off junior year at a party where every single woman in attendance is wearing next to nothing. I never claimed to be smart.

"She's smokin'," I tell Matt. "Go make a move."

"I would, but…" He lets out a grumbling sound. "She's checking *you* out."

"Well, I'm closed for business," I answer with a shrug. "Feel free to go over there and tell her that." I poke him good-naturedly on the arm. "I'm sure she'll view you as an adequate consolation prize."

"Ha! Fuck off. I'm nobody's second choice. If she's not dying to hook up with me, I'd way rather find someone who is. I don't need to compete for a woman's attention."

This is why I like Matt—he's competitive on the ice, but off of it he's really decent. I've been playing hockey my entire life, and I've had teammates who wouldn't even blink at stealing another guy's girl, or even worse, hooking up with her behind his back. I've played with guys who treat our hockey groupies as disposable, who've shared girls like Tic Tacs. Guys with zero respect and terrible judgment.

But at Briar, I'm fortunate to play with some stand-up dudes. Sure, no roster is without a douchebag or two, but for the most part my teammates are good guys.

"Yeah, I don't think it'll be too hard," I agree. "The brunette at two o'clock is already boning down with you in her head."

His brown eyes widen in appreciation as they land on the curvy girl in the short white nightie. Her cheeks flush when their gazes meet and then she smiles shyly and raises her cup in a silent toast.

Matt abandons me without a backward glance. I don't blame him.

The living room is packed with girls in lingerie and guys in Hugh Hefner pajamas. I hadn't known this was a theme event, so I'm in cargo shorts and a white wife-beater, and I'm good with that. Most of the dudes around me look ridiculous in their get-ups.

"Having a good time?" The music is blaring, but it's not loud enough that I don't hear the girl. The one Matt had originally been checking out.

"Yeah. Nice turnout." I shrug. "DJ is pretty good."

She sidles up closer. "I'm Gina."

"Hunter."

"I know who you are." Sympathy creeps into her voice. "I was there for the conference championship against Harvard, when that jerk broke your wrist. I can't believe he did that."

I can. I fucked his girlfriend.

But I keep that to myself. It's not like I did it intentionally, anyway. I had no clue who that girl was when I slept with her. Apparently she knew who *I* was, though. She wanted to get back at her boyfriend, but I didn't know that until he launched himself at me in the middle of the second-most important game of the season, the one that determines who goes to the Frozen Four, the *first*-most important game of a college season. The broken wrist was the result of a tackle to the ice. The Harvard asshole didn't intend to break it, but it happened, and just like that I was out of the game. And so was our team captain, Nate Rhodes, who was ejected for fighting while trying to defend me.

I snap myself out of the past. "It was a shitty way to end the season," I say.

Her hand finds its way onto my right bicep. My arms are looking huge these days, if I do say so myself. When you're not having sex, working out is imperative for your sanity.

"I'm sorry," Gina purrs. Her fingers gently glide over my bare skin, sending pinpricks of heat through my arm.

I almost groan out loud. Sweet fuck, I'm so horny that a woman caressing my *arm* is giving me a semi.

I know I should brush her hand off me, but it's been so long since I've been touched in a non-platonic way. At home my roommates are constantly pawing at me, but there's nothing sexual about it. Brenna likes to mockingly smack or pinch my ass whenever we pass each other in the hall, but that's not because she wants me. She's just an asshole.

"Want to go somewhere quiet and talk or something?" Gina suggests.

I've lived on this planet long enough to be able to decode what "talk or something" means in girl speak.

1) There won't be much talking.

2) There'll be a lot of "or something."

Gina couldn't have made this clearer if she were holding up a sign saying DO ME! She even licks her lips as she voices the question.

I know I should say no, but the idea of going home right now and jacking off in my bedroom while my roommates marathon old seasons of *The Hills* isn't too appealing. So I say, "Sure," and follow Gina out of the room.

------

We end up in a small den that contains a couch, a couple of bookshelves, and a desk against the far wall under a window. It's surprisingly empty. The party gods have taken pity on my celibate ass and provided us with the kind of dangerous privacy I should actively be avoiding. Instead, I'm on the couch and letting Gina kiss my neck.

Her satin camisole rubs my arm and it's almost pornographic how good the barely there friction feels. Everything is turning me on these days. I got a stiffy watching a YouTube ad for Tupperware the other day because the MILF in the ad was peeling a banana. Then she chopped it up into bits and placed the banana pieces in a plastic container and not even that horrific symbolism could dissuade me from jerking off to Banana Woman. Give me a few more months and I'll be fucking the apple pies my roommate Rupi bakes every Sunday.

"You smell so good." Gina inhales deeply, then exhales, her warm breath tickling my neck. Her lips latch on once more, a hot, wet brand against my neck.

She feels good in my lap. Her shapely thighs straddle mine, her satin-clad body warm and curvy. And I have to stop this.

I made a promise to myself, and to my team, although none of them asked me to do it and they all think I'm insane for even attempting abstinence. Matt flat-out stated he doesn't believe that me setting aside my sexual urges is going to impact our hockey games in the slightest. But I think it will, and for me it's a matter of principle. The guys voted me captain. I take that responsibility seriously, and I know from personal experience that I have the tendency to let women mess with my head. Screwing around got me a broken wrist last year. I'm not looking to repeat that.

"Gina, I—"

She cuts me off by pressing her lips to mine, and then we're kissing and my mind begins to spin. She tastes like beer and bubble gum. And her hair, which falls over one shoulder in a thick curtain of red curls, smells like apples. Mmmm, I want to eat her up.

Our tongues dance and the kiss grows deeper, hotter. My head keeps spinning as lust and unhappiness war inside me. I've lost all capability to think clearly. I'm so hard it hurts and Gina makes it worse by rubbing herself all over my crotch.

Thirty more seconds, I tell myself. Thirty more seconds and then I'll stop this from going any further.

"I want you so bad." Her lips are fused to my neck again, and then, *fuck*, her hand slides between us. She cups my cock over my shorts and I almost weep with pleasure. It's been so long since a hand that didn't belong to myself touched my dick. It feels criminally good.

"Gina, no," I groan, and it takes all my willpower to remove her hand. My cock protests by leaking precome all over the inside of my boxers.

Her cheeks are flushed red. Eyes glazed. "Why not?"

"I'm…taking a break from all that."

"From what?"

"Sex."

"What about it?"

"I'm going without."

"Without what?" She looks as confused as I am miserable.

"Without sex," I clarify glumly. "As in, I'm not having it for a while."

Her brows crash together. "But…why not?"

"It's a long story." I pause. "Actually, it's not a long story at all. I want to concentrate on hockey this year, and sex is too big of a distraction. That's pretty much it."

She pauses for a long beat. Then she touches my cheek and sweeps her thumb over the stubble on my jaw. She licks her lips, and I almost come in my pants.

"If you're worried that I'm going to want anything more, don't. I'm only looking for a one-night thing. My course load is insane this semester and I don't have time for relationships either."

"It's not a relationship issue," I try to explain. "It's sex in general. Once I have it, I want to keep having it. I get distracted and—"

She cuts me off again. "Fine, no sex. I'll just suck you off."

I nearly choke on my tongue. "Gina—"

"Don't worry, I'll get myself off while I'm doing it. Blowjobs turn me on so much."

This is torture.

Pure torture.

I swear, if the military needs any ideas on how to break someone? Give them a hard-up college guy, throw a hot chick on his lap, have her tell him how she wants nothing but no-strings sex and offer him blowjobs because it turns her on *so much*.

"I'm sorry," I manage to croak. Then I accomplish the even more difficult feat of easing her off my lap and getting to my feet. "I'm not in a good headspace for…any of this."

She stays seated, her head tipped back to stare at me. Her eyes are wide with incredulity and a touch of…I think it might be *sympathy*. For chrissake. Now I'm being pitied for my celibacy.

"I'm sorry," I say again. "And just so you know, you're the hottest girl at this party and my decision has nothing to do with you. I made myself a promise back in April and I want to keep it."

Gina chews on her bottom lip. Then, to my surprise, her expression takes on a glimmer of admiration. "I'm not going to lie," she says, "I'm kind of impressed. Not many guys could stand by that conviction in the face of my hotness."

"Not many guys are as stupid as I am."

Grinning, she hops to her feet. "Well, I guess I'll see you around, Hunter. I'd like to say I'll wait for you, but a girl has needs. And obviously they don't align with yours."

With a laugh, she saunters out of the den, and I watch her sexy ass sway with each step.

I rake both hands through my hair and then release a silent groan into my palms. I don't know if I should be proud of myself or kick my own ass for this ridiculous path I've chosen.

For the most part, it *has* helped keep me focused on hockey. I take out all my sexual frustration on the ice. I'm faster and stronger than I was last season, and there's almost a desperation in each shot that I snap at the net. The bullets hit their mark, almost as if in tribute to my suffering dick. An acknowledgment that his sacrifice must be honored.

It's only until the end of the season, I reassure myself. Seven more months, which will put me at one full year of celibacy once I cross the finish line. And then I'll reward myself with an entire summer of sex. A sex summer.

A dirty, decadent, endless sex summer...

Oh Christ. I'm so tired of fucking my own hand. Granted, I'm not helping my cause when I do idiotic things like opening myself up to temptation with gorgeous sorority girls.

For the first time in a long time, I'm dying for classes to start. Hopefully I'll have so much work this semester I'll be drowning in it. Homework, extra ice time, practice, and games—that's all I'm allowed to focus on. And definitely no more sorority parties.

Avoiding temptation is the only way to keep my head in the game and my dick in my pants.

# 2
# DEMI

"Lock it," I order as my boyfriend Nico shuts the bedroom door behind us. Just because my sorority is hosting tonight's party doesn't mean my room is open to the public. The last time we threw a party and I forgot to lock up, I went upstairs to grab a sweater and walked in on a threesome in progress. One of the two guys had even committed the atrocity of using my one-eyed stuffed panda Fernando as a pillow to shove under the girl's bottom. You know, to create easier access for the double penetration that was about to commence.

*Never again, Fernando,* I silently assure my childhood friend as I move him onto the nightstand to make room for my boyfriend.

Nico falls backward onto the bed, covers his face with his arm, and releases a weary breath. He missed the party because he had to work, but I appreciate that he made the effort to come over after his shift instead of going home to the studio apartment he rents in Hastings. The little town is a ten-minute drive from the Briar campus, so it's not super far. But I know it would've been easier for him to go straight home and crash.

"Tired?" I cluck in sympathy.

"Dead," is his muffled reply. His forearm shields his eyes from my view, which gives me the opportunity to admire his body without getting teased for it.

Nico has the long, lean build of a basketball player. Although he played point guard in high school, he didn't land any college basketball scholarships, and he was never good enough to go to the NBA. I don't think he cares much. Playing ball was something fun to do with his high school buddies; his real passion is cars. But though he doesn't play sports these days, he's still in great shape. He gets a good workout hauling boxes and furniture at the moving company where he works.

"Poor baby," I murmur. "Let me take care of it."

Smiling, I start at the bottom of his body and work my way up. Pull his sneakers off, slide his belt from its loops, peel his pants down his legs. He sits up to help me with his hoodie, then collapses back down. Now he's bare chested, wearing boxers and socks, with his arm over his face again to protect his eyes from the light.

Taking pity on him, I turn off the main light and flick on the lamp on the bed table, which emits a pale glow.

Then I settle beside him, clad in the black silk nightie I wore for the party.

"Demi," he mumbles as I start kissing his neck.

"Mmmm?"

"I'm way too tired for this."

My mouth travels along the angular line of his jaw, rough stubble abrading my lips. I reach his mouth and kiss him softly. He kisses me back but it's a fleeting caress. Then he gives another tired moan.

"Baby, seriously, I don't have any energy. I've been working fourteen hours straight."

"I'll do all the work," I whisper, but when my hand slides down to his crotch, there are no signs of life down there. His junk is a limp noodle.

"Another night, *mami*," he says sleepily. "Why don't you put on your creepy show or something?"

I swallow my disappointment. We haven't had sex in more than a week. Nico works on the weekends and several nights during the week, but he has tomorrow off so this is one of the rare Saturdays when we could actually stay up late fooling around if we want.

But he hasn't moved a muscle since he lay down.

"All right," I relent, rolling over to grab my laptop. "The latest episode is *Children Who Kill*, but I don't remember if I made you watch the one before that—*Clowns Who Kill*...?"

Nico is snoring softly.

Wonderful. It's Saturday night, there's a party raging downstairs, and it's not even ten o'clock. My hot boyfriend is sound asleep in my bed and I'm about to watch a show about murderers. By myself.

Living the college dream. Woo-hoo.

To make matters worse, this is the last stress-free weekend we're going to have in a long time. The fall semester starts on Monday, and my schedule is intense this year. I'm pre-med, so I need to excel and then some during my last two years at Briar if I want to get into a good med school. I won't have nearly as much time to spend with Nico as I'll want.

I shoot a quick glance at the snoring lump beside me. He doesn't seem bothered by our impending lack of quality time. But maybe he's right not to be. We've been dating since the eighth grade. Our relationship has had its ups and downs over the years, with some breaks along the way, but we survived every single hurdle, and we'll survive this, too.

I crawl under the covers, a feat of skill because Nico's heavy body is weighing down the other side of the blanket. I position the computer on my lap and load the next episode of my favorite show. I want to say I watch this series solely for the psychology component, but...who am I kidding? It's fucked up and I love it.

Ominous music fills the bedroom, followed by the host's familiar British monotone informing me that I'm in store for sixty delightful minutes of children who kill.

---

The rest of the weekend flies by. Monday morning brings with it the first class of my junior year, and the one I'm most excited about—Abnormal Psychology. Even better, two of my good friends are also taking this course. They're waiting for me on the stone steps of the massive ivy-covered building.

"Gawd, you look hot!" Pax Ling throws his arms around me, pulls back to smack a loud kiss on my cheek, and then reaches around to pinch my butt. I'm wearing denim shorts and a striped tank top, because it's a million degrees out today. Not that I'm complaining about the summer spilling over into September. Bring on the heat, baby.

"The *things* those shorts do to your *legs*, babe," Pax gushes in approval.

Beside him, TJ Bukowski rolls his eyes. When I first introduced them, TJ wasn't a fan of Pax's outrageous personality. But he eventually warmed up to Pax, and now they have a love-hate friendship that makes me laugh.

"You look pretty hot yourself," I inform Pax. "I love the shirt."

He flips up the collar of his pea-green polo. "It's Gucci, bitches. My sister and I were in Boston this weekend and spent a little too much money. But hey, worth it, right?" He does a quick spin to show off his new shirt.

"Worth it," I agree.

TJ adjusts the straps of his backpack. "Come on, let's go in. We don't want to be late for the first class. I hear Andrews is a strict prof."

I laugh. "We're fifteen minutes early. Don't worry."

"Did you seriously just tell *Thomas Joseph* not to worry?" Pax demands. "That's his default mode."

He's not wrong. TJ is a walking, talking ball of anxiety.

TJ glowers at us. He doesn't like being made fun of, especially about his anxiety, so I reach out and take his hand, giving it a warm squeeze. "Don't sulk, hon. I like that you're a worry-wart. Means I'm never late for anything."

With a slight smile, he squeezes my hand back. TJ and I met in freshman year when we lived in the same dorm. My roommate had been absolutely unbearable, so TJ's room became sort of a sanctuary for me. He's not always the easiest person to get along with, but he's been a good friend to me from day one.

"Waaaaaiittt!"

The female shriek pierces the breezy morning air. I turn my head to see a petite girl sprinting down the tree-lined path. She's clad in a knee-length black dress with big white buttons running down the middle. One arm is thrust skyward, waving what looks like a plastic food container.

A dark-haired guy pauses near the steps. He's tall and noticeably fit, even while wearing a bulky gray hoodie with the Briar U logo on it. A frown creases his handsome face when he realizes he's being chased.

The girl skids to a stop in front of him. I can't hear what he says to her, but her response is loud and clear. I think she might be one of the loudest people I've ever encountered.

"I made you lunch!" Smiling broadly, she presents the container as if she's handing him the Holy Grail.

Meanwhile, his body language conveys annoyance, as if what she's actually handing him is a bag of dog poop.

Seriously? His girlfriend made him lunch and he's not throwing his arms around her in gratitude? Jerk.

"I hate that guy," mutters TJ.

"You know him?" I can't hide my dubious expression. TJ doesn't hang out with many jocks, and the guy we're looking at is one hundred percent a jock. Those broad shoulders are a dead giveaway.

"That's Hunter Davenport." Pax is the one who speaks, and I instantly recognize that tone of voice. Translation: *oh-em-gee I want to lick that boy up*.

Sure enough, he's got a dreamy look in his eyes. "Who's Hunter Davenport?" I ask.

"He's on the hockey team."

Nailed it. I knew he was an athlete. Those shoulders, man. "Never heard of him," I say with a shrug.

"You're not missing out. He's just some rich prick jock," TJ says.

I arch a brow. "What do you have against him?" TJ doesn't normally bash student athletes. Or anyone, for that matter, aside from the occasional jab at Pax.

"Nothing. I just think he's gross. I caught him banging some slut in the library last year. Fully clothed, but with his pants pulled down revealing half his ass. He had her right up against the wall in one of the study rooms." TJ shakes his head in disgust.

I'm disgusted too, but more so with my friend's rude representation of Davenport's companion. "Please don't use that word," I chide. "You know I'm not into slut-shaming."

TJ is instantly contrite. "Sorry, you're right, that wasn't cool. If anything, Davenport was the slut in that scenario."

"Why does anyone have to be a slut?"

"I want to be his slut," Pax says absently. His gaze remains glued to the dark-haired hockey player, who's still bickering with his girlfriend.

The girl keeps pushing the Tupperware into his hand and he keep pushing it back into hers. I think he's saying he won't have time to eat, because her answering screech is, "There's always time to eat, Hunter! But you know what, fine. Go hungry. Forgive me for trying to offer you nourishment!"

Grinning, I cup my hands around my mouth and holler, "Just take the fucking lunch already!"

Davenport's head swivels my way. He gives me a deep frown.

The girl, on the other hand, beams at me. "*Thank* you!" She shoves the container in his hand one last time and flounces off. Her kitten heels snap like tap shoes against the cobblestones that comprise most of the historical campus.

Hockey Boy is glowering as he stalks toward us. "You have no idea what you just did," he growls at me. His voice is deeper than I expect, with a cute rasp to it. He lifts the container. "Now we set a precedent. She'll be making my fucking lunch all semester."

I roll my eyes. "Wow, forgive her for trying to offer you *nourishment*."

Sighing, he starts to move away. Then halts. "Oh hey, how's it going, man?" he says to Pax.

My friend's jaw drops to his white tennis shoes. They look new too, so I guess the shirt wasn't the only thing he picked up in Boston.

"Hi," Pax blurts out, clearly stunned to be singled out.

"You were in my Alternative Media class last term. Jax, right?"

To my disbelief, *Pax* nods stupidly.

"You in this Abnormal Psych class, too?"

"Yes," Pax breathes.

"Cool. Well, see you in there." Davenport claps Pax on the shoulder before sauntering up the stairs toward the building's entrance.

I stare pointedly at my friend, but he's too busy gawking at Davenport's ass.

"Hey Jax," I mock. "Earth to Jax."

TJ snickers.

Pax snaps out of his trance. He gives me a sheepish look. "He fucking remembered me, Demi. I wasn't going to correct him after he *remembered* me."

"He remembered Jax!"

"That's me! I'm Jax. I now live life as Jax. Hunter Davenport said so."

I smother a sigh and glance at TJ. "Why are we friends with him again?"

"I have no idea," he replies with a grin. "Come on, Jax, let's escort our lady to class."

I enter the lecture hall sandwiched between the two boys, my arms linked through theirs. The bulk of my friends are male, a fact that my boyfriend has come to accept. In high school he wasn't too thrilled about it, but Nico's never been a controlling boyfriend, and I think he secretly likes how well I get along with his friends.

Don't get me wrong, I've got girlfriends too. My sorority sisters. Pippa and Corinne, who I'm meeting for dinner tonight. But my guy friends do outnumber the girls, for whatever reason.

Inside the cavernous room, the boys and I find three seats together in a row near the middle of the room. I notice Hunter Davenport one row ahead of us at the end of the aisle, hunched over his phone.

"Gawd, he is perfection," Pax groans. "You have no idea how often I've fantasized about luring him over to the D-side."

I pat my friend on the arm. "Maybe one day. I have faith in you."

The room fills up, but all chatter dies when our professor enters at nine o'clock sharp. She's a tall, slender woman with short hair and shrewd brown eyes behind a pair of square black frames. She greets us warmly, and goes on to introduce herself, her credentials, and what we can expect to learn this year.

I'm pumped. My father is a surgeon and my mother used to be a pediatrics nurse, so it was inevitable that I'd wind up in a medicine-related field. It's probably programmed into my DNA. But surgery and nursing never interested me. Since I was a kid, I've been drawn to the *mind*. I'm especially fascinated by personality disorders. By destructive patterns of thinking and how they impact an individual when they interact with the world.

Professor Andrews discusses the specific topics we'll be covering. "We're going to see how abnormal psych was dealt with in the past and how modern approaches to it have evolved over the years. Clinical assessments and diagnosis will play a large role in our studies. Also, I believe in a hands-on approach to teaching. Which means I'm not simply going to stand here at this podium and spew facts about stress disorders, mood disorders, sexual disorders, and the like."

I lean forward. I'm already enthralled. I like her no-nonsense tone, and the way she sweeps her gaze over the room and tries to look everyone in the eye. I've had a lot of classes where the prof reads off a laptop in a monotone and doesn't seem to notice there're other people in the room.

She says we'll be expected to write summaries of the case studies she talks about in class, that there'll be a few multiple-choice tests. "All test dates are in the syllabus that was emailed to you. As for your major research project, it requires a partner, and it will be an ongoing partnership, with the final research paper and in-depth case study due before the holiday break. Now this is the fun part…"

I notice several uneasy glances being exchanged throughout the lecture hall. I guess it's a red flag when a prof uses the word "fun." But I'm not concerned. Everything she's described so far sounds interesting.

"You know that old childhood game—playing doctor?" Professor Andrews grins at the room. "That's the gist of this research project. One partner will play the role of the psychologist; the other will be the patient. The former will be provided with diagnostic tools in order to make an assessment and write a detailed case study. The latter will be assigned a psychological disorder that they'll be required to research and, for lack of a better word, play-act for the doctor."

"I love it," Pax says to me. "Please, *please* let me play the patient."

"Why do you assume you're partnering with Demi?" TJ objects.

"Boys, there's plenty of me to go around."

But Andrews throws us for a loop. "I'm assigning partners based on this alphabetized class list." She holds up some sheets of paper. "When you hear your names, raise your hands so you know who you're working with. All right, let's start—Ames and Ardin."

Two arms go up. A girl with bright purple hair, and a girl wearing a Patriots cap.

"Axelrod and Bailey."

There are about a hundred people in the class, but Andrews is efficient. She whizzes through names at a fast clip, and we reach the D's in no time.

"Davenport and Davis."

I raise my hand at the same time as Hunter. He shifts his gaze toward me, quirking his mouth in a half-smile.

Next to me, TJ sighs unhappily. He leans in to whisper, "Do you want me to legally change my last name to Davidson to save you from the hockey asshole?"

I grin at him. "It's okay, I'll survive."

"Grey and Guthrie," Andrews is saying.

"Are you sure?" TJ presses. "I bet you can switch partners if you said something."

"Killington and Ladde."

"Babe, it's fine. I don't even know the guy," I say. "You're the one who doesn't like him."

"I love him," Pax bemoans. "*I* want to play doctor with him."

But then Andrews calls out, "Lawson and Ling," and Pax brightens up when his partner raises a hand. It's a guy with wavy brown hair and a killer jawline.

"He'll do," murmurs Pax, and I swallow a laugh.

"These packages," Andrews says, gesturing to the stacks of orange manila envelopes on her desk, "contain detailed instructions about the assignment. One partner, please remember to grab one after the lecture. It'll be up to each team to decide who assumes which role."

Hunter twists around and gives me a finger gun, I assume to tell me I'm on envelope duty.

I roll my eyes. Already making me do all the work, I see.

Once everyone's assigned a partner, Andrews resumes the lecture, and I take so many notes my wrist starts to ache. Shit, I'll need to bring my laptop next time. I usually prefer writing notes by hand, but there's a lot of material to unpack and she covers so much in such a short time.

After we're dismissed, I head to the front of the room to grab a manila envelope. It's got some heft to it. That might alarm some people, but I'm looking forward to this project. It sounds fun and comprehensive, even if I am paired with a jock.

Speaking of the jock, he wanders toward me, hiking his backpack over one broad shoulder. "Davis," he greets me.

"Davenport."

"Call me Hunter." His gaze does a slow sweep of me from head to toe. It lingers a little too long on my bare legs, still nice and tanned from a summer spent in Miami.

"I'm Demi." I notice TJ and Pax standing near the exit, waiting for me to finish up.

"Demi…" he says absently. He's still checking out my legs, and he visibly gulps before wrenching his gaze back to mine.

"Yes, that's my name." Why is he shifting his stance like that? I narrow my eyes at his crotch. Does he have an *erection*?

"Demi," he repeats.

"Uh-huh. Rhymes with semi." I shoot a pointed look at his crotch.

Hunter glances down. Then he snickers. "For fuck's sake, I'm not rocking a boner. That's just my pants."

"Surrrrre."

He slides one big hand to his zipper area and covers it with his palm, and the tent in the denim does seem to flatten. "New jeans," he grumbles. "They're still kinda stiff."

"Stiff, you say."

"It's the fabric. See? Touch it."

Laughter sputters from my throat. "Oh my God, I am not touching your dick."

"Your loss." Hunter smirks.

"If you say so, bud." I hold up the envelope. "So when should we meet up and go over all this stuff?"

"I dunno. You free tonight?"

I shake my head. "I've got plans. How about tomorrow night?"

"Yeah, I'll be around. When and where?"

"Eight o'clock at the Theta Beta Nu house?"

"Huh, really? I didn't take you for a sorority girl." I shrug. "Well, I am."

Truth be told, I only pledged because I didn't want to live in the dorms. Plus, my mother belonged to the Theta chapter at her college, and I grew up hearing about how her sorority days were some of the best days of her life. She was the life of the party back then, and still is.

"Okay then. I'll see you tomorrow night, Semi," he drawls before striding off.

# 3

# HUNTER

"Ugh. I miss those tits so much."

"They miss you too..."

"Mmmm, yeah? What do they miss most about me?"

"Definitely your tongue."

"Mmmm. Let me see 'em, Hottie. Just a peek."

"What if one of your teammates walks in?"

"Then they'll be jealous of me till the end of time because I'm dating the sexiest woman in the world."

"Fine, I'll play. But only if you show me your dick."

"Deal. You first…aw fuck, baby…wait, maybe you should put the girls away—what if Hunter walks in? You said he was home."

"Oh, it's a non-issue. Hunter's a monk now. My bare boobs won't make an impact."

From the kitchen, I finally release the growl stuck in my throat. I *thought* I was coming downstairs to grab some dinner before my study date with Demi Davis. Instead, I just spent the past five minutes listening to the most nauseating Skype session in the world.

"Yeah, I'm a monk," I holler at the doorway. "Not a motherfucking eunuch!"

I march into the living room without giving Brenna any time to cover herself up. She doesn't deserve it. As a reward for enduring

Brenna and Jake Connelly's video sexing, I deserve to see some boobs outside of porn.

But Brenna is already shoving her shirt over her chest, so all I get is a teasing glimpse of reddish brown nipples before they disappear from view.

"Move over, you evil devil woman." I drop my ass on the couch beside her and shove a forkful of wild rice into my mouth. I glance at the laptop sitting on the coffee table. "Hey Connelly. Nice cock."

The man on the computer screen gives a startled curse. His gaze snaps down to his right hand, as if it's just occurred to him he's gripping a rather impressive erection. A blur of motion and the sound of a zipper, and then Jake Connelly glares at me with intense green eyes.

"Spying on us, Davenport?"

I swallow my food. "Is it considered spying when you're naked Skyping in my goddamn living room?"

"*Our* living room," Brenna says sweetly, reaching over to pat my shoulder.

Right, like I could ever forget. Other men might be thrilled to shack up with three chicks, but it's not my ideal living situation. I like Brenna, Summer and Rupi individually, but throw the three of them together and the world becomes…loud. Not to mention they're always ganging up on me.

My former roommates, Mike Hollis and Colin Fitzgerald, technically still live here too, but they're not around nearly as much as I'd like.

Hollis only shows up on the weekends—he stays with his folks in New Hampshire during the week for his job.

Fitz is a video game designer and has been taking on a lot of contract work since he graduated Briar. Sometimes that means traveling to the game studio's headquarters. Right now he's in New York working on a sci-fi role-playing game, and staying at Summer's family's Manhattan penthouse for the duration of the gig. Lucky

Fitzy. The Heyward-Di Laurentis clan is filthy rich, so he's currently living it up in the lap of luxury.

"Connelly, get a move on. The car's waiting for us downstairs," another voice barks out of the laptop speakers. "We've got that charity photo op thing tonight."

Jake glances over his shoulder. "Oh shit, I forgot about that."

"What are you doing on—oh, hey Brenna!" A huge face appears on screen, a close-up so extreme that I can see up the guy's hairy nostrils.

When the man pulls back, I experience a rare fanboy moment, because holy shit—it's Theo Nilsson, one of the star players for Edmonton. I can't believe Nilsson just casually strolled into Jake's hotel room, and there's no stopping a pang of envy at the notion that Jake is actually out in the world playing hockey with some serious legends.

When I was a kid I dreamed of playing professionally, but as I got older I realized it might not be the best path for me. The lifestyle scares me, if I'm behind honest. So I didn't make myself eligible for the draft. Hell, I hadn't even planned on playing in college. I came to Briar set on earning a business degree and becoming an entrepreneur. But a friend and teammate who graduated a couple of years ago lured me out of my self-imposed retirement, and now here I am.

"I have to go, babe," Jake tells Brenna.

"Have fun getting your picture taken with all those thirsty puck bunnies," she chirps.

Nilsson barks with laughter. "It's a charity event for a senior citizen curling organization," Jake's teammate reveals.

She's unfazed. "Have you *seen* Jake?" she asks Theo. "Those old broads will be all over him. Puck bunnies transcend age."

As Brenna signs off, I shove a piece of grilled chicken into my mouth. "I can't believe that was Theo Nilsson," I say between bites.

"Yeah, he's really cool. We had dinner with him last week when they played the Bruins."

"Don't rub it in.".

Brenna's trademark red lips purse in a saccharine smile. Even when she's home alone, she still takes the time to slather on that fuck-me lipstick. She's evil. "If you're a good boy, I'll invite you next time."

"I'm always a good boy," I protest. "Just ask my dick—poor dude wants to be bad and I ain't having it."

She laughs. "I feel like all this pent-up lust isn't good for your health. What if your balls explode and you die?"

I think it over. "Maybe it'll be like a thousand orgasms all rolled up in one explosion, and who would want to keep living after that? I feel like after you've experienced a thousand-orgasm explosion, there's nowhere to go but down."

"That's a good point." Brenna's dark eyes track me as I get up and head for the kitchen to rinse my plate.

"I gotta go now," I tell her, popping my head back into the living room. "See you later."

"Where are you off to?"

"Study thing at the Theta house."

"Ha! So much for the vow of celibacy."

"Nope. The vow's still intact. I'm just working on a project with a chick there."

"A project," she mocks.

"Yes, a project. The world doesn't revolve around sex, Bee."

"Sure it does." She licks her lips lasciviously and my mouth tingles in response. So does my penis.

She's right. Sex is everything and everywhere. A woman can't even lick her lips without my brain sinking right into the sexual gutter.

So far, I've found only one solution for controlling my libido: marijuana. And I can't even do *that* as often as I'd like, except for the occasional joint at a party. Weed mellows me out and reins in my carnal impulses, but it also makes me tired and slows me down during workouts. And there's no way I want to tempt the NCAA drug-testing gods. So, like sex, it's just another fun activity I get to avoid. My life is awesome.

"Anyway, I'm meeting some of the boys at Malone's afterward to shoot pool. Don't wait up."

"What? No invite?" She mock pouts.

"Nope," I reply and I don't feel the slightest bit guilty about it. I live in the estrogen zone, and sometimes it's imperative I escape it, even if it's just for the night. "No girls allowed. There's enough girls in this house already."

"Oh, you love it. Rupi makes you lunch every day, Summer cooks you breakfast, and I'm always walking around in my underwear. Food and sexy material for your spank bank, Davenport. You're living the dream."

"If I was living the dream, I'd be banging all of you every night. At the same time."

"Ha! You wish. Go have fun with your"—Brenna uses air quotes—"project."

I give her the finger and leave, and fifteen minutes later I'm back on campus, parking my Land Rover on the tree-lined street that houses Greek Row. It's Tuesday night and the area is surprisingly quiet. Usually there's always some nightly party or event happening on Greek Row, but tonight I hear only the faint sound of music from a few of the fraternity houses.

I walk up the flower-lined path that leads to the front door of the Theta house. Nearly every window of the three-story Victorian is lit up. I ring the doorbell and a tall, skinny girl in sweats appears.

She arches an eyebrow. "Can I help you?"

"I'm here to see Demi." I lift the shoulder that's holding my backpack. "We're studying."

Demi's sorority sister shrugs, then turns her head and shouts, "Demi! Door!"

I enter the house, which has undergone a drastic makeover since I was here on the weekend. It's neat as a pin and smells like lemon cleaner, and there's no scantily clad chicks, drunken dudes, or puddles of beer all over the hardwood.

Footsteps echo on the wooden staircase, and the girl from psych class saunters down the steps, a lollipop sticking out of the corner of her mouth. Naturally, I zero in on her lips, which are glossy and tinged red from the candy she's sucking on. Her dark hair is up in a high ponytail and she's wearing plaid pants and a thin white tank top over a black sports bra.

She's really fucking cute, and I have to force myself to stop checking her out.

"Hi," she says, giving me a long appraisal.

"Mel, who was at the door?" someone shouts.

There's a burst of chatter, and then half a dozen girls spill out of the kitchen into the front hall. They all stop abruptly when they notice me. One of them openly undresses me with her eyes, while the others are slightly more discreet.

"Hunter Davenport," the ogler drawls. "Lord, you're even better looking up close."

I don't normally get shy or stupid around women, but they're all standing there appraising me, and it's fucking disconcerting. "Maybe you should give me your number?" I murmur to Demi.

"Why would I do that?"

"So that next time I can text you when I'm here and you can quietly come get me and we could avoid all of…this…" I gesture to our audience.

"What's the matter? Are you intimidated by a few girls?" Rolling her eyes, Demi leads me toward the stairs.

"Nah." I wink. "I'm worried about you."

"Me?"

"Well, yeah. If I keep coming over to see you, your sisters will start getting insanely jealous, and their resentment will eventually make them treat you poorly and you'll lose all of your friends. Is that really what you want, Semi?"

She laughs. "Oh no! You're right. From now on you should climb in through my window. Like Romeo." Her tongue shifts her lollipop to the other side of her mouth. "Spoiler alert: Romeo dies."

She ushers me into a room on the second floor and closes the door.

I examine the bedroom. The walls are yellow and the bed is one of those four-post ones that looks like it should have a billowing canopy but doesn't. The bedspread is purple, and there's a stuffed panda chilling on one of the pillows.

Demi's desk is laden with textbooks. Chem, bio, and a math one I can't read the title of. I raise my eyebrows. If she's taking all of those in one semester, that's an intense course load and I don't envy her at all.

But my gaze is more interested in the large bulletin board over the desk. It's practically overflowing with pictures, and I move toward it to take a closer look. Hmmm, there are a helluva lot of dudes in these photographs. Some girls, too, but Demi's friend group seems to consist mostly of guys. Several photos feature Demi with the same raven-haired guy. Boyfriend?

"So, how are we doing this?" I ask, dropping my bag on her desk chair.

"Well, Andrews said we're supposed to treat these meet-ups like real therapy sessions."

"Right." I waggle my eyebrows. "You ready to play doctor?"

"Gross. I'm not playing anything with you, hockey boy."

"That's hockey *man*, thank you very much."

"Okay, hockey man." Demi digs into her schoolbag and pulls out the manila envelope we got in class yesterday. She sits on the edge of the bed with the envelope on her lap. "All right, so I figured you would be the patient, and I'd be the doctor. That means you'd be doing the easier part of the write-up."

I frown. "What makes you think I need the easy part?"

"Oh, sorry, I don't mean to insult your intelligence," she says, sounding sincere. "But a friend told me you're a business major."

"So?"

"So I'm the psych major in this partnership, and I think writing the case study and doing all the diagnosis work would be more beneficial to me than you, since I want to make a career out of this. But if you really don't want to do the research element, we can draw straws."

I think about it for a moment. She does have a point about the career stuff. And I don't mind doing the research portion. "Sure, whatever. I'll be the patient."

"Perfect. Done."

"See how well we work together?" My gaze drifts to the small loveseat tucked beneath the window. "Sweet, it's like a real shrink's office." I stride over to the couch and cram my too-large body onto it, stretching my legs over the edge. Then I reach for my zipper. "Pants on or off?"

# 4
# DEMI

I burst out laughing at the outlandish question. "Please, for the love of God, keep your pants *on*."

"You sure?" Hunter says, his fingers poised over the button of his jeans.

"Positive."

"Your loss." He winks and shoves his hands behind his head.

Davenport is entertaining, I'll give him that. He's also too attractive for his own good. My sorority sisters left drool puddles on the floor when he walked by them before. Most of them have a huge thing for jocks, so they'll probably burst into my room begging for details the second Hunter leaves.

He stretches out on my little couch and kicks off his shoes. He's wearing jeans that are ripped at the knees, a black T-shirt, and an unzipped gray hoodie. Muscular but not bulky, he's got a great body, and the heart-stopping face to go with it. And when he flashes me a cocky grin, I'm horrified to feel heat rise in my cheeks. That smile of his is dangerous. No wonder Pax is obsessed with this guy.

I open the large envelope and extract a stapled packet with the instructions for our assignment, as well as two other envelopes. One is labeled "DOCTOR," the other "PATIENT."

"Here." I toss the patient envelope at the couch. Hunter catches it easily.

Inside my envelope, I find a stack of papers, and flip through it. It's blank templates that I'm supposed to use for my "session notes." I skim the instructions bundle. We need to log a minimum of eight sessions, but we can do as many as we want. My session notes will apparently be included in the appendix for the case study I'll need to write. My package also includes diagnostic tools and tip sheets.

From the couch, Hunter chuckles softly. I glance over to see him skimming through papers. His stack isn't as big as mine, likely because his part of the project involves more research.

"We probably should've decided on our roles in class," I realize. "I don't know if we can do much of a session before you've brushed up on your fake condition."

But Hunter just shrugs. A wry note enters his voice as he studies his papers again. "It's cool. I know enough to wing it, at least for this first chat."

"You sure?"

"Yup." He slides the paperwork back into the envelope and drops it on his bag. Then he gets comfortable again. "All right, let's go."

As per Andrews' instructions, I'm not allowed to record the session. But I'm confident in my note-taking abilities. I crunch the last bit of my lollipop between my teeth, swallow the candy, and toss the little stick in the wastebasket.

Once we're both settled, we start going through the formalities. "So, Mister…?" I wait for him to fill in the rest.

"Sexy."

"Veto. You can do better than that."

"Big," he supplies.

I sigh. "Smith," I say firmly. "You're Mr. Smith. First name, um, Damien."

"Like the devil kid from that horror movie? Veto. It's bad karma."

"You're bad karma," I mutter. Jesus, it's taking forever just to record his fake name. At this rate, the project will never get done. "Fine, your first name is Richard, you picky dick."

He snorts.

"It's nice to meet you, Dick Smith," I say sweetly. "I'm Dr. Davis. What brings you here today?"

I half-expect another bullshit line, something about how this Dick needs to be sucked. But he surprises me. "My wife thinks I need therapy."

My eyebrows shoot up. Ooh, getting right down to it. I love it. "Is that so... And why does she think that?"

"Honestly? I don't know. *She's* the one who needs therapy. She's always losing her mind over something."

I jot down his phrasing. "What do you mean by that, losing her mind?"

"She overthinks everything. She bitches all the time. For example, if I'm home late from work, her brain immediately jumps to 'he's been screwing around.'" Hunter pauses irritably. "I guess for the sake of full disclosure, I should mention I cheated on her once or twice, and yes, she is aware of this."

Wow, this is like a soap opera. I'm already invested.

"All right...this cheating you mention." I make some more notes. "How long ago did it take place? And was it once, or was it twice?"

"The first affair was years ago, the most recent one this year. I was under a lot of stress at work."

I note that he ignored my question about how many times he'd actually cheated.

"Why do you think you cheated? Is there a particular reason that stands out?"

"It's hard to feel connected to somebody when they're constantly complaining and making demands. She fucking drove me to cheat. I mean, what else did she expect would happen if she kept acting like that?"

Ugh, what a prick. He holds his *wife* responsible for *his* cheating—

I stop the train of thought, reminding myself that I'm not supposed to be judge. I'm supposed to understand.

If I'm going to be a clinical psychologist, I'm sure I'll hear thousands of sordid tales of infidelity. I might even need to counsel someone who physically or emotionally abuses their partner. It's highly likely I'll encounter patients I despise, or who I might not be able to help.

My job isn't to condemn them; it's to hopefully help them reach self-awareness.

"So when you came clean about the affairs, did you and your wife agree to start over? Start fresh?"

Hunter nods. "She accepted responsibility for her part in what happened and agreed to forgive me. That means it's done, in the past. Her being suspicious of me all the time doesn't make me want to spend time with her. Trust me, she's not making it easy to be around her."

"I imagine so. But can you recognize why she might be behaving this way? Let's try to put yourself in her position. How do you think you'd react if your wife was unfaithful?"

"She'd never cheat on me," he says smugly. "I'm the catch in this relationship. She's definitely punching above her weight class."

*You're the fucking worst,* I want to say.

"I see," is what I say instead. And now I understand why therapists seem to cling to those two words. It's code for whatever expletives are ringing in your head.

Hunter and I talk for another twenty minutes about his fictional wife, her nagging, and his infidelity, and I begin to notice a trend in his responses. A complete inability to put himself in her shoes.

*Lack of empathy,* I write down, and draw a little star around it.

As he finishes another long-winded anecdote that paints his wife as the villain and himself as the innocent victim, I can't help but be impressed by how he just threw himself headfirst into this assignment. And he's doing *such* a solid job, which is…ugh, it's sexy as hell, if I'm being honest.

I'm about to ask another question when Hunter sits up. "Let's stop now. I've officially tapped out my knowledge about…my condition," he says vaguely. "Got to do some more research before we keep talking."

"This was fun," I admit. "Don't you think?"

"Yeah, it kinda was." He slides off the loveseat and raises his muscular arms above his head to stretch them out. His T-shirt slides up as he does this, revealing abs of steel.

My jaw drops. "Oh my God. That is so unfair."

"What?" Hunter's dark eyebrows furrow.

"Have you seen your abs? Who the fuck has abs like that?"

His confusion gives way to a smug smile. "I play hockey. Every inch of me looks like that."

Once again, my cheeks feel a bit warm. I'm trying hard not to picture what the rest of him looks like beneath his clothes, but I have a feeling he's not exaggerating. His physique is bonkers.

I notice my phone light up on the nightstand and go over to check it. It's been on silent, and Nico texted twice during the past hour. One message thirty minutes ago, and another just now.

**NICO**: Hey bb I'm gonna have to bail on sleepover 2nite. Car died after work. Battery probs. Gonna get it towed to the garage in Hastings and pick it up in the a.m. b4 class.
**NICO**: R u mad

I type a quick reply.

**ME**: Not mad, babe. Disappointed, tho.

"Everything okay?" Hunter asks as he zips up his hoodie.

I shrug. "My boyfriend canceled on me. He was supposed to stay over tonight but his car battery died. I guess he needs a new one or something."

"Bummer. I'd invite you to play pool with me and the boys tonight, but I need a break from chicks."

"Yes, I imagine all the female attention must be excruciating."
I think about the cute girl from yesterday, the one who went out of
her way to make him lunch and he totally spurned her. "Come on,
I'll walk you downstairs."

But before I can reach the door, Nico calls. "Oh, I need to answer
this," I say as we leave the bedroom.

I have no choice, because whenever I miss a call or text from
Nico, he has a tendency not to answer when I call or text back, even
if it's half a second later. I don't get it. Way too many people do that.
How are they not available five seconds after contacting me? I swear,
it's like they send a text and then hurl their phones into the river.

"Hey," I say hastily. "What's up?"

"Just wanted to check in," Nico says. "I'm gonna shower soon
and then I'll probably crash early."

"Why—oh, right, you need to pick up your car."

"Pick it up?"

"Because you got it towed to the shop…?" I remind him. From
the corner of my eye, I notice Hunter curiously listening in. I urge
him to walk faster as we descend the stairs.

"Oh no, actually, I got a jump from Steve. He had cables in his
truck."

"Wait, so you got the car started?" *Then why can't you drive here?*
I want to ask, but force myself not to.

"Yeah, I did. But I don't want to drive it again tonight in case
the battery dies again," Nico says as if reading my mind. "I'm gonna
get it checked out in the morning. But I'll see you tomorrow night,
okay?"

"Sure."

"Love you, *mami*."

"Love you too."

I'm frowning as Hunter and I reach the front door. "The
boyfriend?" he prompts.

I nod slowly. "I guess he got his car going with jumper cables, but the battery is still messed up? I'm not sure. I don't know much about cars."

"Sounds a bit shady," remarks Hunter. "Using the ol' car broke down excuse to avoid seeing someone."

"Really?" I challenge. "Do you often lie about your car breaking down to get out of a date?"

"Often? No. Have I done it? Yes."

I glare at him. "Well, not everybody is a liar like you."

He doesn't take offense. Just grins. "Gee. I didn't mean to hit a nerve."

"You didn't."

"Uh-huh. Anyway. My boys are waiting. Later, Semi."

I practically shove him out the front door. Maybe if I get rid of him fast enough, that little seed of doubt he created won't take root.

# 5
# HUNTER

I'M THE FIRST ONE TO ARRIVE FOR THURSDAY AFTERNOON'S TEAM meeting. I never used to be early for these things, but now that I'm team captain I'm trying to lead by example, so here I am, alone in the media room.

The Briar hockey facility is top-of-the-line, so we have a sweet A/V set-up. The large auditorium-style room offers three rows of tables with huge padded chairs, and a massive screen to watch game tape on. We've been studying film on Eastwood College all week. They're our conference rivals, and we're matched up against them for tomorrow's first official game of the season.

I'm not too worried. Eastwood's roster is not particularly strong this year—ours is. Even with Fitzy, Hollis and Nate Rhodes gone, the team still has a solid lineup. Me, Matty, an excellent goalie, and some of the hottest high school players Coach Jensen recruited for the freshman class.

After the team voted me to take over for Nate, our former captain, I called him up asking for tips on how to keep morale up, how to motivate the boys, how to actually *lead*, but he didn't have much advice. He said the dynamics change every year with the ebb and flow of new faces, and that I'd learn as I go along. It's simply a matter of navigating your way through thirty-odd egos, and keeping everybody pumped up and focused on the task at hand: winning.

Speaking of new faces, there are quite a lot of them this season. At the end of August we held open tryouts, an event that serves to showcase players who weren't recruited out of high school or those who try out for the hell of it. One of my new favorite teammates is the result of those tryouts—Conor Edwards, who saunters into the room as I'm settling in a chair in the front row.

Con's a self-proclaimed fuckboy, but he's not as douchey as you'd expect. He's actually quite decent, with a dry sense of humor that I appreciate.

"S'up, captain," he says before yawning hugely. He rakes a lazy hand through his sun-streaked blond hair, drawing my attention to the purple hickey on his neck.

He reminds me of Dean, the older brother of my roommate Summer, and a good friend (and former mentor) of mine. Dean was unapologetically sexual when he attended Briar. He didn't care if everyone knew he was constantly hooking up. And his manwhore ways didn't hurt his reputation either, because every chick who met him wanted to get naked with him. But his girlfriend Allie is the only one to ever steal his heart. They've been living together in NYC for the past couple of years.

Conor sits beside me. A few seniors stride in and settle in the top row. "Yo," they greet us, nodding hello.

We nod back.

Matt Anderson enters next. With Fitz and Hollis gone, I guess Matty's my best friend on the team now. He's the only black player on the roster, drafted by LA last year. I hope he officially signs with them, because it's a great franchise to play for.

"Hey," Matt says.

The room begins to fill up. We've got about two dozen starters, and then the rest of the roster is made up of benchwarmers and guys who still need a lot of development. And although Mike Hollis graduated, there is always, without fail, a Hollis type on every team. The lovable idiot, as Brenna calls him. The honor this year goes to a sophomore named Aaron, except everyone calls him Bucky because he looks like that character from the Marvel movies.

Bucky hates it, but the thing about nicknames is, they stick— whether you want them to or not. Just ask our senior left-winger Treeface, sometimes shortened to Tree or T, who one time four years ago got drunk and lamented how sad it is that trees don't have faces and can't see the birds who make nests on them. I'm pretty sure John Logan is responsible for that nickname.

Munching on a bran muffin he probably grabbed from the team kitchen, Bucky approaches the front row. "Did you talk to Coach about it?" he demands while chewing with his mouth open.

I play dumb. "About what?"

"The pig, dude."

"The pig," echoes Jesse Wilkes, a fellow junior. He was on his phone, but now he's focused on our conversation.

Fuck. I was hoping the subject would quietly be forgotten.

"No, not yet." *And I don't plan on it*, I want to add, but I haven't found a way to finagle out of this one yet.

The guys are insisting we need a team mascot, while I personally don't see the point. I mean, if we were somehow able to strap a pair of skates on a polar bear and have him perform double axels on the ice between periods, then, sure, great. Bring it on.

Short of that, who the fuck cares.

Coach's arrival spares me from humoring my teammates. He strides in and claps his hands sharply. "Let's not waste time," he barks. "Eyes on the screen."

Chad Jensen is a total hard-ass—he doesn't mince words or indulge us. When we're in this arena, we're required to be all business or else GTFO.

"Pay attention to Kriska on this first play," Coach orders as a hi-def video pops up on the projection screen. He's at his desk, using his tablet pen to circle Eastwood's goalie, Johan Kriska.

The freshman is rumored to be one of the best college goalies on the east coast. I've been studying the handful of his high school games that were televised, as well as all of Eastwood's preseason games. I need to be prepared when I face this kid. Not to sound cocky, but I'm the best forward on the team. And the top scorer, for sure, judging by last season's stats lines. Nate and I were tied for goals, but my former captain had me on assists. I guess that's another captainly requirement—*Don't hog the glory.*

I'm slowly compiling a list of captain dos and don'ts.

Despite his stellar rep, I'm not overly concerned about Kriska. I've already found a weakness. "His glove is slow," I pipe up. "Kid has trouble with the high shots. Maybe a thirty percent save rate, if that."

"Yes," Coach confirms. "That's why we've been running those concentrated shooting drills this week. But I'm sure they're prepping just as hard, and Kriska knows his own weaknesses. I want to see a shit ton of low shots on goal tomorrow. He'll already be overcompensating for the weak glove, and he may be so focused on stopping those shots that we'll catch him off guard and push one through the five hole."

"Good point."

We watch more of the tape. Someone whistles when Kriska makes one of the most gorgeous stick saves I've ever seen.

"Look at that," Coach says, pausing the game. "No desperation on his face at all. He's diving back into position to try to deflect the puck after getting completely hammered by those shots, and he's cool as a cucumber."

It is kind of impressive. Goaltenders don't use their sticks to make a save if they can help it. Pads, gloves, even their own bodies, are preferable. A stick save tends to be the result of pure luck, with the goalie scrambling like mad. But with Kriska, it appears effortless.

"We just need to find a way to rattle him," Matt speaks up.

I nod in agreement. I'm feeling confident, though. Last season we were killing it. It wasn't lack of skill that cost us. It was a fluke injury, along with Nate's ejection while defending my honor.

Another rule for the captain's handbook: *defend your boys.*

This year we lost a few good guys to graduation, but we gained a lot more. There's no reason why we shouldn't make it to the Frozen Four, not unless we're waylaid by massive team-wide injuries or do something to royally fuck up our chances.

The meeting wraps up when Coach claps his hands signaling that we can leave. Bucky instantly raises an arm and clears his throat. Loudly. He glances over to shoot me a meaningful look.

Shit.

Coach's head lifts from his laptop. "What's going on?"

"The captain has something to say," Bucky announces.

Jensen's shrewd dark eyes shift toward me. Those eyes are uncannily like Brenna's, complete with the perpetual glint of mocking. Then again, he's her father, so...

"Davenport?" he prompts.

"Uh…" Fuck fuck fuck. I'm about to sound like total moron. But I force myself to stand up and say, "Some of the guys want a pig."

Coach's eyebrows rise to his hairline. It's rare to catch the man off guard, but right now he looks flabbergasted. "A fucking what?"

I swallow a sigh. "A pig."

"A teacup pig," Jesse Wilkes chimes in.

"A fucking what?" Coach repeats.

"Here's the thing," I explain stupidly. "Bucky's sister and brother-in-law just got a pig from a breeder up in Vermont. Not a huge one, but a mini version. Apparently they make great pets? They're like dogs, except they eat and shit more."

"What is happening right now?" Coach shakes his head. "What are you saying to me?"

I take another stab at an explanation. "You know how some teams have mascots? The Darby College Rams have that billy goat that lives in the clubhouse behind their arena. Or the Coyotes down in Providence—they have a dog that's half-wolf and everyone takes turns housing him?"

"Tabasco," exclaims a senior D-man.

"I love that dog," Tree says happily.

"Did you know Tabasco can hump on command?" Bucky says, sounding impressed.

"Big fucking deal," Conor drawls. "I can do that too."

Loud laughter rings out.

Coach holds up his hand to silence everybody. "Are you idiots asking me if you can have a pet?"

"Pretty much." I give him a pleading look. "As the new captain, I've been asked to formally put forth the request."

"A room full of grown men are requesting a pet."

I nod.

"It'll be great for morale," Bucky insists. "Think about it, Coach. We could bring the pig out before games and he'll get the crowd all hyped up. Dude, it'll build so much excitement."

"How does a pig hype up a crowd? Is he going to sing the national anthem?" Coach asks politely.

"Come on, Coach, don't be silly," Con mocks. "Everyone knows pigs can't sing."

"You on board with this, Edwards?" Coach is skeptical. "You're Team Pig?"

Conor flashes a cheerful smile. "I literally could not care less."

"We're *all* on board," Bucky argues.

Coach's sharp gaze conducts a sweep of the room. "Jesus Christ. You dumbasses are serious? You honestly think that between the thirty of you, you can actually keep an animal alive?"

"Hey," Matt protests. "I've got two dogs at home."

"And where is your home?"

"Minneapolis."

"And where are you right now?"

Matt shuts up.

"You're all full-time college students with intensive athletic schedules—and don't even get me started on your social lives—and you think you can take care of a living creature? I call bullshit."

He's done the exact wrong thing. A bunch of competitive hockey players being told they can't do something? Suddenly even the guys that were indifferent to the pig are coming to their own defense.

"I could take care of a pet," objects Joe Foster, a new addition to the forward roster.

"Me too."

"Ditto."

"Yeah, come on, bro, give us a shot."

Coach's jaw tightens and twitches as if he's holding back a sea of expletives. "I'll be right back," he finally says, before stalking out of the room without explanation.

"Holy shit, you think he's going to get a pig?"

I turn toward the moron who asked the question. "Of course not," I sputter at Bucky. "Where the fuck would he find one? Hiding in the equipment closet?" I shake my head mutinously. "You just *had* to make me ask him, eh? Now he thinks we're insane."

"There's nothing insane about wanting the love of a pig."

Jesse hoots. "Guys, I know what to write on Bucky's tombstone."

"Fuck off, Wilkes."

My teammates are still bickering amongst themselves when Coach returns. With purposeful strides, he goes to the center of the media room and holds up an egg, which I assume he grabbed from the team kitchen.

"What's that?" Bucky asks in bewilderment.

Our fearless leader smirks. "This is your pig."

"Coach, I think it's an egg," one of the freshmen says hesitantly.

That earns him a look of disdain. "I know it's an egg, Peters. I'm not a moron. However, until the end of the regular season, this egg is your pig. You want me to sign off on a team pet, which, by the way, involves a shit ton of red tape with the university? Then prove to me that you can keep something alive." He waves the egg in the air. "It's hard-boiled. If it cracks, you killed your precious porker. Bring it back to me in one piece and then we'll talk pigs."

Coach grabs a Sharpie from the desk and scribbles something on the egg.

"What are you doing?" Bucky asks curiously.

"Signing it. And trust me, I know when my signature has been forged. So if this breaks, don't even think about trying to swap it out with another one. If this isn't the egg that comes back to me, then no pig." Coach plants the egg in Bucky's hand. "Congratulations, you have a team mascot."

Bucky catches my eye and gives me a triumphant thumbs-up.

If this is what being team captain is all about, I don't know if I really want the job.

# 6
# HUNTER

WE'RE ABSOLUTELY WIPING THE ICE WITH EASTWOOD COLLEGE ON Friday night, and it has nothing to do with Kriska's weak glove. We're simply on fire and they are not. Kriska stops shot after shot, but five—count 'em, five—light up the lamp. I'd like to say I contributed more than one, but the hockey gods decided to spread the wealth. The first goal was mine, but the next four went to various teammates.

I don't know what happened to Eastwood's defense, but the D-men didn't show up to play tonight. Kriska is all alone in the net batting off pucks like Neo dodging bullets in *The Matrix*. Any time a Briar player gets a breakaway, the goalie's face turns snow white behind his mask, because he knows he's in trouble. The Eastwood D-men are either scrambling to keep up with us, or tangled up in the corners providing endless rebound opportunities for Briar.

Our fans scream their approval. This is a home game, so our school colors, black and silver, make up a massive expanse of the stands. Damn, it feels good to be back, to be breathing the crisp air in the arena. The chill tickling the back of my neck only heightens the adrenaline coursing in my blood.

I'm on the bench. Two minutes left in the third period, but there's no way Eastwood is scoring five goals in two minutes. I glance over. Con's beside me. We're on the same line this year, along with Matt, and the three of us are a forced to be reckoned with. This line is going to take us all the way to the finals.

"Je-sus, that was a crazy crosscheck," I praise him.

We're both out of breath. Our last shift was a penalty kill, during which Conor landed a bone-jarring hit on an Eastwood forward.

"Dude, my ears are still ringing from it." His grin gives off a toothy, wolfish vibe thanks to the mouth guard half dangling from his mouth.

"We needed you last season," I admit. "We didn't have a lot of goons." Meanwhile, our biggest rival Harvard had the goon of all goons, Brooks Weston.

But Conor only transferred this year from a college on the West Coast. He's a California boy, with his surfer hair and laidback attitude. Yet there's nothing laidback about him when he's smashing other dudes into the boards.

Coach keeps us on the bench as the clock ticks down, letting our third and fourth lines enjoy the action. We're in no danger of losing the game, and the extra ice time helps to develop them as players. The boys manage to hold Eastwood, and our first game ends in a shutout.

Everyone's in a celebratory mood as we file into the locker room to shower and change. Arrangements are made to go to Malone's, the bar in Hastings where the hockey crowd usually gathers.

"You in?" I ask Bucky.

"Yeah. Just gimme a couple minutes. Gotta make sure Pablo gets his dinner."

I choke back laughter.

On the top shelf of Bucky's locker, the team mascot is tucked away in its brand new coral-pink drink cozy. With the utmost care, Bucky reaches for Pablo Eggscobar.

Jesse, who's wandering by in a towel, spots the egg in Bucky's hand. "What the hell, man! Can't you see Pablo's hungry?"

"*Feed me,*" a singsong voice drifts from across the room, courtesy of Velky, our international student from Sweden.

In the day and a half since Pablo joined us, things have taken an evil turn. A few of the guys decided to be dicks about it and fuck with Bucky, texting him at random times throughout the day and night from the egg's point of view. Usually in all caps. Messages along the lines of: FEED ME! PET ME! LET ME OUT TO TAKE A DUMP!

However, like my friend Mike Hollis, Bucky is rubber and we're glue, and nothing anyone says or does ever bothers him. The fucker decided that sticking to a care schedule actually makes sense. Then he discussed it with Coach, and now we're all sworn by the honor system to treat Pablo like a real pig. Reasoning being that if we don't, then any time he's in our custody we'd toss him in a drawer and forget about him.

Bucky's the only one treating it seriously. The rest of us are just excited to mess with each other.

"Here, Pablo, eat your dinner," Bucky tells the egg.

The egg says nothing because it's a goddamn egg.

"I feel like I've traveled back in time to pre-school," Matt remarks. He shakes his head. "I'm not pandering to an egg, dude."

"Aw, well, that's too bad," Bucky answers smugly. "'Cause tonight's your turn with him."

"No, it's not. It's Conor's," Matty protests.

"Nope. Refer to the schedule." Bucky did a random draw this morning to determine who has custody of the egg and when. My turn is next week.

"This is fucking balls." Matt grabs the plush egg container from Bucky. "Swear to God, I'mma get wasted tonight and eat this motherfuckin' thing."

I'm chuckling as I leave the locker room, with Matt and Bucky in tow. Conor and the others are already gone. We meet up with them again at Malone's, my favorite place in town. Mostly due to its roomy booths, cheap beer, and sports memorabilia all over the walls, which at the moment are shaking from the classic rock song blasting through the bar.

Matt says something, but the loud chatter and blaring music drowns him out. He switches to sign language, nodding toward the bar and making a drinking motion with his hand, signaling he's going over there to order.

My gaze gives the main room a quick sweep, but doesn't land on anyone familiar. I weave through the crowd toward the arched doorway to the adjoining room, which houses the pool tables and some more booths along the wall. I spot a blonde head and then a brunette one. The Betty and Veronica of Briar University.

"There's Brenna and Summer in the middle booth." I raise my voice so Bucky can hear me.

His brown eyes glaze over. "Fuuuuck. She's so hot."

"Who? Brenna? Or Summer?"

"Well, both. But I was talking about Summer. That top she's wearing is...*fuuuuck*," he says again.

Yeah, her skimpy yellow halter top is hot, I have to acknowledge as we near the booth. But I'm gratified that the sight of Summer Di Laurentis no longer elicits a sexual response from me. Even celibate, I don't particularly want to sleep with her.

I had a thing for Summer when she first transferred to Briar, but unfortunately she had a thing for Fitz. And while I still believe my friend was shady in the way he handled the situation, I'm one hundred percent over Summer. She and Fitzy are happy together, and the more time I spend with her living in the same house, the more I realize she's not my type.

Summer's too easy, and I don't mean slutty. She's just not much of a challenge. She's easy to please, easy to figure out. Her transparency was initially why I liked her, but I can't deny it's more fun when a woman poses a bit more of a mystery.

Not that I'm solving any female mysteries any time soon. No sex means limiting my exposure to women, because I know myself. The more time I spend with someone, the more I want to fuck them. My roommates are the exception. And as of Monday, so is Demi Davis.

My new classmate is fun to talk to, but the best thing about her is her boyfriend.

Brenna bolts out of the booth when she spots me. "Hunter! Jesus, what a game!"

"I know, right?"

"You superstar, you." She flings her arms around me, which is way more touchy-feely than Brenna usually is. But then I see the two shot glasses on the tabletop. Ah. She and Summer already started hitting the vodka.

"Seriously, I was on my feet the entire time cheering my lungs out," Brenna raves, and I know it's not just drunken praise. Brenna Jensen is probably the biggest hockey fan (and expert) in this entire bar. She's definitely her father's daughter, even landing an internship at ESPN. She works there on weekends, and afternoons when she doesn't have class.

"That was the ass kicking of the century," Summer agrees. "I wish Fitzy got to see it, but I was live-tweeting the entire time, so he can read the thread later."

I sit next to Brenna. Bucky slides in next to Summer. A minute later Matt reappears with a pitcher and a stack of plastic cups. Malone's has a new Friday night special—half-price pitchers, baby. I don't plan on going overboard tonight, because we have another game tomorrow. But a few beers won't hurt.

"Where's the nutty one?" Matt asks the girls.

"Who? Rupi?" Brenna snickers. "She's at home watching *Glee* reruns."

"Why didn't she come out?"

"She doesn't have a fake ID," I supply. "And she refuses to get one."

Summer speaks up, mimicking Rupi's high voice so flawlessly it's almost like she's in the booth with us. "I can't *break* the *law!* I will wait until I am of *age*, thank you very much!"

Brenna lets out a rueful sigh. "I honestly don't know how Hollis puts up with her. And vice versa."

"For real," Summer agrees. "All they do is scream at each other."

"Or make out," I counter.

"True. They scream or they make out." Summer shakes her head. "There's no in between."

"Is he still coming back on the weekends?" Matt asks, raising his beer to his lips. He takes a sip. "I haven't seen him in ages."

"He's home every weekend," I confirm. "But he spends most of his time with Rupi. Hollis in love is a scary thing to witness, bro. You need to come over this weekend and see it for yourself."

Bucky sets Pablo on the table so he can pour himself a beer. When Summer reaches for the egg, he swiftly smacks her hand away. "Pablo isn't a toy," he scolds.

"It's just an egg."

"*Just* an egg?" Conor drawls, approaching the booth to catch the end of Summer's amused response. "That's our fucking mascot, Di Laurentis. Show some respect."

"Oh, I'm sorry! I didn't mean to insult your *egg*."

He grins, and even Summer can't deny him a response. Her cheeks pinken, and Con's grin widens. Dude's well aware of what his smile does to women. He's probably been harnessing that power since grade school, like one of the X-Men.

But although Summer isn't entirely unaffected, she's still very much unavailable. "Stop smiling at me like that or I'll tell Fitz." She sticks out her tongue. "Then he'll show up at practice and kick your ass."

"I'm not allowed to smile at you? All right, then. How 'bout dancing? Can we dance?"

Summer ponders that. "Sure, that's allowed. But only because I like this song." It's some Taylor Swift track I don't know too well.

She hops up and drags Conor toward the cluster of people gathered near the small stage that's hardly ever used. I don't think I've ever seen a live band grace the stage at Malone's, but the tiny space in front of it is the closest to a dance floor that the bar has.

Brenna's eyes track Conor's easy gait. And his ass. "Geez, that boy is attractive."

"Don't you have a boyfriend?" Matt reminds her.

"So? I'm not allowed to acknowledge someone else is attractive? Come on. *Look* at him."

Matt, Bucky and I turn to scrutinize our teammate. He's got one hand on Summer's slim waist, the other holding his beer as they dance. When he leans in to whisper something in her ear, his gray eyes twinkle devilishly.

I mean, I'm not going to lie. Edwards is hot. We all know it.

"Ugh. Now I feel left out," Brenna whines, and the next thing I know she's shoving me out of the booth and tugging me to my feet. "Come on, hot stuff, dance with me."

Before I can blink, we're across the room and Brenna is squished up against me. And her body is so fire that I forget how to breathe. Skintight jeans are plastered to her long, shapely legs, her dark hair is thick and glossy, and her top is even more indecent than Summer's. So tight it looks like her full tits are trying to escape.

I don't want to touch her. I'm scared that if I do, that if my hands connect with a hint of bare skin or the slightest female curve, I might embarrass myself.

"What's the matter?" Brenna says. "You forget how to move?"

I offer a self-deprecating smile. "Trust me, you don't want me to move."

"Why's that…?" Understanding suddenly dawns. "Ohhh. Because you're out of commission." She purses her lips. "Are you scared that if our bodies touch, you'll get aroused?"

"I already am aroused," I grumble. "*Everything* gets me aroused, Bee. The feel of the wind on my face gets me aroused. Bumping into a table gets me aroused."

She throws her head back and laughs. "Oh, you really are in a state, aren't you?"

I groan. "The worst kind."

"You poor thing." She grabs my hands and plants them on her hips, then loops her arms around my neck.

And yup, my dick cannot distinguish between a girl with a boyfriend and one without. It promptly thickens behind my zipper.

"Fucking hell, Jensen, let's not do this. Please."

"Aw, come on. What's a boner between friends?" She starts moving to the upbeat T-Swift song, except three seconds later it ends and is replaced with that old T.I. track—"Whatever You Like." The one that's all about fucking, with a sultry beat that is way too dangerous for my aching nether regions.

"My boner doesn't understand that you're off-limits," I mutter.

"Can I tell you a secret?" Brenna says, and I almost pass out when she brings her red lips to my ear and seductively whispers in it. "Jake and I have an open relationship."

Immediately, my throat goes dry. "W-what?" I stammer hoarsely.

"I'm just saying..." Her hips sway. "If you ever want to break your vow..."

A bolt of heat shoots up my spine. "What the hell are you saying?"

"You know exactly what I'm saying."

She draws tiny circles on my nape with her fingernails. Meanwhile, T.I. is singing about things being wet and hot and tight and I'm in big trouble.

"Why don't we go home?" she suggests, wrapping her arms tighter around my neck. Our bodies are almost flush now. Her sexy voice is still tickling my ear. "We'll be really, really quiet. Rupi won't hear a thing."

My mouth is sawdust. From the corner of my eye, I catch Summer giving us an odd look. I've given up on dancing because my dick is way too hard. "Are you serious right now?" I demand. Because I don't buy it.

And I'm right not to.

"Oh my God, Hunter. Of *course* I'm not serious." Mischief gleams in her expression.

"So you and Connelly don't have an open relationship?"

"No!"

I stare at her. "What if I'd said yes? What if I'd kissed you?"

"Then Jake would catch the next redeye from Edmonton and your body would probably never be found."

"You're such a bitch," I sigh.

"Sorry." She's still laughing, but she has the decency to sound somewhat repentant. "I couldn't help myself. This celibacy thing of yours is fascinating. But...dude, if you're so hard up that you were actually considering hooking up with *me*? Then I don't know how you're ever gonna survive this."

Me neither.

"Whatever, c'mere," I grumble, tugging her against me. "Let's just dance."

"You sure?"

I nod miserably. "Yeah, why not. What's a boner between friends, right?"

# 7
# DEMI

I FOLLOW NICO INTO THE BUSY BAR. WE'RE MEETING SOME FRIENDS at Malone's, which is the only bar in Hastings.

Nico and I don't come here often; if we're hanging out in town, we usually invite people to Nico's apartment and chill there. But my boyfriend was in the mood to go out tonight, and I wasn't about to complain. Malone's makes the *best* nachos in town. And the best chicken wings. The best burgers. The best—ugh, okay, the entire menu is stellar.

"Do you see Pippa?" I stand on my tiptoes and scan the crowded main room. "She texted that they're in a booth near the—oh, there she is."

Nico follows my gaze. "Who's she with?"

"Looks like Corinne and Darius and—oh wow, TJ actually showed up." I invited him to join us, but I hadn't expected him to come, because TJ's not particularly social. When we go for lunch or to the movies, it tends to be just the two of us. He's not big on crowds or groups.

Nico makes a face at the mention of TJ.

"Be nice," I chide.

"He's a *pendejo*, Demi." My boyfriend always reverts to Spanish when he's dissing someone.

"He is not. He's my friend."

"Friend? C'mon, babe, he's in love with you."

It's not the first time Nico's voiced that sentiment, but I don't believe it to be true. "He's not in love with me."

"Oh really? Then why's he always staring at you with moon eyes?"

"You're imagining it." I shrug. "And even if he *is* in love with me—so what? We both know who *I'm* in love with."

"Damn right we do." Nico curls a hand over the back of my head and pulls me in for a kiss.

To my surprise, he slips me some tongue and the next thing I know we're engaged in a mini make-out session in the middle of the bar. It draws catcalls from a group of guys in hockey jerseys, and I'm blushing as I pull back.

"What was that for?" I smile at my boyfriend.

"Just for being you." Nico takes my hand and brings it up to his lips. Like the Latin heartthrob he is, he brushes a kiss over my knuckles.

He's being extra sweet tonight, and in all honesty I love it. He turned down my sex advances last weekend because he was too tired, and then he bailed on me this week because of his car. I deserve to be spoiled a bit.

"Go join the group. I'll grab us some drinks," Nico offers before heading for the ridiculously long line at the bar.

As I walk toward my friends' booth, I glimpse a familiar face through the doorway that separates the main room with the adjoining one.

Hunter Davenport is dancing with a stunning brunette in a tight tank and blood-red lipstick. He's whispering in her ear. When he lifts his head to look at her, I don't miss the ruddy flush of his cheekbones and his heavy-lidded eyes. Uh-huh. Someone's getting laid tonight.

I wonder how his lunch girl feels about that...

The idea of dating multiple people sounds like a nightmare to me. Although, what sounds even worse is being the girl who is *dating* the guy who's dating multiple people. I'm a possessive bitch, thank you very much. My man's not allowed to see other women when he's with me. And if I ever do wind up having to date again, I'd stake my claim immediately and make sure to have the exclusivity talk before the dude is even allowed to hold my hand.

Like my mom always says, know your worth. Make them work for it.

But to each their own. Hunter clearly has a lot of luck with the ladies. The girl he's dancing with laughs at whatever he just said, and as he shakes his head in amusement, he catches sight of me in the doorway. He dips his chin in greeting.

I blow him a kiss. He grins and refocuses on his date, while I join my friends.

"Demi!" Pippa squeals, jumping out of the booth to throw her arms around me.

"Heya, chica." Pippa is my best friend at Briar. We met at freshman orientation, discovered we both grew up in Florida, and were instantly inseparable.

"Hey," our friend Corinne greets me. "I *love* that skirt."

"Thanks, it's like a million years old." I smooth my hands over the front of my distressed denim skirt. It's autumn, and I'm still wearing short skirts and tank tops. I don't know whether to hate or love global warming.

I lean into the booth to smack a kiss on TJ's cheek. "I can't believe you're here," I tell him. "I'm so glad you came."

He blushes slightly and takes a huge gulp of his beer. Beside him is Darius Johnson, a good friend of mine and Nico's.

"Hi, D," I say.

"Hi, D," he mimics, and we both grin. When we first met, there was a bit of competition about who'd get to keep the nickname, but in the end we decided to share it.

"Where's the rest of the crew?" I ask. Wherever Darius is, there's usually at least three other basketball players not far behind. But they're nowhere to be found tonight.

"Briar won the hockey game," Darius explains. "They didn't want to deal with all the hockey fans. Those guys are nuts."

As if to prove that point, a trio of dudes choose that moment to drunkenly lumber past our booth screaming, "Bri-ar! Bri-ar!" One of them is waving his black-and-silver jersey in the air, which means he's stumbling through the bar shirtless. Classy.

Nico returns with a pink daiquiri for me, and a bottle of beer for himself. It's a Cuban brand that you can rarely find in the States and yet somehow Malone's actually serves it. It makes me smile, because I'm pretty sure my mom is the one who introduced Nico to that beer. I remember she let him taste hers at my fifteenth birthday party. He's been drinking it exclusively ever since.

"What have you been up to this week?" I ask Corinne as I slide in across from her. "You never answered my text about unpacking. Did you still want help?"

"I know, I'm sorry. I was dealing with furniture shit. Moving is the worst," she complains.

Corinne just moved into a one-bedroom apartment in Hastings, only a few blocks from Malone's, in fact. It's rare to find housing in town, but Corinne knew the previous tenant, a fellow Econ major at Briar who abruptly decided to drop out. Corinne had an application in with the landlord of the small building before anyone else even knew the apartment was available.

"Moving isn't *that* bad," Nico teases her. "I mean, especially when you have three strapping young men helping you out." He wiggles his eyebrows.

I snort. Nico and two of his co-workers from the moving company helped Corinne last Sunday, hauling all her boxes and furniture from the house she used to share with five other girls.

"Did the strapping young men take off their shirts and flex their muscles for you?" I ask a blushing Corinne.

She bursts out laughing. "I wish. All they did was drink my beer and get my new carpet all dirty from their boot prints."

"She's lying!" Nico declares good-naturedly. "We wore booties over our shoes."

"And to answer your question," she says to me, running a hand through her mop of dark curls, "yes. I totally need help organizing everything. Maybe one night this week?"

"Sure. Just let me know when." I met Corinne through Pippa, and although we've never been as close, I like hanging out with her. She's a bit guarded, but when she relaxes she's actually pretty hilarious.

Nico takes a swig of beer before setting down the bottle and slinging his arm around me. He's so handsy tonight. He leans in and plants soft kisses on my neck until Pippa releases a loud groan.

"Come on, guys, enough with the PDA. You *just* got here. At this rate you'll be banging on the table by the end of the night."

"Sounds hot," Nico says, winking at me.

Lord, he is so good-looking. Originally from Cuba, Nico and his family came to Miami when Nico was eight. They moved in next door, and all it took was one look at Nico's soulful eyes and big dimples, and eight-year-old Demi was in love. Luckily, he felt the same way about me.

We talk about our classes for a bit, but I don't contribute much to the conversation. Truth be told, I hate all my courses this semester, except for Psych. Today in Organic Chemistry, we discussed organometallic compounds in such detail that my brain almost melted. I didn't mind my science classes in high school, but since I started college I'm slowly beginning to hate the sciences.

As I sip my drink, I absently listen to Nico and Darius chat about the basketball team. D is trying to convince Nico to be their equipment manager because their current one just bailed, but Nico's too busy with his work and class schedule. TJ remains quiet for most of the conversation, only speaking when I draw him out of his shell.

I don't care what Nico says. TJ's a sweetie. He's such a great listener, and he usually dispenses really solid advice. I wish he'd find a girlfriend, but he's so shy and it's hard for him to open up. I tried setting him up with one of my sorority sisters once, and she said he barely spoke a single word during their entire date.

"I'll be your equipment manager," Pippa tells D. "But only if I get to watch you guys shower. I feel like that's a reasonable requirement for—oh my God." She stops midsentence, gaping at the tall guy who saunters past our booth. "Forget it. I want to watch *him* shower."

I only manage to catch a glimpse before he passes. Shoulder-length blond hair, a red T-shirt. I twist around but can't see his face. His body is banging, though.

"Eyes up here," Nico chides, lifting two fingers up to his face.

I grin. "Oh, come on. Look at his butt. It's something else."

My boyfriend peeks out the booth just as the guy disappears through the corridor to the restrooms. "It's a'ight," he relents. "But that doesn't mean you're allowed to check him out."

"What are you gonna do, spank me?"

His chocolate-brown eyes narrow seductively. "Don't tempt me, *mami.*"

Corinne gives a slight cough, while Pippa and Darius sigh dramatically.

"Sorry," I tell everyone. "We'll be good now, I swear."

"I don't want to be good," Pippa announces. "I want to be bad with that hottie. Who *was* that?"

TJ speaks up. "Hockey player, I think. He came from the hockey booth, at least."

"The hockey booth?" she echoes.

He nods toward the other room, where Hunter Davenport and his friends are piled into two huge booths. All I see are gorgeous girls, big athlete types, and a lot of food.

Speaking of food...

"Who wants nachos?" I ask as I grab the menu in front of Darius. "I'm ordering some for me, but I'm also thinking—ooh, there's a new app on here. Deep-fried spinach and mozzarella balls. Oh my fuck, yes. I'm in. I'll get an order of those, and then we're looking at the nachos, and maybe…the boneless wings?"

"Who is she even talking to?" Pippa asks my boyfriend.

He sighs. "Just let it happen, Pips. You know the drill."

I peer up from the menu. "Am I being judged right now?"

"Yes," Pippa tells me.

"One hundred percent, yes," Darius concurs.

"How do you eat so much and never gain weight?" Corinne demands.

"I'd never judge you," TJ assures me, grinning mischievously.

"*Thank* you, Thomas Joseph. The rest of you, guess what? You don't get to taste my spinach balls. You can sit here in envy while—"

"He's coming back," hisses Pippa.

Sure enough, the hockey player in the red shirt strides by again. This time I do see his face, and promptly understand why Pippa is drooling all over the table. He's got vivid gray eyes, and a beautiful smile that curves his mouth when he catches Pippa's gaze on him. He keeps walking, though.

"Oh my," I murmur, and Nico pokes me in the ribs.

"Definitely a hockey guy," TJ confirms with a nod. "But I can't remember his name."

"Hold on, I'll find out." I slide my phone out of my purse.

"What do you mean, you'll find out?" Pippa squawks.

I pull up Hunter's name in my contacts list. We exchanged numbers at my house on Monday night.

**ME**: Hey, hockey man. Who's the dude in the red t-shirt with the fuck-me face and tight ass?

Although I crane my neck toward the other room, I can't pick out Hunter amidst the sea of jocks. But on my phone screen three gray bubbles pop up to indicate a response is being typed.

"Who are you texting?" Nico demands.

"Hunter Davenport."

TJ looks up sharply. "You're texting Davenport?"

"Yeah, we're working on that project, remember? I have his number."

"Who's Hunter Davenport?" Corinne asks.

"Just a hockey player who thinks he's God's gift to the world," TJ tells her, smiling wryly.

"You don't even know him," I tease.

"I had a tutorial with him last year, remember? He treated the library like his own personal motel?"

I don't answer because Hunter's message just appeared.

> **HUNTER**: Conor Edwards. Right-winger, #62. Why? You want his number?? Are we cheating on the boyfriend??? Tsk tsk.

Nobody's cheating on anyone, I type back, and when I sense Nico reading over my shoulder, I hammer the point home by adding, I love my boyfriend very VERY much.

Nico relaxes and drops a kiss atop my head.

> **ME**: A friend of mine is eyeing him. Is he single?
> **HUNTER**: Ya but I think he's already picked his flavor for the night. I'll come over and introduce them if you want?

I glance at Pippa. "You want an intro?"

Her jaw falls open again. "What! *No.* He's way too good-looking."

"You sure?" I wave my phone enticingly at her. "I got you an in."

"Am I *sure?* I've got a zit on my forehead and haven't washed my hair in four days, because I wasn't planning on meeting *Adonis* tonight. Come on, Demi, what the fuck is wrong with you?"

I snicker and text Hunter back.

**ME**: Maybe another night.

He responds with, Okey dokey, and the gray dots disappear.

"Coward," I tease Pippa.

"Whatever. You can't throw something like that on me at the last second. I'm not mentally prepared to hook up tonight."

I hadn't realized mental preparation was required for casual hook-ups, but I suppose I'm clueless when it comes to modern dating. And I'm perfectly okay with that. Look at what's happening around me—Hunter juggling different girls, Pippa squirming nervously at the notion of being introduced to a hot guy. Dating seems insanely stressful.

Relationships, meanwhile, are nice and secure. The world of relationships is where I belong.

I link my fingers through Nico's and thank my lucky stars that I'm not part of that other, terrifying world.

# 8
# DEMI

Nico walks me to class on Monday morning. He'd spent the night, and I feel like we're back on track again as we stroll hand-in-hand down one of the many walkways that weave through Briar. Although the weather hasn't turned yet, the colors on campus are slowly beginning to change. I admire the massive trees that line the paths and dot the lawns, marveling at how pretty and quaint everything is. Sometimes it feels surreal. I lived in Miami until I was fifteen years old, so I'm accustomed to palm trees and colorful beach houses, not stately oaks and ancient buildings.

I remember putting up a huge stink when I found out we were moving to Massachusetts. My father had been offered a position at a prestigious hospital in Boston. Head of neurosurgery. Which is a HUGE DEAL. But I was a bratty, entitled teenager, and therefore I wasn't having it.

Dad, however, doesn't tolerate temper tantrums. Or rather, he lets me stomp and yell and bitch…and then offers a wry smile and pleasantly asks, *Are you done?* Because we all know he's going to get his way at the end of the day. He does the same thing with my mother. Mom personifies the stereotype of feisty Latina, complete with a generations-old family hot sauce recipe and a temper that's even more explosive than mine. But even Mom can't win against my father.

I peer down at the ground. Well, this is a dilemma.

"Hold up there, girly girl." To my surprise, big tough Hockey Man strips out of his long-sleeved shirt, leaving himself in a tight wife-beater. He stretches the thin material of his shirt out on the grass. "My lady," he says graciously.

"Aw, thanks. That was surprisingly nice of you." I sit down, then lean back on my elbows and tip my head to gaze at the canopy of green above me.

"Why surprisingly?" Hunter demands.

"You didn't strike me as the chivalrous type."

"So you thought I was an asshole? Also, why do you think I'm hooking up with three chicks?" He sounds genuinely confused.

"Oh come on, don't play dumb." I proceed to tick them off with my fingers. "The girl who brought you lunch last week and practically begged you to love her. The one you were dancing with at Malone's. The one today, with the blonde hair and supermodel face…?"

Hunter starts to laugh. It's a deep husky sound that tickles my ears. "I'm not hooking up with any of them. They're my roommates."

"Your roommates?" I echo doubtfully.

"Yeah. The loud one is dating one of my friends, the blonde is dating another one of my friends, and the brunette from the bar has a boyfriend. And I live with all three of them."

"You live with three women?"

"Originally it was me, Hollis and Fitz, but they both graduated and somehow it was decided that Summer, Rupi, and Brenna would move in. No house meeting, no discussion, nothing. Nobody even asked for my opinion. Not that I'm complaining."

"You *are* complaining."

Hunter grumbles irritably. "Fine, I'm complaining. The girls are great, but I would've liked it if some of my other teammates had moved in instead. But this arrangement is more convenient for Hollis and Fitz. Hollis comes home on the weekends, and Fitz technically

Grinning, Nico gives me a peck on the lips. "A'ight, I got to go. I'll see you later, *mami*."

"Bye, babe."

"Doesn't *mami* mean *mother*?" Hunter inquires after Nico leaves. He furrows his brow.

"Well, yeah, that's the literal translation, but it's also a term of endearment. Mami, papi—it's like babe or sweetheart or whatever."

"Huh. Okay." Hunter pauses. "I give you permission to start calling me Big Daddy, then."

"Gross. Never."

He's chuckling as we enter the building. TJ waits at the door of the classroom, uneasiness flickering through his eyes when he sees me with Hunter.

"Hey. Where's Pax?" I ask, glancing around.

"No idea." TJ gives me a side hug and a peck on the cheek.

"Let's go in," I say.

Inside the lecture hall, TJ takes the seat beside me, while Hunter flops down on my other side. TJ raises a brow at the intrusion. We don't usually sit with other people. I just shrug and grin at him. I find Hunter amusing.

The room fills up and Professor Andrews arrives. Pax is still nowhere to be seen.

"Did Pax text you?" I ask TJ.

"Nope."

"Who's this Pax?" Hunter butts into the conversation.

"He's a friend of ours," I answer. "You talked to him last week—you called him Jax?"

"Oh, right. Jax. That little dude is hilarious."

"His name's Pax," I say in exasperation.

"Pax," TJ confirms.

Hunter chews on his bottom lip for a moment. "Are you sure?"

"Yes!" I can't control a burst of laughter. "His name is Pax Ling."

"Nah, I'm pretty sure he told me it was Jax. We must be talking about different dudes."

This guy's unreal.

TJ gives a soft snicker. Apparently even he isn't immune to Hunter's weird appeal.

Andrews commences the morning's lecture, which is an overview of personality disorders. Excellent. I'm happy we're starting off with PDs. I'm still trying to diagnose my fictional patient, and based on the notes I made during our first session I suspect I'm dealing with a personality issue.

He could be a sociopath, but the characteristic apathy was missing. Antisocial or narcissistic personality disorders are still on the table, and maybe borderline too, although Hunter hadn't described any mood swings or impulsive behavior, unless you count adultery. But his fake cheating came off as incredibly calculated and not at all impulsive. Hopefully he gives me more to work with in our next session.

Halfway through class, my phone vibrates.

**PAX**: Partied too hard last night and overslept. Take notes for me!

My nosy seatmate Hunter peers over my shoulder. "Is that Jax?"

"No, it's Pax."

"Agree to disagree."

I fight a smile and turn my attention back to Professor Andrews. She's discussing a case involving antisocial personality disorder she once encountered and how she reached the diagnosis. I'm obsessed with this course.

After class, TJ links an arm through mine and says, "Want to grab a quick coffee?"

"Actually"—I glance at Hunter—"maybe we could work on the project for a bit? I'm not meeting Nico till one thirty."

He shrugs. "Sure, let's do it. I'm done for the day."

"Rain check on that coffee," I assure TJ, giving his arm

"No prob. Text me later."

As TJ ambles off, Hunter stares after him, shaking ruefully. "Poor guy."

"What does that mean?"

"It means, poor guy. He's got a major crush on you, b deep in the friend zone it'd take the same rescue team tha the Chilean miners to save him. And even then I think the

"He doesn't have a crush on me," I insist. What is everyo that I'm not? "I've had a boyfriend for as long as I've knowr

"So? I've had crushes on lots of chicks with boyfriends doesn't discriminate."

"Yeah, I've noticed," I say dryly.

"What does that mean?" he mimics.

"It means in the one measly week I've known you, yo hooked up with three different women. Congrats, your pe be extremely pleased."

"Oh, trust me, my penis is nowhere close to pleased." I hand through his dark hair. "You want to go to your house

"Why don't we find a nice spot on the quad?" I suggest. a gorgeous day."

"Lead the way, Semi."

We follow the wide stone path toward one of t manicured lawns that make up Briar's campus. We're not ones taking advantage of the warm weather. There are sever in progress, a soccer ball being kicked around, and a game being played in the distance.

We stop underneath a towering tree, its branches droo one side like a waterfall. It provides a small pocket of shad up by rays of sunlight that slice through the gaps in the Normally I'd plop right down on the grass, but my short shade of beige that won't hide any potential grass stains.

# 9
# HUNTER

I SLIDE INTO MY LAND ROVER AND INSTANTLY CRANK THE A/C. Christ, how is it still so hot outside when we're halfway through September? Don't get me wrong, I hope it never ends, but I'm actually sweating after spending the past hour in the quad with Demi.

I drive out of the student lot and back to Hastings, where I speed past my residential street to another one a couple of blocks away.

I wasn't kidding when I told Demi I wish that someone had consulted me about the girls moving into the townhouse. I have nothing against them, but I'm in college, dammit. I want to hang out with the guys. I'm not in the market for a girlfriend this year and there's no reason why I should know so much about eucalyptus facemasks and what kind of tampons everyone in my house uses. Also, Rupi's and Brenna's cycles somehow synced up so now they get their periods at the same time. They're really mean when that happens.

I park in the driveway behind the beat-up Jeep that Matt shares with Conor. They're housemates, along with our teammate Foster and two seniors named Gavin and Alec.

When Matty answers the door, I welcome the familiar sounds of guys insulting each other and video game controllers clicking, and the aroma of pizza and stale beer when it's barely noon. This is college.

"Hey," I greet everyone in the living room.

Foster is sprawled in the armchair, balancing a beer can on his knee. Gavin and Alec are battling it out in a shooter game. The only notable absence is Conor, who's probably in class.

I'm not sure whose turn it is with Pablo Eggscobar, but he's on the coffee table in the drink-cozy harness that Bucky made for him, and he's rocking a new look. Someone used a black Sharpie to draw eyes and a snout right above Coach Jensen's scrawl, and voila—Pablo now has a pig face with Jensen's signature serving as his mouth.

Truthfully, I'm surprised he's still in one piece. Drunken college guys aren't exactly conducive to egg rearing.

"What's up, Pablo?" I greet the egg. He doesn't answer, because he's not real, but hey, at least I'm trying to make an effort.

Captain handbook rule number a thousand: *pick your battles*.

"Who's playing egg mom today?" I ask.

"Con. But he just went upstairs with some chick, so we're waiting for the right moment." Matt settles on the couch.

I flop down on the other end. "The right moment for what?"

Matt and Foster exchange evil grins. "For feeding time. Pablo is about to be hungry as fuck."

Gavin snorts without looking away from the TV screen.

I stifle a sigh. According to my sources, things have escalated since last week. Jesse Wilkes texted me yesterday bitching about how the other guys wouldn't stop calling him when he was out with Katie. It's officially become a game to inconvenience the egg carrier as much as possible.

"How long's it been?" Alec asks, his fingers moving like lightning over the game controller.

"Only about ten minutes," Foster replies. "They're probably still on foreplay."

"Hers," Gavin guesses.

"Or he's getting blown," Matt counters.

They all go quiet for a moment.

"Nah," Foster finally says, raising his beer to his lips. "He goes down on her first, then she blows him, then they fuck. That's the order of sex."

I start to laugh. "Oh really? Is that what the manual says?"

Matt snickers.

"That's the order I do it in," Alec chimes in. "Why? What do *you* do?"

"I don't fucking know. I don't chart out my sexual encounters like I'm exploring undiscovered islands in the Maldives." I roll my eyes. "There's no set order. You just see how it plays out."

"It always plays out the same way," Alec says stubbornly.

"It's true," Foster agrees. "Usually goes that way for me, too."

"Huh. Weird." When I think back on past hook-ups, they're honestly different every time.

Sometimes we stumble into my room and she's on her knees with my dick in her mouth before I can blink. Once I was with a girl who wanted to kiss for all of three seconds before she turned around and offered me her ass, ordering me to screw her from behind. Longer sessions have begun with me kissing every inch of their bodies, or vice versa. Sometimes we even start with sex and end with foreplay.

"I don't know what you guys are doing, but I can't find a pattern in my hook-ups," I admit.

"Maybe it's a girlfriend thing," Foster suggests. "I dated the same chick all throughout high school and I'm using her as my point of reference."

"Three years with Sasha for me," Alec says with a nod, referring to his current girlfriend.

"Oh, it's definitely a girlfriend thing," Matt confirms. "Like, with Jesse. He and Katie have the most predictable sex life ever. When we were rooming together in the dorms last year, every time they put that stupid sock on the door I knew they'd need exactly forty-seven minutes to bang. I could probably plot out the exact time of orgasm."

"Sounds kinda boring." Although maybe having sex with

someone you're madly in love with feels different somehow? I have no idea. I had a few girlfriends in high school, but none of them were ever *the one.*

"Okay. It's been twenty-one minutes," Foster announces. "He's either balls deep right now or she's got her mouth full. Either way, the dick is in play. I repeat, the dick is in play."

"You jackasses are the worst. As team captain, I should stop this," I warn.

They all wait expectantly.

A slow grin stretches my mouth. On the other hand, Conor gets so much action his ego could probably use some coitus interruptus. "But I won't. Go ahead. Do it."

Foster and Alec sprint up the narrow staircase. A moment later their heavy footsteps thud on the ceiling. Incessant pounding reverberates through the house as their fists attack Conor's bedroom door. It sounds like a SWAT team breaking into a crack den.

"Pablo's hungry!" Foster shouts.

"*Feed me,*" Alec hollers.

On the other end of the sofa, Matt is shuddering from laughter.

An even louder commotion ensues. Angry cursing rings in the air, followed by the frantic footsteps of two huge hockey players racing down the stairs. Conor is on their tail, bare-chested, barefoot, with a pair of plaid boxers haphazardly sagging off one hip. His blond hair sticks up and his lips are a bit swollen.

"You fucking assholes," he growls.

"What?" Foster blinks innocently. He gestures to the coffee table. "Our pig needs his lunch. We have a *pet,* bro. Pet comes before pussy."

"Pet before pussy," Matt echoes.

Gavin tears his eyes off the video game and nods gravely. "The wise words of Thomas Jefferson."

"I fed him this morning," Conor protests.

Foster glares. "He eats three meals a day, you selfish jackass. Look at him—he's starving."

I glance at the egg and his stupid face, then bury my own face in my hands and quiver in silent laughter.

"Davenport!" Conor barks. "You're team captain. I'm filing a complaint against them."

I lift my head, lips still twitching. "What's the complaint?"

He jabs the air with his index finger. "I was fucking."

"That's not a complaint. It's a statement of fact."

Foster crosses his arms over his bulky chest. "Don't forget—you gotta take five whole minutes to make sure he eats all his food."

A vein throbs in Con's forehead as he snatches Pablo off the table. It looks like he's about to whip the egg against the wall, but at the last second he curses under his breath and spins around. Low mumbling comes from the kitchen.

I gape at Matt. "He's not going to prepare actual food, is he?"

"Nah, it's not in the rules."

"What exactly *are* the rules?"

"They're whatever we make them," Foster replies with a grin. "But basically, five minutes are required whenever Pablo is in play."

"But you can't abuse the system," Matt says.

"What system?" I sputter. "It's all nonsense."

"He eats three times a day, shits twice a day, and requires attention whenever one of us is bored and wants to harass whoever has him."

"But you can't play the attention card more than a few times a day," Foster adds. "With that said, texting between the hours of one and five a.m. is highly encouraged."

"This is all very reasonable," Alec tells me. "What aren't you getting?"

"Are you gonna do this to me when I have him?" I shudder. My turn is on Friday.

"Nah, we would never do that to you," Foster assures me.

The others chime in.

"Never."

"Of course not."

"Never do that to our captain."

Goddamn liars.

––––––––––––

On Thursday night, Demi and I manage to squeeze in a second study session for the week. Once again, we convene in her bedroom at the Theta house. She's sitting cross-legged on the purple bedspread, sucking on a grape lollipop. I'm sprawled on her little couch, regaling her with a juicy new tale in the sordid history of Dick Smith.

"So she promised to pick up a strawberry cheesecake along with the usual pumpkin pie. Meanwhile, everything else was coming together beautifully. The catering staff was top-notch. The table was set with the crystal my grandparents gave us as a wedding present. We had family coming in from Palm Springs and Manhattan. Thanksgiving in the Hamptons is always an important event."

Demi observes me carefully. I know she's trying to figure out where I'm going with this.

"But the pièce de résistance was going to be the strawberry cheese-cake," I brag. "That was the first cake my parents ever sold when they opened that original little bakery on Burton Street, which they turned into a massive dessert empire. It was perfect—Mother would be so touched that I remembered, that I'd gone out of my way to please her. God knows my brother Geoffrey doesn't care about her happiness."

Demi's lollipop pokes into the inside of her cheek. "Is this typical for you, taking great pains to seek the approval of your mother?"

"It had nothing to do with approval. I just told you, I wanted to make Mother happy."

"I see."

I huff in annoyance. "Anyway. Dinner was spectacular, and then it was time for dessert, and you know what happened? The servers come out with a fucking pumpkin pie and nothing else. No cheesecake. I was forced to paste a smile on my face, but inside I was seething. Kathryn apologized after dinner and insisted that all the bakeries in the area were either closed or sold out, but a fucking apology didn't help me in the moment. She made me look bad in front of the whole family, and then goddamn Geoff made a joke about pumpkin pie and how original that was, and I wanted to clock him. Happy Thanksgiving, right?"

There's a beat of silence. I glance over to find Demi shrewdly inspecting me.

"Wow," she says slowly. "There's a lot to unpack here. I guess my first question is—if all the bakeries were closed for the holiday, do you think it's fair to blame your wife for not being able to get the cheesecake?"

"She could've picked it up the day before," I say coldly. "There was no excuse."

She shakes her head a couple times, as if jarred out of the charade. "Jeez. You're good at this," she remarks.

I give an awkward shrug. "Right? You think I should quit hockey and get into acting?" It's a lame joke.

The actual punch line is, it's not a joke at all. The story I just told is the unfiltered truth. The only part I left out was how the asshole's son endured weeks and weeks of obnoxious boasting about that stupid strawberry cheesecake prior to Thanksgiving, and then years of bitter griping about the pumpkin pie following it.

Yup, that's my father for you, doesn't give a shit about anybody but himself. He wanted to look good and one-up his brother, and fuck all the closed bakeries and my horrible selfish mother for depriving him of his needs. Poor Mom was walking on eggshells for months afterward. That man is impossible to please.

When I opened my "PATIENT" envelope last week and saw the disorder I'd been assigned, I'd almost laughed out loud. Hardly any research required, as I'm wholly familiar with the symptoms and how it manifests. I've lived with it my entire life.

"Why was it so important for you to look good in front of your family?" Dr. Demi asks.

"What do you mean?"

She rephrases. "What was supposed to be a happy family gathering turned into a competition between you and your brother. I'm simply wondering why you engaged in it?"

"*I* don't turn shit into a competition, *he* does. He's jealous of me because I'm older and more successful. And, what, I'm supposed to let myself be humiliated when he tries to put me down? No way. I'm going to fight back."

"I see." A pause. "Do you feel like you have unreasonably high expectations of the people in your life, or an average level of expectation?"

I wonder what conclusions she's reaching. It's evident that Demi is highly intelligent. That's just one of the many reasons I enjoy hanging out with her. The main reason is that she's easy to talk to, and there's no pressure whatsoever to be anything but platonic. She has a boyfriend who she clearly loves, so there's no temptation on my end. Sure, her body is hot as fuck, and she has a habit of wearing tight tops that hug her perky tits and bare her midriff, but I'm able to admire her without fantasizing about tearing her clothes off.

Demi jots down more notes, then says, "Kay, let's finish up. I've got dinner plans with Nico. But I think I'm starting to form an idea about your diagnosis."

"This really is fun," I admit. The irony is not lost on me that I'm having a good time describing—in detail—the way my father's brain works.

Dad isn't my favorite person, but I don't typically complain about him to anyone. My whole life, I just went along with the cookie-cutter perfect family thing we've got going on. Anything else would've felt self-indulgent. I mean, I'm a rich dude who grew up in Greenwich and attended elite private schools. Other people have it worse. Some of them suffer from actual physical abuse, which is far worse than simply being unable to meet the unrealistic standards of an egomaniac.

Nevertheless, it is fascinating to describe these events of my childhood from Dad's point of view. I don't know if I'm hitting the right notes, but more research on the subject will probably help me zero in on specific thought patterns.

"I'll see you next week," I tell Demi. "But I don't think I'm available on Monday, though."

"How about mid-week?"

"I should be around on Wednesday night. But not the weekend— we're playing three games."

"Okay, possibly Wednesday night," she says, "but that's usually my gym day."

"You go to the gym?"

"Of course. Why do you think I look this good?"

Naturally, my gaze is pulled right back to her tight, petite body. She can't be taller than five-three, but, man, her legs seem endless. Long and tanned and bare in her tiny denim shorts. I bet her ass is taut and perfect, a perfect little handful.

Oh shit.

It's happening.

I'm fantasizing about her.

*Abort, dude, abort!*

"Anyway." I wrench my gaze away, but not before she catches me.

"Oh my God, stop it. You're not allowed to look at me like that," Demi orders. "You're a monk, remember?"

"I wasn't looking at you like anything," I lie.

"Bullshit. You were giving me the Penis Eyes."

"I was not. Trust me, smoldering looks aren't my go-to move." I smirk. "If I was making a real move on you, you wouldn't be telling me to stop."

"You have an actual *move*?" A delighted smile lights up Demi's pretty face. Her skin is incredible. Glowing and flawless, and I don't think she's even wearing makeup. "Show me!"

"No."

"Please?"

"No," I growl. "You're not allowed to see my move."

"Why not?" she whines.

"Two reasons—you have a boyfriend, and I'm a monk."

"Fine. But for the record, I'm betting your move is lamer than lame." Grinning, she opens the top drawer of her desk. After some fumbling, her hand emerges with another lollipop. Cherry, this time. Or maybe strawberry.

"I think you're a sugar addict," I inform her.

"Nah, I just like having things in my mouth."

"Nope, not even touching that statement."

She glares at me. "It's called an oral fixation, Hunter. It's quite common."

"Uh-huh. If you say so."

And despite my best efforts to forget all about this conversation, thoughts of Demi and her oral fixation follow me all the way home and consume my sexed-up brain. And the next thing I know I'm locking the bathroom door and stepping into the shower, a tight fist around an erection hard enough to slice a slab of marble in half.

It's happening again.

I'm fantasizing about Demi Davis, and this time I ain't stopping it.

I picture her plump lips wrapped around that red lollipop, except within seconds the lollipop is replaced with the head of my cock. I'm nudging it between those sexy lips, and her tongue instantly darts out for a taste, because she's so hungry for it.

"*Mmmm*," I imagine her murmuring. "*Tastes like candy.*" And I imagine myself saying that her pussy probably tastes even sweeter, which makes her moan and the throaty sound travels the length of my shaft and tightens my balls.

"Goddamn." My hoarse expletive echoes in the shower stall. I rest my forearm against the tiled wall as I work myself over with fast, desperate strokes. My dick is so hard it hurts. The steam in the bathroom makes it difficult to breathe. As I start fucking my own fist, my forehead sags against my arm and I suck in gulps of heated oxygen.

Oh man, this feels good. My cheesy scripted fantasy has dissolved in the steamy air. Now I'm stroking my cock to random images that flash through my mind—Demi sucking on me, Demi's cleavage spilling from those tight tops she wears, her tanned legs…spreading for me. Ah hell, I wonder what noises she makes when she comes—

I go off like a bottle rocket. Holy *hell*. My hips grow still as a rush of hot pleasure surges through my body. I shoot in my own hand, breathing hard, black dots flashing in my field of vision and my cock tingling wildly.

I feel only slightly guilty that I fantasized about Demi. And I think she'd forgive me if I told her. I mean, it was bound to happen. I'm in dire straits, five endless months without sex. By the end of the month, I'll be jerking it to fantasies of Mike Hollis.

I'm starting to get genuinely concerned for my sanity.

Loud pounding rattles the doorframe.

Startled, I almost wipe out in the tub.

"*Hunter!*" Rupi shrieks. "Get out of there already. You'll use up all the hot water and I want to shower before bed!"

A groan lodges in my throat, which feels raw and achy from all the heavy panting I just did. I'm still gripping my dick, but it's rapidly softening because that's what Rupi's voice does to penises.

"Go away," I growl at the door, but there's no negotiating with terrorists. If I don't submit to her demands, she'll probably go find a YouTube video on lock-picking, bust open the door, and forcibly pull me out of the shower.

I hate my roommates.

# 10
# DEMI

I don't have class on Wednesdays, so I spend the morning studying for a bio test and completing a math assignment. This semester's workload is nearly double the previous year's, so I'm now waking up an hour earlier every day in the hopes that it'll help me stay on top of my classes.

And if I'm not already stressed enough, my father has decided that I should get a head start on studying for the MCAT exam. Last night he even sent a text offering to hire me a tutor. I told him I'd think about it.

Really, though, I just need to think of a diplomatic way to say, *Please, for the love of God, don't make me study for med school yet or I'll never survive junior year.*

In the afternoon, I hang out with Corinne at her new apartment in Hastings, helping her organize her closet. At my house in Boston, I have a sweet walk-in that's categorized by both color and style. My levels of anxiety reduce drastically when everything is neat and tidy.

"Thanks so much for doing this," Corinne says, a bit shyly.

I slide a heavy cable-knit sweater onto a hanger. "Of course. You know this kind of stuff is my jam. Plus we're friends. Friends don't let friends clean closets alone."

Her answering smile is brimming with gratitude.

Corinne's a tough nut to crack sometimes. She's very pretty, and there's a constant stream of guys chasing after her, but she's selective about who she dates. She's antisocial, quiet at times, but her sarcasm is top-notch and when she relaxes her guard she's a lot of fun.

"This apartment is super cute," I tell her. "I love how massive the bedroom is." It's almost as big as my room at the sorority house, and I lucked out in the random draw and snagged the master.

My phone buzzes on Corinne's double bed. I grab it and discover a message from Hunter.

**HUNTER**: Did you watch the Bruins game last night??

In one of our previous text exchanges, he'd been raving about some game on TV, and I'd mentioned I'd be sure to start watching hockey. I don't think he picked up on the sarcasm.

**ME**: Oh ya! It was INTENSE! I can't believe that player scored nineteen points!!!
**HIM**: You didn't watch it, did you?
**ME**: No. Sorry. Told you, I don't care for hockey.
**HIM**: I expected more from my therapist. Goodbye.

There's a long pause.

**HUNTER**: Fuck, wait, I texted for a reason. We still holding our session at the gym today?
**ME**: Yep. After I'm done with dinner. So around 8? Oh, and make sure you're wearing tight spandex pants so I can objectify you.
**HIM**: Obvs.

I grin at the screen.

"The hockey player again?" Corinne asks.

"Yeah." Chuckling, I shake my head indulgently. "He's so full of himself. But really hot. I'd set you up with him, but he doesn't have sex."

"Wait, what?"

"He's practicing abstinence for a while." I hope it's not a secret, but just in case, I don't offer any further details. "Hey, what's your Wi-Fi network? I'm trying to join it."

"Oh, I haven't set up the Wi-Fi yet. They're coming on Friday to do it."

I'm about to put my phone away when another message comes in.

**TJ**: Are we still on for dinner?
**ME**: Oh yeah. Sushi baby!!!!

I punctuate that with three fish emojis. TJ counters with a couple of shrimp, and then we're sending each other random sea-life emojis that make me giggle.

**ME**: Did you realize there's no lobster emoji?? WTH!

TJ doesn't respond, so I set the phone down and begin folding the pile of T-shirts on Corinne's mattress. "I feel like these should all go in your dresser," I suggest. "Hanging T-shirts is a waste of hangers."

"Agreed. Let's hang the stuff that might wrinkle, and then dresses, skirts—"

My phone buzzes again. TJ just sent a picture of a cartoon lobster with hearts in his eyes, and a speech bubble above his head that reads: "I WANT TO GET MY CLAWS INTO YOU!"

I burst out laughing. "Sorry," I tell Corinne. "TJ is sending memes."

"You have like a gazillion male friends. Meanwhile, I can't even deal with one." She shakes her head. "I don't know how you do it. All those fragile egos... They're all just little boys in need of attention."

She gasps in delight. "You know who you are? You're Wendy with all the Lost Boys!"

"Sounds about right," I say dryly. "But I love my Lost Boys. They're a constant source of entertainment." I fold another T-shirt. "TJ and I are grabbing dinner in town tonight. We're trying out the new Japanese place that opened across from the theater. Wanna come?"

"I can't. I'm hosting a study group here later. It's just you and TJ? No Nico?"

"Nico is playing basketball with Darius and then meeting up with some guys from work for drinks. You probably met them when they helped you move."

"I met two." She thinks it over. "One was really cute, and one was really bald."

I snicker. "The bald one is Steve, and I think the cute one…it was probably Roddy? Short for Rodrigo. But I think he has a girlfriend."

"Bummer."

"Yeah right. You don't even want a boyfriend."

"True."

I carry the stack of neatly folded shirts to Corinne's second-hand wooden dresser. "Come on, let's put all this random stuff away and then dive back into the closet. The closet is the fun part."

"The things that bring you joy…" She sighs. "You're so fucking weird, Demi."

I spend a couple more hours with Corinne, then walk the short distance into the heart of town. TJ meets me at the sushi place, which ends up being phenomenal, so naturally I text my boyfriend all about it on the Uber ride back to campus, because good food gets me excited and when I'm excited I must share it with Nico.

**NICO**: I think u devalue the currency of the orgasm whenever u call a meal "orgasmic."

**ME**: Well, I think you underappreciate good food. And that's practically a crime b/c you're Cuban and food is in your blood.

**HIM**: Nah.

**ME**: I'm telling your mom you said that.

**HIM**: Don't u dare.

**ME**: I'm hitting the gym soon. Be home around 9. Wanna come by after you're done with the boys?

**HIM**: Prolly not, bb. Think we're gonna go back to Steve's and have a Fortnite marathon.

I'm only a smidge disappointed. We didn't have plans, so I can't fault him for wanting to continue hanging out with his friends, the people he originally had plans with.

**ME**: OK. Have fun! Love you.

**NICO**: Love u too bb <3 <3 <3 <3

---

"I miss blowjobs," Hunter declares at the gym an hour later.

The forlorn assertion triggers a burst of laughter from me, which nearly results in me tripping on the treadmill. It's been a week since we've seen each other, and obviously his monk status is still solidly intact.

"I'm sorry to hear that," I tell him.

"Don't apologize to me, apologize to my dick."

Snorting, I dip my gaze south. Not gonna lie—his package is kind of impressive beneath his black track pants. I make a magnanimous gesture at his crotch. "I'm sincerely sorry for your recent troubles, Hunter's dick."

Hunter's dick's owner nods soberly. "He appreciates the sentiment."

This fucking guy. He is either the best or the worst. I still haven't decided.

With that said, he's definitely the worst gym buddy. For the past forty minutes, we've been side-by-side on our respective treadmills without altering the brisk pace. But now I'm waning. It's an admission of defeat when I flick my finger on the incline button to make the workout a bit easier.

Mr. Hockey Star has barely broken a sweat. A slight sheen coats his forehead and that's about it. Meanwhile, I'm a sweaty mess. Thank God I'm not romantically interested in him, otherwise I'd be incredibly self-conscious and embarrassed about perspiring this much. Even Nico hasn't seen me at my sweatiest.

"Aww, does someone need a break?" Hunter mocks.

"Nope, just a flatter path."

"Wimp."

"Monk."

"You gotta stop using that as an insult. *Some* people consider my celibacy admirable."

"Says the guy who's moaning about missing blowjobs."

"Oh, like you wouldn't miss it if the boyfriend stopped going down on you."

"Not really," I say before I can stop myself. And I regret it instantly. I'm not a fan of locker room talk, especially involving my boyfriend. So what if Nico isn't an oral genius? That doesn't mean he doesn't possess other exceptional qualities.

Unfortunately, Hunter heard me loud and clear. Even as his head swivels my way, the rest of his body doesn't miss a step, his long legs eating up the treadmill. "Uh oh. My man Nico's not doing it for you with his tongue?"

"No, he is."

"Yeah? Didn't sound like it just now."

"Whatever, not everyone is great at oral," I grumble. "Practice makes perfect, right?"

Hunter appears to be trying not to laugh. "Haven't you guys been together for like ten years?"

"Eight," I say grudgingly. "We officially started dating when we were thirteen."

"And he still hasn't mastered the art of eating pussy?" Incredulity lines his tone.

"Don't be crude."

"Fine, would you like me to call it cunnilingus?"

Ugh, that word is truly unappealing. Who even came up with it? "Look, I'm not saying he's awful at it. Honestly, I think it's me. I'm just not interested in it."

"Have you ever gotten oral from anyone else?"

"No."

"Then how do you know it's you?" Hunter challenges. "A hundred bucks says he just sucks at going down on chicks. How much time does he spend down there?"

My cheeks are on fire. "Not a lot." I hurry on in Nico's defense, "I think he's too impatient to get inside me."

"But the anticipation is half the fun," Hunter protests.

I shrug. "It doesn't matter. Even if it *is* him, he does amazing things when he's in me, and his finger game is pretty sweet. We can't all be good at everything, right?"

"I can," Hunter says smugly.

"Mmm-hmmm, I'm sure you're phenomenal in bed. Men who brag about their sexual prowess always are."

"I am. Too bad you'll never find out."

"Me and every other girl, Monk."

He rolls his eyes. His pace remains brisk. How is he carrying an entire conversation without getting breathless? Me, I'm struggling to talk and run at the same time. Damn athletes.

"Anyway, despite his very disappointing failings, Nico seems like a cool dude," Hunter relents. "He's funny."

"He's hilarious. And yes, he is a cool dude."

"Minus the subpar oral skills, of course."

"They're not subpar. They're par."

"What an endorsement!"

"Oh, shut up."

"You shut up." Hunter flashes that devilish grin of his. "Don't worry, I won't tell him you said that. It would crush his ego."

"Everything you and I talk about falls under doctor-patient confidentiality," I say firmly.

"You got it, Doc."

A woman in tight workout gear meanders over and starts doing squats directly in our line of sight. One might think her choice of location is unintentional, if not for the fact that in the mirror across the room, her thirsty gaze is super-glued to Hunter.

He notices the admirer and gives me a wink. She's not the first female to try to catch his attention this evening, and I'm sure she won't be the last. It's ironic that he's celibate, because any chick in this fitness center would happily have sex with him. In the gym. In front of everyone.

"I can't believe Nico's the only person you've ever slept with," Hunter muses.

"What's wrong with that?"

"Wrong? Nothing. It's just surprising."

"We've been together forever—when would I have had the opportunity to sleep around?"

"You never cheated? Ever?"

"Never. There were some breaks over the years, but I never slept with anyone else."

He cocks one eyebrow defiantly. "You're saying you didn't hook up at all during those breaks?"

"I kissed some guys," I admit with a shrug.

"Because *that* isn't the vaguest response I've ever heard."

"God, you're so frickin' nosy. Fine. I kissed three other guys, and there may have been some petting during one of those encounters."

"Light or heavy?"

"Light. Didn't go beyond second base. He wanted to do more, but I felt like I was betraying Nico."

"Really? You should've gone for it. Because I hate to break it to you, but I *guarantee* that Nico was going beyond second base."

"I know he was. He and I are honest with each other. Plus, on one of the breaks I saw him making out with some girl at a party. That's what led to me fooling around with the light petting guy." I hesitate. "And I know Nico slept with someone else, at least once."

"At least?" Hunter's sneakers slap the treadmill as he increases his pace. Ugh. He's running faster now! And he's still not even breathing hard. It's unbelievable.

I'm moving at a snail-paced walk by this point, and I'm not even on the cool-down setting. "I know there was one hook-up for sure, because he told me about it. But… I think he cheated on me once," I confess, and then chastise myself for it.

It's one thing to critique your boyfriend's oral skills, but opening the closet and letting the skeletons tumble out? That's crossing a line.

"Do *not* tell anyone I said that."

Hunter is smart enough to recognize I'm serious. "You really believe he cheated on you?"

I jerk my head in a nod. This isn't a subject I particularly enjoy dwelling on. "The summer before senior year, I visited him in Miami and a bunch of us went on a camping trip to the Everglades. Well, not really camping. More like glamping."

"Booooo!" Hunter exclaims instantly, giving me two thumbs down.

The woman who's shaking her butt in our faces glances over her shoulder to see what the commotion is, but Hunter doesn't even look her way.

"Nope, nope, nope," he announces. "You're not allowed to be one of those girls, Semi."

"I don't believe in outhouses, okay? I prefer camping in a place with walls and a toilet and Wi-Fi and—"

"That's not camping!"

"Exactly. It's glamping, like I said."

"Boooooo!"

"Will you *please* stop booing me?"

"Just when I was starting to like you, I find out you're a spoiled Miami brat who refuses to sleep in a tent."

"Do you want to hear the rest of the story or no?"

His expression quickly turns eager. "Oh, I really do. But only if you want to tell me."

For some inexplicable reason, I *do* want to tell him. I'd only ever confided in one other person about it: Amber, my best friend in Miami. And she told me I was being paranoid.

"One of our friends brought his cousin Rashida on the trip, and I'm telling you, this chick would *not* stop flirting with Nico. It was starting to piss me off, so I—" I stop abruptly.

"You what?" Hunter demands.

I make a grumbling sound. "I may or may not have told her that if she didn't stop hitting on my man, I'd drown her in the lake and leave her body for the gators."

For the first time in sixty-two minutes, Hunter's gait stutters. He grabs the handrail to steady himself, but the laughter shaking his body doesn't subside. "Fuck. You're a psychopath, Davis. I knew it."

"Nah, I stole that killing method from an episode of *Cheerleaders Who Kill*. I'm not creative enough to plan a gruesome murder. Anyway, this Rashida chick was so predatory and so obvious about it that she needed the reminder that he had girlfriend. God knows he wasn't acting like it. I felt like he was encouraging the flirting, which annoyed me even more. We started arguing about it and Nico got pissy, announced he was taking a walk, and disappeared for a few hours."

"A few *hours*?" Hunter narrows his eyes. "Let me guess, Rashida disappeared about the same time?"

"Good guess. She claimed she drove into town to buy snacks, and the cupboard in the cabin *was* restocked, so maybe she did. But I still found it suspicious."

"Hell yeah, it was suspicious."

"I confronted Nico and he insisted he was alone in the woods and hadn't seen or spoken to Rashida in hours. He told me I was being ridiculous and overreacting, and freaked out on me so hard that I felt guilty for making the accusation and ended up apologizing to him for a whole year afterward." I frown deeply. "I want to believe he didn't do anything, but…"

"But you don't," Hunter finishes.

"I don't. And I feel like an asshole for it."

"You shouldn't. Always trust your gut, Demi. If people are acting shady it's usually because they've done something shady. And the fact that he lost his shit and yelled at you speaks volumes. Guilty people attack. Innocent people don't."

"Maybe, but…whatever, this was years ago. We were kids." I shrug. "We're in our twenties now and it's in the past."

"Is something like that ever truly in the past?" Hunter's voice becomes gruff. "I feel like an incident like that would always lurk in the back of my mind. Like, let's say Summer changed her mind and decided she liked me and not Fitz after all? It'd be niggling at me for our entire relationship—*does she actually want me, is she thinking about him right now*, that kinda shit. I think it's better to…" He makes a snipping motion with his fingers. "Cut it off. Start fresh. If a well runs dry or goes bad, you dig a new one, right? You don't drink from the poisoned water."

I snort. "You know much about wells, Connecticut boy?"

"You don't need firsthand experience with something to use it as a metaphor." Hunter's expression turns pensive. "But, look, Nico does seem like a decent guy, and he's obviously in love with you, if that makes you feel better."

"It does, actually." I appreciate impartial third-party observations. They mean more than the false assurances and platitudes you tend to receive from people who love you.

Another girl passes by. Her stride slows drastically when she notices Hunter. He's finally sweating, his damp shirt clinging to the most impressive chest I've ever seen. His pecs are perfectly defined, and his arms are spectacular. I don't blame any of these women for going gaga over him.

Hunter spares a glance for his admirer, then gravely looks my way. "You have no idea how nice it is to hang out with someone who doesn't want to fuck me."

"Oh my God, that's the most conceited thing I ever heard."

"It's true." He waves his hand around. "Look at them, Semi, look at them all! They're all so fuckable and they all want me. Meanwhile, you're like this beautiful neutral creature with no desire to bang me. It's glorious."

"They're *all* fuckable? I feel like that's an exaggeration."

"We've already established my dick doesn't discriminate. Even you don't have immunity."

I swivel my head. "What the hell does that mean?"

"Ah. Nothing." He's obviously hiding something as he presses a few buttons on the machine to trigger the cool-down setting. When he glances at me again, his expression is sheepish. "I have a confession to make, but you have to promise not to be mad."

"I will never promise that. Ever."

"Seriously?"

"Seriously. Tell me at your own peril."

"Fine. I jerked off the other night—"

"Congratulations. Did your penis tingle when you came?"

"I wasn't finished."

"So you didn't come?"

"I meant I wasn't finished speaking," he growls. "I jerked off the other night…fantasizing about you."

My jaw drops.

Um. What?

"Oh. My. God." I stare at him in utter disbelief. "Why would you ever tell me that?"

"Because I felt guilty about it. Like I needed to go to church and confess."

I can feel myself blushing, and I suspect I'm redder than a tomato. Yes, I have many male friends, but this is the first time one of them has confessed to pleasuring themselves while fantasizing about *me*. I mean…it's flattering, I guess? If TJ or Darius or—

I shudder at the mere thought of it.

Okay. Interesting response. The idea of my other guy friends masturbating to me is extremely unappealing. But the idea of Hunter stroking his cock and fantasizing about me is…

My thighs actually clench together at the dirty image.

Oh my God.

No.

Nope.

In. Ap. Propriate.

Hunter heaves a big sigh. "I feel so much better now that I got that off my chest."

"Well, *I* don't!" I can't get the image out of my mind now, and that is so, so wrong.

His dark eyes twinkle. "Take it as a compliment."

"No, thanks."

He uses the hem of his shirt to mop up the sweat on his brow, which means he literally just flashed his entire chest to me and the rest of the gym. His washboard abs are glistening.

"Anyway, aside from the teeny little hiccup of me yanking it with you in mind, I'm truly digging this thing we have." He gestures between us. "Promise me this will never change."

"That what will never change?"

"That you'll never want to sleep with me," he says dramatically.

The sheer arrogance… I release a sigh of my own and reach over to pat his stupidly muscular arm. "I promise I will never want to sleep with you, Hunter."

# 11
# HUNTER

I'VE BEEN AVOIDING GREEK ROW PARTIES SINCE THE THETA BETA Nu lingerie torture fest, but the boys insist on hitting a frat party after our game on Saturday. We played at Suffolk, so the bus doesn't drop us off on campus until past eleven. Then we have to drive to Hastings, because we all live off-campus and the guys want to change. Or, in Foster's case, grab his weed.

Hard partying during the season is minimal, but drinking and the occasional joint isn't unheard of. I know several hockey guys who do coke, but Coach Jensen runs a clean program at Briar. Every now and then someone hits up a concert and does MDMA, but it's not a frequent occurrence. We're all wholly aware of the NCAA's strict (and random) drug-testing protocol.

Instead of choosing a designated driver, we take an Uber back to campus because everybody's planning on having some drinks to celebrate winning our games this weekend. But our schedule has been light so far. Next week we're facing some tough matchups, including Boston University, and they're undefeated this season. But it's early yet.

Conor is next to me in the backseat, with Foster on his other side. Con's scrolling through his phone. Probably browsing his digital black book.

I'm on egg duty tonight, so I wore a collared shirt with a pocket that I could stick Pablo in. "Look at this manwhore," I tell the egg. "You ever see anything so disgusting?"

Conor's head lifts from the screen. "Oh, can it. I've heard the rumors about you, Mr. I Boned Every Woman on Campus Last Year."

He's got me there. "Who are you talking to?" I ask curiously.

"This chick Michelle. She's meeting us at the party."

He resumes his texting, so I follow suit, because Foster is also on his phone and I'm tired of being ignored. I message Hollis, who's home for the weekend and wanted to party with us tonight. He and Rupi were arguing about it when I left. He wanted to go, she wanted to stay home. Girlfriends, amiright?

> **ME**: Dude, just sling that little hellcat over your shoulder and come out. You know you want to...
>
> **HOLLIS**: I really really want to. Been soooo long since I went to a party :((( Is this what it's like having a gf? Constant snuggling?

I'm typing a response when another message pops up.

> **HOLLIS**: I didn't mean that. Having a girlfriend is the most rewarding experience in a young man's life. Girlfriends are to be treasured.
>
> **ME**: Rupi, did you steal Mike's phone?

NO, is the response, and I start laughing because it's so obvious that she did. Corny words aside, Hollis has never texted in full sentences in his life.

> **ME**: Throw the man a bone, Rupes. He wants to go to a party, not a weeklong EDM festival. Basically means having a beer or two and grinding up all over you to shitty music. Be nice to him for once.

No reply. My phone remains silent all the way to campus, not lighting up until the guys and I are sliding out of the Uber.

**HOLLIS**: U are da fucking man, Davenport! SEE YOU THERE!!!!!!!!

Well. I did my good deed for the day.

A crowd gathers outside the Alpha Delta house. This terrific weather we've been experiencing is still holding up, and although it's almost midnight the air is balmy and people are in shorts and T-shirts. The frat even set up a snow cone machine on the front lawn. I love college.

Conor thumps me on the arm. "Michelle says she's out back." He winks. "In the hot tub."

Foster pales. "Oh, Jesus, no, do *not* go in that hot tub. You're gonna get syphilis of the leg."

"What the fuck are you talking about?"

"Don't you remember that gross rash on Jesse's leg? During preseason? Yeah, he got it from soaking in the Alpha Delt hot tub, AKA Bacteria Central."

"It's true, he did," Bucky confirms. "I don't think anyone ever checks the pH levels or whatever the hell you're supposed to do." He wags a finger at me. "Don't bring Pablo anywhere near it."

"Yeah, you might boil the fucker," Foster guffaws.

"He's already hard-boiled," I argue. "He can't get any *more* boiled."

"So?"

"So I could crack him open right now and he'd be delicious."

"Dude, don't do that," drawls Conor. "That egg has changed so many hands these past couple weeks *it* probably has syphilis."

I snort and pat my breast pocket. "Congrats. You get to live another day, Mr. Eggscobar."

The four of us walk around the side of the house and through the gate. The backyard is massive, housing a kidney-shaped pool, a large expanse of lawn, and the infamous hot tub. Luckily, the tub is full, so even if we wanted to get in, there'd be no room. Chicks are doubling up on guys' laps, and each other's.

Several partygoers let out a huge cheer at our entrance. "Briar hockey!" someone shouts, raising a red cup.

"Briar hockey!" the crowd shouts back.

Not gonna lie—it's awesome being campus celebrities. The football team hasn't done well for nearly a decade, but the hockey program has always been excellent. We kick ass on a frequent basis, and we've got no shortage of fans.

Guys come up to slap me on the shoulder. Girls begin swarming, one of whom makes a beeline for Conor.

The nice thing about Conor is that he's a "one at a time" sort of man. When he sets his sights on a woman, they tend to remain on that woman. Granted, his focus doesn't last more than a week or two. When it comes to hooking up, Con even gives Dean Di Laurentis a run for his money. But for the time being, his interest is directed solely at the cute blonde elbowing her way through the mob.

Conor slings an arm around her shoulder. "Hey babe."

"Hi!" Her lips are stained red from the cherry snow cone in her hand. She raises it to Con's mouth and chirps, "Want some?"

"Fuck yeah." And he growls and chomps off the top of it like a savage.

Michelle giggles, and the other girls disperse unhappily as they realize they won't be reeling in the big fish tonight.

Conor introduces me to Michelle and we chat for a bit, while Bucky and Foster dart off to grab us drinks. Michelle inquires as to why there's a bulge in my shirt pocket, which forces us to explain the Pablo situation. You'd think she'd be horrified by the sheer scope of our immaturity, but instead she laughs in delight and tells Conor how adorable he is. He gives her the Penis Eyes and before long they're making their way inside the house, likely in search of some privacy.

"Hockey man!" a loud voice exclaims, and I turn to see Nico sauntering over.

I blink in surprise. "Hey," I greet Demi's boyfriend. "Fancy meeting you here."

We exchange a macho fist bump. "All these dumbasses here won't quit cheering—I assume you just won a game?" he asks with a grin.

"Yup, yup."

"Nice. I guess Briar's unstoppable tonight—the basketball team won, too. Fucking *destroyed* Yale. We all just came from there."

"Is Demi with you?" I peer past his shoulder.

"Nah, she's at home. It's boys' night." He gestures to a small group a few yards away, and I note that it includes more than boys. Quite a few scantily clad women are hanging all over Nico's friends.

My brain suddenly summons Demi's confession on the treadmill the other night. How she secretly believes, even years later, that Nico cheated on her in high school.

And now, running into him at a frat party with a bunch of chicks in tow, my internal alarm system is triggered.

But maybe I'm being a jerk. Just because he's hanging out with some girls doesn't mean he's stepping out on Demi.

"Anyway, I spotted you from over there and wanted to say hello," Nico says, raising his cup in a toast. Except he does it so abruptly that liquid spills over the edge, and the potent odor of vodka reaches my nostrils. His clumsy hands and hazy eyes tell me he's pretty drunk. "Catch you later, 'kay?"

"Cool. Cheers." I lift my own cup.

Nico strolls back to his friends. I'm mollified to see that he doesn't stand next to any of the girls, but is immediately engrossed in conversation with a short, balding guy in a black tank top. I don't care if Nico catches me watching him—I'm just looking out for Demi. She's a good egg.

"Just like you," I tell Pablo, patting my pocket.

"I. HAVE. ARRIVED!"

The majestic shout is courtesy of Mike Hollis, who emerges onto the patio from the back door, both arms raised in a victory pose. Rupi scampers at his heels like an annoyed kitten.

Despite being incredibly obnoxious, Hollis was quite popular when he attended Briar. Old teammates and a slew of fans wander over to say hello and he accepts their welcome and their praise as if he's Meghan Markle greeting the commoners.

Rupi spots me and marches up. She's clad in traditional Rupi attire: a knee-length, high-waisted skirt and a prim, buttoned tee with a high neckline.

"I *really* wanted to watch *Riverdale* tonight, Hunter," she huffs.

I throw an arm around her tiny shoulders. "Sorry, Rupes. But sometimes we need to make sacrifices for those we love."

A huge smile practically breaks her face in two. "Oh my gosh, that was the sweetest thing you've ever said. I *knew* you were a secret softie."

"Don't tell anyone. You want a drink?"

"I can't. I drove us here."

"I thought you didn't have a license."

"No, I don't have a *fake* license. Ugh, Hunter, you don't know me at *all*."

I suppose I don't, and I gotta admit—I'm A-OK with that. Rupi is exhausting on a good day.

"Is that Pablo?" Her expression brightens. "I didn't know we had him this weekend," she adds, as if discussing the custody arrangement of a human child. "Let me hold him!"

I extract the pink bundle from my pocket and pass it to Rupi. "Go nuts," I tell her.

We mingle for the next hour or so. Foster passes me a joint and I take a deep drag before handing it back. I feel good. Loose, relaxed. Happy to just chill with my buddies and dance with Rupi to the crappy pop music blasting from the outdoor speakers. For the first time in ages, I'm not thinking about sex. Women try to catch my eye. Several come over to flirt with me. But I'm not feeling it. No libido for me tonight. Weed has that effect on me.

"Pablooooo!" Hollis crows. He'd been chatting with some dudes from the lacrosse team, but now he rejoins us near the deep end of the pool. "Hand 'im over, babe."

"Leave Pablo alone," Rupi chastises, protectively holding the egg to her bosom. "You're too drunk to hold him."

"I am not! C'mon, pass 'im to me."

"No."

"Fine, then I'll just…TAKE HIM FROM YOU!" Like a ninja, Hollis snatches the egg from his girlfriend. Only, she's right—he's too drunk to be holding small objects. His big paw fumbles with Pablo, who flies out of Hollis's grip and goes sailing.

Directly into the pool.

Bucky cries out in horror. Hell, even I'm momentarily stunned. We all stare at the little bundle bobbing in the water, which appears blue thanks to the lit-up pool tiles. Nobody moves.

"Did we just kill him?" Foster demands.

"Can pigs swim?" Rupi asks anxiously.

"No idea," I admit. Pablo is still floating in the pool.

"Quick, someone Google if pigs can swim," Bucky orders.

Rupi's already on her phone. "Oh my gosh," she says a moment later, her voice rippling with relief. "They can! It says here that some pigs take naturally to water, like dogs. Others hate getting wet. You can train them to swim." She examines our aquatic egg. "If it was a real pig I don't think he'd be able to get out of the pool by himself, though. There's no steps in the shallow end."

"Yeah, he ain't climbing that ladder," Foster agrees.

All eyes turn to me.

"What?" I say.

"You're in charge of him tonight. You need to get him out."

"Pardon me?" I stare at the empty pool, which an hour ago

was teeming with people. Now it's almost two a.m. and there's no swimming to be had. "I'm not jumping in the pool, you fuckers."

"We never trained him to swim," Bucky argues. "Right now he's treading water. Soon he'll be dead."

"This has gone too far," I say firmly.

Except, to my genuine shock, everyone stands their ground, even Foster. Bucky crosses his arms tightly.

"Fuck's sake," I snap. "You're seriously gonna make me do this?"

I'm cursing up a blue streak as I strip out of my shirt. Shoes and cargo shorts come off too, because I'm not sitting soaking wet in an Uber on the way home.

I step toward the edge of the deck. "You assholes don't deserve me as a captain," I mutter, and then I dive into the water in my boxers.

Luckily, the temperature is like bath water, and as I swim for Pablo, I force myself to think good thoughts about my team.

Captain rule number a million: *Patience. Always be patient.*

With Pablo in hand, I climb up the ladder, dripping water all over the concrete deck. "Here," I mutter to Foster, shoving the egg in his hand. "I'm going upstairs to dry off and change."

Rupi's unhappy gaze fixes on my underwear. "Hunter, I can see the outline of your penis."

Yup, because the boxers are white, and they're soaked and sticking to my flesh. I scowl at Rupi before gathering my discarded clothing and stalking into the house.

It's late and the party is winding down, so there's no line at the main floor bathroom. But the door is locked and when I knock on it, an agonized voice slurs, "Go 'way, I'm busy in 'ere."

So I trudge upstairs and try the one in the hall. Door's shut, but I jiggle the knob and find it's unlocked. I push the door open in time to hear a husky groan and see Conor Edwards fisting both his hands in a tangle of blonde hair.

"Ahhh fuck, I'm coming," he rasps, his hips pumping. And on her knees Michelle swallows every drop.

Jesus!!

I quickly slam the door, not caring if they heard it. I've witnessed friends hooking up before, but never had the honor of staring into their heavy-lidded eyes fuzzy with bliss as they climax. Goddamn Conor. Hasn't he ever heard of a lock?

My gaze turns toward a bedroom at the end of the all. I know the guy who lives there—Ben something or other. And he has a private bath. My wet body is dripping water on the carpet. I need a towel and a wastebasket to toss my boxers in. Ben's bathroom, it is.

But I've only taken one step down the hall when Ben's door swings open and I witness yet another thing I shouldn't.

Only this time it's worse than Conor coming in some chick's mouth.

Much, much worse.

# 12
# HUNTER

I'M UP AT SIX A.M. ON MONDAY. WE HAVE MORNING SKATE AT SEVEN and I need to eat, because I always have breakfast before practice. And then a second breakfast afterwards in the hockey facility kitchen. Like a hobbit.

Hollis is already awake. He needs to make the drive back to New Hampshire today. Sometimes he leaves on Sunday night, but some weekends he simply can't sacrifice one single second with his fair maiden Rupi and leaves early on Monday. I guess this was one of those weekends. But he's in for a bitch of a commute at this hour.

"Hey," I say as he staggers into the kitchen.

He grunts in response.

I head for the coffeemaker. I need a dose of caffeine to jumpstart my brain. "Want some?" I offer.

That gets me another grunt.

I decide to treat it as a yes. A couple minutes later we're drinking our coffee while I scroll through my phone to check the meal plan for the week. Our nutritionist Karly has the team on a strict diet. Granted, we break it all the time, but as Karly always warns, ignoring her meal plans only does ourselves the disservice in the end.

I skim the options on the list and decide on an egg white

omelet loaded with veggies. "You want breakfast?" I ask Hollis. "Omelets."

He nods. "Yeah, one for the road might be nice. Actually, make that two."

"You want two omelets."

"I'm hungry."

"I'll start with one and then we'll see if there's time left. Coach will be pissed if I'm late." I slide a cutting board and a knife across the counter. "Get dicing."

Hollis chops mushrooms and green peppers while I prep the eggs. As we cook, the rest of the house remains eerily quiet and the sky's still dark beyond the kitchen window. The darkness makes it feel like nighttime, and my brain is unwittingly transported back to Saturday night.

Fuck.

Nico absolutely slept with that chick I saw him exiting the bedroom with.

Or at the very least, he had his pants off with her.

And when you have a serious girlfriend, your pants should never come off in the presence of another woman.

The thing is… I didn't actually catch him red-handed. I caught the potential aftermath. And I'm not about to stir up trouble in the relationship of someone I barely know. Demi doesn't trust me enough yet to take my word for it. If I went up to a friend, like Dean, for example, and said, "Hey, Allie's cheating," he would believe me. Because Dean knows I'd have no reason to lie or play games. But Demi doesn't know that. She would question my motivations, maybe even suspect me of trying to sabotage Nico so I could have her for myself, which isn't the case.

"Hey Mike," I say as I pour the first omelet mixture into the hot pan.

"Mmmm?" He's busy chopping up a red pepper now.

"I've got a hypothetical for you."

"All right. Hypothetical me."

"What?"

"You know, like *hit me*, only with the word hypothetical instead of—whatever, just fucking say it."

"All right. Let's pretend someone you know is in a long-term, committed relationship, and you caught their boyfriend or girlfriend cheating on them. Well, *possibly* cheating. You're not a hundred percent certain, but the circumstances were very suspicious and…" I set down the spatula on the counter. "You know what? Screw it. I *am* a hundred percent certain. I know when a dude just got sucked off. I literally saw Conor ejaculating three seconds before that."

"Davenport." Hollis speaks in a voice so ominous that I'm almost nervous to turn to face him.

"Yeah?"

"Are you trying to tell me that you saw Rupi sucking Conor Edwards' dick?" Hollis rumbles like an angry bear, his face redder than the pepper on his cutting board. "When the *fuck* did it happen? Was it at the party? Was it when she went to fix her hair—"

"Relax," I interrupt. "I'm not talking about Rupi. Are you insane? That girl would never cheat on you. She's obsessed with you, Hollis. She's your stalker. You're dating your stalker."

"That's the nicest thing anyone's ever said to me."

"I'm talking about a friend from class, okay? I'm pretty sure her boyfriend cheated on her. The question is, do I tell her?"

"Nope." Zero hesitation from Hollis.

"Why not?" I use the spatula to transfer the first omelet from the pan to Mike's plate, then get to work on my own breakfast.

"Because you don't want to stick your nose in other people's biz. Trust me."

"But he's cheating on her."

"So? That's his biz, not yours."

"It's also her business," I point out.

"It can't be her business when she doesn't know about it," Hollis counters.

I pause. "So you subscribe to the whole 'what she doesn't know won't hurt her' camp? Really?"

"I'm just saying, is some rando from class worth you getting involved in a third-party relationship? Child, please."

"Please don't say *child, please*."

He ignores me, taking a huge bite of the omelet. "Look, if it was one of us," he blabbers with his mouth full, "then I'd say hell yeah, you have a duty to say something. But how well do you know this chick?"

"Not well. We're still getting to know each other."

Hollis finally swallows his food. "There you go. So even if you do tell her, she won't believe you, bro. If someone I'm 'still getting to know'"—he uses air quotes—"accused Rupi of cheating, I'd say child, please—"

"I'm begging you to stop saying that."

"—and I'd think they had an ulterior motive."

Mike Hollis, of all people, is rationally confirming my own doubts. But maybe men are naturally cynical? I'm sure if I polled any of the women living in this house whether they'd want to know, the answer would be YES! In a heartbeat.

"You don't want to get involved," Hollis warns. "Trust me, man. Stay as far away from this situation as you can."

———

Morning practice is fast-paced. I'm sweating like a dog, and panting like one as I skate hard toward the net. We're running two-on-ones, designed for the defensemen to attempt to stop a forward on a breakaway. But I'm way faster than Kelvin and Peters. During the entire drill, I've managed not only to outskate them, but to score on net every time.

Until now. I wind up my slapshot and unleash the puck, only for the goaltender to pluck it out of the air with his glove. It's Trenton, our backup goalie.

He lifts his mask and flashes a toothy grin. "How do you like them apples, captain?"

I whistle in admiration. "That's a wicked glove you got there. If you were a bit faster with the pads, you'd be giving Boris some real competition for the starter job."

Rather than look defeated, Trenton's eyes gleam with fortitude. "Then I'll get faster," he vows.

Oh yeah, he's got that hunger. The kid's gonna be starting games in no time.

I skate toward the bench. Coach blows his whistle, signaling practice is over. Our defensive coordinator O'Shea asks a couple of D-men to stay behind to run one more drill, but the rest of us are free to go. Good, because my stomach is grumbling. Time for second breakfast. But first I need to wash all the sweat off me.

Our showers have the sweetest set-up. Each one is its own individual stall separated by waist-high partitions, so we can see each other's heads but not our junk, just the way I like it. In the stall next to mine, Con is dunking his head under the spray, smoothing his longish hair away from his forehead. He's got a bite mark on his left shoulder. This fucking guy.

"Hey, about this weekend," I start, deciding to poll more people about my dilemma.

But Conor misinterprets. Chuckling softly, he turns to grin at me. "Yeah, sorry 'bout that. I forgot to lock the door." He raises a brow. "You should've joined us."

I'm helpless to stop my dick from twitching. Bad enough that I'm not having sex with the parade of women throwing themselves at me at parties—now I'm being invited to threesomes? The universe has a lousy sense of humor.

"Nah, I'm not talking about the BJ. I needed—"

"*Feed me!*" The anguished shout reverberates in the shower area, making Con and me jump.

"For fuck's sake," Conor says, turning toward the doorway.

Matt and Treeface are standing outside Jesse Wilkes' stall, the latter waving Pablo around in the air. I'm not worried about the egg falling into one of the showers, because it's been established that pigs can indeed swim.

Jesse remains unfazed by the intruders. He simply squirts shampoo into his palms and lathers up his hair. "You can wait five minutes, Pablo," he says cheerfully.

Matt glares at him. "Would you really do that if he was real? If your pet pig was standing in the doorway begging to be fed?"

"Hell yeah, I would. I've got three golden retrievers at home. They eat when I tell them to eat."

Laughter bounces off the acoustics in the room. He's got a point. I had a Jack Russell growing up and he ate twice a day, like clock-work. My control-freak father wouldn't have it any other way.

Man, I miss that dog. I was ten years old when he died, and I remember crying my eyes out in my bedroom until Dad came in to inform me that real men don't cry. Good chat.

"But he's *starving*," Tree says in accusation.

Jesse just gives them the finger before continuing to wash his hair. He's even whistling.

Although…he's shampooing rather fast… In fact, I barely have time to blink before he's shutting off the water and darting through the doorway.

Conor grins at Jesse's retreating backside. "Dude. I think they're actually starting to believe it's a real pig."

"Right?" But I can't deny that Pablo has developed a life of his own. Even I can't be certain he's an egg anymore. I think he might be a real boy.

"Anyway," I say as I rinse off. "I need advice."

"Hit me," Conor replies, because that's a normal response from a normal person. I don't understand why Hollis—annnnd there's no point trying to figure out Hollis. It's like trying to understand the wind.

Toweling off, I quickly outline the situation. Unlike Hollis, Con *does* hesitate. He thinks it over for several beats before providing an answer.

"I'd tell her."

"Yeah? Even though she might punch me in the face?"

"Well, sure, the messenger always risks getting shot, but is it better to leave her in the dark? What if you run into her and the boyfriend? What do you do, pretend everything is cool and that you don't know he's a total douchebag?"

"I'm with Con," Foster pipes up from my other side. He's been listening in this entire time. "You gotta tell her, man. And hey, if it turns out you're wrong? You say *I'm sorry, I was trying to be a good friend and look out for you, and I made a mistake.*"

Which is precisely what this boils down to—me wanting to be a good friend. I hate the idea of Demi being played for a fool. Nico seemed like a good guy the first time I met him, but he was emitting some real slime vibes at the party. On the other hand, I hardly know the dude. Maybe he's just a bit slimy. Doesn't make him a cheater.

I poll a few other teammates in the locker room, and the consensus seems to be to tell Demi the truth. But it isn't until Jesse texts his girlfriend for her opinion that I'm fully swayed to the side of morality. In all caps, Katie texts back a resounding:

TELL HER RIGHT EFFING NOW, YOU HEARTLESS MONSTER!!!!!!

I guess I have my answer.

# 13
# DEMI

There's a text message from Hunter when I step out of Biology class late in the afternoon. He's supposed to come by tonight for a fake therapy session, but apparently now he's cancelling.

**HUNTER**: Need to cancel tonight. Last-minute thing in Boston.
**ME**: Didn't we LITERALLY just talk in class earlier and confirm?
**HIM**: Yes, and then I LITERALLY just got a text from a friend and now I have to cancel.
**ME**: I demand to know why.
**HIM**: Bruins game.
**ME**: Is there really a game or are you just lying to get out of studying? Cuz you were acting super strange this morning. Even TJ noticed.
**HIM**: I wasn't acting strange and there really is a game. Google it.
**ME**: I will choose to believe you. How are you getting there?
**HIM**: Teleporting, obviously.
**ME**: Jackass. Are you driving?
**HIM**: Ya. Why?
**ME**: When are you leaving? Maybe I can catch a ride with you??

I'm hopeful as I await his response. A free ride to Boston would enable me to visit my parents, who I haven't seen since Labor Day weekend. It's already mid-October, but I haven't had much free time to make the trek into the city. I don't have a car, an Uber would be too expensive, and the bus takes way too long.

Rather than texting, Hunter calls me. "Why do you need to go to Boston?"

"My parents live there. Our house is near Beacon Hill."

"Fancy."

"You're one to talk, rich boy. So can I catch a ride with you?"

"Sure. I'm leaving around six, but if you want a ride back with me, it won't be till eleven-ish."

"That's fine. Pick me up from here?"

"Yup yup."

"Please don't say yup yup. I don't like it."

"I don't care. See you in an hour."

He hangs up on me and I grin at the phone. Hunter amuses me. He makes a nice addition to my roster of male friends. The Lost Boys, as Corinne would say.

I take a quick shower and then put on a green sundress and the gold hoop earrings my parents gave me for my birthday in August.

I hate these earrings with a passion. They're big hoops, and if it were up to me, big hoops would be banned in this country. But I slide them on now because I want Mom and Dad to think I wear the hoops on the reg. They have the tendency to act all wounded if I don't fawn over their gifts.

Hunter texts when he's outside, and I'm not surprised to find a shiny black Land Rover parked at the curb. I slide into the passenger's side and settle on the sleek leather seat.

"Hey," he says. He's wearing a black-and-yellow jersey, his dark hair slicked back from his face.

"Are you wearing hair gel?"

"Are you wearing enormous hoop earrings?"

"I asked first."

"Yes, I'm wearing gel."

"Your head is *glistening*."

"Yeah, but at least it's staying in place. Whenever I watch live hockey, I get agitated and run my fingers through my hair until it's fucking falling out—I figured gel would help prevent that. Your turn."

"My turn what?"

"The hoops, Semi. I could probably fit my entire glistening head through one of those monsters." He chuckles faintly. "I guess you can take the girl out of Miami but you can't take Miami out of the girl?"

"Wrong. I despise these earrings. They're more my mom's style," I admit. "She's all about the big hoops, and she thinks everyone should dress and accessorize exactly like her. But I prefer tiny studs—you know, so there's no chance of them getting caught on anything and ripping my ear off, leaving a bloody hole in the side of my head."

"That's a really cynical view of hoops."

"They're a safety hazard. I stand by that."

"So you pretend to like them to please your mommy and daddy?" He's mocking me.

I bristle, but only slightly, because there's truth to that statement. Especially the daddy part. My father is a scary man. The kind of man who is so impressive you constantly feel the need to impress him back.

"Why didn't Nico drive you tonight?" Hunter asks suddenly, and there's a strange note in his voice.

He was using that same tone this morning too. Every time I whispered something to him during Andrews' lecture, he responded in that weird tone and then avoided my eyes.

I glance over, but he's focused on the road and his face is devoid of expression. "Nico's working tonight."

"People move at night?"

"Sometimes, yeah. He actually gets paid more for night moves."

"*Night moves* sounds like the name of a porno."

"I think it might be a song," I say, trying to recall. "I could be wrong, though. Anyway, he gets paid time and a half for any jobs after six, so if a late shift comes up, he always takes it."

"Makes sense." Hunter nods. A few beats of awkward silence ensue. First time it's ever happened to us. Then again, we don't know each other super well, so an awkward silence was bound to make an appearance sooner or later.

"Let me sync up my Bluetooth to your car," I say, reaching for the touch screen on his dash. "I'll find us a fun driving playlist."

He instantly swats at my hand. "No way," he says. "No woman is allowed to have that much control over me."

I laugh. "What control? It's Bluetooth. Bluetooth is harmless."

"Nope. Maybe tonight it's harmless. And maybe tomorrow you'll be remotely controlling my car."

"How would I even do that?"

"By hacking into the system and driving my Rover off a cliff." He sounds smug.

"I want to drive you off a cliff *now*," I threaten. "Just let me sync up, dammit." And then because I'm a jerk, I go through the process of pairing my phone to his car. Whistling the entire time.

When I'm done, I graciously ask, "What would you like to listen to?"

He glowers at me. "I can't believe you just did that."

"If you don't pick something, I'll put on Disney soundtracks."

Hunter capitulates. "Got any old-school hip hop mixes?"

I nod in approval. "Coming right up." I click on a popular playlist and we spend the remainder of the drive locked in a competitive rap battle to Cypress Hill and Run-DMC. By the time we reach the city, my throat is hoarse, and Hunter's face is lobster red from laughing.

"You got mad rhymes, Semi!" he says gleefully. "We need to make a YouTube video."

"Oh God, never. I have zero interest in being in the spotlight. Unlike you."

"Me?"

"You like the spotlight, no? Won't you be playing professional hockey when you're done college?"

Hunter surprises me by shaking his head. "No, I didn't declare for the draft and I don't plan on signing with a team after I graduate. Teams have come knocking on my door since high school, but I always tell them I'm not interested."

"Why the heck not?"

"I'm just not. I don't want that kind of national attention."

I wrinkle my forehead. "But aren't you really talented? The girls at the house said you're the best player on the team."

"I'm okay."

I appreciate the modesty. But all it tells me is that Hunter must be a lot more than *okay*.

"I'm not interested in the pros, Demi. Not everyone wants to be famous."

It's a peculiar answer and I don't quite buy it, but the British lady on Hunter's GPS is chirping that our destination is up ahead on the right.

I smile as we drive down the street I've called home since I was fifteen. Even after six years on the east coast, my mother still isn't in love with Boston, whereas I liked it the moment we moved here.

Miami is loud and colorful and undeniably fun, but just because I'm half Latina doesn't mean I want things to be loud all the time. We lived in Little Havana, a mostly Cuban community full of art galleries and coffee shops and cigar stores on every street corner. It's a bustling area, almost the polar opposite of Boston's conservative Beacon Hill neighborhood.

My new city, while not as IN YOUR FACE as Miami, has its own unique character, from its brownstones and tree-lined streets to Boston Common and Newbury Street. Plus, despite contrary opinion, I find the accents downright charming.

"Here we are. Have fun with your parents," Hunter says.

"Have fun at your game."

I'm pleased to notice that he waits until I reach the front stoop before pulling away from the curb. Real gentlemen are hard to find these days.

My mother shrieks happily when I walk through the door. She's the loudest person on the planet. My friends insist that she's a clone of Sofia Vergara from *Modern Family*, and they're not far off the mark. Although Mom's not Colombian like the character, she's drop-dead gorgeous with a voice that could shatter every plate in a china store.

Blabbering on in Spanish, she hugs me tight enough to restrict my airflow, then drags me down the hall toward the kitchen. "Where's Dad?" I ask.

"On his way home from the hospital. He just finished surgery, so expect Grumpy Papa tonight."

I'm used to Grumpy Papa. Some surgeons ride a high after they operate, but Dad is always exhausted after a long surgery, and he gets cranky when he's tired. Like a toddler. But he deserves to be cut some slack, because—hello—he just saved somebody's life. Brain surgeons are allowed a free bitchiness pass, as far as I'm concerned.

"Are you hungry?" Mom demands, then answers her own question. "Of course you are! Sit down so I can feed you, *mami*. How is school going?"

"Good." I fill her in on my classes and the project with Hunter, while she unloads Tupperware containers from the fridge.

If my visit hadn't been last minute, I have no doubt she would've cooked me a feast. Instead, I'm relegated to the leftovers from whatever feast she cooked for Dad yesterday. And it's *spectacular*. Soon the cedar work island is laden with dishes, most of them Cuban, with a few of Dad's American favorites sprinkled in.

My mouth waters as each new item emerges from the microwave. There's shredded beef seasoned to perfection with veggies and olives and served on brown rice. Cuban chicken stew with raisins to give it a bit of sweetness. Stuffed peppers. Fried beans. The roasted potatoes and garlic carrots that Dad likes.

"Oh my goodness, Mom," I declare while inhaling her food. "I've missed your cooking *so* much." Pieces of rice fly out of my mouth as I talk.

"Demi," she chides.

"Hmmmm?" I mumble through a mouthful of spicy beef.

She flips her glossy brown hair over one shoulder. "Of all the traits you could've inherited from your father, his poor table manners is what it had to be?"

"What? You should take it as a compliment that we both enjoy your cooking."

"Maybe you can enjoy it with your mouth full," she suggests. "And leave some carrots for your father." She slaps my hand when I try to stick my fork in the carrot container.

Speaking of my father, he appears in the doorway without warning. I hadn't heard him come in. Granted, that's probably because I'm chewing so loudly.

"Hi baby," he says happily. Enormous arms encircle me from behind as he places a kiss on the top of my head.

"Hey Daddy." I swallow some more rice.

He greets my mother, which is always a fun sight to see. Standing at six foot five, Dad is a bald black guy with arms like tree trunks, palms like oven mitts, and long but surprisingly delicate fingers. Or I guess not surprisingly, seeing as how nimble digits are required when poking around in somebody's skull. And then there's Mom, who's all of five feet, with huge boobs and shiny hair and the Latin temper she passed on to me. They're the cutest couple ever, and I adore my little family. Being an only child means I don't have to share anything with a sibling, including my parents' attention.

Dad joins me at the counter and digs into the leftovers. Mom, who has trouble staying still, eventually sits down too and nibbles on an olive while Dad tells us about his surgery. The patient was a construction worker whose skull nearly got crushed by a falling steel beam. He wasn't wearing his hardhat, and now he might have permanent brain damage. It's heartbreaking. Which is one of the reasons I'd never want to be a surgeon—that and I don't have the hands for it. My fingers get trembly when I'm nervous, and I can't imagine a more anxiety-inducing situation than sawing into a human being's skull.

The topic once again shifts to my classes, which I list for my father. "Organic Chem, bio, math, and Abnormal Psych."

"Organic Chemistry was always a favorite of mine," Dad reveals, sipping on a glass of water Mom gets for him.

"It's my least favorite," I confess. "Right now I'm having the most fun with the psychology class. It's so fascinating."

"Are you taking physics next semester?"

I grimace. "Unfortunately."

Dad laughs. "You'll enjoy it," he promises. "And then wait till med school! Everything you learn there will be fascinating. Have you given more thought to that MCATs tutor? I have a good one lined up—just say the word."

I swallow, but it does nothing to alleviate the lump of pressure that constricts my throat. "Maybe next semester?" I counter. "I'm worried my grades will dip a little if I add another study commitment to my schedule."

"It'll only be a few times a week."

*A few times a week?* Oh my God, I thought I'd only have to see this tutor once, *maybe* twice a week.

"Let me see how it goes with midterms and then we can reevaluate?" I hold my breath, praying he'll accept the compromise.

Luckily, he does. "All right. But I do think the head start will help you a lot. The med school application process can be stressful."

know the dates. But you should definitely come. Allie showed up to the last game and the girls lost their shit. They love her show." Dean's girlfriend, Allie Hayes, is an actress on a popular HBO show. It even won a bunch of Emmys recently. Allie wasn't nominated for her role, but they won for Best Drama, which is impressive as fuck.

"Is Allie here?" I ask, searching for her blonde head.

Dean nods. "She's up in the box with Grace, chatting up a storm. All the girlie talk got too much for me, so I said I'd wait for you out here." He gestures to the front entrance of the massive arena behind us.

The air is electric tonight, as it always is for a home game. All around us are black-and-yellow jerseys, interspersed with the ed-and-white ones worn by the fans representing Detroit, tonight's pponent.

It's utterly surreal to think that I'm friends with not one, but vo of the men on the ice tonight. Garrett Graham is the star of the am, the leading scorer in the entire league, and arguably one of the eatest hockey players of all time. I can't believe I played one year college with him.

The other friend is John Logan, another college legend. It's gan's rookie season with the team. Before this, he was playing the Bruins' farm team, so this is like his big promotion. So far, done well in the first few games of the season, and I'm excited atch him and Garrett play live again. These days I catch their es on TV, but it's not the same.

'Is Fitz still staying with you guys in Manhattan?" I ask Dean e head inside.

Not at mine and Allie's place. He's at my fam's penthouse, doing for that Brooklyn game studio. He has the whole penthouse to lf this time, which I think is a huge relief for him."

Oh, it is. He told me he was staying there with your dad last ."

an chuckles. "Yup, the two of them living it up in the bache-, while Summer's in Boston and Mom's in Greenwich. Jesus.

"Honestly…" I find some courage, then continue, "Sometimes it feels overwhelming when I think about it. Med school, I mean."

"I won't deny it's a lot of work, and a lot of sleepless nights. But that makes it all the more rewarding when you graduate and start calling yourself Dr. Davis."

"You're Dr. Davis."

"There can be two," he teases.

I hesitate again. "You know, I could still call myself doctor if I got a PhD in psychology rather than med school."

His shoulders immediately stiffen. "Are you considering that avenue?" There's an edge to his voice, along with surprise-tinged disapproval.

*Yes,* I almost blurt out. Because it's the more appealing avenue, in my eyes. What do I care about biology or anatomy? I'd way rather be taking courses like psych theory, cognitive and behavioral therapies, research methods, personality development. AKA far more interesting areas of study.

And yet I can't say any of that out loud. My father's approval matters to me. Maybe too much, but that's how it's always been.

So I backtrack as fast as I can. "No, that was just a joke. Everyone knows people with doctorates aren't *real* doctors. Like, come on."

Dad booms with laughter again. "You got that right."

Then I shovel more food into my mouth so I won't have to keep talking. This doesn't bode well, though. With senior year coming up, I've been giving more and more thought to what I want to do after I graduate. Med school had been the plan, but grad school is also tempting. Truth is, I find psychiatry to be so…clinical. There's such a large focus on medication management of patients, and I can't seem to gather much excitement at the notion of prescribing meds and monitoring dosages. I suppose I could specialize in something stimulating, like neuropsychiatry and treat patients with Alzheimer's and MS. Or maybe work in a psychiatric unit of a hospital.

But I want to focus on treating the behaviors of patients, not only the symptoms. I want to talk to people, to *listen* to them. But my father never would get that. And this proves it. I mean, I just stuck my toe in the water and an alligator bit it off. That doesn't exactly make me want to broach the subject again.

# 14
# HUNTER

"Dude! It's been ages!" Dean looks insanely happy

Dean took me under his wing when I was a fresh~~ was a senior, and I think part of him still views me ~~ protégé. To be honest, he's the one who taught me th~~ that landed me in trouble last season. "How To Pick U~~ Dean Heyward-Di Laurentis should be a prerequisite horny college boys. The guy knows what he's doing.

Of course, it helps when you have supermodel-cl~~ golden hair, sparkling green eyes. Summer is like th~~ Dean, which is a bit unnerving considering I've jer~~ sies of her before.

"It's good to see you," I tell my old friend. "H~~

"Pretty damn good. My roster is *killer* this y~~ a girls' hockey team at a private school in Manh~~ gotten into Harvard Law, but at the last momer~~ ing position instead. I guess you could say he'~~ teacher, but he also coaches hockey and volley~~ where his true passion lies.

"Nice. I should try to catch one of you~~ conflict with my sched. Do you ever have ro~~ Boston?"

"Actually, there's a tournament here r~~

I can't imagine having to shack up with Allie's father. He'd probably murder me in my sleep and bury my body in a block of cement under their brownstone. No one would find it until years later, when someone decides to rebuild the house and jackhammers the foundation."

"Oh come on, I thought you and Allie's dad were cool."

"For the most part. But he still calls me 'rich boy' and always asks me what designer I'm wearing." Dean sighs glumly. "So now I just wear rags when I'm there so that I don't get made fun of."

I swallow a laugh. Stories about Allie's father never fail to entertain me. I haven't met the man, but he sounds hilarious. "Does your dad like Fitzy?" I ask curiously.

"Are you kidding me? Dad will love anybody Summer brings home. She's his princess and can do no wrong. She could legit bring home a serial killer and Dad would be sitting there asking to see pictures of the victims." Dean imitates his father's voice. "Oh, you used a hacksaw to chop off the head? Neat! Can you show me how to do that?"

This time I can't contain my laughter. "You're exaggerating."

"Not exaggerating in the slightest, dude. Remember that guy in high school? You'd know him—you were in the same year. Rickie? Ronnie? The one with the face tattoo?"

"Lawrence," I say with a groan.

"Man, I was *way* off."

"That guy was such a loser. Summer went out with him?"

"It was during her rebellious stage. Mom told her she couldn't do something, I can't remember what, so Summer got all huffy and that weekend she brought Face Tattoo to our family picnic. Mom almost died. Meanwhile Dad's asking him about the inspiration behind the *face tattoo*."

"It was...stars?" I ask, trying to picture Lawrence's tats.

"Birds," Dean corrects with a snort. "Winding around his neck and going up to his cheek and forehead."

"Sounds hot."

Snickering, we take the escalators up to the private boxes reserved for VIPs. I flash the guest credentials Dean handed me downstairs, and the guards wave us through. Our box is the one for Wives and Girlfriends. I love it. We're considered WAGs tonight, but the only actual girlfriend present is Grace Ivers, a senior at Briar. She and Logan live together in an apartment between Hastings and Boston.

I don't know Grace very well. In fact, I don't think we've ever had a conversation. But she greets me warmly and gives me a quick hug.

I know Allie a lot better because of Dean, and her hug is tighter and lasts much longer. "Hunter! You're looking so good! You've gained like fifty pounds of muscle."

"Not quite." I smile. "You look great. I'm digging the shorter hair."

She smooths a hand over her blonde bob. "Really? Dean says it makes me look like a pixie."

"So? Pixies are hot. Did you guys take the train in from New York?"

"Yeah. We were both free tonight and decided, what the hell. Might as well support the boys."

"Good call." I wander over to the massive window overlooking the rink. The players are warming up at the moment. I search the ice for Garrett's and Logan's jersey numbers. I spot Logan first. Grace's eyes are glued on him too, as she comes up beside me.

"How's he doing this season?" I ask. "I haven't studied his stats line too closely."

"He's doing well. Not as well as he'd like to be doing, but he got two assists in the game against Philly. Boston has some pretty amazing defensemen already, so John's not seeing as much ice time as he wants." Grace sounds unhappy. I'm not sure if it's on Logan's behalf, or if there's more to it.

"Uh oh, is he taking it out on you?" Allie demands. Evidently she glimpsed that same flicker of discouragement in Grace's eyes.

"No, not at all. But he's just a bit on edge. And I'm busy at the radio station, so our schedules often conflict." She shrugs before offering a halfhearted smile. "Every relationship has its speed bumps in the road. We'll be fine."

"True," Allie agrees. "But if you need me to knock some sense into him, let me know. I'll get my boyfriend to beat him up."

"Wait," Dean balks, channeling Mike Hollis. "*I'm* your boyfriend."

I snicker.

Dean sets his jaw. "I'd never beat up Logan for you, Allie-Cat. He's my BFF."

"I thought Garrett was your BFF," she taunts.

"I thought *I* was your BFF," I whine.

He sighs. "Jesus fucking Christ, you're all my BFFs, okay?"

"Hey, where's Hannah?" I ask, referring to Garrett's girlfriend, Hannah Wells. The last time I was in the WAGs box, she was also present.

"Holy shit, did you not hear about Wellsy?" Dean demands.

"What about her?"

"You know how she's been working with that famous producer? The one who's also worked with Rihanna and Beyoncé and a bunch of other huge names?"

"Yeah, but I thought she wasn't making her own music. Isn't she writing songs now?"

"She is," Allie confirms. "And one of her songs is going to be performed by—get *this*! Delilah Sparks! They're in the recording studio as we speak, laying down the track. Hannah says it might actually be the single on Delilah's next album."

"Wow. That is impressive." It's really cool seeing what everyone's been doing after college. Dean teaching and coaching. Allie on TV. Hannah rubbing elbows with superstar recording artists.

But…and maybe this is just the little boy in me…for me, watching Garrett and Logan skating in a packed TD Garden, representing our city, trumps everybody else's careers.

All I ever wanted was to play professional hockey. It was my childhood dream. When I first told my parents that dream, I think Dad was pissed, because in his mind he'd been grooming me since birth to work for his company and eventually take it over. But when it turned out I was really damn good and had a more than realistic shot of making a shit ton of money as a pro hockey player, suddenly Dad was on board, encouraging my budding career.

So, yes, I wanted it. Badly. But then… I changed my mind. I realized that the NHL lifestyle is not for me. It's too decadent, too destructive if you're not careful, and I truly don't know if I trust myself to be part of it.

Still, knowing I won't be down on that ice one day doesn't take away from the excitement of watching my friends skate. Everyone in the box is cheering their lungs out, and a wave of screams rocks the room when Garrett creates a rebound that lands on Logan's stick. Logan snaps it up and scores his first goal of the season. Grace is on her feet, screaming herself hoarse, her face shining with pride.

I wonder if I'll ever find a woman who looks at me like that. A woman who, when presented with "speed bumps" in our relationship, works with me to smooth them out instead of simply driving away. I might not want a girlfriend this very second, but I can't deny that I hope to find something—no, someone—real in the future.

On the other hand, some relationships are total shit. I mean, look at Demi. She's head over heels for her boyfriend, and he's going around getting his dick wet at frat parties.

And I *still* haven't told her the truth. I had all day to do it, for chrissake. We sat together in Abnormal Psych this morning. We spent an hour in the car together on the way up here. Yet every time I opened my mouth to tell her, I couldn't get the words out.

I'll say something on the drive home tonight. I have to.

I'm just going to suck it up, blurt it out, and let the chips fall where they may.

Like a coward, I wait until the last possible second to broach the subject with Demi. After picking her up from her parents' house, I let her chat for the entire drive home, nodding and smiling while internally gathering my courage. The last time I found myself in a situation like this, it blew up in my face like a grenade. Every fiber of my being wants me to keep my mouth shut, but I like this girl, and I think she deserves to know.

I guess I'm not a great actor, because Demi finally calls me on my behavior as I turn onto the main road toward campus.

"Okay, what is *up* with you?"

"Nothing," I lie.

"I'd think I was boring you, but I know for a fact that I am *not* boring. I'm a fucking excellent conversationalist and I just told you a story about the time I met Gigi Hadid in South Beach AKA the best meet-cute of the century."

I crack a smile. "You're certainly not boring," I agree.

"So why are you acting weird?" Demi sounds aggravated.

"I..." Inhale. Exhale. Here goes. "I need to tell you something, and I've been debating all day whether or not to do it."

"What is it?"

"Uh."

Silence commences.

"Okay. Cool. Great chat, bro!"

I quickly backtrack. "You know what, it's not important." *It's none of my business*, I tell myself. Whatever Nico's doing is his own business.

"I'm joking," she insists. "Tell me what going on."

"Uh."

Silence recommences.

"Come on, Monk, am I going to have to beat it out of you?"

"I'd like to see you try."

"I'm a lot stronger than I look." She frowns. "Are you really not going to tell me?"

"Nico," I blurt before I can stop myself.

And I instantly want to punch myself in the face, because Demi is like a shark that just caught a sniff of blood.

"What about him?" she demands.

"Nothing." Goddammit, why did I even bring it up? And why is it taking so long to reach Greek Row? I need an escape plan, ASAP.

"*Hunter*," she says sharply.

"Fine. Just…don't shoot the messenger, okay?" I release a quick breath. "I ran into him at a party this weekend at the Alpha Delta house. Saturday night?"

Demi toys with one of her hoop earrings as she thinks about it. "He went out with his work friends Saturday night. I thought they were in Hastings, but I suppose they could've gone to that party."

"They were definitely there. I don't know if it was with the work buddies or not, but Nico was there. He and I even spoke."

"Okay. So he went to a party. Big deal."

"That's not all he did."

Her features sharpen again. "What do you mean?"

"I mean I saw him upstairs with some chick."

Once again, silence falls over the car. Shit. I should not have brought this up at all.

"All right," she says slowly. "You saw him with a girl. What were they doing?"

"They were exiting a bedroom."

"Were they naked?"

"Well, no, they were both fully clothed. But…" I don't want to say it, but I force myself to spit it out. "He was zipping up his pants."

"Oh."

"Obviously that doesn't mean they were doing anything," I add hastily. "Maybe they both needed to use the bathroom and he forgot to do up his fly after taking a leak. But, speaking as a guy—"

"As a fuckboy, you mean."

"Whoa." I'm taken aback by the verbal assault. She must really hate me right now. "Should I remind you I haven't been sexually active in months?"

"Should I remind me how sexually active you were last year? You said so yourself, remember? So maybe you're just associating your own behavior with whatever you think you saw Nico doing." Her lips tighten. "Maybe they were using the bathroom. Maybe they were hanging out or talking or whatever. You don't know for certain that something happened."

"That's exactly what I'm saying to you," I grumble. "I don't know if anything happened."

We reach the fork in the road that leads to Greek Row, and I eagerly flick the turn signal. I've never been happier to see a sorority house and I'm not even banging anyone inside of it.

"Look, I'm sorry," I mutter. "I shouldn't have said anything."

Demi doesn't answer. Her profile is as tense as the current state of my shoulders.

I stop in front of the Theta house. I avoid her eyes as I put the Rover in park. "But I figured I should tell you. You know, just in case."

"Tell me what? That my boyfriend was talking to some girl?"

"No, that he went upstairs with her, that they were alone in a bedroom, and that he walked out zipping up his pants. Get your head out of the sand, Demi. Men in relationships don't do that kind of shit."

I instantly regret my harsh tone. But rather than go silent or meek, Demi's eyes turn molten. "You don't know anything about my relationship, Hunter."

"I know that you already suspected him of cheating on you once."

"Yeah, when we were kids. He's matured since then."

*Has he?* I want to challenge. I keep quiet, but the unspoken question hangs in the air, and Demi hisses in response to it.

"He *has*," she insists. "And you know what? I don't appreciate you jumping to conclusions, and I don't appreciate all your fear mongering!"

"Fear mongering?" I can't help but snicker. "Jesus Christ. All I'm telling you is that I saw the dude zip up his pants. Do with that what you will."

# 15
# DEMI

*He was zipping up his pants.*

Hunter's words buzz in my brain as I stalk into house. Despite the late hour, a bunch of my sorority sisters are still up, watching a horror movie. The living room is dark, and I glimpse bowls of popcorn and hear a lot of shrieking at the screen. But I don't join them. I'm not in the mood.

Instead I go to the kitchen and stick my head in the fridge. I need a snack. Pronto. When I'm agitated, I eat. It's a habit I probably need to squash, because great metabolism doesn't last forever, but my mom is in her forties and can still eat whatever she wants, so I'm hopeful for the future. I grab a block of cheddar and angrily start cutting the cheese into cubes.

I don't care what Hunter says. Nico couldn't have cheated. Yes, he was out on Saturday night with his friends. And fine, maybe they did wind up at a frat party. But that doesn't mean he did anything shady. For all Hunter knows, Nico was hanging out with Pippa. I'm pretty sure Pippa went to that party, too.

I put down the knife and grab my phone, wasting no time texting my friend.

**ME**: Hey, were you at the Alpha Delt party on Sat??

As I wait for Pippa's response, I pile the cheese cubes onto a plate and then rummage through the pantry for a box of crackers. I dump a bunch of those on the plate too.

When my phone buzzes, I dive for it.

**PIPPA**: Ya. Why??

**ME**: Did you see Nico there?

**HER**: No. Was he there?

**ME**: Maybe? Someone says they saw him.

**HER**: Hmmm. Well I did leave kinda early, like around 11. Do you know what time he got there?

**ME**: No clue. But just to be clear, you didn't see him when you were there?

**HER**: Nope.

I bite my lip. All right. So he wasn't with Pippa. That doesn't mean anything.

**PIPPA**: What's going on, D?

**ME**: Call me?

She calls less than five seconds later. I carry my cracker and cheese plate upstairs to my bedroom, balancing the phone on my shoulder. "Do you think Nico's cheating on me?" I demand in lieu of hello.

"Cheating on you? Is that a joke?"

"No. Someone saw him in a compromising position with another girl at the party."

Pippa laughs. "Bullshit."

A tiny sliver of hope pierces into me. "You think so?"

"I know so. Come on, babe. That boy is *obsessed* with you."

"That doesn't mean he's not cheating."

"Trust me, there's no way he would do anything to jeopardize your relationship. He's constantly going on and on about how you guys are going to get married someday. I can't see him throwing everything away for some random hook-up."

I can't, either. And, she's right. Nico does have the tendency to boast about the amazing future we're going to have. Why would he be planning a future with me if he's hooking up with other women?

"Who told you about this?" Pippa asks.

"Hunter," I confess.

"The hockey player?"

"Yes. He was at the party and he saw Nico leaving one of the upstairs bedrooms with a girl. Apparently he was zipping up his pants."

A brief silence meets my ear. Then Pippa says, "No. I still don't buy it."

"You don't?" The hope in my chest grows, joined by a rush of relief. "So, what, you think Hunter is lying?"

"Probably."

"What's his motivation to lie?"

"I bet he wants in your pants."

"We're just friends," I say. And I can't stop picturing the tortured expression on his face when he told me what he saw. It's obvious he didn't want to say anything.

Or…he could've been putting on an act, pretending that it pained him *so much* to tell me, but really it was all a plot to, as Pippa said, get in my pants. I mean, Hunter fully admitted to having a sexual fantasy about me once. *And* he's a self-proclaimed former manwhore. Why should I trust anything he has to say about women and relationships?

On the flip side, I've known Nico since I was eight years old. He's my best friend.

"Nico loves you," Pippa says as if reading my mind. "I think Hunter is lying or else he misinterpreted what he saw."

"So you think I'm being crazy?"

"I think you're being crazy."

"Thanks, chica." I sigh. "Should I say something to Nico?"

"I don't know, babe. It might start a fight, but if you need to do it for your peace of mind, then yeah, you should. But don't frame it like an accusation," she advises. "Maybe treat it more as a joke? Like, *omigosh hon, can you believe that?*"

"That's a good approach."

We hang up a few minutes later, and I'm left sitting on my bed with a snack plate in my lap.

I stare down at the mountain of cheese and crackers, but I don't have much of an appetite anymore.

---

**NICO**: Good morning, bb. Meet for breakfast?

I stare at my boyfriend's message for a good five minutes before assembling enough courage to respond.

**ME**: Sure. But I just woke up, so I need time to get ready. Pick me up in 45?

**HIM**: Sounds good :) I'll msg u when I get 2 campus.

I'm nervous as I get ready. I decided I'm definitely going to confront him about what Hunter told me. I have no choice, because if I don't, it'll eat away at me like a slow-moving cancer, until I won't even be able to look at him without wondering if he cheated.

Hunter has to be wrong, though. Like Pippa said, he's either straight-up lying or he misinterpreted the situation. I'm hoping for the latter, because I enjoy our friendship and I don't like the idea that he's secretly been running a long con to get me into bed. That would be really shitty.

Nico texts when he's outside. I step onto the porch and am

greeted by his handsome face and beautiful dimpled smile. I find myself relaxing. I adore that smile, and I adore that face. He's... well, he's my first love. I'm always going to see him and have this giddy, schoolgirl reaction. And just because I've had some doubts about our relationship, some suspicions along the way, doesn't mean we're not a good couple.

"Hey *mami*." He pulls me toward him for a hug, followed by a deep, tongue-tangling kiss.

I want to say it's a lot of passion this early in the morning, but Nico is always this passionate. It's the Cuban in him. He's all about bold claims and romantic gestures.

"You look good enough to eat." He smacks his lips together comically and I laugh.

"So do you. But I think I want some real food first."

"You always want real food."

"True."

He snickers. "How was Boston last night?" he asks as we step off the porch.

"Good. My parents were bummed you weren't there."

"Me too. But I had to work." He takes my hand. "Hopefully we can get up to see them before Thanksgiving."

"I doubt it. I've got midterms, and in the beginning of November the sorority is planning that fundraiser for the animal shelter."

His fingers loosely clasp mine as we walk towards the curb.

"Nice, you have your work truck," I say. It's one of the white pick-ups from the moving company, with their black and red logo stenciled onto the side.

"I know it's only a ten-minute walk, but do you mind if we drive to Carver? I only have an hour."

"Your first class isn't until two," I remind him.

"I know, but I need to go to work for a few hours. I told Frank I'd do a small job before class." He opens the passenger side door for me, then hurries around to get into the driver's seat.

"You asked Frank about next Friday, right?"

Nico starts the engine. "Next Friday, like two weeks from now?"

"Yeah, it's Corinne's housewarming. You were supposed to tell Frank you couldn't work that night."

"Oh, right." Nico nods, and a hunk of black hair falls on his forehead. I reach over to brush it away. "Sorry, I forgot because it's so far away. But yes, I did talk to him. He promised I'd be outta there by seven."

"Good." I buckle my seatbelt. "Isn't her new place so cute?"

"Honestly? I don't remember what it looks like," he says with a grin. "I've moved boxes into so many houses and apartments that they all blend together in my mind. Oh hey, I got you something."

That piques my interest. "You did?"

"D and I were grabbing burgers in the city the other day, and the place had one of those gumball machines, except instead of gumballs it gave out little toys and trinkets. Cost me a buck, but"—Nico grins broadly—"I knew I *had* to get this for you."

He pops open the small compartment in the center console and sticks a hand inside. Things rustle and keys jingle as he rummages around.

Finally, his hand emerges with a plastic yellow egg. "Here you go."

Highly curious, I pry open the two plastic pieces, and a small baggie falls into my lap. I break out in a grin. The bag contains a pair of cheap, plastic earrings—enormous red hoops with black polka dots.

"Because I know how much you *love* the big hoops," Nico teases.

"Aww, you're the worst." But I can't stop grinning because this gift means Nico was thinking of me when he was out with his friends, enough to stick a dollar bill into some kiddie machine so he could get me these silly earrings.

"I love them," I say, and then dramatically fling my arms around him and kiss his cheek.

"Also, they're plastic," he says helpfully. "So if they do get caught on anything, they'll probably break apart before your earlobe gets ripped off."

This boy knows me well.

He pulls away from the curb and it takes literally a minute to drive three parking lots over to the one behind Carver Hall. I have a meal plan since I technically live on campus, but Nico doesn't, so he has to pay for his breakfast. He gets French toast, and I fill my plate with bacon, eggs and toast from the buffet. Then we find a cozy table in the back of the chalet-style dining hall. The room has an impossibly high ceiling, oak paneled walls, and round mahogany tables scattered throughout.

Ten minutes into breakfast, I finally raise the subject. "Hey, so I wanted to ask you something."

"Hmmm?" He takes a bite of French toast.

"It's just…and honestly, I am *not* accusing you of anything, so please don't take it wrong way."

That gets Nico's attention. His fork snaps down on his tray. "Accusing me? What's going on?"

"Um, well. Someone mentioned something to me and I wanted to discuss it with you."

"Discuss what?"

Shit, what am I doing? Do I really want to discuss this in public? What if it goes horribly wrong?

But I already boarded the train and now I've gotta ride it all the way to crazy town. "Somebody saw you at the Alpha Delta party last weekend. With a girl."

"Somebody saw me with a girl… Can we be a little more specific?"

"They saw you coming out of an upstairs bedroom with her, and you may or may not have been zipping up your pants."

His dark eyes flash angrily. "Who said this exactly?"

"That's not important."

"Like fuck it isn't. I want to know who's spreading lies about me."

I study his expression. He seems genuinely upset, and his denial didn't ring false to me. Yet for some reason I don't want to throw Hunter under the bus, so I lie about my source. "It was a random girl at the party who told one of my sorority sisters, who told me. How I found out isn't important. I just wanted to be sure…you're saying you didn't do anything?"

"Of course not."

I hear nothing but sincerity in his voice. "Were you at the party, though?"

"Yeah, I went with Steve and Rodrigo and a couple other guys from work. I told you I was chilling with them that night."

"Right, but you didn't tell me you were going to a frat party down the street from me."

"I said the boys and I were hanging out, and we were. We went to a few different places," Nico says irritably. "Eventually we wound up there, but it was late and I didn't see the point in calling you. I had a few drinks, joked around with the guys, and the only chick I spent any time with was Roddy's sister Carla—that's probably who they saw me with. I took her up to use the bathroom. The line for the other bathroom was ridiculous, so we snuck upstairs."

This all sounds plausible. I've been in the Alpha Delta house before, and I've seen how popular that lone downstairs bathroom is.

"Carla did her business, I did my business, and then we left the room. I don't remember zipping my fly." His jaw tightens. "But if I did, it's probably because I forgot to zip it up after taking a piss."

He doesn't sound defensive. He's defending himself, yes, but I'm not getting any sense that he's trying to convince me of something.

"Whoever told you this crap obviously read something more into the situation."

"That's what I figured. I only brought it up because…" I shrug. "Well, because it's good to always be open and honest with each other."

"I agree." His body language is still a tad stiff as he picks up his fork and resumes eating. "But I don't like the idea of people talking trash about me."

"There was no trash talking involved," I promise. "Just one friend watching out for another friend."

"One friend trying to stir up shit, more like it. Which chick said this to you?"

"I told you, I don't know the girl at the party."

"But which one of the Thetas said it?"

"It doesn't matter. She brought it to my attention because we look out for each other, but for what it's worth she also didn't think there was anything to the story," I lie.

Nico looks pleased. "Good. And I'm glad you don't believe that bullshit, either." He reaches across the table for my hand, interlacing our fingers. "You know I would never do that to you."

# 16
# DEMI

I'M TEMPTED TO CANCEL MY SESSION WITH HUNTER THE FOLLOW-ing Monday. We haven't spoken since Boston last week, our only contact being when he texted to ask if we were still on for tonight. I feel like he was hoping I'd cancel. But this class is important to me, and I want to do well on our project. That means sucking it up and continuing to see him every week.

Maybe Hunter truly was looking out for me when he threw Nico under the bus, but for the past week everyone I've spoken to has assured me whatever happened with Nico and that girl was completely innocent. When we were at one of the campus bars a few nights ago, Darius had pulled me aside and said, "Listen, I wasn't even there that night and I can still tell you it's bullshit."

I appreciated hearing it from Darius. Nico's work friends all backed him up too, but I don't know them as well as I know D. Also...I'd never say this out loud, but I find Steve and Roddy and those guys seriously douchey. I suspect they'd have Nico's back regardless of his guilt or innocence, because they're all about the bro code. Darius, however, is a good friend to both of us, so I know he wouldn't lie to me.

Meanwhile, Nico has been extra attentive since I confronted him. Coming dangerously close to what I'd consider sucking up. I'm trying hard not to hold a cynical view about it, and even harder to put this behind us. He told me nothing happened and I said I believed him. That means letting go of any negativity, and not mistrusting him or questioning his motives.

I'm on edge as I wait for Hunter to arrive, stress-eating a bag of potato chips.

**HUNTER:** Josie let me in. I'm coming up.

He knocks on the door a moment later. I call out, "Come in," between my loud crunching.

Hunter appears, his thumbs loosely hooked in the pockets of his ripped jeans. They're not skinny jeans, but they're fitted to his long legs, while his black Under Armour shirt is tight to his sculpted chest. His dark hair is tousled, and his cheeks are red.

"It's windy out there," he mutters, dragging one hand through his hair.

"It's supposed to thunderstorm tonight."

"Good. It's mid-October—how is it still so hot out there?"

"Global warming," I supply.

"Yeah, it's a real problem."

Oh boy. This is not going to be fun. We're discussing the climate. And he's not looking at me, but at his Timberland boots. The ease and humor that normally flows between us is nowhere to be found.

When Hunter takes his designated seat on the loveseat, he doesn't lie down like he usually does. His big, muscular body remains seated—and tense. "Whatever, let's do this."

I grit my teeth. "You could sound a little more enthused."

"So could you," he shoots back.

I shove the chip bag on my nightstand. Fine. I guess this is how it is. I flip open the binder I'm using for the project and turn to the latest blank log.

After having done this a handful of times, I think I'm solidly in the Narcissistic Personality Disorder camp. "Dick Smith" fits all the diagnostic criteria from the DSM-5. But the problem with an NPD diagnosis is that narcissists customarily don't *know* they're narcissists, meaning that any analysis is only as useful as the info coming in. And the fact that narcissists have a tendency to rewrite events in their minds makes the whole process even more challenging.

This means the therapist needs to ask the right questions. Weed out important tidbits and search for any emerging patterns, such as the patient describing an interaction that doesn't match their reaction to it. And don't get me started on treatment. I mean, if a narcissist can't recognize he's a narcissist, how on earth do you treat his narcissism?

Ugh. I'm not super thrilled with this one. I would prefer something more straightforward, like an anxiety disorder. At least those suffering from anxiety tend to be aware they have a problem.

"So why do you think you're in therapy?" I ask my fake patient.

"I told you, my wife wanted me to go."

"So you don't think you need therapy."

"Nope." Hunter crosses his ankles and gazes up at the ceiling. "There's nothing wrong with me."

"There doesn't need to be something wrong with you, or anybody, for you to benefit from therapy."

"People who see shrinks are weak. Only reason I'm doing this is to keep my marriage together."

"And why do you want to do that?"

He scoffs. "Because no one in my family gets divorced. Divorce is another sign of weakness. An indication of your inability to work hard enough to achieve a goal."

"The goal here being, saving your marriage."

"Yes."

"Because if you get divorced, you'll look bad in front of your family and colleagues?"

"No, because I love my wife. I want to keep everything together for her and my son."

"Your *son*?"

Oh my God. Plot twist! I've been waiting weeks for a curveball like this.

Instantly, my pen is poised over my paper, ready to take copious notes. "This is the first time you mentioned a son."

"I had no reason to. The problems in my marriage have nothing to do with him."

"Yes, but it would still be fruitful for me to get a better sense of your family unit," I point out. "I need to know all the facts."

Hunter watches me through slitted eyes. "I see. So knowing all the facts *is* important?"

I tense at the jab, which is obviously directed at me, Demi, and not the fake Dr. Davis. "When the facts are true or relevant to the discussion, then yes. When someone is stirring up trouble for no reason, then no."

"For *no reason*?" The muscles in his jaw harden. "Whatever. Fine. You want to hear about my son? I'll tell you about my son. He's a little prick."

I'm taken aback by the vehemence in his tone. "Why do you say that?"

"The kid's a snitch. If it weren't for him, my wife would have no idea about that goddamn affair with my assistant. He's the one who told her."

"I see."

"He showed up at my office one day over summer break. He came by to say hello and caught me banging my secretary on the desk." Disgust twists Hunter's features. "Did he try to get an explanation from me? Ask what his mother may have done to drive me to such extreme actions? Absolutely not. Instead he took off, ran home, and told his mother what he saw."

There is something scarily…realistic about this story.

Hunter's visible resentment tells me this is more than playacting. "How old was he?"

"Fourteen. A fourteen-year-old punk who thought he was a man, the big hero who was gonna rescue his mom. Joke's on him, though. Kathryn didn't care. Of course she wasn't going to leave me. Look at me—rich, attractive. She can't do any better than me. My son thought he was doing the right thing, but as it turns out, nobody gave a shit about his opinion."

Hunter angrily shakes his head. "And it scarred the kid, because it turns out his mom already *knew* about that affair, and the previous affairs before it, and she begged him to just look the other way because his father was *such* a good man and a good dad and a good provider. When he tried to argue, she called him a troublemaker and made him feel like he'd done something wrong by telling her the truth. And so years later, when he saw something else he knew might hurt another woman, he wanted to keep his mouth shut." He's glaring at me now. "And it took a fucking lot for him to say anything. He asked his friends if he should, if they would want to know, and in the back of his mind a little voice was saying *don't get involved, it's only gonna blow up in your face again,* and look what happened—it fucking did."

Silence crashes over the bedroom. Hunter is visibly furious. I don't know if it's with me, or with himself, or with the world. He scrapes his fingers through his hair again, stone-faced.

"Hunter," I start carefully. "You…told your mother that you caught your father cheating? And…so wait…all these things you've been describing during our sessions, they actually happened to you? Your dad is the one who…"

I trail off in confusion, as my brain cycles through our sessions in an attempt to parse out which stories were real and which ones he fabricated to suit the assignment. Obviously his father was the inspiration for the narcissist he'd been pretending to be, but how much of it was an act?

"Whatever," Hunter mutters, rising to his feet. "I was trying to be a good friend, but you know what, screw this. We're done for the day. See you next week."

I'm helpless to do anything as he storms out of my room. I want to go after him, but my mind still feels muddled. Too many facts are scrambling my brain. I flip through my notes, reading over the Thanksgiving story, all the affairs, the wife's lack of a backbone and my patient's cruel dismissals of anyone he views as inferior. Is this Hunter's family? How much of it was embellished?

The one thing I'm certain was real, was the agony in his voice when he recounted telling his mother what he saw, and being told he was a troublemaker for trying to protect her.

And I said the same thing to him, accusing him of stirring up trouble.

Fuck. Sighing, I scrub my palms over my face, as guilt twists my stomach into knots. Maybe Hunter's motives were one hundred percent pure, after all.

But…he's still wrong, dammit.

---

On Friday we go to Corinne's housewarming. She's low-key so she didn't want a party, but Pippa and I talked her into it and she agreed on the condition that we kept it small.

Nico grabs me, Darius and Pippa from campus. As his girlfriend, I'm granted permanent shotgun, which means Darius and his six-foot six-inches frame is banished to the backseat.

"C'mon, D," he gripes. "My body deserves shotgun and you know it."

"If you're nice, I'll let you have it on the way back." I pull out my phone to text Corinne, only to discover it's completely dead. Shit. I forgot to charge it before I left.

I twist around to address Pippa. "Can you let Corinne know we're on the way?"

"On it."

I slide my iPhone back into my purse. Nico drives one-handed, his free hand planted firmly on my thigh. At a couple points during the drive his thumb seductively rubs my bare knee, and at one red light he even slides his fingertips under the hem of my skirt. I give him a look that says, *You're incorrigible*, and he winks in response.

There are already several people at Corinne's place when we arrive. It's an interesting mix tonight: a couple of basketball players, a girl from Corinne's yoga studio in town, and some guys from her math class. She's an Economics major and a math geek, and so are her three classmates. One of them is actually wearing a suit and tie, which makes me grin.

"You know you're at a party, right?" I tease after we're introduced. His name is Kyler and he's a senior.

"The tie's too much?" he says wryly.

"Just a bit."

As Kyler and I chat, Nico appears at my side and takes my hand. He does that sometimes, staking a physical claim when I'm with another guy, as if to say *she's mine*. I used to think it was cute. Sometimes I still do. Other times, like tonight, when I'm trying to walk around the room and talk to people, his being glued to my hip is an encumbrance.

And, frankly, annoying.

Corinne set up a refreshment table in the small dining/living area. The party is BYOB, but she bought a variety of chasers and a couple bottles of tequila. I'm planning on drinking tonight, so I don't waste any time organizing the first round of shots.

"Come on, guys," I urge, waving everyone over.

Nico's all for it. He's more of a rum man, but he happily pours a waterfall of tequila over the row of shot glasses I lay out. I start handing them out, and then the eleven of us raise our glasses. "To Corinne, and her awesome new place!" I toast.

"To adulting!" Pippa adds.

"To adulting!"

The tequila burns a fiery path down my throat and instantly I'm warm all over. Someone turns up the music, and Nico and I drift over to the couch.

Pippa is sitting in Darius's lap, his long fingers toying with her hair. They're not a couple, but they flirt shamelessly when they're together. I tried setting them up a long time ago, but it didn't work out for whatever reason. I think neither of them wants a serious relationship, so their flirty arrangement suits them both.

Corinne stands nearby chatting with Kyler, and the others are gathered near the drinks table. Darius snatches the remote off the glass table when he notices what's on TV.

He swiftly turns up the volume. "Aw shit, I love this movie!"

"You realize it's for chicks, right?" Nico informs him.

"If it's for chicks then why is Scarlett Johansson in it?" D challenges. "Cuz I highly doubt chicks jerk off to ScarJo as often as I do."

Laughter breaks out. Kyler the math guy blushes. He's kind of cute. I wonder if he and Corinne are into each other. He's standing very close to her.

"Where do I know this actor from?" Pippa asks as a handsome guy appears on the screen. "He was in that movie about a cellphone, wasn't he?"

"That's the vaguest shit I ever heard," Darius says, poking her in the ribs.

"You know the movie I'm talking about, right, Demi?"

I peer at the screen. "Is that Chris Evans?"

Pippa nods. "And I swear to God, he was in that cellphone movie. It's an older movie with...that British guy, and that lady, and..."

Darius hoots loudly. "Fuck's sake, P, stop being so vague."

"Wait, I think I know the movie you mean," I tell Pippa. "Shit. I can't remember the title, either. Babe, let me use your phone to look it up?"

Nico reaches into his pocket and hands me his iPhone. It doesn't require a passcode to unlock, which only serves as another reason why Hunter's cheating accusations fall flat to me. Why would Nico willingly relinquish his phone if he were hiding something?

Nico's data plan is shit, so rather than pull up a browser, I open his settings first. "Hey, what's your Wi-Fi network?" I ask Corinne.

"Cwiley22," she calls back. "Password is lower-case A, upper-case F—"

"That's weird," I interrupt, "it connected on its own."

An uneasy feeling tickles my tummy as I glance at Nico.

"Huh." A frown creases his brow. "You know what, my phone must have saved your network when the boys and I were here moving you in," he says to Corinne.

"Oh, that must be it," she replies.

I nod slowly and open a web browser to search for—what am I searching for again? Oh, right. Chris Evans. But my fingers are trembling as I Google his filmography.

Something's bothering me and I can't figure out what it is. I mean, I already knew that Nico and his co-workers moved all of Corinne's boxes from the dorm to the apartment, and transported her new furniture. He never hid that, and neither did she. And of course she would've given Nico her Wi-Fi password if he'd asked. And he would've asked, because his data plan sucks and if he was here for a couple hours and wanted to use his phone, he'd definitely—

Then it hits me, the reason why my stomach is churning and twisting itself into knots.

Corinne didn't have Wi-Fi until nearly a week after she'd moved in. When I came over to help with her closet, it still hadn't been set up.

There's no way it could've been up and running when Nico was there days and days before.

My entire body suddenly feels cold.

"Demi. What's the movie we're thinking of?" Pippa asks impatiently.

My breathing is labored as I glance at the phone screen. "It was called *Cellular*," I mumble.

"Ha! Damn, you were right about it being a cellphone movie," a laughing Darius says to Pippa.

"I told you so."

As everyone starts chatting again, I drop the phone in Nico's lap. His deep brown eyes study me carefully. "Babe?"

I'm having a tough time finding my voice. I truly don't know what to say. Corinne is still talking to Kyler, but for some reason I *know* she's listening to me and Nico.

I draw a shaky breath. Why did his phone instantly connect to her Wi-Fi? That would suggest he's been back here since moving day, but why would he ever need to be? She's my friend, not his. I can see him hanging out with Pippa without me, but not Corinne.

The tequila gurgles in my stomach. Fuck. Am I going to throw up?

"Demi, what's wrong?" Nico urges.

I weakly meet his gaze. "Corinne only set up her Wi-Fi a week after she moved in."

For one fast second, panic flits through his expression. But it happens so quickly that I can't be sure.

"Okay, that is weird, then," he says, pursing his lips. "I wonder why it just connected like that."

"Yeah, I wonder," I say tightly.

Our hushed conversation draws Pippa's attention. "What's going on?" she asks.

"Nothing," Nico says instantly.

But Pippa knows me well. One look at my face and she's already sliding off Darius's lap.

"What's going on?" she repeats, her sharp gaze moving from me to Nico and then back to me.

I open my mouth but nothing comes out. Slowly, I turn my head toward Corinne. She's looking right back, and the guilty cloud in her eyes is all it takes for me to bolt to my feet.

The room spins for a moment. With three shots of tequila swimming in my gut, now I really am in danger of vomiting.

I choke down the bile coating my throat. "You have *got* to be kidding me," I spit out. "How long?"

Corinne takes a step toward me. "It's not what you're thinking—"

"How long have you been fucking my boyfriend, Corinne?" My head swivels toward Nico. "How long have you been fucking her?"

The entire room goes dead silent. On the TV screen, ScarJo is bickering with Chris Evans and suddenly the movie doesn't feel so cute and funny anymore. It feels like a slap in the face, these stupid people falling in love when I've just been blindsided by my boyfriend of eight years.

"Oh shit," Darius murmurs. His voice is low, and he seems as stunned as I feel. I don't think he knew about this. I don't think anyone did, except for Hunter.

Hunter tried to warn me. He found the courage to tell me what he saw at the party and—

I abruptly turn to Corinne again. "Was that you at the frat party?" I demand.

She blinks. "What?"

"A couple of weekends ago, the party at the Alpha Delta house on Saturday night—were you there with Nico?"

She rapidly shakes her head. "No, I swear I wasn't. I'm in a study group with Kyler and Ahmed and we meet Saturday night."

She gestures to the two guys, who are quick to back up her alibi. "We were all together," Kyler says awkwardly.

"Then how long has this been going on?" My voice is cold.

"It only happened once," she blurts out. "Just one time, I swear."

My stomach roils again. I don't want to hear anymore. I'm done.

Gulping hard, I spin on my heel and stomp toward the door. Nico chases after me, his pleading voice echoing through the small apartment.

"Demi, please, stop! Let me explain."

"Explain what?" I roar, whirling around. "You cheated on me

with my friend! And then again with some other girl at the party! Who was she? How many goddamn women are you screwing?"

"I didn't cheat on you. She's lying—"

"Hey!" Corinne flies forward. "I am *not* lying!"

I flick my gaze her way and glimpse a flash of outrage. It's directed at my boyfriend.

"I'm not lying, Demi," Corinne says quietly. "It happened."

And I believe her.

"Pippa," I say in a wobbly voice. "Get me an Uber. Now." I'm fighting tears, because my phone's dead and I'm trapped here in this stupid apartment with my traitorous friend and my cheating boyfriend and I just want to crawl in a fucking hole and die.

"On it," Pippa tells me.

"Demi." Nico tries to grab my arm.

On instinct I swing my other arm and clock him in the face.

His head rears back, a bitter curse ripped out of his mouth.

My fist caught him on his left cheekbone. With a wounded expression, he cups one hand over it. "You hit me."

"You bet I fucking did, and you deserve a whole lot more, you fucking asshole."

"Uber's two minutes away," Pippa announces.

I jab my index finger into the center of Nico's chest. "Do *not* follow me," I warn him, and then I run out the door.

# 17
# HUNTER

It's Friday night and my roommates and I are playing an inane board game called Zombies!™ Exclamation mark included.

Hollis is home for the weekend, which means we get to listen to him and Rupi bicker over the latest development in the game. Hollis just drew a Sacrifice card—this requires him to sacrifice someone in our collaborative group in order for the rest of us to get closer to safety. Only problem is, the most advantageous move would be to get rid of Rupi. If she dies, we don't lose much. Everybody else is too valuable to the group. There are two crossbows in my arsenal, for chrissake. What does Rupi have? Nothing.

"Dammit, Mike, finish her off," Summer bursts out, and damned if I don't crack up hearing someone as angelic-looking as Summer advocating for the fake killing of one of our friends.

"Summer!" Rupi gasps in utter betrayal.

"What?" she says defensively. "The whole point is to get the most people to the research station. There's only one Sacrifice card in the deck. Only one person in the group is gonna die and it has to be you."

"Has to be you," Brenna agrees, taking a sip of the hot chocolate that soon-to-be deceased Rupi prepared for us.

"Mike," Rupi warns. "If you kill me, I swear to God…"

"Babe," he says.

"Mike."

"Babe."

"Mike."

"Babe," he sighs, and then places the Sacrifice card in front of her pile.

Rupi shrieks loud enough to shake the coffee table. "I *cannot* believe you did that!"

"I had no choice," he protests. "It was best for the group."

"What about what's best for *me*?"

"You're being very selfish right now, babe."

"Why? Because I want my boyfriend to protect me from harm? I don't believe this! After we're done with this game, I'm going to—"

"You *are* done with the game," Brenna interrupts dryly. "He killed you."

Rupi huffs and flounces off in traditional Rupi fashion. The girl is a drama queen.

Luckily, she found true love with a drama king. Hollis stands up and throws his frazzled arms up in the air. "Do you see what you made me do?" he accuses the rest of us. "This is why I never play board games!"

He hurries after Rupi.

"And then there were three," Brenna says indifferently, flipping through her arsenal cards.

"We can't go on without him," I tell her. "He's the only one who has the antidote for the second mutation. Oh, and the only one who can skin a rabbit."

"We'll redistribute all the assets," Summer suggests.

"Nah, I think the game's over." I drop my cards on the board and lean back against the couch cushions.

"We need to stop playing games with them," Brenna remarks as she picks up her mug.

"Definitely," Summer concurs. "They're the worst."

I reach for my own hot chocolate and gulp it down. My head wasn't in the game, anyway.

For the past five days, Demi Davis has consumed my thoughts. I feel like shit for snapping at her, but if my severe tone wasn't bad enough, I followed it up by info-dumping my dismal relationship with my father on her. I could practically see the gears in her brain working over all the things I'd told her since the semester started, trying to discern which ones were true.

Sadly, the majority were. I embellished a few details, to be sure. Dad generally isn't cruel to my mother, nor does he speak to her with the same disdain I used during the fake therapy sessions. I was trying to exaggerate certain narcissistic tendencies to make it easier for Demi.

But all the events I described occurred in real life. I did catch my father banging his secretary when I was fourteen years old. I did tell my mom, and she did tell me to not interfere in their marriage. Just be a good boy and stay quiet because Daddy takes care of us and what kind of life would we have without him.

That was the day I realized my mother has no self-worth and my father has too much of it.

Still, an angry trip down memory lane was no excuse to take it out on Demi. I knew there was a chance she wouldn't believe me when I told her about Nico. I shouldn't have mocked her about getting her head out of the sand, insinuated she was a naïve fool.

*She called you a fuckboy.*

Ugh, true. She was as much of a dick to me as I was to her. We're both dicks.

Fuck. I should try to clear the air. I look toward the side table where I left my phone. But no. Texting is garbage. A text conversation about this would feel too impersonal.

"You know what." I hop off the couch. "I have to go."

Summer glances over. "Are you sure? We could start a new game."

"Nah, I think the zombies can have this one. I'll be back later."

"Where are you going?" Brenna asks.

"To see a friend."

"Ha!" Mocking laughter rings out. "I knew the celibacy wouldn't last."

"Not for sex," I clarify. "It's the girl I'm working on that project with. We got into an argument the other day, and I want to smooth things over."

"You know you can just text her," Summer says helpfully.

"You know you can mind your own business."

"All right then."

I haven't been drinking, so I make the ten-minute drive to campus and turn onto Greek Row. I can't find a spot in front of the Theta house, but there's a stretch of empty curb a few houses away. I park the Rover and that's when I hear the yells.

Oh shit.

I quickly jog down the lane, skidding to a stop cartoon-character style when I spot Nico on the lawn of the Theta house, shouting up at the second-floor window.

"Come on, Demi! Please!"

The man sounds utterly destroyed. I'd probably feel genuine sympathy for him if not for the fact that I know precisely what's going on. He cheated on Demi at the party. There's no other reason why he'd be outside Demi's house, begging her to let him in.

"Please, *mami*, I love you! I fucked up, okay!"

I lurk near the hedges that separate the sorority house from its neighbor.

"Go away!" comes a high-pitched voice.

It's not Demi. I peer up and see two girls at the window, their figures backlit by Demi's bedroom lights.

"She doesn't want to talk to you. Go away," one of them yells.

"We'll call the police if you don't," the other one warns. "You're disrupting the peace. People are trying to sleep."

"It's nine o'clock on a Friday and this is Greek Row!" Nico growls. "Nobody is fucking sleeping, Josie! Just tell her to come down."

"She doesn't want to see you, you cheating prick."

Yup. I called this one.

"Demi," he wails. His voice actually cracks, and this time I *do* feel for the guy.

I know narcissists—I lived with one my whole life—and they don't usually experience remorse. If they do show any regret, it's probably an act. Yes, Nico could be putting on that act, but my gut says he isn't. He seems genuinely heartbroken.

*He made his bed,* a voice in my head points out.

"Demi! I'm going to stand out here all night until you let me in! *Please.* We've been together forever! You owe me a conversation. You owe me a chance to explain—"

A shriek of epic proportions slices through the night air. It's shrill enough to give Rupi Miller a run for her money.

Demi appears at the window, shoving her sisters out of the way. "I owe you?" she thunders. "I OWE YOU?"

Nico instantly recognizes his mistake. "No, I didn't mean it in that way—"

She cuts him off. "You cheated on me with one of my friends! And then you cheated on me *again* with some random chick at a party!"

*Oh, Nico, you stupid bastard.*

Any sympathy I had for him is long gone. I'm solidly on Team Demi. I mean, I always was, but now I don't care how gutted the guy appears to be. He deserves it.

"We're done," Demi screams out the window. "Do you hear me, Nicolás? We're *done.*"

"Baby, don't say that."

"You're right—we've known each other forever. I've been loyal to you forever. But you're incapable of reciprocating that loyalty. So please, just go."

"We can work through this," he pleads. "Please, give me another chance. Let me earn your trust back."

"*Dude!*" a random voice shouts from one of the neighboring houses. "You're pathetic! Bitch wants you to leave!"

Demi ignores the interruption. "There's no earning my trust back," she calls to Nico. "We're done. I don't want to be with you anymore. I don't want to be with a liar and a cheater. I'm worth more than what you've given me."

She's right about that. And call me a perv, but I'm disgustingly aroused by the sight of her right now. Her cheeks are flushed and her dark eyes are blazing like hot coals. She's got a hand on her hip as she glares down at Nico. Fierce and confident. Scorned but not defeated.

"We're not done," Nico says.

"We're done," she repeats.

"*You're done, bro,*" someone else hollers, and then other voices from Greek Row chime in.

"*Go home, asshole!*"

"*You're killing my buzz!*"

Nico only has eyes and ears for Demi. "You don't mean it," he informs her.

Idiot. Men really need to stop telling women what they mean or don't mean. The one lesson I've learned over the years is that a woman doesn't appreciate it when you put words in her mouth—or your dick in someone else's mouth.

"Oh, trust me, I mean it." Demi abruptly disappears from the window.

For a moment I think it's over. But then she reappears, her arms full of clothes.

"Let me help you clean out your drawer before you go," she says angrily.

I choke on a laugh as items of clothing come sailing out the second-floor window onto the lawn. A Celtics hoodie. Some T-shirts. A pair of boxers float down.

"You don't deserve a drawer in my house! You don't deserve

anything anymore. I'm done with this. Take all your stuff and get out of my life."

Once again I think it's all over.

But then Nico, stupid *stupid* Nico, utters the dumbest shit he could've ever uttered. "Don't you dare throw my PlayStation out the window, Demi!"

If that ain't a challenge.

She whirls around again, and this time she doesn't come back.

Huh. Okay. Maybe she decided to spare the PlayStation. Nico seems to think so, because his entire body relaxes. He glumly walks forward and begins picking up the clothes on the lawn.

He still hasn't noticed me, and I'm not about to make my presence known. It'd be like approaching a lion with a thorn in its paw.

Just when I decide all is well—when the night is quiet and Nico's scattered items have been collected—the front door of the sorority house flies open and Demi emerges. Holding a tangle of cables, controllers, and a slender black PlayStation.

Nico's head snaps up. "Thank you!" Looking relieved, he holds out his hands as if he truly believes he's getting the game console back unscathed.

"Thank you? No, thank *you*," Demi shoots back. She's spitting fire again. "Thank you for wasting eight years of my life." She hurls one controller to the ground. "Thank you for lying to my face." The second controller smashes on the concrete walkway. "Thank you for disrespecting me."

When she reaches the curb, the only item she's left holding is the PlayStation.

I hold my breath. The other components could easily be replaced. This console itself can't.

"I never want to see you again. You've ruined this. You ruined our friendship, you ruined our relationship, you ruined *everything*."

*Crash*!

The PlayStation collides with the sidewalk, breaking into several pieces.

Nico has the nerve to say, "I can't believe you did that!" Which prompts Demi to take a swing at him, and that's when I jump away from the hedge.

She manages to get one sharp blow in before I haul her away from him, trying to corral her like a wild horse.

She might not be a teammate, but I think this still qualifies for paragraph four, line eight of the captain's log: *Don't let your teammates commit murder.*

"Hey, hey, stop," I order.

"Hunter? What are you doing here?" She blinks a few times before her eyes go feral again. "Let me go. He deserves an ass kicking!"

"Yes, he does," I agree, and Nico scowls at me. "But karma will do that job for you, trust me."

"Hunter, let me go!" Now she's grunting, gritting her teeth, attempting to punch her way out of my grip. So I fling her over my shoulder in a fireman's carry. "Hunter!" she screeches in outrage. "Put me down!"

"No. I'm not watching you get arrested for assault tonight, okay?" I kick away a piece of Nico's PlayStation, while trying to contain a struggling Demi. "You're already guilty of property damage."

"I don't care!" she says stubbornly. "Now I want to do bodily damage."

"I know you do, Semi, but trust me, he ain't worth it."

But the riled-up woman in my arms is still flapping her arms like a trapped bird trying to get free. I spare a dark look at Nico before marching off toward my Land Rover. Only when I reach the vehicle do I set Demi down. The moment her socked feet meet the sidewalk, her steely demeanor seems to crumble. Suddenly she turns into a vulnerable girl, tears welling in her eyes.

"He humiliated me," she whispers.

"I know, babe. C'mere." I open my arms, but she ducks her head shamefully.

"No. I don't want a hug," she mumbles.

"Fine, then get in the car."

"Why?"

"You're coming over to my place and we're getting drunk. You could use the distraction."

Demi hesitates. She glances in the vicinity of the Theta house, where Nico is slowly walking toward his pick-up truck. Then she tears her gaze away and opens the passenger's door of my Rover.

We're on the road a few seconds later. Demi doesn't say a single word. She keeps her gaze straight ahead.

"I'm so sorry," I say gruffly.

She finally speaks, her voice trembling with each word. "No, I'm the one who's sorry. You were right—about everything. And I snapped at you and called you a fuckboy." She sniffles. "I feel horrible about that. Please tell me you accept my apology."

"Of course I do. It's all good with us, Demi. I promise."

She still refuses to look at me. "*He* was the fuckboy. He cheated on me. More than once, with more than one person."

"Yeah, I gathered."

I turn onto the main road that leads to town. It's a straight ten-minute drive, and then I'm pulling up into the driveway behind Summer's silver Audi. The lights are still on in the living room.

"Come on, you look like you need that drink."

Fat teardrops slip out the corners of her eyes. She blinks them back fast. "Okay."

We walk inside. Demi reaches down as if to remove her shoes before realizing she's not wearing any. Pink and gray striped socks cover her small feet. She stares at them for a moment as if questioning whether they even belong to her.

"Yo, Hunter? That you?" Hollis calls from the living room.

"Yeah," I call back.

"Good timing—we're about to start a new game."

I guess he and Rupi ironed out their insane differences. "I brought a friend with me," I answer as I unlace my boots.

"Oooh," teases Brenna. "Is it a sexy friend?"

I examine Demi. All I see are quivering lips, smudges of mascara under red-rimmed eyes, and a shell-shocked expression.

"Fuck off," she says ruefully.

I snicker. "Sorry, but sexy isn't on your side right now."

When we enter the living room, the girls take one look at my guest and jump to their feet. "Are you okay?" Summer blurts out.

Brenna glares at me, then turns to Demi. "What did he do to you?"

"Oh, screw off, Bee."

Demi laughs through her tears. "Be nice to him. He just stopped me from physically assaulting my cheating boyf—*ex*-boyfriend," she corrects.

"Ugh! Cheaters are the worst kind of dirt bags," Summer declares.

"The worst," Hollis agrees.

"You poor thing," Rupi clucks, tugging Demi toward the couch.

In the blink of an eye, she's surrounded by the girls, who immediately start pressing for details.

"If you guys don't mind, I'd rather not talk about it," Demi admits. She gulps a few times, then gives a half-hearted smile and points to the board game on the coffee table. "What are we playing?"

# 18
# DEMI

"I've barely seen you these past couple weeks." Disappointment and compassion war in TJ's eyes, but after a beat he reaches across the table and gives my hand a squeeze, showing that his compassion won out. Which is a relief, because I'm simply not equipped to reassure him right now. My mental health comes first, and I've been AWOL for reasons that have nothing to do with him or our friendship.

"You didn't miss much. I haven't been great company." I pick at the edge of my banana muffin.

"You're always great company," TJ says with a smile.

"That's sweet of you to say."

"It's the truth. How are you doing?"

"Better. I mean, my boyfriend cheated on me, so I'm not throwing any parades right now, but I'm also not tempted to commit violence and blow up his apartment." Which, considering my behavior following Corinne's housewarming, is certainly progress.

I honestly think I blacked out that night. I remember everything I did, but the memories feel removed and are filtered through a red haze. Throwing Nico's clothes out the window, smashing his PlayStation, punching him in the face. The clearest of the memories are the ones involving Hunter and his roommates. That silly board game we played had succeeded in calming me down, and therefore I'm forever indebted to Zombies!™

"Have you spoken to him?" TJ asks. "Or do you still have his number blocked?"

"Still blocked." I had no choice but to do it. Nico was calling and texting so often it was becoming intolerable. "But he did show up at the house last week," I admit.

TJ frowns deeply. "You didn't tell me that."

"There was nothing to tell. He knocked on the door, and Josie and the others threatened to castrate him if he came by again."

"Good. And don't forget, my offer still stands—I'll beat him up for you if you want."

I give a dry smile. "He's not worth it. Besides, I don't want you getting hurt." TJ isn't scrawny, but he's five-eight with a lanky build. Nico would murder him in a fight.

His hand tightens over mine.

"I didn't mean it in a you're-a-wimp sense," I backpedal. "I know you're not. I just mean he's not worth the effort. Besides, you'd have to get in line. Pax is already doing extra arm days at the gym to bulk up, so that he can, and I quote, 'fuck him up and not in the good way.'" We both snicker. "And Darius isn't speaking to him at all."

"Wow. Really?"

"Yep. Say what you will about D, but you know how he feels about monogamy." Darius is also very religious, so he doesn't condone anything that treads the line of immorality. "Oh, and we can't forget about Hunter. He would love to knock Nico around."

Speaking of Hunter, my phone buzzes a minute later with a text from him. I click on it to find a picture of an egg in a tiny hammock. A second message simply says: @PabloEggscobar.

Oh my God.

Pablo has his own Instagram account now.

TJ leans in curiously. "What's that pic of?"

"They have a pet egg." I put the phone down, shaking my head.

"What? Who?" TJ sounds confused.

"The hockey team. Their mascot is a hard-boiled egg that they all take turns caring for. I think it's some sort of team-building exercise? Hunter wasn't very articulate about it."

"Won't it go rotten and start stinking?"

"Already has. These days it's wrapped up in cellophane and kept in the fridge overnight, but the plastic wrap hasn't suppressed the smell completely. Hunter had the egg on him last week and I kept catching whiffs of sulfur."

"That is so weird. I'll never understand jocks."

"Honestly, I don't think it's an across-the-board jock thing. I think it's a Briar hockey player thing. They're all nuts, Hunter included."

"Then why do you keep texting with him?" TJ asks lightly.

"Because we're friends." I shrug. "My friends are allowed to be nuts."

And Hunter, for all his strange habits, has been an amazing friend to me since my relationship was blown to smithereens. Also, his roommates are my new favorite people. Brenna is a total smartass and I love her. Summer and I don't have much in common, but she makes me laugh. And Rupi is…Rupi. Her relationship with Hunter's friend Hollis fascinates me. I truly can't tell if they're madly in love or hate each other's guts. Maybe a mixture of both? Either way, they're highly entertaining.

I'm learning that keeping busy is the best remedy for a bad break-up. This means concentrating on midterms, math quizzes, chem labs, psych readings, anything that occupies my brain. And when my brain gets tired, I distract myself with friends. Drinks with Pippa, movie nights with my sorority sisters, hangouts at Hunter's house. So far, it's helping.

"When does your bus leave today?" TJ asks over the rim of his cup. A teabag string hangs over the edge. He's not a coffee drinker, so it's herbal teas for him.

"Seven-thirty." I groan. "Ugh, I'm not looking forward to Thanksgiving. My parents are going to have simultaneous heart attacks when I tell them about Nico."

"Wait, you still haven't told them you guys broke up?"

"Nope. It'll be a Thanksgiving surprise."

"That sucks. They really like him, eh?"

"Like him? That's like saying frat boys *like* kegs. They're obsessed with him, view him as a son-in-law. They're going to be devasta—" I stop midsentence when a familiar person enters the Coffee Hut.

Corinne.

My spine snaps into a straight, inflexible line. Corinne tried calling several times after her housewarming. When I ignored her calls, she sent a text asking if we could talk. I sent one back saying that when I'm ready to talk, I'll reach out myself.

Well, it's been two weeks and I'm nowhere near ready.

She freezes like a deer in the headlights when she notices me. Then she recovers her composure and—dammit, she's walking toward us.

"Hide me," I plead at TJ, but it's too late. Corinne reaches our little table, a nervous smile on her face.

"Hi," she says softly.

"Hi." My voice is tight.

"I know you said we'd talk when you're ready, but…well, the holidays are coming up, and then we'll be back and it's final exams, and then spring break…" She shrugs wryly. "Maybe we should just clear the air right now?" She lets the request hang in the uncomfortable air between us.

TJ gives me a questioning look, as if to say, *should I step in?*

I respond with a slight shake of the head. "Fine," I tell Corinne. To TJ, I say, "Do you mind? You're supposed to go meet your roommate soon, anyway. Right?"

He nods. "Yeah, it's no problem." He eyes Corinne warily as he stands up.

She goes to grab a coffee, her black curls cascading down her back. She's wearing a puffy navy-blue winter coat, which she takes off as she gets in line.

"I really don't want to do this," I tell TJ.

"I know, but you can handle it."

"I'm not so sure about that."

"You can handle anything," TJ promises. "You're fearless. But if you truly need an out, text me SOS and I'll ditch Ryan and come right back."

"You da best."

He touches my shoulder, his palm lingering before he withdraws it. A moment later, the bell over the door jingles as he exits the coffeehouse.

When Corinne returns, we endure another awkward silence. I stare at her, because I'm not going to be the first person to speak.

"I'm so sorry," is her opening line.

How original. "Yes, you already told me that."

"I know, and I'm just going to keep saying it until maybe you'll believe that I mean it."

"Oh, I believe you mean it. But it's easy to ask forgiveness. What *shouldn't* have been easy for you was sleeping with your friend's boyfriend."

Shame colors her cheeks. She gulps, offering a quick nod. "I know. I made a mistake. And if you want to ask me any questions about it, I promise every word I say will be the truth."

"Okay, I'll bite." My tone is more frigid than I intend it to be, but I can't control it. "How many times did you sleep with him?"

"Once," she says instantly. "It wasn't long after the move. He came by one night to help me hang a shelf."

I strain to recall when that could've been. Probably one of the nights Nico was working late. I wonder how many times he lied to me over the years. God. This entire conversation is so embarrassing.

"We had a beer, and you know I don't handle alcohol very

well—that's not an excuse," she hurries on. "I'm not blaming the alcohol, but I *was* buzzed. And he was, you know, he was Nico. He's charming."

"Yes, he is," I say tersely. It's the dimples. Those dimples never fail to disarm women.

Corinne stares at her hands, wrapped around her coffee cup. "He kissed me, and I knew kissing him back was a bad idea, but I wasn't thinking clearly and then he said—" She stops.

"He said what?"

"He told me you guys were having problems but that you didn't want anyone to know."

My jaw drops.

"And he said…" She blushes. "He said your sex life was non-existent."

"Non-existent?" I'm seething again. "We were having sex regularly." I just didn't realize he was also having sex with everyone else.

"I'm sorry. I really don't want my excuse to be that I was a stupid girl, but I was. I was stupid and insecure, and I hadn't had a boyfriend in so long and suddenly this charming, gorgeous guy was paying attention to me, flirting with me, telling me all these terrible things about you."

"And you believed him?" I'm hurt by the notion.

"No," Corinne admits. "I *wanted* to believe him, because then it'd give me justification to not feel bad. But I did feel bad. I felt awful—before it happened, during, and after. And then he actually tried to see me again, in secret. I felt sick and said no way in hell. I wanted to tell you the truth, but he said he'd deny it if I did, and paint me as a slut who tried to seduce him."

I don't even know what to believe anymore. In his subsequent texts after our showdown at my house, Nico spammed my phone with his explanations, his excuses. And that was precisely what he told me—that Corinne came on to him, and he was too drunk to fend off her wicked advances.

"I don't know if this helps or not, but..." Corinne takes her phone out of her bag. "These are all the text exchanges I had with him."

She slides the phone across the table and I reluctantly pick it up. The first thing I do is click on Nico's contact page to ensure that his name is assigned to the right number. People are liars, and technology is easily, and frequently, manipulated these days. But it's the right number.

I don't want to do it, but I force myself to read the text thread. And there it is, in black and white. Or rather, gray and blue. My loving boyfriend, asking my friend when they were going to have sex again. Corinne's not lying. The entire exchange is disgusting.

**NICO**: Still thinking bout u. when r we gonna do it again? ;)

**CORINNE**: Never. I never want to do it again, Nico.

**HIM**: Srsly? playing hard 2 get all of a sudden?

**HER**: No. I feel sick to my stomach. I want to tell Demi what happened.

**HIM**: WTF? R u kidding me?

**HER**: No, I'm not. I can't sleep, I can't eat. I feel like the worst person on the planet. She's one of my closest friends. I don't have a lot of those. What we did was so freaking stupid and I'm so ashamed of myself. I'm throwing up every night. I have to tell her.

**HIM**: Not gonna happen, Corinne. She's gonna think ur a liar

**HER**: No, she won't.

**HIM**: Ya she will, cuz I'll tell her ur lying.

It goes on for a while longer, and Corinne is right. She insists on coming clean, Nico warns her what he'll do if she does.

I set the phone down. My eyes are stinging, but I refuse to cry.

"I'm really sorry," she whispers. "And I know our friendship is irrevocably changed. All I'm asking for is forgiveness and maybe another chance. When you're ready, of course."

I nod slowly. "I accept your apology, and I will work on the forgiveness part, but…I can't do it right now. I'm not there." Her feeling genuine remorse after she slept with my boyfriend doesn't alter the fact that she slept with my boyfriend.

"I understand."

"But I am glad we finally talked," I say, and I truly mean it. I'm not one of those girls who will blame the "other woman." Yes, Corinne demonstrated poor judgment and total disregard for our friendship, but she wasn't the one sleeping with me, the one professing love for me, the one telling me we were going to get married. Corinne was a bad friend, but Nico's betrayal cuts so much deeper.

"Anyway, I have to go." I scrape my chair back. "I need to pack for Thanksgiving."

"Are you going to Boston?"

"Yes. I'm leaving tonight and coming back Sunday. Are you seeing your family in Vermont?"

"No, we're doing a friends' Thanksgiving in Hastings." She hesitates. "Pippa will be there. I hope that's okay."

I swallow a sigh. Pippa's been walking on eggshells lately, trying not to mention her friendship with Corinne to me. Fuck Nico for complicating everything.

Men are such garbage.

---

My parents are thrilled to have me home, even if it's only for a few days. There's already a full buffet on the table when I arrive, and it's only the three of us tonight. Tomorrow we have a ton of family coming in from Miami. Dad's an only child like me, but Mom's side of the family is enormous. I expect tomorrow to be super noisy. Two of my mother's three sisters are coming with their brood, and all my cousins are younger than me, so there'll be a tiny mob of eight, nine and ten-year-olds running around. Mom's only brother Luis and his wife Liana just had a baby boy, who I cannot wait to meet. I love babies.

Tonight is basically the calm before the storm.

"Oh lord!" My mouth is legit watering when I glimpse the feast Mom laid out. I'll be leaving a trail of drool on the way to the table. "Mom, you are the greatest treasure in the whole world."

"Thank you, *mami*." She plants a kiss on my forehead and then pushes me into a chair. "Now, eat! You look so thin, Demi. What's going on? What's wrong?"

I give a slight frown. My appetite disappeared after the break-up and it's only now returning, but I hadn't thought I'd lost any weight. All my clothes still fit.

Since lying to my mother is impossible, I reply with, "Let's wait for Dad. I'll tell you both at same time."

"*Dios mío!* I knew it. Something *is* wrong. Tell us what!? *Marcus!*" she screams at the doorway, and my eardrums promptly shatter. I'm surprised the paintings don't fall off the dining room walls.

My father takes his time coming downstairs. He's learned to differentiate between Mom's various screams and volume levels, and has clearly deduced this is not an emergency. When he finally strolls into the room, he greets me with a hug and kiss. "Hi, baby."

"Hey, Daddy." I stab a deep-fried crab cake with my fork and plop it down on my plate.

"What's going on?" He glances at Mom as he takes his usual chair at the head of the table.

"Demi has something to tell us."

His gaze swings back to me. "That so? What is it?"

"Can you let me finish this yummy crab cake first?" I chew extra slowly, relishing the taste, then spear some Cuban-style shrimp from one of the serving dishes. I quickly pop a shrimp in my mouth. "Mmmmm. Did you pan-fry this in pineapple? And garlic? It's so good."

I'm stalling and Mom knows it. "Put down the shrimp, Demi."

Ugh. "Fine." I lay my fork on the plate, swallow, and wipe my mouth with a napkin. "Mom, maybe you should sit down too."

They're both alarmed. "*Dios mío!*" she cries again. "You're pregnant! Marcus, she's pregnant!"

My eyebrows shoot up in alarm. "What! No! I'm not pregnant. Jesus. Sit down already." I hastily add, "Please."

Suitably chastised, Mom settles in the chair next to my father.

I clasp my hands on the tablecloth and clear my throat, as if I'm about to deliver a really depressing lecture. "Okay, first of all, to reiterate, I am *not* pregnant." I give them a warning look. "But this does have to do with Nico, and I need you guys to remain calm—"

"Is he all right?" Mom says in horror. "Is he in the hospital?"

"No, he's not in the hospital, and I literally just asked you to be calm. Could you please promise to let me finish speaking before commenting?"

Dad waves a big paw. "Go on."

"Promise," I order.

They both mumble a promise to stay quiet.

I release a breath. "Nico and I broke up a couple weeks ago."

When Mom's mouth snaps open, I slice my hand down to karate chop the air. Her mouth closes.

"I know this isn't something you want to hear," I continue, "and believe me when I say I didn't expect it to happen. As far as I knew, we were happy together and our relationship was on track."

Dad growls. "What did he do?"

I let this particular interruption slide. "He cheated on me."

Silence falls.

"Was it… was it a drunk mistake at a party?" Mom actually has the nerve to sound hopeful.

"Even if it was, that's still unforgivable," I say firmly.

"Well, it's far more forgivable than if he—"

"Three different girls," I interject, and her mouth slams shut again. "One of them was my friend, one was the sister of his coworker, and the third was a random girl he met at a bar when he was out with friends." He fessed up to the third indiscretion via one of his text diatribes. "Four, if you count the girl he cheated with in high school—" Another lovely text confession, although that one was more of a confirmation. "So, no, there's no hope and no forgiveness. I'm officially done with him. Maybe one day I'll be able to be his friend again, and the only reason I'd even consider that is because of our families, not for myself."

"Oh, Demi," Mom says sadly.

"Obviously I'd never ask you guys to stop talking to Dora and Joaquín, but…" I hesitate, wringing my hands together. "I know we invited the Delgados to visit for Christmas, but—and I'm begging you here—maybe we can ask them not to come…?"

Dad, who reacted protectively when I revealed Nico's infidelity, now looks uneasy. "But everything has already been planned, sweetheart." I know my father well—he doesn't want to look bad in front of his friends.

"I get it, but I'm asking you, as your only daughter, to please put my well-being first when it comes to this. I can't spend Christmas with Nico and his family. I just *can't*. The breakup is still too fresh and it would be so awkward. It would…it would hurt me," I say softly, and then avert my eyes because I hate showing vulnerability in front of my dad. He's so strong that falling apart in front of him feels like a crushing failure.

But the words have the desired effect. With tears clinging to her eyelashes, Mom stands up and comes over to hug me. "Oh, *mami*. I am so sorry."

As I hug her back, I watch my father, who's still trying to rationalize Nico's actions. "You truly don't think you'll give him another chance?"

"No," I reply through clenched teeth. "I can't."

Dad's expression flickers with unhappiness. "I've known that boy since he was eight years old. He always had a good head on his shoulders."

"I thought so, too."

"Surely there's more to this story. Perhaps Nico—"

"He cheated on me, Daddy."

"And I'm not excusing it," he says quickly. "I promise you I'm not. All I'm saying is, maybe there's more to the story. Maybe Nico is having emotional problems we're unaware of, or substance abuse issues, or—"

"Or maybe he's just a fucking asshole," I snap.

Dad's eyes narrow. "Language."

"No, I'm not going to watch my language, and I'm not going to stand here while you seriously try to persuade me that my serial-cheating ex-boyfriend is worthy of another chance. No way, Dad. I'm not getting back together with him and I'm not excusing that kind of behavior. We're over."

"Maybe in the future—"

A cry of desperation is ripped from my throat. "Oh my God, no! We're done. And please, *please* don't invite them for Christmas." My stomach churns as I imagine having to spend the holidays with Nico's family. I always thought my father had my back, but at the moment it seems as though he's genuinely torn between me and Nico. And I'm his *daughter*.

Without another word, I stomp out of the kitchen and hurry upstairs to my bedroom. It's not ten seconds later when my mother appears in the doorway.

"Demi, baby." She sees my wet eyes and holds her arms open, and like a little kid I fall into them.

"Why is he being so stupid?" I mumble against her huge boobs.

"Because he's a man."

My answering giggle is muffled.

"Do you want to talk about it some more?" Mom offers, rubbing soothing circles on my upper spine.

"No, there's nothing else to say. But what I'd love for you to do is go downstairs and tell Dad to stop whatever the hell this is. Tell him if he wants Nico back, he can date him himself."

She laughs quietly. "I will pass that message along. And I want you to know, yes, we are having a tough time believing that Nicolás could do something like this, but the pain in your eyes tells me that boy hurt you very badly, and anyone who hurts my baby…" She trails off ominously, her brown eyes becoming deadly slits. "Are you sure we can't invite them for Christmas so I can poison their food?"

"No," I say glumly. "I like the rest of his family too much." A sigh slips out. "And I don't want him dead, either. I think he probably feels terrible about what he did. But that doesn't mean I'd ever take him back. Do you know how humiliating it is knowing he was sleeping with other women? Meanwhile, he was lying to me about it and buying me dumb gifts and making me feel like—" My voice cracks and I stop talking, because there's no point in continuing.

It's over between Nico and me. And I truly don't want him back. In fact, since I blocked his number it's almost like a weight was lifted off my chest.

"Ugh. Mom, I just want to be alone for a bit," I admit. "Do you mind putting aside a plate for me so I can eat it later?"

"Of course, *mami*. If you need me I'm only a shout away, okay?"

Once she's gone, I lie on my bed and stare at the ceiling. The room was dusted and cleaned in anticipation of my arrival, and it smells like pine and fresh linens. Mom knows how to make everything feel homey.

I roll over and toy with the edge of a throw pillow. This truly sucks. I hate how entangled mine and Nico's families are. I'm always going to have this constant reminder of him, when all I want to do is put him behind me. Truth be told, I'm ready to move on. Or, at the very least, I'm intrigued by the idea of being with somebody new.

Sighing, I open Instagram and mindlessly scroll through my feed. I make sure to follow Pablo Eggscobar, who still only has one pic up. I wonder if that little rope hammock was homemade. I can't imagine where they might've bought one. Hastings isn't exactly teeming with miniature egg clothing and accessories boutiques.

Hunter texts during my scrolling session, a welcome distraction from social media.

> **HUNTER**: You make it to the city all right?
> **ME**: Yep. I'm here now. But it was the worst bus ride EVER. The guy beside me kept showing me pictures of his ferrets.
> **HIM**: Ferrets???
> **ME**: Ferrets.
> **HIM**: Semi, I think you sat beside a serial killer. Next time please text me a pic of your seatmate so I have something to show the police.

I laugh to myself, and type, Are you in Greenwich? I know he was making the drive there after his morning practice.

> **HIM**: Yeah. Drove up with Summer and Fitzy. He's spending Thanksgiving with her fam.
> **ME**: And for you, it's just you and your parents? No uncle/aunt/cousins/grandparents?
> **HIM**: Nope. Just the three of us. Oh joy.
> **ME**: Is it that bad?
> **HIM**: My father yelled at the caterer for only putting out one communal gravy boat on the table instead of small individual ones for each person. I heard her crying in the kitchen afterward.

Oh Lord, that's brutal. And I can't believe his family gets *catering* for Thanksgiving. My mother would literally rather face an execution squad than entrust someone else to cook Thanksgiving dinner.

> **ME**: That = fucked up. Though if it makes you feel better, my father's being insufferable right now too. I just told

them about Nico, and Dad tried to convince me to give him another chance!!

**HIM**: Seriously??

**ME**: Yep. He's obsessed with him.

**HIM**: Do you *want* to give him another chance?

**ME**: 100% no. Actually, I was just thinking before you texted that I might be ready for...drum roll please...a rebound.

**HIM**: Oooh exciting. Those are fun.

**ME**: Are you volunteering for the job?

Wait. What?

What the hell did I just type? And to add to my sudden case of agitation, Hunter responds with an LOL.

**ME**: WTF does that mean?

**HIM**: It means laughing out loud.

**ME**: I know what LOL means! But why are you laughing at me?

**HIM**: Because you were joking...?

**ME**: What, rebounding with me is a laughing matter? You don't think I'm cute?

**HIM**: You're more than cute.

I can feel myself blushing. This entire conversation is ridiculous. Of course Hunter wasn't volunteering to be my rebound, and now I'm just fishing for compliments because I'm insecure that my ex-boyfriend couldn't keep his pants zipped. Literally and figuratively.

**HIM**: Can we be real? Are you legit asking me to be your rebound?

My thumb hovers over the letter *y*. I could just press it, and then the letter *e*, the letter *s*. But that means opening the door to something that could blow up in my face. Hunter and I are friends. I find him attractive, but this is the first time I've considered being more than friends.

I don't get the chance to type those three letters, as Hunter sends a follow-up.

**HIM**: Because you know I'd have to say no, Semi. I'm out of commission.

I don't even try to make sense of the disappointment that flutters through me. My emotions are all over the place these days.

**ME**: I know. I was basically joking.
**HIM**: Basically?
**ME**: 60/40 joking.
**HIM**: So 40% of you wants to get with this?
**ME**: Get with what?
**HIM**: With me. You want to get all up in my dick biz.

Laughter sputters out of my mouth. Suddenly I don't feel so disappointed anymore.

**ME**: If you say so. Anyway, pointless discussion. Like you said, you're out of commission.

I put the phone down and slide into a sitting position. Interacting with Hunter never fails to cheer me up. I'm still grinning, and my appetite has officially returned. Luckily, there's a feast downstairs with my name on it.

It isn't until much later, nearly midnight, that I hear from Hunter again. I'm just getting into bed when the message lights up my phone.

**HUNTER**: If I wasn't, I'd be all over you, Demi.

# 19
# DEMI

I FEEL SURPRISINGLY REFRESHED AFTER THANKSGIVING WEEKEND. It was nice to see all my cousins and my crazy family, and Dad eventually did calm down about the Nico situation. He said he was sorry for not acknowledging my feelings, and I accepted his apology. Then he spent nearly an hour trying to badger me into hiring an MCATs tutor for next semester, until finally I flat-out told him I wasn't interested in even *thinking* about that exam until next year. He didn't like that idea one bit. So I appeased him by saying I'd take another science class over the summer to free up next year's schedule for med school studying. That idea, he *loved*.

I get it, I really do. My dad had a tough upbringing. He grew up dirt poor in Atlanta and worked his ass off to climb out of the gutter. Because he's genius-level smart, he excelled in high school, graduated early and got a scholarship to Yale. That's when he met and married my mother, who was originally from Miami. She wanted to move back after graduation, so Dad went with her, working at Miami General for nearly two decades before we moved to Massachusetts.

Dad's intense drive and unparalleled work ethic got him to where he is now, and he's instilled in me the value of hard work since the day I was born. When I was a teenager, he insisted I do volunteer work and community outreach so I could see how many people go without the privilege I was born into. He wanted me to understand how blessed I am. And I do understand, absolutely.

But the pressure of living up to my father's high standards can be exhausting.

And although Dad didn't bring up the Nico subject again this weekend, that didn't stop him from dropping several subtle comments over the weekend about how people are flawed, how human beings make mistakes. It was never specifically about Nico, but I knew exactly what Dad was trying to imply.

Well, too bad. Dad will just have to get over it. His boner for my ex-boyfriend will eventually deflate and hopefully get hard again for whoever I date next—and if *that* isn't the grossest analogy I've ever used, then I don't know what is. I don't want to think about my father getting hard over anyone. I don't want my father to have a penis, period.

As for the rebound idea I floated with Hunter via text, I'm finding myself more and more open to the idea. In fact, I'm kind of excited about it as I walk to class on Monday morning.

I'm wearing a parka with a fur-lined hood, an oversized messenger bag over one shoulder, fur-lined boots, and holding a steaming coffee cup in my hand.

You know that saying—dress for the job you want? Well, I dress for the *season* I want. It's the end of November and it still hasn't snowed, and I'm growing tired of this weird in-between period where there are no leaves on the trees but no snow on the ground. It's eerie and I hate it.

Pax, TJ and I chat about our Thanksgivings until Professor Andrews arrives. Hunter texted early this morning that he wouldn't be in class today. Apparently he has a physical with the team doctor.

I see him later that night, though, when he comes over for our—sob—final therapy session. My session logs are filled with notes. Hunter's done with all his research. Now it's just a matter of him writing the technical paper, and me writing the case study and detailed diagnosis, but those aren't due for a few more weeks.

"Since we're officially done, am I allowed to tell you your diagnosis?" I ask him.

"Hit me," Hunter says with a grin. He's sprawled on the loveseat, his hands propped behind his head, his arms bare. He runs hot, according to him, so every time he's in my room he strips down to a wife-beater or T-shirt, showing off those sculpted arms.

"Congratulations, you suffer from Narcissistic Personality Disorder, with a hint of antisocial PD."

"You're good."

"Thank you. I figured it out after like the second session, but NPD is actually super hard to diagnose properly," I say, which leads to a short discussion about the disorder and what Hunter learned during his research. He concurs that NPD cases are tough, especially because narcissists are so skilled at manipulating people, including psychologists.

"My father had our therapist eating out of his palm," Hunter admits.

I try to mask my eagerness. I hadn't wanted to bring it up myself, but I've been thinking a lot about our last session. Hunter's breakdown. His revelation that we'd been discussing his own father this entire time. My breakup with Nico had dominated my thoughts after that session, but now it's in the forefront of my mind as I cautiously study Hunter.

"I'm really sorry you had to go through all that crap with him," I say in a quiet voice.

He shrugs. "Whatever. Other people have it worse."

"So? My boyfriend cheated—other women might have a husband of thirty years who cheated and six kids at home. Does that diminish my own experience, because someone has it worse? There's always someone with a shittier life than yours. That doesn't turn the shit in *your* life into roses."

He exhales sharply. "That is very true, and you're too smart for your own good."

I chuckle. "I know. And I mean it, I'm sorry for everything your father has put you through."

"Thank you." His tone ripples with…awe, maybe? I can't tell. But it's evident he's genuinely appreciative of my words.

Then I realize what he'd said before—*our therapist*—and surprise jolts through me. "Wait, your father actually went to therapy? Willingly?"

"Willingly, hell no. It was one of those extremely rare times when Mom tried to stand up for herself. She told him if he didn't change his behavior, she would leave him. I mean, nobody bought that, but I guess she sounded serious enough that he capitulated. So we went to family therapy. Mom thought Dad and I also needed to clear the air between us, so I was forced into it. Christ, the whole thing was a shitshow."

"Why's that?"

"He completely manipulated the therapist during his individual sessions. I don't know what he told her, but when we saw her as a family, she was squarely on Team Dad. She spoke as if Mom and I were the evil perpetrators and he was the victim. It was unreal."

"Wow. I'm so sorry, babe. I can't even imagine having a parent like that. Parents aren't supposed to be the selfish ones. I mean, we're the kids. *We're* the selfish ones."

Hunter offers a sad smile. "In my house, my father is the only person who matters. You're lucky—your dad might want you to get back with your ex, but at least he doesn't treat you like a piece of property."

That is a very good point. Empathy continues to swell in my belly. I want to go over and give him a big hug, but I suspect he'd feel embarrassed.

"What's going on with all that, anyway?" Hunter asks, changing the subject. "Have you spoken to Nico?"

"Nope, and I don't plan on it, not for a long time."

"And the rebound situation?"

My heart skips a beat. "Well. You won't give me one, so I guess I'm on the hunt."

He looks startled for a second and then he laughs. "Come on, you said you were basically joking about that."

"Right."

But was I?

I suddenly find myself staring at him. With his classically handsome features, Hunter Davenport is objectively one of the best-looking men I've ever met.

If we're talking *sub*jectively, then...ugh, then *yes*. I think he's incredibly hot. He has a sexy mouth and a killer smile. And dimples. What is it with me and guys with dimples? It's like my sexual kryptonite.

My gaze travels the length of his body. He's wearing jeans, and I wonder what he's packing underneath them. Considering women are constantly throwing themselves at him, he must have some good dick game. And check me out, talking about dick games as if I know what good dick actually entails. My list of lovers is a resounding ONE.

"So. Just because we haven't checked in for a while—you're still a monk?" Somehow I muster up a casual tone.

"Yup yup."

"*Don't* say yup yup."

"I can't believe I've lasted this long." His expression becomes tortured. "We're at seven months, almost eight."

"When does this celibacy vow expire? I mean, you don't plan on keeping it forever, right?"

"Nah, till the end of the season."

"And then what? You'll go wild in the summer? You still have your senior year at Briar," I remind him.

"I know." He groans. "Honestly, I'll probably go nuts in the summer and fuck anything that moves." Another groan. "My balls hurt all the time, Semi."

I grin. "Aw, do you want me to make it better?"

"Stop teasing."

"I'm not teasing."

Am I? Lord, I don't even know anymore. What I do know is that I desperately need that rebound.

"I need that rebound," I say out loud.

Hunter purses his lips. "I don't know if I like the idea anymore. You hooking up with some random dude is…worrisome." He holds up a hand. "And stop saying you want me to do it because we both know you don't mean it. Besides, this dick's broken." He points to his groin as if I don't know where a penis is located.

"Well, then it has to be a random guy. I can't hook up with one of my friends—that's just a recipe for disaster."

"Exactly!" Hunter says triumphantly. "Ergo, stop trying to rebound me."

"Is that a verb?"

"It is now."

"Anyway, so you're out because of the broken dick. Pax is gay—"

"Yeah, Jax isn't a good candidate."

I roll my eyes. "TJ is too—"

"—in love with you," Hunter finishes.

"He's not in love with me. But he's too good of a friend and he's super sensitive. I could see him getting emotionally attached."

"Got it. So you want a guy who won't get emotionally attached."

"Pretty much."

"Are you on Tinder?"

"I've been dating the same guy since I was thirteen. Of course I'm not on Tinder."

"Then you should be. It's the easiest way to find a no-strings hook-up or friend with benefits. Come to think of it, that's probably a better fit for you. You need a FWB."

"Why's that?"

Hunter offers a shrug. "I think you'd feel sleazy after a one-night stand. Like you said, you were with the same guy since the age of thirteen. You're used to a certain level of intimacy."

He has a point. "So you think I need someone who I'll see more than once."

"Yup yup—"

"Don't say yup yup."

"—this will be fun. Come on, let's download the app." With a wolfish grin, he climbs onto my bed and flops down beside me. A moment later, we're downloading—ugh—Tinder.

"I only have an hour or so for this," I warn. "I'm meeting TJ for dinner tonight."

"In town or on campus?"

"Carver Hall."

"Then we have plenty of time. Carver's like down the street from you." Hunter watches as I load the app. "Oh, this is so exciting. I get to live vicariously through you."

"When your dick was functional, were you ever on any of these apps?"

"Nah. Do you realize how easy it is for me to get sex, Semi?"

"You're such an egomaniac."

"No, I'm a hockey player. I could literally walk out my front door and there'd be a woman standing there ready to screw me."

He's probably right. I'm still not much of a hockey fan, but I have been making an effort to pay attention when it's on. My favorite part of hockey is when the half-naked men get interviewed in the locker room after the game. So I can definitely see the appeal.

"Also, we're in college. Dating apps aren't really necessary since everyone's always partying and being social. It's easy to meet people on campus."

"Then why am I setting this up?" I grumble.

"Because we're fishing for a specific kind of meeting. When you want a particular thing, you filter out everything else. Yeah, you could sit in a bar, wait for different guys to approach you, and try to figure out what they're looking for. But this way you go into it knowing exactly what they want."

"Fair enough." Excitement tickles my belly as I set up the account. I use my phone number to log in, because I don't want my social media linked to this craziness. When it's time to load my profile picture, Hunter slides closer and watches me scroll through my camera roll.

He smells fantastic. It's a woodsy, masculine scent and I'm tempted to bury my face in his neck and inhale. However, I think that could be construed as sexual harassment.

"How about this one?" I click on a photo that I think I look super cute in.

Hunter balks. "Seriously? Who are we trying to attract here? Young Republicans? No. The first profile photo needs to show some skin."

"What do you mean, skin? Like a nude?"

"Of course not, dumbass. I don't think that's even allowed. But you sure as shit can't use *this* picture. You're wearing a turtleneck— and that long flowy skirt? You look lumpy, Semi. Do you want the first picture potential suitors see of you to make them say, *hey, who's this lumpy chick?*"

"You are *such* an ass."

"No, I'm realistic. I'm not trying to be skeevy, but come on. These dudes don't care about your personality. They care about your looks. They're literally swiping through photographs deciding if they want to meet you based on those photos."

"Okay, fine. How about this one?" In this next photo, I'm clad in a tight tank top and denim shorts. My boobs look great and my hair is loose and flowing over one shoulder.

"Better." Hunter nods his approval. "Stick that one in for now and then we'll rearrange the order." He steals the phone from my hand and takes over scrolling duties. "Ah, fuck yes, you definitely want to include this one."

"No way. I'm in a bikini."

"Exactly. And you look goddamn edible. You're searching for a guy to fuck you, Demi. *This* would make me fuck you."

Heat rises in my cheeks. Oh lord. He is sitting way too close to be dropping F-bombs like that. And why does he smell so good? Has he always smelled like this? I don't think we've ever sat this close before. Our thighs are touching, and one muscular arm is pressed up against the sleeve of my thin sweater. I can feel his body heat through the material.

"You would really fuck me if you saw this picture?" I study the bathing suit I'm wearing. It's a red string bikini that reveals *a lot* of skin. The picture was taken in South Beach, courtesy of my friend Amber.

"Oh yeah," Hunter confirms, and I notice his eyes have actually glazed over.

"Are you trying to picture what I look like underneath the bikini?" I accuse.

"Yes."

I lightly punch his shoulder. "Hey, I already offered you the rebound. You declined. Therefore you're not allowed to fantasize about me now."

"Fine," he grumbles.

We select a few more pictures. Hunter insists I need a full-body shot, a face shot where I'm staring directly at the camera, and a shot in which I'm smiling with teeth, because apparently not showing teeth means I've got the mouth of an old British man. He also lays down the law about Snapchat filters, and any selfies taken from above. According to Hunter, that's the "deception angle."

"For the last photo, how about this one with me and my friends?" I suggest. "That way the guys can see I'm a social person."

"You can't use that picture. You're with a bunch of guys. It's intimidating."

"Why?"

"Are you joking? They look like huge basketball players."

"Well, yeah. Because they are."

Hunter rolls his eyes. "By posting this, you're pretty much saying these are the kind of guys you can pull. Any guy who doesn't look like that will be way too scared to swipe on you."

"You are scarily good at this," I inform him.

"It's common sense, Semi. Now let's write your profile. We want to keep it short. My recommendation? Three letters. D. T. F."

"No way."

"Uh-huh. So I'm wrong about your intentions?"

"No, but I'm sure if we put our heads together we could find a more diplomatic way of saying it," I say dryly. "How about this?"

I write:

Recently single. New to this and not looking for anything serious right now.

"Not bad," Hunter relents. "And maybe we should add a few interests. Here, let me." He snatches the phone again, chortling as he types.

When he passes it back, I can't stop a laugh.

Fascinated by child psychopaths, unhealthy relationship with food, will break your PlayStation if you f*%k with me.

"That makes me sound like a lunatic," I say.

"Look me in the eye and tell me that *none* of those things are accurate."

"I fucking hate you."

Then I delete what he wrote and change it to: crime show enthusiast, food lover, all-around awesome person.

Once again, Hunter concedes. "I like it. All right, hit *next* to finalize the account."

I obey his command, then offer a nervous grin. "Now what?"

"Now we swipe."

# 20
# DEMI

I HAD NO IDEA THERE WERE SO MANY MEN IN THE WORLD. Obviously, I was aware the global population is in the billions, but how are there *this many* guys on this app, all within a sixty-mile radius of me? It's way too much data. I'm on sensory overload as my finger flicks past profile after profile.

Like Dan, who enjoys kickboxing.

Or Kyle, who's here for a good time, not a long time.

Or Chris, who wants me to "just ask."

Or another Kyle, who describes himself with three eggplant emojis. And another Kyle! This one likes to eat out. Hint hint, nudge nudge.

"Ewww! Why are all the Kyles so repulsive?" I demand.

Hunter thinks it over. "Coincidence," he finally answers.

"Coincidence? That's your best guess?" I can't stop laughing. This is the most fun I've had in ages. I swipe to the next profile and gasp. "Oooh, I like *him*. Let's swipe right on Roy."

Hunter examines the potential suitor's photos. He whistles softly. "Fuck yeah. Check out those obliques. I'd do him."

"Glad we're in agreement." I grumble in disappointment when Roy and I don't match. The last three guys I swiped right on, I matched instantly with.

"Don't let it get to you," Hunter says helpfully. "A guy with a body like that has options."

Literally two seconds later, a bubble pops up announcing I matched with Roy.

"Ha!" I say in triumph.

Hunter grins. "Looks like you made the cut."

"What about this guy?" I ask about the next profile.

"He's wearing sunglasses and a hat in every picture. He's either bald and ugly, or a murderer. Though I'm sure the latter would be enticing for you."

"Oh, for sure. I'd sell my firstborn to be able to psychoanalyze a killer."

"It worries me that I can't tell if you're joking."

We swipe for a bit longer, but all the faces are melding together. I'm starting to get bored and the messages are starting to pour in. "Let's talk to some of these matches and weed out the ones we don't like," I suggest.

But it doesn't take long to realize we're dealing with a quantity over quality situation.

"Christ, these messages are lame," Hunter groans.

What's up beautiful?

You're so hottttt.

9 inches, at your service.

"Hard pass," I declare, and promptly unmatch Mr. 9 Inches. I open the next message and give it a skim. The guy, Ethan, wrote an entire paragraph introducing himself. "Jeez. Check this one out."

Hunter reads the message and whistles. "No way. He's too thirsty. I don't like him."

"Me neither." We seem to be on the same wavelength when it comes to the vibes we're getting from these men.

Finally, I reach Roy's message.

Hey Demi! I know this sounds cliché, but you've got beautiful eyes. How's your night going?

"I like him," I announce.

Hunter chuckles. "Isn't it sad that all they have to do to gain our approval is possess basic conversational skills and not talk about their cocks? Shows how low of a bar we're dealing with here."

"You're right—that's sad as fuck. What should I say back?"

"Tell him you like his man-vee."

Ignoring the suggestion, I type, Thanks! Your eyes are pretty nice too. So is the rest of you ;)

Hunter mock gasps. "Demi, you hussy!"

I grin and send a follow-up message.

**ME**: My night is okay. Doing some schoolwork. How about you?

**HIM**: My night would be a lot better if we were having a beer together :)

"Oh, he is good," Hunter remarks.

**HIM**: What do you say? Should we meet up for a drink tonight?

"Ask him to go to Malone's," is Hunter's advice.

"What? Right now? We've literally exchanged three messages."

"So? You're not looking for a pen pal or a sexting buddy. The point of this is to get a date, right? You need to meet in person to know if there's any chemistry."

"But does it have to be tonight?"

"Why not?"

"I have plans with TJ."

"Then ask to meet up tomorrow. But trust me, a guy with an ass like that doesn't last long on the meat market. I'd marry him in a heartbeat."

I chew on my bottom lip. I suppose I could reschedule with TJ—he and I see each other all the time. And it might be nice to go on a date with someone new. I haven't done that since high school, during one of my breaks with Nico.

"Okay," I decide. "I'm meeting Roy tonight."

"That's the spirit!" Hunter raises his hand.

We high-five, and then I nervously type out a response to Roy. We make arrangements to meet at Malone's in an hour. Hunter offers to drive me.

Next, I message TJ.

> **ME**: I need a rain check on dinner. I have a......DATE. Gasp! Can you believe it? How's tomorrow night?

I see him typing, but it takes almost a full minute before the message arrives.

> **TJ**: No prob. Tomorrow works.
> **ME**: Okay perfect. You da best.
> **TJ**: xoxo

There's an army of butterflies wreaking havoc on my stomach. "Oh God," I tell Hunter. "I'm so nervous! And I only have an hour to take a shower and figure out what to wear."

"Go take the shower. I'll pick an outfit for you." Hunter's already striding toward my closet.

"Clothes," I warn, wagging my finger at him. "Please pick *real* clothes, Hunter."

He's cackling as I close the bathroom door.

———————

By the time we arrive at Malone's, my palms are sweaty and my heart is beating dangerously fast. Am I actually doing this? Suddenly I don't feel so ready.

Hunter parks the Land Rover in the tiny lot behind the bar. He cuts the engine and turns to appraise me. "I do good work," the jackass says with a pleased nod.

I'll allow him the outfit—he picked a pair of dark blue skinny jeans, a soft gray sweater that hangs over one shoulder and shows some skin, and black suede boots with short heels. It's a cute outfit and I look cute in it.

But the accessories? He doesn't get any credit for those. "I hate these earrings," I gripe, carefully arranging the big hoops so that they don't catch in my hair. "You *know* this. And yet you still peer-pressured me into wearing them."

"Because you look hot in them," he protests. "Trust me, they up the outfit's hotness factor from a nine to an eleven. Just quit complaining and wear them for tonight. One night."

"Ugh. Fine." As I slide out of the SUV, I'm surprised to see Hunter do the same. "You're coming in with me?"

He gives a nod. "Don't worry, I'll sit at the bar. I'll stick around until I'm sure he won't murder you. Just pretend I'm not there."

I'm genuinely touched. "Thank you. You're a good friend."

We round the side of the building toward the entrance. I can't believe I'm going on a date. A Tinder date, to boot. That's pretty much code for "*maybe I'll have sex with you tonight.*"

Wait, tonight? I can't have sex with anyone tonight. I just realized I forgot to shave my legs.

Dammit, why didn't I shave my legs?

*It's fine, it's only a drink*, I reassure my panicky self.

We enter the bar and I conduct a quick scan of the main room. It's busier than I expected for a Monday night, but college students go out drinking any night of the week, I guess. My pulse accelerates when I notice a tall, muscular guy pushing away from the bar.

His eyes widen appreciatively when he spots me. "Demi?" he calls out.

"Roy?"

"That's me." He smiles, flashing a pair of dimples. Oh no, he has dimples. I'm in trouble. "There's a free table over there," Roy says warmly. "Shall we?"

"We shall." Ugh, that was *so* dorky. I'm bad at this.

A smattering of high, standing tables make up the main room. Two are empty, and we choose the more secluded of the pair. I glance over my shoulder. Hunter winks and nods in encouragement, then wanders toward the bar stools.

"Sorry for being so forward, but you are even hotter in person." Roy openly checks me out, so I don't feel bad doing the same.

His shirt is outrageously tight, probably tighter than any piece of clothing I own. I can clearly see the outline of every muscle, and his nipples. Hard little beads poking out for all to see. I'd always been indifferent to man nipples, but Roy's body-hugging shirt brings so much attention to them that I can't look away. I force myself to redirect my gaze to the TV screens above our heads. One is playing Monday night football, the other shows an NHL game.

"Do you like sports?" Roy asks.

"I'll watch football if it's on. I'm not too into hockey, although I have a friend who plays. And my ex-boyfriend played basketball, so I had no choice but to pay attention to the NBA." Dammit, you're not supposed to bring up another guy when you're on a date. That feels like a major no-no.

Okay, I'm *really* bad at this.

But Roy doesn't seem fazed. "I never played any sports." He gestures to his huge, muscly body. "I know, I know, doesn't look like it, but I got this physique from working out."

"So you're, like, a gym guy?"

He nods vigorously. "Seven days a week. How about you? Do you go to the gym?"

"I use the one in the student fitness center a couple times a week. But I don't do more than use the treadmill, lift some weights, nothing fancy."

A waiter comes up to take our order. Roy asks for a Bud Light. I'm not in love with beer, but I don't feel comfortable drinking anything harder. My nerves are tickling my tummy and making my fingers tremble.

"I'll have a Bud Light too," I finally decide.

Once the server is gone, Roy picks up where we left off. "Have you used the pool in the fitness center? It's great for swimming laps."

"No, I haven't. Like I said, my workouts are pretty mild." I shrug. "I have a great metabolism."

"Working out has nothing to do with metabolism. Fitness is about health. Healthy heart rate, healthy mental state, healthy bones." He goes on about the benefits of exercise for several minutes, until my eyes start glazing over.

Finally, I interrupt him. "You kind of lost me there, bud."

Roy offers a sheepish smile. "Sorry. I'm really passionate about fitness."

"I can tell."

"Let's talk about other stuff." He rests his forearms on the table. A heavy silver watch adorns his left wrist, and it sparkles under the light fixtures. "So you're looking for something casual, huh?"

Oh boy. This topic is even more awkward. I'd way rather talk about his biceps curls. "Um, yeah. I mean, I recently broke up with my long-term boyfriend, so…"

"So you're on the rebound," he supplies.

I nod.

"Me too," Roy confesses.

"Really?" His profile bio didn't mention that. "When was your break-up?"

"A couple days ago."

A couple *days* ago? And he's already on Tinder? At least my break-up can be measured in weeks.

"That's very recent," I say carefully. "Are you sure you should be, you know, doing this?" I gesture between us.

Roy's right hand fiddles with his bulky watch. "Truthfully? I don't know. But I need to get over her, and I figured this is the best way. Putting myself right back out there, you know?"

Uneasiness trickles up my throat.

"Can I ask why you and your ex broke up?"

I answer truthfully. "He cheated."

"Oh man, that sucks. Were you together long?"

"We've known each other since we were eight. First kiss at twelve. Officially boyfriend and girlfriend at thirteen." As I recite the details, I'm startled to notice the lack of accompanying emotions. My heart didn't even clench when I listed each Nico milestone.

"Wow," Roy marvels. "That's a lot of history."

The server returns with our beers, and I gratefully accept my bottle. I'm not entirely sure how this date is going, but I'm leaning toward *not well*.

We clink our bottles together. "Cheers," I say.

"Cheers." He takes a long swig.

I do too, and it requires all my willpower not to blanch. I hate the taste of beer. Why did I even order this? What a stupid decision. I wonder if I should flag down the waiter and ask for a glass of water.

"So we're both unlucky in love." Roy observes me over the rim of his bottle.

"Guess so. What happened with your girlfriend?"

"She said I didn't spend enough time with her." He swallows another quick sip. "She thinks she should be my number one priority and that I focus on trivial shit instead of her."

I think it over. "Well, she has a point and she also doesn't.

Obviously your partner needs to be a top priority, but we're in college. We also need to prioritize our classes, our assignments, our social lives—"

"No," he interrupts. "She means the gym. She thinks I'm addicted to the gym."

I can't stop my gaze from lowering to his pecs. The ones that are straining against his shirt, fighting to break free. *This shirt cannot hold me!* those pecs are screaming.

I think maybe Roy's ex is right.

"But screw that," he says irritably. "She should be proud of all the work I put into looking like this. Other dudes pump themselves full of 'roids, HGH. They poison their bodies. But me? This is *all* natural. My body is a temple."

A snort rings out from behind me. For fuck's sake. Is someone eavesdropping on us?

I turn my head—and sigh when I recognize the familiar profile. It belongs to Hunter, who's lurking at the neighboring table. He was supposed to be at the bar, dammit.

My discomfort only grows at the knowledge that my friend is listening in. But maybe it doesn't matter, because it's also becoming painfully obvious that Roy and I will *not* be entering into a Friends with Benefits arrangement.

"I don't get why I have to choose," he's grousing.

I fix him with a serious look. "Did you love her?"

"With all of my heart," he says passionately.

"Then how is it even a choice? Cut back on your gym time, you dummy."

Another snort.

"It *is* a choice," he argues. "An impossible choice."

"Oh, come on now. That's an exaggeration. You can't love the gym more than a woman. You can't get married to the gym, Roy. You can't have babies with the gym."

The floor beneath my feet is vibrating, and I don't know if it's from the heavy bass track blasting from the speakers, or because of Hunter shaking uncontrollably with laughter.

"You have a point," Roy says, albeit begrudgingly. "But I don't see why I should give up my passion."

"She's not asking you to give it up. She's clearly asking you to find a balance," I answer pragmatically.

"A balance," he echoes.

"Yes. Listen. What's your girlfriend's name?"

"Kaelin."

"I think Kaelin has a point. If you truly view her on the same level as the *gym*, then she's right to be upset. Kaelin is a human being, Roy. The gym is just a room full of machines."

Behind me, Hunter howls.

I ignore him. "I think you need to examine your priorities," I advise. "A rebound isn't the right move for you. Granted, it'll be a rebound with a ridiculously hot woman—"

"The hottest," he agrees, and my ego takes comfort in that.

"But it's not the right move," I repeat.

He sips his beer. "What's the right move then?"

"Calling Kaelin and asking her to get together and talk. And maybe actually *listen* to what she's telling you. She's not trying to control you. She simply wants to be with you." I really hope I'm not misinterpreting this, and that Kaelin didn't dump him because he's clearly in love with the gym, and I do mean in love in a sexual way. But heck, it warrants a conversation, seeing as how he's obviously not over her.

"I know this is totally rude…" Roy reaches into his back pocket and pulls out a twenty-dollar bill, way too much money for two shitty beers. "But do you mind if I bail on you?"

"Absolutely not. Go get 'er, Tiger." I accept the twenty. Might as well use it to buy me and Hunter a round.

Speaking of Hunter, he appears at my side the moment Roy disappears. "That was the craziest fucking date I've ever spied on," he declares, his jaw half open.

"Tell me about it. Is this what it's like to be back in the saddle? You just have to ride a bunch of donkeys?"

"Dude. First of all—the way that man was jacked, he's a majestic steed, not a donkey."

"And second of all?"

"Oh, I don't have a second point."

I sigh. "I can't believe that just happened."

"Well, you didn't do yourself any favors by being such a *therapist.*"

"How is that a bad thing?"

"It is when you're trying to hook up. You're supposed to ride the man's dick, Semi, not convince him to get back together with his girlfriend."

"You're right. I really do suck at this," I moan.

Hunter pulls the Bud Light out of my hand and sets it on the table. "Let's get this garbage out of the way. We will *not* be drinking Bud Light tonight."

"We?"

"Your date bailed. I'm all you got, babe. I'll go and grab us some actual beer."

Hunter is gone all of three seconds before another guy approaches me. He has a shaved head, an oversized hoodie, and very white teeth.

"Hey, beautiful. Want some company?"

I'm about to say no, but he's already sidling up beside me.

"What happened to your friend?" White Teeth asks.

"He's getting our drinks. So if you don't mind—"

He leans in closer, and I instinctively lean back. I don't like it when people infringe on my space cushion.

"What's the matter?" White Teeth drawls.

"You're in my space cushion," I retort. "I'd appreciate it if you moved."

He furrows his brow. "What do you need space for? We're getting to know each other."

To my sheer relief, Hunter returns with our drinks. He takes one look at the intruder and levels him with a hard glare. "No," Hunter says coldly.

"No what?" White Teeth sounds annoyed.

Hunter widens his stance. "This ain't happening. Get lost."

I smile at Hunter's menacing pose. Apparently he's my new protector.

My very attractive protector.

Dammit, I need to stop thinking about how hot is. He doesn't want a rebound with me. He already made that clear.

It would be *so* much easier if he agreed to it, though. I'm attracted to him, and, more importantly, I trust him. But I'm not making a play for my friend, especially when he explicitly stated he's not into it.

The Space Cushion Encroacher stalks off in a huff, while Hunter stares after him in amusement. "That was easy." Then, with an extravagant gesture, he presents me with a tall can of beer. It's called Jack's Abbey House Lager.

"It's in a can," I remark.

"Yeah, cans are making a big comeback in craft beer circles. You're really living now, babe."

"Ergh. I probably should've told you to grab me a vodka cran or something fruity. I'm not a fan of most beers." I pause in thought. "Actually, I can't think of a single beer I like. They all taste the same to me: bad."

"Trust me, you'll like this one. It goes down *so* smooth. Just try it."

As Hunter watches expectantly, I take a big swallow of his magical beer.

"Well?" he demands.

My gaze drops to my suede boots. "It tastes exactly like the other one."

"Are you *joking* right now? You think Abbey House and Bud Light taste the *same*? I'm so ashamed of you right now."

"I told you, I'm not a beer girl."

"You're a disgrace."

"*You're* a disgrace."

Hunter grins as I stick out my tongue at him. He sips his own can of pretentious beer, then says, "I'm sorry it didn't work out with Mr. Muscles."

"It's fine. To be honest, it was nice to get out of the house. And it's good practice, right?"

We do some people-watching as we savor our beers. Well, Hunter savors. I just hold my nose and swallow. We crack each other up by creating fake backstories for various bar patrons, and in no time at all I've forgotten all about being ditched by Roy. I have more fun with Hunter, anyway.

Around nine-thirty we leave the bar and head for the parking lot. As I'm zipping up my parka, one of my earrings nearly gets caught in the hood and I curse under my breath.

"I hate these stupid things," I complain as I move the hoop aside. "They're a menace."

"You're a menace."

Yes, this is our thing now. It makes us snicker every time, which I suppose indicates that either our shared sense of humor is immature, or we are.

Hunter starts the Rover and reverses out of the parking spot. "I'm taking you home?" He glances over.

"Yep, thank you." I buckle my seatbelt, laughing when I notice that *my* Bluetooth is the device that connects to his car.

"You didn't un-sync!" he accuses. "You promised me you did."

"I lied to you, Hunter." Chortling, I load a playlist that includes a bunch of Whitney Houston ballads, which I know he doesn't like.

"You're evil," he says as he drives us away from town.

"Sorry, I can't hear you. Whitney is singing."

Then, just because I can, I sing along to "Greatest Love of All" until Hunter threatens to leave me on the side of the dark, deserted road if I don't shut up.

"Hey, could you turn off my butt heater?" he asks. "My ass is on fire."

"Sure." I'm holding my phone, so I go to plop it into the cup holder. But the Rover hits a pothole at that exact moment and the phone slips from my hand and tumbles to Hunter's feet.

"Chrissake, Semi. Grab that before it gets stuck under the gas pedal."

"Chill out. Hold on." I lean toward him and stretch out my arm, but the moving car sends my phone skittering across the floor mat. "Dammit, I can't reach it. Can you try to kick it toward my hand?"

"No. I'm fucking driving."

"Just try."

Groaning, he tries to poke the phone with his left foot, and the SUV swerves slightly.

"Okay, no, stop doing that," I order. "Focus on driving. I'll do it."

I unbuckle my seatbelt and crawl over his lower body. My hand begins wiggling around in the vicinity of his calves. The car swerves again.

"Pay attention to the road!"

"Trying to," he grinds out. "But you keep bumping my leg." I bend over as far as I can, until my head is squished in Hunter's lap. I stretch out my arm again, and—yes! My fingers collide with the phone and I swiftly close a fist around it.

"Got it!" I announce, and then I move to sit up and—

I can't.

"Demi," Hunter orders. "Move." The car rocks slightly to the right.

I try to lift my head again, and a jolt of pain shoots through my ear. "Oh my God," I wail. "I told you. I fucking *told* you."

"Told me what? Jesus, get up—"

"I can't!" My voice is muffled against the fly of his jeans. "My earring is stuck."

"Stuck on what?"

"On you! On your jeans! I don't know what." The position I've found myself in has my head wrenched to the side, so all I can see is Hunter's knees, and his foot on the gas pedal. Rather than attempt an escape, I keep my head planted flat on his thigh.

"Try to unsnag yourself," he pleads.

I refuse to budge. "No. It'll rip my earlobe off, Hunter."

"It won't."

"It will." Honest-to-God tears well up in my eyes.

He growls in frustration. "It's not gonna rip your—fuck, you know what, hold on. Let me pull over," he says.

And that's when we hear the sirens.

# 21
# HUNTER

This is a disaster. I'm getting pulled over by the cops, and Demi's head is stuck in my lap. She's draped over me like a blanket, her face inches from my crotch, and I know that the second the officer reaches the driver's side window, he's going to think...

Jesus Chris, he's going to think she's blowing me.

"Why did they pull us over?" she hisses.

"Must've seen us swerving all over the road." Shit, this is a nightmare.

I shut off the engine. As I wait for the cop to approach the window, I make a frantic attempt to pry Demi off me.

"Ow!" she wails.

"Sorry," I mumble. "I'm trying to get you free." Her earring is caught, all right, but I'm not sure on what.

I think it's one of my belt loops? But how the hell did it get embedded like that? Maybe it snagged on a thread? I'm not making a lick of progress, and every time I try to tug the hoop free, Demi whimpers in pain. I can't believe I'm even thinking it, but...she might lose that ear.

I don't know whether to laugh or cry.

"Someone's coming," she whispers as footsteps thump on the pavement.

"License and regist—"The police officer stops midsentence.

I sigh in resignation.

"What in the hell is going on here? Sit up, Miss," he commands. "Now, please."

"I can't!" moans Demi.

The cop's stern eyes fix on me. "I'm going to need you and your girlfriend to get out of the car and place both your hands on the hood."

"I'm not his girlfriend," Demi says, as if *that's* our most pressing concern, being mistaken for a couple.

"We can't," I answer through gritted teeth.

"Look, kid, I realize this is a cool thing you college boys like to do—"

A *cool thing* we do?

"—but lewd behavior is grounds for arrest. Not only that, you were driving recklessly and endangering other drivers."

I peer out the windshield at the dark and completely empty road. "What other drivers? There's nobody here but us. A single car hasn't driven by since you pulled us over."

"And we're not being lewd," Demi protests. "I'm stuck!"

"Stuck," he echoes dubiously.

I sigh. "She dropped her phone and tried to pick it up, and now she's stuck."

"Stuck," he says again. Then he shakes his head as if deciding he doesn't want to buy what we're selling. "Miss, this is the last time I'm going to ask—please sit up."

"I can't."

The officer reaches for his belt.

"Jesus!" I blurt out. "You don't need your weapon!"

"What weapon!" Demi starts wiggling in my lap, renewed in her efforts to set herself free.

If the officer wasn't there and it was the two of us, all that wild undulating would summon a heated response out of my dick. But the cop *is* here, so my dick is limp and I'm seconds away from breaking out in manic laughter. Which won't go over well with the increasingly irritated officer.

Turns out, he was only reaching for a radio. "I'm going to need some backup on Ninth Line and Highway Forty-eight. Suspects were pulled over for reckless driving and performing oral sex while in a moving vehicle and are now resisting arrest." Static crackles.

"I'm not performing oral sex!" Demi growls. "Trust me, I would *love* to perform oral sex on him, but he's celibate."

I'm sorry, what?

Did she just say she would love to perform oral sex on me?

"Seriously, Demi? You're saying you actually want to bl—do that?" My mind spins like a carousel. During all this talk about rebounds, I truly believed she was joking when she suggested me as a candidate. That's why I never let myself...get my hopes up, I guess?

"I told you I want a rebound, and I wanted to have it with you." Her voice is muffled and her fingers continue to fumble with her ear.

But we'll need to discuss Demi's desire to blow me later. I need to get through to this stubborn officer first.

"Sir," I say calmly. "Please. I understand what this looks like, but we are not engaging in lewd behavior. We're both clothed. My dick's in my pants."

"Where is your license and registration?"

"In the glove box, but I can't reach—"

A shout of triumph echoes in the car, and suddenly Demi's head pops up like a jack-in-the-box.

"I did it!" She's frantically rubbing her left ear.

"Holy shit," I say when she moves her hand. Her earlobe is bright red and swollen to three times its size, and there's blood staining her fingertips.

She's right. Hoop earrings should be banned.

"See!" Relief lines her voice as she gazes imploringly at the officer. "His pants are zipped. We weren't doing anything wrong. And we only drank a beer each. Well, two for me."

I swallow a groan.

Goddammit. Drinking hadn't even been part of this equation. And now, thanks to her, it is.

The cop is officially done humoring us. "I'm going to need both of you to get out of the car. Now."

———————

"*This* is the drunk tank?" Demi asks an hour later.

She looks thoroughly unimpressed with the holding area of the only jail in Hastings. The large cell currently houses three people—us, and a middle-aged man with a bushy beard, sleeping on one of the benches. He's twitching in his sleep, and one foot taps against the bars every few seconds.

Yup, we're behind *bars*, and it's all thanks to the big hoops.

"Maybe it's nicer when you're actually drunk?" she hypothesizes.

I laugh as I slide my back down the cement wall and sink onto the metal bench. Beneath my feet is a dirty linoleum floor. Above my head the fluorescent lights are way too bright.

"You know this is all your fault," I say cheerfully.

"*My* fault?" Her brown eyes fill with indignation.

"I told you what would happen if you synced your Bluetooth to my car."

"This is *not* my Bluetooth's fault."

"Oh really?"

"Really. I dropped my phone."

"Still your fault."

"Oh shut up."

"You shut up." I scoot closer to her, until we're sitting about a foot apart. "How's your ear?" I ask gruffly.

From what I can see, it's still pink and swollen, but it doesn't seem to be bleeding anymore. The dried blood caked onto the lobe triggers a pang of guilt, because I'm the one who talked her into wearing those earrings tonight.

"It's sore," she admits. "But at least it's still attached to my head."

"At least that," I agree. "I'm sorry I made you wear the big hoops."

"It's all right. Now you know." She releases a bleak sigh. "Sometimes you must witness the tragedy firsthand in order to understand it."

"Yes," I said gravely.

My lips twitch until finally a laugh slips out. She joins in, stretching out her legs and tapping her suede boots on the linoleum.

"I wish I had a lollipop," she says.

"I wish I had my freedom."

That summons another laugh from her. "God. I can't believe we're in jail. For lewd behavior, of all things."

"And my dick wasn't even out!"

"I know, right?"

The lone deputy in the holding area glances in our direction, and I glimpse a glimmer of amusement in his eyes. He's been at his desk for the past hour, typing on a computer.

I have no idea where the arresting officer disappeared to, although we weren't technically arrested. Nobody read me my Miranda rights, anyway. No Miranda rights? Ha! I've seen enough *Law and Order* reruns to know that any judge in his right mind would dismiss this case in a heartbeat. Unless the judge is having a bad day.

Personally, I think Officer Cranky was having a shitty night. Demi and I didn't do anything wrong and he knows it. Our breathalyzers barely registered a thing.

"What's the punishment for lewd behavior?" she asks curiously.

"No clue."

"Excuse me—sir?" She hops up and approaches the bars. "What's the punishment for lewd behavior? Is it death?"

Once again, he seems to be fighting a smile. "For first-time offenders, usually a fine."

"Perfect," she chirps. "My co-conspirator is filthy rich. He can write you a check."

"Hey, don't look at me," the desk jockey says with a grin. "Wait until Officer Jenk returns—he's the one you need to talk to."

"Officer Jerk, more like it," Demi grumbles.

I snicker. "Nice."

She addresses the deputy again. "Aren't we supposed to get a phone call?" she challenges.

"She's right," I say, sauntering up to the bars. "I'd like my phone call, please."

"Sure. Whatever." The young cop walks over and unlocks the cell door. He gestures for me to step out before sliding the bars back into place with a sharp click.

"Who are you calling?" Demi demands.

I turn to answer her, but the sight of her gripping two iron bars and peering at me from inside a cell… It's too good. I'd regret it my whole life if I let this opportunity pass.

"Am I allowed to take a picture?" I beg the cop.

"Don't you *dare*," Demi warns.

He grins. "Go for it." I think this is the most fun he's had in a while. Riding a desk is probably boring as fuck.

I fish my phone from my pocket and snap a picture of Demi, who looks like she wants to murder me. Then, to rub salt in the wound, I turn around to take a selfie, with Demi's outraged face in the background, her fingers curled around the bars.

"That's my Christmas card, right there," I tell her, giving a finger gun.

"I hate you."

*No you don't, you want to blow me.*

I can't stop the wicked thought. And I can't quite fathom it, either. Was she actually serious about wanting me to be her rebound? She's so sarcastic that I assumed she was messing with me.

Maybe it's a good thing I was in the dark about it. Hell, it'd probably be better if I still was. I promised myself I wouldn't hook up this year, and the temptation to break that vow for Demi is overwhelming.

The deputy leads me over to his desk and points to the landline.

"Can't I use my own phone?" I hold it up in reminder. I mean, he literally just allowed me to take a picture.

He shakes his head. "Against protocol."

"Okay, well, that doesn't make any sense, but whatever." I shrug and grab the handset off its cradle. Then I dial one of the few numbers I know by heart.

"Hey Coach," I say after his brusque hello.

"Davenport?" he asks suspiciously.

"Yeah. I hope I didn't wake you." The digital clock across the room reads 10:37. Not crazy late, but we have a six-thirty a.m. morning skate, so there's a chance he was already in bed. "What's going on?" he barks in my ear.

"Not much." I stall, wondering the best way to frame my predicament.

"Is this about the fucking egg?" Coach sounds annoyed. "Did something happen to it?"

"Nah, Pablo's good, thanks for asking. Well, at least I think he's good—he's with Conor tonight, so…yeah…anyway…" I exhale. "There's no easy way to say this, so I'm just going to Band-Aid it. I'm in jail right now and I'm hoping you might be able to come here and talk to the officers and, you know, do your thing?"

"My thing?"

"Yelling at people," I clarify.

There's a brief silence, followed by, "Is this a prank? Because I don't have time for that shit."

I swallow a laugh. "I'm dead serious. A friend and I got pulled over in Hastings tonight. It was a total misunderstanding—we weren't drunk and there was no lewd behavior despite what Officer Jerk might say—"

The desk cop chuckles softly. Man, I wish he was the one who pulled us over. He probably would've high-fived me and let us go.

"Coach?" I prompt.

Another silence trickles by.

"I'm on my way."

# 22
# HUNTER

"Where is he?" Demi asks impatiently. "I thought you said he lived ten minutes away."

"He does. And it's literally only been *one* minute since I called." Rolling my eyes, I rejoin her on the uncomfortable metal bench. Our cellmate remains fast asleep, now snoring softly. His foot keeps twitching, and there's no mistaking the odor of stale booze that wafts our way.

Demi presses her lips together, as if trying not to laugh. "This is the best date I've ever been on," she says sarcastically. "I mean, the romantic ambience alone…"

A snort slips out. "Only thing missing is the Whitney Houston ballad. Oh, and your actual date—you know, the dude who ditched you for his girlfriend. Or maybe the gym. I honestly can't be sure. It was such an impossible choice."

It's her turn to snort. "Meh. Whatever. You're a way better date."

Grinning, I sling one arm around her and tug her closer, and she rests her head on my shoulder. The sweet scent of her hair floats up into my nostrils. I breathe deeply, trying to pinpoint the scent. Jasmine, I think. She feels nice and warm pressed up beside me. I wonder what she's thinking about right now. If her thoughts align with mine.

I almost groan in disappointment when she lifts her head. "I really mean it," she informs me.

"Mean what?" Shit, my voice sounds way too husky. I promptly clear the gravel from my throat.

"You're a fun date."

"This isn't a date."

She tips her head in challenge. "Then why are you giving me the Penis Eyes?"

"I'm not."

"I know Penis Eyes when I see 'em."

A laugh tickles my throat. This girl is something else. She cracks me up. And she's so fucking beautiful. Her skin always looks so soft and luminous that my fingers itch to stroke it. Her hair looks silky to the touch too. It falls in a straight, shiny curtain over her shoulder, the one that's bared by her loose sweater. A few dark strands fall over her left eye.

My lips feel dry. I lick them, and heat flares in Demi's expression.

"You've got hair in your eyes," I say roughly.

I reach out to gently brush it away. My thumb lingers on her cheekbone as I tuck the hair behind her ear, the one that's normal-sized.

She gives a sharp intake of breath. "Oh my God. Was that it?"

My eyebrows crash together. "Was what it?"

"Was that your move?" Delight dances in her eyes. "Licking the lips, brushing hair off my face, that little thumb rub. That's totally the move. Right?"

I flash a cocky smile. "Depends. Did it work?"

"Yes," she says frankly, and now it's my breath that hitches.

Her honesty is such a turn-on. And although I didn't plan on busting it out tonight, that *was* my move. It just happened naturally.

"Davenport," booms a loud voice.

My head snaps toward the bars. Footsteps thud down a hallway and then Coach's thunderous face appears in the doorway. Officer Jenk tails him.

"Unlock that door." Coach issues the order to the desk jockey, who jumps to his feet at the arrival of Coach and his colleague.

Weirdly enough, the younger deputy actually reaches for his heavy key ring before remembering that Coach is not his superior, nor a cop. "Jeff?" he says, glancing at Officer Jenk.

His name is Jeff? Jeff Jenk?

Poor bastard. Maybe that's why he's in such a bad mood.

"Do it," Jenk says curtly.

Coach gives me and Demi a brisk once-over as we emerge from the cell. "You all right?" he says curtly. "Did anybody manhandle you?"

"No," I assure him, touched that he'd asked. "Nobody knocked us around at all, but thanks for worrying."

"I'm not worried about you, you idiot. I'm worried about your fucking shooting hand. We have a game in four days." His accusatory eyes shift toward the officers. "If his slapshot is even a tenth of a second slower than usual, I'm going to hold you personally responsible, Albertson."

"Sorry, Coach," the desk jockey mumbles.

I stare at them both. "You two know each other?"

"Yeah, kid used to play for me. Sammy Albertson, class of 2012."

Damn, now I really wish Albertson was the one who pulled us over. I could've just name-dropped and gone on my merry way. Just my luck that I got the cop with the chip on his shoulder.

"And you," Coach says, turning to a sour-faced Jenk. "Unless the kid's dick is out and inside someone's mouth, it ain't considered lewd conduct. Make wiser choices next time."

"Tell your player that," Jenk says snidely. "He can't be swerving all over the road."

"I was stuck," Demi pipes up. "Hunter was trying to—"

Coach raises a hand to silence her, and, like all of his players, Demi falls in line. "Any paperwork we need to sign?" he barks at Jenk. "Any fines to pay?"

"No, I'm letting them off with a warning as a courtesy to—"

"Good, let's go," Coach interrupts. He nods his head, and Demi and I scamper after him like baby geese following their mommy.

Outside the tiny station, Coach zips up his coat. It still hasn't snowed once this winter, but the temperature is finally turning frigid. Coach's breath escapes in white puffs as he says, "Your Land Rover wasn't impounded because the tow truck's ETA was a couple of hours, so it's still on Ninth Line. I'll drive you over to it."

"Thanks, Coach."

"And I want you to go straight home, you hear me?"

"Demi lives on campus," I say, shaking my head. "I need to drop her off first."

"I'll do it," he snaps before stalking toward the curb, where his Jeep is parked.

Demi turns to me in alarm. "Should I be worried he might murder me on the drive home?" She pauses. "I can't remember if my show has an episode called *Coaches Who Kill*."

"You're probably okay."

"*Probably?*"

I shrug. "He's more pissed at me than you. I'm the one who dragged him out of bed."

"True." She flips up the fur-lined hood of her parka, and plants one hand on her hip. "And for the record, none of this would have happened if you'd agreed to rebound me."

"It still would've happened." I smirk at her. "Only difference is, you would've actually been blowing me." I instantly regret saying that, because the thought of my dick stuffed in her mouth is so torturously enticing I almost groan out loud.

"No," she counters, "we wouldn't have been anywhere near your car. We would've been warm and cozy in my bedroom, with no Tinder profiles and no distractions. Just you and me and a big comfy bed and my mouth on your penis. I want you to think about that!" she taunts as she flounces off to Coach's vehicle.

Right. As if now I'll be able to think of anything *but*.

———

And think about it I do. All week long.

Normally I'd be pumped and focused on the upcoming game, but by the time Friday rolls around, I can't even remember who we're playing against. My concentration is shot, not only because Demi's gotten under my skin, but from the constant ragging I've been getting from my teammates all week.

I had no choice but to fess up about the jail incident, because Brenna had breakfast with her father the morning after and Coach Jensen decided to be an ass and told his daughter. And obviously Brenna opened her big mouth, and now I'm Hunter Davenport, the guy who got arrested for receiving a blowjob while driving. The worst part is, I didn't even get the blowjob.

Demi's also been teasing me about it, only she's taking things a step further than my teammates. Since experiencing my "move," she's launched a campaign to end my celibacy, as evidenced by the text she just sent.

> **DEMI:** Have a good game tonight! I hope you score! Speaking of scoring, have you considered breaking your vow?

I sigh at the phone. See? I should be mentally prepping for the game right now. I'm in the visitors' locker room at…Boston College. Right! That's who we're facing tonight. I should be thinking about the game, not Demi Davis.

> **ME:** I told you, it ain't happening.
> **HER:** You wouldn't even consider it? For lil ole me?

Someone smacks me between the shoulder blades. "Hey, now. Stop fantasizing about the road head, captain."

I turn to find Matt grinning at me.

"Seriously, though, *nice*," he praises.

"You've said that to me at morning skate every day this week."

"Yeah, because it's *nice*. Always wanted road head."

"Me too," I say dryly. "Like I've been telling *you* every day, nothing happened. Demi's earring got stuck on my pants."

"I've gotten road head," Conor drawls as he unbuttons his white dress shirt.

"You've gotten head everywhere," I shoot back.

"That's not true. I've never gotten…" He strains his brain trying to offer up a blowjob-free location.

"Having a little trouble there?" Matt hoots.

Chuckling, I peel off my own clothes and begin to suit up. My phone dings again and I realize I didn't respond to Demi.

> **HER**: Sorry. I'll stop talking about this. I know it makes you uncomfortable.
>
> **ME**: No, sorry, I'm just gearing up. Gotta go, talk later.

I add a kissy face and then tuck the phone in the pocket of my discarded pants. Once I'm in uniform, I sink down on the bench to put on my skates.

Conor sits beside me. "What are you doing after the game? We were going to have some people over. You in?"

"Sure. I've got nothing else going on."

He slants his head pensively. "Are you seriously not doing this sex thing or are you fucking with all of us?"

"Not since April," I confirm.

"Christ. That's intense. I'd probably lose my mind if I couldn't bust a nut."

"I never said I'm not busting nuts." I release a gloomy sigh. "I'm just doing it solo."

"Still. Sounds like a hellscape."

I can't help but snicker. "It's not that bad. I'm actually getting used to the perpetual blue balls."

"Jesus!" Bucky interrupts, walking over with a Saran-wrapped stinky Pablo in one hand and a cellphone in the other. "Have you *seen* this shit? Pablo's Insta account reached ten thousand followers. Someone just DM'd asking if we'd do a sponsored post for an age-defying moisturizing cream."

My jaw drops. "Is that a joke?"

"No joke." Bucky shakes his head in disbelief.

"Age-defying cream?" Alec pipes up, looking confused. "How do you defy age?"

"And what the hell does that have to do with an egg?" Conor cracks. "Are we supposed to slather moisturizer on his little pig face and pose him for a photo shoot?"

Bucky grins. "I'll message them back and find out."

Coach strides into the locker room to deliver his pregame pep talk, which typically consists of a sentence or two, tops, before he turns it over to the captain or assistant captains to pump everybody up. This evening's "pep talk" offers the usual sentiments—kick their ass, don't embarrass me, don't bring shame onto your house, et cetera et cetera. Then I give a little speech and we all file out onto the ice.

The crowd is deafening, and I don't even care that only a third of the seats consist of Briar fans. The screams and cheers and even the boos fuel my blood. I fucking love this sport. I love the ice, the speed, the aggression. I love the physicality of it, the way every bone in my body jars and my teeth rattle when I'm slammed into the boards. Those are messed up things to love, but that's hockey.

I remember the game Fitz and I watched in our living room last night. Edmonton versus Vancouver. Jake Connelly scored one of the most beautiful goals I'd ever seen. And I remember the longing I felt, an ache that actually tightened my throat, because while college hockey is great, it's nowhere near as fast and competitive as professional hockey.

And if the pros were simply about being out there on the ice, I'd sign up in a heartbeat. But that life comes with strings I'm not interested in. It comes with women and glamour and press conferences and constant travel. Constant temptation. And Davenport men don't fare well in the face of temptation.

So I'll just have to content myself with *this*, right now, skating out on the ice with my friends, kicking ass. Because this is what it's all about.

---

The bus drops us off on campus around eleven, and from there I hop into my Rover and drive myself and a few teammates back to Hastings. I deliver them to Matt and Con's house, then head home to park my car. I'm planning on walking back to Matt's. That way I can drink more than a couple of beers.

At home, I change out of my dress clothes—we're required to wear jackets, ties, and trousers for all away games. It's almost a shame to strip out of my suit, because I rock it like nobody's business. I can thank my father for that. He pulls off the CEO look better than anyone. Probably why he's so popular with the ladies.

A little *too* popular.

"Hunter, you heading out?" Brenna pokes her head into my bedroom. As usual, there was no knocking involved.

"Yeah, I'm going to Matty's. Want to come?"

"I might pop over later. I'm Skyping with Jake first."

"Tell him I said hey. Oh, and tell him I'm jealous of that goal he scored yesterday. It was a beauty."

"Right? I've never been more turned on in my life."

"I honestly think Edmonton has a shot of winning the Cup this year."

"Same. They're unstoppable."

I zip up my hoodie. "When I was in Boston last month, Garrett was saying he hopes they don't have to face each other in a playoffs series." Christ, I don't even know who I'd be rooting for in that scenario. Garrett, I guess. No. Jake. Or maybe Garrett. Fuck, it's an impossible choice. Like picking between the gym and your girlfriend.

Brenna wanders off, and I go downstairs to put on my coat and boots. I'm about to slide my phone in my pocket when it beeps in my hand. I check it and find a text from Tara, a girl I hooked up with last year.

**TARA**: Hey, sorry for texting out of the blue like this—random, right? Nice win tonight. Just wanted to give you a heads up, tho. Some guy was asking about you.

**ME**: I might need more details than that LOL

**HER**: After the game, some guys came over and one of them was grilling me and my girls about where you were. I said probably on the team bus.

**ME**: Wait, this happened in the city?

**HER**: Yeah, outside the BC arena.

**ME**: OK, that's weird. Thanks for the heads up.

**HER**: No prob, hon.

She punctuates that with three hearts. *Red* hearts. Every guy on the planet is aware that red hearts mean business. An invitation to start something up if I want to. But I don't.

I walk out the front door, and I'm nearing the sidewalk when my phone beeps again. This time I find a message from Grady, the little brother of one of my teammates.

**GRADY**: Hey. Hunter. Got your # from Dan. He told me to text about this—some dude was looking for you at BC.

**ME**: Yeah, I just heard. Any idea who it was?

**HIM**: Never seen any of them before. The main guy kinda looked like a young Johnny Depp?

**ME**: Doesn't ring a bell.

**HIM**: Anyway, I heard someone mention to them that you

might be at Matt Anderson's house tonight. Wanted to let
you know in case he tracks you down.
**ME**: Thanks. I appreciate it, man.

Okay. I don't like this at all. Two different warnings that a bunch
of strangers were asking about me? Strangers who raised enough
alarms that Tara and Grady both felt the need to reach out to me.

And fuck, I'm glad they did, because when I reach Matt and
Con's street, I immediately notice the group twenty feet ahead,
loitering by the curb. If I hadn't been forewarned, I might've waltzed
right up to them thinking they were partygoers.

Instead, I slow my gait, giving myself time to scope out the
guys. There are five of them. They're not particularly huge in terms
of height, but they're all pretty beefy. One is bald and stocky and
appears vaguely familiar. The tallest one has his back to me, but he
turns around when he hears my footsteps.

"Nico," I say guardedly. "Hey."

I haven't seen or spoken to Demi's ex since the night she went
all Carrie Underwood on his stuff. And on closer examination, he
kind of does resemble a young Johnny Depp, but with a darker
complexion.

"What's going on?" I ask when he doesn't return the greeting.

"You tell me."

I resist the urge to roll my eyes. "I'm not sure what you mean."

"Really? Because rumor has it you were out with Demi on
Monday night." Barely concealed rage reddens his face. His fists are
clenched at his sides.

Nico's friends creep forward. Not close enough to pose a physical threat, but enough that my shoulders snap into a rigid line.

"Yeah, we went to Malone's for a drink." I omit the part where
Demi was going there to meet another guy. Nico is already on edge.

"I heard it was more than a drink." His voice trembles with
anger. "Heard you got thrown in lockup together."

Fuck's sake.

I open my mouth to respond, but Nico hisses like a venomous snake. "Heard you got pulled over with your *dick* in her mouth."

"That's not what happened." My tone is calm, even.

"You feel like a big man, Davenport, disrespecting my girl like that?"

"I'm not disrespecting anyone—"

He's still talking. "Using her? Forcing her to blow you?"

"I didn't force her." I quickly amend that when I realize what it implies. "Nothing happened, man. It was a misunderstanding, and the cops let us go. But even if something *did* happen, you'd have no right to be pissed. You guys aren't together anymore."

"We're not together right now," he qualifies. "We'll get back together. We always do."

"Is that so," I drawl.

"You don't know a damn thing about our history."

"I know you cheated on her at a frat party."

Nico's eyes flash. "She tell you that?"

"Nah, I saw you, man."

A brief silence travels between us. Then Nico hisses again. "Wait, it was you? You're the asshole who told her about the chick at the party?"

"What the hell does it matter? She was going to find out anyway, Nico. She was already going to find out about your *other* screw-up because you're too stupid to delete a Wi-Fi password."

"Who the fuck you calling stupid?"

He charges at me, and I dodge him, taking several steps back. "I'm just saying, you did this to yourself. If you want someone to blame, go look in the mirror."

"You ratted me out." Nico glances over his shoulder at his buddies, each of whom has his arms crossed. "This *puta* ratted me out, can you believe that? You're a real prick, Davenport."

"I'm the prick? You cheated on your girlfriend."

"You broke the bro code," he spits back.

"You're not my bro." I take another backward step. "Are we done here?"

Before I can blink, his arm shoots out. He grabs the collar of my winter coat, tugging me toward him. His face is inches from mine, the white puffs of his alcohol-scented breath chilling my face.

"Nico," I warn.

A spiteful smile stretches across his angry face. Beyond his shoulders, I spy his buddies closing in on us.

"Get your hands off me," I say in a deadly voice.

His smile widens. "Or what?"

# 23
# HUNTER

"The way I see it, there's five of us and only one of you." Nico chuckles, his dark eyes glinting with impending violence. "Sure, you're the hockey guy. I bet you can fight real good. But can you take all five of us?"

I know I can't. I glance toward Matt's front door. It's closed, and the pulsing music thudding in the house tells me that even if I shouted for backup, nobody would hear me. My best hope is that someone decides to brave the early December chill, come out to smoke a cigarette or a joint, and throw me an assist.

But what I'd prefer happen is that I defuse this bomb before it goes off in the first place.

"Look, Nico. You seem like a cool guy. You made a mistake, and there's no need for violence, okay? Even if I didn't tell Demi about the party, she would've found out through her friend. But you're right—what I did went against the bro code. I should've kept my mouth shut."

"Damn right you should have."

"So I'm sorry for that, okay? With that said, you *really* need to take your hands off me." Adrenaline is already surging in my bloodstream. Nico's right—hockey players are no strangers to fighting. I've gotten into scraps on the ice, and off of it. I can hold my own in most physical confrontations.

But not when it's five against one.

"Sorry, jock boy, but you're not getting off that easy." Nico chuckles.

"For chrissake, man, you're gonna punish me when *you're* the moron who cheated on your woman—"

The first blow cuts me off and sends my head rearing back. His fist crunches against my jaw, a jolt of pain shooting down my neck. Just as I straighten out, two of his buddies are suddenly behind me, locking my arms behind my back. Presenting me like a juicy carcass to a pissed-off hyena.

Nico cracks the knuckles of his right hand, then the left. "All I'm saying is, us men need to stick together. And the fuckers who don't, deserve to get their ass whupped."

His second punch collides with the corner of my mouth.

I taste blood. I spit it out onto the pavement. "Get your punches in," I tell him in a resigned tone. "If that's what makes you feel better. But it's not gonna bring Demi back and it's not gonna change the fact that you're a sack of shit—"

The next blow gets me in the ribs.

*Fuck.*

My side is already sore from a hit I took in the game tonight, and now my entire ribcage is throbbing and I'm goddamn pissed. The anger brings another jolt of adrenaline that enables me to scramble out of the iron-hold on me. I elbow one of Nico's friends in the throat, manage to land a punch in another one's stomach, but then my body is thrown back like a rag doll, and they all swarm again.

"What the hell!" someone shouts from the porch.

The cavalry has arrived.

Matt comes tearing down the frost-covered lawn. More shouts and angry curses fill the night as six more hockey players race toward the curb. Someone grabs me and shoves me aside. Nico and his cronies retreat, creating about three feet of distance as the two groups face off with each other. My bottom lip is caked with blood. Nico's ragged breaths exit his mouth in rapid puffs.

"Go home," I tell him.

"Fuck you," he snaps.

"You really don't want to stick around, Nico. You're the one who's outnumbered now, and there's already been enough violence tonight, okay?" I drag my forearm over my mouth to sop up the blood. "Just get out of here."

"Stay away from my girl."

*She's not your girl*, I want to say, but I resist the urge to provoke him.

Beside me, Conor takes a slight step forward. "Leave," he drawls, and despite the laidback tone, his expression is deadlier than I've ever seen it.

It has the desired effect. Nico spits on the ground, and then he and his friends stalk off toward a nearby truck. I watch them go, hoping that the shitshow is truly over and this wasn't just the first act.

---

I'm cleaning my face in the hall bathroom when I hear the commotion beyond the door. My shoulders instantly tense. Nico had better not be back—

"Is he in there? Hunter, are you in there!"

I relax at the familiar voice. "In here," I call out.

I'd left the door slightly ajar, and Demi wastes no time pushing it open. She appears in all her fierce glory, hands on hips, eyes on fire.

"I'm going to *kill* him!" she thunders when she sees my face. "Are you okay? I cannot *believe* he did this!"

"How'd you find out what happened?" I frown. "And how'd you get here?"

"I called a campus taxi right after Brenna called."

Frickin' Brenna. With impeccable timing, she'd shown up just as we were all trudging inside after the fight. She must've phoned Demi before she'd even taken off her coat.

"You're bleeding," Demi frets. "Brenna said you weren't badly hurt."

"I wasn't," I assure her. "My lip split open again because I was laughing at something Conor said."

Guilt floats through her expression. "I am so sorry. How did he even know you were here?"

"Apparently he was at Boston College earlier, asking random people where I was. I think he and his friends were drunk."

Demi's entire body vibrates with anger. "I'm unblocking him so I can yell at him."

"Don't. You blocked him for a reason. And it's fine, I'm fine."

"Are you sure?" She reaches for my face. I try to swat her hands away, but she's not having it. "Let me look at it, dammit." Her fingertips tenderly graze the side of my mouth.

A shiver runs up my spine.

Her bottomless brown eyes lock with mine. "This is it? Just the busted lip?" Her hand sweeps up my face to gingerly examine my cheekbone.

I wince. "He got me there too, but that one'll just be a small bruise."

"I can't believe he did this," she says again.

"Nah, I get it. He heard about our dalliance with the cops last night and jumped to conclusions."

Her jaw drops. "How on earth did he find out about that?"

"It's gotten around," I admit. "Coach told Brenna, so now the entire team knows about it, and people talk. He lives in Hastings, right? Hell, he could've heard someone talking about it at the diner."

"Maybe." She curses. "Ugh. You're bleeding again. Sit down, will you?"

I dutifully lower myself onto the closed toilet lid. If she wants to fuss over me, then I'm going to let her.

She shoves some toilet paper under the sink faucet, then presses the wet wad against my lip to soak up the blood.

"Let's leave this on here for thirty seconds or so," she murmurs. "Hopefully the pressure will stop the bleeding for good."

I try not to smile. "You know I could be doing this myself, right?"

"Just let me do it, Hunter. Please. This is all my fault."

"It's not your fault."

She kneels on the floor and damned if that position doesn't send a flurry of dirty images to my brain. If a woman's on her knees in front of me, it's usually because she's about to undo my pants and take my cock out. My eyes dip to Demi's pink lips. I imagine the tight suction of them around the head of my cock and suddenly it becomes difficult to swallow.

I jerk my gaze away from her mouth.

"What?" she says urgently. "Are you okay?"

"I'm fine," I croak. Christ. My dick is harder than stone.

"What's wrong? You look like you're in pain! Is this hurting?" She reduces some of the pressure.

"It's all good. Don't worry about it."

Demi bites her lower lip. Fuck, I need to stop fixating on those gorgeous lips. But I can't. They'd probably feel so soft and warm pressed against mine.

We should not be alone together right now. I'm still hopped up on adrenaline from the game, from the fight.

"I don't know whether to believe you or not," she mutters.

"I'm fine. Trust me, I've suffered worse from playing hockey."

She removes the toilet paper from my lip. It's soaked red, and she makes a face before tossing it in the wastebasket. "The bleeding stopped," she says.

"That's good."

Her fingertips run over my cheek again.

"Demi," I say thickly.

"Yeah?"

"Please stop touching me."

She looks startled. "Why?"

"Because no one's touched me like that in ages. You realize this is essentially torture?"

She presses her lips together as if resisting a smile. "It's turning you on?" Her knuckles graze my cheekbone, the one that isn't bruised. "This? This is turning you on?"

"Yes," I say through gritted teeth. "Therefore—please stop."

My protest sounds hollow to my own ears, so I'm not surprised when an impish glimmer fills her eyes. "What if I don't want to?"

"Well, it's not about what you want, now is it?" In one swift motion, I lock her wrist with my right hand and move it away from my face.

Only, I make the mistake of putting it near my knee, and now her fingertips are centimeters from my thigh. I almost expect her to move her small palm in a caress, but she keeps it still. A slight crease appears in her forehead as her gaze fixates on my mouth.

"Am I bleeding again?" I ask hoarsely.

She slowly shakes her head.

"Then why are you staring at me like that?"

"You got beat up because of me. I feel bad."

I study her preoccupied expression. "Really, that's why you're staring at me?"

Her brown eyes abruptly come into focus. "Well, no. That's just me feeling bad. I'm staring at you because I want to kiss you."

I inhale sharply. "You shouldn't do that."

"I'm not going to, not unless you're into it. But that doesn't mean I'm not thinking about it. We're making out hardcore in my head right now." She blinks innocently. "It's amazing, in case you're wondering." Her eyes twinkle. "I urge you to reconsider."

A beautiful girl is begging me to kiss her. How is this even a quandary? But I promised myself I wouldn't hook up during the season. It might not be the most noteworthy vow any human being has ever taken. I'm sure others have made sacrifices for much nobler causes. But this was important to me. *Is* important to me.

"Is that a no?" she prompts when I remain quiet.

"It's a…" I trail off helplessly.

Demi leans toward me. "If you don't want it, stop me," she whispers, but I'm powerless to stop her, because I want it as bad as she does.

"Just one taste," I mumble, and holy fuck, I was right—her lips *are* soft. They feel like heaven as she gently rubs them against mine in the sweetest of kisses.

The moment our mouths make contact, a hot shiver rolls through me and settles between my legs. My dick is thick, heavy against my thigh. Motherfucker. This kiss is *everything*.

She moans, and the throaty sound creates tiny vibrations that quicken my pulse. Her tongue tentatively prods the seam of my lips, and like an idiot I part them to let her in. The meeting of our tongues summons desperate noises from both of us. Hers is a whimper of happy surprise, mine is a tormented groan. Demi's hand curls over my cheek as her tongue teases and explores. She tastes like candy, literally, and I wonder if she was sucking on one of her lollipops earlier. I savor the sweet flavor and thrust my fingers through her dark hair.

I officially forget my surroundings. I register the faint sound of music, but my pounding heart drowns it out. I am so turned on it's not even funny. The kiss goes on and on, a tangle of tongues and the mingling of heated breaths, not ceasing until the moment I taste copper in my mouth.

"Ugh." This time I groan unhappily. "Demi, stop." When she pulls back, I see her lips are tinged with my blood. "I'm bleeding again and now it's all over you."

"Really? I didn't even notice." Her voice is breathy. "Oh my *fuck*."

"What?" I grab more toilet paper from the roll and dab my lips. "Is it terrible?"

"No, I'm saying oh my fuck because…" She shakes her head in wonderment. "That was a good kiss."

I can't disagree. "It was."

"I want to do it again."

I haul her up to her feet. "Bad idea."

"Come on, Monk, let's do it again. I know you enjoyed it." She directs a pointed look at my crotch.

"Of course I enjoyed it. I haven't been with anyone in like eight months."

A part of her seems to deflate, and I realize I'd said the wrong thing. "You're saying you would've enjoyed kissing anyone? I'm nothing but a pair of lips?"

I let out a breath. "No. You're much more than that. But you can't pressure me into being your rebound."

"I'm not trying to pressure you," she argues.

"Seriously? You just stuck your tongue in my mouth and now I'm harder than stone. You knew it would tempt me."

"Oh my God, you *gave* me the green light. You said you wanted a taste, and I can't help it if kissing me gets you hard. Jeez, it's okay to get a boner every now and then."

A loud guffaw echoes in the doorway. I glance over to find an amused Conor watching us. "Yeah, captain. A boner's not gonna kill you."

Demi is smug. "Exactly."

I'm grateful for the distraction, until I notice Conor assessing her with his trademark Penis Eyes. "And you are?" he asks slowly.

"The reason I look like this," I answer for her, jerking a finger at my face.

"Ah, the ex-girlfriend and infamous provider of road head."

"Oh, give it up," I grumble. "There was no road head. It was a misunderstanding."

"Uh-huh. That's what they all say, bro."

Demi grins at Conor. "Sadly for him, this time it's true. Nothing happened except that I was nearly the victim of ear mutilation. I could've died."

"Chrissake, Semi, you wouldn't have died."

"There are important arteries in your ear. What if I bled out?"

"I don't think there is a single motherfucking artery in an ear," I growl.

Chuckling, Con gives her another flirtatious appraisal. "All right. So if you're not with my captain and you're not with that loser who beat him up, that mean you're single?"

"Yep," she says, flicking a mocking look my way.

"Excellent. Then how about I get you a drink?"

"Sounds great." She steps toward him, then glances over her shoulder, as if expecting me to stop her from grabbing a drink with Conor.

But I just lift one shoulder indifferently.

And she walks away.

# 24
# HUNTER

**DEMI**: Did you win your game today?

**ME**: Yup yup.

**HER**: Don't say that. But good. I'm glad you won.

**ME**: You were worried we'd lose?

**HER**: I thought maybe you'd be too banged up from Nico.

**ME**: Ribs were a little sore, but I powered through.

**HER**: Are you home now?

**ME**: Ya, but not for long. Heading into the city soon. Friend of mine coaches girls hockey and they have an exhibition this weekend.

**HER**: You played hockey all day and now you're going to watch hockey all night?

**ME**: Got a problem with that?

**HER**: You need a life.

**ME**: I have one. It's called hockey.

I type a follow up, but hesitation ripples through me. My fingers hover over the *SEND* button. I can still taste her on my lips, and I'm afraid to be around her again.

But we're friends. If I actively avoid her after one kiss, what the hell kind of friend am I?

I hit *SEND*.

**ME**: Wanna come?

She clearly struggles with her own moment of hesitation, because she takes equally long to respond.

**HER**: Sure? Anyone else coming or is it just us?
**ME**: Just us. Unless you want me to invite Conor...?

Is there a font for *snide*? I'm fully aware that nothing happened between them last night, but watching Con flirt with her still grated. And Demi was flirting back. She'd mauled me in the bathroom and then gone off with my teammate and took a tequila shot off his abs.

Although in her defense, I'd all but shoved her into Conor's arms by pretending I couldn't care less what she did with him.

**HER**: Invite whoever you want. I'll Uber to your place so you don't have to make the drive to campus. It just started snowing.

Demi shows up forty-five minutes later, bundled up in her parka, gloves and a bright-green scarf. I'm guessing her favorite color is green, because she wears it frequently. It looks good on her. Brings out the flecks of amber in her dark brown eyes.

"So who's this friend we're meeting?" she asks as I flick on the windshield defroster in the Rover.

She was right about it snowing, but sadly it's only light flurries. Nothing's sticking to the ground, and I find myself wondering if winter might skip New England altogether this year. So far we've received only one major snowfall and it all melted away by the morning. If we don't get a white Christmas, I'm going to be bummed. It's the only thing that makes the holidays in Connecticut bearable.

"Dean Di Laurentis," I answer. "He's a former teammate, graduated a couple years ago. Oh, and he's Summer's brother."

"Eek. Does that mean he's as…dramatic as Summer?" Her tone is the epitome of tactful.

"Nah, he's definitely more chill. They could be twins, though."

For once, Demi lets me listen to my own music library during the ride. I think we're both remembering what happened the last time we used her Bluetooth. Still, she makes sure to skip any song she can't dance to or doesn't know the words to.

Neither of us brings up the kiss. I'm thinking about it, though. I wonder if she is. I sneak glances at her, but she's too busy singing along or bopping her sexy torso to the beat. She's the cutest fucking thing and I want to kick myself for rejecting her.

Dean's girls are playing at a community center near Chestnut Hill. The parking lot is surprisingly packed *and* costs twenty bucks to enter. I can afford it, but it's the principle of the matter.

"*Twenty* bucks," I mutter under my breath as we get out of the Rover. "That is a travesty."

"You're a travesty."

Snickering, I check my phone to read an incoming text from Dean.

**DEAN**: G and Logan are here too. Behind my bench.

Huh, really? How are they swinging *that*? Garrett is one of the most recognizable hockey players in the country. Last time I saw him, he admitted he scarcely goes out anymore because he's constantly getting recognized. Logan is in his rookie season, so he can probably still maintain a low profile, but G's the star of the team.

When we arrive at our seats, I discover that the two Boston players are terrible at disguises. They've opted for baseball caps, and

Garrett's wearing a pair of square hipster glasses on the bridge of his nose.

I burst out laughing. "Fake glasses? Seriously?"

He smirks. "Worked, didn't it? You did a double take."

"Not because I didn't recognize you—because you look stupid."

Logan snickers.

I introduce them to Demi, who, thanks to her complete ignorance of the sport, doesn't make a big fuss over them.

"Are Hannah or Grace coming?" I ask. I hope the answer's yes, because it would be nice if Demi had some chicks to chat with during the game. I doubt she'll pay a lick of attention to what's happening on the ice.

"Gracie's writing a paper," Logan replies. "She wanted to get it done before winter break so she doesn't have to work over the holidays."

"And Hannah's still at the studio," Garrett says. "She said she'd try to meet up with us afterward, if we go out anywhere. What have you been up to?"

"Oh, Hunter's been super busy," Demi answers for me. "He got arrested, got his ass kicked…busy busy bee."

Logan snorts. "I didn't want to ask about your lip, but now that the subject's been brought up…"

"My ex-boyfriend beat him up," Demi informs him. "I take full responsibility for it."

"Yeah, and you should take full responsibility for the jail thing, too," I say in accusation.

"*You're* the one who made me wear the big hoops!"

"This is confusing to me," Garrett says frankly.

We don't get a chance to elaborate—Dean just spotted us and he's slapping a palm on the Plexiglass to say hello.

"That's Dean," I tell Demi, who for once is speechless.

"Oh," she finally remarks. "Wow."

I narrow my eyes. "What does that mean?"

"It means he's insanely attractive."

"Yeah, and he knows it," Garrett says with a sigh.

The first period kicks off, Dean's army of fourteen-year-olds taking the ice. The puck drops, and the center wins the faceoff, deking out two opponents before passing to one of her defensewomen. Dean's girls are good. Very, very good. The refs, on the other hand, are hot garbage.

"What the hell was that?!" Logan shouts, flying to his feet. "They were offsides!"

On the bench, Dean is red-faced from outrage. "Offsides!" he thunders, but the ref merely skates past him.

"Lord, he's even beautiful when he's angry," Demi breathes. "Guys, how are you not acknowledging this?"

"We lived with him for four years," Garrett says dryly. "We're well aware of his appeal."

"Do you think life is different when you're that attractive?"

I lean over to pinch her side. "We should ask *you* that. You're the supermodel."

"Aw, thanks, Monk."

"Monk?" Garrett echoes.

"Because he's celibate," Demi clarifies.

G grins. "That's still going on?"

"Yup yup—"

"Don't say yup yup," Demi interjects.

"—you know me, willpower of steel."

The rest of the game, while fast-paced, is not at all competitive. Dean's team crushes their opponent, scoring five goals to the other team's one. I note that Dean is a terrific coach, praising his players each time they return to the bench. With one girl, he leans in to whisper in her ear for a long time between line changes, dispensing his wisdom. When she's back on the ice for her next shift, she almost scores off a teammate's rebound. Even without a goal under her belt, she's beaming at Dean when her line skates off. That's the mark of a great coach—he can make you feel invincible whether you win or lose.

After the ass-kicking, we meet up with Dean in the lobby. "I'm just coordinating with the other teachers about getting the girls back to the hotel," he says. "I gotta ride the bus with them, but I want to go out afterward. I can meet you guys somewhere."

"You don't have to stay with the girls?" Garrett asks.

"God no. Parent chaperones, baby. I've done my job, and now I need to get the fuck out. I've been surrounded by teenage girls for the past two days." Yet he says it jokingly, and I know he's proud of his team's performance this weekend. "You in?"

"Where are you thinking?" Demi asks him.

"Hmmm. Well, Saturdays are Latin night at the Exodus Club."

She rolls her eyes. "Why did you look at me when you said that? Because I'm Latina?"

He rolls his eyes back. "No, because you asked me the question, baby doll. So what do you say?"

Demi glances at me with an unspoken *Can we?*

"Sure." I shrug. "Why the hell not."

---

Hannah Wells meets us outside the club. There's a line down the block to get in, but Dean has no qualms about striding to the bouncer and dropping a name in his ear. *Dude, you can't make Garrett Graham wait in line*, I suspect he's saying. And a second later we're waved past the velvet rope.

Our little group follows a nearly pitch-black corridor toward the sounds of thumping bass and Spanish guitar. There's a coat check at the end of the hall, which we make use of, handing over our winter gear.

"So I hear your songwriting career has taken off," I tease Hannah with a smile.

"I'm doing okay," she says modestly.

"You were in the studio with Delilah Sparks tonight. That's more than *okay*."

"Right? I can't even. It's still so surreal."

When we enter the club, an array of strobe lights assaults my vision. The music blares and the temperature is scorching. Three seconds in, and I'm already sweating through my Under Armour T-shirt.

Demi links her arm through mine. "Do you salsa, Monk?"

"Nope." She's wearing a skimpy tank top, and the heat of her body sears into me. Christ. I wish she'd never kissed me. I've been horny as fuck ever since.

"Let's grab some drinks," Garrett suggests.

"Shots?" Logan says hopefully.

"*One* shot."

"C'mon, G, we've got four days off. Let's take advantage."

Garrett throws a muscular arm around his long-time girlfriend. "Oh, trust me." He winks. "I'll be taking advantage of it."

Hannah grins.

They do one round of shots, but I abstain. I'm the DD, so I want to keep a clear head tonight. What if we get pulled over again? What if this time Demi decides to suck my dick in the car for real?

A man can hope.

We spend the next few minutes shouting to each other over the music. When the current song changes, Demi shrieks in delight. It's "Despacito," the Bieber version, and the entire club goes wild.

"Come salsa with me," she begs, tugging on my arm. "This is my song!"

"Nope," I say firmly. "I don't salsa."

"I do," Dean announces, holding out his hand.

"You salsa?" She gawks at him before turning to me. "He's beautiful *and* he salsas? What on earth am I doing here with *you*?"

She's joking, but I still glare at her. "He's taken."

"Super taken," Dean confirms. "But I'm a salsa master thanks to my girl. Allie-Cat and I took lessons."

Demi takes his hand, and I swallow a sigh as I watch them saunter toward the dance floor.

"She's cool," Logan tells me.

"I know. We're good friends."

"Just friends?"

I shrug. "She got out of a relationship a month ago."

"So?"

I twist the cap off my water bottle and take a hasty sip. I'm not sure why I put that out there. Then I shift my gaze to the dance floor and almost choke on my water.

Goddamn Dean. Since when does he salsa dance? And he looks damn good doing it. Dean might've skipped out on law school to become a gym teacher, but the man still oozes money. He's wearing khakis and a crisp white shirt, its top two buttons undone and the sleeves rolled up. His blond hair falls onto his forehead as he spins Demi around as if they're on *Dancing with the Stars*.

"Check out that footwork," Garrett marvels.

They're even drawing stares from the other dancers. Demi's in leggings, leather boots, and a red tank, but the way her hips are moving, I can totally envision her in a bright sundress and high heels, the ones with straps that wrap around a woman's ankles. Maybe a flower in her hair. Red lipstick painted on those pouty lips.

Annnnd now I'm acting out my own salsa-themed porno in my head. Which Dean brings to life when he lifts one of her legs and props it on his hip, and they do a sexy little grinding move before he spins her around again. Demi's cheeks are flushed, her eyes bright with joy. Dean whispers something in her ear and she starts giggling.

Jealousy constricts my throat. Obviously I'm being ridiculous. There's always chemistry when two hot people are dancing, it's inevitable. But the sight of Dean's hands on Demi's body makes my blood boil.

"What the hell is a *despacito* anyway?" I grumble. "Is it like a desperado?"

Hannah bursts out laughing. "It means slowly."

"Whatever. It's a shitty song." I don't really believe that. If anything, I'm indifferent to the damn track. I just wish it would end already. I promptly glare daggers at the dance floor again.

"Just friends?" Logan asks knowingly.

The sigh I've been holding slips out.

"Aw, he has a crush," teases Hannah.

"Nah," I lie. "I'm putting sex and dating on the backburner this year. I want to focus on hockey."

"I get it." Garrett nods a couple times. "But there's more to life than hockey, Davenport." He's gazing at his girlfriend as he says that. Hannah is his entire world. I have no doubt he'd give up anything for her, even a flourishing career.

"I know there is, but I made myself a promise. You know, to try to grow as a person and all that shit."

The guys laugh loudly, while Hannah offers an admiring smile. "I actually think that's commendable," she says. "We get so caught up in sex and relationships, sometimes it's good to take some time for yourself."

"But sex is so good," Logan protests.

He's right. Sex is goddamn incredible, and right now Dean and Demi are engaged in a vertical version of it on the dance floor. My stomach twists again.

"You should cut in," Garrett suggests.

I'm about to maintain that I can't salsa, when the DJ changes up the music again. A slower, sultry beat reverberates through the club. "Havana" by Camila Cabello. I can work with that.

"I'll be right back." I stride forward, leaving my companions in the proverbial rear view mirror.

I can hear them laughing behind me, but I don't give a shit. I make a beeline for Demi. "Beat it," I tell Dean.

It's a joke.

But also not a joke.

And he knows it. Grinning, he slaps my shoulder and goes off to join the others.

Demi stares at me, one eyebrow quirked. "Wow. Was that a show of dominance?"

"Nah."

"Really? So you banished my dancing partner for no reason? What am I supposed to do now?" She snaps a hand on her hip. We're surrounded by other dancers, but neither of us moves.

"Well. I guess I'll just have to do," I say, extending a hand toward her.

She breaks out in a smile. "Took you long enough."

I yank her toward me, grabbing hold of her waist. Demi rests one hand on my shoulder, and places the other one at my nape, her fingers curling loosely around my neck as we begin to move to the beat.

Luckily, our lower bodies aren't touching, so I'm spared the agony of feeling her rubbing up against me. The experience would be too confusing for my dick.

Except great. Now she's rubbing up against me.

Cue: dick confusion.

I try to ease my hips away from her sexy body, but that earns me a huff of exasperation. "You have to actually dance back, Hunter. You can't just stand there."

"I'm dancing back," I protest.

"Your body is two feet away! Where did you learn to dance? Puritan camp? Why did you even bother cutting in?"

I shrug.

Demi thinks it over for a second. Then she releases a triumphant laugh. "Oh my God, you were jealous! You didn't like seeing me dancing with Dean!"

Another shrug.

"Ha!" She's so much shorter than me that she has to tug my head down to bring her lips to my ear. "Admit it," she whispers.

My lips travel toward *her* ear. "Fine," I whisper back, and I'm gratified to feel a shiver run down her body. "Maybe a little jealous. But it wasn't real jealousy."

"What the hell does that mean?"

"It was body jealousy."

"That's not a real thing."

"Yes it is. Bodies get jealous when they see other bodies close together."

"Right. Keep telling yourself that."

I kind of need to, to preserve my own sanity. I can't let myself develop feelings for Demi. I mean, obviously, I like her. She's amazing and we have fun together. As *friends*.

I don't want our friendship to be ruined.

But Demi seems hell-bent on setting it on fire.

"I have a secret," she teases, gesturing for me to lower my head again.

"Yeah?" My voice comes out stupidly husky.

Her breath tickles my earlobe. "I'm about to do something you're not going to like."

Like a fool I ask, "What's that?"

And rather than answer, Demi angles her head and slants her mouth over mine.

The kiss is as delicious as the last time. She tastes like tequila and a hint of cherry, probably from the red candy she had in her mouth at the game. Her tongue had kept poking it into her cheek, making it look like she had a creature moving around in there.

I laugh at the memory.

She pulls back breathlessly. "What is it?"

"Nothing. I was just thinking about your candy obsession and… forget it." I just kiss her again, and her tongue eagerly slides into my mouth.

Just feeling it touch the tip of mine unleashes a greedy, caveman side I never knew I possessed. I shove my hand in her hair and drive the kiss deeper. She gasps against my lips. I'm fully aware we're in the middle of the dance floor sucking on each other's tongues. I hear music. I register people around us. I don't know if they're dancing or staring at us. I don't care. All I care about is kissing her. And touching her.

I slide a hand down her slender back and cup one firm ass cheek. Ah Christ, I want to rip off those leggings. I want to smack her perfect ass. I want to slip a finger inside her and find out how wet she is for me.

Demi breaks the kiss again. "Let's get out of here," she pleads.

The sheer desire swimming in her eyes brings me back to my senses. "No," I croak, abruptly leading her away from the dance floor.

"Why not?" is her frustrated response.

"Because I don't want to complicate our friendship."

"We've been making out for the past five minutes, Hunter! It's already been complicated!"

"No, it hasn't. That was…just kissing." The best kissing ever. My body is still throbbing from it.

Accusation sharpens her face. "I feel like you're purposely trying to be difficult."

"I'm not," I say unhappily. "Look, I made this decision before I even met you. And I want to stick by it. I want to prove to myself that I can actually stick to a goal I've set and not let sex blow up my whole life again."

"That won't happen," she insists. "The team is doing great. You're winning all your games."

"Yeah, because my head is clear. And now it's about more than celibacy. I *like* you. This friendship is everything to me and we both know damn well that sex would screw it up. So I'm sorry, okay? I'm not giving in to temptation again." I shake my head in defeat. "I can't."

Unhappiness flickers in her eyes for a moment. Then it transforms into a glimmer of determination. "Fine. I won't hit on you anymore. But only if you make me a promise."

"Demi—"

"After the season ends—" She slants her head, defiant. "*I* get to be the one you cross the finish line with, friendship be damned."

# 25
# DEMI

A FEW DAYS BEFORE THE BREAK STARTS, I MANAGE TO SQUEEZE IN a coffee date with TJ, who meets me at the Theta house. It's chilly outside, but we both agree a winter walk through campus would be lovely, so we set off in the direction of the Coffee Hut.

"Are you mad at me?"

TJ's wounded tone has me glancing over in surprise. "Of course not. I've just been crazy-busy. I'm working on the case study, cramming for finals, planning the sorority's holiday party with Josie, organizing a Secret Santa for everyone in my Biology tutorial. Life is nuts right now."

"No, I know. I just miss you."

"Aw, I miss you too." I link my arm through his.

"Are you around tonight?" he asks. "There's this skating thing at the rink in Hastings."

"What skating thing?"

"It's, like, a winter fair? It's the first year the town is holding it. I thought it would be cool to go. Drink some hot cocoa, skate for a bit, get our picture taken with Santa."

"That sounds fun. I love fairs. Oh—but I have Hunter's game tonight."

"Hunter's game?"

I nod. "Briar's playing against…you know what, I didn't even ask who they're playing. But it's a home game, and I promised him I'd go. It'll probably end around nine-thirty, ten? How long is the fair open until?"

He opens a browser on his iPhone, and I notice the Town of Hastings webpage is already loaded up. "It says here it goes till midnight."

I brighten. "Okay, that works, then. I should be done by ten-ish, and that'll give us a couple hours at the fair. Sound like a plan?"

"Sounds great." He smiles, a rare sight to behold.

I can't deny that TJ isn't the easiest person to get to know. He keeps his emotions locked up tight, but once he warms up to people, he's actually super sweet. He can be moody at times, which is probably why I can't spend long chunks of time with him. That doesn't mean I don't like him, though. I also can't spend an inordinate amount of time with Pax, whose melodramatic nature eventually drains my patience.

TJ and I navigate the winding path, snow crunching beneath our feet. The ground is icy, and he tightens his hold on my arm as we encounter a particularly precarious section of the path.

"They need to salt this," he gripes.

"Right? I nearly face-planted just now."

We're about fifty yards from the Coffee Hut when TJ brings up the subject of Hunter. "You two hang out a lot," he remarks.

I can't decipher his tone. I feel like it might contain a hint of disapproval, but I'm not certain. TJ can be so hard to read sometimes. "Well, yeah. We're friends."

*Friends who kiss.*

I keep that tidbit to myself. Hell, I don't know why I'm even still thinking about it. I kissed the guy twice and would happily kiss him a hundred more times. But Hunter rejected me twice and doesn't want a single kiss more.

Ugh, and he wouldn't even promise that we could resume the kissing when the hockey season ends. He just reiterated that our friendship is too important, and we proceeded to spend the rest of the night hanging out with Dean and his other friends, pretending we hadn't just sucked each other's faces off.

It's so vexing. Frustrating. I don't believe it's an ego problem on my end, because I'm confident I wouldn't have much trouble finding someone to have sex with me. Half the men on Tinder would offer themselves up.

But I don't want those men.

I want Hunter Davenport.

I haven't allowed myself to delve too deeply about precisely *what* I want from him. To keep kissing him, for sure. And sex, absolutely. The mere thought of our naked bodies tangled together gets me hot.

I'm not looking beyond that. But I do think he's wrong—I think we *could* be friends with benefits without it complicating anything.

Couldn't we?

"I just think it's weird," TJ says, jolting me from my troubled thoughts.

"Why is it weird?"

"I dunno. He's such a fuckboy."

"Not really."

"Yes really. I told you about catching him in the library last year, remember? Any guy who fucks chicks in public is slimy."

"One, that's not at all an accurate barometer of slime—lots of very respectable people possess exhibitionist tendencies. Weren't you paying attention to Andrews' lecture about sexual compulsions? And two, that happened last year. Hunter's different now. He's not even dating at the moment."

"Yeah, probably because of the herpes."

I give TJ a sharp look. "That's a rude thing to say."

He shrugs. "The truth isn't always pretty."

Now I roll my eyes. "What truth? You're saying Hunter Davenport has herpes?"

"I think that's what it was? I don't remember exactly, but I'm friends with this chick in my dorm and she said Davenport gave her an STI this past spring. She used the word outbreak, so I just assumed herpes—but do the other ones give you outbreaks? What do chlamydia and gonorrhea do?"

"I don't know." I frown. "Are you being serious right now?"

"Honest to God."

My stomach does a queasy little flip. TJ is a decent guy, and he doesn't typically spread rumors, so I'm predisposed to believe he did hear something. But there's no way it's *true*. Hunter doesn't have a sexually transmitted disease.

Well, I mean…he could.

Something else suddenly occurs to me. Is *that* why he's not sexually active? Because he's embarrassed about having something and passing it to someone else?

It's possible, I guess. Either way, I'm uncomfortable discussing Hunter's private business with TJ, who clearly doesn't like him.

"Whatever. This is not a conversation we should be having," TJ says before I can. "It's really none of our business."

"You're right," I agree.

"I shouldn't have even said anything. But I wanted you to be aware, just in case. Since you're spending so much time with him."

———————

Later that night, I drag Pippa to the hockey game with me and Brenna. Mostly because I'm worried Brenna will be so absorbed in the game that I won't have anybody to talk to. Like me, Pippa isn't a hockey fan. Neither of us could properly explain what's currently happening on the ice. I just see big hulking boys skating very fast and wielding sticks.

Hunter told me his jersey number is 12, so I attempt to track those two digits with my gaze. I think he's doing well? Then again, he hasn't scored any goals, so maybe he's doing poorly?

I truly don't know how to measure hockey success. Nico played basketball in high school and used to score a ton of points in every game. But when I ask Brenna why nobody is scoring, she explains that hockey isn't as point-laden as basketball. Apparently some games might end with only one goal between both teams. Or even a tie of zero.

Speaking of Nico, Pippa asks about him during the first intermission. "Did you ever hear from Nico after he attacked Hockey Boy?"

"Nope."

"Has he tried to contact you?" Brenna asks curiously.

"No idea. I told you, I blocked him on everything, even email. I'm sure he's figured that out by now."

"Oh he has," Pippa confirms.

I look over sharply. "You've spoken to him?"

"Me, personally? No. But Darius is speaking to him again."

That brings a frown to my lips. I was texting with D the other day, and he didn't once mention he's back in contact with my ex.

"Darius said Nico is losing his shit. The guys had to forcibly stop him several times from showing up at your house. D told him it was asking for trouble."

I make a mental note to call Darius later for more details.

"But yeah, he's definitely not over you, or handling this breakup well." Pippa gazes at the ice, where the Zamboni is shuffling along to smooth out the shiny surface. Then she switches gears from my cheating ex to the friend he cheated with. "Corinne says you two are texting again."

I nod. "She sent me a funny meme the other day and we had a short convo."

"For what it's worth, she still feels terrible about everything."

"She should," I mutter, but my anger toward our friend isn't as powerful as it used to be. Even my anger at Nico has dimmed.

"I really hope you two can be friends again one day, so we can hang out the way we used to. Maybe over the holiday break the three of us could have a girls' night?"

A sigh flutters out. "I mean, we could try."

"Hold up—you're *texting* and making *hangout* plans with the chick who slept with your boyfriend?" Brenna demands. Her mouth is wide with disbelief, drawing attention to her trademark red lips. It's the only splash of color amidst her black turtleneck, leggings and leather boots.

Pippa shakes her head wryly. "Seriously, Demi, you're so fucking forgiving and understanding it makes me want to punch you."

"Really? Those two wonderful qualities of mine make you want to *punch* me? Also! You literally just suggested we do a girls' night. You're encouraging me to be friends with Corinne again."

"Yeah, but by agreeing to it you're setting a bad example for the rest of us. You know, the grudge holders."

Brenna grins. "I hold a mean grudge, I'll tell you that."

I roll my eyes at both of them. "I want to be a psychologist. That means I ought to practice what I preach, right?"

The second period gets underway when the referee skates up to the faceoff and drops the puck.

"How does he not get hurt?" Pippa demands.

"Who, the ref?" Brenna asks.

"Yes! Look at that little guy! He's way too close to the action. One of those huge monsters could smash into him at any second and break every bone in his body."

"I know it looks dangerous, but the refs know how to stay out of the way," Brenna assures her.

A cheer rocks the arena and I squint hard, trying to understand what I'm seeing. #12 is flying past the blue line at the center of the rink. "Oooh, that's Hunter! And he's all alone."

Brenna supplies the hockey lingo. "He's on a breakaway."

Oh gosh, he's tearing toward the opposing net, his stick snapping up in preparation for his shot. As my heart lodges in my throat, I find myself shooting to my feet.

"Holy shit, you're into hockey!" Pippa accuses, staring up at me in shock.

"Into it? No. But did you see that shot?" Hunter missed, but it was still ridiculously thrilling to watch.

Pippa narrows her eyes. "Ohhhhh," she finally says. "I get what's happening. You're not into hockey. You're into the hockey *player*."

"No," I lie. Then I groan. "Well, maybe a little."

Brenna lets out a hoot. "That means *a lot*. Have you found the key to his chastity belt yet?"

A laugh pops out of my mouth. "No, sadly. It's still locked up tight." I hesitate for a beat. I haven't told anybody about kissing Hunter, but I suspect that's about to change. I need advice, and there's no better time like the present.

So while Brenna and Pippa sit there grinning at me, I confess to the two kisses, which I think of as Bathroom Kiss and Salsa Kiss. "Salsa Kiss involved a butt squeeze," I confess. "But then he stopped it from going any further. I think I might need to accept he's not interested."

"Bullshit," Brenna says.

Pippa nods in agreement. "If he wasn't interested, he wouldn't keep kissing you back."

"And then *stopping* it," I reiterate. "He's dead set on trying to be a good team leader and make hockey his priority."

"Sleeping with you isn't going to destroy the team." Brenna rolls her eyes. "That's just nonsense."

"Maybe, but I can't force someone to sleep with me. There's this thing called consent?"

"Nobody's telling you to force him," Pippa says. "But it couldn't hurt to give him a nudge?"

"I've done more than nudge. I kissed him twice. He shut me down twice. And after Salsa Kiss, I told him I wouldn't hit on him again until he's done with the season."

"Then don't hit on him." An evil glint lights Brenna's eyes. "You need to change your tactics here, babe. Stop going after him. Make him come to *you*."

"How?"

"Make him jealous. Flirt with one of his buddies."

"Oooh, Operation Jealousy!" Pippa chimes in. "That's totally what you need to do."

Make him jealous... I guess I already did that, the night I danced with Dean. And it worked, I realize. I wasn't openly flirting, but the mere act of dancing with another man triggered Hunter's possessive instincts.

"Isn't there always a party after these games?" Pippa asks. "You should do it tonight."

"I can't. I have plans with TJ. Oh shit, that reminds me! I need to text him my ETA. When is the game over?" I ask Brenna. I'm worried I'll end up being late, because even though we got here at seven-thirty, they didn't drop the puck until past eight. There was a lot of preamble first, including a ceremony honoring a middle-aged alumnus who supposedly set a bunch of records back in the day.

"The second period just started. So you have at least another hour, hour and a half. And maybe another half hour for the boys to shower and change?"

Shit, that puts us closer to eleven. And if I want to say hi to Hunter once he's out of the locker room, it becomes even more unlikely I'll get to Hastings at a reasonable time. Shit.

I unlock my phone and pull up my text thread with TJ.

**ME**: Hey, so I totally got the times wrong. Apparently I'm not out of here til 11. I don't think there's a point in showing up at 11 if the fair closes at 12. Is it on tomorrow night too?

**TJ**: Not sure. Can't you duck out of the game early?

**ME**: I would, except I'm here with Pippa and Brenna, and I promised Hunter I'd come find him after the game.

There's a long delay. And still no response.

**ME**: I'm so sorry. Please don't be mad. Our meet-up was a last-minute thing, anyway, remember? I already had plans to go to the game.
**HIM**: I know. It's fine, D. Have fun at the game.

He's clearly annoyed. I don't blame him for it, either. But I'm also growing weary of reassuring him all the time. TJ asks me to hang out nearly every single day. We're friends, sure, but I don't even see Pippa every day, and I consider her my bestie. Hell, I didn't even see Nico every day and we were a *couple*.

Regardless of all that, I do feel bad about not being able to make it to the fair. I shouldn't have agreed to two sets of plans in one night. Any time you do that, timing always overlaps in some stupid way, and now I've disappointed one of my good friends.

**ME**: I'm really sorry, hon. This is on me. I shouldn't have made plans on top of plans. It turned into a dumb double-booking thing, and I apologize for that. I'll call you tomorrow and we can plan a friend day that fits both of our schedules, okay?
Xo

He responds with xoxo followed by an, Okay.

Whew. I'm glad I patched that one up. Now it's time for more pressing matters.

"I'm not meeting TJ," I tell the girls. "So I guess I'm good to party later. What's my game plan?"

"Flirt and seduce," Brenna advises. "Pick his hottest friend—I'm thinking that's Conor, or Matty. Get your flirt on, and make sure Hunter's watching."

"Then what?"

She shrugs. "If he takes the bait, hopefully there'll be a chastity belt on your bedroom floor tonight. If he doesn't…hell, hook up with Conor or Matty, then."

I balk. "But I hardly know them."

Pippa snorts. "You are the most sheltered college woman on the planet. It's okay to fool around with guys you haven't known since you were eight years old, D."

I stick out my tongue at her.

"I'm serious. You're allowed to experiment. For all you know, you were having the worst sex of your life with Nico, only you thought it was mind-blowing because you didn't know any better. Let yourself know better."

"Nico and I had good sex." I pause. "Well, aside from the subpar oral." Because who am I kidding? It was never even close to par. "But I never really saw the appeal, anyway. With oral, I could take it or leave it."

"But that's the most important part!" Brenna says in outrage.

"If I do end up with Hunter tonight, should I be worried about… um…you know, sexually transmitted diseases?" TJ's warning continues to lurk in the back of my head like a cat burglar.

"As in, does Hunter have one?" Brenna thinks it over. "Nobody's ever said anything to me about that, but obviously I can't know for sure." She wrinkles her forehead at me. "But that's why you have the conversation before the clothes come off."

"The conversation?"

"Disclosure," she explains. "Diseases, birth control, any weird kinks you want to disclose. Like, if a guy has a foot fetish, I need to know about that shit up front so I don't throw up on him."

Pippa breaks out laughing. "Oh God, that's a great point. All foot fetishes must be disclosed prior to sexual relations. And don't even get me started on the guy in sophomore year who wanted me to pee on him."

I resist the urge to bury my face in my hands and moan in despair. I am so out of my element here. I've only slept with one person. I lost my virginity to him, and we were in a long-term relationship for years. There was never any need to have "the conversation."

And I never, ever had to wonder if he *wanted me to pee on him.*

I never thought of myself as naïve or inexperienced. I thought I was a ballsy, smart-talking chick from Miami who owned her body and her sexuality. But maybe it's time to grow up a little. I *do* need to think about things like STIs and new partners.

And if everything goes my way tonight, that new partner is going to be Hunter Davenport.

# 26
# DEMI

THE AFTER PARTY IS HELD AT CONOR'S HOUSE. I KNOW FROM MY last visit that he's got four roommates and they're all hockey players. In fact, most of the male bodies in the townhouse tonight belong to hockey players, which means there isn't much space to maneuver. I'm talking muscles galore.

A crappy EDM song blasts in the air, making my temples throb. Never been a fan of electronic dance music. Nico and I attended a couple of raves in Miami, but it wasn't my thing. When we were there, he tried to convince me to do MDMA, and I said hell no, which surprised most of his friends.

It's funny, but people expect me to be more reckless than I actually am. I mean, I'll dance at the drop of a hat, no matter where I am. I'll talk to strangers in the CVS checkout line. And sure, if someone asked me to go skydiving or bungee jumping I'd consider it. But I've never cared for the drug scene or the kind of dangerous activities our Miami friends were into. Whenever I visited, Nico spent a lot of time racing cars. Illegally, of course, which meant I was looking over my shoulder the entire time waiting for the cops to show up.

So no, recklessness isn't a trait I usually possess. But I'm going to be reckless tonight. I'm going to tease my friend and hopefully convince him to break his vow. I guess that probably makes me a jerk, but a part of me wonders if Hunter is overcompensating for something. Last year he acted in a self-destructive manner, hooking up with random girls, drinking too much. But I don't believe that's inherently his nature. I think he was simply reeling from Summer's rejection and the perceived betrayal from his friend.

If you ask me, sex isn't the reason his hockey season imploded last year, nor do I think the *lack* of it is responsible for the team's success this year.

I'm starting to believe it's a matter of trust. As in, he doesn't trust himself to make good decisions in the moment. But I don't think avoiding any situations that require difficult decision-making is the solution.

My gaze drifts in Hunter's direction. He's across the living room, deep in conversation with Matt Anderson. Meanwhile, I'm in the corner like a loser, sucking on one of the many lollipops stashed at all times in my purse. Hunter left me to my own devices once we got here, but this isn't my crowd and I don't miss all the dirty looks I'm receiving from the hockey groupies, as if I'm trespassing on their property.

I don't particularly understand the sports groupie mentality. The fact that they make it seem like I'm trying to *steal* something from them tells me that they don't care about the men they're coveting, only the status those men bring to the table. I look at Hunter and see Hunter. They look at him and see HOCKEY PLAYER.

"What's the matter? Not having fun?" Conor wanders over and joins me in the doorway.

It's impossible to look at Conor without noticing how incredibly attractive he is. He sort of resembles Hunter's friend Dean, except in a surfer-dude way whereas Dean should be posing in cologne ads or underwear spreads.

"Eh, I just don't know anyone." I shrug, absently twirling the stick of my lollipop between my thumb and index finger.

"You know *me*." He flashes a crooked grin.

"True."

He nods toward Hunter. "And Davenport."

"Also true. But he's busy at the moment."

"Well, I'm not." Conor slants his head. "Come dance with me. We can entertain each other."

Normally I wouldn't turn down a dance offer, but my bladder is full from the two sodas I drank at the game and the vodka cranberry one of Conor's roommates made for me.

"I would, but I have to pee so bad," I admit. "If we dance I'd probably pee all over you." Then again, maybe that's his kink. As I learned tonight, that's actually a *thing* people do.

He laughs. "All right, how 'bout you take care of that little problem first, and then we'll reevaluate."

I check behind us, noting the line for the downstairs bathroom. "How 'bout you keep me company while I wait in line?"

"I'll do you one better." He winks and holds out his hand.

I take it.

And when I notice Hunter frowning in our direction just before we exit the room, I can't fight a smug smile. I hadn't intended on it happening right this second, but looks like Operation Jealousy has officially commenced.

Upstairs, Conor opens a door and gestures for me to enter. "I've got the master bedroom with the ensuite. My toilet is yours, milady."

I snicker. "Thanks, milord."

In the bathroom, I toss out my lollipop, then lift up my dress and do my thing. I feel slightly stupid wearing a short dress in the middle of winter, but we stopped off at Brenna and Hunter's house after the game, where Brenna convinced me to ditch my leggings and sweater for one of her dresses—a long-sleeved, ribbed sweater dress that barely reaches my knees. Black, of course.

As I wash my hands, I hear the murmur of voices beyond the bathroom door. A female one, and more than one male. I emerge to find Matt sprawled on the bed next to a girl with dark braids. "Hi!" she says when she spots me. "I'm Andrea."

"Demi."

"Come sit down," Conor calls from the small couch. The master is big enough to contain a double bed, a dresser, sofa, and huge flat screen TV. Conor's on one end of the couch, fiddling with a video game controller. Hunter is on the other end, uncapping a bottle of amber-colored liquid.

"Whiskey?" I say, wrinkling my nose. "We're drinking whiskey now? What happened to your precious beer?" When we got here, he'd made a big deal about how Matt had picked up a case of Dampf Punk for them. Obviously, I inquired as to why anyone would pick such a stupid name for a beer, at which point he'd given me the finger.

"We're all out. The only thing that's left is the watery keg." He makes a face. "Come do a shot with me, Semi."

I hesitate. If I start doing shots, I might lose my head. On the other hand, I could use the liquid courage. Truth be told, I have no clue how to go about seducing somebody.

"Is it still cool if I crash on your couch tonight?" I ask him.

Hunter nods. He removes his baseball cap to run his fingers through his dark hair, then shoves the cap back on.

I join him on the couch. "Okay. Let's do it."

While Conor is busy setting up a skateboarding game, Hunter pours a shot and swallows it back.

I watch the strong column of his throat as he gulps the whiskey. I want to kiss him right there—right at the base of his throat. I wonder if I'd feel his pulse fluttering beneath my lips.

He passes me the shot glass. I eye it suspiciously. "What? I don't get my own?"

"There's only one up here. If you want your own, go downstairs and get one." Hunter lifts an eyebrow. "What, you afraid of catching my cooties?"

"Your tongue's been in my mouth. If you have cooties, I'm already infected."

That makes Conor chuckle. "Pour me a shot, too."

"Me first," I say, lifting the glass to my lips.

I drink, and the alcohol instantly makes my eyes water. Eeek. I'm not used to whiskey, I guess. I can sling back tequila like a pro, but something about this whiskey is getting me buzzed harder and faster than usual.

Hunter pours another one, and I pass the shot to Conor. He swallows it, then starts a game. I watch as his skateboarder performs a series of tricks on a concrete half-pipe.

"Hey, that's in Jacksonville!" I exclaim as I study the familiar setting on the screen.

"Kona Skatepark," Conor confirms. "You been there before?"

"A few times. My ex"—Lord, it's still so weird saying that—"was friends with a lot of skaters. Have you ever been to Florida?" I ask him.

"Nah, I'm a West Coast boy."

"California?"

Conor nods. "Huntington Beach."

"Never been," I admit.

"You should come visit me this summer. I'll show you around."

Hunter rolls his eyes. "Watch out, Semi. He's making his move."

"I'm not making any moves," protests Conor. "I'm just sitting here like a good little boy, playing my game." He presses a few buttons on his controller, then gives me a cocky smile. "Unless you want me to make a move?"

I think it over. "Maybe."

Hunter makes a grouchy noise. "Demi. I think I'm gonna have to cut you off."

"I've literally had one shot!"

"And it's clearly clouded your judgment if you're openly flirting with this dumbass."

On the bed, Andrea overhears him and giggles. "Um. You can't *not* flirt with Conor Edwards. He just brings out that side in women."

"What about me?" Matt complains, and I notice they've inched so close to each other they're practically cuddling. "What side do I bring out in you?"

She whispers something in his ear. Matt chuckles in response, and I lose interest.

Conor passes the controller to Hunter, who leans forward and rests his forearms on his thighs. His forehead creases in concentration as his player performs a series of kick flips. I don't recognize this next course, and to be honest my patience threshold for watching video games has officially exceeded its limit.

Meanwhile, I don't miss that Conor has moved closer to me. He smells good, like sandalwood and citrus soap. His hair's slightly damp from the shower he must've taken after the game. He's wearing a T-shirt and cargo shorts, and he's barefoot.

A perpetually high body temperature must be a hockey player thing—Hunter stripped out of his hoodie almost the second we arrived at the party, leaving him in his trademark white wife-beater.

"So." Conor sounds thoughtful. "We've established that you want me to make a move."

"I said maybe," I remind him. Coyly.

"'Kay... What'll it take to turn the maybe into a hell yes?"

"I don't know. Make me an offer and let's see what happens."

"Hmmm." His long fingers travel up my sleeve and toy with a strand of my hair. "How 'bout the best sex of your life?"

Hunter snorts. His focus remains on the screen.

"What else you got?" I lightly rest my hand on Conor's knee, and this time Hunter's gaze flicks over.

"How about the best massage of your life?"

"Dude, you gotta stop using superlatives. Only sets you up for failure." Hunter tosses the controller in Conor's lap. "You're up. I have to take a leak." He staggers to his feet and ducks into the bathroom.

Conor doesn't start a new game. Rather, he sets the controller on the floor and angles his body toward mine. His silvery eyes glint knowingly. "So, you and the captain have a thing going on?"

"We kissed a couple times," I confess, my tongue loosened by the whiskey. "But he doesn't want to do anything more."

"Ah right. The vow of celibacy."

"Yep."

"Is this why you're hitting on me?" He cocks his head, and his lips are curved in a mocking smile. "You're hoping he'll be jealous enough to cave?"

"I'm not hitting on you."

"Let's not do that."

"Do what?"

"Lie to each other." Chuckling, Conor captures my chin with his thumb and forefinger, forcing eye contact. "You want my help or not?"

My throat goes dry. I swallow a few times, but it doesn't help. "You think we can get to him?"

"Baby," he drawls. "I can get to anyone."

# 27
# HUNTER

WHEN I STEP OUT OF THE BATHROOM, DEMI AND CONOR ARE still on the couch, but Matt and Andrea are gone. I'm not particularly thrilled about Demi and Con's proximity to each other. She's sitting so close to him she might as well be in his lap.

I can't say anything, though, because I made my own position clear last week. I told her I just want to be friends. Which means, if she wants to flirt with my teammate, I'd be a real asshole to try to stop her. And I'd be a selfish team captain if I cock-blocked one of my guys.

That's rule number five thousand, draft three of the captain handbook. *Your teammate's dick comes first.*

Despite their blatant flirting, they don't ask me to leave. And like a chump I don't leave, despite the fact that I'm very noticeably the third wheel.

Conor murmurs something that makes Demi giggle.

I bristle. "What are you whispering about over there?"

"Nothing. Pass the bottle?" Con holds out his hand.

I look at Demi. Her cheeks are flushed, but whether it's from too much alcohol consumption, I can't be sure.

"It's for me," Con says knowingly.

I lean over to hand him the whiskey and he takes a swig directly from the bottle.

He hands it back to me, and I take a swig too. Maybe that's what I need to do—get stupidly drunk. Because it's inevitable that Demi will find her rebound tonight and if it's not with Con I'll eat my hat. And why not? Despite his ladies' man reputation, I've never heard a single woman express she felt used by him or didn't have a good time.

"So you guys have kissed," Con says suddenly, his gray eyes fixing on me. "How'd that go?"

*Phenomenally.* "It was all right," I say out loud.

Demi's outraged gasp makes me smile. "Just all right? Fuck off, Monk. My kissing is more than all right. I'm an excellent kisser." Her eyes dare me to defy her.

"She's an excellent kisser," I admit.

She beams at me. "And you want to do it again…?" she prompts.

"Nope."

Conor snorts. "Damn, dude, you're no good for a woman's ego."

"Trust me, her ego is doing just fine."

"It is," Demi confirms. "I'm very confident in my overall awesomeness as a person."

"Yeah?" Conor has his arm around her now, while the fingertips of his other hand teasingly stroke her bare thigh.

Despite its long sleeves, Demi's black dress is indecently short. I don't remember her wearing it at the game. When did she have time to change?

It's getting hard to breathe. I'm not drunk enough for this. And I'm definitely not drunk enough when Con's hand slides upward, his knuckles grazing Demi's right breast on the way to her neck. He starts stroking that, too.

Her breath hitches. "Did you just cop a feel?"

"No." His tongue is caught between his teeth as he offers a lewd grin.

"You grazed my boob."

"Yeah, a graze, not a feel."

"Same thing. Right, Hunter?"

I don't answer. My mouth is bone-dry. I remember making out with her in the club in Boston, how badly I'd wanted to cup her tits with both hands, tease my thumbs over her nipples until they were harder than icicles. But we were in public and I didn't do it. And even in private, I still can't do that.

Maybe watching Conor do it will provide me with some sort of satisfaction? Is secondhand boob-groping a thing?

But Con's focus is no longer on Demi's perfect tits. He lowers his mouth, and Demi squeaks in surprise.

I stiffen at the sight of his blond head buried in her neck. She, on the other hand, softens like warm butter. Her body practically melts into Con, and she even slants her head to grant him easier access to suck on her neck.

It's no longer difficult to breathe—it's impossible. Jealousy pounds a steady drumbeat in my blood. But so does arousal. I should get up and leave, ASAP. Anything short of that is self-torture.

But my ass remains glued to the couch cushion.

Conor lifts his head, his eyelids heavy with lust. "I want to kiss you," he whispers to Demi, who inhales deeply.

I curl my fingers over my knee to stop them from clenching into a fist.

Con flicks me a brief look, winks, and then lowers his mouth to Demi's.

Mother*fucker*.

She welcomes the kiss, parting her lips for him, and I almost curse out loud when I see his tongue enter her mouth.

I grit my teeth. Finally finding my voice. "I'm just gonna go…"

Demi breaks the kiss and plants her hand on my thigh. "Stay."

Oh sweet Jesus. Yeah, there's definitely no oxygen in this room anymore. "Nah," I grind out. "I feel like you guys might need some privacy."

Conor licks his bottom lip. "When you were in the can, I was telling Demi about that time you walked in on me getting sucked off. She said it was the hottest thing she'd ever heard."

I glance sharply at Demi, whose lips curve seductively. "The hottest," she says in a throaty voice. "Why didn't you join them?"

"That's what I said!" Con nuzzles her neck again. I know the moment he sucks on her flesh, because she gasps in delight.

When he raises his head again, he quirks up an eyebrow and his gaze locks with mine, as if to say, *I'm down for anything. How about you?*

I don't know what the hell I'm feeling. I know that I'm hard as a rock and that I shouldn't be.

I know that Demi is threading her fingers through Conor's shoulder-length hair and pulling on the blond strands to tug him forward.

I know that when I see their tongues touch, I want to rip his out of his mouth and wear it around my neck like a war trophy while I fuck Demi right in front of him.

And that's when I snap. The scorching jealousy in my blood rivals the primal need flooding my body. I snarl like a territorial dog and jump to my feet, forcibly pulling Demi up with me.

"Nope. Nope nope nope nope *nope.*"

Her eyes widen. "What the hell!"

Conor merely chuckles.

"We're leaving," I bark at her, as my pulse careens and my breaths come out ragged.

"But—"

I silence her protest with a growl. "You want your rebound? I'll give you your fucking rebound. Let's go."

# 28
# DEMI

I DON'T REMEMBER GETTING TO HUNTER'S HOUSE. NOT BECAUSE I'm drunk and unaware of my surroundings, but because I'm so full of anticipation I can't think or see straight. Hell, I can't hear straight, either—the only sound registering is the incessant thudding of my heart.

Getting Hunter to cave was so easy. Although I won't lie—for a moment there I was worried I'd crossed the line from making him jealous to completely driving him away. I can't deny it felt good kissing Conor, but nothing rivals the dizzying excitement of stumbling into Hunter's bedroom and glimpsing that ravenous look on his face.

He kicks the door closed. Locks it. Then he's advancing on me like a predator. He stops when our bodies are less than a foot apart. "Are you sure about this?" His voice is low. Husky.

"Yes." I swallow. "Are you?"

A ragged breath puffs between us. "Yeah, unfortunately."

My jaw drops. "Really, Hunter? The idea of having sex with me is *sooooo* unfortunate—"

He cuts me off with a kiss and I've already forgotten what I was bitching about.

I am obsessed with this guy's kisses. Hot, passionate, just enough tongue to not be overpowering or slobbery. He knows how to draw moans from my throat, how to seduce me with his firm, talented mouth. And as his tongue slicks over mine seductively, his big hands drift down to my ass, caressing the line of flesh where the hem of Brenna's dress ends.

"This dress is way too short," he hisses in my ear before sliding his hands underneath and squeezing my ass. My butt cheeks might as well be bare, with that dental-floss thong between them.

"Short is bad?" I ask breathlessly.

"It is when you've got Conor Edwards' hand on your thigh."

"Jealous?"

"Yes." No denial, just pure hunger in his dark eyes as he yanks the sweater dress up and over my head. He whips it aside, then steps back to admire my thong and skimpy bikini bra.

"Take the bra off," he rasps. "Show me those tits."

My fingers shake as they undo the front clasp. The bra flutters to the floor. Now I'm standing topless in front of him, my heart pounding.

He admires me for a moment. Then he licks his lips and moves close again, filling his palms with my aching breasts. When his thumbs sweep over my nipples, I whimper. They're so hard they actually hurt.

"Your tits are perfect, Demi."

I can't speak. I'm too busy watching his face as he plays with my breasts. Each caress makes my heart beat even faster. I'm sure he feels the rapid *thump-thump* beneath his exploring hands. I almost weep when he stops, but then those rough hands travel lower to grip the thin strap at my waist. He shoves the thong down my legs. I'm naked now. Hunter's still fully dressed.

He's just staring at me, and the need burning in his eyes is too much. My core clenches tightly. "Do something," I whisper.

"I shouldn't," he says gruffly, and yet he grabs his shirt by the collar and pulls it off.

His bare torso taunts me. Smooth golden flesh with a smatter of hair between his heavy pecs. Sculpted abs tapering into a trim waist. He has a treasure trail that disappears into the waistband of his black cargo pants and I want nothing more than to follow that trail with my tongue and see what it leads to.

I want to kiss his chest, drag my tongue over every ridge, every tight sinew. But I'm too scared to move. Scared that if I break the spell, he'll put a stop to this.

Without a word, he undoes his pants and lets them drop on the floor. His belt buckle jangles when it hits the hardwood. Next, he tugs his white boxers down his muscular legs. His dick swings up, long and thick.

Like one of Pavlov's dogs, saliva floods my mouth. "Oh my goodness. That thing's been under there this entire time?"

He gives a choked laugh. "Yeah. A man's cock is typically attached to his body."

I can't take my eyes off it. It's a lot bigger than Nico's.

Hunter takes a step closer, then another one. When our bodies are almost flush, his dick brushes against my stomach, leaving a streak of moisture near my belly button.

He looks down sheepishly. "Just realized something."

"What is it?"

"I'm going to come the second you touch me."

I narrow my eyes. "You're being hyperbolic."

"Trust me, I'm not. I haven't been with anyone since April."

My lips twitch in humor. "So you're saying I'm not going to enjoy this?"

"That's not what I'm saying at all." And before I can blink, he lifts me up in his arms.

My legs instinctively close around his hips, arms looping around his neck. He kisses me deeply as he stalks to the bed and lowers me onto the mattress. My head collides with a pillow. I blink again and suddenly his calloused hands are roaming my body. When he cups my pussy, a jolt of pleasure ricochets through me.

"*Fuck.*" Hunter moans against my neck and I wonder, is there any sound sexier than a man moaning? If there is, I can't name it.

The hoarse sound is so frickin' hot, and I can't help but compare this encounter to any of my encounters with Nico, who was so quiet during sex that sometimes, if the room was pitch black, it felt like I was in the bed alone.

But Hunter makes noise. He whispers how sexy I am. Groans when his palm glides over my very wet core. Hisses when the tip of his finger slides inside to feel even more wetness. I love how vocal he is. I love the needy haze in his eyes as he raises himself up on his elbow and peers down at me.

"You're so beautiful." His lips find my breasts again, and one nipple is drawn into the hot, wet suction of his mouth.

I shiver. "Feels nice," I murmur.

"That's the goal." He continues to suck my nipples until I'm gasping in pleasure.

It feels so ridiculously good, and I get impossibly wetter. By the time his muscular body shifts down the mattress so that his head is positioned between my legs, I almost apologize for how aroused I am. I'm pretty sure I left a wet spot on his bedspread. That's fucking embarrassing, but he doesn't seem to mind.

He absently rubs my clit, watching me from beneath surprisingly thick eyelashes. "I'm not getting up until I make you come," he informs me. "I'm going to lick every goddamn inch of you, and I'm going to do it right." A sexy smile curves his lips. "That means you telling me what you like…"

"I already told you," I say awkwardly, "oral isn't that important to—"

He kisses my pussy, and my hips buck off the bed.

"That," I gasp. "I like that."

He gives me another soft kiss, then another, and then his tongue joins the mix and the sensation of it gliding over my clit is both pure torture and exquisite ecstasy. "Start slow," I whisper. Then brace myself, because this is usually the moment when an overeager tongue flicks hard and quick over my clit until I'm squirming to make it end.

But Hunter proceeds to bestow the sweetest, slowest licks upon my delighted pussy. Kissing, teasing, exploring. His palms sweep over my quivering thighs in a soft caress before snaking underneath me to squeeze my ass. He lifts me up slightly and brings me closer to his greedy mouth. Oh my *God*. I think I like oral sex. It was never me at all.

His low groan vibrates in my core. "You taste so fucking good. I could do this for hours." He starts going faster, laving my clit with his tongue, and I ease away a bit. "Not good?" he murmurs.

"Not yet," I mumble. "Too much too soon."

He resumes the slow pace, whispering dirty words against my core. "Got it. How about I suck on this for a bit," he gently rubs my clit with his thumb, "I think that'd feel really, really good, baby. What do you think?"

"I don't know," I croak. "Why don't you give it a try?"

He gently captures my clit between his lips, gives a light suck, and oh my *goodness* it's the best feeling in the world.

Hunter continues to tease me with long, languid licks, interspersed with open-mouth kisses that always end with the sweet sucking of my clit and me rocking my hips in sheer desperation.

"Hmmm," he chuckles against my pussy. "That's how we do it, then."

"Do what?" I'm too turned on to think.

"That's how we make you come. Slow and steady, and just when you can't take it anymore, I suck on this hot little clit and your body fucking sings…" He lifts his head and grins up at me. His lips are shiny and swollen. "I figured you out."

I want to say it's not that difficult, but I know from previous experience that my body is a hard nut to crack.

Humming with satisfaction, Hunter goes back to driving me crazy. As he works me over with his tongue, I slide my hands through his hair. I'm not the girl who can come in three seconds. It takes time for me, but he doesn't complain. If anything, the noises he's making grow hungrier and hungrier, and when his finger slides inside me and my pussy eagerly clamps around it, he groans loudly.

I gaze at his long body stretched out before me, his muscular thighs, his taut ass. I catch a flash of movement and realize he's got his dick in his free hand. It's rock hard, but he's not stroking it. He's squeezing it, as if he's trying not to come. Knowing he's *that* turned on from going down on me triggers a rush of hot pleasure. My hips start moving faster.

"Oh fuck, baby, yes. I want to feel you coming on my tongue. Give it to me."

The command is hoarse, dirty. "Finger," I choke out, and he pushes one finger back inside as his lips close around my clit.

The orgasm sweeps through me in a scorching wave of pleasure. It's the first time I've climaxed with someone other than Nico, and that's scary and exhilarating and I can't stop moaning as I grip Hunter's hair and shake with release.

When I go calm and still, he plants a soft kiss between my legs and whispers, "Ah fuck, that was so hot." Then he kisses his way up my body and nuzzles the crook of my neck.

His dick is heavy against my hip, the heat of it branding my flesh. I reach down to grip it and Hunter's agonized groan makes me laugh. "You're going to have to let me touch it eventually," I point out.

"I know. I'm just already embarrassed about what's gonna happen."

"You can do it," I encourage. "I believe in you."

He trembles with laughter. Then he starts to roll over, and for a second I wonder if he's going to slide his dick inside me without protection. But no, he's just rising to his knees and leaning over my body to grab a condom from the nightstand.

The square packet is a sobering reminder of the conversation we didn't have before ripping each other's clothes off.

"Um." I gulp. "I know this is awkward, but...I don't have to worry about any diseases on your end, right...?" I let that hang.

His response rings with reassurance. "I'm one hundred percent clean. I get tested regularly on the team. I can show you my latest results, but they're a month old."

"We should get tested together," I suggest. "Actually, I—" I halt, suddenly horrified. "Oh my God, I should've gotten tested immediately after finding out about Nico. Dammit, Hunter! He was sleeping with other girls. What if I'm the one with the disease?"

He chuckles ruefully. "Well, there's nothing I can do about it now, because I just went down on you for a half hour. But tell you what, we'll use a condom now and then if we ever want to do this again, we'll take a trip down to the health center together."

"Sounds like fun! Couples STD testing!"

He barks out a laugh. I'm glad he found that amusing and didn't comment on the word *couples*. It was just a figure of speech, anyway. I know what this is and what it isn't.

As Hunter grips the base of his dick so he can roll the condom on, I begin to applaud. "Look, you didn't come from doing that!"

"Yeah, well, you know, the diseases talk usually kills some of the mood."

"So you're saying you're not in the mood anymore?"

He secures the condom, and his erection sticks out like an iron spike. "Does that look like I'm not in the mood?"

I giggle.

"I'm just saying, now I might be able to last a little longer."

"Good. Get in me already." And then we're kissing again and he's on top of me. I'm still wet, and more than ready, when he enters me.

The moment his full length is buried deep, Hunter releases a streak of desperate curses against my lips. "Oh, fuck, you feel so good."

He withdraws, then plunges back in.

"Fuck fuck fuck fuck *fuck*. Why is sex so good?" His lust-soaked expletives heat the air between us.

"Sex or sex with me?" Yep, apparently even during the act of copulation, I resort to fishing for compliments.

"Sex with you," he says hoarsely.

"So it wouldn't be this good with anybody else?"

His head jerks as he shakes it, his dark hair tickling my cheek. "I don't know if it's ever been this good."

I'm sure that's probably his eight-month drought talking, but I like to think maybe it's me.

He starts to move, and I meet him thrust for thrust by lifting my ass. As he plunges into me over and over and over again, we kiss frantically and make helpless, tortured noises against each other's lips. It feels amazing. I don't think I'm going to come again, but I already got my orgasm and now I get to watch Hunter as he comes apart before my eyes.

Anguish creases his forehead. He bites his lower lip, then slowly releases it. He curses. He groans. His eyes are hot with lust.

He fucks me for longer than I expected, and I realize that his chest is trembling and his features are taut because he's trying desperately not to lose control. So I scrape my nails down his back and squeeze my inner muscles around his dick. "Let go," I urge.

He moans. "You sure?"

"Uh-huh. There's nothing hotter than watching you right now. Give it to me."

Heat flares in his eyes and then his hips snap forward. The tempo quickens. His breaths come out in short pants, until he gives a final thrust and I can feel the orgasm shudder through his body. When he peers down at me, he looks sleepy and sated and it's so damn sexy.

"That was good," I mumble.

"So good." His head drops again, his mouth prodding at me as his lips seek any sort of contact. They connect with my chin, and he kisses it before burying his face in my neck.

"I'm sorry I made you break your vow," I whisper sheepishly, as I hold him tightly against me.

"I'm not," he whispers back.

# 29
# HUNTER

"Hey, is Matty here?" I ask when Conor opens the door the next afternoon. It's one-thirty, Demi left my house thirty minutes ago, and I'm in desperate need of advice.

Con shakes his head. "He went home with Andrea last night. Hasn't come back yet. The rest of the guys are still passed out. And I'm about to lift some weights. Come on, you can spot me."

"Sure, what the hell." I step inside and take off my coat and boots.

"How was last night?" Conor asks with a knowing grin.

Incredible, I want to say. Magnificent. Tremendous. Mind-blowing. Stupendous. There aren't enough adjectives to describe how good last night was. It was the best sex of my life, hands down.

When I woke up this morning and saw Demi lying naked in my bed, so sweet, so irresistible, I couldn't help myself again. I made her come with my tongue, and then she gave me a handjob that made me see stars. After I spilled into her hand, she winked, brought one of her fingers to her mouth to lick it up, and I almost came again.

That girl is...incredible. Magnificent. Tremendous—okay, not enough adjectives again. She's so sexy, and I'm attracted to everything about her. And yet as much as I want to sleep with her again, I'm also pissed at myself. I walked over here to talk to Matt about it, but looks like Conor will have to do.

We go down to the basement, where the guys have a makeshift gym. It's not much—treadmill, a bench press, a rowing machine, and some free weights and resistance bands. Con heads for the bench and strips out of his T-shirt.

Groaning, he slaps his rock-hard stomach and says, "Do I have a booze belly? I feel like I'm bloated."

"Are you fishing for compliments? Because your abs are tighter than a gymnast's ass," I grumble as I help him get the weights. I raise a brow when I see what he's lifting. "A hundred pounds? Slacker," I taunt.

"Hung-over," he grunts. "I'm starting off slow."

I snicker. "Hung-over how? I'm pretty sure I drank all your whiskey."

"I cracked open another bottle after you left," he says with a grin. "Stayed up till three in the morning drinking with a really hot redhead."

"Uh-huh, I'm sure all you guys did was drink."

"Well, no. I got laid—obvs."

I roll my eyes. "Obvs."

It doesn't surprise me that he went from kissing my girl to hooking up with another one. And I doubt he did it to soothe his bruised ego—Con's ego could sustain a direct missile hit. If he hooked up, it was because he was horny from kissing Demi, not because he needed a confidence boost after Demi went home with me.

"How about you, captain?" he asks.

I play dumb. "How about me what?"

"You never answered how last night was for you. Am I the only one who got laid?" He lies down on the bench and holds up his palms so I can deposit the barbell into them.

When I don't answer, Conor barks out a laugh. "Come on, man, it's not a trick question."

"Fine. I got laid," I admit.

"Shocking! Never saw that coming!"

"Fuck off," I sigh.

He lifts a brow. "Why so glum? Did you blow your load too fast because of the celibacy thing? Or was it just bad sex in general?" He frowns. "That's surprising, 'cause she looked like she'd be a lot of fun." As he lifts and lowers the barbell, all the muscles in his arms bulge and flex.

"She is fun. And the sex was great," I say roughly.

"Then why do you look so pissed?"

I gaze down at him unhappily. "Because I broke my vow."

"Fuck the vow."

"I wanted to stick by it," I say in a tired voice. "You weren't here last year. My partying is the reason we didn't beat Harvard."

Conor rolls his eyes. "If you truly believe that, then you're an arrogant prick. One player doesn't make a team."

"It wasn't one player, it was two. Our captain was out, too. Nate and I were the top two players on the team."

"Well, shit happens. Some teams lose their top three, four, five, to injuries. It's just bad luck."

"I guess." I'm still unconvinced. I release another sigh. "I just wanted to be a good captain this year."

"Dude, you are a good captain. I mean, look at the shit you tolerate. Bucky and Jesse wanted a *pig*, and you made yourself look like a complete idiot in front of Coach to make it happen for them. Cut yourself some slack."

"You're just saying that because you cut everybody slack. You're a surfer dude—your whole life is slack."

He laughs, which trips up his even breathing for a second. He inhales deeply and resumes lifting. When he's done with his set, I put the bar back in place and give him a second to catch his breath.

"I'm just worried it'll fuck us over," I confess. "I'm worried we'll go on a losing streak now."

"You really need to chill, dude." Con's tone grows serious. "Look, Demi's cool. I like her."

I narrow my eyes.

That gets me another laugh. "I don't like her like that. I mean, don't get me wrong, if you weren't in the picture, I'd be all about her. But—one, you are in the picture. And two, I'm not looking for a relationship."

"I was in the picture last night too," I say darkly.

Con looks like he's trying not to roll his eyes again. "Do you honestly think I'd mack on your girl?"

"You did mack on my girl."

"Yeah, to light a fire under your ass, you idiot."

I falter. "What do you mean?"

"I was never going to go through with it. Neither was she." Conor is chuckling as he stretches out on the bench and gestures for me to spot him again. "I'm surprised you let it go as far as you did. She and I figured there'd be some flirting and nothing more. Didn't realize I'd need to stick my tongue down her throat for you to get the memo."

"You guys *planned* it?" I feel outraged, but at the same time, I'm also…touched? Yeah, I think I'm actually touched. But I guess that makes sense after what happened with Summer and Fitzy. I told Fitz I was into Summer and he made a move anyway. It's kind of a relief to know Conor wouldn't do that to me.

"Like I said, Demi's really cool," he tells me. "Women like that don't come along often, so trust me when I say you need to lock it down, ASAP. If you don't make an effort to keep her, you'll lose her. She'll have a boyfriend again in no time, and then you'll look back on it and realize what a total dumbass you were for letting her go."

———

I last about six hours before I cave and shoot a text to Demi.

**ME**: Want to hang out tonight?

To my relief, she answers immediately.

**DEMI**: Come over?
**ME**: Be there in 20.

It's difficult not to break every traffic law on my way to campus. I force myself to stick to the speed limit, which means I'm twitching with impatience by the time I reach the Theta house. The sorority president, Josie, lets me in. She doesn't look surprised to see me. The Thetas are used to me being around, thanks to mine and Demi's psych project.

When I walk into Demi's room, I find her on the bed, sitting in front of a mountain of schoolwork. The mattress is covered with textbooks, papers, notes, binders, and highlighters.

"Did you rob a school supplies store?" I ask pleasantly.

"Studying for my bio exam," she moans. She peers up at me with big brown eyes. "I hate science, Hunter. I hate it."

Sympathy rises inside me. "I'm sorry." She's visibly distressed, a drastic contrast from the way her face lights up when we're working on our psych project.

"I think I'll do okay on bio and math. I'm more worried about Organic Chem. The exam is the day before winter break, and I'm nowhere near ready for it. I need like ten thousand more study sessions in order to ace that class."

"You'll ace all of them," I assure her. "I have faith in you." And I have faith in her work ethic. This girl works her ass off. I've seen how invested she is in psychology, and I know she puts the same amount of effort into all her classes.

"Are you sure you have time to hang out?" I ask. I'm standing awkwardly at the foot of the bed, because there's no room for me on there. "Should I even be here right now?"

Demi glares at me. "I'll kill you if you leave."

I can't tell if she's joking. That's the problem with being into a chick who's into murderers.

She gets up and methodically gathers her study materials. She stacks the textbooks on her small desk, then the binders, the pages of notes. All in neat little piles. Her organizational skills are as cute as the rest of her.

When the bedspread is clear, she glances at it for a moment before turning to me, a blush on her cheeks. "I've been thinking about you since the second I opened my eyes this morning," she admits.

"Obviously." I grin, cocky as fuck. "You opened your eyes this morning to my tongue between your legs."

"Mmmm yeah." She shivers happily. "I'll rephrase—I've been thinking about you since I left your house today." She hesitates. "Have you been thinking about me?"

"God, yes." No hesitation on my end.

Her expression brightens. "Really?"

"Oh yeah."

"Oh. Okay. That's good. Because I wasn't sure if you wanted last night to be a one-time thing."

Our eyes lock.

"I don't think once will be enough," I confess.

"Me neither," she agrees solemnly, and the next thing I know, our mouths are fused together.

The kiss makes my head spin. I fucking *love* kissing her. I love how eager her tongue is, how warm her lips are. I love the way she whimpers when I tug her body close to mine.

I break the kiss to lick my lips. "Have you been sucking on something cherry? Or is that strawberry?"

"Cherry gummies," she confirms. "But…I'd way rather be sucking on something else now…"

Grinning broadly, she pushes me onto the bed and starts pulling my clothes off. A second later, I'm buck naked and sprawled on my back, while Demi crawls down my body.

She kisses her way south, her lips leaving shivers in their wake.

My cock rises in full salute, pleading for her attention, and when she curls her fingers around the base, a bead of moisture pools at the tip.

With a devilish smile, Demi laps at the pearly drop with the tip of her tongue.

The tortured groan she draws from my throat is so loud I half expect an army of Thetas to bang on the door asking if everything is okay.

Demi lifts her head. "You make the hottest sounds in bed."

"That's because you do the hottest things in bed." Then I watch from under heavy eyelids as she sucks on the tip of my cock before lavishing wet kisses on my shaft.

Eventually my eyes flutter closed and I lose myself to sensation. The sweet scrape of her tongue, the hot suction of her lips. The blowjob is slow, tentative, as she determines what I like.

I guide her with husky commands. "I like it rougher than that," I whisper, and I reach for her fist, wrap my hand around it, and tighten her grip.

"Really? Like that?" she says in surprise. "I feel like that would hurt!"

"It doesn't hurt," I assure her.

She tests her grip again, squeezing hard, and I shudder in pleasure. "What if I break your penis?"

A choked laugh flies out. "You're not going to break my penis, I promise."

Demi gives a hard stroke, then sucks on my tip again and it's the best feeling ever. I thread one hand through her hair and start thrusting upward. This is way too good. My balls draw up tight and my vision wavers. *Way* too good.

"I need to be inside you," I grind out.

She gets up and crawls toward the nightstand, and the sight of her on her hands and knees is too tempting to ignore. I rise up on my knees behind her and slip a hand between her legs. She's so wet. When I slip a finger inside, her pussy clamps tightly around it.

Moaning, Demi bucks back against my touch. I add another finger, and now there's two moving inside her, summoning breathy noises from her lips. "Oh my God. Feels so good."

I finger her with lazy, teasing thrusts until my body can no longer take it. "Condom," I mutter, and Demi slaps one into my palm.

My dick throbs as I roll the latex onto it. I stop for a second to admire Demi's perfect ass. It's jutting in the air, practically begging for me to—

"Eek!" she exclaims when my palm connects with her smooth flesh.

"Sorry," I say, quickly soothing the sting with a soft caress. "Your ass is so smackable, you don't even know, babe."

"Do it again."

A grin lifts one corner of my mouth. "You like to be spanked?"

"Maybe?" She wiggles that sexy ass and my palm once again lands in a sharp smack.

"Oh my *goodness*," Demi mumbles. "Do it again—but this time when you're inside me."

This girl is incredible.

I'm harder than steel as I position my dick at her opening. I slide inside her and spank her ass at the same time, and Demi moans loud enough to wake the dead.

My heart pounds an erratic beat as I start fucking her. One hand grips her right ass cheek, the other curves over her left one, squeezing, kneading, spanking each time she begs for it. My hips piston, pushing my dick inside her. Deeper, faster, until we're both groaning in desperation as we hurtle toward the finish line.

She's still on all fours when the orgasm hits her, but by the time she's finished shuddering, she's flat on her stomach, moaning happily. I curve my body over her sweat-soaked back and angle my hips, driving into her with shallow thrusts. Fast, desperate strokes, while my heart threatens to give out and my balls tingle wildly.

"Coming," I grunt.

The pleasure slams into me, stealing the breath from my lungs. I collapse on top of her, only rolling over when she informs me she can't breathe.

I have no words as I yank her closer. She snuggles beside me, her chin on my shoulder. She doesn't speak either. There's nothing to say.

We both know how good that was.

We both know it's going to happen again.

And we're both perfectly okay with that.

# 30
# DEMI

My parents betrayed me.

I'm talking Benedict-Arnold-screwing-over-America level of betrayal.

No—even worse. Brad Pitt cheating on Jennifer Aniston.

*That's* how deep the well of betrayal runs.

I was under the impression that we would not be spending the holidays with Nico's family. My father never outright stated it, but the subject hadn't been brought up again after the night I told them in no uncertain words that having Nico around for Christmas would, and I'm quoting myself here, *hurt me*.

But I guess my feelings don't matter, because as we're driving away from the airport in our rental car, Dad informs me that the Delgados will be joining us tonight.

Yep, my parents waited until we arrived in Miami to drop this bomb, probably because they knew I'd never board the plane at Logan Airport otherwise.

With a family as large as mine, the holidays are always a huge production. Christmas Day is spent with my mom's enormous brood, but Christmas Eve is a quieter affair—just us, and Nico's family. It's been a tradition since I was eight years old.

This year, however, it'll be like the plot line of some awkward holiday comedy. *Christmas with the Delgados*, starring my cheating ex-boyfriend and my disloyal parents.

As I fume in the backseat, Dad explains that breaking our annual tradition is something he thinks I'd regret in the future. Awesome. Now even my life's regrets are being decided for me, and they haven't even fucking happened yet.

I find this absolutely egregious. I don't care that they're family friends. My parents could have compromised. They could've gone out for dinner with Nico's parents on their own, sparing me from having to spend any time with Nico. But *noooooo*, God forbid we break *tradition*. The world will end!

We arrive at Aunt Paula's house in the early afternoon. She's the only one of Mom's sisters who isn't married yet, and she owns a gorgeous beachfront property. Some people think there needs to be snow on the ground in order for it to be a real Christmas, but having grown up in Florida, for me the holiday season is sunshine and palm trees and the salty spray of the ocean on my face.

I'm still fuming by the time it's time to leave for Nico's house. As Dad searches for where he left the car keys, Mom notices my face and pulls me aside. "*Mami*, I know you don't like this—"

"You're right, I hate it," I growl.

"But your father made his decision, and you need to make the best of it. Dora and Joaquín are going to be in our lives regardless of whether you and Nico are dating. Dora is like a sister to me, and Papa views Joaquín as a brother." Mom's tone softens. "It's not easy for you, I know. But this is what happens when families are woven so tightly together. So, please, let this be your first test—a test to see if the two of you can be around each other without hostility. Nico is willing to try. He told Dora he was fine with this."

Of course he's fine with it. He probably thinks we're getting back together. That's what he's been saying to Darius since the second we broke up.

But Mom is right. The Delgados are their closest friends. They're family. I have no choice but to suck it up.

I'd debated looking extra hot tonight, but I didn't want Nico getting any ideas. So I did the opposite—I dressed down. A plain white dress, knee-length and with a modest neckline, paired with flat brown sandals, not even a hint of a heel. My hair is tied in a low ponytail with a red bow. I look like a child who's going to perform some cringe-worthy song for the adults after dinner.

Perfect.

Fifteen minutes later, we're entering the familiar house where I'd spent so much of my time. I honestly never envisioned Nico and me *not* being together for the holidays.

Or that I'd be sleeping with another guy.

On the regular.

My rebound with Hunter didn't stop after Conor's party. We slept together again the next day. And the day after that, and then the day after that. Yesterday we stayed up all night having sex, even though I had to get up early to meet my parents at the airport.

My body is already craving him again. I'm addicted to it. I never thought I'd be sleeping with a jock, but I kind of understand now why so many women love athletes. God. All those rock-hard muscles. The sheer strength of their bodies. Yesterday Hunter lifted me onto his dick and fucked me standing up against my bedroom wall. Apparently everyone in the house heard the wall banging, and my sorority sisters teased me mercilessly about it this morning. But they're happy for me. Hell, *I'm* happy for me. I deserve good sex with a man who isn't sexing up everybody else too. Every woman deserves that.

Nico's family greets me warmly. His little sister Alicia flings her arms around my neck and shrieks, "Oh my God, it's been *forever!*" She's thirteen and has always viewed me as a role model of sorts. I'm the one she called when she got her first period last year.

Dora greets me with smacking kisses and a bear hug, and then Joaquín steps forward to give me a hug.

"Damn fool," he mutters.

I frown slightly. "What?"

His expression turns wry. "My son's a damn fool." He says the words softly, so only I can hear him.

My frown dissolves into a faint smile. "Yep."

Nico still hasn't come downstairs, thank the Lord. I hope he's cowering in his bedroom. My family is ushered into the living room, where I'm fussed over by Dora and Alicia while Joaquín prepares drinks for my parents.

Then I hear his voice. "Demi."

I turn slowly. Unlike me, Nico did make an effort with his appearance. He chose black trousers and a white shirt with the top button undone. His hair is slicked back and he's fully clean-shaven. He looks really good, but the sight of him only evokes mild indifference. I haven't seen or spoken to him since the night we broke up. I thought it might be awful when we eventually came to face to face. That my heartbeat would accelerate, that I'd experience a pang of longing.

But I don't. If anything, I feel sorry for him. He almost looks like a little boy as he steps forward. He starts to open his arms, and I give a quick shake of my head.

"Let's not do that," I advise.

Disappointment clouds his eyes. "Come on, Demi."

The next thing I know there's a glass in my hand. Granted, it's just a soda, and not the full-to-the-brim glass of tequila I would've preferred. But still. Mom to the rescue!

"Let's help Dora with dinner," she chirps as she whisks me toward the kitchen.

I follow her without a backward glance at Nico.

---

Dinner is awkward, at least for me. If it is for our parents, they're not showing it.

Each time Nico speaks to me, I answer politely. But I don't

engage or elaborate on anything he asks. He reveals that he quit the moving company, and I don't even blink because I don't care. Then he talks about his new job as a line cook at Della's Diner. I don't care about that either, except to make a mental note to not eat there anymore. He'll either spit in my food or mix a love potion into it.

After dinner, the men go outside on the bricked patio to smoke their Cubans, and the women tidy up. Old-fashioned, maybe, but that's how it's always been. Alicia and I load the dishwasher and then wash the bigger dishes by hand. She chatters on about the eighth grade and her friends as I pass her pots and pans to dry.

"I can't believe you and Nico aren't together anymore," she whines. "I'm so sad."

"I know, hon, but things don't always work out the way you want them to," I answer ruefully. "Go grab that huge salad bowl from the table, will you? I think it's the last thing we need to wash."

As Alicia dashes off, Dora comes up beside me. "Nicolás told me what he did," she says softly. "I want you to know how disappointed in him I am, Demi. I raised him better than that."

I meet her unhappy eyes. "I'm surprised he actually told you the truth and didn't conjure up some story that painted him as the victim."

She snorts. "That boy is incapable of lying to his mama, you know that."

True. Nico is a total mama's boy. Besides, Cuban women are scarily perceptive—they can read minds. Even if he tried to lie, Dora would've known.

"It's his loss, Demi. I mean that, even though he's my son. And you know you'll always be a daughter to us, no matter what."

"I know." I give her a warm hug, and for the first time all evening I experience the rush of longing I hadn't felt with Nico earlier.

I do love his parents, and it elicits genuine sorrow, the reminder that things will never be the same now that Nico and I are no longer together.

But things change. Relationships evolve. The same people could remain in your life, people you've known for years and years, only they play a different role now.

I blink back tears as I turn off the faucet and dry my hands on a dishrag.

Dessert is served in the living room, where Alicia demands we play a board game. "I got this new one called Zombies!" she exclaims, and I burst out laughing.

"Oh, I'm quite familiar with that one," I inform the thirteen-year-old. "I've played it numerous times at a friend's house. He killed me off the last time."

She gasps. "You got sacrificed!"

"Yep."

"What friend?" Nico asks suspiciously.

I want to tell him to mind his own damn business. But I can't be rude in front of his family. "Nobody," I say vaguely.

He raises an eyebrow. "Really? Nobody?"

For some reason, Dad decides this is a hill he wants to die on, too. "Which friend is this?" he asks.

I roll my eyes at his stern tone. "My friend Hunter."

"The hockey player?" Nico demands, eyes flashing.

"Yes, the hockey player. You know the one that you and your little buddies—"

"I know who you mean," he interrupts, a warning note in his voice.

Aw, he doesn't want me to rat him out to his parents. Of course not. Dora wouldn't like it one damn bit if she knew her baby boy was beating people up for no reason.

Our eyes lock for a beat. Nico looks worried I might tattle, and relaxes when I don't.

"Hunter and his roommates are hilarious," I say instead, glancing at Alicia. "They have a board game night a couple times a month, and this is their game of choice at the moment. But I don't think it's a good Christmas Eve game, hon. Maybe we should just play charades?"

Mom claps her hands. "Yessss! Let's do it!"

Dora smiles at her daughter. "Go find those charades cards we wrote up last year, *mami*. They should be in the game drawer in the family room."

Alicia hurries off excitedly.

I get up from my perch on the leather sofa. "I'm going to steal some candy from the bowl in the dining room. Anyone want some?"

"I'm surprised your teeth haven't rotted off by now," Nico's mother chides with a sigh.

"Good genes," I say, flashing my pearly whites. I'm a sugar fiend, yet I've never had a single cavity.

I pop into the other room and rummage through the bowl for something cherry-flavored. I'm barely gone five seconds before Nico's gruff voice comes from the doorway.

"Can we talk?"

I've been dreading this. "There's really nothing to say."

He steps into the room. "Look, I'm not going to try to win you back, if that's what you're worried about. I get it, we're done."

"Thank you. I appreciate that."

"But I did want to say I'm sorry. Not just for what happened with us, but for what I did to your hockey friend. I was drunk that night." He shifts his feet, looking sheepish.

"You can save your apologies for Hunter. As for me, no apology is going to make up for what you did to me." I suck in my cheeks as anger ripples through me. "We were together for so long and you played me like that?"

"I know. I'm sorry, D. I was an idiot, okay?"

"A horny idiot."

Nico shakes his head. "No. It was about more than just sex. I..."

"You what?"

He makes a frustrated sound. "I can't explain why I did it. It's just...it's hard to live up to your expectations sometimes, okay?"

My eyebrows fly out. "My expectations? Nico. The only

expectation I ever had of you was to not stick your dick in anyone else. I hadn't realized that was an impossible standard to meet," I say sarcastically.

He scrapes one hand through his black hair. "You don't get it. You're so smart and you've always known exactly what you want to do with your life. And I'm just a fucked-up loser from Miami."

"That's not true."

"You're too perfect, Demi. Even back when we were just friends, I always felt this need to impress you. And then we started dating and the pressure got even worse. I felt like I was trying to live up to something. And those other chicks, they threw themselves at me, made me feel like a big man, and I just ate it up, okay?" He avoids my gaze. "Whatever, it's pathetic, but it's the truth."

"Yeah, it's pathetic," I agree, but my psychologist brain has already kicked in. Never in my wildest dreams had I thought that I was emasculating him. "I'm sorry if I made you feel that way, Nico. All I ever wanted was the best for you."

"I get it. And I tried to be that dude you wanted. I worked my ass off to get into an Ivy League—"

"I never asked you to do that," I protest.

"I felt like I had to. I knew I'd lose you if we went to different colleges. But…" He sounds frazzled. "But it's so goddamn hard, D. I study so fucking hard. And I work even fucking harder because my family's not as well-off as yours."

"I never asked you to do any of that," I maintain. But the guilt trip is having an effect on me. "You pushed *yourself*, Nico. Whatever urge was pushing you to do it, you still created that pressure within yourself. But if I gave off the impression that I needed you to be some perfect specimen, I'm sorry. I didn't mean to do that. I always liked you exactly the way you were."

"Liked?" he says sadly.

"Yeah. That's usually what happens when you sleep with someone who isn't me."

"I'm sorry, okay? I'm disgusting. There's no excuse."

"Nope. But here's a tip for next time, with the next girl—maybe you could talk to her about any insecurities you might be having, instead of needing to go out and get an ego boost from other women."

"You make me sound even more pathetic when you phrase it like that."

I sigh quietly. "The fact that you couldn't talk to me about how you were feeling only shows that our relationship was never going to work. We were kids when we started going out. We were naïve to think it was going to last forever."

"It would have, if I hadn't screwed up."

"But you did, and now we'll never know what would've happened." I brush past him, heading for the doorway. "It's Christmas, Nico. Let's go spend time with our families."

"Demi."

I glance over my shoulder and find remorse swimming in his dark eyes. "What is it?"

"There's really no chance, is there?"

"No. There isn't."

---

On the car ride home, I send Happy Holidays! texts to TJ, Pax, and the other Lost Boys, and then I finally get a chance to text Hunter, who's spending the holidays in Connecticut. Apparently his father's company held a holiday party tonight, which Hunter and his mother were expected to attend because, well, because they're nothing but props for his father.

> **ME**: How'd it go tonight?
> **HIM**: Not terrible. Open bar, good food. Danced with my mother to a live version of Baby It's Cold Outside, which was awkward.

**ME**: Awkward? More like hot!

**HIM**: FFS! We're talking about my mother here.

**ME**: Was your dad on his best behavior?

**HIM**: Of course. He's gotta put on a show for his adoring fans.

"Demi," Dad says from the driver's seat. "Could you please close your window? Your mother's cold."

"Mmm-hmmm." I absently hit the automatic button, but I press it the wrong way and end up opening the window fully rather than doing the opposite. "Oh shoot. Sorry, Mom." I drop my phone on the seat beside me and click the button again.

"Who are you texting with?" she asks curiously.

"Just a friend."

Dad pounces instantly. "This Hunter boy you mentioned earlier?"

I wrinkle my forehead. "Yes. Is that a problem?"

He doesn't answer for a moment. When he does, suspicion colors his tone. "Nico doesn't think much of him."

Interesting. Looks like Nico had more to say when the men went out for their second round of cigars.

"I see." I nod politely. "Because Nico's opinion is the mantle by which we measure all wisdom and purity."

"Demi," Mom chides from the passenger side.

"What? It's true? His moral compass isn't exactly in working order." I meet Dad's eyes in the rearview mirror. "When you were outside talking about my friend, did Nico also tell you how he beat Hunter up?"

Mom gasps. "He didn't! Did he?"

"Oh yeah. Hunter was the one who gave me the heads up about the cheating. Nico didn't like that, so he tracked Hunter down and roughed him up with four of his friends. Five against one, Dad. That's how mature adults deal with their problems, right?"

Dad's cheeks hollow as if he's grinding his teeth. "Well. That aside, I wonder if perhaps you should keep your distance from this Hunter."

"Why? This is coming out of nowhere. You don't even know him, and I don't think you should be taking Nico's word for anything, please. He's a liar."

"He lied to you, yes. But that doesn't make him a liar."

"Daddy. If I murdered you, I'd be a murderer. He lied to me, therefore he's a liar."

"Semantics."

I heave a sigh. "Look, I like Hunter, all right? He's great."

"Are you dating him?" my father demands.

"Not really."

Mom twists around in her seat, her meddlesome instincts kicking in. "'Not really?' *Dios mío!* You *are* dating him! When did this happen?!"

"We're not dating." *Just having sex. Repeatedly.* "But if we were, I'd expect both of you to give him a fair shot. Nico isn't my boyfriend anymore, you guys. Eventually someone else is going to fill that role, and I need you to accept that and be open-minded about it." I shrug. "As for Hunter, he's a good guy and I like him a lot." I meet my father's eyes again. "And if you met him, you'd like him too."

# 31
# DEMI

**NEW YEAR'S EVE**

Hunter has me on the bed before I can even say hello. His greedy mouth latches onto mine, the kiss stealing the breath from my lungs.

"I missed this," I whimper, and I feel his answering groan vibrate through my body. I wrap my legs around his trim hips and shamelessly grind against his very prominent bulge.

"Missed you too," he mumbles. His lips are exploring my throat now. He sucks on the side of my neck, then rolls us over so that I'm straddling him.

His hands slide underneath my shirt to cup my boobs. I'm not wearing a bra, so his calloused palms are a delicious scrape over my sensitive flesh. My nipples instantly pucker and strain against his touch.

"Fuck," he groans. "Take this infuriating thing *off*." He peels the shirt off me and whips it across the room.

A laugh flies out. "Hey, now, my shirt didn't do anything wrong."

"It was covering these perfect tits. I'm furious at it." The hot whisper fans over my nipple and I moan when he draws it into his mouth and sucks deeply. *God.* I can't believe it's been two weeks since I've seen him. How have I gone without this for two weeks?

I roll my hips, grinding his covered erection. He cups and squeezes my breasts, then curls one hand behind my neck and tugs me down for a kiss. His tongue touches mine and it's like a bolt of lightning directly to my core.

In an unplanned synchronized frenzy, we fumble at each other's waistbands. He shoves my PJ pants down. I try to do the same with his jeans, but the denim snags on his thighs. He grins and lifts his ass to help me out. He's still wearing a shirt, but naked below the waist, and his cock springs up, long and thick. My mouth actually waters.

"Fuck," Hunter chokes out as his gaze roams my nude body.

Our gazes lock. A second ticks by, two, three.

And then we're mauling each other again. I find a condom and put it on him. He pulls me back onto his lap. I impale myself on him, and off to the races we go.

I don't know how long I ride him. It could be seconds, minutes or hours. All I know is that the knot of pleasure between my legs is almost painful, unbearable. My breathing is shaky. So are my hands. My fingertips tingle as I stroke them over his sculpted pecs. Lord, I know I'm close.

Pippa was right when she posited that maybe I've been having sex all wrong. Or maybe sex simply becomes predictable when you've been having it with the same person for years. With Hunter, it's completely unpredictable, and right now I'm relishing the newness of it, all these firsts with him.

First kiss.

First fuck.

First orgasm while I'm riding his dick.

I come first, collapsing onto him, and he thrusts his hips, digging his fingers into my ass. He bites my shoulder as he comes, and I laugh breathlessly against his damp chest. We lie there for a moment, his arms wrapped snugly around me, his dick still buried inside me.

"Oh my gosh," I say dreamily. "That was so good."

"So good," he mumbles.

We stay in that position for nearly a minute before he reluctantly withdraws. I sit up and help him remove the condom. "Here, let me get rid of this. I need to pee anyway."

I return to the bed a minute later and we snuggle up, still naked. Hunter reaches for the fleece throw at the foot of the bed, pinches the corner and drags it up to cover us.

"It's New Year's Eve," he remarks.

"Are you just realizing it now? Did you not see all the decorations the girls are setting up downstairs?" Theta Beta Nu is hosting one of the many parties on Greek Row tonight. Which means my presence is mandatory.

I'm touched that Hunter chose to come here tonight instead of chilling with his boys. His teammates are throwing a huge party in Hastings.

"Are you sure you don't want to go to Conor's?" I fret.

"No." He kisses the top of my head. "I'm never leaving this room."

"Well, we have to leave it at some point to make an appearance downstairs."

"Fine. We'll go down once every hour for twenty-minute intervals, then come back up here and fuck. After midnight, all bets are off and we stay in here forever." His hand slithers down to pinch my bare butt.

"You're insatiable."

"Babe. I'm literally coming off a nine-month sex drought. If it was possible, my dick would be permanently inside you for at least three weeks."

"Three *weeks*?" I yelp. That sounds exhausting. Fun, but exhausting.

"You're right. That's completely unreasonable. I'll need at least three months inside you before my balls return to normal. It takes a while for semen production to regulate."

I snicker loudly. "Gross."

Voices echo outside my door as several of my sorority sisters pass by.

"Well, if you do want to go and party with your friends, I wouldn't fault you for it," I say, carelessly stroking his ridged abdomen.

"Not going anywhere, Semi," he says stubbornly, his arm tightening around me.

"Can I ask you something?"

He snorts. "You'll ask regardless of my answer to that."

"True." My grin fades as I broach the subject I'd been avoiding since we first had sex. "Are you mad at me for pushing you to break your celibacy vow?"

"No." Nothing but sincerity there.

"Are you mad at yourself?"

"I was the morning after," he reveals.

"Really?" I say in surprise. This is the first time he's admitted to having any doubts or regrets about us.

"Yeah, for all of five minutes." His calloused fingertips tease my shoulder. "Then I saw you lying there naked in my bed, and I wanted to keep breaking the vow, over and over again."

"But it was important to you," I say guiltily.

"It was, but…" His hand continues roaming my bare skin. "This feels more important."

He doesn't elaborate, and I don't push him to. We lie there for a while, neither of us in a hurry to join the party, which has already started judging by the music that's rocking the house.

"Did you have a good time in New York?" After Christmas he spent a few days in Manhattan with Dean and his girlfriend.

"It was fun. The Bruins were playing the Islanders, so Garrett got us into the box. Fucking amazing game."

I reach up and run my fingers through his hair. "None of your hair seems to be missing," I tease.

"It's the gel, man. Stops me from pulling it out."

"What do you like better—watching live hockey, or playing it?"

"Playing, obviously." He doesn't even hesitate.

"Have you ever played in front of a crowd as large as the one in TD Garden?"

Hunter chuckles. "No college arena even rivals that. Now *that* would be a thrill, eh?"

I furrow my brow. "I still don't get why you can't do it. From what Brenna's told me, someone would sign you in a heartbeat. She says if you announced your interest, half the teams in the league would be courting you after your graduate. But you keep saying you're not interested and it makes no sense to me. You said you don't want to be famous, but I don't believe that's the reason. I mean, maybe it's tied into it, but what's the real reason?"

"It's the lifestyle, Demi. I have a problem with debauchery."

"No, I think you *think* you have a problem with debauchery," I correct. "But from what I've gleaned, you don't drink to excess, you don't have any harmful sexual compulsions that interfere with your regular life, you don't do drugs. You're charming, so you could easily handle being interviewed or doing press." I inject a note of challenge into my voice. "So what are you really afraid of?"

Hunter is silent for a long time. He absently strokes my shoulder. When he finally speaks, his voice is rough. "If I tell you, do you promise not to make fun of me? Or judge me?"

I almost laugh until I realize he's serious. So I put on my best neutral tone. "I promise I won't make fun of you. And I'd never judge you, Hunter."

"Okay." His chest rises as he draws a breath. "I'm afraid I'll cheat," he confesses.

"Cheat? Like in the game?"

"No, the other kind of cheating." He exhales in a slow stream of air. "All those road games, all those hotel rooms and hotel bars, all those women throwing themselves at me. I know I don't have a sex addiction, but I've got my father's genes and they don't exactly have the greatest track record."

"Your father's a narcissist. You're not." I plant a reassuring kiss on his shoulder. "You're nothing like him, baby."

"He'd disagree with you on that. A few years ago he told me we're two of a kind."

My eyes narrow. "Why on earth would he say *that*?"

Hunter sighs sheepishly. "The summer before college, he caught me fucking a chick on our kitchen counter. Mom was visiting my grandparents that weekend, and Dad was supposed to be away on business, but he came home early." An edge hardens his tone. "You should've seen how proud he looked to find me buck-naked and going to town on a girl I wasn't even dating. I met her at a party the night before and she stayed over."

I try to imagine what my own father would do if he walked in on me having sex with someone in our kitchen. Commit a double homicide, obviously.

"He was genuinely *proud* to think his son was a depraved cad. But I guess that's not much of a surprise. I know Dad slept with at least three of his assistants—one I witnessed firsthand. And I just…I think about all the business trips he took over the years. I bet he had a woman in every city. I'm sure there were more affairs than Mom and I could even imagine."

"And you're worried you'll have a girlfriend or wife, and you'll be away a lot and cheat?"

"Pretty much."

"So you're punishing yourself for something you haven't even done."

His bare chest tenses. "That's not it."

"That's exactly it. You're preemptively punishing yourself—depriving yourself of something you love, for fear you might do something you hate, some vague point down the line. That's not a healthy way to look at things."

"No. I mean, maybe? Maybe that's it, or maybe it isn't. All I know is that when I decided not to enter the draft after high school, I felt relieved."

"And yet every time I see you watching Garrett and Logan play, there's envy in your eyes."

Hunter's ragged breath tickles my head. His chest rises and falls again. "Let's put this on the shelf for now. It's hurting my brain. Tell me about your holidays."

"I already did—we texted every day," I remind him.

"I know, but I like your voice and I want to hear you talk."

I smile against his left pec, then offer a more detailed recap of my visit to Miami. I tell him about my new nephew, about my crazy aunts and my excitable cousins. Being a very Catholic community, Christmas is very much celebrated in Miami, and one of my family's favorite traditions is a visit to Santa's Enchanted Forest. I took my younger cousins there, and five-year-old Maria peed on one of the rides. While sitting in my lap. Fun times.

"Do you speak Spanish?" Hunter asks curiously. "I just realized I don't even know if you do."

"I understand it better than I speak it. Dad has a terrible ear for languages, so he only speaks English at home. Mom used to speak both to me because she didn't want me to lose the Spanish, but I kinda have," I say glumly. "Not entirely, though. I mean, I'd be fluent again in a week if I was around people who spoke it exclusively."

"I'd love to learn another language. You should teach me Spanish, and then we could practice together."

"Deal." I snuggle up closer to him. "Oh, and on the flight home, I tried bringing up the med school thing to my dad again. Mom is staying in Miami for another week, so it was just me and him. But he wasn't having it," I admit.

Hunter strokes my hair. "You still having doubts about that?"

"More than doubts." I inhale slowly. "I don't want to go."

It's the first time I've ever said that out loud.

"Then don't," Hunter says simply. "You shouldn't go to med school for your father—you should go for yourself. You need to walk your own path, and that means following your own dreams, not his. Your first priority should be pleasing yourself, not him."

A laugh tickles my throat. I try to hold it in, but it ripples out.

"What is it?"

"I just realized what a sad pair we are." I can't stop giggling. "Here I am sacrificing my aspirations to be like my father, and you're sacrificing your aspirations to *not* be like your father. That is fascinating."

"Jesus. You're *such* a psychologist. Is this what it's always going to be like? Lying in bed naked while you psychoanalyze us?"

I prop up on my elbow, biting my lip. "Does it actually bother you?"

"Nah." He flashes his dimpled smile, and I lean down and kiss one of those adorable dimples. "It's funny," he continues. "Most of the time, you analyze and rationalize and try to find solutions. And then other times, you're batshit crazy."

"I am not!"

"You have a violent streak, you maniac. You smash people's game consoles." He grins up at me. "Quite the dichotomy, Demi Davis."

"Both crazy and sane," I say somberly. "A rare condition, indeed."

"Anyway." He strokes his knuckles over my cheek. "You don't need to chase your father's approval—you already have it. I don't think he'll disown you if you choose grad school over med school."

"You don't know how he feels about PhDs, Hunter. For the rest of my life he'll be making wisecracks about how I'm not a real doctor." My buzzing phone captures my attention. "Shit, that's probably Josie ordering me to come downstairs and hang more decorations."

I stretch across his muscular chest to grab my phone from the nightstand. Hunter uses the opportunity to slide one palm between us to cup one of my boobs.

I shiver in pleasure, but my arousal dissolves when I see my father's name. Speak of the devil.

I click on his message, and my eyebrows soar. "Oh, this is interesting."

"What?" Hunter lazily caresses the swell of my breast.

"My father is inviting us to New Year's Day brunch tomorrow."

Hunter's hand freezes. "Us?"

"Yep." I sit up and grin at his panicky expression. "He wants to meet you."

# 32
# DEMI

A FEW DAYS AFTER NEW YEAR'S, HUNTER AND I ARE BACK ON campus walking toward the Psych building. It's the final lecture of the semester and we're supposed to be receiving our case studies back, but while I've got a spring to my step as we amble down the path, Hunter's long gait is stilted and his expression is sullen. He's been sulking non-stop since we had brunch with my father.

"God, could you try to smile?" I demand. "It's such a beautiful day."

"It's minus-fucking-twenty and your dad hates me. It's *not* a beautiful day."

I suppress a sigh. "He doesn't hate you. He liked you."

"If by liked, you mean loathed, then you're right."

"I see. Now he doesn't just hate you—he *loathes* you. Someone's been drinking the drama juice."

"And someone's refusing to face the truth," Hunter grumbles. "Your father did *not* like me."

I want to argue again, but it's getting harder to find a solid defense for my father's behavior.

I refuse to say it aloud, because I don't want to injure Hunter's pride any further, but brunch was...awful.

It did *not* go well.

I really wish Mom had been there to create a parental balance, but she's still in Florida, and it was me and Hunter versus my father from the get-go. After a whopping two questions about Hunter's background, Dad determined he was dealing with a spoiled rich boy from Greenwich, Connecticut. Which is absolutely not the case—Hunter is the most down-to-earth person I know, and his work ethic is stellar.

But my father is incredibly biased and impossible to please. He grew up poor and sacrificed so much to get to where he is now, so needless to say, anyone born with a silver spoon in their mouth already has one strike in my father's eyes.

And he wasn't even impressed by Hunter's athletic achievements. I thought for sure that would win him over. I not-so-subtly brought up how much work is required in order to excel in a sport, but I think by that point Dad was just *trying* to be difficult because he waved my comment off. Which is bullshit. He's a big football fan, and I've heard him say numerous times that football players possess an incredible work ethic.

Clearly, Dad is still on Team Nico. But I'm hoping he switches his loyalties, because I'm Team Hunter all the way.

"He'll warm up to you," I say, giving Hunter's hand a squeeze.

He slants his head. "Will he? Because that implies I'll be seeing him often."

I hesitate. We haven't formally declared ourselves as "dating," so I'm not entirely sure if he'll see my dad again. Also, until we define our relationship, I'm trying to avoid PDA, so I drop Hunter's hand as we reach the building, because Pax and TJ are waiting on the steps.

"Ah! New boots!" Pax shouts when he spots me. His envious gaze devours my footwear, which is indeed new—black leather boots with brown fur, to match the hood of my parka. "I *love!*" he announces.

"Thanks! I'd like to say I feel the same way about your hair, but…what the hell is going on there?"

Hunter snorts. "For real, Jax. I'm not into it."

I roll my eyes. He's well aware what Pax's real name is, but now it's just a running joke, and Pax plays along because he thinks Hunter is hot.

"When did you get that done?" I ask.

"And why?" TJ says, looking like he's trying not to laugh.

Sighing dramatically, Pax smooths a hand over the green streaks in his black hair. "This past weekend. And why? Because my little sister is in cosmetology school and her exams are coming up, so she was practicing her dye skills on me."

"I'm not going to lie," I inform him. "It looks terrible."

"Gee, thanks, bestie." He winks. "The guy I hooked up with last night didn't seem to mind."

"*Nice.*" Hunter holds his palm up for a high five.

Jax—dammit, now *I'm* doing it. *Pax* returns the high five, and then the four of us escape the January chill and enter the building. I notice TJ slide a curious look between me and Hunter, but he doesn't say anything.

We take our usual seats in the middle of the row, only this time Hunter usurps Pax's place beside me. Once again TJ's gaze takes note.

Anticipation ripples inside me when Professor Andrews arrives with her two TAs in tow. *Yes!* Either my eyes are projecting what they want to see, or the teaching assistants are carrying our graded assignments.

"Morning, ladies and gents. So… The previous times I taught this course, I used to return these at the end of the final lecture, with the simple goal of torturing everyone. I'm not certain what that reveals about my own psychological makeup—" Andrews grins at the class. "With that said, I'm in the mood to be nice today."

She's behaving atypically goofy, but perhaps that's because this is our last day. The TAs who ran our tutorials approach each aisle and begin calling out names. One by one, students get up to accept their assignments.

Although everyone worked together on the projects, each paper was handed in and graded separately. I practically dive out of my seat when my name is called. The moment the envelope that contains my submission is in my hand, I waste no time slicing it open. Beside me, Hunter does the same with his.

A cover page is stapled to the front of my submission, and I almost shriek out loud when I see my grade.

A-plus, baby.

Hell yeah.

Curious, I peer over at Hunter's sheet. "What'd you get?"

"B-plus." He looks pleased with that. I had proofed his research paper and thought it was excellent, but I probably would've gone more in-depth about certain things, so I think the grade is fair.

I flip through the pages of my case study to find that Andrews scribbled notes in the margins. The praise I find is ludicrously good for my ego. Things like:

*Terrific insight!*

*Highly perceptive!*

*Provocative...*

*GREAT angle*, she writes in the section where I discuss possible counseling tactics to try to help the narcissist reach the rare self-awareness. The slew of compliments has my ego swelling to monstrous proportions. This feels way more satisfying than the A-plus I got in Organic Chem. This one feels *right*.

Hunter leans closer to whisper in my ear. "You look so hot right now."

I wrinkle my forehead. "Really?"

"Oh yeah." His breath tickles my cheek. "It's that cocky look in your eyes. Never thought I'd get turned on by an academic, but *fuck*, I've got a semi, Semi."

I snicker softly. But I realize he's not kidding when he straightens up and I glimpse the hot lust swimming in his eyes.

I gulp through my suddenly parched throat, turning toward TJ as a distraction. "How'd you do?"

"An A," he replies, and Pax got a B, so all in all I'd say Abnormal Psych was a smashing success.

Since it's the last class, Andrews rewards us with a topic that I could probably spend a solid twenty-four hours listening to: serial killers. In fact, if you tally all the time I've spent watching crime shows, it probably adds up to a depressingly long portion of my life.

Andrews begins to discuss a case that's so macabre I'm on the edge of my seat. Ten minutes in, although she still hasn't named the killer, I grab Hunter's arms and hiss, "She's talking about Harold Howarth!"

"Who?"

"He was the subject of the episode *Brain Surgeons Who Kill*." I remember calling my dad immediately after watching that episode. I told him he's never, ever allowed to inject poison into a patient's frontal lobe, and he asked me if I was high.

As I resettle in my chair, I almost rest my hand on Hunter's knee, a habit I have when we're sitting together on his couch. This morning I forcibly have to stop myself. PDA isn't allowed until I know what this is. But my gaze keeps flitting toward him. I wish I could touch his leg. Or even better—slide my hand inside his pants and wrap it around his cock. I find myself wanting to touch this man all the time.

And I mean *all the time*. Sometimes I want him so badly I can't even wait for him to close the bedroom door before I'm mauling him. Today is one of those times, except we're not in a bedroom and my throbbing body is furious at this predicament.

By the time Andrews dismisses us, my core is one dull ache. I barely hear Andrews thanking us for being so attentive this semester, wishing us luck with our future. Any other day, I'd linger after class to express my own gratitude, but I think I'll need to settle for sending a lengthy email.

I'm so aroused, I'm practically leaping out of my own skin as we exit the lecture hall. My impatient gaze darts around the wide corridor. We didn't drive, and there's no way I can last the long walk back to my house. So, as Pax and TJ walk on ahead of us, I grab Hunter's hand and drag him around the corner.

# 33
# HUNTER

Demi shoves me through the nearest doorway. Luckily, it leads into an unlit room with tables and chairs arranged in a semicircle. The blinds are shut, but the room isn't pitch black. Just shadowy, with thin stripes of sunlight peeking in from the slats.

"What are you doing?" I ask in amusement.

She hurriedly shuts the door. "I was going crazy not being able to touch you in there. You have *no* idea how close I was to just taking off your pants and riding your dick, right there in front of everyone."

My groin clenches. Oh Jesus, that sounds hot. The two of us are all over each other, all the time. It's almost become an addiction. And I'm embarrassed to say it hasn't affected hockey whatsoever, which means my vow of celibacy was completely fucking pointless. If anything, I'm playing even *better* these days.

I've avoided talking about it with Demi, because I'm afraid she'll tease me, tell me I'd been acting out a scene from *Wizard of Oz* or some shit. Like, *you had the power to be a good captain and teammate all along, Hunter! It was your guilt, and your fear of being a selfish jackass like your father, that stopped you from seeing that.*

I can totally see Demi using a cheesy analogy like that.

But I guess it's a lesson I needed to learn. Last season's fuckery had scarred me. And I started this season wanting to put my team— and not my dick—first. I wanted to be a good captain. I wanted to prove to myself that I'm not a selfish narcissistic asshole whose needs are the only ones that matter. When our season went up in flames last year, it was a wake-up call for me. The first thing I thought after we lost that game was, *maybe we are two of a kind*. My father and I.

The first time he'd said that to me, I blanched inside. I felt dirty. Spooked by the notion that I could actually be anything like him. A dirt bag. An egomaniac.

But sex with Demi hasn't resulted in anything but me going to bed sated every night and killing it in practice every morning. Not to mention the playoffs—we're dominating the other teams.

Demi loops her arms around my neck and yanks my head down for a kiss. Christ. I love kissing her. I love fucking her. I love doing everything with and to her.

We both know this thing between us is more than a rebound. More than sex. But I don't know what that *more* is. And I'm enjoying it too much to rock the boat by asking.

I laugh when she pushes me against the door. She clicks the lock into place, and her hand is at my belt before I can blink. She undoes my jeans and tugs them and my boxers just low enough that she can reach inside and pull out my hot, heavy cock.

"Oh my God, I wanted this so badly the past two hours," Demi mumbles in anguish. "I want it all the time."

"Take it," I say huskily.

She sinks to her knees and my body tightens in anticipation. When her mouth engulfs my dick in one wet glide, I hiss in pleasure. So does she, and her brown eyes shine happily as she releases me to say, "I *love* having this in my mouth."

"You and your oral fixation," I mock, all the while trying to nudge my cockhead through her sexy lips again.

She laughs at my pathetic attempts. "So when I need my candy, it's, what did you call it the other day? A *serious problem*. But when I'm craving your dick, my oral fixation is just fine and dandy?"

I grin. "Now you're gettin' it."

Demi sticks out her tongue, and I take full advantage of that. Within seconds, I'm in her hot mouth again.

"Oh yeah." I hold the back of her head with both hands, guiding her along my shaft.

There's a murmur of voices out in the hall. I don't care. Demi makes me forget that other people inhabit the world with us. We're the only ones in this room, in this building, on this planet. When I'm inside her, nobody exists but us. When she's petting and rubbing and sucking on my dick, nobody exists but her.

She swallows me up, her eager tongue curling around the head of my dick. She gets it nice and wet, while her fist moves up and down the length of me. Squeezing the tip on each upstroke, sucking me to the root on the way down.

I rock my hips, restless, aroused, my balls beginning to tingle. When she pulled me in here, I assumed I'd fuck her against a wall. But this blowjob is so criminally good, I won't last long enough to get inside her.

"Baby," I groan, trying to still her.

She peers up at me with big eyes. Her lips are wrapped tight around my cockhead. It's the sexiest thing I've ever seen, and I trace that naughty O with my thumb, rubbing the corner of her mouth.

"I'm close," I warn. "If you came in here wanting to fuck, you'd better stop that."

Her wet mouth slides off me, and my cock emerges with a *pop*. "No, I want to make you come right now. I want to hear you moan my name when you shoot in my mouth."

*Jesus*. This girl will be the death of me.

She resumes her wicked task, and in less than thirty seconds I'm giving the woman what she wants.

"Demi," I groan when my climax breaks the surface. Her lips remain firmly around me as she swallows everything I have to give. I'm dead. She's killed me. She's perfect.

Demi plants soft kisses on my still-hard shaft as I float down from the high. Smiling, she tucks me into my cargo pants. Primly wipes her mouth with the back of her hand as she rises to her feet. She zips me up and stands on her tiptoes to brush her lips over mine.

I can't help but deepen the kiss, and when I taste myself on her tongue I'm damn near raring to go again. I shiver.

"You okay?" she teases.

"Peachy," I croak.

She snickers, then gives me a long appraisal before unlocking the door. We reenter the hall, and the bright fluorescent lighting blinds me for a moment.

"Are you coming over tonight?" she asks as we fall into step with each other.

"I can't. I'm having drinks with Hollis. But I can come over now and hang out with you till I need to meet him?"

"Boooooo."

"Don't boo me."

"Why not? You boo me all the time."

"Because I'm a child, Semi. You're far too mature for that nonsense. Have some respect for yourself."

She bursts out laughing and I smile. I like making her laugh.

"I'd bail," I say, "but Hollis stressed that it was important."

Demi stops walking. "I'm sorry. Mike Hollis implied that something was *important*?"

"Implied? More like explicitly stated. He pulled me aside this morning and asked if we could talk tonight."

"Why was he even home? It's Monday."

A frown touches my lips. "He called in sick to work, but he didn't look sick to me."

"I hope everything's okay with him."

"I'm sure it is. Hollis is indestructible. I bet he just wants to talk about something random, like what to get Rupi for her birthday."

"Is it coming up?"

"Oh, you're going to love this. The girl was born on...wait for it...February fourteenth."

Demi gasps. "Valentine's Day! Oh my God. Poor Mike. He's going to have to go all out. Maybe even buy her a pony."

I snort.

When we enter the lobby, I notice TJ standing a few feet away chatting with one of the TAs. A frown twists his mouth when he spots us. It seems like an extreme response for no reason, until I realize that his gaze is on my crotch.

I look down and swallow a curse. Demi must not have zipped me up all the way, because my fly slid right back down. I discreetly do it up, but that does nothing to erase the distrustful look on TJ's face.

———

Later that night I slide into the booth across from Hollis, signaling the waitress as I settle in. Hollis didn't order yet, despite the fact that he's already been here for ten minutes. I was late driving over because there was four feet of ice on my windshield when I left Demi's house. Nearly froze my balls off scraping it all away.

"Sorry, I was scraping ice," I grumble.

"Fuckin' ice. It should be banned."

"I'll be sure to let the climate know you feel that way, Michael."

I smile in gratitude when the waitress returns with my lager. Hollis ordered a can of Boom Sauce, which I think he likes just because of the name. We tap our drinks in cheers.

"So what's going on?" I ask my buddy. "Why did you drag me to Malone's in the dead of butt-fuck winter when we live in the same house and could easily have talked there?"

Hollis plays with the rim of his beer can. "Needed to get out." He shrugs. "How's it going with you? You still seeing Demi? Did Coach approve the pig yet?"

He's stalling, but I play along for the time being. Hollis is so dramatic that pushing him could potentially result in him storming out in a huff, and I'd really like to finish my beer.

"I'm fine. Did well in all my courses last semester. Still seeing Demi. And no, Coach hasn't green-lit the pig yet." I mull it over for a moment. "But I just realized—once he does, that means Pablo has to go." Shit. I don't know if I'm ready to say goodbye yet.

"Dude, it's about time. Do you know how much that little dude stinks? Eggs aren't meant to be out in the wild."

I chuckle. "I don't even notice the smell anymore, to be honest."

"We should get a pet for the house," Hollis says.

"Ha. Sure. Rupi would never let you have a pet. It'd mean less attention for her."

"True. It's hard enough only giving her attention on the weekends." Hollis rubs his eyes, and I notice that he looks deeply exhausted. I knew the two-hour commute to New Hampshire was taking its toll on him, but it appears it's gotten even worse. His eyes are actually puffy, as if he hasn't slept properly in years.

"You heading back to your folks' place tomorrow or calling in sick again?" I ask carefully.

"I'm heading back." He takes a quick sip. "Honestly, I don't want to sell insurance anymore, Davenport. I hate it up there. I hate living at home again, and I hate working with my dad. That dude's crazy."

"Mmm-hmmm, *he's* crazy."

"He is! And he tells the stupidest jokes all day long."

I stare at Hollis. "I truly cannot conceive of the kind of torture you must be going through."

"Right?"

Whoosh. Right over his head. "Why don't you try to find work in Hastings?" I suggest.

"I have, but nobody is hiring. Or at least hiring for positions I'd actually *want*. There's a job opening for a graveyard-shift clerk at the gas station, but what's the point of that? I'd just sleep all day and work all night, and the pay is shit."

"If I hear of anything, I'll let you know."

"Thanks."

"And I guess for now you just keep your full-time job of selling insurance during the week and your full-time job of Rupi on the weekends."

"Dude, she really is a full-time job." Yet he's grinning broadly as he says it.

"I don't understand your relationship at all."

"Of course you don't. It's transcendent."

"What does that even mean?"

"Exactly," he says smugly. But it isn't long before his blue eyes grow serious again. It's not an expression you often see on Mike Hollis's face. "She's only a sophomore, bro."

"Rupi? So?"

"So she won't graduate for two and a half more years. That means two and a half more years of me making this God-awful commute so I can sell insurance with my crazy father."

I put down my beer. "Are you considering…breaking up with her?"

He's utterly aghast. "What! What the fuck is wrong with you? Of course not. Did you not listen to the part where I said we're *transcendent*?"

"Right, sorry, I forgot." I study him again. "So what exactly are we talking about here? You hate your job. You hate living at home again. You hate commuting. You hate that Rupi has a couple more years of school left. But you love Rupi."

"Yes to all that."

I purse my lips. "Okay, answer me this. If none of those things you listed as hating were in the equation, what would you be doing?"

"I'm not following."

"Pretend you don't have to worry about jobs and commutes and all that crap—what would you want to be doing?"

"I would—" He stops. "Nothing. It's stupid."

"No, tell me," I order. "Let's figure this out, man."

Hollis gulps down some more Boom Sauce. "I'd travel," he finally confesses. "Like, dude, do you realize how many other countries there are in the world? Dozens!"

"Hundreds," I correct.

"Don't be crazy now. There's only seven continents, why would there be hundreds of countries? Your math is erroneous. But yeah, that's what I'd do. I'd travel all over the motherfucking world and meet new people and experience new cultures and eat weird food and—*oh*, Rupi and I could bang on trains and airplanes and camels if we go somewhere with camels—"

"Wait, Rupi's on this trip, too?"

He nods fervently. "Where else would she be?"

I nod back, but slow and thoughtful. "You want my advice? You should talk to Rupi about all this. Be honest about how exhausted you are, and tell her you'd love to go on a trip with her. Maybe you can plan something for the summer? It'd give you something to look forward to while you make that long commute to New Hampshire..." I trail off enticingly.

Hollis narrows his eyes at me.

"What?" I say.

"Have you always been this smart or have I just always been this stupid?"

I grin at him. "I choose not to answer that question."

# 34
# DEMI

By the end of January, Hunter and I still haven't defined our relationship. We're just sort of floating along, having sex on a consistent basis, cuddling, texting, giving each other advice. I attend his hockey games even though I still don't care about hockey. He watches crime documentaries even though he finds them disturbing.

As Brenna likes to say, we're in a situationship. But according to Pippa, we're a married couple who won't even call themselves boyfriend and girlfriend.

Pippa's right. He's my boyfriend, and I'm his girlfriend. It's funny—for two people who communicate extremely well, neither of us has raised the subject. I know why *I* haven't, but I wonder what's holding Hunter back.

Me, I'm scared to make that commitment. What if things change the moment I call him my boyfriend? What if suddenly he decides I'm tying him down or cramping his style, and starts looking elsewhere? It's an irrational fear, and the bitter memory of Nico's cheating isn't helping matters.

The ambiguity of our relationship is a constant source of anxiety for me. Human beings have a compulsion to define things. Definitions provide us with comfort. But I'm torn about what I want more—to label us, or to avoid possible rejection. For now, I simply don't bring it up, and neither does Hunter.

His team is in the midst of playoffs and he's been working hard this past week. Practices are grueling, and he's covered in bruises every time I see him. Tonight he was feeling particularly sore, so I decided to go out with my friends and give his body some time to recover. It's impossible for me to see Hunter without climbing all over that hard body and banging his brains out.

Hunter, however, is grumpy about being alone tonight. He keeps texting pictures of various parts of his body, some bruised and some not, begging me to come over and kiss them. Eventually, I interrupt Pippa midsentence and say, "Hold that thought. Let me just tell him to eff off."

**ME**: I'm with my friends, Monk. The world doesn't revolve around you.

**HIM**: Sure it does.

**ME**: I see. Are you channeling your father?

**HIM**: OMG you're right. I'm sorry. The world is not my oyster. I'm just one pearl floating in a sea of pearls.

**ME**: That analogy is nonsensical. Now go away. I'm with my friends.

**HIM**: Fine!

I put the phone down. "Sorry, that needed to be done," I tell my friends.

Pippa, TJ and I are in a cramped booth at one of the campus bars. Corinne is on her way to meet us, and this will be my third hangout with her since everything exploded back in November.

The first time was beyond awkward. We had a movie night at Pippa's and I couldn't bring myself to utter a single word to Corinne. Every time I looked at her I pictured her naked with my ex-boyfriend. The second time went better, because there was drinking involved. But then I had one too many tequila shots, which tipped me into Scorned Woman territory and I may have made a snide comment or two. I'm vowing not to do that tonight.

When my phone lights up again, I flip it over facedown. "This guy," I grumble.

"Hockey boy?" Pippa says with a laugh.

"Yes. He's all bruised up and sore, so he's taking it easy at home and he's bored. When he's bored, he gets annoying."

"Don't they all?"

"Hey, I don't annoy anyone when I'm bored," TJ protests. He casually swirls his straw in the strawberry daiquiri we forced him to order.

Originally this was supposed to be girls only, but TJ sounded glum when he realized he couldn't come, so I told him he could join us as long as he honored the rules of Girls' Night. AKA ordering lots of brightly colored drinks.

"What's going on with you guys, anyway?" he asks curiously. "It seems like it's evolved from just hanging out…"

"Um yeah," Pippa answers for me. "They're frickin' married."

TJ looks stunned. "For real?"

A snort slips out. "No, not for real. But we do spend a lot of time together." I pick up my obnoxiously pink drink with its gaudy purple umbrella. "I guess that means we're dating. I'm not entirely sure, though. We haven't even had the exclusivity talk."

"You haven't?" Pippa raises a brow. "It's been months, D. What if he's having sex with other women?"

"He's not."

"Of course he is," TJ says, rolling his eyes.

I scowl at them both.

Pippa objects. "Hey, don't look at *me* like that. I didn't say he was. That's all this one." She pokes TJ in the arm.

He raises both hands as if surrendering to enemy soldiers. "Hey, don't shoot the messenger. Of course he's sleeping with other people. I'm telling you this as a college dude who lives in the dorms surrounded by other college dudes. If you don't make it clear to a guy that you want to be exclusive, I guarantee he's seeing more than one woman."

"I mean…TJ has a point," Pippa says slowly.

"And he was out with all those girls, like, a week ago," TJ goes on. "He's definitely hooking up with other people."

A chill runs up my spine. "What girls? And how do you know what he was doing?"

"I saw something on Instagram."

"You saw something on Instagram," I echo uncertainly.

TJ nods. "I follow a shit ton of Briar people. Someone posted a picture of the hockey team at a party, not sure where it took place. Davenport was in the picture kissing some chick."

*Bullshit*, I want to retort.

But doubt creeps into me like strands of ivy and tightens around my throat. Hunter did go to an after party last week that I didn't attend, but that doesn't mean anything. Moreover, we're not even an official couple.

I bite the inside of my cheek. Hard. The pain triggered by my teeth doesn't even compare to the shooting pain in my heart. My stomach lurches. With shaky fingers, I flip over my phone. The last text from Hunter was a kissy face.

I ignore it. Suddenly wondering how many other kissy faces he's sending and to whom.

"I took a screenshot for you," TJ admits, "but I deleted it."

"What! *Why?*" Pippa thunders.

Misery clouds his eyes as he looks at me. "Because I didn't want you to think I was trying to cause trouble. I remember how much it annoyed you the last time we talked about Hunter behind his back."

"Thomas Joseph," Pippa snaps. "Get your phone out and recover the picture from the deleted folder. I bet it's probably still in there."

My heartbeat is erratic as TJ scrolls through his photo roll. I'm almost hoping he doesn't find the picture. I don't want it to exist. I want it to be a figment of TJ's imagination.

"Here it is!" he says, and my stomach plummets like a shot-down missile.

TJ slides the phone toward me. Pippa practically drapes herself over the sticky tabletop to get a good look.

The photo features half a dozen guys and a few girls. I recognize several faces: Matt Anderson, that Jesse guy, and I think that's Mike Hollis in the corner but it's hard to tell. Matt has his arm around a smiling redhead, and Jesse is posing next to a girl I think might be his girlfriend Katie. But I don't see Hunter—

Oh. There he is.

TJ's right. Hunter *is* in the photo.

And he is absolutely kissing someone else.

# 35
# DEMI

My heart jumps to my throat in horror, tightening my windpipe and making it difficult to breathe. In the photo, the blonde's mouth is fused to Hunter's in a frozen kiss captured for all of eternity. Permanently documented for me, Demi Davis, to see.

Jealousy and anger form a pretzel in the pit of my stomach. I'm allowed to feel the former, but not the latter.

"D?" Pippa says.

I paste on a careless expression. "We never had the are-we-exclusive talk."

She sees right through me. "Oh, babe. We don't know when this was taken," she points out.

TJ speaks up. "It was posted like six days ago."

"That doesn't mean it was *taken* six days ago," argues Pippa.

"Why would someone post an old picture?"

"Are you serious? People do it all the time! Throwback Thursday? Flashback Friday? Way-back Wednesday?"

"The caption doesn't use any of those hashtags," TJ counters.

"Maybe they forgot. I don't know."

"You don't know what?" a third voice joins in.

I glance up at Corinne's arrival. She's wearing an oversized sweater and skinny jeans, her curly hair pulled back with a yellow scrunchie. She climbs into the booth beside me, and now it feels even more cramped.

"We're just arguing about this picture of the guy Demi is dating," Pippa explains.

"Hockey boy?" Corrine asks.

"Yeah." That awful cold sensation keeps fluttering through my body.

She picks up the phone. "Which one is he?"

I point at Hunter and the blonde. They're still kissing in the picture.

Dammit. I was kind of hoping I'd look at it again and they'd be standing on opposite sides of the frame.

Corinne studies the image. "This is the guy you're seeing?"

"Yep."

"Oh. I'm sorry." She seems genuinely upset on my behalf. Or maybe it's just pity. *Poor Demi, the girl who keeps getting shafted for other chicks.*

Pippa grabs the phone again and spends an inordinate amount of time examining the screen. "No, this is *definitely* an old picture," she finally announces. "I recognize this girl." She taps the face of the redhead beside Matt Anderson. "That's Jenny."

"Who's Jenny?" asks Corinne.

"She was in one of my acting classes freshman year." Pippa appears both relieved and triumphant. "It's an old picture, D. I promise."

"How can you be sure?" I'm almost embarrassed by the balloon of hope rising in my chest.

"Because she doesn't go here anymore. She transferred to the drama program at UCLA more than a year ago."

"Seriously?"

"How do you know it's her?" TJ asks. "It's not the clearest shot. Or maybe she's in town visiting friends, you don't know."

"Hold on. Let me find her Insta account so we can compare pics.

Amuse yourselves for a minute, girls and boy." She bends over her phone, a woman on a mission.

I try to focus on Corinne as she chats about her new classes this semester, but when Pippa gives a shout of satisfaction, my focus ricochets back to her in an instant.

"See!" She lays down her phone, side by side with TJ's. "That's Jenny."

I compare the pictures. It's the same girl.

"And she's not visiting," Pippa adds. "According to her Insta, she's been in Hawaii with her family for the past few weeks."

Relief courses through me, so overpowering that I feel faint. And sick. And afraid.

Not defining a relationship is a terrible place to be in. But what's even more terrible is the current state of my mind and heart. I went from zero to infidelity in a nanosecond. Instantly succumbed to suspicion and assumed Hunter had made out with someone else at a party.

I force myself to drink my entire daiquiri. To listen to Pippa and Corinne, to express interest when TJ talks about how he's visiting his brother in England this summer. But I can't concentrate. I'm too riled up from that false alarm. I feel stupid and uncertain.

I need to talk to Hunter.

"Hey, I'm going to take off," I say when Pippa suggests ordering another round. "My head's not in this."

TJ looks disappointed. "It's only nine-thirty."

"I know. I'm sorry. But I'm emotionally exhausted."

"It's cool," Pippa says, waving a hand. "I'll see you tomorrow anyway. Dinner with Darius, remember?"

"Right." I say my goodbyes, then zip up my parka and exit the bar.

Greek Row is a three-minute walk from here, but I'm not headed home. I order an Uber, and fifteen minutes later I'm in Hastings, ringing Hunter's doorbell.

Summer lets me in. "Hey. I didn't know you were coming over." She greets me with a dazzling smile, because that's the default mode for her face. Dazzling.

"Last-minute thing," I answer vaguely.

Beyond her shoulder, I spot her boyfriend Fitz walking past the kitchen doorway in gray sweatpants and no shirt. He backs up when he catches sight of me, and lifts one tattooed arm in a quick wave. "Hey Demi. There's leftover pizza if you want."

"No thanks. I'm good. I'm just going to go up and see Hunter." My heart beats faster as I climb the stairs and approach his bedroom door.

When I knock, he responds with a loud growl. "Go away, Rupi. I don't want to watch *Riverdale*. It's fucking stupid."

"It's me," I answer with a laugh.

"Semi? Why did you even knock? Get your cute butt in here."

I enter the room to find him sprawled on his bed. A hockey game flashes on the TV, but I can't tell who's playing. Hunter's head is propped up on a pillow, his dark hair rumpled, and stubble shadowing his jaw.

Those dimples appear as he smiles at me. "I thought you didn't want to come over."

"I wasn't going to, but then—"

"—but then you realized you wanted to get all up in my dick biz. Wise decision."

I crack a smile. "No. I just…" I trail off.

I suddenly feel ridiculous for showing up like this. What am I supposed to say? *I was out with friends and saw a picture of you kissing some girl and I thought it was recent and then I felt sick but it turned out to be old and yet I couldn't stop freaking out so I raced over here for no good reason.*

"What's going on?" he asks, his forehead creasing. "What's wrong?"

To my utter horror, hot tears fill my eyes.

"Demi." He sits up. "What's going on?"

"Nothing. Just…ah, I'm an idiot."

"No you're not. But I'll bite—why do you think you're an idiot?"

I exhale in a rush, and then the entire story spills out. Hunter listens without a single interjection, visibly bewildered.

"I'm sorry," I blabber on. "I'm not saying you did anything wrong, because you didn't—it was an old picture. But when I thought it *wasn't* old, my brain immediately jumped to you cheating on me. That's where my idiocy comes in, because how could you cheat on me if we're not even officially together?"

"Sure we are."

I falter. "We are?"

"Of course. Just because we haven't labeled this doesn't mean we're not together. When anyone asks, I refer to you as my girlfriend."

"You do?" I angrily swipe at my wet eyes. "Why the fuck don't you refer to me as your girlfriend when *I'm* there?"

He snorts with laughter. "I don't know, why don't you ever call me your man?"

"Because I didn't want to rush into things." I release a heavy sigh, trying to articulate the emotions swirling inside me. "I'm so embarrassed," I finally admit. "I like to think of myself as level-headed and mature, and yet I immediately jumped to conclusions and assumed you were sleeping around. And it made me realize that Nico really messed with my head. I thought I was over it, but apparently I'm not. Apparently now any time anything even the slightest bit sketchy happens, I'm going to assume the person I'm with is sleeping with someone else."

I finish with an anguished groan.

"C'mere," he says gruffly. He moves toward the foot of the bed where I'm lurking and pulls me into his lap.

I rest my chin on his shoulder, inhaling a weak breath.

"You didn't jump to conclusions, Demi. You saw a picture of me kissing another woman. Yes, it was taken last year, but you didn't know that at first. Believe me, if I saw a picture of you kissing another man, I'd lose my shit."

"You would?"

"Yes. Look, I know we kind of did this backwards. We didn't have any of those big relationship talks, or set any ground rules, but…" Hunter captures my chin with his hands and lifts my head so we're eye to eye. "I promise you, I'm not seeing anybody else. I'm not sleeping with anybody else. I'm with you, and I'm all in." His voice cracks. "I love you."

# 36
# HUNTER

No one has a harder job than the man who comes after the cheater.

To be honest, I'm surprised Demi didn't experience a breakdown like this sooner. Yes, she had her violent breakdown, her fit of rage when she hurled Nico's stuff out the window and clocked him in the face. But I don't think she ever fully dealt with the emotional implications of what Nico did.

I know all about the aftermath of infidelity. I remember how my mom acted following the revelation of another one of Dad's affairs. She'd be jittery and suspicious for weeks and months afterward. Whenever he bent over his phone, her shoulders would stiffen. *Who is he texting?* she'd wonder. Whenever he had to go to the office, anxiety would flood her eyes. *Who is he going to fuck on his desk today?*

I used to have a lot of sympathy for her, but over the years it faded away. People are in control of their own lives and their own decisions. They're not powerless victims to some cruel overlord who keeps them trapped in a misery loop. Mom made the decision to stay with him. I can't sympathize anymore, not when there are so many other solutions available to her. She doesn't have to be miserable, afraid, distrustful. She doesn't have to be a pushover. She chooses to be.

But Demi, unlike my mother, doesn't want to be stuck in this situation. She came directly to me to seek reassurance, and I'm going to give it to her.

"You love me," she echoes.

My pulse speeds up as I study her expression. It's impossible to decipher. I don't know how she feels about what I'd just said. Hell, I don't know how *I* feel about it.

I've only said those words to one other person, a high school girlfriend. And if I'm being honest, she said them first and I felt awkward not returning the sentiment. Teenage boys are stupid cowards sometimes. I wasn't actually in love with her, the girl from high school.

But *this* girl, the gorgeous woman in my lap—I'm definitely in love with her. I love everything about her. Her intelligence, her sassiness, her craziness. She has the most dynamic personality. There are so many different facets to Demi Davis, and the more I learn about her, the more I love her.

So yes, I'm going to take on this challenging task and face the brunt of the damage that Nico caused. I'm going to be patient and help Demi regain her trust in my foolish sex, which has been given a bad rap thanks to men like Nico and my father. I'm going to stick by her and shower her with assurances that I love her, until she realizes she doesn't ever need to worry about what I'm doing or who I'm doing it with—because she's the only one who matters to me.

A strange, unexpected sense of empowerment rushes through me. And I realize something. The same way my mother is in control of her own happiness, I'm in control of my own impulses. I'm not enslaved by my genetics, and I'm *not* my father.

"Fuck," I marvel.

"What?" She still looks a bit dazed by my admission that I love her.

I gape at her. "I would never cheat on you."

She snorts softly. "Don't sound so surprised."

"But I am. I'm thinking about the conversation we had a while ago, about my hockey career. About how I don't want to be like my dad, how I'm worried about being on the road, lonely and horny and giving in to temptation. But I can't even imagine being tempted by anyone else. Maybe that's damn naïve of me, but ten chicks could walk in here right now, buck naked, and I'd still only have eyes for you. Even with your face all puffy like that."

"Who are you calling *puffy*?" she objects.

"You. You're a terrible crier, Semi. You don't look good crying."

She punches me in the shoulder. "You're supposed to be acting romantic right now."

"I just told you I loved you! Trust me, I'm fucking romantic."

"True." She licks her lower lip. Then bites it. "I don't know if I'm ready to say it back," she confesses, and I chuckle because she looks so cute nervously nibbling on her lip like that.

"I didn't say it so you would say it back. I said it because I felt it. I'm in love with you. And I don't want to kiss anybody but you." I bring my lips to hers, and she wraps her arms around my neck and kisses me back.

We fall onto the mattress, kissing eagerly, and we're breathless by the time we come up for air. Now I'm propped up on my elbows, though, which puts strain on my sore body, sending a jolt of pain to my ribcage.

"I can't stay in this position," I groan. "My side is throbbing. I'm sorry, baby."

"Don't ever be sorry. About anything."

I grin. "About anything?"

"No, wait, I take that back. I'm sure you're going to be sorry for tons of things that deserve your sorryness, but this is not one of them. Lie back. Let me make you feel better."

"I'm supposed to be making *you* feel better."

"Then why have you been texting me pictures of your boo-boos all night?"

"Just to annoy you when you were out with your friends."

"Jackass. But, what, does that mean you're going to stop me if I start kissing all the boo-boos?" She lifts the hem of my shirt and plants a teasing kiss on my hip.

It sends a hot tremor up my spine. "Only a chump turns down free kisses."

"That's what I thought." Very methodically, she removes my shirt. She winces when she spots the bruises coloring my ribs. "Aw, those do look bad. Maybe I shouldn't be doing this." She runs a tentative palm over my abs, torturously close to my waistband.

"You should *always* be doing this," I disagree.

"Are you sure your body can handle it? Because I…really need this." Sheepish, she casts her eyes downward.

"We both do," I assure her.

Demi takes off her sweater and hops up to unbutton her jeans. She leaves me on the bed only to get a condom, and then she's back, tugging on the waistband of my sweatpants. I'm commando underneath and she moans happily. She grips my dick and gives it a slow stroke.

I'm hard, primed, ready to go. As she rolls the condom on, I reach between her legs and find her equally ready. Her wet pussy glides beneath my palm, and when I cup her, a dizzying rush of pleasure spirals through me. I can't get enough of this girl. She turns me on something fierce.

"Come here and fuck me already," I mumble.

Laughing at my impatience, she gingerly climbs onto my lap. She grips the base of me and guides my cockhead to where we both want it most.

"Fuck," I wheeze when she's fully seated. "Your pussy feels so good." Then she starts to move, and it feels even better.

She rides me, taking care not to jostle me. "Is this okay?" she murmurs.

As the pleasure rises, black dots flash in my vision. "More than okay."

Her hips roll seductively. My breathing quickens. I cup her ass, then skate my palms up her delicate spine, reaching around to squeeze her tits. I love touching her. Love the breathy sounds she makes as her body strains against mine, seeking her own pleasure.

I thrust my fingers through her dark hair and urge her head down. "Kiss me," I rasp.

And she does, whimpering when our tongues touch. We stay in that position forever, her mouth exploring mine, her body draped over me, slowly fucking me into oblivion. And when I come, white-hot pleasure engulfing my body, I know without a doubt that I truly am in love with this girl.

# 37
# DEMI

**TJ**: You and hockey guy straighten everything out?

THE MESSAGE POPS UP WHEN I'M ON A BUS HEADED FOR BOSTON. I would've preferred taking the train, but none of the departure and arrival times lined up with my schedule for today. I wanted to visit Boston all week, but my dad's been in surgery nearly every day. Now it's Friday and he's available, but Hunter's team is playing tonight, so I'm squeezing in a quick trip to the city and then racing back to Hastings.

I can't miss this game. Apparently it's a crucial game in the playoffs. If they win, they go to the semi-finals? I think? I'm not entirely sure how it goes, but I know Hunter would appreciate it if I came to cheer him on.

I'm at the front of the bus, curled up in a window seat. Luckily, there's nobody with ferret pics sitting beside me. No seatmate at all, in fact, so my purse gets its own seat.

**ME**: Yep, it's all good. We talked at the beginning of the week.
**HIM**: Oh. You didn't mention it.
**ME**: You didn't ask :)
**HIM**: I'm sorry that pic upset you. Wish I never showed it to you.

**ME**: No, I'm glad I saw it. It was actually the catalyst we
needed to have THE TALK. Anyway, how are you doing? Is
your Lit prof still being an ass?
**HIM**: Sort of, but it's nbd. I'm more interested in your TALK.
How'd that go?
**ME:** Well, we're officially together now, so I'm gonna say it
went pretty well. Guess who has a boyfriend again lol I'm on
my way to Boston right now to tell my parents.
**HIM**: Seriously? You're going all the way to Boston to tell
your family you're dating some guy?
**ME**: Yep.

A wry smile tickles my lips. It's true, a phone call would have
sufficed. A text, even. But my parents are a huge part of my life. It's
always been just the three of us, and in my family we talk things out
in person. Our little unit took a hit after Nico and I broke up, but
Dad isn't pushing me to get back with Nico anymore. Granted, now
he's regularly dropping hints about how I should stop seeing Hunter.

I honestly don't know what his problem with Hunter is, other
than Hunter's wealthy background, which is a non-issue. Dad is just
being extra protective, and I'd like to get to the heart of that.

And because I'm feeling so emboldened, I'm also going to tell
him I'm not applying for med school.

Which means I'll either be at Hunter's game tonight, or I'll be
dead.

**TJ**: Well, good luck with that. Doesn't your dad hate him?
**ME**: Don't know if he hates him, per se. But he does
disapprove.
**HIM**: Same thing.
**ME**: No it's not. But it doesn't matter. Hunter is my bf, and
Dad will just have to deal. Anyway, gotta go! Just got to the
station xo

I tuck my phone away and slip on my parka in preparation of leaving the warmth of the bus. The air is frigid as I walk through the bus station toward the taxi and ride share lines outside. There's a taxi right there and it's too cold to wait for an Uber, so I hop into the back of the cab and provide my address.

Mom told me that Dad had pulled an all-nighter at the hospital and only got home at ten-thirty this morning. That means I'll most likely be dealing with Grumpy Papa today. It's not ideal, but I can't schedule my life around my dad's various moods.

When the taxi reaches my brownstone, I take a deep breath before getting out of the car. I need to gather every ounce of courage I possess, because my father won't be happy to hear what I have to say today. But Hunter was right—Dad's not going to disown me. I know in my heart he won't. He might huff and puff, but he's not blowing any houses down.

I just need to stick to my guns, and not let him bulldoze me, especially about medical school. It's time for me to stop being Daddy's Little Girl and be my own woman.

As usual, numerous aromas greet my nostrils when I stride into the house. "Mom?" I call.

"In here." She's in the kitchen, where else?

I pop through the doorway and almost collapse in a puddle of ravenous drool. She's pan-frying chicken with peppers and peas, and the spicy smell draws me toward the stove.

"Oh my God, Mom. Please move into the Theta house with me," I plead. "You could cook for us every single day. Breakfasts, lunches, dinners." I shiver in pure joy. "I'd be living the dream."

Mom snorts.

I wrap my arms around her from behind, giving her a kiss on the cheek. Then I try to steal a piece of chicken and she smacks my hand with her spatula.

"Go away! Shoo!" She flaps her arm around like she's trying to get rid of a pesky fly.

"You're mean," I gripe.

She rolls her eyes and continues cooking.

Because the food looks and smells so delicious, I make an executive decision to wait until after dinner to start dropping truth bombs. Dad looks exhausted when he joins us in the dining room. His dark eyes are lined with fatigue, and he keeps rubbing them throughout dinner.

"Tough surgery?" I sympathize.

"Surgeries, plural. I performed back-to-back craniotomies—one biopsy and one tumor removal. And just when I thought I was done, a third patient was airlifted in with a subdural hematoma." He goes on about each case in depth, which includes a shit ton of technical details. I don't understand half of what he's saying, but he seems content to just chat with me about it.

"I can't imagine being in an operating room for so long," I confess. "I'd probably fall asleep on the patient."

"It requires great discipline." He chuckles. "It's funny—this was indeed a long night, but I'm nowhere near as wiped as when I was completing my residency or going through medical school."

It's the perfect opening.

*Take it, Demi, take it!*

But I'm a wimp. So I don't.

Instead, I bring up the other reason I'm home. Better to start small, right? Revealing that I have a new boyfriend isn't as extreme as telling them I'm switching career paths.

I clear my throat. "I wanted to talk to you guys about something."

Mom scrapes back her chair and starts to rise. "Let me put everything away first."

"No, Mom. Come on, sit down. We can do that after."

"After?" She sounds horrified. Because in our house, you eat a big meal and then you clean it all up. But then she sees my grave expression and sinks back down, concern flickering in her honey-brown eyes. "Is everything all right?"

"Everything is more than all right," I confess.

At the head of the table, Dad's expression clouds over. Dammit. I think he knows what I'm about to say.

"I wanted to let you know..." I blow out a hasty breath. "I'm officially dating Hunter."

Silence.

"Um. This is good news...?" I prompt, looking from one parent to the other.

Mom is the first to speak. "Okay. Marcus. What are your thoughts on this?"

"You already know my thoughts. I don't think he's good for her."

She nods deliberately before turning back to me.

"And that's it?" I exclaim in disbelief. "He says that and you just nod along like a little puppet?"

Mom frowns. "Demi."

"It's true. You haven't even met Hunter!"

"If your father says he's not good for you, then I agree with him."

"You. Haven't. Even. Met. Him." I spit out each word through clenched teeth. Then I suck in several breaths, trying to calm myself. "Seriously, Mom. I'm so disappointed in you right now."

Indignation darkens my mother's face. She opens her mouth and I know the Latina temper is about to be unleashed. But mine beats her to it.

"You're constantly letting Dad dictate how you think! You yell and scream and throw temper tantrums when it's about your stuff. *Your* kitchen, *your* wardrobe, *your* interests. But when it comes to important things, he has the run of the house—and the run of your brain, apparently."

"Demi," my father rumbles.

"It's true," I insist, angrily shaking my head at her. "You haven't even given Hunter a chance. I expected better from you. And you," I turn toward Dad, "you did meet him, and he was nothing but nice to you. He wasn't rude, he listened when you spoke, tried to pay for lunch—"

"Because he's a rich boy," Dad says snidely.

"No, because he's a nice person. And I'm really, *really* into him." Anguish rises in my throat. "You guys don't have to like him if you don't want to—that's fine. But he's going to be in my life either way. We're dating now, and it's serious between us. We've talked about going away for spring break, and maybe Europe this summer. Hunter will be in my life whether you like it or not."

Dad is frowning. "You're supposed to take Molecular Biology in the summer," he reminds me.

Frustration seizes up all my muscles. For a moment I find myself too tense to move, let alone speak. I inhale again, willing myself to relax. I know from experience that temper tantrums don't work on my father. He's impenetrable to yelling. If you want to get through to my father, you need to use logic.

"I'm not taking that class," I tell him. "I'm not interested in taking any more sciences."

His brow furrows. "What are you saying?"

"I'm saying my brain is going to explode. I don't care about bio or chem or any of the pre-med courses I've been taking these past couple years." I lick my suddenly bone-dry lips. "I won't be going to med school after I graduate."

The ensuing silence is deafening. Nobody says a word, and yet my head is a cacophony of noise thanks to my shrieking pulse. Dad's shock is unmistakable, but I can't tell if he's angry.

"I'm not going to med school," I repeat. "This is something I've been thinking about since…well, pretty much since I started at Briar. I want to go to grad school, get my master's, get my doctorate. And while I do that, I can get a counseling degree and actually see patients—"

"Clients," he corrects stiffly. "There's a difference."

"Fine, whatever, it won't be patients. It's still *people*—people I'll be able to help. That's what I want to do," I finish, and when I realize my shoulders have sagged in defeat, I force myself to straighten up. Because fuck that, why should I be defeated? I'm proud of this decision.

Dad flicks up one bushy eyebrow. "What does your new boyfriend think about this?"

"He supports me one hundred percent."

"Of course he does," Dad sneers.

"Marcus," Mom says sharply, and I look over in gratitude. Maybe what I said got through to her a little.

"Is he the one who talked you out of going to med school?" my father demands.

"No. I told you, I've been struggling with this forever. I make my own decisions—Hunter just supports them. Unlike you." My chest clenches with disappointment. "Anyway. This is why I came home today. I wanted to tell you guys, in person, about the two very important life changes happening for me right now. I'm with somebody new and I'm pivoting career-wise. I'm sure there are lots of interesting specialties within psychiatry, but that's not the path I want to take." I pause. "Oh, and since I'm being extra honest right now—I don't like hoop earrings and I gave Pippa your birthday present because I'm never going to wear those earrings."

The dining room falls silent.

Mom rises and starts gathering up the dishes. Without a word, I help her. As we trudge silently into the kitchen, I notice that her eyes look moist.

"Are you crying?" I ask in concern.

She blinks hard, and her long eyelashes shimmer with tears. "I'm sorry, *mami*. I didn't realize… I…" She pauses, then tries again. "You know your father, Demi. He's an alpha male. And you're right, I defer to him a lot and I'm sorry for that. I should be forming my own opinion of your new boyfriend."

"Yes," I agree.

She rubs her knuckles beneath her wet eyes. "The next time you're in the city, why don't you bring him and we can go out for lunch or dinner?" she suggests, her voice soft. "How does that sound?"

"It sounds wonderful. Thank you," I say gratefully.

"As for the rest of it, you know I'll support you no matter what career you choose." She winks at me. "You could be a stripper and I'd be in the front row cheering you on—but please don't choose that path because I think your father might actually kill you."

I let out a shaky laugh. "Do you think he'll kill me for the med school thing?"

"He'll come around."

"You really believe that?"

"Absolutely." She sighs. "But I don't know if he'll ever forgive you for giving away your birthday gift. He picked those earrings out himself, Demi."

---

The journey home is timed perfectly. Hunter's game starts at eight, and the bus pulls into Hastings just before seven. That gives me plenty of time to go home, shower, and make my way to the hockey rink to meet Pippa, and Hunter's roommates. Well, except for Hollis and Rupi. They're away on a weekend trip, which is a relief because the arena is already loud enough without adding Rupi Miller's voice to it.

I do have one more task to complete, though. I've been thinking about it for days now, ever since Hunter told me he loved me.

I feel like a jerk for not saying it back, but I didn't want him to think the only reason I was saying it was because I was upset, or simply grateful that he wasn't cheating. When I do say it, I want to be calm and centered. I want him to look into my eyes and see the sincerity shining there when I tell him I love him. Because I do love him.

And when I love someone, my first instincts are to protect them, support them, encourage them to embrace their strengths and combat their weaknesses. I heard the confidence in Hunter's voice when he announced that he would never cheat on me, and it told me something important.

It told me he's starting to trust himself.

Sure, it helps that his season didn't fall apart after we started sleeping together, as he feared it might. But even if it had, I still think he would've learned these same lessons. That he's capable of staying faithful. He's capable of playing hockey and having a girlfriend, a sex life.

I truly believe he can succeed in the NHL without letting the lifestyle corrupt him. Don't get me wrong—I can see how it would freak him out. Garrett Graham can't leave his house without a disguise, for God's sake. And Garrett's girlfriend told me at the nightclub that there's a woman who lurks outside their city brownstone hoping to catch glimpses of him.

So yes, it's a daunting life. It's long stints away from your loved ones. It's sex on a platter. But I have faith in Hunter. And although he's finally starting to have faith in himself, he still needs one last push.

I pull up Brenna's number and gaze out the window as I wait for her to answer. The bus is about ten minutes from the station in Hastings.

"Hey," Brenna greets me. "Are we still good for tonight?"

"Of course. I'm going to take an Uber to campus and stop off at home first to shower and change, though. But I just had a quick question for you."

"What's up?"

"Do you have any way of contacting Garrett Graham?"

A beat. "Um. Yeah, I should be able to do that. Why?"

"I'm planning a surprise thing for Hunter," I answer vaguely. "I could use Garrett's help."

"Sure. I don't know if I have his cell saved in my phone, but Fitzy would definitely have it, or Summer's brother. I'll ask them."

"Thanks, chica. I'll see you in a bit."

The moment I get home, I strip off my clothes and take a hot shower, hoping to inject some warmth back into my bones. We've reached that hideous part of the winter where you can never, ever feel warm. February in New England is a glacial hellscape, the time of year when my mother and I are in wholehearted agreement. She hates the winter from start to finish, I hate it in February. It's like a Venn diagram and we're finally in the same circle, clinging to each other for body heat.

I bundle up in my terrycloth robe and approach my closet, debating what to wear. I'd like to look cute for Hunter if we're hanging out afterward, but the arena is so damn cold. Sure, there are heaters and enough bodies in the place to generate some heat, but it doesn't completely eliminate the chill.

I finally settle on thick leggings, thick socks, and a thick red sweater. Key word: thick. I look like a marshmallow, but oh well. Warmth trumps cuteness.

I'm about to start doing my makeup when my phone lights up. I hope it's not Hunter calling to ask how it went in Boston. He needs to focus on the game tonight, and hearing that my father and I aren't speaking right now probably won't pump him up for the playoffs. I'll tell him later.

But it's not Hunter; it's TJ. "Hey," I greet him. "Are you coming to the game? You never gave me an answer."

"No. I'm not."

"Ah. Okay. That sucks." I open my makeup case. "It would have been nice to see you."

"Really? Would it have?" His mocking voice ripples into my ear.

I furrow my brow. "Are you all right? You sound a bit drunk."

He just laughs.

My frown deepens. "Okay, then. Well. I'm getting ready right now, so tell me what's up, otherwise I'll call you tomorrow."

"Mmm-hmmm." He's still laughing, but it's tinged with hysteria.

"TJ." A queasy feeling tickles my stomach. "What the hell is going on?"

Silence. It lasts about three seconds, and just when I'm about to check if the call dropped, TJ starts babbling. He talks so fast I can barely keep up, and my constant interruptions—*"wait, what?"* *"What are you saying?"* *"What does that mean?"*—only agitate him further. By the time he winds down, I'm on the verge of throwing up.

I draw in a fearful breath. "Stay where you are. I'm on my way."

# 38
# HUNTER

EXCITEMENT SIZZLES IN THE AIR AS MY TEAMMATES AND I GEAR up. Whoever wins tonight will progress to the conference finals, so we're all feeling the pressure. Last season we made it to those finals, and I suffered a broken wrist thanks to a scorned boyfriend. This season my wrist is perfectly fine and my dick hasn't gotten me into an iota of trouble.

Beside me, Bucky is shoving his pants up to his hips, while babbling to Matt and Alec about some new radical therapies being used on athletes these days.

"Swear to God, this chamber looks like something they'd torture James Bond with. They blast you with liquid nitrogen to like minus-a-hundred-and-fifty degrees."

"And then what?" Alec sounds fascinated.

"Well, in theory it stimulates healing. In reality I think it just gives you frostbite?"

I glance over in amusement. "What's this you're talking about?"

"Cryotherapy," Bucky replies.

"Sounds intense," remarks Conor, who's sitting on the bench beside me. He lifts a hand and tucks his blond hair behind his ears.

"Dude," I tell him. "Not sure if anyone's told you this, but... you're treading pretty damn close to mullet territory."

From his locker, Matt hoots. "Bizness in front, party in the back, yo."

Conor just gives that easygoing shrug of his. Even being informed he's rocking a mullet doesn't faze this guy. I wish I could bottle up his confidence and sell it to pimply-faced teenage boys. We'd make a killing.

"You should cut it," Jesse advises. "It's a lady-boner killer."

Con rolls his eyes. "First off, there's nothing I could *ever* do that would kill a lady's boner."

He's probably right about that.

"And secondly, I can't cut it. Otherwise we'll lose the game."

"Shit," Jesse says, paling. "You're right."

Hockey players and their superstitions. Looks like Con ain't getting a haircut till April.

"Jesus *Christ*, what is that stench?" Coach demands from the doorway. He strides into the locker room, his nose wrinkled in repulsion.

I exchange a look with the guys. I don't smell anything, and everyone's blank expressions say they're equally stumped.

"It smells like a sulfur factory exploded," Coach growls.

"Oh," Bucky realizes. "Yeah, that's Pablo."

"The egg?"

I can't help but snicker. "Yup yup—"

"Don't fucking say yup yup, Davenport."

I ignore him. "—because that's what happens when you ask someone to take care of an egg for like five months. It goes rotten. We're all used to the smell now." I glance at Bucky, who's pulling Pablo Eggscobar out of his locker. "I thought you were keeping him in that zippered pouch to try to contain the stink."

At the current moment, Pablo is wrapped in numerous layers of cellophane, his pink drink-cozy stretched tightly around the plastic bundle. You can't even see his little pig face anymore because the odor-suppressing plastic wrap is an inch thick.

"I took him out because I felt bad for the guy, always being locked up like that. He's not a criminal."

Snorts and chuckles ring out in the locker room. Coach, however, is not amused.

"Give it to me," he orders, sticking out a meaty paw.

Bucky looks alarmed. He checks with me as if to ask, *should I?*

I shrug. "He's the boss."

The second Coach has our team mascot in hand, he marches over to the wastebasket by the door and unceremoniously dumps Pablo in the trash.

A strangled cry bursts out, courtesy of Bucky, followed by a widespread hush that lends a spooky air to the room.

I feel like the wind was just knocked out of me. Pablo's been a part of us for so long that I don't even know what to say. My teammates' stunned faces confirm they feel the same way.

Coach Jensen crosses his arms. "Congratulations, you passed the absurd task I didn't want to assign or think you'd remember to carry out. But—" His voice becomes gruff. "—you all showed some real teamwork and responsibility passing that egg around. And I'm a man of my word—I spoke to the dean and he said we might be able to make something happen with the pig."

Bucky looks ecstatic. "Seriously? We get the pig? Guys, we did it."

"Pablo the Pig," Jesse says slowly. "Doesn't have the same ring to it. We need a new name."

"Pablo Pigscobar," Conor and I blurt out in unison, then turn to each other, grinning.

"Oh Jesus," Matt says with a wail of laughter. "That's it, everybody stop talking. Nothing you say could ever top that."

The rest of the team is cackling their asses off. Even Coach's lips are twitching. But then he claps his hands to signal that Happy Time is over, and everyone resumes getting ready.

I'm about to slide my chest protector over my head when my

phone buzzes. I peer into my locker to see an incoming call from Garrett.

"Hey Coach," I call out. "Your favorite child Garrett Graham is on the line. Mind if I take this?"

He glances at the clock. We have thirty minutes before the puck drops. "Yes, but make it fast, Davenport. And tell him that was a brilliant play at the end of the third during yesterday's game against Nashville."

"Will do." The locker room's too damn loud, so I step out into the hallway, where I nod at the security guard standing there. Briar takes the protection of its athletes seriously.

"G," I answer, raising the phone to my ear. "What's up?"

"Hey, glad I caught you. I was worried you'd already shut your phone off."

"Aw. Calling to wish me good luck?"

There's a snort in my ear. "Nah, you don't need it. BU doesn't stand a chance."

Damn right they don't. They've been our toughest competitor this year, but I'm confident we can beat them. Granted, I would've preferred playing a softer opponent. Like Eastwood College, who, just as I suspected, couldn't pull their shit together despite their amazing goalie. Kriska can stop a thousand goals, but it won't help if his forwards aren't scoring any on the other net.

"Anyway, I'm with Landon in his office right now. He's headed for LA tonight and will be gone for two weeks, but he wanted to touch base with you before he leaves."

"Landon?" I have no clue who G is talking about.

"Landon McEllis? My agent—but that word isn't allowed to be spoken right now, so pretend I never said it. In fact, we're not having this conversation at all, okay?"

"Okay? Why are you calling exactly?"

"Because I was just talking to Demi and she said you were hoping to sign with a franchise after graduation."

I almost drop the phone. "What?" When the hell did he speak to Demi?

"Yeah, she and I spoke at length about it. She was wondering if you'd need an agent in order to do that, and I explained that technically you can't have an agent while you're in an NCAA program. But I was with Landon when she called, and he wanted to have a quick chat with you. Just remember—this conversation ain't happening."

I understand his need for secrecy. NCAA athletes aren't allowed any contact with sports agents. Even guys who've already been drafted are required to officially end their player-agent relationship for the duration of their college careers.

That's the official party line, anyway. In every sport, there's a fair bit of shadiness behind the scenes. But it's important to be careful.

"I'm putting you on speaker now," Garrett says. "Cool?"

"Sure." I'm still a tad dazed.

"Hunter, hey. This is Landon McEllis."

"Hello, sir."

"Can it with the sir stuff—call me Landon." He chuckles. "Listen, when G mentioned you might be in the market for an agent next year, I just about jumped out of my chair and dove for the phone."

Damned if that doesn't puff up my chest a little.

"I wanted to introduce myself," he goes on. "Unofficially, of course."

I try not to laugh. "Of course."

"And I won't beat around the bush—you're one of the top college players in the country. If you're interested in going pro, I can put together a deal for you without even lifting a pinky."

"Really?" I know it's far easier for the eighteen-and nineteen-year-old guys to land somewhere big. But I'll be twenty-two when I graduate. Yup, I'm getting up there in my years, an old man at the current age of twenty-one. But athletic careers have short life spans.

"Absolutely. And look, I can't sign you right now, and we can't speak again after tonight. But I just wanted to gauge your interest, find out which other agents you might be considering."

"I'm not considering other agents," I admit. Hell, I didn't expect to hear from *this* agent. I don't know whether to be pissed at Demi's interference, or eternally grateful for it. I could get in trouble with the university if anyone found out Landon and I were even having this conversation.

"Then you're interested," he says.

"Definitely." Even if I had a dozen agents knocking on my door, Landon McEllis would still be at the top of the list. His client roster is staggering, and Garrett's said nothing but good things about him.

"Perfect, then we're on the same page." He chuckles again. "I'll touch base with you next year."

"Sounds great. Thank you, sir—Landon."

"Kick ass tonight," Garrett's voice chirps in my ear. "I'll talk to you later."

"Later, G." I hang up. Once again I feel winded, as I stand there staring at my phone. Fuckin' Demi. That woman is literally the best thing that's ever happened to me.

"Davenport," booms a deep voice.

The universe has a real sense of humor, because the moment I think about Demi, her father appears like a scary apparition.

I stare in confusion, because either I'm hallucinating it, or that's actually Marcus Davis at the other end of the hall.

A second security guard is preventing him from entering. The university started taking more precautions after one too many troublemakers snuck into the team locker rooms. It never happened in my day, but Dean said that when he was a freshman, a rival team smuggled in a duffel full of chocolate syrup containers and sprayed the brown sauce all over our locker room. When the Briar players showed up before the game, they thought there was actually diarrhea dripping down the walls.

"Hey, it's okay," I call to the guard. "I know him."

The guard steps aside, and Dr. Davis comes stalking toward me in all his terrifying glory. Jeez, he is a *big* man. Ironically, he's only two, maybe three inches taller than me, but he's built like Dwayne the Rock Johnson, and looks twice my size. It boggles the mind that this enormous man spends his days performing delicate surgeries in an operating room. But never judge a book by its cover, right?

"Hello, sir." I brace myself for his response—I suspect it won't be pleasant. I haven't seen him since our very short, very awkward brunch back in January, when he made his dislike for me crystal clear.

"It's time we have a talk," Dr. Davis retorts. "Man to man."

I swallow a sigh. "I would love to do that, sir, but I've got a game starting in about twenty minutes. Maybe we could postpone this until tomorrow?"

"No. We can't. I take matters regarding my daughter very seriously."

"So do I," I say simply. "She means a lot to me."

"Does she? Is that why you're encouraging her to throw her future away?" Ice hardens his tone, and his harsh features are even more forbidding when he's pissed.

Evidently Demi's trip to Boston didn't go as well as she'd hoped.

"She's not throwing her future away," I reply in a careful tone. "She's staying in the same field, just taking a different direction to get there."

"Do you know how much a psychiatrist makes on average? Over two hundred K annually. Two seventy-five, on the top end. Want to compare that to a clinical psychologist? Or better yet, a run-of-the-mill therapist? There's one of those on every street corner."

"Demi doesn't care about money. And she doesn't want an MD. She wants to get a doctorate."

"Look, son, where do you get off dictating my daughter's life choices?"

"I'm not dictating her life choices. If anything, *she's* the dictator in our relationship." I can't help but snort. "Have you met your daughter? She's the bossiest person on the planet."

For one fleeting second a flicker of humor lights his eyes, and I think maybe, just *maybe*, he's softening. But it's gone in a flash, and his face turns to stone again.

"I don't trust you," he says tightly.

I let out a tired breath. "With all due respect, sir, you don't even know me."

"You and my daughter are too different. She's—"

The door behind me flies open without warning. I expect Coach's furious face to appear, so I'm already uttering, "I'm sorry, I—" when I realize I'm looking at Matt.

Matty is startled to find a beefy bald man looming over me, but then he shakes himself out of it. "Dude, you need to get in here right *now*." He waves his phone under my nose. "It's fucking chaos."

I knit my brows. "What is?"

"Shit's going down at Bristol House. There's two people up on the roof, and it looks like they're going to jump. Someone's live-tweeting it, and a chick on the top floor of Hartford House managed to snap a picture." Matt thrusts the phone in my hand. "One of them is your girl."

# 39
# DEMI

NONE OF THE DORMITORIES ON CAMPUS OFFER ROOF ACCESS TO their residents. In fact, it's explicitly disallowed, which is understandable. The administration doesn't want raucous parties up there. Drunken kids accidentally falling to their deaths.

Or, in rare cases, *not* accidentally.

Most schools have safeguards against this shit. Locks that only the maintenance staff has keys for. Some of the newer dorms require keycards to access the roofs. But Bristol House is known for its lax security. The door to the roof is old, and the lock is easy to pick. If you live in the dorms, as I did in freshman year, it's common knowledge how easy it is to sneak up to Bristol's roof. Most residents stay under the radar, usually going up there to smoke weed or have sex. It's widely understood that if you use Bristol's roof, you don't make a big production out of it.

TJ, however, apparently never got the memo.

And I've never been more afraid in my life as I stare at my friend standing up on the ledge, his thin body silhouetted in the dark night.

"TJ, please." My voice cracks. It's been difficult to speak since I got here. No, even before that. Since he called twenty minutes ago and informed me he was going to kill himself.

How the *fuck* did I not see the signs?

I'm planning on becoming a psychologist and I couldn't fucking tell that one of my close friends was *suicidal*?

I want to cry. I truly hadn't realized TJ was suffering. Yes, he gets moody every now and then, but not once since I've known him, not even *once*, has he expressed feelings of hopelessness or talked about suicide. He might've displayed anxious tendencies, but not suicidal ones.

So far, all of my attempts to talk him off the ledge have failed. I don't know how to get through to him.

"TJ," I plead. "Come down from there."

"Why do you care?" he spits out. "You don't care about anyone but yourself."

His harsh words sting, but I banish my own emotions from this equation. This isn't about me. TJ is clearly going through something.

*Going through something?* a voice in my head shrieks. *Understatement of the fucking year!*

My heart is jammed in my throat, liable to choke me. The rooftop is covered in ice, because nobody ever comes up here to lay down salt. To make matters exponentially worse, it's starting to snow, and the wind is picking up. One misstep and he'll—

*Do NOT even go there!*

"TJ, please get off of there and come back," I beg. "Come talk to me."

"No. I don't want to talk. I fucking hate *talking*, Demi."

"I know you do," I whisper.

I edge closer to him. The synapses in my brain are firing in total panic mode, trying to catalogue the red flags I'd missed.

TJ's always been antisocial, but he also made an effort to go out with me, to socialize with my friends. He didn't isolate himself from everyone, so I didn't consider it a red flag. He barely drinks, doesn't abuse drugs, so no red flag there. He has trouble opening up to people, expressing his emotions—but that's not unique. Corinne is equally guarded, and I didn't peg her as suicidal either.

God. I don't know what to do.

I truly don't.

This isn't a class project, or a fucking true crime show. This is real life, and I'm utterly helpless.

I try again. "Listen, it's obvious you've been drinking—"

"No, I haven't." His voice is unnervingly composed.

I bite my lip. Shit. He's sober? He's literally standing on a ledge, four stories off the ground, and he's stone-cold sober?

I suddenly hear the wail of sirens in the distance. My heart jumps. Is this about us? Did someone spot us up here and call the police? God, I want the police to come. I want them to bring one of those negotiators who talks to potential jumpers and convinces them not to commit suicide.

I'm not equipped to handle this.

The wind snakes under my hair and makes it flap around me like a panicky bird. I didn't even grab a coat when I ran out of my house. I'm in my red sweater and leggings and boots, and it's so cold outside I feel the chill in my lungs. I can't even imagine how cold TJ must be—he's in a thin T-shirt. His slight build could get knocked over by a strong gust. And judging by the snowflakes falling and swirling wildly in the air, that gust could come any second.

"Okay," I say weakly. "Okay. If you're not going to come down, then I'm coming up."

"Stay away, Demi." TJ's shoulders set in a tense line. "Seriously. I'll do it."

I clench my teeth, in fear, not anger, and inch closer to the ledge. "I don't want you to," I tell him, as my heart drums a terrified rhythm on my ribcage. "First I want to talk to you. After that, we can discuss your next move."

"There's nothing to talk about. Go back to your new boyfriend."

I reach the ledge. And almost throw up when I glimpse the thin layer of white frost spanning the cement. At least I hope it's just frost, and not a solid stretch of ice.

"Is that what this is about, then?" I ask quietly. "Me and Hunter?"

"Yes, I'm standing here about to jump to my death because of you and Hunter. Christ, Demi! You are *so* fucking self-absorbed."

I flinch. Then I suck in a gulp of frigid air and lift one foot onto the ledge. It slips on my first attempt. Fuck, that *is* ice. Oh Lord. What am I fucking doing right now?

*Saving your friend. He needs help.*

Yes. TJ needs help.

I take another breath.

The second time, I manage to climb up. And then I'm standing beside him, and I make the mistake of looking down and oh my fuck, looking down was a *terrible* idea.

I inhale through the rush of dizziness that hits me. Inhale. Then exhale. I force myself to keep breathing. I don't look down again. But the image has already been branded in my brain. That huge drop. No grass or bushes down there, either. Nothing but pavement.

My breath escapes in frantic white puffs. That was legit the scariest sight I'd ever seen.

But what's even scarier is the thought of losing TJ. I may not have heard his cries for help before, but I sure as hell am hearing them now.

"Get *down*," he snaps at me, but the anger has left his voice. It's been replaced by worry. Desperation. "You could get hurt."

"So could you. And I'm not getting down until you do."

"Really? Suddenly you care so much about me?"

"I've always cared about you, TJ. You're one of my best friends."

*Do not look down again, Demi. Do not—*

I glance down again and almost puke. Four stories is, what, fifty feet? Why does it seem so much higher from where we are? I never thought fifty feet was so fucking high.

"Best friends," TJ scoffs. "Do you know how patronizing that is?"

"What, calling you my friend? I've known you since freshman year, TJ."

"Exactly! Freshman year! That means I waited almost three years for you to wake up and see what a douchebag Nico was."

The wind ruffles our hair. This time I refuse to take another peek over the edge.

"And then you broke up with that asshole, and I gave you space and time to heal. I thought, just be patient, man. We have this connection and I thought, she's finally going to see what was in front of her fucking eyes for *three years*." Anguish clouds his face. "I thought you would come to *me* after you dumped Nico and instead you go for that fucking hockey asshole?"

I don't defend Hunter. I'm scared it will trigger TJ to take drastic measures. But I do hedge in with a soft observation. "I thought you said this wasn't about me."

"Fine, I guess it is. Not entirely, but part of it. I'm just tired of being fucking invisible. Invisible to you, invisible to my family. My parents are obsessed with my brother and his big fancy job in London and I'm just an afterthought to everybody, if I even cross their fucking minds. Which I highly doubt."

"That's not true." I met his parents once and they seemed to really love their son. Appearances can be deceiving, I know that. But my gut says that TJ's parents would fly into a panic if they knew what their son was considering doing right now.

"I don't think you're giving yourself enough credit," I tell him.

The sirens get louder.

TJ stiffens. He shifts his feet and I instinctively brace myself for the worst. But then he rights himself, and I'm so dizzyingly relieved that I nearly lose bladder function and pee my pants.

I have literally not moved an inch since I climbed up here. I'm a statue on this ledge. It's two feet wide, so it's not like my toes are dangling over the edge, but I feel like I'm balancing on a paper clip.

"Why didn't you ever talk to me about any of this? Feeling ignored by your parents, feeling inferior to your brother, feeling like you wanted to…" *Die.* I don't say it out loud. I bite hard on the inside of my cheek. "You know I would've been there for you. Why didn't you ask for help?"

"Why did you pick him?" he says instead of addressing my question.

"It wasn't a matter of picking." I sigh wearily. "It's not like you and Hunter were both there in front of me and I needed to choose between you. He and I were friends, and it just developed into something more—"

"You and I are friends—why didn't *we* develop into something more?" Hurt and betrayal darken his eyes.

Fuck, that was the wrong thing to say. "I don't know," I say simply. "Chalk it up to chemistry, I guess. I have chemistry with him."

"And not with me?"

What do I do now? Lie? Get his hopes up just to get him off this ledge?

But that feels disingenuous and cruel. Also, I think he'll be able to see through me. I don't have romantic feelings for TJ. I never have.

I decide to be honest, because that's who I am. "I don't feel any sexual chemistry with you," I admit. "I think you're attractive—"

"Bullshit," he spits.

"I do," I insist. " You have the kindest eyes, and a great butt."

He hesitates, as if trying to assess whether I'm lying.

"But I also objectively think Liam Hemsworth is gorgeous and I have no desire to sleep with him. I can't explain chemistry. Some people have it, and some don't."

"Chemistry," he echoes. Pain twists his features. "Why don't I have it with anybody?"

"Can I hazard a guess?"

He gives me a sharp look.

"You just said that for the past three years you've been waiting for me to break up with Nico. Stands to reason, then, that you haven't been putting yourself out there. In almost three years, you've only gone on one date, as far as I know—the sorority sister I set you up with. If you're closed off to the potential of dating anyone, you're not going to find anyone."

"I'm not closed off." But he sounds unconvinced.

The wind rustles my hair again, and shivers break out at the nape of my neck and scurry down my spine like rats fleeing a sinking ship. I wish I could flee, too. It's so cold up here. But I'm not leaving this roof without TJ. I'll stand up here all night if I have to.

"Yes, you were," I tell him. "And I get it, okay? Pining over a girl with a boyfriend sucks. Even worse, it means you're not giving out the vibes you should be transmitting. You wasted almost three years, TJ. But, and here's the good part, you still have a year and a half left of college. You've got plenty of time to put yourself out there."

"I'm done putting myself out there," he argues. "Not after you."

I swallow my frustration. It doesn't seem to occur to him that he never actually put himself on the line for me, never once expressed his emotions to me—he just stood there passively waiting for me to notice that he had a crush on me. I guess that was easier for him than putting his feelings out there.

But why didn't I notice, dammit? Misery crawls up my throat as I think back to all the times Nico, and even Hunter, told me that TJ liked me. I didn't see it.

Or maybe I didn't *want* to see it.

Maybe, like TJ, like everyone else in this world, I chose to take the easy way out. Subconsciously, anyway. Maybe it was easier to remain blind to TJ's true feelings, categorize him as a needy friend, instead of processing what those feelings might mean for our friendship.

"TJ," I say softly, and for the first time in five minutes—I move. I hold my hand out to him. My fingers are shaking harder than they've ever shaken. I'm so afraid I feel like it's inevitable I'm going to pee my pants.

He stares at my visibly trembling hand, unhappiness in his eyes as he brushes snowflakes off his face. "You're scared," he mutters. "I don't want you to be scared."

"Then come down from this ledge with me," I plead.

He doesn't answer.

I let my hand drop, pressing it tight to my side once again.

The faint murmur of voices drifts up toward us. A crowd has gathered below. I can make out uniformed officers, and I wonder if the one who arrested me and Hunter is down there. Officer Jenk. That jerk. An ambulance and several police cruisers have pulled up to the small parking lot in front of the dormitory.

"There's nothing for me here," TJ mumbles. "I'd rather just be dead than deal with this stupid shitty life anymore."

"You might not die," I point out.

"We're four stories up. That's like a fifty-foot drop."

"A fall from four or five stories has about a fifty-percent chance of survival. A hundred feet, sure, you'd probably die." I arch a brow. "But most falls from this height aren't fatal."

His eyes flash. "I'm not in the mood to listen to your bullshit statistics, Demi."

"It's not bullshit. I was literally just talking about this with my father tonight."

"Why the hell would you be talking about that?"

"Because Dad operated on a man who fell about sixty feet from an apartment window. He was trying to sneak a cigarette without his wife finding out, so he was leaning out the window and lost his balance. Fell headfirst to the pavement." I swallow. "Do you want me to tell you what happened to him?"

"He survived his big adventure and even though his wife divorced him for smoking behind her back, he's now living happily ever after with the hot nurse who gave him sponge baths," TJ says sarcastically. "Moral of the story: life is always worth living. Nice try, Demi."

I give a humourless laugh. "No. He survived the fall, but suffered a skull fracture, which led to a subdural hematoma. My father operated but the damage was too severe. He's still alive, but he's badly brain damaged. He'll never live a regular life again. Oh, and he's blind in one eye because the fall severed his ocular nerve. It's still too early to tell the extent of cognitive damage, but Dad isn't hopeful."

TJ looks stunned. He goes scarily silent, his gaze glued to the ground below us.

The flashing red and blue lights slice through the darkness. Thick clouds obscure the moon, and the falling snow is a blinding array of white against the backdrop of the inky sky. Despite the crowd gathered in front of Bristol House, it feels like TJ and I are the only two people in the world right now.

My stomach is in knots as I rack my brain wondering what else to say. How to help him. "So," I say softly. "Here we are."

Pain flickers across his face. "Here we are."

# 40
# HUNTER

I HAVE NO FUCKING IDEA WHAT'S GOING ON AS I CHARGE INTO THE locker room. The guys are all suited up. I'm the only one half-dressed and I don't give two shits right now. Demi's father is on my heels, startling every single one of my teammates by his appearance.

Coach's eyebrows fly up. "Who's this?" he demands.

"This is Demi's father," I explain. "Dr. Marcus Davis."

"Wow," Bucky blurts out, gaping at the newcomer. "You got here fast! This news literally just broke."

"What exactly is going on?" Dr. Davis demands, ignoring everyone but the other adult in the room.

Jensen sticks out a hand. "Chad Jensen, and I'm afraid I can't answer that for you. All we have is a grainy picture on a phone."

"It's Demi," I say through gritted teeth.

Dr. Davis nods grimly. "That's my daughter. Where is this place exactly? Bristol House?"

"It's a dorm on the west side of campus," Matt supplies. "Ten-minute walk, two minute drive."

Dr. Davis is already back at the door. "Davenport," he barks. "I need you to show me where it is."

My feet stay rooted to the floor. Because…the team's about to hit the ice. This game determines who goes to our conference finals, and from there it's on to the national tournament. The Frozen Four.

But I can't play hockey right now. My girlfriend is up on a goddamn roof in the middle of February, trying to talk down a *suicide jumper*. I skimmed several tweets in the stream Matt showed me, and it doesn't sound like it's just two people simply hanging out up there. TJ is clearly threatening to jump.

I rake both hands through my hair. My fingers are shaking wildly. I'm geared up in my lower pads, hockey pants, and socks. But up top I'm in a wife-beater. My shoulder and elbow pads spill haphazardly out of my locker. My chest protector is on the bench.

Swallowing hard, I sweep my gaze around the room. I'm about to break every rule in the captain's handbook.

I wanted to be a good captain. I wanted to put the team first, support my guys, be patient with them, follow all the rules I've been compiling since the season started. I promised myself I wouldn't let girls interfere with hockey, and now I'm about to throw the rulebook out the window…for a girl.

But there is literally no other choice here for me. Guys like Garrett, Dean, Logan—I think they'd understand. I think they'd never put sports ahead of their women. So if my team hates me, so be it. All I know is, if Demi's in trouble, then she comes first.

"Guys." My voice is rough. "I'm sorry. I can't play tonight."

Nobody utters a word.

Guilt spirals through me and forms a tight pretzel in the pit of my stomach. "Trust me," I continue desperately, "I don't want to miss this game, but even if I went out there right now and played, I would only be a detriment to you. My head isn't here, it's with Demi. I won't be able to concentrate until I know she's safe and—"

"She just climbed onto the ledge," Matt blurts out, his eyes glued to his phone screen.

Dr. Davis freezes in the doorway. I'm sure the sheer terror in his eyes reflects my own.

"She did what?" I demand. "What's happening now?"

"I dunno. This tweet just says there's now two people up on the ledge. No other deets."

My heart pounds so fast I feel faint. I suck in an unsteady breath, then scrub my hand through my hair again. I want to tear it out. "I'm sorry," I tell my team. "I need to go."

"Dude, why the fuck are you sorry?" Matt demands.

"And why the fuck are you still here?" drawls Conor. The lazy tone is belied by the serious glint in his eyes.

I wearily glance at Coach, who offers a brisk nod. Then I snatch my sneakers off the floor and race out of the locker room.

---

"This is it," I announce five minutes later, concern and impatience warring inside me. "The lot entrance is up there on the right."

But when we try to turn into the parking lot, we find the Hastings police sectioned it off. Across the lot, I spot an ambulance and three police cruisers, along with two campus security cars.

I curse in frustration. "Just stop here on the side of the road. If you get towed, I'll just give you my car, okay?"

He's as impatient as I am as we dive out of his BMW. The winter chill slaps me in the face, same way it did when we'd barrelled out of the arena. It's freezing out. Yet it's not the temperature that's making my bones ache. It's fear. Pure, paralyzing terror.

When I gaze up at the roof of Bristol House, a hiss of horror flies out. "Jesus."

"Oh my God," Dr. Davis says at the same time. He lets out a tortured moan, and when I look over he's covering his eyes with the back of his hand, as if he can't bear to look again. Then his arm drops limply and he gives a determined nod. "Let's go."

We hurry forward, but the police roped off the scene. The *scene*. Christ, I'm already viewing this as the scene of a crime. Or rather, a potentially devastating accident.

I stare up again, my throat tightening to the point of asphyxiation. Although Demi's dark hair is blowing in the wind, she stands as motionless as a statue. She's in a red sweater and black leggings, and she looks so small and vulnerable up there. I wish I could hear her voice or see her eyes.

Beside her, TJ is in a T-shirt and sweats, his skinny arms planted firmly at his sides.

They're talking. I don't know what they're saying. I don't *care* what they're saying. I want to go up there and pull that little asshole off the ledge—and then throw him the fuck over it for endangering Demi's life.

I force myself to take a breath. Then I notice that Demi's father is about to hurl himself over the blockade, despite the protests of the young officer who's attempting to stop him.

"You can't go beyond this point, sir!"

My gaze flies toward the cop's face. I *know* that guy. What was his name again? Alberts? Albertson!

"That's his daughter," I explain, stepping between the two males. Albertson's eyes widen when he recognizes me. "And she's my girlfriend. You know her, Albertson—she was the one in the holding cell with me."

Dr. Davis turns to glower at me. "What holding cell?"

I wave off the question. "Please. Albertson." Somehow my voice sounds calm.

The uniformed man throws a discreet glance over his shoulder, then dips his head in a tiny nod and allows us to rush past him.

We skid to a stop about twenty yards from the entrance of the dormitory. Near the front doors, several officers are engaged in intent conversation with a man in a suit. The dean, I realize. Other faculty members are also present, along with a small crowd of observers that the cops are trying to corral to one area.

Dr. Davis grabs my arm suddenly. I flinch, because his steel grip is definitely going to leave a bruise. "Do you know how to get up there?" he demands.

I hesitate. Because I *do* know. It's not a well-kept secret that Bristol is the place to go if you want to hang out on the roof and smoke J's. But the wild look in his eyes tells me it's not a wise idea for him to be anywhere near Demi right now. Hell, I can barely keep my own cool, and she's my girlfriend. I can't imagine how I'd feel if I was looking up there at my *daughter*.

Fear and desperation form a lethal cocktail in my bloodstream. My hands won't quit shaking. I can barely stay upright without stumbling, and my bare arms are covered with goose pimples.

"Even if I did, there's no way the cops are letting us enter that building. I think we're gonna have to stay out here."

Rage burns hot in his dark eyes. "And you claim to give a shit about my daughter?"

"I do give a shit." I exhale weakly. "Dr. Davis. Marcus. Look at her—look at them."

His anger dissolves into agony as he tilts his head back. His scalp is shiny under the glow of the streetlamp at the foot of the path.

"Trust her," I urge.

He blinks. "What?"

"Just trust her. I know you want to run up there and storm the roof, but all you're going to do is scare the shit out of TJ. Trust me, if I was up on that ledge and *you* came out…?" I shake my head in warning. "You'll make things worse, I promise you that. I know how much you love your daughter—I mean, you drove all the way from Boston to order me to stay away from her. Which I still don't understand, by the way, because I've done nothing but love that girl with all my heart. And because I love her, I have faith in her."

He visibly gulps. His massive Adam's apple bobs like there's a whole other entity in his throat.

"She's so smart," I tell him. "And she knows what she's doing—she and I spent the entire semester working on a project that required her to pretend to be my therapist. If anyone can get through to TJ, it's her. Trust her."

All the fight seems to drain out of him. His massive shoulders sag.

After a second of hesitation, I reach over and touch his arm reassuringly.

His eyes narrow at first, but then his expression softens. "You do love her," he says brusquely.

"Yes."

We both turn our attention back to Demi. Time ceases to exist. It's frozen like the air. Frozen like the ground beneath my feet. Frozen like the fear in my heart. Minutes pass, or maybe it's hours. Days. I don't know.

What I do know is that I don't breathe easy until Demi finally takes TJ's hand and safely helps him off the ledge.

# 41
# DEMI

I'M IN SHOCK. MY ENTIRE BODY IS ICE-COLD AND TREMBLING LIKE a leaf in a windstorm. My eyes are blinking and in focus, but I don't see anything. My ears are working but no sounds register. When I exit the front doors of Bristol House and spot Hunter and my father standing off to the side, I assume they're not real. A figment of my imagination, a product of my shock. So I keep walking with my arm around TJ.

"Demi."

I stop. Because that *did* sound real. That sounded like my father.

But the cops are now closing in on us, distracting me from my dad. TJ looks as shocked as I feel, panic swamping his eyes when one of the officers tries to lead him toward the ambulance.

"I don't need to go to the hospital," he protests. "*Demi.*"

"Yes, you do," I say quietly, giving him a tight squeeze. "You need to talk to somebody about what happened tonight."

"I talked to you."

He did, but I've done as much as I can. The fact that he seriously contemplated suicide and took action to try to implement it, is beyond my capabilities. Plus, he has no choice but to go to the hospital. They'll probably admit him into the psych ward and keep him under observation for seventy-two hours to ensure he doesn't harm himself or others.

"I'll come and see you the moment I can," I assure him. "I promise."

That gets me a weak nod. He's in a total daze as he follows the cop toward the waiting ambulance.

I turn around, and the next thing I know, my father's huge arms envelop me whole. I was already having trouble breathing. Now I'm choking.

"Dad, please," I wheeze desperately. "I can't breathe."

It's with great reluctance that he releases me and sets me on my feet. I blink and then I'm being hugged again, not as violently as before but with an equal amount of emotion.

"You have no idea how worried we were," Hunter says hoarsely.

Dad makes a guttural noise as he nods in grim agreement.

"I don't understand," I say slowly. "Why are you here?"

"Someone snapped a picture of you on the roof and a bunch of people are tweeting about it," Hunter explains.

"No, not you." I stare at my father. "Why are *you* here? Why aren't you in Boston?"

"I came to…" He stops for a beat, and Hunter smoothly finishes his sentence.

"To see you."

My dad smiles wryly. "No, kid, I don't need you to cover my ass." He shrugs. "I came here to tell him to stop seeing you."

"*Dad.*" My jaw drops.

"I know, sweetheart. I'm sorry. I just…" He drags a hand over his bald skull. "You're my baby girl. You'd just had your heart broken and I didn't want it to happen again. Nico hurt you, and then I saw who you went out and picked right afterward?" He tips his head at Hunter. "Rich boy, hotshot athlete? In my experience those two qualities indicate a player. Seemed like a recipe for another broken heart," he growls protectively, "and I wasn't gonna let that happen to you."

"I'm sure you had the best intentions, but Hunter's not a player. And like I told you earlier, we're together now, and you're just going to have to deal with it. You could either make this hard on everyone, or you could accept that this is my new boyfriend. And yes he's a rich hockey player, but—*oh my fucking God*!" I suddenly burst out.

"Demi, language."

My upset gaze swings toward Hunter, and for the first time in five minutes I realize he's wearing the lower half of his hockey uniform. "What are you doing here? What time is it?" I scramble to get my phone out of my pocket. "It's eight-thirty! Your game started at eight!"

"Yeah, I know."

His careless shrug triggers another rush of panic. "Then why aren't you playing? What the *fuck* are you doing here?"

"Language."

"Dad, I swear to God!"

Hunter's lips twitch as he reaches for my hand. "Babe. Do you honestly think I would just suit up and play hockey while you're standing on a ledge a hundred feet off the ground—"

"Fifty feet—"

"—A *thousand* feet off the ground, with a dude threatening to jump? One, that speaks volumes about how little you think of me. And two…well, I don't have a two, okay? One is bad enough. Fuck's sake, Demi."

"Language," my dad chides.

Hunter dons a sheepish smile. "Sorry, sir."

"You need to get to the arena," I order. "We need to get him to the arena." And then I'm hurrying past them. "Where's your car, Dad?"

He leads the way to his silver BMW, and I'm amazed to discover that the engine is still running, both driver and passenger door are thrown open, and the vehicle's back bumper is sticking out toward the road. Wow. They must've *really* been worried.

Dad slides behind the wheel, with Hunter next to him, and me in the middle of the backseat.

"I can't believe you're not on the ice right now," I say in dismay.

"You mean more to me than hockey," he says simply, and damned if that doesn't make my heart expand. "Get it through your stubborn head."

I lean toward him and reach for his hand. He grips mine tightly, and I know he must feel how icy my fingers are.

"You have no idea how scared I was," he says roughly.

"Not as scared as I was," I admit.

Dad peers sharply at me. "Are you sure you don't want to go to the hospital and get checked out?"

"I'm fine. Just in shock." I bite hard on my lower lip. "I was so afraid he was going to do it. You have no idea."

Briar's hockey facility comes into view. Dad bypasses the parking lot and stops directly out front. To my dismay, Hunter doesn't immediately dive out of the car.

Instead, he twists to meet my eyes. "I knew you'd be able to help him."

"Help him?" Anguish clogs my throat. "I didn't even see that he needed help, Hunter. How did I miss all the signs? And what kind of shrink am I going to be if I can't even see the warning signs in my own friends?"

"A brilliant shrink," Dad replies, his tone stern. "Human beings aren't infallible, sweetheart. Sometimes we make mistakes. Sometimes we fail. I've lost more patients on that table than my conscience can handle, but you? You didn't lose your friend tonight. You saved him." Dad gestures toward Hunter. "And he's right—he knew you'd be okay. I was seconds away from scaling the building like Spider-Man to rescue you, but your boyfriend here convinced me to have faith."

"In what?"

"In you," Hunter answers, and he and Dad exchange an awkward smile.

I'm touched to see it. "Mom says she wants to take me and

Hunter out the next time we're in the city," I say after a beat of hesitation. "Maybe you could join us and we'll have a redo of the brunch?"

My father nods. "I'll be there."

"Thank you." I turn to Hunter. "And thank you for coming to save me. With that said—get out of this car, Monk. Now. If you hurry, you could probably get ready in time to play in the second period." My teeth dig into my lip again. "Would you be horribly upset if I didn't go in and watch the game? I need some time to process what happened tonight. Just...decompress, you know? And I want to call my mom."

Hunter cups my cheek. "It's absolutely fine. Maybe you and your dad can grab a coffee and get you warmed up? Your hands are freezing." He glances at my father expectantly.

Dad replies with a firm nod. "I'll take care of her. Go play your game, kid."

"I'll come find you afterward," I promise Hunter.

He leans in to plant a chaste kiss on my lips, then hops out of the car. Tears fill my eyes as I watch him dart toward the entrance of the arena.

"It's fine," Dad says gruffly. "I'm sure his absence didn't hurt his team too ba—"

"I'm not crying because of that," I interrupt between sniffles. "I don't even know why I'm crying. The tears just started pouring for no reason."

"Not for no reason. The shock is wearing off, and it's finally hitting you—the gravity of what happened tonight." My father's smile is tinged with sadness. "Come up here in the front, sweetheart, and we'll go somewhere and talk. Okay?"

I rub my tear-streaked cheeks, then nod and reach for the door handle. "Thanks for being here, Daddy."

"Always."

# 42
# DEMI

I FEEL LIKE I'VE RUN TWO MARATHONS AND GONE TO WAR ALL IN one night by the time Hunter and I walk through his front door later.

His team won the game, so everybody is out celebrating tonight. But we decided to bail on the after party, along with Summer and Fitz. And Brenna, who said she'd rather Skype with her boyfriend than "deal with a bunch of horny drunk boys slobbering all over her."

The house is pitch black and dead silent as the entire group files inside.

"Okay, this is fucking creepy," Brenna remarks.

"It doesn't feel right when they're not here," Summer agrees.

"Who?" I ask. "Hollis and Rupi?"

"Yeah." Summer vaguely waves a hand over the shadowy hallway. "Listen to it."

I wrinkle my nose. "To what?"

"Exactly!"

As we enter the living room, the haunting, albeit tinny notes of a familiar song waft out of Brenna's phone. It's Simon and Garfunkel's "The Sound of Silence." I burst out laughing as she solemnly holds it up for all to hear.

She has a point, though. This is the quietest I've ever heard this house. "Where did they go, anyway?" I ask.

"No idea," Hunter replies. "Hollis said it was a surprise."

"A surprise for who?"

"For Rupi."

"So then why couldn't he tell the rest of you?" I counter.

"Because it was a surprise."

I let out a sigh. "I don't understand that guy."

"Nobody does," Brenna says frankly. "Don't waste any more brain cells trying to."

"Anyway, if you'll excuse us," Hunter announces, "Semi and I are heading up to bed. She's had a tough night."

"I'm so sorry you had to go through that," Summer says sympathetically. She and I aren't super close, but she surprises me with a hug tight enough to steal the breath from my lungs.

"Thank you. It was terrifying, not gonna lie."

"I hope your friend is going to be okay," Fitz says gruffly.

"Me too." I wonder what the shrinks at the hospital will make of TJ's mental state. I think he's suffering from depression, and he definitely has dangerously low feelings of self-worth. I hope whoever he talks to will provide him with the help and guidance he needs.

I'm sure the school or the police already contacted his family, and I'm planning on seeing him the moment he's allowed visitors. TJ was always there for me when I needed to talk, when I needed someone to listen, and I plan on doing the same for him.

But tonight I don't want to spend another second reliving what happened on that roof. Dad and I discussed it at length over a cup of coffee in my kitchen, and the pride shining in his eyes when I described talking TJ off the ledge made my heart clench with emotion. I hope he eventually accepts my decision to forgo medical school. Maybe one day he'll be proud of that too.

I check my phone as we enter Hunter's room. A million messages await me. Pippa, Corinne, Darius, Pax, my mom, and even one from Nico, who I unblocked after Christmas. It says he heard about TJ, he's glad we're both all right, and that I'm a very good friend. It's a sweet message, and I make a mental note to reply to him, and everyone else, tomorrow.

"Congratulations on your win," I tell Hunter.

"Congratulations on saving someone's life."

"I feel so awful for him," I admit. "He's always been shy, reserved. But I didn't think he was suicidal, Hunter. I truly didn't."

"I know, baby."

"I wish he'd spoken to me about it and shared his feelings, instead of letting things get so bad that he felt like his only option was to kill himself." I swallow the lump of sorrow in my throat. "I just...you know what, I can't talk about this anymore tonight. Just distract me. Please."

"Sure." He flicks up an eyebrow. "Want me to tell you about the call I got from Garrett's agent today?"

Panic flies through me. "Oh my God! No!"

"What do you mean, no?"

"Garrett says you're not allowed to have an agent. It's against NCAA rules—"

"Don't worry, it's okay," Hunter interrupts with a smile. "He just called to say hello. A very unofficial hello. And, well, perhaps there was also an unofficial expression of interest on both our ends."

"*Both*? You're interested?" I try valiantly not to break out in a satisfied smile. I knew calling Garrett would be the push that Hunter needed.

He nods. "I mean, we don't even know if any teams will want me after I graduate—"

"They will."

"—but if one does, and it's a good deal..." He trails off.

"You'll sign?" I prompt.

"I'll sign. But..." He curls his arm around my waist and pulls me toward him. "That means you need to apply to grad schools in whatever city I land in. Or," he mulls it over, "I suppose we can see where *you* land and then I'll tell G's agent to get me in with that team."

"We'll figure something out." I love how we're already making plans for the future. And why not? I'm excited for it. I want nothing more than to work toward my master's and open up a counselling practice, while the man I love plays—

"Oh fuck," I blurt out. "I forgot to tell you I love you!"

Hunter's startled gaze snaps to mine. Then he starts to laugh. "I'm sorry, what?"

"I forgot to tell you I love you. I wanted to say it the night you said it, but—"

"You weren't ready, I get it." His voice comes out husky.

"It wasn't the right moment, given the circumstances. But I do love you." I feel my cheeks heating up. I never thought I'd fall for Mr. Hockey, with his cocky dimpled smiles and strange sense of humor. But life is full of strange surprises. "I love you, Hunter Davenport."

"I love you, Demi Davis." He leans down to kiss me. Meanwhile, his warm palms slide underneath the back of my shirt to stroke my back—and then he squawks in horror. "Holy shit, you're like a block of ice, baby. C'mere."

I grin as he begins to expertly tug off my clothes. "If you're trying to warm me up, you should be putting *more* clothes on me."

"Nah, I should be putting *me* on you." He wiggles his eyebrows playfully and nudges me toward his bed. Then he lifts the corner of the comforter and we crawl underneath it, our naked bodies tangled together.

He slips one hand between my legs, probing, stroking gently. "How are you already so fucking wet?"

"That's what happens when you're around," I mumble, and then my fingers find his dick. Big, thick, so warm.

Except he robs me of enjoyment, shoving my hand away with an outraged shout. "Oh my fucking God, Demi! Never touch my dick again."

I let out a howl of laughter. "Hands are too cold?"

"*Too cold* is an understatement. Nope. Nope nope nope nope.

You're not allowed to touch me tonight." Hunter pushes me onto my back, locks both my wrists with his left hand, and thrusts my arms over my head. "Don't move," he warns.

"Or what?"

"Or I won't fuck you."

I pout. "That's mean."

"No, what's mean was that war crime you just committed against my penis."

Gales of laughter shake my body. I love this guy. We have so much fun together, no matter the circumstances. We could be studying or sitting in a jail cell or lying naked in bed, and he'd never fail to crack me up.

His grip tightens on my wrists. "I'm warning you…"

"Oh fine. Go ahead and do your thing."

Grinning, he lowers his head to kiss me, and I let him seduce me with his mouth, his tongue, his calloused fingertips. Eventually he releases me, but I keep my hands over my head, letting him have his way with me. His mouth is warm, wet, as it closes around my nipple. He sucks gently, swirls his tongue around that aching tip, and my hips move restlessly, seeking relief.

Hunter reaches between us, his knuckles grazing my clit before one long finger slides inside me. "Aw, fuck," he groans. His hot mouth stays latched onto my breast as he starts fingering me. "Jesus motherfucking Christ, babe, I need to be inside you." He's grinding shamelessly against my bare leg, his dick leaving stripes of precome on my flesh.

I grumble impatiently when he leaves the bed to get a condom. "You should have done that first!" I scold.

He responds cheerfully. "Please don't lecture me when I'm about to give you an orgasm."

"Who says you're going to give me an orgasm?"

He grips his dick and wags it at me. "This guy."

Another laugh shudders through me, but it transforms into a

throaty moan when Hunter climbs on top of me and enters my pussy in one smooth glide. He fills me completely, my body stretching to accommodate him, and I stroke the sinewy muscles of his back as he fucks me in slow, sweet strokes.

"I love you so much," I whisper.

"Love you too." His hips retreat, then flex forward in a deep thrust that makes me see stars.

Pleasure forms a tight knot in my core and then slowly unravels, ribbons of heat traveling through my body. I'm not cold anymore. I'm on fire. Hunter's body is a furnace. His tongue is hot and eager. His dick elicits the most incredible sensations inside, stoking my arousal.

When the orgasm reaches the surface, I cry out and cling to him. He swallows my moans with greedy, desperate kisses, and then grunts huskily as he gives in to his own release.

"I'm never gonna get tired of this," he croaks. He rolls us over so that I'm lying on his warm chest.

"Good thing you never have to," I tease, still shivering from the aftershocks of release.

His strong arms wrap securely around me. "Oh really. So what are you saying? We're going to be together forever?"

Smiling, I peer down at his gorgeous face. Then I brush a light kiss over his lips. "That's exactly what I'm saying."

# EPILOGUE
## DEMI

IT'S ELEVEN P.M. ON SUNDAY AND WE'RE ON HUNTER'S COUCH watching my favorite show. Tonight's episode: *Magicians Who Kill*. Summer is fast asleep on the other end of the couch from us. Brenna's curled up in one armchair, watching the screen in fascination, while Fitz takes up residence in the other armchair, still on the fence about the episode. We're only ten minutes in and he's already said the words "this is fucked up" half a dozen times.

"Swear to God, if her severed head appears in his magician's hat, I'm getting up and leaving," Fitz warns.

Hunter leans forward when his phone buzzes on the coffee table. "Hey, it's Hollis."

"Answer it," Brenna orders. "Find out when they're coming home."

"But it's a FaceTime call," Hunter complains.

"So? What, you need to touch up your makeup?" she mocks.

I giggle.

"Whatever." He presses a button, and a moment later an explosion of noise rocks the living room.

"AHHHHHHHH! YOU GUYS!"

Summer shoots up into a sitting position, wide awake in a heartbeat. "What the fuck? What's wrong?" she demands, rubbing her eyes in alarm.

"Guys! Can you hear us?!" It's Rupi, shrill and worried. "Mike! I don't know if they can hear us!"

"They can hear us, babe!"

"We can hear you!" Hunter says in exasperation. "What the hell? Where *are* you? Why is it so bright?"

I peer at his phone, but I can't figure out where they are either. It's daylight, that's for sure. What time zone are they in?

Brenna hops up and settles on the arm of the sofa to get a better look, while Summer peeks over my shoulder. Fitz doesn't leave his chair, although I can tell his interest is focused solidly on the conversation.

"We're in Nepal," Hollis reveals.

We all freeze.

"What do you mean, you're in Nepal?" Brenna demands.

"I mean we're in Nepal. Dude, we're staying in the coolest place ever! It's like on top of a mountain and there's a Buddhist monastery right *there*, and, oh, Davenport! There's actual monks here, and these dudes don't have sex at all! A lot of them took a vow of silence, so I can't really get any deets for you, but—"

"Hollis," Summer interrupts. "Why are you guys in Nepal?"

Rupi re-enters the frame, her perfect white teeth sparkling in the sunshine of the Nepalese mountains, or wherever the heck they are.

"We're on our honeymoon!" she shrieks.

Summer gasps. The rest of us gawk at the phone.

"Is this a joke?" Brenna asks, her dark eyes narrowing.

"Nope!" Hollis replies. His and Rupi's faces fill up the whole screen, and I can't deny I've never seen two people look happier. "We got married on Friday! I'm sorry, I know you guys would've wanted to come. And Fitz—I know, I know, you've always dreamed of being my best man—"

"Always," Fitz says dryly.

"I'm sorry, man, I'll make it up to you. We're having a real wedding this summer. It's in India, and you're all invited."

"What is happening?" Summer sounds utterly baffled.

"You seriously got married?" Hunter asks incredulously.

"Yeah, we did it in a courthouse in Boston. Our witness was a dude trying to get out of a traffic ticket."

I tamp down a laugh.

"And now you're on your honeymoon in Nepal," Brenna says, each word coming out slowly and lined with bewilderment. "But you're having an official wedding this summer. In India."

"Yes!" Rupi say proudly. "Isn't this *amazing*?"

Nobody answers.

The brief silence summons a shriek from her throat. "Are none of you going to say congratulations?" she demands, her eyes on fire.

That snaps us into action, and soon we're all blurting out our congratulations.

"We're so happy for you! I promise!" Summer assures them, and there's nothing insincere about it. "We're just stunned. We didn't expect you to elope."

"That's why people elope, because nobody expects it!" Rupi chirps happily.

"So how long are you in Nepal?" Fitz calls toward the phone. "When are you home?"

"We'll be back in a year," Hollis says.

"A year?" Summer echoes in amazement. "But…"

"What about your job?" Hunter asks Hollis.

"Rupi, what about school?" I pipe up.

"I quit." Hollis.

"I dropped out." Rupi.

I gape at both of them.

"I haven't even picked a major," Rupi says, waving an indifferent hand. "I don't care about college."

"And I don't care about my job," Hollis chimes in. "Davenport said we should travel, so that's what we're doing."

I glance at Hunter as if to say *what the fuck?*

"I advised him to take Rupi on a weekend getaway or a summer trip," Hunter retorts. "Not to elope and run off to India!"

"Nepal," Hollis corrects. "Jeez, pay attention, dude."

"Well." Summer clears her throat. "We're all thrilled for you. I can't believe you're married."

I can't either, but Rupi and Hollis seem over the moon about it, and who am I to judge?

"Okay, you guys, it's like eight in the morning here and we have a big day planned," Rupi announces in her shrill, bossy *voice*.

"We'll call back in a few days," Hollis assures us. "Or a month. Whatever. Love you guys! Be back in a year!"

The call disconnects.

And we all exchange mystified looks.

"She dropped out of college," Brenna says, sounding impressed.

"They got married," Fitz says, sounding horrified.

"She's only nineteen," I realize.

"Yeah, but in Rupi's defense, she knew she was going to marry Michael Hollis the second she met him," Summer points out.

"True," Brenna agrees.

"They'll either be divorced in a week, or they'll be together forever," Hunter predicts with a sigh. "There's no in between with those two."

Summer tucks her golden hair behind her ears. "I'm happy for them, I really am. But holy shit, that came out of left field."

Hunter shakes his head a few times, as if trying to come out of a daze. "Okay, then. That was…fascinating." He picks up the remote control. "Should we keep watching? We were about to find out if the dismembered head winds up in the magic guy's hat."

"I'm going upstairs to play Fortnite," Fitz grumbles.

"I'm going to sleep," Summer says.

Brenna stands up. "I'm going to see if Jake's still awake so I can tell him about this latest development."

"Party poopers," I accuse.

As Hunter's roommates scatter and disappear, he tugs me closer to his warm, muscular body. "What do you say, babe? Shall we?"

I slant my head and grin up at him. "Yup yup."

# The End

# 1

# TAYLOR

IT'S FRIDAY NIGHT, AND I'M WATCHING THE GREATEST MINDS OF MY
generation get destroyed by Jell-O shots and blue concoctions served
from ten-gallon paint buckets. Sweat-beaded bodies writhing half-
naked, frenzied, hypnotized with subliminal waves of electronic
arousal. The house is wall-to-wall psych majors acting out their parental resentment on unsuspecting future MBAs. Poli-sci students plant-
ing the seeds of the blackmail checks they'll be writing in ten years.

AKA your typical Greek Row party.

"Have you ever noticed how dance music kind of sounds like
listening to drunk people having sex?" Sasha Lennox remarks. She's
standing beside me in the corner, where we've wedged ourselves
between the grandfather clock and a standing lamp to best blend in
with the furniture.

She gets it.

It's the first weekend back from spring break, and that means
the annual Spring Break Hangover party at our Kappa Chi sorority
house. One of the many events Sasha and I refer to as mandatory
fun. As Kappas, we're required to attend, even if that means our
presence is more decorative than functional.

"Like it wouldn't be so offensive if there was a melody, at least. This…" Sasha crinkles her nose, and her head twitches to a siren wail that blares through the surround sound system before another shattering bass line thunders in. "This is some shit the CIA used on doped-out MKUltra test subjects."

I cough out a strangled laugh, almost choking on the cup of whatever YouTube party punch recipe I've been nursing for the last hour. Sasha, a music major, has an almost religious aversion to anything not performed by live instruments. She'd rather be front row at a concert in some dive bar, the reverb of a Gibson Les Paul ringing in her ears, than be caught dead under the flashing techno kaleidoscope of a dance club.

Don't get me wrong, Sasha and I certainly aren't fun-averse. We hang out at the campus bars, we do karaoke in town (well, she does, while I cheer her on from the safety of the shadows). Hell, we once got lost in Boston Common at three in the morning while stone-cold sober. It was so dark that Sasha accidentally fell into the pond and almost got molested by a swan. Trust me, we know how to hang.

But the ritualistic practice of college kids plying each other with mind-altering substances until they mistake inebriation for attraction and inhibition for personality isn't our fondest idea of a good time.

"Look out." Sasha nudges me with her elbow at the sound of shouts and whistles from the foyer. "Here comes trouble."

A wall of unabashed maleness crashes through the front door to chants of *"Briar! Briar!"*

Like Wildlings storming Castle Black, the towering goliaths of the Briar University hockey team trample through the house, all thick shoulders and broad chests.

"All hail the conquering heroes," I say sarcastically, while Sasha smothers a snide smirk with the side of her thumb.

The hockey team won their game tonight, putting them into the first round of the national championship. I know this because our Kappa sister Linley is dating a benchwarmer, so she was at the game snapchatting rather than here with us cleaning toilets, vacuuming, and mixing drinks for the party. The privileges of dating royalty. Although a fourth-stringer ain't exactly Prince Harry, but maybe somewhere closer to the coke-addict son of someone prince-adjacent.

Sasha pulls her phone from the waistband of her skin-tight faux leather leggings and checks the time.

I peer at the screen and groan. Oh man, it's only eleven p.m.? I already feel a migraine coming on.

"No, this is good," she says. "Twenty minutes flat and those goons will have the keg killed. Then they'll blow through whatever's left of the liquor. I'd say that's quitting time for me. Half hour, tops."

Charlotte Cagney, our sorority president, didn't explicitly mandate how long we had to stay to fulfill our attendance requirement. Usually, once the drinks run dry, people go looking for the afterparty, at which point it's easy to sneak out unnoticed. With any luck, I'll be back in my apartment in Hastings and in my pajamas by midnight. Knowing Sasha, she'll drive into Boston and find a live show.

Together, she and I are the outcast stepsisters of Kappa Chi. We each came to be among their ranks for our own ill-conceived reasons. For Sasha, it was family. Her mother, and her mother's mother, and her mother's mother's mother, and so on, were all Kappas, so it was never a question that Sasha's academic career would include carrying on the legacy. It was either that or kiss something as "frivolous and self-indulgent" as a music major goodbye. She comes from a family of doctors, so her decisions are already heavily contested.

For me, well, I suppose I had grand designs of a college glow up. From high school loser to college It Crowd. A reinvention. Total life makeover. Thing is, joining their clubs and wearing their letters and enduring their weeks of sacramental indoctrination didn't have the desired effects. I didn't come out the other side all shiny and new. It's like everyone else drank the Kool-Aid and saw the pretty colors, but I was just left standing there in the dark with a cup of water and red food coloring.

"Hey!" a bleary-eyed guy greets us, staggering to sidle up next to Sasha while openly talking to my tits. We tend to make one perfectly desirable female when standing side-by-side. Her exquisite facial symmetry and slender figure, and my enormous rack. "You wanna drink?"

"We're good," Sasha shouts back over the pounding music. We both hold up our mostly full cups. A strategic device to keep the horny frat bros at bay.

"Wanna dance?" he then asks, leaning toward my chest like he's speaking into the box at a fast food drive-thru.

"Sorry," I retort, "they don't dance."

I don't know if he hears me or understands my contempt, but he nods and strolls away just the same.

"Your boobs have a gravitational force that only attracts douche-bags," Sasha says with a snort.

"You have no idea."

One day I woke up and it was like two massive tumors just erupted on my chest. Ever since middle school I've had to walk around with these things that arrive everywhere ten minutes before I do. I'm not sure which of us is the greater hazard to each other, me or Sasha. My boobs or her face. She causes a stir just walking into the library. Dudes stumbling over themselves to stand in her presence and forget their own names.

A loud *pop* bursts through the house, causing everyone to cringe and cover their ears. Silence ensues in the confusion while our eardrums drown in the lingering echoes of tinnitus.

"Speaker's blown!" one of our sisters yells from the next room.

Boos fill the house.

A mad scramble ensues as Kappas scurry to find a quick fix to save the party before our restless guests revolt. Sasha doesn't even try to hide her excitement. She eyes me with a look that says we may get to escape this party early after all.

Then Abigail Hobbes happens.

We see her sashay through the tightly packed crowd in a skimpy little black dress, platinum hair curled into perfect tendrils. She claps her hands, and in a voice that could cut glass, demands all attention fall on her bright red lips.

"Listen up, everybody! It's time to play Dare or Dare."

Cheers erupt in response as the living room swells with more bodies. The game is a popular Kappa tradition, and it's exactly what it sounds like. Someone dares you to do something and you do it—no truth option. Occasionally amusing and often brutal, it's resulted in more than a few arrests, at least one expulsion, and rumor has it, even a couple babies.

"Now let's see…" Our house vice president puts one manicured finger to her chin and turns in a slow circle to survey the room, deciding on her first victim. "Who shall it be?"

Of course her evil green eyes land squarely on where Sasha and I are plastered against the wall. Abigail strides up to us with pure sugary malice.

"Oh, sweetie," she says to me, with the glassy stare of a girl who's had a few too many. "Loosen up, it's a party. You look like you just found another stretch mark."

Abigail's a mean drunk, and I'm her favorite target. I'm used to it from her, but the laughs she elicits every time she uses my body as a punchline never fail to leave a scar. My curves have been the bane of my existence since I was twelve years old.

"Oh, sweetie," Sasha mimics, making a show of flashing her the bird. "How about you eff right off?"

"Aww, come on," Abigail whimpers in a mocking baby voice. "Tay-Tay knows I'm just kidding." She punctuates her statement by poking my stomach like I'm a goddamn Pillsbury Doughgirl.

"We're keeping your thinning hairline in our thoughts, Abs."

I have to chomp down on my bottom lip to stop from laughing at Sasha's retort. She knows I disintegrate amid conflict and never shies away from a chance to trade barbs in my defense.

Abigail answers with a sarcastic laugh.

"Are we playing or not?" demands Jules Munn, Abigail's sidekick. The tall brunette saunters over to us, donning a bored look. "What's the matter? Sasha trying to back out from doing a dare again like she did at the Harvest Bash?"

"Fuck off," Sasha shoots back. "You dared me to throw a brick through the dean's window. I wasn't about to get expelled over some juvenile sorority game."

Jules arches a brow. "Did she just insult an age-old tradition, Abs? Because I think she did."

"Oh, she did. But no worries, here's your chance for redemption, Sasha," Abigail offers sweetly, then pauses. "Hmm. I dare you to…" She turns toward her spectators while contemplating the dare. She's nothing if not in it for the attention. Then she snaps back around to face Sasha. "Do the Double Double then sing the chapter symphony."

My best friend snorts and shrugs, as if to say, *Is that all?*

"Upside down and backwards," Abigail adds.

Sasha curls her lips and sort of snarls at her, which gets the guys in the room hooting in amusement. Dudes love catfights.

"Whatever." Rolling her eyes, Sasha steps forward and shakes out her arms like a boxer warming up for a fight.

The Double Double is another Kappa party tradition, which entails downing two double shots of whatever's lying around, then a ten-second beer bong followed by a ten-second keg stand. Even the sturdiest drinkers among us rarely make it through the gauntlet. Throwing a handstand on top of it while singing the house song backwards is just Abigail being a spiteful bitch.

But as long as it won't get her expelled, Sasha is never one to back down from a challenge. She ties her thick black hair in a ponytail and accepts the shot glass that materializes out of nowhere, dutifully tossing back one shot, then the next. She powers through the beer bong while a couple Theta guys hold up the funnel for her, the crowd around her screaming their encouragement. To a cacophony of cheers, she muscles her way past the keg stand with a six-three hockey player keeping her legs in the air. When she's right-side up again, everyone's impressed to see her even able to stand, much less looking mean and holding steady. That girl's a warrior.

"Stand back!" Sasha declares, clearing people from the far wall.

With a gymnast's flourish, she thrusts her arms in the air and then sort of half-cartwheels so that her backside is flush against the wall in a handstand. Loud and confident, she belts out the words to our house song in reverse while the rest of us stupidly try to keep up in our heads to make sure she's getting it right.

Then, when she's done, Sasha completes an elegant dismount back to her feet and gives the crowd a bow to resounding applause.

"You're a fucking robot," I say, laughing when she prances over to resume her spot slouching in our losers' corner. "Beautiful dismount."

"Never met a landing I couldn't stick." Freshman year Sasha was on her way to Olympic qualifiers as one of the best vaulters in the world before she busted her knee slipping on some ice, and that was it for her gymnastics career.

Not to be outshined, Abigail sets her gaze on me. "Your turn, Taylor."

I take a deep breath. My heart races. Already I feel my cheeks burning red. Abigail smiles at my discomfort like a shark alerting to the vibrations of a wriggling seal in distress. I brace myself for whatever evil endeavor she's concocting for me.

"I dare you to…" She drags her teeth across her bottom lip. I see my impending humiliation in her eyes before she even opens her mouth. "Get a guy of my choice to take you upstairs."

# ACKNOWLEDGMENTS

This book was a joy to write! Hunter and Demi's friendship, banter, and sparks kept me on my toes during the entire writing process, and I couldn't be happier with how their story played out. With that said, please note that I took some liberties with the college semester/hockey season schedule, extending them for plot purposes.

I've said it before and I'll say it again, but this book (and life in general) would be a real bummer without the love and support of some amazing people:

My editor Lindsey Faber—reunited and it feels so good! And my agent Kimberly Brower for making sure I stay on top of things, and serving as my occasional relationship therapist.

The beta reading skills of Nikki Sloane ("suck his $#&! why don't ya!"), K.A. Tucker (winery champ and all-around hottie), Robin Covington (THANK YOU!) and Sarah J. Maas (Garrett Graham's #1 fan, and—finally!—someone as dorky as I am!).

Sarina Bowen, just because I love her. She's so sa-weet!

Vi Keeland, my frenemy, who lives vicariously through my love life. You're welcome.

Monica James, my Australian soulmate. You are so genuine and wonderful, and I know your dad was so very proud of the woman you are. I'm lucky to know you.

Nina, my publicist and wifey, who loves me so much she wouldn't even divorce me after finding out I've never read Harry Potter.

Aquila Editing, for proofing this book (Sorry for all the typos!)

Nicole, lifesaver extraordinaire.

Heyyyyy, Natasha. Set it free!

Damonza.com, for bringing Demi to life with this stunning cover!

All my author friends who shared this release and offered their love and support—it's truly remarkable how supportive this community can be. So many big hearts and talented writers!

And as always, the bloggers, reviewers and readers who continue to spread the word about my books. I am so thankful for your love and kindness. You're the reason I keep writing these crazy stories!

Love,
Elle

# ABOUT THE AUTHOR

A *New York Times*, *USA Today* and *Wall Street Journal* bestselling author, Elle Kennedy grew up in the suburbs of Toronto, Ontario, and holds a BA in English from York University. From an early age, she knew she wanted to be a writer and actively began pursuing that dream when she was a teenager. She loves strong heroines and sexy alpha heroes, and just enough heat and danger to keep things interesting!

Elle loves to hear from her readers. Visit her website www .ellekennedy.com or sign up for her newsletter to receive updates about upcoming books and exclusive excerpts. You can also find her on Facebook (ElleKennedyAuthor), Twitter (@ElleKennedy), Instagram (@ElleKennedy33), or TikTok (@ElleKennedyAuthor).

# ASK FOR ANDREA

## NOELLE W. IHLI

Published 2022 by Dynamite Books

www.dynamitebookspublishing.com

© Noelle West Ihli

ISBN: 979-8-9878455-0-9

Any references to historical events, real people, or real places are used fictitiously. Names, characters, and places are products of the author's imagination.

Cover design by Elizabeth Mackey

First printing, April 2022.

Dynamite Books, LLC

*For Nate.*
*I'll haunt you (but only because I love you).*

# 1. MEGHAN

## OQUIRRH MOUNTAINS, UTAH

### 1 YEAR BEFORE

Despite the crushing weight of him, my brain screamed at me to run.

*Run,* it demanded as he grunted and pulled the scarf—my scarf —tighter around my neck.

Instead I lay frozen, like a mouse under a cat's paw, until the vise of pressure and pain suddenly released.

He looked at me for a few seconds as he got to his feet, his mouth turned down in disgust. He was breathing hard. His pale face hovered above me in the darkness, the distinctive mole on his cheek a stark punctuation mark.

He let the limp, pink-and-green scarf fall to the ground beside me.

*Run,* my brain roared again. *RUN!*

I still didn't move. I didn't even blink.

He turned toward the car he'd precariously parked on the shoulder of the rutted dirt road.

I could only imagine what he'd left in the trunk. But if I didn't move, I knew I'd find out.

So that's when I finally ran, bolting into the shadows of the pines that beckoned with hiding places, if not safety.

I scrambled down a steep embankment toward a dry stream bed, pushing myself faster and willing myself not to fall, no longer even conscious of the pain in my throat.

I wasn't sure where I was going. All I knew was that I needed to put as much distance as I could between myself and the spotless blue Kia Sorento. And more importantly, I needed to get away from the soft-spoken, fine-as-hell man who drove it: *The needle,* I'd called him when I told Sharesa about our upcoming date. As in, the needle in a deep haystack of bachelors on the MatchStrike app: divorced dads with kids, complicated custody agreements, and cringey gym-bathroom selfies.

Jimmy was different. With his dark amber eyes, a close-shaved beard along his angular jawline and a hard-part haircut, he was a dead ringer for Chris Hemsworth.

When I showed Sharesa his photo, she'd actually squealed.

I, on the other hand, had kept my expectations in check. I wasn't new to the online dating scene. I'd taken an Uber to Gracie's Spot in Salt Lake after my shift and braced to meet Chris Hemsworth's creepy cousin. I even texted Sharesa on my way. *Call me in an hour with an out?* I could see the text bubbles appear immediately after I hit send. *Whatever, you know you're thirsty.* I rolled my eyes. More bubbles. ... *I'll call <3.*

We talked in the back booth of Gracie's until last call at eleven. I texted Sharesa from the bathroom that there was no need to rescue me after all.

She'd replied immediately, like always: *Thirrrrrsty.*

As I washed my hands, a paper sign taped to the bathroom mirror caught my attention. "On a date that isn't going well? Do you feel unsafe or just a little uneasy? Ask for Andrea at the bar. We'll make sure you get home safe." I smiled as I dried my hands, grateful I didn't need to ask. Not tonight. Not with him.

I stopped looking at the sign and studied myself in the mirror. I'd taken extra time with my hair, which I usually let fall in a blunt line across my shoulders. Earlier, I had coaxed it into waves that looked like spun gold in the restaurant lighting. I reapplied some of the deep pink lipstick that had become my signature accessory over the years and pressed my lips together, wondering if he'd kiss me later.

I had two beers over the course of the evening. Not enough to get me drunk or anything. Just enough to take the edge off my nerves. Because he did not in fact look like Chris Hemsworth's creepy cousin. He was thoughtful and funny. Even the large mole on his cheek somehow made him all the more attractive.

He drank ginger ale. It didn't faze me. I lived in Utah, after all.

The last thing I remember was feeling a little bit too warm. And really, really happy. The syrup-colored lights blazing in the trendy sputnik chandeliers suddenly had these little auras surrounding them. So when he suggested that I let him drive me home instead of waiting for an Uber in the cold, I didn't even hesitate.

The car had those crinkly paper covers on the seats, like it had just been cleaned.

That's the last thing I remember. Until I woke up with his hands—and my scarf—around my neck. The warm lights of Gracie's were gone, replaced with the bite of pine needles and dirt under my hair and the swirling dark of the freezing night air.

For a few seconds, I couldn't understand what was happening. I couldn't scream. I couldn't move. I couldn't even tell where I was. All I knew was that everything hurt.

The memory of our date crashed through the haze when I saw his eyes glinting above me. They weren't warm or even amber-colored anymore like they had been in the booth at Gracie's. These eyes were cold. Wide. And full of rage.

I thought about the sign in the bathroom at Gracie's. *Ask for Andrea.*

Andrea couldn't help me now. No one could.

I moved faster than I'd ever moved in my life, the pounding in my head and my chest and the crushing pressure of the scarf forgotten.

I didn't care where I was going. All that mattered was putting as much distance between us as possible, even if it meant running headlong into the looming woods.

I thought I heard someone call out as I dove down the rocky slope of the shallow stream bed. It sounded like a woman.

I ignored it and kept running.

He didn't follow me.

He didn't need to.

Because when I finally stopped running, I realized to my amazement that I wasn't out of breath.

Just as quickly, the amazement turned to horror.

I wasn't breathing hard because I wasn't breathing at all.

# 2. BRECIA

## BOULDER, COLORADO

### *2 YEARS BEFORE*

I first realized I was dead the same way you realize you've been dreaming. Except backwards, I guess. Because the bad dream was real.

I didn't know it had happened at first. Not for a few seconds. Not until I stood up—while my own body stayed put. I looked at the soft chambray pajamas I'd changed into after getting home from work, now dirty and damp. One of my slippers was kicked off, so you could see the chipped peach polish on my bare toes. My long, dark hair was streaked with something darker and sticky. I couldn't feel the throbbing in my head or the awful pressure on my neck anymore.

He was looking at me, too. Not at *me,* me. At my body. At my unblinking, bloodshot hazel eyes. He was breathing hard, expressionless. He was still holding the extension cord.

He'd grown out a Joaquin Phoenix beard that nearly—but not quite—obscured the dark mole on his cheek. It made him look ten years older than the last time I'd seen him. If he'd been sporting the beard back then, we probably wouldn't have gone out in the first place. Don't get me wrong: I'll swoon for a good five-o'clock shadow, but this thing was fully bird-nest material. It took him from a comfortable nine to a very solid three.

A year earlier, we had dated for exactly one week. How do I know that? Because he was upset when I spent our "one-week anniversary" with my girlfriends. I couldn't understand why it bothered him so much. It was Lanelle's birthday. And like I said, we'd been dating for *one week*. Still, I talked about him the whole time. I hadn't dated much since my last breakup a couple years earlier, and it felt good to say the word "boyfriend" again. It felt good to answer all the juicy questions over watermelon margaritas about whether he was a good kisser (yes), good in bed (no idea, early days), and how we'd met. That one, I fudged a little. I wasn't proud I'd finally gotten desperate enough to make a profile on MatchStrike. So I dodged the question. I decided that if we lasted, I'd fess up.

When I ran into him on my way out of the restaurant after Lanelle's party, I didn't know what to think at first. He smiled his pretty smile and acted like it was a wild coincidence. That's how I played it off to Lanelle and the rest of my friends. I could tell that they thought he was cute. That I'd done well. So I pushed aside the uncomfortable feeling in my gut as I tried to remember whether I'd mentioned the name of the restaurant to him earlier. I was pretty sure I hadn't.

I let him drive me home, even though that meant leaving my car in the Barbacoa parking lot. At first, he just seemed happy to see me. But when I asked who he'd met up with at Barbacoa, he sort of dodged the question. So I asked again. That was when he just kind of blew up.

He went on and on about me brushing him off to hang out with my friends. Then he ranted about me not even being glad to see him at the restaurant.

I texted him later that night to tell him I thought we should break up. He tried to call me immediately. When I didn't pick up, he called again. And again. And again. I put the phone in airplane mode and went to bed, still feeling the watermelon margs and wishing I hadn't told Lanelle or the girls about him yet.

When I woke up the next morning, I had twenty-two text messages waiting for me. They started out sort of sweet. He'd had a terrible day yesterday and just really wanted to see me. He understood why I was upset. Could he have another chance? By the last text message, I was a fat bitch. A fat bitch who had wasted his time. As soon as I had finished reading that one, another text came through. He could see that I had read his texts, so why wasn't I responding? I'd wasted his time, broken his heart, and now I wouldn't even write back.

The texts trickled in for the next three days, even though I didn't respond. I finally blocked his number and reported his profile on MatchStrike, figuring that maybe I'd save other girls the trouble.

When the texts stopped, I pretty much forgot about him.

I redecorated my duplex. I got a new job and a raise. I got bangs and highlights in my hair. I deleted MatchStrike after a handful of duds who didn't even make it past a second date. And I adopted a cat: a fire-point named Frank.

So when I took the recycle bin out to the side yard in my pajamas that night, he was the last person I was expecting to see.

I didn't even recognize him at first with that awful beard. He was standing there almost casually, like maybe it was some kind of coincidence. Just like he had that night at Barbacoa. Except this time he was standing in my side yard. Behind my fence.

I almost screamed. I only caught myself when I recognized his eyes. Honestly, I was a little relieved that he wasn't a stranger.

Then I got mad. It had been an entire *year.* What the *fuck* was wrong with him, showing up like this? Scaring me like this? Did he think I was going to take him back now?

That was when he pulled out the extension cord. My extension cord. I recognized it in slow motion as he came toward me. I hadn't bothered to bring it inside yet after using it to plug in the Christmas lights I'd finally goaded myself into putting up.

If you want to know, it takes a long time to strangle somebody. I'd heard that on an episode of *Investigation Discovery* once. I can tell you it takes even longer when you're the one being strangled. My throat was on fire. My head was on fire. My chest was on fire. Even my eyes felt like they were burning. I couldn't make a sound. I couldn't even see, as the tears poured down my cheeks.

I guess it was taking too long for him, too. Because in the end, he smashed the side of my head against the pavement. After that, everything went dark. The unbearable fire was suddenly gone, along with the chill in the air and the feel of the wet, rough pavement.

When I caught my first glimpse of, well, I still didn't know what to call it—my soul? My spirit? My echo?—it was sort of like looking at my reflection in a mirror. I wasn't wafting in the breeze or anything. I wasn't see-through. I just wasn't alive anymore. I was still wearing my pajamas and slippers, but they looked clean, the way they had a couple minutes earlier.

As soon as he realized I was dead—which was a hot minute after *I* realized I was dead—he booked it through my back gate. I was left standing beside my own body and the recycling bin I'd just wheeled out of the garage.

I followed him, finding that I could keep pace with him easily—something I never could have said of myself while alive. I actually grabbed his arm and watched as my own fingers rested lightly on top of his shoulder. I sort of expected them to slide right through.

He didn't react, exactly. However, he did walk faster, down the dark driveway, down the sidewalk, until he reached the blue Kia he'd left at the end of the street.

When he opened the driver's side door, I dove inside the car headlong with him. I wasn't going to risk letting him go if that car door slammed shut in my face.

As I watched him hurry into the car, I knew that I couldn't do anything for the girl who was lying on the pavement with blood in her hair. I couldn't do anything for Frank, who was probably still asleep on the big tufted chair in my bedroom.

Nobody else was looking out for me tonight. Nobody else was going to realize that I was missing, let alone dead, until I didn't show up for work tomorrow. Nobody could do anything to help me now.

Before he drove away, he used a packet of wipes to clean his hands. Carefully. Almost lovingly. Like he hadn't just used them to wrap a dirty extension cord around my neck by my recycle bins in my side yard until I finally stopped fighting.

In hindsight, that was when I decided I was going to haunt him.

I studied him from the passenger seat while he drove. His amber eyes, black in the darkness of the car, stayed fixed on the road while we made the twenty-minute drive back to his place.

It wasn't the apartment he'd told me about last year—down to the roommate who left his socks in the kitchen. Instead, it was a little brick 70s-style rambler in Broomfield with one porch light burned out.

I followed him up the front walkway of the house, past a Big Wheel bike tipped over into an overgrown flower bed and a tangle of half-naked Barbies on the steps.

The lone porch light flickered a little as he turned the knob and went inside the house, shutting the door behind him and leaving me standing on the porch for a little while longer, staring at the toys and the riot of azaleas in the flowerbeds I just knew he hadn't planted.

I found that I couldn't just walk through the front door, once he went inside. So I was glad I'd gotten into the car when I had the chance.

I stood outside on his porch for a while. Because despite all the scary movies I'd watched, I had learned zero useful information about being dead. Could I make the doorknob move if I focused really hard? No. What would happen if I screamed? I tried it. I could hear myself just fine, but based on the reaction of the guy walking his dog across the street, nobody else could.

Well, that's not totally accurate. The dog—a little gray schnauzer—stopped walking and looked straight at the front porch.

I got my hopes up. "Hey, buddy! Hey!" The schnauzer growled a little. He sniffed. Then he kept walking. The owner didn't even look up from the blue glow of his smartphone.

I turned away from the useless dog and sat down on the porch. I studied my hands—the reflection of my hands. I watched the way they rested on the reflection of my knees. The way my feet rested on the cracked concrete. Barely touching, as if I were made of something just heavier than air.

I swiped hard at a leaf on the step and watched it move so imperceptibly it was impossible to tell whether it had been the night air.

*You're dead,* I told myself firmly. *Feel sad.*

When my favorite aunt had died in a car accident, the cushion of denial lasted a solid hour. It was too big. I couldn't take it in. When it finally hit me, I felt like the wind had been knocked out of me. It felt like that. Only this time, the impossibly awful thing had happened to me.

I could see blurry shapes moving behind the pebbled glass of the kitchen window above the flowerbed. I stepped into the azaleas and watched my reflection scatter through the spaces between the leggy blooms. The plants didn't move. *I* did.

It would have been completely fascinating if I hadn't just been murdered; however, it did give me an idea. I couldn't walk through walls. Or grab anything. I seemed to have had all the power of the night air. Not the wind, even. *The air.*

I sat with this idea for a while, watching the azalea leaves shiver in the slight breeze. I lifted my hand toward the nearest flower and reached for a cluster of blooms. This time I watched more carefully as my hand slipped, sort of like smoke, between two large magenta blossoms.

I wasn't wind: I was air. But air could go places. And that gave me an idea.

I walked around the house until I got to the side gate, which was closed. I could see the side yard—and his recycle bins—through the slats. I focused on the air between the slats and moved forward.

Easily enough, I scattered right through the fence.

My gaze settled on a cat door, slightly ajar, leading into the garage. I went through that too. No problem.

The light was on, illuminating a neat garage and a few rows of stacked boxes on one side, a minivan on the other. I gave the boxes a cursory glance. They were labeled with kitchen, bathroom, bedroom, etc. A stack of labels and a permanent marker sat on the topmost box.

He was moving.

I heard a clattering noise behind me and turned in time to see a little calico cat scurry into the garage through the cat door.

"Hi, kitty," I said softly, and I swear he sat down and stared right at me for a few seconds—then settled in front of a bowl of cat food. I followed him and crouched beside him as he ate. I thought of Frank with his chirping meow. He was probably tearing up the carpet at the bottom of the stairs in protest that I hadn't fed him yet.

I knew I couldn't cry actual tears. Even so, I felt the familiar prickling feeling in the back of my eyes and sadness that spread through the center of me. I wouldn't ever feel the downy fur underneath Frank's chin or his rumbly purr as he flopped down on the bed beside me with his eyes closed again.

As the feeling got bigger, I heard a quiet pop that plunged the garage into sudden darkness.

I froze, listening to the quiet tinkling of the filament in the bulb.

"I think I did that," I whispered to the cat, who continued crunching away.

There were little pinpricks of light surrounding the door to his house. I moved toward them and the sound of the muffled voices inside.

An hour ago, he had taken everything I had.

I didn't know how, but I planned to return the favor.

# 3. SKYE

KUNA, IDAHO

## NOW

He came into the Daily Grind coffeehouse a lot when I was on shift that summer.

It didn't bother me. I looked forward to it, actually. He tipped. He was cute. He was one of the few white folks in Idaho who didn't try to make small talk about where I was *really* from or take the opportunity to test out their fledgling Spanish. (Much to my mom's disappointment, I had taken exactly one year of Spanish elective in middle school.)

He called me "Dolly," on account of me wearing a Dolly Parton shirt the day he first came in for a hot chocolate. Never coffee. Always hot chocolate. That was a little unusual, so I remembered his order. I started adding a little smiley face on the cup, next to his name. *James.*

"Thanks, Dolly," he always said with a grin that made me blush. So of course I mumbled something awkward and turned around to prep the next order. His amber eyes—I swear, they looked like dark, liquid gold—lingered on me while I pretended not to notice.

My manager, Ken, teased me about him once in a while. He told me I should write my number on his cup next time he came in. "The hot chocolate dude that looks like Chris Hemsworth is totally flirting with you," Ken said, wiggling his eyebrows. "Ball's in your court, honeybun."

I almost did. I rolled the idea around in my head sometimes while I was toasting somebody's bagel or adding exactly 5.5 pumps of caramel syrup to a Frappuccino. I was embarrassed to admit—even to myself—that I had never been on a real date, let alone made the first move. I told myself that's what college was for. When I got there in the fall, somehow I would shed my skin and lose my awkwardness when I crossed the threshold of campus at Idaho State.

It wasn't unusual for me to see him three or four times a week that summer; however, a few weeks before I was set to drive to ISU, he suddenly stopped coming by. I felt weirdly sad about it. Like I had missed my chance or something. I pictured his face while I worked, feeling wistful that I'd probably never see him again. He was older than me by a lot—late twenties, if I had to guess. Honestly, he was so good-looking with those caramel eyes, dark hair, and dramatic celebrity-style beauty mark that I didn't really care.

It felt like fate when, on my last day at work before I left for ISU, he walked through the doors with a big smile and ordered his usual. I could feel my cheeks go red as I tried to bully myself into writing my number on his hot chocolate cup. I told myself it was practice, I guess. To prove I was ready for college (I wasn't). But I chickened out. I reasoned that I was leaving for school in two days, so what was the point?

I told him in a mumbled rush that today was my last day. He probably wouldn't see me at the Daily Grind again. He looked genuinely disappointed and then sort of shrugged. "Well, I'll miss you, Dolly."

My cheeks flared even hotter, and I pretended that the espresso machine was spilling over until he left. *Idiota,* I thought to myself. I remembered the curse words.

I finished my shift at four and turned in my apron and employee door tag. I gave Ken a hug, promising I'd text him. Then I walked to the bus stop. I was about to hit *send* on a text to my mom about dinner—pupusas at our favorite food truck? I had skipped lunch and was starving—when I saw a car slow down beside me in the shopping center.

It was him.

He gave me that smile, like he was as surprised as me. Like it was serendipity. Then he said, "Hey, Dolly. Want a ride?"

I didn't even hesitate. The universe had given me a second chance after I'd punted earlier—and all those other times. I easily batted aside the voice that quietly piped up to wonder why he was still in the sleepy shopping center two hours after I'd last seen him.

"Sure, why not?" I said, pleased that my voice sounded so easygoing, even when I could feel my heart pounding hard against my chest. *It's not a big deal,* I told myself. *It's not like he's a stranger.* I smoothed down my curls, which were a mess like they always were after work.

Then I got into the blue Kia and buckled my seatbelt.

"You maybe wanna grab something to eat first?" he asked. I felt my heart calm down a little.

"Sure, I'm starving," I replied, blushing and making eye contact with the dark mark on his cheek. This meant it was a date. I couldn't wait to text Ken later. He'd be so proud of me.

He grinned. "Well, then I'm gonna take you to my favorite place, okay? It's kind of out of the way, but it's worth it."

The voice in my head piped up again. I'd lived in Kuna all my life. There weren't many places I'd never been. Especially when it came to food. "What's it called?" I asked.

He shook his head. "You'll see."

As we drove, he asked me questions. Questions about my family. Whether I'd ever visited El Salvador (once, when I was a baby). What kind of music I liked. What I wanted to study. Whether I was a morning person or a night owl. Question after question. Like I was the most interesting person in the world. All with that smile. Stealing glances at me while he pulled onto the interstate toward Boise.

I told myself to relax. Boise was a thirty-minute drive, but it did have more restaurants.

I focused on what he was saying and tried to enjoy myself. He was telling a story about one of his roommates, who had gotten a growler instead of a pony keg for their last party. I laughed, not really sure what the difference was either but unwilling to reveal that. He seemed kind of old to still be partying, but what did I know?

Five minutes later, he signaled to leave the interstate. I looked up at the sign. Blacks Creek. Kuna-Mora Road. My stomach turned over. He didn't miss a beat as he continued telling the story. I had been on Blacks Creek Road once, on a hike. As far as I knew, there weren't any restaurants this way. Just hills and canyons.

My stomach started to hurt. "Is this the right exit?" I asked, as lightly as I could. I was still worried I would blow it. Hurt his feelings. Disappoint him. Reveal that I was a baby who had never even been on a real date or kissed a boy. That Ken—who himself had a boyfriend— was the only boy I ever spent any amount of time with.

"You haven't been to Moe's?" he asked, glancing at me with genuine surprise. "And you grew up here?" He shot me a sly smile, and I believed him.

Just in case, I decided to send a text to my mom. "Oh, Moe's?" I bluffed. "Oh yeah, I've always wanted to try it." I swallowed as I pulled my phone out of my jacket pocket. "I'm just going to text my mom, let her know. I told her I'd be home soon."

As I said it, I looked at the screen and saw zero bars.

My thumbs hovered over the text message box as I read my mom's last text message again and again. *Te quiero, mi'ja.*

The sick feeling came back. And when I looked up at him, I saw that he had been watching me. I plastered a fake smile on my face.

He took it in stride. "There's no service for a couple miles—but just past that hill, you'll get three bars. No problem. You want me to stop there so you can text her?"

The whiplash from dread to relief made me feel dizzy, and I mustered up a real smile. Maybe Moe's *did* exist. Maybe everything was fine. I was getting worked up over nothing. Like I always did. "Sure," I said, as casually as I could. "She'll worry if I don't."

A few minutes later, we took a bend in the road. There was a "Ranch exit" sign just ahead, and he slowed the car and signaled onto what looked like little more than a dirt trail. I looked down at my phone as the tires crunched and rumbled along the uneven, rocky surface.

Still no service.

He spoke as if he had read my mind, pointing outside the car. "If you still aren't getting bars, that spot down by the creek should do it." He smiled. "Found it by accident when my friend Greg had to take a leak on the way out here."

I laughed a little and got out of the car, my eyes on my phone as I walked toward the creek.

Still no bars.

I held the phone up and took a few steps forward and tried again.

Nothing.

And that's when he grabbed me from behind. One hand roughly pulled my head back by my hair. The other closed around my throat as he pushed me to the ground. I landed hard on my stomach, but the only sound I could manage was a muffled grunt as his knees pinned me down.

I tried to scream. Tried to twist my body around to get him off me. Tried to fight.

All I could focus on was trying to get his hands off my throat.

When I was in fourth grade, the little boy next door—his name was Dewey—drowned in the hot tub on his back patio. He tried to get in it while his mom was making lunch, and the cover shut on him. After that, I sometimes had a hard time falling asleep at night. I couldn't stop thinking about what it must have been like for him.

Drowning was the worst way I could imagine dying.

Until now.

It couldn't have been more than a couple minutes before I lost consciousness, but the seconds seemed to expand as I tried—and failed—to find a way to make him stop.

When the darkness finally closed in, the pain and the pressure disappeared with the light.

When the light reappeared, I could still hear him grunting behind me. I could still see the dirt and gravel beneath my face. Everything else had gone numb.

To my amazement however, I rolled away from his grasp.

To my horror, he didn't even notice. Because the girl with the dark, messy curls lying face down in the dirt didn't move at all.

I'd seen those *Dateline* specials about people who had out-of-body experiences. Near-death experiences. I quickly decided that's what was happening.

"GET OFF ME," I screamed, launching myself at him.

My fists landed on his back with all the force of a butterfly wing.

"Stop, stop, stop," I cried. I knew he couldn't hear me. I wasn't sure I could even hear myself.

The girl on the ground—me—wasn't putting up a fight anymore. Her lips were a deep lavender. There was a long line of drool coming out of one corner of her mouth. Her eyes weren't closed, but they weren't open, either.

The distant sound of a vehicle on the interstate was what finally made him let go. It wasn't close, but there was no cover out here, aside from some scrubby sage and the shallow creek.

I watched as he finally stood up and inspected his hands then walked back toward the blue Kia.

He didn't look back at the body on the ground.

As I heard his tires crunch along the road, I waited for it to happen. For my soul to reunite with the lifeless, dusty body in the dirt.

I sat down and got as close as I could to my body. "He's gone," I whispered. "You can wake up now."

I imagined reuniting with my body, focusing as hard as I could on what it had felt like in the moments before everything went dark. I lay down next to myself, hoping that all of a sudden, I'd feel the pain again, the desperation to breathe. That was what happened in the *Dateline* episode. You saw yourself outside your body, and then wham, you came roaring back. Or some kind of loving being appeared to tell you it wasn't your time to meet God yet.

"Come back," I whispered. I thought about my mom, already home from work and wondering why I hadn't beat her home. Why I hadn't texted. Whether I wanted two or three pupusas.

My phone was lying in the dirt beneath me. I could see one corner, pinned underneath my thigh.

It was still and silent.

Just like me.

# 4. MEGHAN

## OQUIRRH MOUNTAINS, UTAH

### 1 YEAR BEFORE

It took all night for me to find my way back to my body in the dark forest.

The thumbnail of a moon provided just enough light to get me back to the rocky gully. From there, it was an impossible guessing game of sagebrush, crumbling limestone, and hundreds of scrawny pine trees that looked exactly alike.

There were no stumbles or falls to slow me down as I moved through the darkness. But as it turned out, being a ghost didn't come with a maps app. And it didn't make me any less afraid of the dark. The night was full of snapping branches, and unearthly muttering noises. I screamed in terror and frustration every few minutes. The sound didn't echo.

Despite my best efforts to move like the spirits I'd seen on TV, my feet stayed on the ground, in the lace-up coral flats I'd been wearing earlier.

Above me, the stars were brighter than I'd ever seen them. Everything else surrounding me was swallowed up in inky blackness.

I'd always enjoyed camping—the few times I'd gone anyway. Still, I was quick as anyone to park myself around the campfire or zip myself up in my tent when the sun set. Nature was beautiful, at a distance. Up close, it was usually terrifying.

With every new twig snap or rustling branch, I froze. Or screamed.

From somewhere in the distance, I could hear the excited chorus of coyotes.

It wasn't that I was afraid something bad would happen to me. The worst thing had already happened. Fear felt different than it had while I was alive. My heartbeat didn't speed up. My breath didn't speed up. I just felt the terror of being alone, of being lost, of being dead, in every part of me that was left.

When I came around a bend and saw a huge pair of glinting eyes staring back at me from a rocky outcropping, I shrieked.

The eyes didn't disappear. If anything, they moved a little closer before I ran. The pinpricks of stars swirled in front of me as I moved faster and faster, still screaming for help I knew would not be coming.

\* \* \*

It was the coyotes that led me back to my body as the sky turned steel gray above the rocky horizon.

They had stopped calling to each other. But as I climbed up an embankment that looked vaguely familiar, I could hear growls and snarls coming from just beyond the ravine.

The first thing I saw was one of my coral shoes: the battered mortal twin to the pristine reflections on my feet. It was lying in the dirt, smears of something dark crusting the tongue.

There were five coyotes just past the shoe. They were skinny and small enough that I wouldn't have been afraid of any of them in the daylight. In the darkness, it was a different story. Backs hunched together, eyes flashing green as they snapped and chattered to one another, and jaws dark with what I knew was blood, they were something else entirely.

I felt the terror expand until it was too big for me to contain it. "Get away!" I screamed, taking a step toward them.

To my amazement, five heads swiveled toward me as the chattering snarls stopped.

The coyote nearest me, who had a dark patch on her head, drew back her lips to bare needle-like teeth.

"Get out of here," I screamed again, stepping toward them.

Their ears went back slightly, and they sniffed the air, taking a few shuffling steps away from my body.

I took a step forward, still screaming.

They didn't flinch, exactly. However, they didn't turn back to their meal, either.

The coyote with the dark patch made a muttering noise in her throat and moved to circle the rest of her companions—allowing me a glimpse behind her.

I'd never seen a dead body before, except on TV.

Let alone my own dead body.

The dread and disgust shot through me like a massive bolt of electricity, and I drew back from the mangled, bloody corpse on the ground. One of my legs from the knee down was in tatters, hanging on by dark threads. They'd ripped open my stomach, letting the glinting entrails spill partway out onto the ground.

My face had been spared. But the skin on my neck that was visible where the pink-and-green scarf lay open was a mass of bruises that could be seen even in the dim light.

The coyote with the dark patch on her head circled back around in a wide loop, sniffing the air. Her muzzle was wet with blood, and she was still making that muttering noise in the back of her throat.

In a daze, I reached out a hand to touch her, and she gave a sharp bark then loped toward the ravine with her ears pinned against her tawny head.

The others followed her into the steel-gray darkness.

I sat down in the dirt, a few feet away from where the ground turned black and slick, until the sun finally came up on my remains.

# 5. BRECIA

## BOULDER, COLORADO

### *2 YEARS BEFORE*

These were the things I had learned after three days of living in his house:

The naked Barbies in the front yard belonged to his two daughters, Emma and Kimmie. I had never been good at pinpointing exactly how old kids were. If I had to pick a number, I'd say that the two little girls with duck-down, white-blond hair were six and four. Still babies. For the most part, I kept my distance from them, wary of anything he'd touched.

The scraggly azaleas beneath the kitchen window had been planted by his wife, April, who was the opposite of everything I'd been while I was alive. She was quiet. Blond. Rail-thin. Endlessly patient and doting. When I wasn't following her husband from room to room, brimming with hatred, I watched her. She washed the dishes, folded laundry, picked up toys, fed the cat, read a book, and made breakfast. She snuggled up next to him at night and kissed him in the morning. At first, I was sure that if I looked hard enough I'd see that she was his match: rotten at the core. But the more I looked, the more confused I felt. To be honest, I hated her at first—maybe even more than I would have if she'd been awful. Because she seemed so blissfully, doggedly unaware. Just like I had been when I'd dated her husband a year ago. Except this woman had been married to him for years.

The cat in the garage was named Oscar. Out of everyone who lived in the little brick rambler in Boulder, he was the only one who seemed to have the sense to hate the man of the house as much as I did. When the garage door opened, he sat up in his kitty bed in the corner by the bikes, craning his neck to see who it was. If it was April or one of the girls, he made a chatty little noise in his throat and hurried over in hopes of being scooped up and taken inside the house. If it was him, Oscar stayed put. Or slunk out of the garage.

To be fair, Oscar didn't like *me* much, either. Whenever I approached, the cat stopped what he was doing and stared for a few seconds. If I tried to touch him, he shrank back and moved the other way. I found this strangely reassuring. It seemed to mean that somebody knew I still existed. Even if it was just an orange tabby.

The boxes in the garage, stacked in neat rows and meticulously labeled with black sharpie, were destined for Herriman, Utah. The U-Haul had already been paid for.

I followed him like an invisible shadow that first day. While he ate breakfast at his mid-century-style kitchen table. While he shaved off the Joaquin Phoenix beard that I wondered if he'd grown for the sole purpose of making himself less recognizable. And while he tickled Kimmie and Emma on his way downstairs.

I tried everything I could think of to do the things ghosts were supposed to be able to do. And I'm here to tell you that either *Ghost Whisperer* was a bunch of BS, or there was a different brand of ghost involved. Because I couldn't slam any doors. I couldn't (as far as I could tell by his reaction, anyway) make the temperature in the room suddenly drop. I couldn't be heard.

I really couldn't do anything.

For a hot second, I thought about trying to find my way home. I quickly discarded the idea. I didn't know my way around Boulder. I couldn't have found my way, even if I'd wanted to.

Part of me felt homesick for Frank and my apartment. But I knew that the only thing waiting there for me was my dead body. Probably not even that. Robin, my manager, would have been the one to report me missing when I didn't show up for work. Knowing Robin, she had taken it upon herself to check on me before calling the police.

I hoped she took Frank.

\* \* \*

He did normal stuff for most of the day. He had a home office in the basement, where he disappeared right after breakfast.

To my surprise, he hadn't lied about his job. He actually was a programmer—for a tech startup called TreeHaus. I couldn't tell exactly what he was working on. Code, and more code.

He was still on MatchStrike, with a new profile broadcasting the same alluring, blurry photo—and the same lies that had reeled me in:

That he was single.

That his name was Jamie Carver.

That he was looking for his soulmate.

By this point, I had pieced together that his real name was James Carson.

He compulsively opened up the MatchStrike app on an incognito browser to check on the messages he'd gotten since he'd last logged in.

He was chatting with four different girls.

Nicole. Allie. Tena. Danae.

Nicole was his clear favorite. She responded the quickest and the most often. He spent the most time crafting his messages to her—which he then copied and pasted into the other chats, when he came up with little tidbits he liked.

I thought about all of the messages he'd sent me on MatchStrike last year and wondered how many of them had been copied and pasted into other chats—or from other chats. How many other lines he'd had in the water when he decided to meet up with me for the first time.

I wondered what he'd told his wife, April, during the week we'd dated. He'd never stayed the night at my apartment or anything. But we'd spent hours across from each other in the dinette on the corner near my house. I'd been planning to invite him to my place.

Finally, he used the incognito browser to look for me. First, he typed "Brecia Collier." Then "Brecia Collier murder."

The first headline read, "Woman found murdered in backyard of her Denver home."

I read fast, not wanting to miss a word if he suddenly clicked out of the article.

*When police arrived at the home of Brecia Collier, the Colorado woman who was reported missing on Friday afternoon, they found Collier strangled to death in her side yard.*

*According to court documents published online Saturday, Collier had been reported missing by coworkers when she failed to appear at work.*

*Chilling details reveal that forensics has confirmed that the murder weapon was an extension cord likely taken from Collier's trash. According to the court documents, the cause of death has been confirmed as asphyxiation by strangulation and blunt force trauma to the back of the head.*

*Police are asking for potential witnesses or anyone with information about Brecia Collier's murder to come forward immediately.*

*"There was no evidence of sexual assault. We believe that Brecia was surprised while taking her recycling bins out to the side yard at approximately 8:30 p.m. on Thursday evening," read the probable cause statement.*

*No one answered the door when police arrived at Collier's home Friday afternoon when a coworker notified police that Collier had not appeared at work. However, Collier's car was parked outside, and she didn't answer her cell phone.*

*Collier's sister, in a statement to the press made Saturday morning said, "Our family is devastated by this horrific and senseless tragedy. Brecia was so loved by her friends and family. We are desperate for any information. Please, if you know anything, come forward."*

I had time to read my sister's statement twice before he closed the tab and went back to MatchStrike. They were desperate for any information, which meant they had no information.

They didn't know who had done this. Red-and-blue flashing lights would not be appearing at the window.

I tried to remember who I had even told about Jamie's/James's erratic texts after I broke things off with him. My sister. Lanelle. Robin. A couple other friends, maybe. Life went on. And by the time he showed up in my side yard, he was old news.

The disturbing truth was, James's texts were par for the course. I'd heard worse stories from plenty of friends. Online dating was a roulette of men who didn't like to hear the word "no." I never could have imagined any of them showing up in my side yard with an extension cord.

"What the fuck is wrong with you," I hissed in his ear. He didn't react. Instead, he crafted a new message to Nicole: *Saturday night? Meet at O'Michaels?*

Nicole responded almost instantly in the affirmative.

The piece of paper on the top of his neat office mail filer was a receipt for U-Haul. The truck was rented out for Sunday.

I studied the thumbnail photo of Nicole in the chat window. She had gorgeous auburn hair with perfectly blended highlights. Subtle makeup. Stunning smile. If I knew anything, I knew that right now she was hanging on every word "Jamie Carver" said.

Because he was beautiful, too. He was the kind of beautiful that drew you in before you even considered the fact that beautiful things can be poisonous.

As he read her response, his lips turned up in the barest smile—which disappeared as the sound of little footsteps clattered across the office ceiling, accompanied by shrieks of laughter.

The anger that had been simmering inside me for the past three days bubbled into something white-hot as I watched him close the incognito browser and put in headphones. If I still had a body, it would have been shaking. Since I didn't, the whole world sort of turned fuzzy and charged.

That's when I heard a quiet pop, and his computer screen went dark.

He pulled the headphones out of the computer jack and flung them onto the desk in annoyance, as if they were the source of the problem.

I stared at the dark computer screen as the fizzy feeling disappeared. It was replaced by something like hope.

Had I done that? Computers fritzed out all the time. So did light bulbs. It might have been a coincidence.

But I didn't think so.

# 6. SKYE

KUNA, IDAHO

## NOW

It was my useless phone that led them to my body in the foothills off Blacks Creek Road. Three days after I was supposed to be driving to college.

Even without service, the phone had pinged off cell towers in Boise and Kuna. Once the police finally started searching, I wasn't exceptionally hard to find.

I kept a vigil by my body for at least half an hour before giving up hope that I would wake up.

Obviously, I didn't. Because it wasn't a near-death experience. It was just death.

My skin was already turning ashy and a sort of sickly grayish brown. I reached out to touch the dusty black curls framing my half-closed eyes, then drew my hand back. That wasn't me anymore. That was just a dead girl.

Even after I admitted to myself that I was fully dead, I still waited a little longer. Would God beam me up? Where was the light everybody talked about?

*Tonta,* I berated myself for hoping.

Finally, I just started walking. Back the way we'd driven into the foothills on Blacks Creek Road. I knew the way.

Dead or alive, I just wanted to go home to my mom.

I stayed on the crumbling shoulder of the narrow, two-lane highway that wound through the barren hills. I was pretty sure I could walk right down the middle of the road if I felt like it. I wasn't confident what would happen to me if I were to get hit by one of the few cars that passed in the gathering dusk. Was there another level of death that I'd reach if I got squashed? Was death like a video game with different levels? If so, how many levels were there?

I wasn't interested in any more surprises related to my mortality. So I stayed on the shoulder.

It was already late afternoon when I started out. Before long, the sun dipped down over the canyon walls. I kept walking.

At one point, a family of deer stepped out of the hills and into my path, in the semi-darkness. The big doe raised her head as I approached and stared through me, her long ears twisting forward and back as she listened. Her babies—a couple of yearlings with knobby knees—flanked her tightly on either side. I didn't move through them, exactly. Not the way I might have expected, anyway. I sort of scattered around them, into the pockets of air between their flanks and legs.

They watched me do it. I swear they did. Then they went right back to picking through the patches of tender green blades poking through the thistly brown stalks along the road.

I kept walking, as the sun completely disappeared and it got difficult to see anything except the road in front of me.

I thought about my body, lying in the dirt near the shallow ravine, and felt guilty for leaving it behind so easily.

I thought about him. The sounds he made. The way he brushed his hands on his jeans as he hurried back to his car, away from the girl on the ground.

I thought about what I would find when I finally made it through the silent, endless hills. Had my mom called the police yet? Would Ken tell them about the single guy who came in without fail for his hot chocolate—and to flirt with me?

I wasn't really sure how many miles I was from home. Maybe fifteen, if I had to guess. All I knew was that it would have taken me all night and probably into the next day to walk this far if I were alive.

Since I didn't have to stop, or rest, or worry about staying hydrated or picked off by any of the glowing eyes I saw farther back in the hills, I found my way back to the main street in Kuna after what I guessed was just a few hours.

The streets were quiet in a way I'd never seen them before. A stray cat darted out in front of me as I crossed the shopping center parking lot and stood looking at the Daily Grind's bay windows, dimly lit by the lights under the register. It didn't look up when I called out.

In a few hours, Ken would be arriving to open up the store for the early risers, filling the quiet lobby with the sound of machines perking up and the smell of new espresso.

Part of me hadn't wanted to leave my safe corner of the world. Even if it meant a small life in a small town, where I'd managed to graduate from high school never having even kissed a boy.

And now I never would.

The house was still and quiet when I finally made it home. The sight of the familiar front door, with the only porchlight still on, filled me to the brim with a mix of longing and despair.

I wasn't sure how to get into the house at first. However, after a few minutes, I realized I could scatter through the cracked dryer vent, slipping through the narrow opening. It felt kind of like sneezing. Except I was the sneeze.

I found my mom asleep in my bedroom, in the same sweater she'd been wearing Thursday morning, the last time I saw her. Her ISU sweatshirt, a twin to the one she'd gotten me after I got my scholarship letter.

Her face was crumpled, like it was frozen on the verge of tears. Forehead furrowed. Eyes scrunched tightly shut. Mouth pressed into a thin line. But her breathing told me she was really and truly asleep.

I lay down beside her on my bed, wrapping one arm around her waist and burying my face in her hair. Then I closed my eyes and tried to recall the exact smell of her hair. The faint mix of spices from whatever dish she'd been cooking earlier. Ivory soap. And something I didn't know how to describe. Just her.

She made a quiet moaning sound, and I could hear her teeth grinding.

"It's okay, Mom," I whispered.

The noise stopped.

The idea that maybe some part of her could hear me made the despair well up until it was so big it felt like I was made of it. "Don't be sad. I'm still here. *Te quiero*," I tried again. "Can you hear me?"

She jolted upward in bed with a scream, knocking the glass of water off my nightstand as she fumbled for her phone. I leaped up off the bed and moved into the corner of the room, where I stood frozen.

She stared at the blue glow of her cell for a few seconds, her face still tightly crumpled. Then she set the phone carefully back on the nightstand and lay back down on my bed, mumbling something in Spanish.

I took a few steps closer to the bed. "Mom?"

She stared at the ceiling for a few minutes. Even when I leaned in close enough to see the freckles on her wet cheeks.

Then I sat down where I was, letting myself sink to the carpet as I listened to her snuffling sobs until she finally turned off the light.

Growing up, I didn't get noticed much. To be honest I preferred it that way. I was the quiet Latina girl who never raised her hand in class. The one who avoided eye contact at all costs on the bus. I was pretty content to let people look right through me. She was the one exception.

Not anymore.

# 7. MEGHAN

## OQUIRRH MOUNTAINS, UTAH

### 1 YEAR BEFORE

The scavengers with wings showed up after the coyotes. Crows, magpies, hornets, flies. Even a skinny eagle.

I stayed where I was because I didn't know where else to go. I wasn't eager to spend any more time weaving through the endless trees and rocks in the darkness. And I couldn't bring myself to risk getting lost in the woods again.

It didn't take as long as I would have imagined for the shock of seeing my mutilated body to wear off. I watched with interest as the scavengers did their job, jockeying for a corner of the spoils in their own way.

By the time the sun set on the second day, my body had mostly been reduced to bones. Not the white, bleached kind. More like soup bones. Red and raw and stripped clean of the skin and muscles. The animals left my clothing alone, except where it prevented them from accessing what they wanted. The gauzy pink-and-green scarf had blown into the base of a prickly bush, where it waved like a flag when the wind kicked up.

A glossy raven had taken a particular interest in one of my shoes. With some effort, she hopped and dragged it away from the rest of the mess, out of sight behind some rocks.

At first, I tried shooing the crows and the hornets away—like I had with the coyotes. But it only seemed to work when I was able to drum up a lot of feelings.

It worked when I thought about waking up in the dark, with his hands on my throat.

Or when I thought about my parents, who by now surely knew I wasn't okay.

Or when I thought about the fact that I was dead and lost in the woods while the coyotes and crows ate my body.

I tried to keep my big feelings bright for a while. There was something comforting about the idea that I could still influence the world around me. Even if it was just bees, or a bird who was interested in stripping my leg clean.

I wore myself out after a while. It was impossible to feel very angry or sad or disgusted for long—just like when I was alive. So as the days passed, I settled into a weird acceptance.

I tried flying.

It's a little embarrassing to admit, but I just assumed ghosts could fly. This was a given in every movie I'd ever seen. First, I just sort of willed myself to float. Nope. Then I leapt up and flapped my arms around like I had in dreams. Nothing. I even climbed up onto a fallen log—and then a scraggly pine—to see if a little extra height would help with liftoff. I just floated back down to the ground like a balloon that had lost all of its helium.

For some reason, this made me feel an especially strong current of despair. Which I used to scatter a couple of ravens who were picking at my arm.

When I got too bored and restless (and tired of jumping off logs and trees), I made a loop around the clearing in the opposite direction I had run before. I found the narrow dirt road he must have driven on. There were still faint tire tracks in the dust.

I tried walking down the road for what I guessed was a few miles. The path forked—and forked—and forked again until I was sure that if I kept going I might not be able to find my way back.

The one sign I came across, a wood, unofficial-looking way-post, stated "Ophir Canyon—10." The name didn't ring any bells. And I didn't hear the sound of a single car all that day.

So I stayed where I was.

The ants made their big debut after the bigger winged animals had lost interest in my remains. I watched them for days, finally willing to get closer to my bones in order to see them better as they scurried in organized chaos from their tunnels. There was something hypnotizing about them as individuals. Even at close range, I could barely tell what they were doing. Their little jaws were so tiny, they appeared to be scurrying back and forth without accomplishing anything at all; however, over the next few days, the soup bones were picked clean. It was a relief to see my remains that way. Just dingy gray and white. No more blood.

I appreciated the ants for that.

The nights still scared me. Once the sun set, I left my perch near the ants and backed myself into a rocky overhang where the ravine dipped down into the dry creek bed. A wide rock shelf hung over a couple of larger boulders, and when I lay back I could look at the stars, while knowing that nothing could sneak up behind me.

I thought about him a lot. About how warm and kind his eyes had been while we were talking at Gracie's. About how cold and angry they looked, flashing in the moonlight as I regained consciousness in the dark, in the woods, in the spot I had never gotten up from.

He'd either carried or dragged me quite a way from the car. The spot where my body lay was at least 100 yards from the edge of the dirt road. It would have been impossible to park in the rocky, tree-tied terrain. Even if another car did come up the dirt road, they weren't going to see anything unless they wandered to the right spot and noticed the bones that were becoming just another part of the landscape, more and more every day.

\* \* \*

I didn't sleep, exactly; however, after a few days, I learned that I could zone out. And it was a little like falling asleep.

When I cleared my mind and relaxed, I could drift. It reminded me of dreaming, except I could choose what I saw. I discovered that I could call my memories up at will more easily than I ever had been able to while I was alive, in vivid detail. Everything I had ever done or seen was all there waiting for me to re-experience in a dream.

I spent a lot of time in the backyard of the house I'd grown up in. In an effort to avoid homework and bedtime, I had sometimes grabbed a blanket from the couch and slipped out the back door to the trampoline where I lay on my back, wrapped myself up, and watched the porch lights come on while the first stars twinkled to life. I could almost hear the crickets and the shuffle of our neighbor next door as he cleaned his grill, the smell of char still drifting through the air.

I thought about my last birthday, when Sharesa and I had rented an Airbnb and jet skis at Bear Lake. The way the wind felt on my face while we raced across the lake, laughing and then screaming when I stopped too quickly and the jet ski rocked then tipped us both into the freezing cold lake. We laughed so hard I was worried we weren't going to be able to pull ourselves back up onto the jet ski.

I thought about my parents, who I hadn't really been in touch with since I'd moved out on my own. I drifted through Christmas mornings, family dinners, movie nights, bike rides, and even some of the times I'd gotten lectured about my grades or getting home late. Even those memories felt comforting.

It was a good way to pass the time.

But once in a while, I felt myself drifting so far into a memory that it took a few seconds to reorient myself to the stark rocks and the blood-soaked ground at my feet, where my bones were scattered across the clearing.

I wasn't sure what would happen if I wandered too far or let myself go into those memories too long or too completely. So I explored carefully.

On day five—I think it was day five anyway, there was really no way for me to tell aside from my own memory—I heard the first car. Distantly. But definitely a car.

I ran as fast as I could. In other words, I would have impressed the crap out of myself running at that kind of speed while I was alive, but it was still sort of disappointing when compared with flying. Which I still really felt like I should be able to do.

I made it to the dirt road in time to watch it crest the switchback a little farther down the hillside. The car was headed in my direction.

I stayed where I was, right in the middle of the road. Against any kind of logic I hoped that maybe they would see me, I guess. Or that I would stop the car. Or at the very least, that I would feel some kind of sensation when the car drove through me.

None of the above happened. The car kept driving—a little too fast for the bumpy dirt road. I didn't stop the car. And it didn't drive through me. Instead, when the car hit me, the force sort of flipped me to the side of the road. Gently. Like I was a tumbleweed or a plastic bag.

I caught a glimpse of the car's passengers before the forest-green RAV4 disappeared into its cloud of dust. A woman and a man. Not *him*, thankfully. The couple were about my age. Mid-twenties. They were listening to their music turned up loud, their laughter even louder on top of it. I saw the way she looked at him as the car bounced over a rut in the dirt. Adoring. Safe. Happy to be alive and together.

The sadness filled me up. That feeling, that connection was what I had been chasing at Gracie's. It had gotten me here. This was where my life had ended. This was what I had left. A well full of memories that stopped at twenty-three.

And that was when I saw it.

The shoe, on the side of the road.

*My* shoe: the one the raven had taken.

It was half propped up in a bush, the coral color already turned a dirty tan streaked with a little bit of rust that I knew was blood.

It was lying in the dip that counted as a shoulder for the road. It wasn't exactly in plain sight. But it wasn't hidden, either. Not like the rest of me.

Which meant that if someone looked at just the right time, they could see it too.

# 8. BRECIA

## BOULDER, COLORADO

### *2 YEARS BEFORE*

I fucked up his computer twelve times over the next few days.

He spent an hour on the phone with Apple support and ultimately got a new computer overnighted because of it.

When that didn't fix the problem, he brought out an electrician, who poked through the wiring in the basement and the garage, fixed a couple of loose connections, then told him it would be another $600 to dig any further.

He declined. He was moving soon. Let the next owners deal with it.

The popping sound and black screen happened when I channeled the anger, the hate, the disgust until it felt like the wave was crashing over me. It wasn't hard to do. Not at first, with the piece of human garbage right in front of me, holed up in his basement with a Diet Coke, pretending to be buried in his job with a browser in MatchStrike open at all times. All while the little blond girls played upstairs and their mother made him food and took his empty dishes away.

Kimmie came to the basement door after the screen had gone dark for the twelfth time. Dinner time had already passed. He'd stayed in the basement, insisting he needed to catch up on work because of his "stupid computer."

She knocked. Then she jiggled the door handle. "Daddy, will you read? Mommy says you will."

When he didn't respond, she tried again. Louder. "Daddyyyyyy! Mommy said to come get you—"

He stood up and flung the door open while her little hand was still on the handle. She fell into the room and banged her elbow on the doorframe.

"Tell *Mommy* she knows I'm busy," he replied between his teeth, ignoring her wide blue eyes filled with tears and the way she pulled her lower lip in hard.

"Okay," she whispered, then hurried back up the stairs.

I stopped for a while after that, filled with guilt instead of anger.

Maybe it wasn't fair for me to poke the bear, when the bear couldn't hurt me anymore.

He messaged Nicole back just once while I was messing with him, muttering under his breath and raking a hand through his short, freshly cut hair about the "frickin' computer."

I tried to bring the emotion back. To stop him. But the harder I tried to summon the rage and horror, the more I felt like a wrung-out rag. The way you feel after you've been sobbing for hours and suddenly hit a wall and you just stop. I couldn't feel anything anymore. I just felt worn out and empty.

I watched long enough to see that he was writing to tell her that they were still on for Saturday—and that he was sorry he hadn't been in touch because he'd been having computer trouble.

Then I went upstairs to be with April and the girls.

April and Emma were doing a puzzle in the empty living room, while Kimmie skipped in circles on the carpet in the spaces where the couches had been the day before. The moving truck would be here Sunday. Nearly everything was packed.

Oscar the cat was sprawled across April's lap, watching her hand move pieces of the puzzle into place. When I entered the room, Oscar turned his head and looked in my direction but stayed where he was.

"Fifteen," Kimmie proclaimed as she completed another circuit. "Sixteen." She stopped to catch her breath. "Mommy, do you think I can get to a hundred?"

April smiled. She looked tired but happy. She'd been up late packing, while James "worked."

I realized she was younger than I'd thought when I saw her that first night. Like the girls, she had soft, wispy white-blond hair that fell in light waves around her shoulders. Her hazel eyes narrowed as she studied the pile of puzzle pieces on the floor. I watched her pick out the edge pieces and nudge them over to Emma, who squealed, "Mom! I found another piece."

April nodded and continued sifting through the puzzle pieces, giving Oscar a pat on the head with her other hand. "I think we're going to be finished with this one before we leave."

I closed my eyes and tried to shut out the rage and foreboding that filled me every time I saw his wife and his two babies.

He didn't deserve this. They sure as hell didn't deserve this. They just didn't know it yet.

I watched Oscar stiffen and raise his head as the feelings welled up and then crashed over me like a wave. He had stopped purring and looked ready to leap out of April's arms.

I backed away and stood at the top of the basement steps for a few minutes before going back downstairs. I couldn't help myself.

\* \* \*

Nicole took a while to respond. I was starting to hope that maybe she'd lost interest—or gotten the message that he was flaky, if not a murderer.

Then on Friday morning, he refreshed his MatchStrike web app for the 100th time, and there it was: a new unread message from Nicole.

I shut down his computer again as soon as the screen popped up. Then again when he rebooted the computer. I already felt worn out by the third time he restarted the computer. So I let it happen, hoping that the message would be a brush-off.

It wasn't.

*Sorry about the technical issues. I was starting to think it was me!! Hah. Meet at Twiggs tomorrow? 7 still good? I swear if you are 4'10" and 600 pounds in person though ...*

I saw his smile. He wouldn't disappoint her. With the weird beard shaved, he was as good-looking as the day I'd first met him.

He spent a few minutes composing his reply to Nicole. He finally went with,

*Starting to sweat a little. Is 5'2" and 590 ok? If so, 7:00 is great.*

She responded almost immediately with a bunch of laughing-face emojis.

His smile got wider.

She was back in.

When he went upstairs for lunch, he told April that he had to meet with a contractor who would be taking on some of his workload while they moved. He didn't want to be too distracted.

April, who was wrapping cups in bubble wrap and placing them into a box alongside the rest of the dishes in the kitchen while the girls skipped around the finished puzzle, nodded. "Thanks, babe. You want to watch a movie or something afterward? If it's not too late? I can't believe it's our last night here." Her face fell a little as she looked past him and down the hallway. "I'm going to miss it. I keep remembering bringing Emma and Kimmie home from the hospital."

He squeezed her arm and took one of the unwrapped cups from the cupboard to pour himself a glass of water. "Yeah, lots of memories. But we'll make new ones."

I felt sick. April just smiled wistfully and kept packing while he took his glass of water downstairs, whistling a little to himself. Probably thinking about his date with Nicole.

The lightbulb in the kitchen flickered above April's head.

I decided then that I was going on his date too.

I wasn't sure what I could do. As far as I could tell, I wasn't very powerful. A flickering light and a messed-up computer weren't going to stop him from hurting someone.

But I had to try.

# 9. SKYE

## KUNA, IDAHO

## NOW

Before it was light outside, my mom was awake and making calls at the kitchen table with a cup of plain black coffee. I sat next to her at the table, watching the wisps of gray light build over the horizon through the patio windows.

I hadn't really started drinking coffee until I'd gotten the job at the Daily Grind a year ago. To my mom's delight, I'd started recreating the drinks at home. In the mornings before I left for school, we'd drink soy lattes or caramel macchiatos together until I had to leave.

The despair washed over me in a wave, and I wondered how long it would last. Mourning every detail of the life I would never experience again.

There were so many little, beautiful things. The feel of the late-afternoon sun filtering through the windows after school as I did my homework. Fresh coffee to my lips. The smell of my mom's hair when she gave me a hug. Things I'd taken in stride as part of my day. Let alone the things I'd never get to experience now. The things I'd been telling myself I dreaded about going to college but was really just nerves.

My mom called the police station first.

I could hear both sides of the conversation as well as if I were on the phone myself, when I squeezed in close to her.

I quickly gathered that they weren't looking for me. Not really.

I was eighteen. I wasn't legally required to come home to anyone.

The fact that my phone was going straight to voicemail wasn't enough of a reason to pull in the resources that would be necessary to track me down.

"The paperwork for the missing persons report has been filed," the woman on the other end of the line replied patiently. "That's all I can tell you for sure right now. I know how difficult this is, but an officer will be in touch as soon as possible. If you learn anything else, please keep me updated."

I watched as my mom's fingers curled into a fist. She gritted her teeth. "She's never done anything like this. Ever. She was supposed to be driving to ISU with me today. Her first year of college. Something is really, really wrong."

There was a brief silence on the other end of the phone. "I understand. An officer should be in touch shortly, you should be hearing from someone today. This morning."

My mom's hands shook as she ended the call and then dialed my dad.

My parents had split up when I was in fifth grade. My dad moved to Oregon with his girlfriend, Sandy. I saw him maybe twice a year after that. We weren't especially close. Still, when he answered his phone on the first ring, I felt almost dizzy with the clash of joy and sadness that filled me to the brim.

"Marisa? Are the police looking for her? Has she come home," he started before she could speak.

The bulb above the kitchen table flickered wildly, and my mom looked up and frowned. She turned the light switch off and stood to dump her coffee down the sink in the semi-darkness of the kitchen.

"They aren't doing much of anything." Her voice wavered. "I'm going over to her work as soon as it opens at six. I couldn't get a hold of anybody last night."

My dad swore under his breath then cleared his throat and said, "I'm booked for the 10:00 flight. I should be there by noon. We'll find her, Mari. We'll find her. Have you been able to log into her computer? See if she was getting cold feet about college or something."

I could hear the desperation in his voice. The hope that maybe there was some kind of non-awful explanation. That maybe I was somewhere safe—if not especially responsible.

They both knew me better than that, even if the police didn't. I'd never not come home.

My mom shook her head. "I tried and tried. I can't figure out her password."

"There's nothing to find there," I told her. "Don't bother." But even as I said the words, she was grabbing a scrap of paper to jot down "1025" and "Mickey." Mickey was the name of the dachshund we'd had when I was five. And 1025 was the pin I'd chosen for a joint bank account I'd had with my mom when I was in elementary school. My actual password was a combination of letters and numbers I'd created from the chorus of a Britney Spears song. She'd never guess it.

When she hung up with my dad, my mom sat at the kitchen table staring at her phone. I sat and stared too, willing it to ring.

It wasn't like finding out what had happened would bring me back.

Even so, I wanted to be found as much as she wanted to find me.

And I wanted the police to hunt James down more than I had ever wanted anything.

"Ask Ken about the hot chocolate guy. His name is James," I told her, knowing she couldn't hear me but unable to stop myself. I was pretty sure nobody had seen me get into James's car; however, he'd been in that coffee shop at least three or four times a week all that summer.

*Ken thought he was a nice guy. He wanted you to ask him out,* I reminded myself as the despair settled over me in the dark kitchen like a lead blanket.

My mom's eyes slowly filled with tears. I wondered if we were wrapped up in that blanket together.

\* \* \*

We pulled into the Daily Grind parking lot at exactly 5:58 a.m.

I sat shotgun on top of a flattened breakfast sandwich wrapper that had been there for at least a month. My mom got teary-eyed to a country song about family and God while she drove. And as she parked the car and swiped at her eyes with the sleeve of her hoodie, I suddenly realized that I was haunting her.

There was hardly anybody on the sidewalks or roads yet. One lone jogger. Someone standing in front of the cookie shop across the strip mall in the dim street light. A dark figure scurrying across the intersection near the bus stop. I wondered whether all of them were alive. Or if I could see dead people now that I *was* one. Did everyone turn into a ghost when they died, or was I an anomaly? Would I disappear after a while? Did I have a choice in the matter? Or was this my personal eternity? Was it limbo, or was this hell? What would happen when they caught James? What would happen if they didn't? Was I still around because I had unfinished business?

I shut down that train of thought and focused on following my mom up to the front door.

Like I'd hoped, Ken was on shift to open up. When he heard the knock on the still-locked door, he walked to the counter and glanced into the lobby. He looked puzzled when he saw my mom's beat-up red Buick Century—which I had sometimes borrowed on weekends if she wasn't working at the hospice center—but he hurried to open the lobby door.

Before he had even finished with, "Hey, are you Skye's mom?" she was in tears and telling him that I hadn't come home.

Ken didn't make her stand in the doorway. He flipped the front-door sign to open and called back to whoever was in the employee area. "Hey! You're on lobby, okay? I need a few minutes." Then he ushered her toward the comfy green chair in the corner of the room where they couldn't be seen from the front counter. It was where the really serious freelancers came to snag a spot to work—and where we sometimes found kids making out after school.

He sat down in front of her and laced his hands together carefully the way he had when I forgot to clean the espresso machine over the weekend and it clogged. "Tell me what happened."

\* \* \*

When my mom told Ken what she knew—which wasn't much—he looked increasingly worried. I hadn't come home, I wasn't answering my texts or calls, and the police weren't exactly racing to find me. Ken pulled out his phone to show her that I hadn't answered his text the night before either. I looked at his screen.

*Drive SAFE. If hot chocolate guy ever asks about u, I'm gonna send him to your dorm.*

It felt like I'd been turned into ice water.

My mom's expression darkened. "Who's hot chocolate guy?"

"Yes," I prompted, standing up. The can lights in the lobby flickered, and the espresso machine blinked erratically. "That's right. That's him."

Ken side-eyed the flickering lights. "Just one of our regulars. Inside joke. I teased her that she should ask him out all the time, write her phone number on his cup, but she never did."

My mom's face fell. "You don't think he has something to do with it?"

Ken shook his head. "He was a really nice guy. She never asked him out though."

The lights were flickering so much now that Ken turned to squint at them. "Sorry. I think we have a bulb about to go out. I can fix it—" he stood up, and my mom shook her head.

"No, it doesn't matter. Please, do you have any ideas about where she might have gone after she got off work? Anywhere she talked about?"

I forced myself to focus on the little packets of sugar and the newly appointed coffee stirrers that Ken had set out for the day before they were destroyed by the first customers. I was pretty sure that

I was the one making the lights flicker. I needed to calm down if I was going to let them talk. Because if I got any more upset, I was worried I might blow up something in the kitchen or at the register. Then Ken really would have to pause this conversation.

I forced myself to count the Stevia packets, then the Sweet n' Lows while I half-listened. Ken was telling her that for all he knew, I was headed to the bus stop to go home like I always did.

Then I heard him say the words, "But we can check the security footage."

The lights flickered again as I felt the excitement fizz through me. "Yes!" I shouted, and the light bulb above us made a popping sound, then went dark.

Ken frowned apologetically. "The wiring is fucked." He glanced up sharply at my mom. "Uh, I mean it's messed up."

My mom didn't even acknowledge it or the fact that the lobby had been plunged into semi-darkness. "Can we look at the footage on the security cams now? Please, I know you have to work. But you know she wouldn't disappear like this."

The tears started to well up in her eyes again, and Ken's jaw tightened. He put a hand on my mom's shoulder. "I know she wouldn't. And it's no problem. I can have Amy cover me." He gestured toward the back room. "Let's go."

# 10. MEGHAN

## OQUIRRH MOUNTAINS, UTAH

### 1 YEAR BEFORE

My clothes were changing.

I realized it when I saw the shoe on the side of the road. When I looked down at my feet, I was no longer wearing the coral shoes I'd worn to Gracie's. Instead, I had on my old gray-striped slip-on flats. The comfy ones I wore while padding around the apartment before bed.

I wasn't sporting the gray culottes or the navy crop hoodie that were a dirty mess beside my bones anymore, either.

They had been swapped for sweats and my John Lennon t-shirt. The clothes I wore when it was just me, bumming around the house.

I couldn't say why. Only that I didn't really want to be wearing the coral shoes or the outfit I'd carefully chosen for my date at Gracie's anymore.

When I imagined myself in my fuzzy bathrobe, I could suddenly see it.

Changing clothes was fun for a few minutes. I tried on my old prom dress from high school. The high heels I'd bought but never worn last year. Even my swimming suit. But without a mirror or anyone else to see my outfit, I kept the sweats and the Lennon shirt.

I thought about going fully nude for a hot second. But even dead, I wasn't quite comfortable with the idea of being a nudist ghost. Not to mention, my actual body had been stripped bare in a way I'd never in my wildest dreams imagined I'd see. So the idea of clothes was comforting, and I kept them.

While I might not have been wearing the coral shoes anymore, they did become the new epicenter of my existence.

I spent most of my time on the dirt road, where the fading side of the shoe could be seen sticking out behind a small collection of pebbles and sticks on the dusty shoulder.

I drifted in and out of memories while I kept vigil, listening for any sound that might be an approaching car.

At first, I worried I would reach the end of the memories. That I would run out. But the more I drifted the more I realized that the memories I had at my fingertips were like an enormous library had been unlocked. The book of my life, every word and image perfectly clear. It felt like the one beautiful gift I still had left.

On day two of my vigil, a flurry of movement nearby took me out of a memory I'd been savoring from when I was two and saw my first caterpillar. I hadn't known I could go back that far. I quickly learned that even those memories were available in crystal clarity if I reached for them. I watched the little black speckles on the caterpillar's back and the way its sucker-cup feet moved rhythmically across the twig in the grass. I could still feel the perfect awe I'd felt then, as clearly as anything. My chubby little fingers, dirty from the crackers I'd just shoved into my mouth, eagerly reached for the caterpillar. "Gentle, Meghan," my mom said beside me. The sunlight that filtered through our big catalpa tree leaves turned her hair into ribbons of gold as she picked up the twig that the caterpillar was climbing and carefully placed it in my outstretched fingers.

Back on the dirt road with the coral shoe, a shiny black raven landed right beside me with a little gray rock in her beak. I tucked the memory of the caterpillar aside as the raven hopped closer to the pile of pebbles and sticks, then set it down on top of the shoe.

"Thank you," I told her. She cocked her head and studied her treasures, then spread her wings with a little mutter of satisfaction.

She landed in one of the taller pines a few yards away, in what appeared to be a sizable tangle of sticks but must have been a nest.

Three days later, the same raven visited her treasure box again with a shiny red berry. If I hadn't seen her gently lay her treasures down near one another, I wouldn't have seen anything other than debris. But knowing it had all been carefully arranged by the bright-eyed, glossy black bird made me feel good.

At first, I was worried that she might move my shoe again. Each time she visited, she fussed over her little collection, moving a twig a few inches or taking one of the pebbles into her beak again before carefully placing it atop the little mound. But more days passed and more pebbles, and then what appeared to be part of a dried fish tail appeared, I accepted that this was simply where she had chosen to keep her treasure box.

I started to look forward to what she would bring next while I waited and drifted.

* * *

On the seventh day of waiting, I heard the sound of a car in the distance.

When it passed me—and my shoe—I mustered all the emotion I could, hoping it would be like the coyotes and the eagle. That the driver—a hunter, by his faded tan-and-olive camo—would sense something and at least stop.

He didn't even slow down.

The tailgate of his beat-up tan Suburban hit the ruts hard, and I watched as he popped a piece of gum into his mouth during the few seconds I could see his face, peppered with black-and-white stubble and etched with craggy lines.

So I waited and drifted further, through slumber parties I'd attended and books I had read. Conversations I'd had. The feeling of being tucked into bed and even the dreams I'd had while I slept at night. My first kiss. Learning to tie my shoes. Journal entries. Breaking my arm at summer camp in the sixth grade. Sneaking out of my second-story bedroom to meet up with Nolan, my first boyfriend, in tenth grade. The week my grandma Rosie—or "Bubbie Rosie"—had come to stay for a week when my mom was in the hospital for back surgery.

She'd taught me how to make braided challah bread one day while we listened to the radio and she told me stories about my mother as a child that I'd half-listened to at the time but now I hung on every word.

It was the last time I'd seen her alive. Grandma Rosie had died three months later when an aneurism she'd known about since she was in her twenties burst.

"When your mama was a little girl, she begged me not to kill the spiders even though she was terrified of them," Grandma Rosie was saying. There was a thin streak of flour powdered along her jaw-line. Her eyes were just like mine, only set deeper in lines that nearly hid them from view when she laughed. "She'd stand there with a cup in one hand and a sheet of paper in the other, just shaking like a leaf as she gently, gently scooted that spider onto the paper and into the cup."

I watched myself laugh, finally listening fully to this story. I hated spiders too. My mom still scooped them up instead of smashing them into a wad of tissue, and I loved her for it.

Grandma Rosie chuckled louder. "One time, she'd trapped this big old wolf. Big as a quarter. It was too heavy for the paper, and as she was carrying it to the door it fell right off onto the front of her shirt. I'd never heard a child make a noise like that before. She stayed there frozen and screaming her head off until I managed to get it off her."

I watched myself fidget on the barstool while Grandma turned the dough out of the bowl and started to tell me about the importance of putting the flour on your hands instead of the dough. I saw her smile falter a little as I asked if I could watch TV while she kneaded the dough. But then the corners of her eyes crinkled and she nodded. "Yes of course, *Bubbelah*." *Little doll.* "Go and watch your show. We'll finish later."

As ten-year-old me hurried upstairs to watch *Sabrina the Teenage Witch*, I wondered where Grandma Rosie was. She had died more than ten years ago. If death for her had been like death for me. "I miss you, Bubbie," I whispered.

I heard her reply as my ten-year-old self reached the top of the stairs.

"I'll be right here when you're ready."

I abruptly stopped drifting and blinked at the quiet, dusty road in front of me. Had that always been part of the memory? Something I hadn't paid attention to when I was ten? There were plenty of details I'd missed in the moment.

Still, it sounded as if she was speaking to *me*.

Not the ten-year-old me.

*Me*, Meghan on the side of the road by a dusty, bloodstained shoe.

A jolt of excitement—followed by a wave of terror—ran through me.

What would it mean if she *was*?

Part of me wanted to drift back then and there. To find out. To see if I could talk to Bubbie. To know whether she would talk back.

But the part that had been sitting by the side of the road in the middle of the woods wasn't ready to find out. Because the part of me that thought just maybe she was speaking to me couldn't quite process the disappointment if she wasn't.

I wanted to hug the possibility for a while before I tested it.

And that was when I heard the sound of another car.

Distantly droning. Smacking the potholes with muted, faraway thunks.

As the sound got closer, I reached deep for the emotions bubbling at the surface. The surprise and hope at hearing Bubbie and wondering if maybe she wasn't gone, just like I wasn't gone. The terror that had brought me here. The rage I felt when I remembered falling asleep in his car and waking up to his black eyes above me in the darkness.

The mix of happy and sad and anger and terror felt effervescent and tight. Like a pop bottle that's been shaken up.

I couldn't feel the dead brown pine needles and dirt along the bank where I stood anymore.

I couldn't feel the temperature drop as the sun set in the hills around me.

But I could feel this, and as the soda bottle burst I watched the car come around the curve in the road, toward me.

The driver was a woman in her twenties. Hair was piled on top of her head in a messy bun. A "coexist" bumper sticker was peeling off the front of her beat-up Jeep. Her lips were moving, like she was singing. But her eyes were sad.

"Stop," I screamed as I watched her eyes flick to the barely noticeable fork in the road ahead, where the shoulder of the road dipped then branched into the sorry excuse for a road. Where my bones were slowly becoming part of the earth.

The girl with the messy bun drove through me and my tidal wave of feelings, crashing invisibly around us both.

"Please stop," I whispered as the despair crashed harder.

And then, even though I couldn't quite believe it was happening, she did.

# 11. BRECIA

## BOULDER, COLORADO

### *2 YEARS BEFORE*

He got ready for his date while April took the girls to McDonald's for dinner.

"Bye, Daddy!" Kimmie called as she and Emma skipped down the hall toward the garage door.

He popped his head out of the bathroom, where he'd been shaving. Then he lifted his hands above his head and growled. "You'd better get in your booster seats before the tickle monster can catch you!"

Kimmie and Emma squealed with delight, and April laughed as he chased the girls out the door and caught them in his arms when the wall of labeled boxes blocked their path, tickling them both until they begged him to stop and promised to eat all of their Happy Meals.

I watched in disbelief.

Grudgingly, I admitted to myself that I understood a little better why April didn't know.

Because if *I* didn't know what he had done—100% for sure, because well, here I was—I never really would have believed he was capable of hurting someone.

It made it worse, somehow. That he could be the tickle monster *and* the monster waiting with an extension cord in my side yard at the same time.

I wanted him to be one or the other. Not both.

When the garage door had shut and the house was silent, he opened his phone and turned his music up loud. A playlist called "60s party."

Neil Sedaka.

Roy Orbison.

Paul Anka.

Again, not what I would have expected. Metallica, yes. Korn, definitely. But peppy 60s hits? I watched his eyes as he tapped a razor on the side of the sink and ran a hand over his freshly shaven face, then practiced his smile in the mirror.

Satisfied, he checked his in-app messages—nothing new from Nicole—and grabbed the keys to the blue Kia in the garage.

But as his fingers closed around the doorknob, he suddenly shook his head and turned around.

I followed him downstairs and into his basement office, where he opened the latched top drawer of his desk and pulled out two containers of Tic Tacs.

He opened one of the containers and tapped a few white capsules into the mostly full second container.

I took a few steps closer to get a better look. He whistled "Pretty Woman" as he closed the Tic Tac container, gave it a little shake, and inspected it from the side.

That's when I realized that the capsules he had added weren't shaped like the others. They were round and white instead of oblong and white. And they were scored down the middle.

*Rohypnol.* I'd seen enough episodes of *SVU* to know the name by heart.

It was one of the most common date rape drugs.

I felt a sort of fuzzy numbness as he tucked the Tic Tac container into his corduroy jacket. Whistling to himself, he hurried back upstairs and into the garage.

When he opened the driver's side to the Kia, I brushed past him and sat in the passenger side. From atop the neatly stacked boxes in the semi-darkness of the garage, Oscar sat perched, flicking his tail back and forth.

James/Jamie connected his phone to the car's bluetooth and joined in with the last chorus of "Sweet Sixteen" by Neil Sedaka as we pulled away from the house, east toward Denver.

I studied his face, looking for any indication of a red flag. Anything that would tell Nicole not to leave her drink alone. Not to take her eyes off it for a second. Not to trust the chiseled, clean-cut jawline or the warm smile.

There was nothing. Not right now.

It had been exactly one week since he'd slipped through my side gate and waited for me to appear. And it had been almost one year since I had screened his last call.

I never could have imagined the price I'd pay for rejecting him.

That little bottle of Tic Tacs was apparently the price she would pay for inviting him into her life. The price for hoping that maybe he would be the one.

Were there more people like me who had paid that price? More women who didn't want him? Or who didn't realize they wanted nothing to do with him until it was too late?

I forced myself to focus on the road in front of us and kept the rage bubbling inside me at a simmer.

I couldn't afford to waste it.

# 12. SKYE

## KUNA, IDAHO

### NOW

There were seventy-two hours of security footage saved on the camera.

Ken removed the memory stick and popped it into a thumb drive on his keychain. "It's good you came today. The camera loops over itself after seventy-two hours. So there's a lot. If we don't get through all of it, I'll make you a copy." He glanced at the door to the small office, and I knew he was thinking about what Don, the owner, would say about giving out a copy of the security footage. Don said no to everything. Thankfully, Don was almost never around.

Ken hit the "backup" button on the camera, which resulted in a ping to his phone. I wished I could give him a hug.

A few minutes later he pressed play at 8:00 a.m. on Friday, when I'd first arrived for my shift. He and my mom watched in silence as I moved into frame at the east edge of the parking lot, walking quickly but glued to the screen of my phone. I was smiling, watching some video or meme I couldn't remember now. It was just a normal day. A happy day. The last time I'd have to work a morning shift before my first weekend at college.

After I went inside and out of frame, Ken scanned forward in the security footage. Each time a car entered the parking lot or an employee exited the building, he hit play.

"That's him," I screamed when a blue Kia appeared on the screen, in the far side of the lot. The footage stopped zooming forward and froze momentarily, and I tried to tamp down my nervous excitement. "That's him," I whispered again as the video resumed at normal speed.

"That's him," Ken said as if repeating me. "That's the regular I was telling you about."

James walked into the Daily Grind then re-emerged a few minutes later with his hot chocolate. My mom frowned when he got back into the car and drove away. It was slow-going. "I can go through this later, I don't want to take up any more of your time. I know you need to work. I just thought maybe you'd recognize something out of the ordinary better than I would. Will you go forward to the end of her shift? She was supposed to get off around four."

Ken nodded and kept scanning the footage in fast-forward. Cars zipped in and out of frame. The mail arrived. A couple of high schoolers made out in front of their car. A flock of seagulls descended to eat someone's discarded bagel remains.

The blue Kia appeared a second time, pulling into the lot at the very edge of the video frame. Nobody got out of the car this time.

When I saw it, the jolt of emotion shut down Ken's phone. My mom panicked. "Did you lose it? Where did it go?"

Ken shook his head in frustration and pressed his phone's home button. "No, the backup is saved. I think it's just a big file." He frowned at the black screen.

Just as the phone rebooted, someone knocked at the office door and a petite brunette who had started the week before—Allison?— poked her head into the room. "Hey, uh. It's getting kind of busy out there—should I call Don about getting someone else on shift or ..." She smiled sweetly, and Ken blanched.

"Um, no. I'll be out in just a second, okay?" he said, throwing my mom an apologetic look. I didn't blame him. It was almost eight. But I tried my darndest to slam the door on Allison as she left. I did not succeed.

"You've been really, really helpful," my mom said. "You get to work, and I'll watch it at home." She stood up and turned her head before he could see her get teary-eyed again, but her voice couldn't hide it. "I just feel so helpless. Like there's nothing I can do. This gives me something at least."

Ken awkwardly patted her shoulder. "Let me know if you need anything else. And please let me know when you find her. I'll ask around to anyone else who was on shift yesterday to see if they noticed anything." I wished again that I could hug him as I followed my mom back to her car.

She kept it together as she drove out of the parking lot then pulled over on a side street that turned into the strip mall to cry.

Her phone pinged once, announcing the incoming email from Ken with the footage. Then again, with a text from my dad. His flight had just taken off. He'd be there in two hours.

\* \* \*

The blue Kia cruised through the footage five times before my shift ended, on the hour. Each time, he pulled into the back corner of the lot, facing the front of the building. Stayed parked for a while. Then drove away.

He had been waiting for me to get off shift.

Each time I saw the blue car, the video briefly froze as my excitement and horror bubbled up.

At first I was hopeful that the freeze-frame would make it easier for my mom to recognize the car as the same one that kept appearing in the parking lot. But of the hundreds of cars that moved into the lot in fast-forward, she didn't notice the Kia. She just got panicky that the video was doing something trippy and started muttering a prayer that it wouldn't crash.

Every few minutes, she checked her phone and felt for the ringer to make sure that it was turned on and that she hadn't missed a call.

She hadn't.

\* \* \*

My dad looked like he hadn't slept.

When he saw my mom's puffy face, his own eyes got red but he grimaced and waved her off. "It's gonna be okay, Mari. Let's not waste time getting emotional."

My mom bit her lip but said nothing as he dragged the suitcase through the front door, intentionally not looking at the photos of me lining the hallway.

I suddenly remembered in stunning clarity the time we had to put my cat Snickers to sleep. It was right before he moved away. When I was in third grade. I hadn't understood what "putting Snickers out of her misery" meant, even though I was old enough that I should have. Especially given that Snickers had just gotten caught in the garage door. I guess I thought they were going to help her. Put her out of her misery and make her better again.

She cried pitiful frail mewls while my dad wrapped her in an old beach towel and my mom hurried to call the vet to see if they were still open. I stroked her black-and-white head, careful not to touch the line of dark red coming from one ear.

When my dad came home from the vet without the cat an hour later, I couldn't stop crying. I had told her it would be okay. And I hadn't said goodbye. Not really.

My dad had taken me by the shoulders, looked me in the eye and said, "I'm sorry, Skyebird. But what's done is done."

The words echoed in my memory as I watched my parents—who hadn't seen each other for at least a year now—sit side by side, scrutinizing the rest of the security footage.

*What's done is done.*

\* \* \*

When the footage showed a timestamp of 4:00—the end of my shift—the blue Kia reappeared at the far edge of the parking lot.

Then at 4:09, as I walked into frame after gathering my things, the car pulled through the open space and into the long, narrow strip mall.

I studied my parent's faces, waiting for them to connect the dots.

But a gray Honda pulled out at the same time. Just as a blue Ford sailed past. I knew I wouldn't have noticed the Kia either except for the fact that I was looking for *him*.

A sinking sense of panic took me like a riptide as I saw myself walk toward the other edge of the video frame. Toward the second entrance from the parking lot to the strip mall. The blue Kia wasn't visible anymore. He'd pulled out of the other parking lot entrance.

I was about to walk out of the camera view.

Which meant that they wouldn't see me get into his car or even talk to him. I'd gotten into the Kia when I passed the FroYo, at least twenty yards away. I remembered wondering if that's where he'd been.

But right before I stepped out of frame in the security footage, my hand went up.

My mom saw it too. "Did you see that?" She leaned forward and nearly toppled the computer off the kitchen table.

My dad shook his head and righted the computer. "What? What was it?"

"She waved. She was waving to someone. Or starting to wave, anyway. Her hand went up and—" My mom quickly rewound the footage back a few seconds and they both watched in silence as I stepped to the edge of the security footage and started to raise my right arm. My mom hit pause.

It was hard to see my expression in the footage. It wasn't crystal clear. But even from a distance, you could tell that I was smiling at someone.

The panic receded, replaced by a fizz of excitement. "Yes, I was waving. At him, at the blue Kia," I exclaimed to zero reaction.

My dad leaned in closer and studied the screen for a few seconds. Then he pulled out his phone. "She's definitely waving at someone. What's the number the police gave you? They should know."

My mom unlocked her phone to pull up the number, rubbing her forefinger and thumb together like she always did when she was nervous. "They'll just say it's one of her friends." She paused then added hopefully, "Maybe it was?"

My dad nodded slowly but wouldn't meet her eyes as he dialed the police. My mom rewound the footage one more time before pressing play to keep watching the rest. Just in case I showed up back at work, I guess. I knew I wouldn't. Not alive, anyway. So I listened to my dad's conversation with the police instead.

To my surprise, the woman who picked up—the same one my mom had spoken to earlier—told him that she had passed on my mom's comments from earlier. Officer Willis was the name of the officer who would be looking into what had happened to me. There was no official investigation yet. But Officer Willis would look at the video they had—and anything else my parents felt like was important—to determine next steps and evaluate the level of likelihood that I was indeed missing.

My dad thanked the dispatcher and hung up. "An officer will be here this afternoon. They're gonna 'evaluate' the case. Which means we need to figure out whatever we can before he gets here. She's in trouble, Mari. I know she is." His voice broke a little, and he cleared his throat. "I know I haven't seen her every day like you have, and I know it's been a while and I feel like shit about that, but she's my daughter and I know her. She wouldn't disappear like this for no good reason. She wouldn't. What else can we do before that officer gets here?"

My mom shook her head and wiped at her cheeks. "I was really hoping we'd see something on the video. I guess—I guess we could go back to the coffee shop and see if anyone else saw anything? A regular? Maybe that hot chocolate guy who came in every day will be there?"

I perked up at this. Maybe he *would* be back. I felt sick at the idea of my parents running into him. But maybe, just maybe he'd come in. Maybe he'd let something slip. Or maybe someone else who had been on shift or on a smoke break noticed me getting into his car.

There were only so many threads to follow when someone disappeared into thin air.

I thought about my body, lying still and broken off Blacks Creek Road. I both longed for and dreaded being found. It would snuff the light right out of my parents' eyes. But seeing the flickers of hope was worse, when I knew without a shred of doubt that there was no chance I was coming back.

# 13. MEGHAN

## OQUIRRH MOUNTAINS, UTAH

### *1 YEAR BEFORE*

I watched in amazement as the woman with the blond messy bun abruptly pulled onto the sloping shoulder of the dirt road, her front bumper just a few feet away from the shoe.

As I watched her through the windshield, I could see that she was crying. Crying hard. Her shoulders shook a little as she lay her head against the steering wheel.

I didn't know why she was crying. Or whether I had anything to do with it—like what had happened with the coyotes and the eagle. But regardless of why, she had stopped.

I couldn't cry with her, but I let the waves of grief flow through me while she cried, letting them crash over me. I mourned my parents. I mourned Sharesa. They knew by now that I probably wasn't coming back. I was dependable to a fault. I never left voicemails or texts unreturned. Unless there was something very wrong.

I called up the faces of the people I loved and felt the sadness settle around me like a heavy blanket. I'd never considered the fact that mourning might go both ways. Instead of mourning one person, I was mourning everyone I had ever cared about. They were all gone now.

Inside the vehicle, the girl cried harder. Loud, ugly sobs that I could hear as well as if she were standing next to me.

I tucked away my memories and just watched her for a few minutes. In the passenger seat was a purple-and-blue backpack with a water bottle strapped onto the side. As I peered into the window, I could see that she was wearing hiking boots. There wasn't any camping gear that I could see anyway, which pointed to a day of hiking. Perhaps a day away from whatever was behind the tears coursing down her cheeks onto the steering wheel.

I watched anxiously as she finally sat upright with a shuddering breath. She studied her reflection in the rearview mirror and wiped her eyes.

"Please don't go. Please get out," I coaxed.

She didn't react.

But a few minutes later, she took the car keys in one hand and stepped out of the car.

She closed her eyes and turned her face to the sun that was streaming through the branches and took a deep breath.

I watched, mesmerized.

The shoe was right in front of her.

She sniffed and wiped at her eyes again, gazing at the scraggly trees, her eyes landing on the mostly hidden fork in the road that led to my body.

She took a few steps forward and I urged her on. "Yes. Keep going, okay? Please."

She put her car keys in her pocket and walked far enough to see that the sorry excuse for a road did indeed continue in that direction, rutted and mostly overgrown.

The raven's dark form circled overhead, and she made a sort of muttering cackle.

The girl stopped and watched, then looked back at her car. Somewhere over the hill, in the brush, a twig snapped.

She frowned and wrinkled her nose. "Nah," she muttered, then turned on her heel, heading back toward her car.

I reached out for her retreating shoulder. My hand rested lightly on top of her kelly-green tank top. "No, don't go. Please. Nobody else will stop."

She kept going.

When she reached the driver's side of the car, she pulled her keys out of her pocket and looked behind her, as if someone were following her.

Technically, she was correct.

I backed up a few steps, wondering if it was my fault. Had I scared her?

The despair came back, and I felt myself sinking under it as she turned the key in the door.

I closed my eyes.

But the door didn't slam shut. And the car didn't pull away.

When I opened my eyes, she was still standing by the open driver's side door, looking right at me.

I really thought she could see me for a second by the confused look that slowly spread across her face.

She took a few steps toward me then crouched in the dirt.

That was when I realized she had seen the shoe—and the little altar the raven had built.

The girl with the messy bun frowned as she studied the bleached coral shoe with the dark stain. She didn't touch it.

After a few minutes, she shook her head again and returned to the car.

This time, she rummaged in her backpack and pulled out a cell phone. She took two photos. One up close, and one a little way back that showed the sign for Big Eddy Campground in the distance.

I told myself that it didn't mean anything. That the photos couldn't possibly mean anyone would ever find me. For all I knew, she was planning to post the images to her Instagram account with the hashtags #pickupyourtrash and #protectourplanet.

But as the engine turned over and she drove away I still whispered, "Thank you," before I could no longer hear the sound of her engine.

# 14. BRECIA

## BOULDER, COLORADO

### 2 YEARS BEFORE

He pulled into the parking lot at 6:50. Enough time to request a "private" corner booth from the hostess at Twiggs before Nicole—all smiles and nervous energy, but playing it cool—arrived, scanning around the upscale bar for the person she hoped was waiting for her.

Her bright red hair was longer than it was in her photos on MatchStrike. It cascaded down her back in beachy waves that looked effortless but, I knew from firsthand experience, had probably taken a long time to get just right. She was wearing a seafoam green sundress and a cropped jacket with a little fringe along the bottom. She'd managed the perfect subtle cat-eye. She was beautiful.

A smile played across her lips when he spotted her and waved from the booth, then hurried over to meet her. The smile widened as he placed his hand on the small of her back to walk her back to the booth. He smiled too. He knew exactly what he was doing.

They talked until nearly closing. He told her all about his ridiculous roommate—"Steve." About his job, which he sort of alluded might be related to government security. I scoffed unheard in the booth beside her, studying his hands. Waiting for him to reach for the Tic Tac container. I wasn't a technical person, but after watching him work in his basement for the last week I could confidently tell you that he was managing the website of a multi-level marketing company selling energy drinks.

I thought about April and Kimmie and Emma, who were probably finishing the puzzle before bedtime. Or playing with whatever magical plastic surprise they'd gotten in their McDonald's Happy Meals. The anger began to percolate, a white-hot slow drip. I pushed it down. Not yet.

He told Nicole stories he'd told me while she listened and nodded and laughed and stroked his ego. Just like I had. Because he was charming and handsome and he asked her about her life, too. And when she told him about it, he listened with a kind of intensity I'd mistaken for generous attention.

I knew now that it was the kind of rapt attention that a cat paid a mouse before it struck. I'd seen that look before, in Frank's eyes before he pounced on the feather toy. In Oscar's eyes when he stalked a fly through the house a few days earlier while April and the girls watched in delight.

Nicole's first drink was almost empty. It was a Moscow Mule, in one of those pretty copper cups. She kept one hand lightly on the handle, taking a tiny sip every few minutes. She'd been nursing that drink for more than an hour now; from the sign on the door, the bar would be closing soon. "You're doing amazing," I told her. "Don't get another drink."

When the waitress appeared at the table to ask about refills, he quickly said, "I'll have another. I'm not ready to go quite yet, are you?" He turned to Nicole with a 1,000-watt smile.

She faltered a little and glanced at her drink. I wondered if maybe she was a lightweight, like I had been. If maybe she was feeling tipsy enough already and didn't want to risk looking silly on a first date.

Whatever it took.

I leaned in close to her ear. As close as I could get. "Do not get another drink." I repeated it again. And again.

I heard her say, "Um, sure. I'll have another too, I guess."

While the waitress disappeared with the drink order, Nicole excused herself to the restroom.

I watched her walk away. So did he. When he saw the restroom door close, he pulled the Tic Tacs from his pocket. Casually. He didn't look around the room. Or try to hide the container. He just popped it open and shook it until three capsules fell into his hand. There were two oblong Tic Tacs—and one round pill.

The panic and rage bubbled up, and I frantically grabbed at the emotion. I focused all of it on him and on the objects in his hand. The way I had with the computer.

The light above us flickered wildly.

He glanced at it, unworried. Then closed the lid, popped the two real Tic Tacs into his mouth, and palmed the Rohypnol.

I watched in horror as the waitress appeared, striding across the bar with the two drinks in her hand.

Nicole wasn't back yet.

The waitress placed both drinks in the middle of the table. "Enjoy!" Her smile faded as she squinted at the light, which was still flickering. "Sorry about that. I can get another bulb."

He returned her smile and waved her off. "It's no big deal."

As the waitress walked away, he reached first for his drink, then Nicole's, deftly slipping the white pill over the edge of the copper cup as he slid it toward her side of the table.

I watched numbly as the little white circle dissolved. I hadn't been able to do anything. It was done. When Nicole returned to the table a few minutes later, she was wearing fresh lipstick. The pill had dissolved. All that remained was a tiny white speck.

The clock on the wall showed 10:15. The bar would close in forty-five minutes. He took a long pull of his drink and flashed her a smile. "You know, I think you have the prettiest eyes I've ever seen. When I first saw you on MatchStrike, I thought maybe it was a fake account. Nobody has eyes like that in real life."

Her pale skin turned a deep shade of pink, and she sipped at the drink. "I kind of wondered the same thing about you."

"You should," I muttered angrily, scooting closer to her in the booth. "He just roofied your drink."

He laughed and shook his head. "Online dating is such a mess. I bet you've got some stories to share."

She giggled, but didn't take another sip of the copper mug. In fact, she nudged the drink back just a little and moved her water glass forward. His eyes flicked between the drinks. She didn't notice, and instead started telling a story about the last guy she'd gone out with on MatchStrike, who wasn't even divorced yet despite listing himself as single. He'd even brought one of his kids on the date as a "chaperone" when he couldn't find a sitter.

He laughed at the story in all the right places. But his eyes kept flicking to her drink, which sat mostly full on the table in front of her. Then over to the clock on the wall. Closing in twenty minutes.

"Okay, that was a doozy, but I know you have more," he teased. "Maybe the kind of stories that unlock when you take a few more sips of that Moscow Mule?" He nodded toward her drink while taking a sip of his own. "I'm dying to hear them, so you'd better drink up. The night's young, pretty girl."

Nicole's cheeks flared red once again, and she leaned forward to take another sip of her drink.

I leaned in with her, pressing my ghost lips closer and closer until I was pretty sure I was actually inside her ear canal. "Listen to me, okay? Do not keep drinking. You're not safe. This drink isn't safe. He isn't safe."

I watched her take a small sip of her drink, her freshly lipsticked mouth puckering around the bright pink straw. Then another tiny sip. She looked up at him as she did, and I could see in her eyes how much she wanted him to like her.

I scooted closer to her and tried again, as loud as I could, desperately grabbing at the feelings of powerlessness and inevitability. Trying to somehow make the message go through.

"Stop. You don't have to drink it. I know you don't understand why, but stop. Stop drinking. Something is wrong. Something is very wrong."

Above us, the lights flickered again, almost imperceptibly this time. Nicole wrinkled up her nose. "Are you trying to get me drunk?" she teased. "I'm a lightweight. I'm already kind of buzzed." She reached for her water glass and drained nearly half of it.

"Yes, drink all the water!" I cheered. He chuckled in reply, but the smile didn't reach his eyes.

I draped myself over the table until I was right in front of his face. "Fuck you."

He shifted his body closer to me as if in response and nudged Nicole's drink back in front of her. "I kind of want to see what 'fully buzzed' Nicole is like. Because 'kind of buzzed' Nicole is seriously adorable."

Her smile stayed put, but she didn't reach for the copper mug again. "So is sober Nicole," she replied playfully, but I could see that he'd struck a nerve.

So could he.

He tried to backpedal. "Oh yeah, definitely."

The change in the air was palpable.

At least, to me it was.

As a ghost—or whatever I was—I had lost the majority of my senses. I couldn't feel the smooth surface of the table where my arms were resting lightly, I couldn't smell the half-eaten plate of fries on the table, and I certainly couldn't taste them. I could see. And I could hear. But what I had lost in physical senses I seemed to have gained in metaphysical ones. It was like a current, circling the table. And it had turned heavy and tense.

He didn't try to push her into finishing her drink again.

And she didn't take another sip.

He tried to coax back the flirtatious, eager energy. He tried asking her about her favorite movies, her family, her friends, even the sundress she was wearing. She smiled and answered. But when she didn't giggle and lean into him like she had before, he stopped trying and started to pout. As if she was the one who had ruined this date.

I was ecstatic.

When the waitress brought the check, Nicole took a long drink of water then pulled out her phone. "Hey, I'm actually not feeling great. I'm going to get an Uber headed my way, okay? It was nice meeting you."

No hug. No "let's do this again." No "do you want to come back to my place."

I cheered. Loudly.

His jaw clenched slightly, and he shrugged. "Cool. I'll just get the check, I guess."

She smiled and stood up from the table. "Thanks. Looks like there's somebody right outside, so I'd better hurry out there. Sorry to run!" I looked at her phone. She hadn't even opened the Uber app; however, she had typed out a text to someone named Jen. "It was going really well, but I'm getting bad vibes. Headed home. Want to watch *Criminal Minds*?"

And then she left, while he waited impatiently for the waitress to return his card, then snapped at her for waiting until closing time to bring the check.

The waitress's face crumpled. "Oh, I just—it looked like you guys were on a date, and I didn't want to rush you—"

He gave her a withering look. "She was a bitch." Then he signed the receipt, no tip, and walked to the parking lot.

# 15. SKYE

KUNA, IDAHO

*NOW*

Nobody saw anything.

And the blue Kia didn't show up.

My parents stood near the lobby entrance for two hours, watching for anyone they thought they recognized in the parking lot while my mom sent texts and Facebook messages to anyone who appeared in my "friends" list. Asking if anyone had seen me. If I'd said anything that might offer any kind of clue as to where I was now.

Nobody knew anything.

My parents asked every single person who walked through the door to get coffee if they had seen me yesterday, while my dad flashed them my senior photo on his phone.

Everyone shook their heads sadly and told my parents that they hoped I showed up soon. One woman, who looked familiar, said she remembered me but hadn't seen me leave work yesterday. A couple of college kids who I had definitely kicked out of the lobby for making out nodded and said they remembered me too. But nobody had seen me leave work.

As the afternoon wore on, I could see that even Ken was getting antsy inside the lobby. He brought my parents a couple of iced lattes and asked if they'd seen anything on the video footage. But he quickly added that he wouldn't be able to give them any additional security footage, glancing back inside the store as he said it. Someone had clearly narked to the owner about the security tape this morning. Even I could feel the desperate, frenetic energy in front of the store. It wasn't good for business. People just wanted their Americanos.

Officer Willis finally called around 2:00 p.m., and my parents agreed to meet him back at the house, in case he needed any of my things. The unspoken understanding being if search dogs were needed.

We piled back into the car. My dad driving, my mom still glued to her phone, copying and pasting the same message to my 541 "friends" on Facebook. "I'm sorry to bother you, I'm Skye's mom. She didn't come home last night, and we're so worried. Please message me if you can think of anything that might help us find her, even if it doesn't seem very important."

I sat watching over her shoulder as the replies poured in, some of them almost instantly. Mostly people whose names I only vaguely recognized responding with some variation of, "Oh no! I'm so sorry. I can't think of anything." I cringed as I saw David Hauser's name pop up. We'd had classes together all through high school. He was an entirely different level of popular, aka people knew who he was. But he was also funny and genuinely nice. I'd heard he was going to ISU in the fall too. Sometimes I thought about what might happen if I, you know, stopped being a social caterpillar and transformed into a social butterfly.

Instead I was dead and my mom was messaging him on Facebook, her tired eyes flicking back and forth between the new message she was typing and the replies coming into her Messenger app.

I didn't realize the car had stopped—and that my dad was saying something—for a few seconds. "Mari, hello? MARISA. Do you see that?"

I tracked where he was pointing and saw the entrance to the FroYo. It was mostly empty, with one older guy hunched over at a patio table, concentrating on eating his frozen yogurt.

My mom frowned. "No, what? I think we need to hurry so we don't miss Officer—" She stopped talking.

I leaned forward over the jockey box in the car and finally saw what my dad was pointing at.

Above the door of the FroYo was a security camera.

Angled out, toward the parking lot.

If that footage still existed, I was on it.

And so was the freak in the blue Kia.

# 16. MEGHAN

## OQUIRRH MOUNTAINS, UTAH

### *1 YEAR BEFORE*

For several days after the girl with the messy blond bun drove away, I stayed where I was, sitting shiva by the shoe. Waiting. Hoping that the photos she took would lead someone to this place. To find me. To take my body—and what was left of my soul—home.

I still couldn't have explained why. I didn't know what good that would do. I would still be dead. I would still be invisible to everyone I loved. But at least maybe I could be near them. For reasons I couldn't really articulate, every part of me wanted to be found.

A few more cars passed me on the rutted dirt road on the way to Ophir Canyon. None of them stopped. The raven returned every few days with new tiny treasures to add to the collection by the shoe. A piece of glass. A little white slice of quartz. A black pebble.

I drifted carefully while I waited, treading lightly through memories of my first job, some of the lectures I'd attended in college, a campout with my church group in high school. I re-read my favorite book, *The Bean Trees* by Barbara Kingsolver. I got drunk with Sharesa in San Diego during spring break.

The sun rose and set in the dusty hills, and rose and set again. The darkness still scared me when the shadows finally overtook my corner of the woods each night. I saw the coyotes every once in a while, their eyes flashing green and white when the moon caught them right. They gave my little shrine by the side of the dirt road a wide berth. I didn't approach them again, either.

When the sun had risen and set at least five times, I ran my hands—which I had given an intricate rainbow manicure—over the raven's altar. The shoe had bleached even further and was covered with a new layer of dust from a windstorm two nights earlier. It was getting hard to recognize as a shoe at all, unless you saw it from just the right angle.

As the days wore on into weeks, I couldn't bear to be alone with the shoe any longer. And I couldn't bear to leave it.

So finally, I drifted back to the memory of Bubbie Rosie.

If this was all I had left—this dusty road and the raven and the coyotes and the bleached shoe and the precious memories I turned over and over in my mind like a worry stone—I needed to know.

I started at the beginning of the memory. To the challah dough, to the sound of my grandmother's delicate laughter and the way the bowl clinked against the counter as Bubbie tipped it out onto the countertops and dipped her hands into a little hill of flour.

I watched Grandma Rosie's eyes as ten-year-old-me asked if I could watch TV while we waited for the dough to rise.

I watched her mouth form the words, "Yes of course, *Bubbelah.*"

And then, while the younger version of myself hurried up the stairs, I tried to hold onto Bubbie.

"I'm sorry I left you to make the bread," I told her.

I felt myself grasping at the edges of the memory. Ten-year-old me didn't have any more memories of Bubbie here. She just had memories of *Sabrina the Teenage Witch.* Specifically, the episode where Sabrina tells her friends she's a witch.

The threads were unraveling quickly. "I wish I had more memories with you," I whispered before I lost them.

Bubbie's soft, rosy cheeks turned up in a slight smile. "Ah, but here you are *Bubbelah.*"

I felt a jolt of electricity as the threads stopped unraveling, the focus suddenly clear again.

I wasn't drifting anymore.

Instead of watching myself sprawl out on the bed and watch Sabrina tell her friends the truth about being a witch, I was still in the kitchen with Bubbie.

It was more than that, though. Before, I had been a fly on the kitchen wall—a voyeur, I guess—watching the interaction. It had been kind of like a movie.

Now I was *in* the kitchen. And Bubbie Rosie was looking at me intently, her hands still covered in flour.

The feeling spread through me like sunlight, and for the first time since I'd disappeared into the hills, I felt a spark of joy.

"Bubbie? You can hear me?" I'd expected the words to sound choked, like they would if I were trying to squeeze them out through all my feelings if I were alive. Instead, they seemed to drift into the memory with me, perfectly clear, caught by the current that surrounded me and Grandma Rosie.

"I can hear you, *Bubbelah.* I've been waiting for you." Her eyes crinkled with joy and then softened with sadness. "I had not expected to see you so soon."

"You're alive? I mean, not alive, but—I don't understand any of this. Is this heaven or something?"

Bubbie Rosie's face broke into a smile. I wasn't sure whether we could hug. I doubted it. Not like before, anyway. Physical sensation had died when I died. But the joy that filled me to the brim and the love that radiated from Grandma Rosie's voice was as warm and as comforting as any hug I'd ever had while I was alive. "I don't know the answer to that question, *Bubbelah.*" She looked down at her hands, covered in flour. "All I know is that we are here together, in this memory. That somehow it still connects us."

"How ..." I struggled to put the pieces together. "Is there like, a god or something? What have you been doing all this time? What happens now?"

Bubbie's smile softened. "I don't know the answer to those questions either, *Bubbelah*. What I know is that the people we loved on the other side are gone. I mourned you, like you mourned me when I died. But I have learned, as you know now, that the people we love are not gone forever. That everything we ever loved, ever did, ever said, ever read, ever experienced, comes back to us. See, here we are together." She gestured around the sunlit kitchen.

"So, you live here now, in this memory?" I asked. "And some of my other memories?"

Bubbie nodded. "In a way, yes. Like you live in mine. It's the tapestry we wove together. The threads still bind us."

I felt a shadow of despair creep into the joy. "We can't make any more memories together, though. It's just ... like a movie?"

She shook her head. "Ah, that is what I wondered at first too. But *Bubbelah,* there are so many movies you have not seen."

I stared at her in confusion. She continued, "Those threads, they branch out forever, if you know the way to go. Lifetimes of threads. Mine, yours." She gestured around us. "So many threads. *Ima* is here. *Satva* is here. I will show you."

*Ima.* Mother. Her mother, my great grandmother who I had never met. *Satva.* Son. Ben, my uncle who had died of an overdose when I was a baby.

I stared at her in amazement. "I don't have any memories of *Ima*, though. She died before I was born. And I really only met Uncle Ben once, right after I was born."

Grandma Rosie nodded. "That doesn't matter anymore, *Bubbelah.* We couldn't see so many of the threads that tied us together while we were alive. Those threads are visible now." She paused, then added, "If you know the way."

I shook my head. "I don't understand."

Grandma Rosie brushed off her hands, and a cloud of flour sifted through the air in front of her. She looked thoughtful for a moment. "We can follow the threads together. The story I told you about your mother, when she was a little girl carrying spiders from the house under paper cups? We can visit that memory together. I can show it to you. Because I was there. Even though you were not."

I suddenly understood what she meant, and the shadow of despair disappeared. So many memories. An eternity of memories stretching backward forever. "Show me," I told her excitedly. This meant I could meet my uncle Ben. I could meet Ima. I hadn't lost my family forever. Yes, I'd lost some of them—for now. But in a strange way, I'd also just found the ones I'd lost.

Grandma Rosie nodded and her smile softened. "When you are ready, *Bubbelah.* I can't show you until you are ready."

I shook my head, confused all over again. "I'm ready, though. What do you mean?"

Bubbie gestured around the kitchen. "Even now, this memory is changing. You are following my thread—instead of yours. In this kitchen, where you never were but I was. It will be hard to go back, after. If you continue, if you follow my threads, it will be impossible."

"Go back?" I let her words sink in. I thought of the coral shoe. The forest road. My body moldering in the rocky ground, disappearing into bleached bones as the ants and the hornets did their work. "You mean, I won't be able to get back to the other side. The side where my body is."

Grandma Rosie nodded. "Yes, *Bubbelah.* And where your mother is. And your friends."

"But I'm lost out there," I told her, the despair sweeping back in. "I'm alone. I don't think anyone is coming for me. He dumped me in the woods."

The joy that had filled the air suddenly went flat. Grandma Rosie's expression crumpled. "Oh, *Bubbelah.* Oh no."

"I thought you knew," I whispered.

She shook her head. "I can't see the other side anymore. I stayed for a long time in the 'real' world. With you. With your mother. But when Ben died, it was time. Time to be here. To find each other in a way we could not while we were alive. Because this is real too, *Bubbelah.*"

I no longer felt like I was drifting. I just felt like I was here. All of me, here. I wanted to tell Bubbie about Jimmy Carlson. For someone to know what had happened to me in the woods. To meet my great grandparents. To see, through Bubbie's eyes, my mother carefully and fearfully carrying spiders safely outside.

Part of me wasn't ready though. Not yet.

"I think I need to go back for a while," I said softly, trying to soak in all the love in the room, buoying me up. "I can find you again, here?"

Grandma Rosie nodded. "Yes, *Bubbelah*. You can always find me. Here or anywhere our lives touched. I love you, little doll."

"I love you too, Bubbie." The threads I'd tried to grasp so tightly earlier now felt like they were pulling snug. Falling into place.

For a moment, I panicked. Grandma Rosie and the sunlit kitchen with the challah bread rising on the countertop didn't disappear like they had before. I thought of the shoe. I thought of the little shrine the raven had assembled. I thought of the Ophir Canyon campground signage, trying to piece together the place that suddenly felt far away. As if it were now the dream.

Then I found myself back on the shoulder of the rutted dirt road, beside the pebble and the little shard of glass, the coins, and the shoe.

I was reminded of the feeling of waking up from a too-late nap in the afternoon, when you sleep until dinnertime and aren't sure, for a few moments, what happened.

The sound of crunching footsteps hit me before I recognized there was someone there with me.

Someone standing over me, looking directly at me.

Looking at the shoe.

The man had a thick auburn beard. He was in his fifties, and wearing a tan shirt and pants.

In one hand, he held a radio.

My gaze drifted in slow motion to the lapel of his shirt.

*Forest Service.*

# 17. BRECIA

## 18 MONTHS BEFORE

I took great delight in watching his face when he saw that Nicole had blocked him on MatchStrike. And not only blocked him, but reported him to the website's admins who suspended his account.

He got the notifications in the moving van around the time we crossed the border into Utah. He pulled into the next rest area, April right behind him in the car with the girls. Then he opened the MatchStrike app.

An error message appeared. *This account has been suspended and banned for violating our terms of service agreement. Please contact admin@MatchStrike.com or call 1-800-MatchStrike for support.*

"Bitch," he hissed through his teeth then slammed the car door and walked to the bathroom, ignoring Emma and Kimmie waving from the car.

He called the number for customer service when we got back on the road. He was down-to-earth and charming at first. It had all been a big misunderstanding, you see. He hadn't pressured Nicole to do anything. They'd had a great time. But he'd declined a second date, and she'd seemed upset. This was apparently her way of sending a pointed message.

The customer service rep—her name was Donna—sounded like she'd heard this line before a few times. She patiently explained that if he would like to appeal the decision, she could escalate his request. It would require a phone interview with both him and Nicole—as a first step.

His tone changed abruptly and he hit the gas a little too hard, making the big van lurch forward. "Are you serious? This is ridiculous. You'll cancel my account just like that, but you'll make me jump through hoops just for the privilege of being part of the worst dating site I've ever been on? What about 'innocent until proven guilty?'"

"I'm sorry, sir, but we are not a court of law. Our user agreement laid all this out, I'd be happy to send you a copy," Donna replied.

I wanted to hug Donna.

He hung up and stared straight ahead at the road.

I studied the set of his jaw and the white of his knuckles on the steering wheel. Remembering how they'd held the extension cord around my neck so tight, not letting up for even a second.

I wished I'd reported him too.

\* \* \*

For the first few months in Utah, he was a normal dad and husband. He unpacked. He took Kimmie and Emma out for ice cream at the adorable little shop around the corner from the new house with the big yard at the base of Lone Peak. He divided his time between a new home office and a tech startup twenty minutes from the new house in Salt Lake. He went for a walk around the block with April and chatted with the neighbors who emerged from the rows of beautiful brick homes lining the streets. He went to church and raised his hand in Sunday school to offer a thought about Jesus' Sermon on the Mount while April beamed.

He didn't appeal the decision from MatchStrike.

He didn't even try to find Nicole online.

But after three months, on a slow Thursday afternoon while he was supposed to be starting a new project for work, he created a new gmail account—and then a new MatchStrike profile.

Jimmy Carlson.

This time, he was a widower. He didn't mention kids. I guessed he was getting to the age where women got suspicious about why he'd never been married.

I shut down the computer three times in a row. Each time, he clenched his jaw and restarted it.

Finally, I left the room and sat down in the hall, across from Oscar. I imagined myself going on more dates with "Jimmy" and felt a crushing sadness and dread.

Oscar stared at me intently. Then cautiously took a few steps toward me until he was right at my feet.

He closed his eyes and flicked his tail a little. "Good kitty," I whispered. He very quietly began to purr.

\* \* \*

I went on every date with James/Jamie/Jimmy for nine months.

I followed him while he worked. While he ate. While he mowed the lawn. While he cleaned his car. While he watched TV—*Chicago PD* and *Chicago Fire.*

Sometimes, he spent hours on the MatchStrike app, flirting and arranging new dates—always a little ways out of town. Other times, he abruptly stopped and turned into a real dad to Emma and Kimmie for a few days, weeks, or even a month. Sometimes, he was cold and dismissive with April. Other times, he could be scarily thoughtful and even funny. Even as his shadow, it was all too easy to believe he was a normal person.

Even on some of his dates.

Sometimes, he eagerly planned to meet the women who responded to his messages. Other times, he ignored them.

Sometimes, he brought the Tic Tac bottle on his dates. Other times, he didn't.

When he did, I could feel it in the way the air churned with sparks and sickness that something was building, the way you feel the barometer start to drop before a storm. The only question was when it would hit.

On those nights I spent the evening whispering—or scream-ing—into her ear.

Sometimes, it seemed to work.

Other times, it didn't.

When it didn't, no amount of flickering lights or hunches helped. Not once he managed to convince her to go on a second date somewhere out of the way. To finish her drink. To let him drive her home instead of calling an Uber. To trust him just enough that he could draw her beyond the reach of potential help. Mine or anyone else's.

He went out with Kelly, who insisted on calling an Uber when she started to feel lightheaded at the end of the night. As she got into the black Honda Civic that pulled into the parking lot of the tiny restaurant, he put on a concerned expression and told her to feel bet-ter. But while the car pulled away, he swore under his breath then blocked her on MatchStrike with the reason from the dropdown menu, "made me uncomfortable."

He'd spent a fair amount of time combing through Reddit on an INCEL forum that offered advice to men "navigating the cesspool of dating apps." It advised blocking women who weren't receptive to advances quickly or who had "misinterpreted advances." Not only did this "teach them a lesson," but on certain apps (including Match-Strike) it made it virtually impossible for that woman to block or re-port his account in return.

He met Liz at an outdoor concert in Deer Valley, about half an hour outside of Salt Lake. I relaxed when he didn't bring the Tic Tac container with him. But between the good music and the string lights flickering like hundreds of fireflies in the cool mountain air, both of them downed four beers a piece no matter how much I screamed and the stage lights flickered. After the show, he walked her to her car and kissed her in the parking lot. She let him—until his hand started wandering up the front of her shirt. When she tried to pull away, he grabbed her by her ponytail and pulled her roughly against him.

I couldn't watch. I also couldn't leave her.

I focused on the dark gravel underneath my feet, imagining I was somewhere else. I chose to be back with Frank, in my apartment, petting his downy head while he purred. The memory was so real that I wrapped it around me like a thick cloak to block out what was happening a few feet away.

Because I couldn't do anything to stop him. Not really. Not enough.

When a car a few rows away chirped and its lights flashed in the dark, I dragged myself back from the memory of Frank to see Liz push him hard, fumbling with her purse while she loudly told him it was time for him to go.

He stared at her, then in the direction of the crunching footsteps approaching from the direction of the car with its headlights blazing.

As he slunk into the darkness, he pulled up the app on his phone to block and report her before he'd gotten back to his own car.

\* \* \*

He chatted with Elle on the MatchStrike app for two months. They exchanged photos and even a video chat one night while April was out to dinner with a new friend and the girls were asleep.

Elle told him about her brother's overdose. Opiates. She'd blamed herself. He shared his grief over his late wife's death. Cancer. It had been really awful. He showed her the photos of Emma and Kimmie hanging on the office walls and cleared his throat like he was regaining his composure. The girls were his world, he said. Everyone was in a good place now. They'd healed. He was a little shy about dating again, but he was feeling strong.

I shut down his phone. Then his computer. Again and again. He patiently waited for them to restart each time, until I went numb.

Elle let him pick her up at her house for their date.

Earlier, in addition to placing the Tic Tac container in his front pocket, he had tucked a long phone charger into the back pocket of his jeans. First, he had wrapped it around the basement banister. Tighter and tighter, to see if it would break.

It didn't.

As the car slowed in front of the address Elle had given him, I dove through the cracked window and made it to the front door before he could get out of the car.

I pleaded. I screamed. I even tried to shove her—which did absolutely nothing. Elle tucked her short blond hair behind one ear and gave him a long hug. Then she got into the car with him, chattering excitedly about the new bar they were going to.

I focused all my fear and horror at the car itself, hoping the engine would die the way the computer had. It didn't work.

He was the perfect date—aside from the little white pill that he tipped into her second drink before they left the bar. When he placed his hand on her back as she stumbled in the parking lot, she looked up at him with a grateful smile and reached out for his hand.

She invited him into her house for a drink when he arrived. Her eyes looked bleary but happy as she shrugged off her jacket.

He followed her inside. They made out in the dark room on her expensive-looking cognac leather couch.

I waited for him to pull the phone charger from his back pocket. To turn into the person who had hidden in my side yard in the dark.

Instead, he waited until her kisses grew sloppy and she mumbled, "I might call it a night, I'm feeling pretty tired." He ignored her. And she didn't protest when he pulled out a condom.

I made myself stay. Because I couldn't bear to leave her alone with him. Because I felt responsible. Because I couldn't find a way to stop him. The air in the room churned dark and electric. In the kitchen, I heard the microwave make a beeping notification, like mine did when the power turned off then on.

When he was finished, he looked down at her in disgust. Then he zipped up his jeans and reached for his back pocket.

In the dim light from the hallway skylight, he trailed the long phone charger across Elle's neck. Back and forth. She didn't move.

I watched in horror. The microwave beeped again, and my horror shifted to anger. After the first few dates, I'd felt sure I could find a way to stop him every time. That maybe this was the entire reason I had been left in limbo. My unfinished business. He had taken my life. And now I was entitled to haunt him, to thwart him.

I'd been wrong, though. The only thing I could actually do now was restart the damn microwave.

Elle's eyes were closed. She was breathing softly, almost peacefully, one arm flung across her partially clothed chest while the other arm hung over the edge of the couch.

He watched her intently for a few minutes until the sound of a muted text notification broke the silence in the room.

It was April. "Sorry to bug you. I know it's a big deadline. But will you be back soon? Emma is sick. She threw up."

He sighed. Then he rolled the phone charger around his hand and traced a thumb slowly over Elle's neck before pulling her skirt back into place and arranging her comfortably on the couch with an afghan.

Before he let himself out of the house and into the dark summer night, he opened the MatchStrike app. He looked at her profile, then scrutinized her sleeping form on the couch in the dark.

He was clearly trying to make a decision. About what, I didn't know. But finally, he sent her a message. "Hope your headache went away. Would love to see you again sometime. I haven't had this much fun since ... well, it's been a long time."

The microwave beeped a third time in the dark room as he sent the message. He rolled his eyes, but his teeth glinted in the dim light as he smiled.

* * *

He went out with Elle one more time.

She didn't invite him into her house again. And when he offered to pick her up at her place, she demurred, saying that she was planning to swing by her dad's place afterward: He was sick.

When they met at the bar, the look in her eyes told me she was studying him. That she knew—but didn't know—that something was wrong. That something had happened the last time they went out.

I pushed on that feeling as hard as I could, leaning close to her ear when she studied him during dinner. When she finished her drink before visiting the ladies' room. When she told the waitress she just wanted a glass of water instead of a second drink. And when she, almost shyly, asked him about what they'd done at her place the night he dropped her off. Because—it was weird—she couldn't remember much.

He smiled in response, but his eyes shifted sideways. *He's lying,* I told her. *He did something really bad to you. He's not a good person.*

"You don't remember?" he asked in response, looking hurt. "I guess we really did have too much to drink." Then he grinned, like he'd said something funny.

Elle laughed and didn't press any further. But when she left the restaurant—long before closing time—she stopped responding to messages.

I expected him to block her, like he had the other women as soon as things started to go tits up. Instead, he sent her message after message. He pretended to be worried at first. Then a little annoyed. Then a little irritated. Like he'd done with me when I told him we were over. He refreshed the app constantly while he worked in the basement at home. He even called customer service at one point, certain that something in the messaging feature was broken. Because Elle wasn't writing back. Why wouldn't she write back?

On the third day with no response, he told April he'd been called into another last-minute work project, despite the fact that there was a church activity that night he'd been talking up to the girls.

I had sort of been looking forward to the church activity myself. They were going to have a bonfire at the base of the mountains, and Kimmie and Emma were dying of excitement. April looked hurt but didn't say anything. She never did.

He brought the phone charger with him in his back pocket and drove to Elle's house.

I studied the expression on his face, eager and agitated as he sat in the car a few houses away, just beyond the glow of a street light. He opened up the app and typed and retyped another message to Elle. In this one, he stopped with the pretenses.

*At least tell me what I did? You SLEEP with me and then pretend like it never happened and ghost? What kind of person does that? No wonder your brother needed those drugs.*

He hovered over the send button for a few seconds, then shook his head and erased the message, peering toward the house. There was a light on in the kitchen. A few minutes passed before Elle appeared at the kitchen sink. She appeared to be rinsing dishes and turned to say something over her shoulder with a smile on her face.

She wasn't alone. He saw it too.

He opened the car door and shut it carefully, quietly—but not before he'd grabbed the seatbelt cutter tool tucked into the dash. I could feel myself panicking, the fear and terror turning the air charged and heavy as I scrambled after him. What could I do?

The street light a few yards away blinked rapidly then went out, if anything making it easier for him to approach the house unseen. I screamed after him, unheard and unnoticed.

He glanced around the empty street then continued toward Elle's driveway.

I rushed to the window, where I could see Elle inside with an older man. Maybe her dad. They were sitting down at the table, watching a basketball game while they ate pizza. "Don't answer the door, don't go outside," I shrieked, knowing they wouldn't hear. As far as I could tell, the only time anyone stood a chance of listening was when I was closer than humanly possible. Basically inside their ear canal. Even then, it only seemed to work if they were open to the suggestion. Screaming never did a thing.

I screamed anyway.

As I turned around, I saw his dark form standing in the driveway at the edges of the porch lights.

He glanced around one more time, then knelt down and pressed the blade of the seatbelt cutter into all four of her tires.

"Bitch," he whispered softly.

Then he turned back around and walked toward his parked car down the road.

I followed him. Because I didn't know what else to do. Because I had chosen this path and wasn't ready to give up yet.

Before he drove away, he blocked Elle on the dating app. *Made me uncomfortable.*

When he got home, he went straight downstairs and started sending out new messages on MatchStrike before even saying hello to April, who must have just gotten home from the bonfire with the girls since their bedroom light was on.

When the first woman responded, he eagerly opened up the app to read the full message.

She had shoulder-length light-brown hair and was wearing bright pink lipstick. Her lips were quirked in the kind of grin that told me she had a sarcastic side.

Her name was Meghan.

# 18. SKYE

## KUNA, IDAHO

### NOW

My dad spent so long in the FroYo first asking, then demanding the security camera footage, that they nearly missed Officer Willis—despite almost getting the police called on to the FroYo.

The kid working at the counter reminded me of a boy I'd had to partner with in science one year. Rail-thin, expressionless, and uptight to the point of total unreasonableness. He just kept repeating, in monotone, that he would have to speak to a manager—who wasn't in right now—about the security footage. At one point, when my dad finally thundered, "We're going to meet with the police right now, goddammit, can you please just help us out?" the kid calmly plucked his cell phone from his apron pocket and threatened to call 9-1-1.

At that point my mom dragged my dad out of the FroYo, promising that Officer Willis would help.

"What if it's only twenty-four hours of footage, Mari?" my dad kept repeating, looking at the clock on the dash and then dragging his hands through his thinning brown hair. "That gives us less than two hours."

My mom stared straight ahead but drove ten over the speed limit back to the house, where Officer Willis was standing in the driveway. Across the street, I could see Mr. and Mrs. Schmalz sitting on their porch, trying not to appear too interested in what was going on.

My dad was out of the car before my mom put it in park. "David, be calm," she whispered, hurrying to unbuckle her seatbelt.

I watched the officer's eyes while my dad frantically explained about the footage they'd seen from the Daily Grind. And the FroYo next door. And the fact that the kid behind the counter had threatened to call the police. The officer didn't look skeptical, exactly. Definitely wary though. I imagined he heard a lot of things on any given day.

When my dad was finished, Officer Willis turned to my mom, who was tearing up again.

She repeated what she'd told the dispatcher earlier, about how I didn't come home like I was supposed to yesterday even though we had plans. Even though I always came home. How I was a good girl and not involved with anything dangerous. I was supposed to be leaving for college today. She swiped at the tears. "I know you're trying to figure out whether this is worth the resources to investigate. I know she's eighteen. I *know.* But she did *not* disappear. Not on purpose. Someone or something kept her from coming home. I know that in my gut." My mom looked at the clock on the microwave. "Please, can you get the footage from the yogurt place?" Her voice broke. "I think it might show what happened."

The officer nodded, and I watched his eyes soften. "Yes, ma'am. We don't usually devote a lot of resources when a non-minor goes missing. Not unless there's some strong evidence of foul play. Still, it sounds like there's reason to believe we should check out that security footage to find out how concerned we need to be as a place to get started, at the very least."

My dad's face crumpled in relief, and my mom bit her cheek and nodded while the tears continued to drip down her cheeks. Then my parents followed the police cruiser back to the FroYo, where my dad was instructed in no uncertain terms to wait outside while the officer talked to the employee.

While he waited, my dad watched the clock. It was 3:39. When he cracked the window, I climbed into the front seat with him and pressed myself against it, finding to my surprise that I could easily move through the small space. Impressed with myself, I hurried over to the door of the FroYo and eyed the hairline space between the door and the doorframe. I moved through it just as easily.

The FroYo employee was on the phone with his manager. He didn't look nearly as smug as he had earlier while talking to my parents. While the officer watched, he said, "Okay, yeah, I got it. Sorry, yeah. Sorry. I know how to do it. It's all okay. Yeah I know. Okay, bye."

Then, calling over his shoulder to the officer, the kid rushed to the back of the shop. "Um, I'm getting it now, okay?"

The officer waited patiently for the kid to return with a thumb drive. He was out of breath. "Okay, you said you wanted to look at around 4:00, right? I've got since 3:42 yesterday onward."

The kid's triumphant expression crumbled when the officer looked less than impressed. "If you ever get a request like this again, which I really hope you don't, I want you to back up the footage *before* I show up. If we'd gotten here twenty minutes later, these poor people would've been out of luck. And that would have been your fault."

"But my manager doesn't—"

The cop took the thumb drive and walked back out to the parking lot, where my parents were waiting. I followed on his heels.

\* \* \*

"Is he going to let us watch it?" My mom fretted while she drove from the strip mall back to the house for the third time that day. She looked utterly exhausted.

Before my dad could answer, she shook her head. "I don't want to step on his toes, but we have a right to know, don't we? If you hadn't seen the camera, it would be too late. We'll know if there's something weird going on better than he will, right?"

I could see the relief on both their faces when the officer asked for a laptop as soon as he got out of his car.

This time, there was no needle-in-a-haystack search.

Clear as day, at 4:07 p.m., they watched me wave at the driver in the car—it wasn't possible to tell the vehicle color, since the security footage was in black-and-white—and get inside of my own free will.

I felt disgusted with myself. I had voluntarily gotten into a stranger's car. Because he didn't feel like a stranger.

My mom turned pale while she watched me talk to the dark figure inside the vehicle. "No, baby," she said as I took a step closer and he flung open the door.

The cop paused the footage, and my parents panicked. "Keep going," my dad growled.

"Do you recognize that man?" the cop asked firmly, pointing at the man's shadowy face in the poor-quality camera footage. "And do you recognize this car?"

My mom shook her head frantically. "No. I mean, I don't think so. I can't tell. Why would she go with him, why was she talking to him at all?"

The officer made a note in his phone then asked, "Is it possible she was seeing someone you didn't know about?"

My dad made that growling sound again. "I don't think Skye had ever been on a real date." He looked at my mom. "Right, Mari? She was shy."

This statement stung, somehow, even though it was true. The officer nodded again slowly. "Can I see the other security footage?"

\* \* \*

It was the officer who noticed the same Kia Sorento cruising through the parking lot every couple of hours that afternoon.

He zoomed in on the plate. *2C 3405.* I felt a fizz of excitement that I wrestled under control as I watched the computer screen blink erratically.

There was no license plate visible in the FroYo video. The officer shook his head in frustration. "I'm ninety percent sure that's the same car. But since we can't see the color in either video, and we can barely see the driver in the Daily Grind footage, I can't say for certain."

I waited for the blow that would follow. The bad news. There was nothing he could do here.

Instead, he said, "I do think we have something, though. Your daughter doesn't sound like the type to disappear. And I'm pretty sure that is the same car. I'm going to need both of you to come with me into the station so we can get a written statement about any details that might be relevant. I'm going to update the status on Skye's case to a 'missing person, possibly endangered.' We'll start by pulling her phone records and finding that car."

The relief on my parents' faces was tainted with a pallor of fear. And my excitement was tempered with a sense of dread.

I wanted them to find him.

I wanted them to find *me*.

But there would be no relief in revealing what had happened.

# 19. MEGHAN

## OQUIRRH MOUNTAINS, UTAH

### 9 MONTHS BEFORE

I stared in disbelief when I saw the police car slowly crest the dirt road.

The man wearing the Forest Service uniform hadn't stayed longer than it took him to snap a few photos of the shoe, make a note in his tablet with the coordinates, and trudge back to his dusty white truck bearing the Forest Service decal. He didn't look around. He didn't follow the nearly invisible fork in the road through the over-grown sagebrush and bent pines. He was doing his job, and nothing more.

Still, I stayed by the shoe like a sentinel after he left. I missed Grandma Rosie. I wanted to meet my uncle. To meet my great grandparents. To see my friend Kiley who had died in a car accident in the fourth grade. To be seen by people who could see me. But I was afraid to drift. Afraid I wouldn't be able to get back again, like Bubbie had warned.

For now, I wanted to be here. I wasn't ready to leave without the option of returning. I knew my resolve wouldn't last forever. I wasn't even sure what I was waiting to feel when someone finally found me. *If,* I reminded myself. *If* someone found me. All I knew was that I wanted to be found.

It was four, maybe five days after the Forest Service employee left that I heard the sound of the police cruiser's motor in the distance.

As it came to a stop in front of the shoe and the raven's stash, I braced myself for a cursory check.

The officer, a woman with a tight, graying brunette bun at the nape of her neck, pulled on gloves and grabbed a clear bag from the front seat of the car as she matter-of-factly opened the door and walked toward the shoulder of the road, scanning until she spotted the bleached-out shoe.

I watched her face closely. She hunched to get a better look and then carefully bagged the shoe before standing up and looking around her. Some of the leaves had already begun to turn brown and gold. The scarce vehicle traffic that ventured this far into the hills had all but disappeared, and in the mornings the edges of the scrubby brush and grass were tinged with a bite of frost. Summer was over. Soon fall would follow, and everything at this altitude would be covered by a blanket of snow.

The woman—whose name was Officer Domanska from her badge—placed the bagged shoe in the cruiser and made a note on her phone. Then she reached into the car's dash and extracted what appeared to be the report the Forest Service had filed.

*Brenda Maxwell, 28. Reported a shoe and what looked like old blood at 38°01'18.5"N 105°41'18.5"W near Ophir Canyon, on the shoulder of the road. Says she thinks something might have happened here. Four-wheel-drive needed, big ruts this far out.*

I thought of the girl with the messy blond bun and silently thanked her. I hoped that whatever she'd been crying about wasn't making her cry anymore. That she was smiling. I felt something like relief well up in me. If I could, *I* would have been crying.

Detective Domanska read the report then scanned the shoulder of the road and farther ahead, where it continued toward Ophir Canyon.

"It's the other way," I told her. "Please don't drive away." I moved until I was close enough to hug her. I reached for her hand,

and I felt a little spark as she reflexively moved the hand to place it on the gun in her holster. Encouraged, I reached up to put my hand on her shoulder. "Please look around. It's not dangerous. Not anymore."

Keeping her hand on the gun, Detective Domanska took a few steps away from me in the direction of Ophir Canyon. The spark of hope faded to dull disappointment as I watched her walk farther down the road, scanning the brush and the rocky shoulder, using a long branch to prod into deeper thickets of sagebrush so she could see better.

My numbness gave way to despair as she reached the bend in the road, stopped, then strode back to the car. If she couldn't find me, who would? I remembered episodes of *Cold Case* I had watched where bodies were unearthed years or decades later. *By accident.* By sheer coincidence. Or sometimes never. That was going to be me, I told myself. I wasn't going to be found.

I let the hurt and the sadness wash over me. If she left with the shoe, would they test it? Did she know my name? Was my disappearance even on her radar? It's not like I was a minor child. How much did anyone care, aside from my parents and friends, that I hadn't come home. Was Detective Domanska thinking about me now and wondering whether this shoe might be mine? Would this be some kind of macabre Cinderella story? Or was I just a name among so many other names of people who never came home? For all I knew she was a junior detective who had been given the unsavory assignment of driving all the way out here to retrieve a shoe.

The despair coalesced into something sharp and black as Detective Domanska sat down in her cruiser and retrieved the keys from her pocket.

I glanced inside the cruiser at my shoe for a few seconds, feeling the sting of loss that it was leaving. It had become my Wilson. It had kept me company here as a castaway for God-knew how long. I was surprised about how upset I felt to see it go.

The only thing left here with me was my bones.

As Detective Domanska put her keys into the ignition and shut the door, I headed toward the hidden fork in the dirt road.

I would say goodbye to my bones. To the last thing that tied me to this place. To this life.

And then I would find Grandma Rosie and the others.

The despair softened into something tender and deep. I heard the cruiser start up behind me.

I studied the skinny, clumped trees reaching toward the cloud-filled sky overhead. They weren't particularly beautiful. The elevation wasn't high enough for the kind of dense forest I remembered camping in when I was younger. Still, they were the last trees I'd see on this side of consciousness. I tried to take in everything I passed for the last time. The sunlight filtering across the branches I couldn't feel but would miss anyway. The hazy blue peaks in the distance that I knew were the Rockies. The sound of the slight breeze in the aspen leaves.

The muffled crunch of footfalls on the carpet of dry pine needles behind me.

I froze and turned around.

To my disbelief, I saw Detective Domanska at the fork in the road. She peered through the weedy brush that nearly obscured the dirt road from view. Then she stood scanning the path of the overgrown road until she was looking directly at me.

If she kept walking, she'd run right into my body. Or what was left of it. I hadn't been to visit my remains in weeks.

I raced ahead, wanting to see what she would see. As I approached the place where it happened, the place where the blue Kia had pulled away while I ran toward the ravine, I panicked. The rusty blood that had been visible while the animals picked apart my bones was gone. And the bones that had once prominently lay on the surface of the rocky ground were covered with a thin layer of pine needles. Weeds were growing in and among my scattered, dirty remains. A section of my ribcage jutted up through the pine needles, and the dull gray of my skull appeared as an unusually smooth rock, an island in the pine needles and debris.

Unless she knew what she was looking for, it was highly unlikely that the officer would see me.

I braced myself for her to turn around again. To get back in the cruiser and report that she had retrieved the shoe. Instead, she moved toward me, closer and closer, peering into the sagebrush and at one point kneeling beside a larger pine to probe at a thin stand of mushrooms growing in the shade.

"Are you here, Meghan?" she said so quietly I might have imagined it.

Even so, the equivalent of a bucket of ice water crashed over me. She wasn't looking at me. Or my body. In fact, she was looking in the opposite direction, toward the ravine that led down to the dry creek bed.

But it didn't matter. She was looking for me. She thought the shoe might be mine. Someone knew that something bad happened. Which meant that for the first time, I wasn't alone.

"I'm here," I screamed. I knelt next to the skull and ribcage in the dirt as if I could dig them free, to show her where to look.

She moved to a crouch and turned in a slow circle, ducking her head to see the small clearing from a different angle.

As her gaze crossed my pathetic pile of bones, I cried out again. "Look, please look at me."

She stopped scanning and stood up. Stopped again, squinting her eyes a little. Then walked with purpose to where I lay prone across my own bones.

I watched her expression harden into one of recognition and then determination as she bent to see the top of my skull.

# 20. BRECIA

## SALT LAKE CITY, UTAH

### 1 YEAR BEFORE

They stayed in the back booth of the cozy pub until last call at eleven.

By that time, her eyes were getting glassy. She made a comment about the room being too warm as she fumbled with her jacket and took a sip to drain her tainted glass of red wine.

"Can I take you home? Or do you want to come to my place to get sobered up?" he asked her, managing to look concerned instead of eager. "We can leave your car here. I'm sure it happens all the time."

"I took an Uber," Meghan replied, slurring slightly.

He made his eyes wide. "Okay, then I am *definitely* going to help you get home. Don't you listen to any true-crime podcasts? You're never supposed to get into a car with a stranger if you're tipsy."

*No,* I said firmly in her ear. *No. He's the stranger you need to worry about. You don't really know him. He put shit in your drink. Do not leave with him.*

Meghan's eyes widened as well, and he laughed. "I'm sure you'd be fine. I also just want to spend a few more minutes with you, and we can't stay here." He smiled shyly.

She took the bait and smiled back, her whole face lighting up at the compliment. She tugged at the scarf around her neck and leaned closer to him. "Okay, but can you take me home? I think I just need to get some sleep. I'm such a lightweight."

I leaned as close as I could, knowing from too many other dates that she was lost to me now. She'd made up her mind to go with him. And I couldn't stop her, even if I turned off the power to the entire restaurant (not that I was strong enough to do that).

Meghan leaned against his shoulder as they walked out of the bar to the parking lot. He gently stroked her shiny chestnut hair. He winked at the waitress closing the place down and said, "I can't believe eleven feels so late! This means I'm old, right?"

The waitress smiled at him and shook her head. "Nah, I'm about to crash, too. You two have a good night."

I tried with the waitress, too. "It's not what it looks like," I cried in her ear before hurrying to follow him into the night. I looked back to see the waitress still watching through the glass door for a moment. Then she went back to wiping down countertops.

Meghan mumbled something about her phone as she reached the car. As she unzipped her purse and opened the bag wide, the phone tipped out along with a tin of mints. The phone landed with a quiet thud on the ground by the car. She didn't notice.

He glanced at the phone for a moment then reassured her it was in her purse as he guided her into the passenger seat.

"Do you need my address, yeah?" Meghan mumbled. "Oh my god I'm so tired."

"Don't worry. I've got it, you texted it to me when we were leaving a second ago," he soothed.

I felt heavy and numb as I climbed past her into the backseat and he turned on the car.

As we pulled out of the parking lot, I stared out the window at the dark rectangle just visible on the blacktop under the street light.

She'd been texting her friend Sharesa about the date earlier.

Someone knew she'd been here. Here with "Jimmy Carlson"— who would disappear like a ghost as soon as he blocked her on MatchStrike and created a new profile.

What he planned to do in the app likely depended on what he planned to do tonight.

He didn't actually have her home address. So I braced for him to pull into a dark parking lot or alley or park. Anywhere without street lights.

I steeled myself to stay with her. I promised myself, like always, that at the very least I wouldn't leave her alone.

This time was different.

As Meghan's head lolled back in the passenger seat of the Sorento and she curled against the plasticky seat cover, he just kept driving through the dark streets.

When he turned onto the highway, headed south, I was mildly puzzled, but as far as I was concerned, it didn't matter where he was taking her. The only thing that mattered was that I kept looking for a way to stop him.

When he signaled to exit in Toole, I stared at him in surprise.

He couldn't be taking her home. Surely April and the girls were there, preparing for bedtime.

My puzzlement dissolved back into dread when he turned toward Cedar Fort.

I managed to make one of his headlights go out as we drove through the small town.

As the beam of light disappeared, he swore softly and cut his eyes to Meghan in the passenger seat.

She didn't stir.

Try as I might, I couldn't make the other headlight budge.

I watched through the windows for any sign of a patrol car. My mom had been pulled over once for a broken headlight. It was a long shot, but there was nothing else I could do.

I tried to wake Meghan up. I snatched at every thread of fear and disgust and anger I could find, directing them at the car's engine. I screamed in his ear.

I had no idea what I was doing. There was no instruction manual. No one to ask for advice. So I imagined myself as the Dark Phoenix, invisible sparks coming from whatever electricity and consciousness still held me together until I was numb.

No matter what I tried, the car kept running. The lone headlight remained. And no blue-and-red lights appeared behind us.

We kept driving farther into the darkness as the towns disappeared and signs for the Oquirrh Mountain pass appeared.

The paved road turned into a dirt road as we climbed. Meghan mumbled something about her phone once as the car hit a deep rut, and he glanced at her then turned his eyes back to the dark road.

When he finally stopped the car along a fork in the road that was barely more than a trail meant for vehicles far more capable than the Kia, I should have known what would happen.

After all, he had killed me.

But that was different, I told myself. He was furious with me. I had rejected him. I had dumped him. He liked this girl, in his own disgusting, duplicitous way.

He turned off the headlights then opened the driver's side door and listened. For the sound of a car's engine, maybe. But aside from the crickets, it was utterly quiet.

Then he walked around to the passenger side and unbuckled Meghan's seatbelt.

He said her name once. Then again, louder. This time, she blinked at him, her eyes bleary and glassy. "Jimmy?"

Before she could say anything else, he was dragging her out of the car.

Down the trail. Away from the car. She didn't put up a fight. She mostly tried to keep up, lifting her head to look at him, her face a mask of confusion and glazed terror.

I followed at a distance.

Because I wouldn't leave her.

But there was nothing else I could do.

She screamed just once, as his hand moved to her throat and snatched at the scarf she was wearing.

Then the sound went quiet, replaced by frantic thrashing.

I carried on screaming for both of us, the night air swirling with dark electricity that had nowhere to go.

I screamed until suddenly I heard her voice again, screaming with me.

He was standing up, from where he'd been kneeling over her on the black, scrubby ground.

When I saw her stand up and run, I almost cheered.

I know. You'd think I would have understood.

I called her name again, not expecting her to turn around—until she did. She heard me. I could see it in the twist of her body as she heard her own name but kept running anyway, toward the inky tree-line.

He brushed past me on his way to the car. When I looked down at the spot where he had been kneeling, I could see the dark shape of Meghan's body, her scarf still tight around her neck, her eyes half-closed and bloodshot.

I nearly went after her into the woods.

I wanted to. I wanted to tell her I was sorry. That she wasn't alone. That she wasn't invisible—not to me, anyway. I didn't want to haunt him anymore. What was the point if I couldn't stop this from happening. Maybe there was no rhyme or reason to why I was still here in limbo, following him around like a puppy.

A darker thought crept in: Maybe I just hadn't figured out how to stop him in time. I had failed her.

I called Meghan's name again as I heard the car's engine start behind me.

The fact was that I couldn't help her. Not anymore. That much I knew for certain. She was dead. Like me.

I had nothing to offer her.

And I couldn't face her.

The only thing I could do was follow him back to the car before he disappeared again.

# 21. SKYE

## KUNA, IDAHO

### NOW

It was my useless phone that led them to the foothills off Blacks Creek Road. Three days after I was supposed to be driving to ISU.

Once the officer ordered the phone records, things moved quickly. And once the police started searching in the right area, I wasn't exceptionally hard to find.

My phone had pinged off cell towers in Kuna, South Boise, Robie Creek, and then Prairie, Idaho, where the signal pinged until it disappeared. Together, along with a GPS signal that had briefly connected along Blacks Creek Road, the little dots created something like a Bermuda triangle, where I'd been swallowed up.

My parents didn't see the constellation of cell phone pings or the GPS data. I drove with them to the police station. But then I followed Officer Willis while a different officer took my parents' detailed statement in separate rooms.

I couldn't be with my parents and their hope. Not when it was about to be shattered.

While my parents were being questioned, Officer Willis requested cell phone records from Verizon. Before he called the customer service number and pressed 8 for law enforcement requests, he printed and faxed a signed affidavit on letterhead stating that the

Kuna Police required the records as soon as possible as part of an endangered missing persons investigation.

I waited with him until the cell phone records were emailed half an hour later. When the cell data report came, I studied the map of tower pings and the long GPS timestamp along Blacks Creek Road over his shoulder. His brow furrowed as he traced a finger along the list of final pings coming from Prairie, Idaho. There was nothing but foothills and canyons anywhere near the area.

The license plate number on the Kia Sorento wasn't immediately useful. It was a Utah plate with a Utah address, registered to James and April Carson. There was no record of either April or James in Idaho yet.

The fact that he was married surprised me less than the fact that he had a living, breathing wife. I tried to imagine her. What did she look like? Beautiful, probably. Did she have any idea who she had married? I wasn't sure whether I should be terrified of her or for her.

Officer Willis barked at someone to create an ALPR report, which I gathered was some kind of license plate monitoring database. Then he pulled up a map of Blacks Creek canyon and left the station in his patrol car.

\* \* \*

I sat shotgun as we drove up Blacks Creek Road. The radio spit codes and meaningless snippets of information as we turned off the highway exit.

I watched the sagebrush and rocky hills fly past outside the car window. The last time I'd seen them this way, I'd been alive. But not for long.

Officer Willis turned onto an unmarked dirt road, a camping site with two cars and a tent visible along the creek bed. He spent a few minutes questioning the man and woman who emerged from the tent then spent some time studying the area. I followed him. And even though I knew he couldn't hear me, I talked to him. "It's farther. Not here. It's farther up the canyon." I glanced at the sun, hanging heavy in the sky. There were only a few hours of daylight left. If he spent this long searching every dirt road that branched off Blacks Creek, this was going to take a long time.

He pulled off the road several more times, each of them the wrong exit. He was drawn most to the pull-offs with camping sites. I tried to gauge how far we were from the spot he'd left my body. Would I recognize the pull-off? I hadn't realized how many dirt paths snaked off the main road. I focused on the memory and found, with surprising clarity, that I could see the horizon and the pull-off as if it were a photo in my mind.

I wasn't sure exactly how far away we were.

But I'd know it as soon as I saw it.

* * *

The horizon was just turning pink when I saw the pull-off.

The officer had skipped the last two dirt roads, marking each on his paper map to check later. I couldn't tell if that decision was influenced by the fact that it was getting late or if he was following some kind of hunch I'd contributed to. Either way, I felt like we were getting close.

Then suddenly, there it was. The scrubby weeds and tall grass covering the little rise at the shoulder in the road stood out in relief against the darker treeline beyond the road. The shape of that rise was burned into my mind.

"There it is," I called frantically, willing him to stop.

His eyes flicked to the exit. The area past the rise wasn't easily visible. In fact, it sort of looked like the turnoff dead-ended before it snaked deeper into the hills.

"Stop," I called again desperately, sliding over until I was nearly on his lap, my hands resting uselessly on the steering wheel as if maybe I could turn it myself.

He wasn't slowing down.

"Stop there," I said again, louder.

Nothing.

His ears weren't picking up what I was saying. I needed to tap into his brain somehow.

I thought about how I'd been able to slip through the crack in the FroYo shop earlier. That's when I had the idea to get as close to Officer Willis's brain as possible.

So I leaned into that hairy ear canal and thought about hitting the brakes hard and pulling off that little dirt road while I looked at the inside of his eardrum.

To my amazement, the car slowed down.

His eyes flicked over to the dirt road. Then he hit the brakes harder and exited.

I felt like cheering. I couldn't say for certain whether he'd heard me, but I was confident he hadn't planned to stop. And yet here we were.

My excitement evaporated as he got out of the car and started poking through the brush.

It took him less than two minutes to find my body, unhidden by the dry creek bed.

The animals had found me over the past three days. One of my arms had been separated from my torso, the gray skin torn from muscle and bone in raw strips.

The rest of me wasn't much better. It was the kind of scene that would have kept me awake at night if I'd seen it in a movie. But this time I couldn't look away. Because this wasn't a movie. This was me.

Officer Willis didn't waste any time in calling for backup.

At first, he hurried to secure the area, pulling caution tape from the trunk of the cruiser and putting on gloves.

There were no other headlights on the road. Everything was still and quiet. We were going to be here for a minute before anyone else arrived. And I wasn't going anywhere.

So after a few minutes, he paused and sat down in the driver's seat of the police cruiser, staring toward the spot where the ground sloped toward the creek bed and my body.

I sat next to him while we waited. After a few seconds passed, he cleared his throat and started to sing softly.

I'd only been to church a few times, but I recognized the hymn immediately. They'd sung it at my granddad's funeral two years earlier.

*Abide with me; 'tis eventide.*
*The day is past and gone;*
*The shadows of the evening fall;*
*The night is coming on.*

\* \* \*

I wasn't there when they told my parents.

By the time Officer Willis drove back down Blacks Creek, it was well after midnight.

My body had been photographed. Evidence—including my cell phone, a cigarette butt, some candy wrappers, and a partial tire track —had been cataloged and tucked into plastic bags.

A tech wearing booties, a mask, and a hair net had carefully pulled down my jeans and underwear to insert a long swab between my legs.

That was the part that finally made me look away. It had to be done. But I didn't want to remember seeing any of it.

I felt weirdly grateful when he pulled my purple-striped underwear back up, careful to re-button my jeans, afterward.

My parents weren't at the station anymore when Officer Willis let us inside the still-humming office. A couple of men were being hauled through the reception area in handcuffs, and a woman was standing at the counter, holding her head in her hands while she sobbed incoherently.

Officer Willis, who looked bone-tired, still took the time to write a report of what had happened. A female officer entered the room at one point to tell him that the missing persons report had been canceled and that a press conference had been scheduled for first thing in the morning. A detective from homicide, someone named Kittleson, would take over from here. He needed to be brought up to speed as soon as possible. The license plate was still a dead end.

Officer Willis nodded. A few minutes later he emailed the report for Detective Kittleson, printed off a copy to be filed, and turned off the light to his office.

When he got into his patrol car, I didn't follow him. Instead, I headed down the main road, then the side streets, until I got home. Miles no longer meant anything. And at this point I knew the way.

As I passed through an overgrown lot at the edge of my neighborhood, a large fox appeared from the brush, carrying some small rodent in her mouth.

She froze.

"Hey," I said, crouching.

She flattened her ears against her head and sniffed the air. Still holding onto the rodent, she crept forward with her head turned toward me, giving me a wide berth. When I stood up, she made a little muffled yip then scurried into the cover of a lilac bush.

\* \* \*

My parents were asleep when I finally slipped into the house through the crack in the back door.

My dad was sitting on the couch, his head leaning at an uncomfortable-looking angle against the wall on account of the too-short backrest. My mom slept with her legs curled up against her chest on the cushion beside him, her head against his leg.

Like most kids of divorced parents, I'd secretly fantasized about all kinds of scenarios that would bring them back together. Or at least bring my dad back to Idaho. I'd never been very good at it. It was easier to imagine them apart than together. Both of them were happier. And my dad's girlfriend was actually pretty nice.

Apparently this was what it took.

"I'm sorry," I whispered, feeling the sadness and love expand in my chest.

My mom whimpered in her sleep, then sat upright on the couch in the dark room. "I can find her," she cried, her eyes still shut. "I'll find her."

My dad reached for her hand. "It's okay, Mari," he murmured and readjusted his head against the back of the couch. "Just sleep. Keep sleeping."

She obediently lay back down on the couch, still holding onto his fingers tightly.

# 22. MEGHAN

## SALT LAKE VALLEY, UTAH

### 6 MONTHS BEFORE

As strange as it sounds, I missed the mountains: my burial grounds.

I didn't think twice about jumping into the front seat of Detective Domanska's police cruiser. But as the rutted, narrow road finally spit us out onto a paved road with signs directing us toward Cedar Fort, I wished I had at least said goodbye to the raven. She wouldn't have known. I knew that. I missed her anyway, though.

Grandma Rosie's words echoed in my memory as we drove. *I'll be here when you're ready.* I wasn't sure what I would learn at the police station, exactly, but I no longer felt a gnawing desperation.

I wanted to be found. I wanted to see him arrested—maybe he already had been? I wanted to say goodbye to my family—surely there would be a funeral now. And then I wanted to pass on.

\* \* \*

Detective Domanska hadn't drawn the short-straw to answer the Forest Service's request to check out the suspicious shoe by the side of the road. I quickly learned that she was the detective assigned to my missing persons case—which was rapidly recategorized as a murder case. She'd been hoping to find me when she got the tip from the Forest Service.

She'd been looking for me for four months, ever since Sharesa had reported me missing the morning after my "date."

I read the call transcripts in my missing persons report as Detective Domanska flipped back through her notes and records. Sharesa had been described as "hysterical." I smiled. It faded when I read the transcript of my parents' calls and interviews.

My mom's first phone transcript was marked "unintelligible" every other line. They'd been on a rafting trip on the Salmon River in Idaho when it happened. Which meant that they hadn't learned of my disappearance for a full five days. They'd been talking about that trip all year. My mom had gifted it to my dad for Christmas.

The waitress at Gracie's had remembered me. She'd remembered Jimmy, too: how handsome he was, mainly. And the fact that we'd stayed until last call. She remembered me being off-my-face drunk as he helped me to the parking lot. "I thought they were a couple," she'd said in her interview.

They'd found my phone in the parking lot. Which was the main reason—in addition to Sharesa's hysteria—that they had escalated my search so quickly.

There were dozens of newspaper articles printed and filed among Detective Domanska's notes. I read all of them. Each article used the recent headshots I'd taken when I got my last work promotion. I'd been so proud of those headshots. They looked like a professional, kickass modern woman who knew what life owed her. But in black-and-white, splashed across the front page of local papers, I had a hard time looking at them. I didn't know her anymore. She looked naive instead of badass. Like she had no idea what was coming for her.

I learned that Jimmy Carlson was a ghost.

He'd never actually existed.

It didn't matter that Sharesa knew his name. Or that she had provided Detective Domanska with a link to his—now defunct—profile on MatchStrike, which I'd sent her before the date to get her approval. He'd registered the account with a fake name, a fake email address—and a VPN. The best MatchStrike could do, even with his messages in my defunct account, was to confirm that his bogus account had been created a year earlier, on July 15th. The last time it had been accessed was the day I disappeared. He'd deleted the account soon after.

They did recover his profile photo—which was zoomed out far enough that it was hard to see a lot of detail, especially in the low-res web upload. I remembered the feeling of relief when I met him at Gracie's: He wasn't a Neanderthal. His photo didn't do him justice. Not even a little bit. Usually it was the opposite situation with MatchStrike. But not Jimmy. Jimmy was handsome. I'd said as much to him on our date. He really needed a better photo. Secretly, I'd been thrilled by this. I'd found a diamond. So what if his photo skills were subpar? It was better than the up-close gym selfies on every other profile.

Domanska ran the photo through facial recognition software, but even enhanced, the photo was too low-res and zoomed out to deliver any matches.

My phone had been bagged as evidence. A partial print from his car—not mine—had been recovered. It wasn't in the database. Detective Domanska's file included my call logs going back six months, as well as transcripts of all my chats.

There was nothing from "Jimmy." We'd only ever communicated through the MatchStrike app. The detectives had combed through those messages, which weren't any more telling than his photo. When I re-read them I wondered how I'd ever found them so sparkling and charming. Now, they just sounded like the opening lines of a horror story.

* * *

During the day, I followed Detective Domanska around like a puppy. I wasn't her only case. But, as a commenter in one article stated bluntly, I was a pretty white girl. And now that I'd been found, the missing persons case turned into a manhunt.

After some debate, Detective Domanska turned his photo over to the press, asking for anyone with information about his identity to come forward.

The next morning, his photo appeared next to mine in the articles. I learned from Detective Domanska's reports, they received more than 500 tips by phone, email, and even the police department's Facebook page that day. The tips continued to pour in the following day from a woman who had been out with a creep from MatchStrike who fit his description. Dark hair. Dark eyes. Tall. Handsome.

There were so many calls.

Some of the women were in tears on the phone. One woman in Wyoming had been assaulted on her date. Another had narrowly escaped.

I rode along on every follow-up that Detective Domanska made personally.

I didn't expect to actually find him.

When I'd told Sharesa he was a needle in a haystack, I hadn't known how fitting that expression would become.

# 23. BRECIA

## 1 YEAR BEFORE

After Meghan, he deleted his MatchStrike account.

He erased his browser history. Cleared his cache. Deleted the messages he'd sent her and anyone else. Scrubbed every trace of Jimmy Carlson from the Internet that he could.

I knew it wasn't that easy to erase yourself. Nothing on the web was ever really gone. But only if someone was looking for it.

A few weeks later, he announced to April that he was quitting his job at the IT company in Salt Lake. They'd treated him like dirt, he said. Underpaid him. Underutilized him. It was time to move on. Plus, the office manager and most of his coworkers were worthless.

April stared at him in shock. Her eyes welled up with tears as she gestured to the house around them and the living room she'd just finished decorating. I'd been there when she opened a package containing new fuzzy throw pillows a few days earlier. Emma had insisted on building a fort with them immediately.

"What are you talking about?" April asked in disbelief. "We're finally settled in. We finally have a nice house. We have friends. The girls have friends. We talked about staying here until they graduated from high school. Why is it always like this?"

His eyes flashed with annoyance. "I've thought about this a lot, and I don't expect you to understand. But since you're not exactly paying the mortgage, I do expect you to support me." He snorted then pointed at the throw-pillow fort Emma and Kimmie had constructed the day before. "I don't criticize *you* for how you do your 'job.'" He lifted his fingers in air quotes. "When you do it, anyway. This place looks like a mess."

April stiffened like she'd been slapped. She quickly swiped at the tears that had escaped down her cheeks and knelt to pick up the pillows and blankets on the floor. The light in the dining room flickered once, then twice as the rage trickled through me. April, however, looked like she'd just been unplugged. He stood over her in the living room for a few minutes in silence as she cleaned up the fort, muttering something under his breath about realtor fees. Then he left the room.

I didn't follow him.

I knew exactly why we were moving. And I knew why we would move again. And again. And again.

To be honest, I sort of felt like I'd been unplugged too. Since that night in the mountains—the night he killed her—I had stopped following him. Instead, I spent my days watching the girls play. Watching April make their lunch and give them baths and tell them stories about fairy queens and pony pals. I was too numb to do anything else.

For all my efforts, I was powerless. Powerless to stop him. Powerless to leave (I had nowhere else to go. How the hell was I going to find my way home now?). Powerless to bring Meghan back.

So I shut down and just existed, wrapping my focus around the bright spots in the void: April and the girls.

April was extra quiet for a few days after he told her he was quitting. But when he didn't mention it again, she gradually softened and carried on like normal. I understood that she'd heard this before.

Three months later, when he abruptly announced that he'd found a new job in Idaho, she smiled weakly then went into the bedroom to lie down with the girls and Oscar for story time.

I lay down on the bed next to Emma. I savored this nightly tradition, when we shut the door and April read to the girls. Oscar glanced at me then settled down beside April and continued purring.

April told the girls the story of the fox and the hound, reading from a bent paperback Disney book tucked into the shelf by the door.

Unlike the pony pals and the fairies, this was a bittersweet book. Two friends from different worlds. You knew right from the start that it wasn't going to end particularly well. But you kept hoping anyway.

When April got to the part about the old dog—Chief—breaking his leg during a hunt for the fox, Kimmie chimed in. "The fox didn't want that old dog to get hurt, Mama."

April nodded. They'd clearly had this conversation before. "That's right, baby. The fox was just trying to get away. He was scared."

Emma sat up in bed. "But that dog *wanted* to hurt the fox. *He* meant it."

April hesitated. Then she nodded again. "Yes. That's just his nature, though. He can't help it, honey."

I stayed at the foot of Emma's bed as April turned off the lights and closed the girls' bedroom door.

There were foxes, and there were hounds.

And then there were the animals who didn't fit into the natural order of things at all. Who meant the hurt they caused every time.

# 24. SKYE

## KUNA, IDAHO

### NOW

It took three days for the police to release my remains to my parents. During those three days, the coroner confirmed my official cause of death as strangulation. The lab results came back. I hadn't been sexually assaulted. And there was no organic matter under my fingernails. In other words, I hadn't fought back.

"I wanted to," I told the coroner as she carefully studied my purple fingers. "I couldn't do anything."

My parents decided to hold my funeral at Hulls Gulch Park, at the base of the foothills in Boise beside the lake where we'd caught tadpoles every spring when I was little. That was back before my parents split up. It was still one of my favorite places. I was glad they'd chosen it.

It was a short funeral. My mom gave a eulogy but had to stop part way through when the words started coming out as little gasps through her tears. My dad took the piece of paper she'd been clutching tightly in her hand and finished, clearing his throat again and again.

There wasn't much talk of God or heaven. My mom and I had stopped going to church a long time ago, and neither of my parents wanted to cold-contact a local church now. Several priests and pastors had offered anyway when the story hit the news the day after my body was found.

After the eulogy, my parents, a few of my friends from high school, and some of my coworkers from the Daily Grind took turns saying nice things about me and scattering wildflower seeds around the scrubby lakeshore. Ken gave my mom a long hug after he scattered his seed packet. He'd been watching for the hot chocolate guy every day, he said.

My mom pressed her lips tightly together and then thanked him for everything. She didn't tell him that the police knew that hot chocolate guy's real name was James Carson. Or that she called the police station every day, asking if they'd found him yet. Detective Kittleson couldn't tell her much. And she'd been given strict orders not to reveal any details that could compromise the investigation. But there had been no arrests.

The news of my kidnapping and murder had blazed hot and bright throughout Idaho for a few days. My senior photo stared back at me from the front page of the Idaho Report, which my mom had neatly folded and tucked beside the computer in her office. In the short amount of time it took for our funeral procession to make its way to Hulls Gulch, a story about a local murder-suicide had taken over the front-page news. I wasn't surprised. I was a brown girl from a poor neighborhood in Kuna.

Sometimes, when I sat beside my mom in the car as she drove to work or picked up dinner for herself, I watched the faces of the people on the street, wondering if there were other ghosts like me. If there were, would I even know it? Or were they tucked into houses and cars like I was, haunting the people they loved most?

Daily Grind corporate had sent my parents a check for $1,000 and a surprisingly touching letter of condolence. My dad fumed that they didn't want to get sued. This was blood money. But my mom tucked the letter into her desk drawer.

Before we left Hulls Gulch to drive to the cemetery, my dad closed the funeral by reading the words to a Celtic funeral blessing. I remembered it from the book he'd sent me a few summers ago for my birthday. He'd left a note inside saying that it was the only book that had ever made him cry.

*Thou goest home to thine eternal slumber.*
*Thou goest home to thine eternal bed.*
*Thou goest back to thy home of winter,*
*Thy home of autumn, of spring, and of summer;*

*Sleep thou, sleep, and away with thy sorrow,*
*Sleep thou, sleep in the calm of all calm,*
*Sleep now, beloved in the shade of high branches*
*Sleep, O sleep in the love of all loves;*

*Sleep this night in the breast of thy mother,*
*Sleep, thou beloved, while she herself soothes thee;*
*Thy face is turned to thine old home, beloved*
*Thou goest back to the womb whence thou sprang*

*The sleep of the seven lights be thine, beloved,*
*The sleep of the seven joys be thine, beloved,*
*The shadow of death enfolds thee, beloved,*
*But in nearness thy father stands by and by*

*Sleep thou, sleep, and away with thy sorrow,*
*Sleep thou, sleep, and away with thy pain.*
*Sleep, O sleep in the guidance of guidance,*
*Sleep, O beloved, the rest of all rest.*

# 25. MEGHAN

## SALT LAKE VALLEY, UTAH

### 6 MONTHS BEFORE

I decided not to attend my own funeral.

My parents both made the drive from Wyoming to retrieve what little remained of me. Detective Domanska had already interviewed both of them over video chat. When they arrived at the morgue, she met them there and stood vigil while my mom signed the release forms with shaking hands.

It hurt to see my parents. Almost as much as it hurt them to see me.

I wanted to tell them that I was okay. That I loved them. That it wasn't their fault it had happened while they were on their trip. That I'd found Grandma Rosie. That someday they'd find me again, too.

But for now, I couldn't tell them anything.

And I couldn't stay with them.

There was no going back. I was still here for one reason and one reason only.

\* \* \*

Ninety-five percent of the tips that trickled in through the tip line were obvious duds.

Detective Domanska followed up on the remaining five percent herself.

Some were simple cases of mistaken identity. Just guys who looked really similar to the low-res profile photo on MatchStrike. I felt sorry for them.

Others gave me a distinctly sick feeling. One, a line cook who lived about three blocks away from Gracie's, agreed to meet us at his home. I watched Detective Domanska's hand go to her hip, a few inches from the holster of her gun, as he welcomed us inside with a smile. A girl from MatchStrike had called into the tip line. He'd gotten way too aggressive at the end of the date, grabbing her arm when she told him she was leaving early.

He wasn't the guy we were looking for, though. His alibi was solid: He'd been at a party with at least a dozen witnesses for the entire night. But there was a flicker of something familiar in his eye as Detective Domanska interviewed him. Like he wasn't really surprised that he was being interviewed—but didn't anticipate anything to come of it.

* * *

Three days after the tip line went live, we got a message from a woman who spoke so quickly that it was hard to tell what she was saying at first. Detective Domanska listened to the message twice. The woman rattled off an address just outside Salt Lake. Her friend's husband worked there, she said. He looked just like the photo she'd seen in the newspaper.

"His name is James," she said, then hung up without giving her own name.

Detective Domanska looked up the address. It was one of those enormous shared-suite buildings that housed dozens of offices. "Dromo" was the name of the company in the suite number the woman had given. She drummed her fingers on the keyboard as she stared at the screen. Then she headed for the patrol car. It wasn't a great tip, but there was something about the woman's voice.

When we walked into the office suite, an older receptionist with kind eyes and a tight gray bun greeted Domanska. "How can I help you?" she asked, smiling. She glanced at the detective's badge. "Everything okay?"

"I'd like to speak with one of your employees," Detective Domanska began.

In my peripheral vision, I saw someone come around the corner, toward the reception desk.

"James Carson," Domanska finished as the receptionist laughed and called out to the man who had almost disappeared into the office.

"Speak of the devil, he's right here."

The shock and disgust rippled through me. The computer on the receptionist's desk suddenly froze as the lights flickered once, then twice.

Nobody seemed to notice.

James smiled and stuck out his hand. He looked puzzled. Slightly concerned. And as handsome as ever.

Detective Domanska took his hand. "Is there an office where I can ask you a few questions?" she asked. "It'll just take a few minutes."

He winked at the receptionist then waved Domanska toward a conference room a few yards away. "No problem, am I in trouble or something?"

I flew at him, knowing I couldn't hurt him any more than the gentle breeze coming from the air conditioning vent above our heads. I couldn't just stand there, though.

I clawed and hit and fought like I wanted to before.

And, like before, I accomplished nothing—aside from the erratic flickering of the fluorescent lights in the conference room.

I still couldn't believe it was him.

We'd found the needle, after all.

But he didn't look worried.

Detective Domanska started out with the easy questions. Where had he been on the night of Friday, June 14th?

He furrowed his brow and pretended to think. "I really don't know." He had the balls to chuckle. "That's so long ago, I'm sorry—

did something happen? I'd have to check back through my phone or ask my wife. She'd know."

He had a wife. It didn't surprise me, exactly. I had no illusions about the kind of human being he was. It just added a new layer of horror. I tried to imagine her. What she looked like. How she had married this monster. Whether she had any kind of inkling of who he was. Whether she was the woman who had called with the anonymous tip.

Detective Domanska nodded. Then she showed him the profile photo the newspaper had run. His profile photo. "Is this you?" she asked him casually.

He took the paper and studied the image. "I can definitely see the resemblance, but no, that's not me. But I saw this in the news yesterday, isn't that the guy they're looking for?"

The detective studied his eyes. I studied her eyes. Could she tell he was lying? Would *I* have been able to tell he was lying if I were in her shoes? I remembered the taped-up sign I'd seen in the bathroom at Gracie's Spot. *On a date that isn't going well? Ask for Andrea at the bar.* I thought of the confidence with which I had ignored that sign and walked back out to my tainted drink and my soon-be-murderer, imagining that this was the start of something beautiful.

Then I remembered the girl with the messy bun. The one who had stopped to take a photo of my bleached shoe on the side of the dirt road. I remembered the forest ranger who had called Detective Domanska.

I leaned in as close as I could to her ear, watching the fluorescent lights continue to flicker as my frustration built. "He's lying," I told her. "It's him. He's the one who killed me. Don't believe him."

Domanska's expression didn't change. I'd learned that her poker face was something to be reckoned with. It might mean that she believed him. Or it might mean that she was playing it cool. There was really no way to tell. She ignored his question and asked, "Have you ever been to Gracie's Spot?"

He looked thoughtful again. Then he finally said, "Yeah. I think I have. It's not too far from here."

Domanska nodded. "Were you there on the night of June 14th?"

He shook his head. "I don't think so. But like I said, I'd have to ask my wife. My brain is like a sieve, I can't even remember what I ate for lunch yesterday." He laughed. "I'm getting ready to move in a couple weeks. This is actually my last day here. You're lucky you caught me."

His eyes crinkled up at the corners. *Lucky you caught me.* He was making a joke.

Domanska's expression stayed impassive. "Good to know. I'll need your new address, then. In case I have more questions." Her jaw tightened just a little. She wasn't buying it. I cheered. The lights overhead continued to flicker like candles.

Domanska placed the newspaper article on the table. "To answer your question, yes. I'm investigating this case." She tapped on my photo. "Do you recognize her?"

He made that stupid, pretend-thoughtful face again. "No, but I recognize the photo from the article I read. Scary stuff."

I leaned in closer to her ear again. "Keep going. Ask him about the waitress. She'd remember him."

To my shock and delight, she did.

"There was a waitress at Gracie's who remembers a man with Meghan that night. She gave us a pretty good description of him. What would happen if I put you in a lineup in front of her?"

The air in the room suddenly felt tense and charged. Something in his eyes went dark. "Excuse me?" He made a show of shaking his head like he couldn't believe what he was hearing. "That photo is blurry as crap. I don't want to be rude, and I hope you find the jerk who did this, but do I need a lawyer or something here? I don't want to end up like that guy on the Netflix documentary."

Domanska didn't budge. "Could you answer the question, please?"

"*No.* The waitress wouldn't recognize me. Am I free to go now?"

"No!" I told Domanska. "It's him. You can't let him leave. Keep asking him questions."

It didn't happen.

"You're free to go," the detective told him slowly. "But like I said, I'm going to need your new address and your contact information. I may have more questions for you."

I lagged behind Domanska by a few seconds. When the door to the conference room shut and the sound of her footsteps disappeared down the hallway, he lifted his middle finger.

"Incompetent bitch wolf," he murmured.

\* \* \*

I felt like I was floating away as I followed Detective Domanska back to her car.

We had found him. But nothing had happened.

The detective turned the key in the ignition and picked up her cell phone.

*Keep going, Bubbelah.* I pictured Grandma Rosie standing across the floury countertop and the bread dough. The wrinkles around the detective's eyes disappeared as I pictured the smile lines in Grandma Rosie's.

Domanska's voice drifted through the memory with me, like background music, getting softer.

*". . . but something about him . . ."*

The sun-soaked kitchen disappeared as I snapped back into the car. Domanska was driving now, her phone on speaker in its cradle. "Maybe I'm wrong, but I got the feeling that he was expecting someone to show up and ask him those questions. He wasn't nearly as surprised as someone in his shoes should've been. And he's a dead ringer for that photo."

The person on the other end of the line cleared their throat. "Want me to circle back with the woman who called in the tip? It was anonymous, but we have her number."

"Yes, call her back. Push hard. Then find this James Carson guy online. See if you can find a good photo so we can send a lineup to that waitress. If she identifies him, that's enough to get a warrant to search his car."

Domanska paused. Finally she said, "He's leaving the state in two weeks. We need to lock this down before then. I don't want to deal with extradition."

My heart—or whatever still held me together—soared. It was impossible to know how much I had contributed to Domanska's hunch. But I decided to believe that this gut feeling she had was partly my doing.

Grandma Rosie would still be waiting for me in two weeks.

I could stay in limbo a little longer.

Because I really wanted to see this bastard go down.

# 26. BRECIA

## KUNA, IDAHO

### *6 MONTHS BEFORE*

I didn't find out that the police had questioned him about Meghan's murder until we were settled into a sprawling 70s rambler in Kuna, Idaho, that he'd managed to rent for cash under the name "James Carlson."

April and I had just gotten back from a "Mommy Meetup" group she'd found on Facebook. I didn't love the idea of leaving Emma and Kimmie home alone—even tucked into their beds. But I couldn't stand to be near him anymore. There wasn't anything I could do to help the girls anyway.

So I followed April to a trendy restaurant in Nampa and listened halfheartedly to the small talk about "gifted and talented" preschoolers, leggings with pockets, and organic snacks. April smiled the whole time and chimed in when she could. But when we got back to the car, she swiped at a tear that escaped down her cheek. She was starting over. Again.

So was he. I just didn't want to know anything about it.

He was hardly ever home anymore, which was a significant change from the days we spent together in his basement computer room in Colorado.

When April pulled into the garage and turned off the car, we could already hear him through the wall.

He was raging at someone.

April froze, then scrambled out of the car. I flew past her, thinking he was screaming at the girls. The bulb in the garage popped, and April yelped as the room went black.

I slipped through the crack in the door and stood facing him.

He'd heard the garage door and was already halfway down the stairs.

The girls' bedroom door, a little ways down the hall, was closed. He wasn't yelling at them. He was talking to somebody on the phone.

He lowered his voice as he disappeared down the stairs, but I caught up to him easily. "You'll be hearing from my lawyer. Don't call me again. I already told you everything I know, which is nothing," he hissed.

I moved closer to him, so I could hear the response on the other end of the line.

"So to be totally clear, you have never met Meghan—"

He hung up the phone and threw it.

The phone cracked hard against the wall and landed face up on the carpet. *Salt Lake City Police* was still displayed on the screen.

Someone in Salt Lake suspected him. Enough that they were pursuing the lead to Idaho.

I backed away from him and stood in the doorway, glancing around the basement den. It was the first time I'd set foot inside since we'd moved three weeks ago.

The room was more man-cave than office. There was a PlayStation hooked up to a TV on one wall and a desk at the other, with a plush brown recliner in one corner. He picked up the phone from where he'd thrown it and shoved it into his hoodie pocket. Then he sat down in the chair and turned on the PlayStation.

My eyes settled on a Daily Grind coffee cup poking out of the trash can next to the chair. "Hot chocolate" and the name "James" were written in careful cursive with a little smiley face at the bottom of the cup.

I'd never seen him—or April—drink coffee before. I'd sort of been under the impression that it was against their religion.

I stood in the hallway, still staring at the smiley face. It wasn't one of the scribbled, hastily drawn ones. It was a whole, cute little face. With eyelashes and everything.

I told myself it meant nothing. It was a coffee cup.

I moved my gaze to the computer. Its screen was black. If the police were questioning him, maybe he was lying low. Staying off MatchStrike. Maybe they'd even catch him for what he did to Meghan. And to me.

There was a creak from the basement stairs. April was coming down. He made an exasperated noise and scanned the room. Then he plucked the empty coffee cup from the trash can and shoved it into a desk drawer, out of sight.

I backed into the hallway. April was hovering at the bottom of the stairs. She appeared to be trying to decide whether to ask him about the yelling. She must have heard the phone hit the wall.

Instead, she padded back upstairs and peeked inside the girls' room. When she saw that they were sleeping soundly, she closed her eyes and let out a sigh of relief.

Then she scooped Oscar up from the floor, made her way to the master bedroom, and tucked the covers around herself.

I generally didn't pay much attention to what April did with her phone. The few times I'd looked, she was arranging playdates for Kimmie or Emma, playing KandyKlash, or scrolling through her endless Instagram feed. But tonight, the look on her face—as she glanced toward the bedroom door, then peered at her screen with a furrowed brow, made me slide over to see what she was looking at.

She'd pulled up a news article about Meghan's murder.

With her thumb and forefinger, she was zooming in and out on a grainy, black-and-white image of her husband.

I watched in disbelief as she opened a new browsing window and typed in, "Can childhood trauma lead to violence."

She stared at the search results without clicking on any of them. A quote from a research article was displayed at the top of the results:

*It is widely accepted that childhood trauma increases the likelihood of violent behavior.*

After a few seconds, April opened up a text thread from three weeks earlier—right before they'd moved. It was a message from someone named Nina that had been left unread. The message was long: it filled up almost the entire screen. It was an apology. Nina thought that the man in the newspaper article looked just like James. She'd "mentioned it" to the Salt Lake Police. It was probably nothing. She should have told April first before contacting the police. She was so sorry. But she couldn't stop thinking about how similar they looked. Maybe he had a brother?

I had no idea who Nina was. At the end of the text she mentioned seeing the girls on Sunday, so I assumed she was a fellow church member.

April read and re-read the text message.

She finally closed the messaging app, erased her browsing history, and placed her phone carefully on the nightstand, burying her face into Oscar's furry, rumbling side.

# 27. SKYE

## KUNA, IDAHO

### NOW

They found him a month after my funeral.

An officer pulled him over on a traffic stop in Meridian. He had a tail light out. When the officer ran his plates—flagged in the database in connection to my murder—she brought him into the station for questioning.

I wasn't there when they questioned him about me. He was in and out of the police station in twenty minutes. Detective Kittleson called my mom later the following day.

James had refused to answer any questions without a lawyer present. Then he'd calmly asked if he was free to go.

And he was. They wrote him a ticket for driving without a valid vehicle registration and plates. Since it was a first-time offense, he left with a $50 ticket.

Detective Kittleson told my parents that the district attorney had significant reservations about pursuing him as a suspect at this time. The Daily Grind security footage that showed the license plate on the dark-colored Kia didn't show me anywhere near the vehicle. And the FroYo video that showed me actually getting into a dark-colored sedan didn't show the license plate. Not to mention that the driver was hardly more than a dark blur. A positive ID was almost impossible.

All they could say for certain was that James Carson had been at the Daily Grind that day. So had hundreds of other dark sedans. James worked nearby: Why wouldn't he grab something to drink on his breaks? His lawyer had communicated this. There was no way to prove that I had gotten in the car with him.

James said he'd never seen me before—outside of my photo in the papers, anyway.

When my mom learned they'd found him—without arresting him—she was getting ready for work, carefully applying eyeliner in the bathroom. I was sitting on the countertop next to her. I'd become her shadow. And I'd realized over the past month how little I actually knew about my mom while I was alive. I had always called her my "best friend." I knew her favorite Salvadoran dish—sopa de res— and her favorite TV series—*El Número Uno*. I loved her. There was no question about that. But I hardly knew anything about her as a person. The focus had always been on me: What I liked, who my friends were, how work was going, what I wanted to do after college, what I was thinking about, what I was reading.

In some ways, I felt like I was seeing her for the first time. The way I might have after a few years at college, or maybe after having a baby of my own. As I listened to her talk to her best friend Lucrecia on the couch, I pretended that she was talking to me sometimes. Especially when the conversation drifted into topics that didn't relate to my kidnapping and murder.

I learned that she'd tried pot when she was fifteen. That part of the reason she'd been so excited about me going to college was that she had dropped out her senior year. That when I was six days old, she'd shown up at a pediatrician's appointment without a bra on, because she hadn't gotten any sleep since I'd been born. That she secretly prayed at night, despite telling Lucrecia that she still didn't believe in God. That she wanted to move away from Idaho. That she still thought about my dad a lot. That she wished she'd had more kids.

I listened and watched and wished I could tell her that I was still here. That in some ways, despite the chasm that I'd fallen into, I felt closer to her now than I ever had.

I didn't try to whisper in her ear at night anymore while she slept. Not after what had happened that first night. But sometimes, while she was applying her eyeliner with shaky hands in the mornings and the bathroom was silent except for the ceiling fan ticking, I talked to her. About what foods I missed the most. About my favorite memories of her and my dad. Every once in a while, she talked back. To her reflection in the mirror—but also to me.

"Skyebird, remember when you learned to crawl and I found you camped out behind the toilet in the bathroom with a toilet cap in your mouth?"

I laughed. She laughed. And to my surprise, I found that I could remember exactly what she was talking about if I picked my way back through the memories. They were all there, as clear as crystal. "Do you remember the little fish drawing you taped to my bathroom mirror when I was two, when you were trying to get me to go number two? So it would 'feed the fishes?'" I said.

She lifted the eyeliner pen to complete a stroke. Then she put her hand down as her eyes crinkled up in laughter. "I remember when you were teeny and terrified to poop in the potty. I told you it would feed *los pescaditos*, and you got right on board after that. I even made you a little drawing to help you visualize it. Lucrecia told me about that one."

\* \* \*

A few days after they found James, Detective Kittleson finally managed to get a search warrant for the blue Kia. I was sure it would have taken him even longer, if not for my mom's repeated phone calls.

They were looking for blood, fingerprints, hair, and fibers. Any evidence that I'd ever been in that car.

My mom was ecstatic. I was hopeful, too. I'd touched the door handle and the inside of the car. Surely, he couldn't have scrubbed every trace of me from it.

The warrant was served on a Tuesday morning, after he'd left for work.

I fully intended to watch. I wasn't sure what I'd see or if there was anything that I could do, but where else did I have to be?

The part where they actually served the warrant wasn't anything like what I'd seen on movies or TV. Detective Kittleson—and a scrubbed-up tech—stood on the porch and knocked politely.

A woman answered the door, flanked by two of the most adorable blond girls I'd ever seen.

When she saw the officers standing on her doorstep, she looked like she had seen a ghost. Which she had. Because I was standing right there. She didn't know that though.

As Detective Kittleson announced the warrant's scope: the keys to the Kia and the Kia itself, I shifted my gaze to the two little girls. Unlike April, they were totally oblivious to the magnitude of what was happening on their front porch. The taller of the two, whose blond bangs stuck up at an angle that made me think she'd just gotten out of bed, hopped from one foot to the other while she tapped on her mom's leg, pointing at the police car in the driveway. The younger girl looked between her mother and older sister, patiently waiting for someone to tell her what was going on.

I was so busy looking at the three of them, that I didn't even notice the fourth person standing a few feet behind them in the hallway until she stepped forward.

She had straight brown hair and wide hazel eyes with the thickest set of eyelashes I'd ever seen. She was wearing a comfy-looking burgundy velvet tracksuit. She appeared to be about the same age as April. Was this a sister? A nanny? From the expression on her face, my first thought was that she looked like she'd seen a ghost too.

And she had.

Because she looked right at me and whispered, "Are you dead?"

# 28. MEGHAN

## SALT LAKE VALLEY, UTAH

### NOW

Domanska listened to her hunches.

Which was good. Because that's all I could contribute—aside from making her Weimaraner Joey uneasy when I got too close.

So when the nervous waitress from Gracie's couldn't conclusively identify James Carson in the photo lineup of dark-haired, handsome men in their late twenties, Domanska didn't give up.

She watched patiently while the skinny, blue-eyed woman scanned each photo, then nodded her head vigorously. "That one could be him. I think that one, maybe? I remember he was cute. He also had brown hair. So that guy fits the bill." Then she moved on to the next photo, frowned, and said the same thing.

I yelled at her. I sat on top of the desk with the photos and got right up in her eardrum when she scanned the actual photo of James —which had been plucked from his LinkedIn profile. "That's him. You *talked* to him! Look at it harder. That's the one. Remember."

All it seemed to do was increase her anxiety. By the time she left the police station, she was visibly shaking. There was no way that a judge was going to grant Domanska a warrant based on that ID.

Domanska, however, was unfazed. She thanked the waitress for her time, placed the photos back into a folder, and asked her assistant to find out whether the traffic cameras in Salt Lake and Cedar Fort still had backup footage stored in the system.

When James Carson had moved to Idaho, he'd gotten himself a bus-bench lawyer who ripped Domanska a new one and made a blistering call to her supervisor about harassing his client. She had patiently made a note on his file—but kept it open on her desk.

She wasn't going to let this go.

Which encouraged me to hold on a little longer, too.

When I wasn't peering over Domanska's shoulder at the computer or riding along on calls, I drifted. I spent more and more time with my memories as the days turned into weeks and Domanska worked on other cases. Twenty-six years holds a lot of memories. So there were still plenty of static worlds to explore that allowed me to come back to the land of the living. I savored each one like a rerun of a beloved TV show. But binge-watching memories or TV by yourself gets lonely. I thought about Grandma Rosie—and the others who had passed on—almost constantly.

At first, I stayed at the police station when Domanska went home at night. It never really closed down. There was always something happening. Always somebody waiting for the next bad thing to happen. It was interesting for a while. I saw a lot of things up close that I'd never seen—or wanted to see. A lot of screaming. A lot of crying. A little blood. A lot of phone calls. And a lot of questions with unsettling answers.

I went home with Domanska for the first time the night they got a call from West Valley about an endangered child—and arrested her parents. I didn't want to be in the same building as the quiet, bespeckled man with salt-and-pepper hair who had raped his ten-year-old daughter. Or the mother who knew about it. So when Domanska left for the night in her unmarked cruiser, I got into the passenger seat with her.

I wasn't comfortable staying at her house when she wasn't there. In large part because Joey, the Weimaraner, peed on the carpet then barked until I went outside the one time I tried.

The comfort of going home—to any home—at the end of the day was just enough to keep me going. At the end of every day, we microwaved one of those frozen meal subscription dinners. Then we took Joey for a walk (he tolerated me if Domanska was nearby), came back home, and watched an episode of *Parks and Recreation*. Sometimes Domanska's daughter dropped by with dinner, and we all went for a walk and ate dinner together.

I thought about my parents a lot. About whether I should have spent my last days haunting them, instead of Domanska and the Salt Lake City police department. I missed my mom and dad, but knowing that I'd see them again—that they would find me in their memories someday—kept me where I was. Grandma Rosie had made it clear that once I made the decision to cross over into that universe of untapped memories, I couldn't come back.

My unfinished business was here. And after months of being alone with my own bones in the mountain, Domanska's place felt like a home of sorts.

* * *

After a few months had passed, I finally won Joey over. When I sat down next to Domanska to watch *Parks and Rec,* he sometimes sat on my side of the couch, snuggling against the pillow and wedging me into the crack between the cushions. I loved it. It was the only thing that still made me feel like I still existed on this side.

The traffic cams had proven useless. And the woman who had called in the tip about James Carson the previous year didn't have anything more than a hunch to offer, either. She knew James's wife from church. She got a bad feeling about him and thought he looked like the photo that had run in the stories about my murder. But that was all. April Carson—James's wife—wasn't talking either. When Domanska called, she said she'd been advised not to answer any questions by her husband's lawyer. So that was the end of that.

All we had left were hunches. But hunches could only take us so far. Domanska kept my file on her desk. She followed every single new tip that trickled in periodically. She didn't know what I knew, though. And I couldn't tell her.

\* \* \*

We were leaving the station for the night when the call came through on the tip line.

I knew it was different when Domanska's assistant Carly ran outside to the parking lot. With all of the previous tips, she'd sent an email with the information to be filed. The caller was still on the line, Carly said, raising an eyebrow and tilting her head toward the station. "I think you should talk to him if you have a second. He's calling about the KTVD article he saw."

I was out of the cruiser and back inside the station before I saw whether Domanska had decided to follow. Carly didn't get excited easily. And the KTVD article, which had been published a couple of days earlier, had already brought in a new trickle of dead-end tips. It happened any time something new was published about my case.

I watched the blinking red light on the phone in the empty room, waiting for Carly and Domanska to catch up to me and take the held call.

It was a 208 number: Idaho.

Domanska got there before Carly. Her expression was impassive, but I knew her well enough by now that she wouldn't have taken the call if she didn't sense the same electricity in Carly's voice that I had.

"Detective Domanska," she said evenly as she picked up the call. I leaned next to the phone and her ear.

The person on the other end of the line cleared his throat. "Um, hi. I'm really sorry to bother you. It's probably nothing. But I figured you're following up on everything. It might be a waste of your time . . ."

"Spit it out, man!" I yelled into the receiver.

Domanska patiently allowed him to finish then prodded, "You're not bothering anyone, and we are definitely following up on all tips. I appreciate the call. Can you tell me what prompted you to call in?"

The caller let out a rush of air. "Oh, okay. Cool. We got KTVD here a couple months ago—you know the buy-and-sell site? You probably know that. But they have articles in the sidebar, and most of them are total clickbait, but the rest are mostly about Utah—I swear I'm getting to the point—" He cleared his throat again nervously, and I imagined myself banging the phone receiver on the desk in frustration.

"Yes, I'm familiar with KTVD," Domanska responded. "You said you saw the article about Meghan?"

"Yes," he replied, sounding relieved. "And I think I've seen that guy before. I—I think maybe he murdered my friend."

I saw Domanska glance at Carly, who was listening in and recording the call on the other side of the room with a headset. She frowned. He was starting to sound crazy.

"Okay. Can you tell me your friend's name? And your name also, if you don't mind?"

There was another sharp intake of breath on the phone.

"Yeah, my name is Ken. And my friend Skye was murdered three months ago."

# 29. BRECIA

## KUNA, IDAHO

### NOW

*Are you dead?*

I asked her the question in the same way I sometimes asked Oscar if he was going to kill the mouse or play with it all day: I didn't really expect a response.

I didn't pay much attention to her at first. I was focused on the fact that there was a detective on the front porch. With an actual search warrant for James's car.

Then the young woman standing next to the detective stepped forward and poked her head into the house.

April didn't even glance at her. Neither did the girls.

Oscar did, though. He made that soft, scary noise in the back of his throat that he sometimes made when he saw the neighbor's cat in the front yard. Then he slunk into the kitchen.

I'd thought she was a tech or an assistant. She was young: couldn't be older than twenty. She had chestnut brown skin and curly black hair that dipped past her shoulder blades. She didn't smile at anyone. Instead she darted her wide, hazel eyes around the room as she stepped forward and peered past April at Kimmie and Emma.

For a split second, I bristled. Who did this girl think she was?

Then I watched as she brushed past April's arm.

She scattered. Like I did.

When I spoke to her, she snapped her gaze toward me.

The lights in the living room flickered as the cocktail of shock, excitement, and horror hit me at once.

"Oh my god," she whispered as she looked at me with an intensity I hadn't experienced while dead or alive. "You're …" She trailed off. There was no question anymore.

I almost missed the fact that April was leading the male detective into the living room to retrieve the keys to the Kia.

"Come on," I told the girl with the black hair. "I'm not missing this."

\* \* \*

Skye and I sat in the backseat of the Kia while the detectives towed the car to the station.

We discovered we had a lot to talk about.

April stood in the driveway with Kimmie and Emma as we pulled away, her face a mask of dread and fear. Maybe I was imagining it, but I thought I saw a trace of something else: doubt.

After the detective from Utah had called a couple of months earlier, James had less-than-patiently explained to April that he was the target of a witch hunt. And it was April's fault. The woman in their old congregation in Utah—the one who had sent April those texts and called the police when she saw the similarity between James and the photo in the news—had opened this can of worms. April hadn't done shit about it. She hadn't even shown him the text messages until he "stumbled" across them while looking for a photo on her phone.

So they had to hire a lawyer they couldn't really afford.

I knew they could afford it. Easily. April didn't, though. She had almost nothing to do with the finances. He transferred a few hundred dollars into a checking account she used for groceries and the occasional outfit when the girls needed new clothes. That was it. So when the detective from Utah had called her cell a few days after she called James, April stayed on the phone for less than thirty seconds. Just long enough to repeat the line she'd been instructed to deliver about all questions going through their lawyer. But afterward, while Emma was at school and Kimmie was taking a nap, she opened an incognito browser and searched for "Meghan Campbell murder." She read every article. She scrutinized the photo of him up close. She shook her head as if exasperated with herself for even entertaining the idea that her husband—her James—could be involved in anything like that. Then she shut the browser and went to pick Emma up from school.

I told Skye all of this as we sat in the towed Kia at the impound lot, waiting for it to be processed that evening. I told her what he had done to me two years earlier. And she told me what he had done to her two months earlier.

He had killed her while I was at home with his wife and kids, pretending that maybe he had stopped because he wasn't using MatchStrike anymore. Pretending like April was.

"I'm so sorry," I told her in the dark car. There were no tears. I didn't have those anymore, and neither did she. But the electric weight of the sadness in the car reached even the lone streetlight at the corner of the impound lot that had just blinked on in the storm rolling over the hills. "I tried so hard to stop him. I followed him everywhere. Like his shadow. In the end, I couldn't do anything to stop it from happening. There was another woman: Meghan. Before you. I was there when he did it … I stopped following him after that."

Her eyes looked like deep pools in the dark Kia. She nodded. "It's not your fault, you know. It's nobody's fault. Just his."

\* \* \*

The car was pretty clean. There was no blood. No hair. No fibers of significant interest.

There was, however, a fingerprint. Just one that didn't match with April, the girls, or James himself. It was on the front passenger side of the vehicle, where the seat connected to the base of the car.

Skye and I looked at each other. Both of us knew that it could mean anything. That justice wasn't guaranteed. That sometimes bad people got away with doing bad things and never paid the price. After all, he'd gotten away with my murder for years now. He'd gotten away with Skye's murder for months. He'd gotten away with all of it.

There was a very small chance that the fingerprint was hers. Zero chance it was mine. The only time I'd been in his car was as a ghost. Most likely, it was from one of the many other women he'd met up with on MatchStrike. The ones he had wowed and terrified and annoyed—but not murdered.

So we didn't grin at each other the way I might have before. Skye just followed the tech to the lab while I stayed with Detective Kittleson.

Because a small chance was still a chance. And small chances were all we had left.

# 30. SKYE

## KUNA, IDAHO

### NOW

The tech said it would take about two hours to run the fingerprint they'd found in his car.

I sort of expected them to be able to pop it into a computer. That we'd know immediately whether or not it was a match. But as I watched the tech carefully prepare and clean up the image she had digitized, I was impressed it was only going to take two hours. The fingerprint card, up close, was a dense maze of ridges, furrows, and channels. And on the other side of that maze was—maybe—the key to an arrest.

The tech was young—not much older than me. Probably just a few years out of college. Her dark hair was tucked into a neat braid, and her brown eyes darted back and forth across the print slide with a focused determination. When someone knocked on the lab door, she ignored it.

She was amazing.

When my mom gently asked about what I might major in, I'd said "maybe science?" But I'd actually given the idea quite a bit of thought. I had loved my chemistry and biology classes. The idea of spending my days in a lab with samples and slides— instead of try-ing to make sales or manage people or participate in "team-building" activities—appealed to every part of my introverted brain. Maybe, if things had turned out differently, this could have been me.

As I watched the tech work, my mind drifted back to everything Brecia had told me. She'd been living with him for two years.

When the tech was finished digitizing and cleaning the print, she quickly uploaded it to something called AFIS—a fingerprinting database.

She frowned and tucked a piece of hair back into her braid as the algorithm scanned through millions of prints and the little blinking bar at the top of the screen announced its progress.

I expected this part to take a while too; however, once the print was in the system, the progress bar speedily moved from zero to one hundred percent in a matter of minutes. The search was over before I knew it.

There was no match.

The tech made a note of the results and strode out of the room. I knew where she was going. Because there was still a chance it was my fingerprint.

My fingerprints hadn't been on file before I died. And the one's they'd taken from my body had to be cleaned up substantially to account for decomposition.

Another tech was cleaning up my post-mortem fingerprints, accounting for the decay and degradation. If it was my fingerprint on the car, we weren't going to get a perfect match. But we'd get close.

I tried not to hope as I watched the analyst compare the two prints an hour later.

But when she overlaid the images, even I could see that they weren't the same.

The light flickered in the office as the disappointment hit hard.

It wasn't my fingerprint. It could be anybody's fingerprint, since whoever it belonged to wasn't in the system.

I walked down the hall toward Kittleson's office in a numb haze. I'd been there with my mom enough times that I knew the way. I wasn't particularly fond of him as a detective. He made a lot of big promises and reassurances then took a long time to follow through.

He should have had my post-mortem prints finished long before now. But even I could tell that he didn't really think he had a case against James Carson. Or anyone else.

So I was pretty sure that this was the dead end that would turn the case truly cold for him. It had never been all that hot.

Brecia was sitting in the office chair, talking to Detective Kittleson when I walked in. He wasn't responding, of course. He was on the phone with my mom, letting her know that the fingerprint wasn't a match to me. He sounded curt and annoyed.

"Watch your tone," Brecia growled as Kittleson sighed loudly then told my mom that he would—like he had already promised—tell her if there were any new developments. The car had already been processed. This had been their best lead. It would be released from impound tomorrow.

I sat down next to Brecia. She clearly already knew about the print results. "He's kind of a prick," she told me, then flashed Kittleson the finger. "What do you want to do now? Are you ... are you going to go back to your mom's house?"

She said it like it was a casual question. But there was no way to hide the undercurrent of sadness that accompanied the words. She'd been alone for a long time.

I hadn't been a ghost for nearly as long as Brecia had, but I couldn't imagine walking away from the one person who could see me. The first person in months who could hear me talk—and talk back to me. The one other person who really understood what had happened to me.

No matter how much I loved my mom and wanted to stay near her, she couldn't see me anymore. And that was the loneliest thing I'd ever felt, alive or dead.

"No," I whispered. "Can I stay with you?"

Brecia smiled and nodded, and the current shifted to relief. She pointed at Kittleson, who was scowling at an email he'd just received. "Should we shut it down?" she asked.

I frowned. "What do you mean?"

Her eyes went wide. "Watch." She closed her eyes, and suddenly the air was electric with rage.

Kittleson's computer screen went black. He swore under his breath and rapidly pressed the on/off button.

Brecia smiled, and the angry electricity fizzled. "Cool, right?"

By the time he managed to get the computer booted back up, his face was red with frustration. "Piece of crap," he muttered under his breath.

As the password lock screen finally flickered back to life, the phone on the desk rang.

He glanced between the computer and the phone.

"Answer it!" Brecia instructed, sliding across the desk until she was right in his face. Then burying her face in his ear.

I flinched. I knew he couldn't see her, but it looked awkward as all hell. "Does that really work?"

"Sometimes." Brecia sat back on the desk as Kittleson walked out of the office without answering the phone. Her expression darkened. "Not always."

I scooted in with her, to listen to the message in the empty room.

The blinking red light flashed as a woman's voice responded to the recorded prompt.

"Detective Kittleson? I hear you have James Carson's car impounded. This is Detective Domanska, in Salt Lake City, Utah. I need you to call me back as soon as possible."

# 31. MEGHAN

## SALT LAKE VALLEY, UTAH

### NOW

By the time the detective from Idaho called Domanska back, it was nearly dinner time. She'd given him her cell—which rang right as we were about to walk out the door with Joey.

I'd never seen Domanska lose her cool before. Not with the eggheaded waitress from Gracie's. Not even with James Carson himself when she'd questioned him face to face.

But when she heard that Detective Kittleson had released James Carson's car out of impound—before even calling her back to report on the fingerprint he'd found—she ripped him a new one.

He tersely agreed to make sure my fingerprint was run in the lab that night.

When he muttered something about overtime and staff shortages, Domanska blew up at him again.

Kittleson hung up without saying goodbye, and all of us—including Joey—made a beeline back to the office to send over the file with my fingerprints.

# 32. BRECIA

## KUNA, IDAHO

### NOW

When James picked the car up from impound, the air felt like a powder keg.

Kittleson still hadn't returned Domanska's message. He was busy with two new cases: the suspicious death of a blue-eyed, blond-haired toddler that had been making front-page headlines for a week straight, and an officer-involved shooting that was sending shockwaves through the community.

When he saw the blinking red light on his phone, he listened to it—and made a note to call her back—then busied himself with another case that had been assigned to him that morning.

We shut down his computer twice that afternoon. It only made him take an early lunch. And then, because neither of us could stand to look at him anymore, Skye and I caught a ride with an officer and waited at the impound lot.

When James arrived at the impound lot to pick up the car, he looked different since I'd last seen him. Less at ease. Less interested in pretenses. On high alert.

April had driven him there. Kimmie and Emma were with her. None of them got out of the car.

James didn't know what detectives knew—or rather what they *didn't* know—but he knew the net was closing.

Skye and I looked at each other as James put the keys in the ignition. We both felt the pull to follow the officer back to the station. But there was something in James's eyes that told me I should jump into the back of his car.

Skye wavered at the threshold of the police station. She saw it too. "I'm going with James, okay?" she said hesitantly. "If somebody needs to mess with Kittleson's computer, I'm not sure I can do it."

I didn't want to leave her. Not now. She was right: Someone needed to follow James. I nodded. "If anything happens, get back to the station as fast as you can, okay? You know the way back there?"

She nodded. Then she jumped into the back of the Kia as he pulled out of the parking lot, behind April and the girls.

# 33. MEGHAN

## SALT LAKE VALLEY, UTAH

### NOW

My fingerprint was a ninety-eight percent match.

When we got the news, Domanska's office turned into a hive of activity.

The warrant for his arrest by the state of Utah was secured in less than two hours. Domanska's assistant arranged for an agency assist from Officer Kittleson in Idaho to make the arrest.

Early the next morning, I was riding shotgun on the way to Idaho to find him—which wasn't going to be as easy as it should have been, since the car had already been released out of impound.

Detective Kittleson insisted they'd let him walk out of the impound lot because they had nothing concrete to hold him in Idaho. No evidence to connect him to the murder that had prompted Ken to call in after seeing that KTVD article.

Not yet.

But now that we had physical evidence that I'd been in his car, we could get a warrant to search his house. His computer. His online activities.

Which meant they were finally going to find not just James Carson but Jimmy Carlson—and whoever else he had been over the years.

# 34. SKYE

## KUNA, IDAHO

### NOW

He tailgated his own wife and kids all the way home, cursing under his breath about how stupid April was. How this was her fault.

I stared at him in disbelief, wondering how I'd ever gotten into the car with him all those months ago. How I'd ever thought he was handsome, or worth two seconds of my thoughts. He darted his eyes back and forth from the tail lights of the minivan to the rearview mirror, and I wondered if he was waiting for the police to suddenly show up behind him with flashing lights.

I hoped they would. But I wasn't holding my breath—so to speak—anymore.

The clock in the car showed that it was almost 10:00 a.m. I wasn't sure how old his girls were, but it seemed like they should be in school.

Suddenly, he grabbed a cell phone that had been lying next to me in the passenger seat. I flinched as his hand fumbled around on the seat. The car radio made a little blip, and I wondered if I'd done it.

He pulled a folded piece of paper out of his pocket then dialed the phone number, slamming on the brakes to keep from plowing into the back of his own minivan. I watched April's wide eyes flick to the rearview mirror. I could only imagine what she was thinking right now. Part of me sympathized with her. She was married to a murderer. And she had no idea.

Another part of me was angry with her. And still another part hated her. Because how could she not know? From what Brecia had told me, she'd looked up the article that had run in Utah about the murder he'd committed there.

I thought back to the months before my parents' divorce. The screaming. The crying. The bad vibes. The pre-emptive, "You know that when Daddy and I fight, it's not your fault, right, Skyebird?" heart-to-hearts. But even after all that, when they finally sat my third-grade self down at the table and told me my dad was moving away, I refused to believe it was real. I didn't want it to happen. So it wasn't happening.

Still, I'd been in third grade.

I leaned closer as the call picked up and a woman answered the phone. "This is Marjorie."

Her voice sounded old—and suspicious.

"It's James," he said flatly.

Her suspicion melted into surprise. "James? My goodness, I didn't recognize your number. It's wonderful to hear from you. It's been such a long time. I didn't think I'd hear—"

He didn't match her tone when he cut her off. "We need to come stay at the cabin."

The radio blipped again as what he had said hit me. I missed Marjorie's response as I frantically looked back at the city behind us, where the police station—and Brecia—had long since disappeared from view.

He was going to run.

I couldn't panic. I had to focus. I had to listen. Marjorie sounded slightly confused but mostly pleased when she responded. "The cabin? Oh yes. Yes, wonderful memories there. It's been so long. When do you want to visit? I'll check my calendar."

He rolled his eyes and hit the brakes hard again as April stopped for a red light. "Wonderful memories?" He laughed bitterly but didn't elaborate. "April and I need to get out of town. I don't have time to explain, but I need you to keep quiet about it—and this phone call—if anyone asks. Can you do that? I damn well kept quiet all those years. Now it's your turn to return the favor."

Marjorie was silent on the other end of the line. I could feel the disgust and irritation coming off him in waves. Who was this woman? And what did he mean about keeping quiet?

James floored the gas as the light changed and April continued through the intersection. The neighborhoods were starting to look familiar. If I remembered correctly, we were almost back to his house.

"All right," Marjorie finally responded flatly. She didn't sound happy anymore. "It's dusty out there, though. Do you remember where we kept the key?"

"I remember," he replied in a clipped voice. "It was my cabin before it was yours."

There was a long pause. Then, "All right then. Glad you remember."

"I remember everything," he spat.

As he ended the call, I slipped through the car's air vents and hightailed it back toward the station as fast as I could go.

# 35. MEGHAN

## BOISE, IDAHO

### NOW

Domanska didn't even stop for a bathroom break. We left just before the sun had broken the horizon and made the drive from Salt Lake to Boise in five hours flat.

When we pulled into the station, I expected to be met by a flurry of momentum that matched the no-pee-breaks-energy in the car. But even after Domanska had returned from the bathroom in the station, Kittleson kept us waiting.

I did what Domanska couldn't and wandered through the building until I found him—talking with another detective outside his open office door about another case.

"Get out here, and let's go arrest his ass!" I called. Today was finally the day we brought him in. The day he finally faced the music for what he'd done to me and god-knew how many other women.

That was the moment a woman poked her head around the corner of the office door.

She was wearing fuzzy pink slippers and the comfiest-looking purple pajamas I'd ever seen.

She looked right at me.

But my surprise that she could obviously see—and hear—me turned to total shock when she whispered, "Oh my god. Meghan."

I took a step back, and the expression on her face crumpled. "I'm so sorry," she said, and the fluorescent lights in the hallway outside of Kittleson's office flickered wildly.

I shook my head, trying to take it all in. "What? Hold on, you can see me?" Was she some kind of psychic? Did that also explain the pajamas somehow?

She nodded. "I'm Brecia. And I'm so sorry. I tried to stop him that night. I wanted to come after you, but you were moving so fast, and I didn't want to let him go . . ."

The lights flickered around us again, and suddenly I understood. I remembered the sound of the woman's voice as I ran through the trees and down the embankment, thinking I was escaping.

She'd been there that night too. Because he'd gotten to her first.

I stared at her in disbelief. She flinched at my gaze, as if I might be gearing up to scream at her.

Instead, without really thinking about it, I brushed past Kittleson—who was still yammering on about something that didn't sound very important at all—and leaned in to give her a hug.

When I did, I learned the answer to every question that had crossed my mind in the past thirty seconds—and every question I might possibly ask in the future about Brecia. As our arms touched and we embraced, I saw with crystal clarity everything she so badly wanted me to know about her own murder. About what she'd tried to do the night I died. And about what she'd done afterward. Everything words couldn't ever have summed up no matter how hard we'd tried.

When we stepped apart, I could see that the same had happened for her. That she understood what I desperately wanted her to know, too. Where I'd been all this time. What it meant that I knew she'd tried to save me, even if it hadn't worked out. Everything I wanted to say.

The fluorescent light overhead finally popped, and Kittleson cursed. "Damn it," he muttered. His phone was ringing yet again—like it had been ever since Domanska arrived. He finally hurried into his office to answer it.

That was when another voice—frantic and shrill—became audible above the sound of the phone.

Brecia and I turned at the same time to see a young Latina woman with curly black hair flying down the hall toward us.

"He's running!" she cried.

And from the way she brushed past desks and around doorways, I knew that she was dead too.

# 36. BRECIA

## KUNA, IDAHO

Meghan, Skye, and I left the police station just as Domanska had—finally—begun to coordinate with Kittleson's Boise agents, who would be assisting with the arrest.

Meghan hung back at first, not wanting to leave Domanska—and clearly not wanting to see him again.

But there was no time to debate. In the end, Meghan came with us. Domanska had things covered. She'd be right behind us. And if we were somehow going to stall him, we needed all hands on deck.

We couldn't fly. Not in the way I would have imagined, anyway. But we ran like champions, the city a blur of color around us as we cut across busy streets without stopping for traffic and through the slats in fenced yards. If I had to guess, we ran about five miles. There was no real way for me to measure time anymore, of course, but before I knew it, we were standing in his front yard.

As if on cue, the garage door opened when we reached the driveway.

The minivan was already running, with April and the girls buckled inside. James Carson was putting a suitcase into a trunk that was already full of loose belongings.

I knew by now this wasn't his usual style. James was neat. He was organized. He was methodical. If the van looked like this, he was leaving sooner rather than later.

The three of us looked at one another. We were so close.

I could feel it in every part of me. And so, apparently, could he.

"Maybe we can stop him," I tried. I'd never had much luck messing with cars. But maybe with Meghan and Skye here, we'd be able to blow something.

It was worth a shot.

I let the panic expand, scrambling to find the cumulative fury and fear of the past two years. Sometimes it felt like the well was running dry. It was getting harder and harder to harness that raw emotion that had been so easy to access in the first weeks and months.

But I could feel the energy coming off Skye—and Meghan too —in waves that made the air around us crackle with electricity.

Skye's eyes were shut tight, her dark curls falling forward as she held her hands out in front of her.

Meghan stared straight ahead, hugging herself hard as she stood at the bumper of the van, turning herself into a mini transformer.

It was all weirdly beautiful. I focused my attention back on him, so I wouldn't dilute the weak current I'd managed to tap into.

James hopped into the driver's seat, oblivious to the fact that both of his tail lights—and probably the headlights too—had suddenly just popped.

Since I wasn't much help, I dove into the minivan, sandwiching myself into the gap between the front seats. April's face was pale. She was looking at the black screen of her phone, pressing the home button again and again to show the time.

I pulled myself to her in a sort of desperate hug. "Get out of the car, April! Call the police. Get the girls away from him. You *know* what he did. He's not running because he's been wrongly accused. He's running because he's guilty."

April turned the phone over on her lap as James got in the driver's side. He looked at the phone sharply. "You can't fucking bring that. Did you not hear anything I told you? Leave it in the house. They'll trace it."

When April didn't move, he snatched it out of her hands and jumped out of the car again. Emma started to whimper in the backseat, and April snapped out of her daze, turning around to comfort the girls. "Everything's okay. Daddy is just having a hard day. We're going to sort everything out and have a fun adventure too."

When James got back into the van, he shifted into reverse and started backing down the driveway.

The lights were shot. But the engine was fine. The car was drivable.

I looked back helplessly at Meghan and Skye, still standing outside the van.

There was nothing left we could do.

As James backed the van down the driveway, first Meghan then Skye slipped through the passenger side door.

Domanska wasn't going to get here in time.

# 37. SKYE

## CASCADE, IDAHO

Aside from the *Sesame Street* soundtrack that April put on for the girls, the van stayed mostly silent for the first half hour on the road.

Brecia, Meghan, and I hadn't said much either. From what he'd said on the phone earlier, we were headed to Cascade—about a two-hour drive. But we didn't talk about that much. Instead, we stayed quiet, waiting for the moment we'd finally hear sirens in the background.

By now, they had to know he'd made a run for it.

James was clearly thinking the same thing, by the number of times he glanced in the rearview mirror. He drove exactly the speed limit, keeping a white-knuckled grip on ten-and-two.

It was only after Kimmie and Emma nodded off to the sound of Cookie Monster jamming out about healthy food that April finally spoke up.

She turned to look back at the car seats, where the girls were sleeping—and where Meghan sat between them, looking out the window at the hills that were giving way to tall lodgepole pines.

April's eyes wandered over the boxes of canned food, camping supplies, and suitcases that had been tucked into every bit of floorspace in the van. Then she whispered, "Will you at least tell me what the detective said to you when you picked up the Kia? If you're innocent—" She caught herself, then started again. "Since you're innocent, why can't we just talk to them? Make them understand you never even met that girl. Why do we have to—" She gestured behind her at the packed minivan. "I feel like I'm in *The Fugitive* right now." She cracked a tentative smile, but it faltered when he didn't smile back.

I heard Brecia sigh in frustration from the back of the van, where she had tucked herself against a pile of sleeping bags. "He's not Richard Kimball, April. He's the one-armed man."

James—I still thought of him as James, even though I knew that person had never existed—narrowed his eyes slightly and didn't respond.

April shook her head. "I mean, they gave us the Kia back. They wouldn't have done that if they'd found something, right?" It was impossible to hide the desperation in her voice.

He pursed his lips and kept his eyes on the road. "That lady detective in Utah has wanted to pin this on me ever since your BFF *Nina*,"—he spat out the name like it was a bad word—"got so bored with her life she decided to ruin mine." He cut his eyes toward April. "And now yours, too," he added in a tight-lipped singsong.

April clutched the seatbelt with one hand as he braked for a tree branch that had fallen into the one-lane road. We'd turned off the paved highway a few miles back and onto a narrow dirt road. We hadn't passed another car since. The treeline around us was getting thicker as we climbed in elevation. I'd been through Cascade once when I was ten, when my mom took me camping in Ponderosa. I had no idea there were cabins on this part of the mountain.

April tried again. "Did you tell your lawyer we were leaving town? How long are we going to be staying? If Emma misses more than a few days of kindergarten, I'm going to have to give the school a doctor's note, or she'll be truant."

He glared at the road. "Can you shut up, please?"

April looked like she'd been slapped. She was quiet for a few seconds. Then she softly asked, "Is there anything you're not telling me?"

He ignored her. After a few minutes, she took a deep breath and tried again. "The last time Marjorie tried to get in touch—after your dad died—you told her that if she ever called the house again, you'd get a restraining order. You didn't even go to the funeral. And now we're going to stay at her cabin?"

His jaw twitched, but he stayed silent. April kept going in a halting voice. "I've never pushed you to talk about her, because I know how you get when her name comes up, but I always wondered if she might have ..." She trailed off and studied him apprehensively. Finally she whispered, "... had something to do with your scars."

He stared straight ahead, his knuckles white on the steering wheel.

"Please talk to me," April choked out. "I'm scared."

He took one hand off the steering wheel. For a second, I thought he was going to hit her. She must have wondered the same thing, because she recoiled against the passenger seat.

He sent her a withering look, as if he couldn't believe how dramatic she was being, then snatched a bottle of water from the cupholder, letting go of the wheel with both hands to open it.

"Is he going to hurt them?" Meghan suddenly asked in a small voice from behind me. She had turned away from the window and was watching Kimmie while she slept, fuzzy purple blankie in hand.

Brecia slid down from the pile of sleeping bags and squeezed into the space on the other side of Emma's car seat. "I don't think so. He brought all their stuff."

"So April would go with him," Meghan responded listlessly. "He didn't buy me drinks because he wanted me to enjoy them." She closed her eyes, and I noticed the same reflective shimmer I sometimes saw in myself when I looked in the mirror. "We shouldn't have come," she whispered. "Whatever's going to happen, I don't want to see it."

\* \* \*

The sun was shining brightly, blazing noon by the time we reached the overgrown dirt driveway that led to the cabin.

There had been no sirens. There had been no other cars on the road.

He'd made it.

The girls woke up when the minivan came to a stop, and April put on her happy mommy mask. While James searched for the key then dragged suitcases and bags into the old cabin, she played pinecone soccer with the girls under the big pines in the front yard.

I followed him inside the cabin while Brecia and Meghan hung back. It was a tiny two-bedroom log structure that looked like it had been furnished in the 70s. Orange shag carpet, dusty yellow lamps, and lime green Formica countertops. It was pretty clear that nobody had been to visit for a very long time. When James turned on the tap, the water was rust red at first.

It looked a little like blood.

# 38. MEGHAN

## CASCADE, IDAHO

When Domanska had finally brought me back to civilization after months on that damn mountain where he'd dumped my body, I never would have imagined that fate would lead me back into the wilderness—with him and his wife and kids, no less.

It was a real trip, let me tell you.

Even in the hours and days after my own murder, as I watched my bones get picked apart by the birds and the coyotes, I didn't feel anxiety like this.

I already knew I wasn't going to stick around if he did something to them. If things went south—more south than they already had, that is—I didn't want to watch. I was going to find Bubbie and disappear for good.

I sat down beside Brecia on a fallen log. "I can't believe you've been following him this long. I feel so helpless. How did you stand it?"

A few feet away, Emma brandished a moss-covered stick at a hornet then ran squealing back to April when it gave chase. Kimmie shrieked and burst into tears as the hornet approached, still clutching her purple blankie.

Brecia shook her head as Skye walked out of the cabin toward us. "I didn't. I gave up."

"So why didn't you leave?" I asked. "Like, for good."

Brecia gave me a look. "I didn't know that was an option."

I glanced between her and Skye, who looked equally confused. They didn't know.

Skye lay down on the carpet of pine needles then closed her eyes. "Tell us your magic, Meghan."

So I told them about the challah and the memory of Bubbie that promised to blossom into a million more memories as soon as I was ready. People I'd never met, places I'd never seen, an expanding universe of connected consciousnesses. I felt a little like a preacher extolling heaven as I watched Brecia's expression shift from disbelief to astonishment.

"I had no idea," she whispered. "If I did, I don't think I would have stayed."

"I almost didn't, a few times."

Skye sat up. "I don't really know anybody else who's died. I doubt anyone's anxiously waiting to show me around the other side. My grandparents are all still alive. I can't think of anyone." She looked thoughtful for a moment. "Except maybe my gym teacher from middle school. He died of cancer last summer. I doubt he's all that excited to see me. I always pretended to have my period to get out of whatever we were doing."

I felt her sadness seep into the air around us. With her skinny frame and big, dark eyes she looked even younger than eighteen. She'd be the one waiting to greet her loved ones when they found her in their memories. "You said you were headed to college at Idaho State, right? Where you didn't know anybody?"

Skye shrugged. "Yeah. Maybe it'll be like that."

I reached for her hand and felt her sadness like it was my own. "Except you'll be meeting your family. The people who raised your grandparents. And the people who raised them, all the way back. Even though you don't know them yet, they're gonna claim you."

She looked thoughtful. "I always meant to do one of those 23andMe kits. My mom tried to get into family history once. Just once, after she saw a commercial. She got all excited and wanted to know if we had, like, Aztec royalty in our blood. It didn't last very long. The line stopped hard at my great, great grandparents in El Salvador during the civil war." She closed her eyes and lay back in the pine boughs again.

Brecia and I lay down beside her. "They're going to be so happy to meet you," I said. "And when your mom gets there and finds you waiting, I bet you're going to introduce her to royalty after all."

Skye smiled. "Yeah. I bet you're right."

The delicate leaves of hope pushing up through the thick sadness curled back in an instant as James suddenly came barreling out of the house.

"Where's the black backpack?" he barked. "I swear to god if you didn't bring it—"

Kimmie went silent, and Emma instinctively reached for April's hand. April tilted her head a little and marched over to the van, where she grabbed a big black backpack that had been shoved under the passenger seats. As she handed it to him, she hissed, "It's right here. Don't talk to me like that in front of the girls. You're scaring them."

"She's all bite when it comes to them," Brecia mumbled. "Come on, let's go see what's in the damn backpack."

# 39. BRECIA

## CASCADE, IDAHO

The backpack was loaded with survival tools—and wads of cash. The exterior looked familiar, and when I searched my memories I found it on the top shelf of the hall closet, next to a pile of random-looking camping supplies and an enormous bucket packed full of Mountain Meals.

I hadn't paid much attention to it until one of April's church friends—a "visiting teacher" who was assigned to deliver a monthly inspiring message—brought over a plate of blondies and read a passage about "food storage." April had proudly showed her the closet with the backpack, camping supplies, and Mountain Meals. "I'm not perfect at anything else, but I'm pretty darn perfect at emergency preparedness," April had said with a grin.

The visiting teacher had oohed and ahhed while April told her all about the wide variety of survival tools and shelter items in her collection. They had six months' worth of food in those buckets, she said. Supplemented with a few fresh items, they could last a year in any number of emergencies.

The three of us watched as he counted the bundles of cash and laid out a knife, a small ax, a handful of lighters, several types of rope, matches, rain ponchos, mess kits, batteries, flashlights, a crank radio, can opener, water purifier, and a few other things I didn't even recognize. The backpack was like a clown car of survival supplies.

"Holy shit," Skye whispered. "Why does he have all this stuff ready to go?"

I sighed. "This was all April. I don't think this is what she imagined it being used for. I think it's part of their religion. Emergency preparedness."

"Looks like he's got the prepping down," Meghan said drily. "Just needs a little work on 'thou shalt not kill.'"

\* \* \*

When April finally brought the girls inside the cabin as the sun started to dip below the horizon, the cabin felt almost cozy. The girls helped her light a fire in the creaky potbelly stove, and they took turns tossing twigs into the open door as the flames licked at the big chunks of firewood they'd taken from the impressive pile under a tarp outside.

With no sirens and no indication that anyone had a clue where he'd gone, James had finally relaxed. He'd apologized to April for the blowup over the backpack—and the car ride. And the chaos that morning. He even took the initiative to make up one of the Mountain Meals for dinner on the ancient electric stove. Beef Stroganoff.

The apologies didn't faze me. I'd been watching him do this dance for two years now. But Meghan and Skye both retreated outside, disgusted. How could April believe him? Why couldn't she see through him? How was she going along with this plan?

I stayed at the table next to the girls, while they ate their dinner, got ready for bed, and said their prayers. *Please bless Mommy and Daddy and Oscar and the bee on the pinecone even though he scared Kimmie.*

April recited the story of *The Fox and the Hound* from memory as they snuggled into a sagging full bed, covered with a shoddily constructed quilt. The teddy bears on the quilt squares hadn't been matched up, so they had been sewn into Frankenstein versions of themselves at the edges. Arms and legs poking out of heads, four pairs of legs, and so on. The girls didn't seem to notice.

"Mommy, Oscar misses us," Emma said matter-of-factly as April finished telling the story and leaned in for hugs.

April turned on her "Everything is okay" smile and smoothed down Emma's hair. "I bet he does, sweetie. Kitties aren't like people, though. He'll be happy to see us when we get back. For now he'll stay busy and happy hunting mice. We left him lots of food, and he can always drink from the creek in the neighbor's yard."

The girl's hadn't asked about Oscar's survival situation. It seemed like April was trying to soothe her own worries as much as Emma's. Emma seemed satisfied though, and I was glad to know that Oscar was okay too.

\* \* \*

I sort of hoped April would try for another conversation with James after the girls went to bed. But I could see on her face that she didn't have much left. I understood.

Skye and Meghan wandered in as she washed her face, brushed her teeth, and crawled into the queen bed in the other tiny bedroom. The checked blue quilt wasn't as bad as the teddy bear monstrosity, but the bed was just as old and creaky.

April lay in bed for a few minutes, staring at the ceiling. Then she got out from under the covers to kneel by her bedside. I knew this routine well and knelt beside her. Sometimes I tried to talk to her while she said her prayers. I had this theory that maybe, while she was trying hard to clear her head and listen, she'd hear me too.

"You need to get the girls out of here," I told her, leaning in close to repeat everything I'd said earlier in the car.

Meghan and Skye watched silently. April closed her eyes harder, focusing.

Skye suddenly asked, "Have you tried talking to her while she's asleep?"

I frowned. "No, why?"

Skye shrugged. "When I made it home—the first night—my mom was already asleep. I talked to her. Got right next to her in bed.

She woke up screaming. I wasn't sure if I did it or not, but I didn't try again. It was intense."

Meghan looked at her in awe. "That's brilliant. Let's try."

\* \* \*

While we waited for April to fall solidly asleep, we stayed up with James. In the dark, in the glow of the potbelly stove in the corner of the room, the room felt almost cozy.

Almost.

He took inventory of the survival tools, freeze-dried meals, and firewood yet again. He wrote the numbers down on the back of a receipt that he'd found in the black backpack.

There were one hundred and eighty meals. Each of them served two people. He wrote down 180 days. Then he frowned, tapping his pen on the receipt in front of him.

He turned over the receipt to look at the date. It was from eight years earlier. He swore softly. "You had one job," he muttered, cutting his eyes toward the closed bedroom door where April was sleeping.

"What's wrong?" Meghan asked anxiously. "Why is he suddenly upset again?"

I shook my head. "It's not actually that much food. I think they made the emergency kit before the girls were born. If they all ate three meals a day, it would only last ..." I did a quick calculation. "Thirty days. Not six months."

He flicked the pen back and forth in his hand, staring at the bedroom door.

"Talk, you piece of shit," Skye spat, right in his ear.

He didn't flinch. And he didn't talk. Instead, he walked over to the pile of camping supplies on the floor near the door and picked up one of the two tarps next to the sleeping bags. He opened it, spreading the tarp wide between his hands, then holding it up to his own body. It reached his chin, and was wider than his arms could stretch. He studied the surface, holding it up to the light. Looking for holes.

"No," Meghan cried. "No. What is he doing?"

"I don't know," I whispered. "It could be anything. Maybe he's going to cover the firewood."

"He's going to kill them," Meghan cried, and the lights in the kitchen flickered wildly.

James looked back at the kitchen light in irritation then turned around to fold up the first tarp and place it back on the pile. We all watched in horror as he picked up the second, larger tarp. He did the same thing he'd done with the first.

"You said he's never hurt them before, right?" Skye asked as she and Meghan turned toward me, as if I could reassure them.

I nodded slowly. "Yes. I mean . . ." I trailed off, remembering the times he'd screamed at April and the girls and thrown his phone against the wall. The time Kimmie had hurt her elbow when he'd flung the door open into her as she tried to enter his office. He'd sent her back upstairs without so much as an apology. There were times April cringed away from him so hard that I knew she was bracing for the verbal blows to land on her skin at some point. Maybe they already had. I hadn't seen everything.

He walked out the cabin door, and we scrambled to follow.

He didn't go far. Just the side of the house, where a shovel leaned against the woodpile. He picked it up and tested the heft of it. Then, seemingly satisfied, he set it back against the woodpile and went back inside.

Meghan sank to the living room floor. In front of us James was brushing his teeth in the kitchen sink. "He's going to kill them," she repeated again.

Skye sat down beside her. "Maybe. But he hasn't yet. So come on. We're going to talk to April." She grabbed Meghan by the hand, and I watched as first surprise then a flood of other emotions—compassion, sadness, horror—played across her features. "Come on, sis. I feel that. And I'm with you. Stay with us, okay?"

Meghan shook her head but followed Skye to the back bedroom, still holding her hand.

# 40. SKYE

## CASCADE, IDAHO

I didn't expect it to work—even though it was my idea.

Brecia did the talking. She knew April and the girls best. And neither Meghan nor I were going to fight her for the pleasure. She had to lie right between April and James—who had stripped off his jeans and crawled into bed twenty minutes earlier.

I knew Meghan was right. He might have dragged his wife and kids here in a panic; after all, they were his family. Even psychopaths held some things dear, right? Even so, my cynicism reminded me that leaving them behind at the house in Boise would have been a liability. April knew him better than anybody else. Which wasn't saying much.

If I was judging the way he was calculating the balance of resources and risks, April and the girls were quickly becoming liabilities here, too. I didn't know how soon he planned to act. Or what he planned to do. All three of us had seen what he was capable of, even when he wasn't cornered; however, unlike Brecia, I'd never imagined myself capable of stopping him. He'd done what he did to me. And he'd keep on doing it.

All we had were whispers and flickering lights.

Or that was what I thought, anyway.

Brecia didn't mince her words as she curled up next to April on the quilted, sagging bed and got right up next to her ear.

"When you wake up, you need to find a way to take the girls and get the hell out of here. You can't wait. He's going to kill them. He's going to kill you, too. Just like he killed me." She paused for a second then said, "I'm Brecia, by the way. And I've been following him—and you—for the past two years. Do you remember the nights he came home late from 'work?' The story you read about the girl who was murdered right by your hometown in Utah. The girl police are asking him about. Remember the photo Nina sent you. Do you remember—"

That was as far as she got. April's eyes had been twitching back and forth the whole time she talked, in the dim light from the little bedroom window. Then, suddenly, she was sitting upright in bed, crying and stumbling out of the covers, flailing to find her phone on the nightstand.

The phone wasn't there. She backed into the corner of the room, staring at James's still form, breathing hard and swiping at her eyes.

"Damn," Meghan whispered, turning toward Brecia and me. "That worked fast."

Brecia was still staring at April. "I can't believe I could have been doing that the whole time. I never thought ..."

I stepped forward and took her hand, just like I'd done with Meghan a few minutes earlier. I knew, even before I touched her hand, that she was headed down a rabbit hole of what ifs. That if she'd somehow figured this out earlier, she could have stopped him.

"No," I told her. "No. Don't carry that. It won't do her any good." I nodded at April, who was carefully shutting the bedroom door behind her and padding into the hallway. "Come on, let's go."

I'd hoped that April would be wrapping the girls up into blankets. That she'd tuck their sleepy little bodies into the minivan, find the keys, and drive until she found the police. That they'd all arrive back here before it was even light outside. Before he knew what was happening.

Instead, she sank to the floor next to their bed, staring at the creepy-ass teddy bears on the quilt in the darkness. Tears were still streaming down her cheeks, glinting silver in the wash of moonlight through the window. She sat on the floor with her hands clasped tight in her lap, shaking her head.

The three of us sat down next to her on the floor. It was impossible to know what she was thinking or how Brecia's words had made their way into her dreams.

I was glad it had been enough to get her out of bed.

I just hoped it was enough to finally wake her up.

# 41. MEGHAN

## CASCADE, IDAHO

Around 4:00 a.m., April finally wiped her eyes, tucked the creepy bear quilt around the girls' shoulders, then climbed back into bed.

I felt my last bright inklings of hope slip away from me, into the darkness beyond the closed bedroom door.

It was just a waiting game now.

Even so, we tried again the next night. And the next night. With about the same results.

Once, after the "dream talking" as Skye had started calling it, April wound up thrashing and screaming so loudly it woke the girls in the other room. James rolled over and shook her roughly to wake her. When she kept whimpering, he pushed her hard enough that she tumbled off the bed in a tangle of sheets and quilt.

As the covers came off the bed in a pile, he swore loudly and stretched out across the bed to snatch them back, ignoring the girls' thin wails from the other room until April slowly picked herself up off the floor, gingerly touching her head.

"You woke them up, you deal with it," he muttered. Then he rolled over and went back to sleep.

As his breathing turned slow and deep, Skye spoke up. "Let's do it to him."

I stared at her, not quite following. "Do what to him?"

"The dream talking thing. The worst nightmare we can come up with."

Brecia shook her head. "*He's* the worst nightmare I can come up with. What scares a fucking narcissist who gets his kicks from killing women?"

Her question hung in the darkness between us for a long moment.

"April," I finally whispered. "And the kids. That they'll see through him and turn him in. That they'll eat all his food and mess up his insane fugitive-on-the-run game."

Skye closed her eyes and nodded. We couldn't send him those nightmares.

He smiled and murmured something in his sleep, as if being rocked to sleep by the waves of simmering rage building and crashing around him.

\* \* \*

The days ticked by even more slowly than they had when I was alone in the mountains. There wasn't a lot to do. No TVs or tablets to distract the girls. Just a few books and toys that were already in the minivan. And the Mountain Meals, which had been a novelty at first, were getting old fast—even at two meals a day. Everyone had the runs, which meant that the one tiny bathroom with the door that didn't fully close was in constant use.

It would have been sort of funny if it weren't so awful.

James stayed in the cabin most of the time, increasingly irritable. He snapped at the girls whenever they asked about mealtimes or said they needed to use the bathroom. He paced the floors back and forth, eyeing the backpack and the neat rows of survival gear and meals he'd arranged into rations and days.

Even at two meals a day, the food was going fast. So was his patience.

April managed to keep the girls occupied with what she dubbed "nature school." Little hikes and lessons about birds and fauna. Stories and art projects made from fallen leaves and rose hips. Kimmie managed to turn a long, skinny pinecone into a doll and named it Pippa. Emma coaxed a chipmunk into eating a little granola from her hand. April smiled brightly and praised the girls' ingenuity. She hadn't asked about school or truancy again. And she hadn't asked about the plan. Or the police. Or when they were going back.

On the third night after April went to sleep, James sat at the kitchen table, staring at the supplies. He stood to look at the food and touch the tarps. Then he walked to the bedroom where April was asleep. But instead of getting undressed for bed, he turned off the hall light and stood in the semi-darkness, listening to the cadence of her breath.

"He's done. He's getting rid of them," I said matter-of-factly like the dread wasn't pooling around me. "Look at his face."

Brecia and Skye were already staring at him. His eyes were different. Calculating. He didn't appear to be anxious, though. Just resolved.

April rolled over in her sleep, but her breathing was even and deep.

He closed the door softly and walked back to the living room, where he extracted a headlamp from the backpack, put on his jacket, and slipped out the front door.

"Where is he going? Is he leaving?" Skye asked hopefully. "Maybe he'll take the van and go."

But the beam of the headlamp had stopped on the shovel near the woodpile.

I watched in horrified silence as he picked it up and started walking into the forest.

* * *

He chose a spot about a quarter mile from the cabin, along a deer path. The ground was soft and mulchy enough beneath the cover of the pines that it didn't take long for him to complete the first hole to his liking.

The three of us stood along the deer path, trying to make it make sense.

The hole was about three feet wide, six feet long, and three feet deep.

He dug in silence, looking up only when the crackle of twigs from some creature broke through the still night and the soft *thunk* of a shovel hitting dirt over and over again.

We stayed long enough to let the reality of what he was doing sink in. Long enough to see that the hole was, unmistakably, a grave —and that he was starting on a second.

Then we fled back to the cabin.

# 42. BRECIA

## CASCADE, IDAHO

It didn't take long to wake April.

Waking her wasn't the problem. Getting her to listen was. And we were running out of time fast.

I had no idea exactly what happened when I spoke to her while she slept. Could she see the images of the shallow graves as I described them urgently in her ear? Could she hear me talking, distantly? Did she even remember what had happened when she woke up, or was I just a night terror, delivering a shot of pure and nameless adrenaline in the dark?

As she awoke with a jolt to an empty bed, I turned to see Skye and Meghan hovering behind me.

I already knew that these might be our last moments together. Meghan wasn't staying. And now that I knew I had a choice, I wouldn't be either. It was too much. And the window to do anything at all was closing. If it came down to it, I couldn't watch. I'd already decided who I was going to find in my memories when the time came: my Aunt Nelly. She'd taken care of me when I was a little girl, and I loved her fiercely. Fresh out of college, she'd moved in with us when I was five and took care of me after preschool until she found a real job a year later. We splashed in the kiddie pool at the YMCA, made necklaces out of cereal and macaroni, brushed the manes and tails of my plastic horses, and watched cartoons together. She'd died in a car crash when I was six. Right after she moved out.

I dragged myself back to the present, in the dark room with April. If there had been any lights left blazing in the little cabin, I had no doubt they would be flickering wildly. The dark room was full of invisible sparks with nowhere else to go. I no longer had any doubts. He was going to murder his own family. He was going to leave them in the woods.

April was breathing hard, blinking to get her bearings in the dark room and rickety bed. I could see that she was biting her lip, trying not to make a sound, until she cautiously felt beside her in the bed and realized that James wasn't even there.

She sagged forward, clutching the quilt in her hands to stop them from shaking and trying to calm her breathing.

And then she listened.

We listened with her.

There was the quiet, steady hum of the old fridge in the kitchen. The chorus of crickets that swelled then faded. The soft, papery flutter of aspens. The slight squeak of the bed frame as she pulled the quilt up farther around her knees.

Then, there it was: the distant, repetitive thunk of something hitting the ground. Even I hadn't realized that the sound would carry this far. If we hadn't been nestled deep in the forest, it probably wouldn't have.

The sound came again: that quiet clank of metal on dirt.

April didn't move for a long time.

She stayed sitting where she was in bed, no longer shaking. Not moving at all. Just listening. Then she wrapped the quilt around herself and padded to the kitchen, where she stared outside into the blackness.

The sound continued, erratic and ominous.

"Does she know what he's doing? Do you think she understands?" Skye whispered, glancing back at the girls' bedroom door.

None of us answered. There were no answers yet. We watched, transfixed, as April walked to the entryway, picked up her shoes, put them on. She ran her fingers over the girls' shoes. James's tennis shoes conspicuously weren't there.

She stood motionless with her hand on the doorknob for at least a minute. The invisible sparks surrounding all of us swirled faster.

"She can't go out there. If he knows that she knows, he'll do it right now," Meghan blurted. In the darkness of the cabin, I could see her hugging her arms around her waist.

Heedless of the warning, April carefully opened the front door and stepped onto the porch.

She stared into the thick bramble of trees surrounding her for a moment. And then, so slowly I knew she was bracing for what she might see, she looked over at the woodpile.

The shovel wasn't there.

Distantly, we could all hear the soft *thunk*, pause, *thunk*.

April walked to the other side of the woodpile, scanning every inch, as if she might have missed the bulky shovel the first time. Her face was expressionless, but her fingers were clutching the quilt so hard that the tips glowed faintly white in the darkness against the embroidered pattern.

*Thunk*, pause. *Thunk*, pause.

*Pause. Pause. Pause.* The muffled crack of a twig came from somewhere in the distance. April took a step back toward the open cabin door.

"Oh shit," Meghan gasped. "He's coming. He's coming back for them now. I can't—"

Skye quickly reached out and grasped her hand as she went to follow April, who was hurrying back inside the cabin. "Come on. She finally gets it. Stay with me, sis."

While Meghan and Skye followed April inside, I raced down the deer path to meet him.

He had the shovel tipped over his shoulder, as if he were returning from an honest day's work—instead of picking his way through the woods in the dark like a wolf.

I couldn't stop myself. I knew it wouldn't help, but I leapt at him anyway. I tore at his ugly plaid jacket and tried to gouge the golden-brown eyes I'd been so entranced by when we first met in person. I screamed like I'd wanted to scream in my backyard, the night my voice was cut off with the extension cord in his hands. I thrashed and kicked and pummeled him with my fists the way I'd imagined doing all these years but never had. Because what was the point?

His shirt and hair whipped wildly in the sudden gust of wind that blew through the deer path but left the aspen leaves above us fluttering peacefully in the mild breeze. I knew it was me. I had done that. But, of course, it hadn't stopped him. It was just a random burst of wind.

He shook himself a little and readjusted the shovel.

Then he kept walking.

When he reached the cabin, the front door was closed. April was nowhere in sight. Neither were Meghan or Skye. He carefully brushed a few flecks of dirt off the plaid jacket, gently leaned the shovel against the woodpile, and quietly opened the front door.

I brushed past him into the room as he sat down and took off his shoes.

From the dark hallway, I saw Meghan and Skye appear, standing like sentinels as all three of us watched him. Meghan backed up slowly into the kitchen as he stood up and surveyed the tiny living room, his eyes resting on the collection of survival tools. Skye held her ground, glaring at him with a fury I could feel from across the room.

He stood where he was in the living room for a few seconds, clearly weighing his options.

"Where's April?" I called to Meghan softly, hoping she wasn't gone yet. I couldn't see her anymore.

"She's in the bedroom," came the quiet reply from the kitchen. "She's pretending to be asleep."

A wave of despair pulled at me like a riptide. "What about the girls? Did she at least grab a knife or something?"

Skye shook her head miserably. "No."

James was on the move again, but he was walking toward the kitchen and Meghan—not toward the bedrooms.

He stopped in front of the wall clock, squinting at the cracked plastic in the darkness. It was 3:00 a.m.

He was standing just a few feet away from Meghan. She stood facing him, her arms still wrapped tightly around her middle as if to keep from flinging herself at him.

"If you want to jump him, do it," I told her. "I couldn't stop myself. It felt good for a second, even though it didn't do anything."

She nodded tightly but didn't look at me—or move to attack him the way I had on the trail. "We heard you out there."

He rubbed a hand along the back of his neck and stretched. Then he yawned and sighed heavily. Skye made a disgusted noise. "Poor baby. Tired after staying up late digging holes."

It was true: He looked exhausted. "Maybe he'll wait," I said hesitantly, still feeling the despair threaten to pull me under. If he didn't do it tonight, he would do it tomorrow. Or the next day. There was still no indication as to what his plans were long-term, but those plans clearly no longer included his family.

It made me think of the hamster I'd had as a little girl who, when I forgot to feed her for a couple of days, ate her three babies. All that was left when I looked into the cage was a few droplets of dark blood.

I shook my head. *No.* He wasn't like an animal at all. At least with the hamster, there was survival on the line. He killed because he wanted to. Because he felt like it. Because he liked it. No animal I knew of did that.

He hesitated in the hallway, looking from the stash of survival objects to the bedroom door. I tried not to imagine what he was thinking about but couldn't stop the mental image of the different deadly objects at his disposal. The knives. The rope. The shovel out by the woodpile. If he wanted to do it tonight, he had plenty of tools available.

He yawned again and rolled his neck, turning to look at the neat piles of meals. He hadn't counted them for a couple of days. But the buckets still looked relatively full. Nobody was eating with the vigor they had a few days ago, given the effects on everyone's digestive system.

He sighed heavily then padded down the hallway to April's room. Skye and I followed, while Meghan hung back. Neither of us prodded her to follow.

He quietly opened the bedroom door, casting a dim square of light across the bed where April lay on her side, turned away from him. I watched her chest rise and fall. Deep breaths like clockwork. If I had to guess, she was counting with each inhale and exhale.

He stared at her for a few seconds. Then he carefully shut the door, pulled off his jeans and plaid shirt, and got into bed on the other side.

# 43. SKYE

## CASCADE, IDAHO

I really missed sleeping. The ability to just turn your brain off for a while was something I'd really taken for granted while I was alive. Without a body that needed sleep to physically recharge, my thoughts never turned off. Except for the times when I got caught up in a memory.

Meghan called it "drifting." That was how she'd found her grandmother, the one who was waiting to welcome her at the end of this horror show.

The three of us gathered around April, speaking the truth about her husband in turn.

April's eyes, wide in the darkness, gave no indication that she sensed any of it. She was finally awake to the gravity of her situation. But only time would tell if that awakening would be enough.

I knew that look in her eyes. It was that same wild-animal feeling I'd gotten when I realized I might have made a terrible mistake getting into his car. And that my choices were now limited to whatever mercy the universe would grant me. In my case, there had been none. But maybe things would be different for April and the girls. I hoped so.

Once James's breathing grew deep and measured, April scooted to the far edge of the bed, clutching the quilt and no longer trying to feign sleep.

The seconds ticked by like hours as we waited for her to move. To do something. To run.

"Move, girl," I kept telling her. "He's asleep. Move."

Brecia shook her head. "The girls are too heavy to carry. And if she wakes them up, they'll wake him up too. They're too little to listen when they're tired and cranky. It's too risky."

So we all just sat there, gathered around April, listening to the whistling sound of his breath, in and out, in and out.

I pulled my thoughts back toward me again and again, like a puppy on a leash, refusing to allow myself to drift. It was excruciating to stay present. And from the feeling in the room, I knew I wasn't alone.

Suddenly, I had an idea. "Brecia, you know that thing that happened in the impound lot when we were talking?"

Brecia nodded. "The same thing happened with Meghan when I hugged her." She looked at Meghan, whose confused expression dissolved into understanding.

"Could we try that again?" I asked, feeling weirdly shy. I was asking for a literal glimpse into their souls. "It wasn't the same as drifting in my own memories. I didn't feel all deep and dreamy. I just kind of, I don't know, got a really clear picture of the story you were telling me. Like you'd shown it to me."

"It was like a movie," Meghan said. "A super high-def movie with a D-BOX. I could actually sort of feel it."

Brecia burst out laughing. "A D-BOX. If my dad knew that you got your own personal D-BOX theater when you died . . ." She stopped herself. "Sorry, Meg. I'm not making fun of you. I know what you mean. It's the perfect way to describe it."

"Can I show you my cat?" Brecia asked softly. "I know that's weird. But I miss him. He's really cute. His name is Frank."

"Please baby Jesus, yes," I told her. "Show us."

We shuffled closer together on the floor, on April's side of the bed. Then we held hands. It was like a seance in reverse, all of us making contact with the land of the living.

As soon as we touched hands, I saw the memories like a living movie in stunning detail. I could almost feel that sweet little furball with the downy white fur and orange ears purring on Brecia's lap. And when I whispered, "Oh, he's a doll," the Brecia inside the memory looked up at me, her eyes full of joy at the cat sleeping on her lap while she watched Netflix before bed.

It was just a cat. But in that moment, it was everything.

We drifted together like that all night, trading memories. Some sweet, some shallow, some heartbreaking, some that filled up the room with a sadness so thick we swam in it. I wasn't sure how it was happening, but I understood now what Meghan had been saying about her Bubbie: The memory wasn't static anymore, but rather a little secret doorway.

All the while, April stayed where she was, frozen, her breaths shallow and fast until the first rays of sunlight finally hit the window in the little bedroom.

At that first clear sign of morning, she carefully swung her legs over the side of the bed and padded to the kitchen. The girls were still asleep, and she didn't wake them.

Meghan, Brecia, and I watched eagerly as she scanned the countertops, felt in his coat pockets, and quietly opened drawers in the tiny kitchen.

"She's looking for the keys," Brecia said in disbelief. "She's going to do it. Oh my god."

"But where are they?" Meghan fretted. "I didn't see where he put them down. Did any of you?"

None of us had. And as April's search grew more creative—under the dusty pot holders by the stove, beneath the tattered rug, in the back of cupboards—all while pausing at the slightest noise from the bedrooms, the hope that the keys were here to be found seemed increasingly unlikely.

He'd tucked them away somewhere he knew she wouldn't look. Because, like all three of the ghosts standing in this kitchen, she might have gotten into the car willingly at one point. But once she did, the chances she'd get out alive went down astronomically.

The lid to the coffee maker slid onto the floor with a loud clatter as April tilted it to see behind the ancient plastic pot.

She froze as the sound was followed by a muffled creak—then heavy footfalls—from down the hallway. She grabbed the coffee pot and ran to the sink to fill it with water.

"What the hell is she doing?" Meghan cried. "They don't even drink coffee."

When he appeared around the corner from the hallway with a sour expression on his face, rubbing sleep from his eyes, he looked at her in irritation. "Are you serious right now? It's barely morning. Why are you banging around in here?" His eyes focused on the coffee pot in her hand, and he scowled. "What are you doing?"

She looked up at him with a thousand-watt smile, turning off the sink as the water reached the brim of the pot. "Babe, I'm so sorry. I remembered we had a couple of hot chocolate packets, and I was trying to do something fun for breakfast. Surprise the girls before they woke up." She made a face at the coffee pot. "I thought this might heat the water up faster than the stove. I'm so sorry I woke you!"

"Damn, April," Brecia said. "Good save."

I was impressed too. I almost believed her myself. But did he?

I studied his face as the scowl softened into irritation. He was mad. He clearly thought she was a moron. But not enough to fly off the handle. April latched onto it and laid her hand on his arm. "I'm really sorry, hon. Go back to sleep, okay?"

He didn't move. "Just use one packet," he muttered, eyeing the lines of food.

She followed his gaze. Then I saw something light up in her eyes. "What would you think about me making a quick trip into town today? I could get us some canned food and maybe some fresh stuff that will last a while? Apples, beans—"

"Yes," Meghan encouraged her. "Yes, girl. Get out of here."

I didn't have time to cheer. The scowl was back on his face. "Are you kidding me right now, April? How stupid can you be? You think you're just going to go *shopping* and then toddle back here?

Someone will recognize you. Someone will recognize the van. Unless maybe that's what you want?" The scowl deepened into something even uglier. It was the first time I'd seen him seriously consider the idea that she might run. Despite berating her at every turn since they'd gotten to this miserable little prison, he'd clearly never really thought she'd turn on him. She wasn't real to him. She and the girls had never been more than accessories to his life. Worth keeping around when they were useful. No reason not to discard them when they became inconvenient.

April tried again, raking her hand through the back of her thin, blond hair to fluff it up in a nervous tell I'd started to recognize. I could hear the desperation bleeding into her voice now. "They're looking for you, not me, and I'll park way before town and walk in. Nobody would see the license plate or anything. I could wear a hat, and without makeup I really don't look like myself—"

He cut her off, snatching the coffee maker out of her hand and splashing water down the front of her shirt. "You have to plug it in, you moron. And no, we are not taking the risk for apples and beans. I'm sorry we aren't eating high on the hog, but you're the one who packed all these meals. Maybe if you'd done the math right, or figured out that they all tasted disgusting and would give everybody the runs, things might be a little nicer."

She stared at him in stunned silence, and I prayed to God that he couldn't tell as well as I could that his wife was hearing every word he said with a new filter. No more rationalizing. No more pretending. He was a ticking time bomb about to blow up in her face.

He stared back, as if daring her to try again. From down the hallway, there was the sound of a door opening and little-girl voices.

April snapped her mask back in place, grabbing a threadbare towel from above the stove to press against her soaked shirt. "You're right," she told him apologetically. "I'm sorry. It was a stupid idea. I'll clean all this up and have the girls help me with breakfast. I'm sorry," she repeated, reaching out for his arm again.

He shrugged her away and turned toward the hall, not bothering to respond to the excited chorus of "Hi, Daddy!" as he walked back to the bedroom.

The long fluorescent bulbs in the kitchen light overhead blinked erratically for a few seconds. They seemed to be less susceptible to our emotions than the halogen variety. I knew the halogen variety would have popped a long time ago.

April glanced at the light then turned on a smile as the girls burst into the kitchen. "Is Daddy angry again?" Emma pouted.

Kimmie's eyes landed on April's wet shirt. "You have an accident, Mommy?"

"God, find a way to get these babies out of here," I mumbled, watching Kimmie pat April's hip comfortingly. I still didn't know what I thought about God. I'd really expected to have some answers by now. I prayed anyway, though. Because there wasn't much else to do.

"It's okay, Mommy," Kimmie assured her, echoing the words I'd heard April say when Kimmie herself really did have an accident once in a while.

For a split second, it looked like April's mask might come down. Her lip trembled slightly as she looked at the girls and around the small kitchen, her gaze resting on the hallway where he'd disappeared a few seconds ago. The babies were awake. There were no car keys to be found. They were trapped.

She pursed her lips and grabbed Kimmie's hand, directing her to the meals along the living room wall. "Oh, I just spilled, baby! I was trying to surprise you guys with hot cocoa. Will you help me find the packet? We'll share it and drink little tea party cups."

The girls eagerly helped search through the buckets while April took steadying breaths and quickly swiped at a tear that had managed to escape down one of her cheeks.

# 44. MEGHAN

## CASCADE, IDAHO

She actually brought him a little cup of the damn hot chocolate.

I wasn't sure I could have done it myself. But she did, and he looked grudgingly grateful and didn't try to stop her when she told him that she was going to play out front with the girls to build more "pinecone people."

The three of us followed her into the clearing by the cabin, where the girls always played. Kimmie and Emma, still riding the hot chocolate high, were so engaged in a conversation about whether the pinecone people would eat pine needles or moss that they didn't realize April had led them past the clearing and onto a trail until she took the two girls by the hand and pulled them behind a tall pine with boughs that dipped thick and low enough to obscure the view of the cabin a hundred yards away.

"Mommy!" Kimmie started to argue, her rosebud lips already headed for a frown. This wasn't the right spot.

"Listen to your mama," Skye hissed in her ear, and she went silent before April could hush her.

Kimmie paused mid-word and frowned.

April looked momentarily startled by Kimmie's seeming mind-reading but didn't stop to ask questions. Skye and I looked at each other. "Whoa," I whispered.

April reached out to stroke both girls' cheeks. Her expression was serious, but with a little conspiratorial smile. "You guys know how Daddy has been kind of grumpy and we've all been feeling kind of yucky in our tummies?" She held one finger to her lips to cut short any overly loud replies.

The girls nodded.

"Well, you know how I surprised you with the hot chocolate this morning? I want us to surprise Daddy again."

Everyone leaned closer to April, dying to know the plan.

"Well, we're going to find a whole bunch of berries to bring back to Daddy for dinner."

Emma looked skeptical. "Berries?"

Kimmie, on the other hand, was gleeful. Nobody had eaten anything fresh for way too long now. "Oh, Mommy, good idea," she whispered. "Where are they?"

"They're really far, and we have to be really quiet so we don't give away the surprise," April whispered back.

"Oh shit," Skye said, her voice barely a whisper too. "Yes, girl. Yes. Go now."

Brecia moved to the edge of the tree to look back at the cabin. "He's still inside," she called. "Go! Hurry!"

As if they could hear her, both Kimmie and Emma took April's outstretched hands.

"We don't want Daddy to see us leave, or he'll know we're up to something," April told the girls, showing them how to duck down slightly beneath the brush level along the deer path. Her smile was looking manic to me, but the girls didn't seem to notice. "Step quietly, until we're a little farther away, okay? We won't have to be quiet anymore after a bit."

The girls followed her directions exactly, and the three started moving down the deer path with Skye and me right behind.

Brecia stayed where she was, in view of the cabin. "I'll catch up with you, okay? I know it won't change anything, but I need to know how far behind he is. I'll head downhill until I find you when he realizes something is up."

The sound of birds among the trees had dropped to a quiet chatter. The air felt charged with danger and uncertainty and the barest sliver of hope.

I lagged behind just a little too, taking one last look at the cabin. *Be there soon, Bubbie,* I thought to myself, feeling for the first time like maybe I'd get to leave this limbo on my own terms. Like maybe I'd be able to finish this business after all. I could just see the top of April's blond ponytail bobbing in the distance above the brushline, when the trail curved around the bend and downward. The sound of snapping twigs was getting fainter, and Brecia's back was still turned as she kept vigil on the cabin. I hurried to catch up with Skye and April.

April was walking the opposite way from the three graves waiting with open mouths farther up the trail. I was glad she wouldn't see them. I knew what it felt like to look into your own grave. And the farther she moved away from them, the better her chances of not ending up in one.

I examined the memory of the drive here as we moved through the forest, scrambling over logs and through brush as the deer trail turned more narrow. I could remember every detail in crystal clarity, but I hadn't looked at the clock on the car after we'd turned onto the main road. It was difficult to tell exactly how fast we'd driven and how far. It had felt like forever at the time. I didn't even know how far the little town of Cascade actually was from the dirt road turnoff. Was it five miles? Ten? Twenty? I felt the flicker of hope start to fade. With two little girls in tow, even my most optimistic estimate was impossibly far.

Skye searched her memory, too, grabbing my hand so I could see. "I looked at the clock in the car when we parked at the cabin," she said. "We got there just before lunch. At 11:58. When was the last time you looked at the car clock?"

I sorted through the memories from before we'd turned off onto the dirt road. "The last time I looked before we made the turn, it was 10:32. We drove another ten minutes, maybe, before we made the turn."

"Hold on, we can figure this out," Skye replied. "He was going the speed limit, because he was worried about cops. It was fifty until we hit the dirt road. So, it would have been about 10:45 when he made the turn. So, about an hour."

We were both silent for a moment, thinking the same thing. It had taken us an hour *in the car* to travel from the turnoff to the cabin. It was going to take forever on foot, with kids.

Skye kept going. "We were going pretty slow along the road. It was curvy and bumpy. I remember thinking I could run next to the car if I'd wanted to. How fast is that?"

I laughed. "I'm a lot faster now than I was before. Maybe ten or fifteen miles an hour?"

Skye nodded. "That sounds right. So, if it took us forty-five-ish minutes to get to the cabin, that means it was about six miles."

I decided to take Skye's calculation as gospel. In part because it sounded better than what I'd imagined. And in part because math wasn't among the limited powers I seemed to have inherited in death. "Can they make it before it starts to get dark?" I asked, not really expecting an answer.

Skye nodded firmly. "Even if they go really slow, one mile per hour, they'll make it. They just have to keep going."

As she said it, Emma let out a shriek as a hornet landed on her arm. She batted at it hysterically and stumbled over a root in the ground while April frantically turned around to calm her down.

"Shit," I whispered, looking behind us. There was no sign of Brecia. Not yet. But I remembered the way the sound of the shovel had carried from the night before. If we could all hear the *thunk* of that shovel hitting the ground in the cabin, the sound of a shriek like that was going to carry far enough.

Like she'd done before, Skye reached out to put a hand on Emma's shoulder. "Honey, stop crying," she said over the sound of April's pleading and shushing.

Whether from April's efforts or Skye's, Emma tearfully bit her lip and stopped wailing.

At first, I thought maybe we'd gotten away with it. Maybe he hadn't heard. Maybe we were far enough away. We'd been walking for at least an hour. But it wasn't five minutes later that Brecia caught up with us.

"He's coming," she said simply. "He's in the van."

Skye and I looked at each other helplessly. "He's in the van?" I'd imagined him chasing us down through the trees.

As if on cue, we heard a distant rumbling sound that had to be tires on the dirt road, somewhere through the trees. I'd wondered how close we might be to the road we'd driven in on, but April didn't seem to be in a hurry to find it. Not yet.

"I think he's trying to get ahead of them," Brecia replied. The even kilter of her voice did nothing to make the forest feel like less of a tinderbox.

We all looked at April, who clearly heard the distant sound too. The girls hadn't noticed yet. She scanned the tangle of tree trunks and scattered clearings and then called softly to the girls. "I think the berries are a little farther that way!" She motioned to a fork in the deer path that led farther away from the road and the sound of the vehicle in the distance.

Kimmie and Emma followed her, but I knew it would be just a matter of time until they started to ask about going home for lunchtime. Before someone slipped on the carpet of pine needles or tripped over a fallen branch littering the trail, or before the three of them drifted far enough from the road that April lost her bearings of how to get back to the road at all. She kept squinting up at the sun, trying, I imagine, to stay on track. But between shepherding the girls around obstacles, tracking the ominous sound of the tires on the road, and offering one long pep talk to keep going, it couldn't be easy.

They hadn't even brought water with them. Or jackets. It was pleasant enough outside right now, but it wouldn't be once nightfall fell. I remembered every detail of that first night I'd spent alone in the mountains. The glowing eyes of the coyotes. The sounds of twigs snapping in the darkness. The feeling that I was completely and ut-terly alone. And I'd been *dead.* Nothing could touch me anymore. I kept my eyes on the sun too, willing it to stay high in the sky. Willing them onward.

April's smile was already showing the strain of stress. And we still had hours to go before there was any hope of finding our way out. That is, if he didn't find us first.

The sound of the tires got closer, although it was impossible to know just how close with the way sound carried.

Then, suddenly, the sound stopped.

April ushered the girls along yet another branch in the scraggly trail, in the opposite direction of the road.

We weren't making any progress toward town, but suddenly that didn't matter. I could imagine the ugly set of his jaw and the rage in his eyes. I didn't know what he'd thrown into the trunk with him, but I knew that he was moving toward us with single-minded, deadly intent. And he wasn't towing two little girls along with him as he ran.

April closed her eyes and set her jaw. She let the mask fall for a moment as she stared at the little blond heads in front of her, still moving diligently—if slowly—along the path.

There wasn't time. They needed to move faster, somehow.

"Girls," she called to them seriously, and they stopped dead in their tracks and turned around. It was clear, even to me, that April didn't use this voice with them.

"Mommy?" Kimmie started, and April cut her off.

April shook her head. "I need you to do something for me, and we don't have time to be scared. Because that will slow us down."

Both Kimmie and Emma were staring at her with wide, fearful eyes now. Brecia and Skye wore about the same expression as we tried to guess what she was about to tell them.

April took a deep breath. "There's a bear behind us. So we need to run as quickly and as quietly as we can, okay?"

Instinctively, Skye moved beside Kimmie while Brecia stepped next to Emma. "Listen to your mama," Brecia told her, and Skye murmured the same words.

To their credit, neither little girl stopped to cry or ask questions. They knew about bears from the songs they sometimes sang while they played with the pinecone people and the stories April told them in their beds.

So if April said run, they would run.

# 45. BRECIA

## CASCADE, IDAHO

I was honestly impressed by how quickly the girls moved after that.

If I knew anything about April, she was beating herself up right now for lying to the girls. For scaring them into running. For not running before. For inventing a bear.

But I wanted to hug her. She'd done exactly the right thing.

There was no time to explain to two little girls that something far worse than a bear really was hunting them along the trails as they scrambled farther into the forest, panting and gasping but not stopping.

I looked back every few seconds, just waiting to see him behind us. Waiting for the snap of the branch that would mean the end of the chase. But little by little, the treeline became less dense and the slope of the mountain mellowed into a rolling terrain. More daylight filtered down through the treetops, and it was easier to move without fear of tripping on fallen logs.

April finally grabbed the girls' hands and told them to stop. They had to rest. Their faces were red, and streaky wet trails cut lines through the dust on their cheeks.

"Is the bear still behind us, Mommy?" Emma asked fearfully, glancing back and forth through the trees behind them.

April squeezed her hand and took a ragged breath. "We're outrunning him, baby. I'm so proud of you. We're going to get help from somebody, okay?"

"And then go back for Daddy?" Kimmie asked tearfully, clearly distraught that they'd left the bastard behind to fend for himself.

Skye shook her head and turned around, scanning for any sign of the road in the distance. I had no idea how far we'd run, but I told myself we had to be getting close. The sun was dipping farther toward the horizon, and the girls had been running off and on for more than an hour now, after walking plenty before that.

April nodded confidently and raked her sweaty hair back with one hand. "You don't need to worry about him, sweetheart. Rest a few more seconds, and then we'll keep going."

\* \* \*

It was Skye who finally, jubilantly, announced that we were almost to the main road. The turnoff to the paved Highway 55 was still at least a mile away—she'd run ahead—but it was just within reach. Another half an hour, if we kept up this pace. We were going to make it. The girls were exhausted and soaked in sweat. Every time they took another short rest, April's hands shook while she scanned the trail they'd traveled. I knew she was practicing her speech for if he found them. But I knew as well as she did that there was nothing she could say. James wouldn't buy the bear line. He knew he was the bear.

"I kept going to see how close we are to town, and it's not far at all," Skye said. "Maybe another five miles along the road? She's a white lady with kids. Someone will stop and give them a ride. She'll flag someone down, right? Then call the police?"

I smiled, ready to celebrate. And that was when April suddenly fell, landing flat against the dirt while Kimmie and Emma turned to her in shock.

At first, I thought she had passed out. It would have made sense. She hadn't had anything to drink—while running for her life—for hours now.

She wasn't lying still, though. She motioned for the girls to lie next to her, hissing for them to be quiet in the same voice she'd used to tell them about the bear. In a tone that I imagined mothers have used in dire moments for as long as they have gathered their children under their wings when death approached. A tone that said, *There is no room for questions. The worst is coming, and these words combined with your exact obedience are your only hope for safety.*

I stopped listening to April and the girls and turned my attention to the danger. The sound of cracking branches and heavy footfalls was approaching fast. It would have been futile to run when he was this close. If he stopped and listened, even for a second, he was close enough to hear them now. Maybe he'd already heard them.

I went out to meet him, while Meghan and Skye stayed with April and the girls. When I glanced back over my shoulder, the only person I could see was Meghan, her arms wrapped around her stomach as she watched me go. The others were completely hidden from this vantage, next to a toppled tree trunk that butted up to a couple of mossy boulders.

He was coming from the direction of the road. When I caught sight of him, I could still see the minivan perched precariously along the narrow dirt shoulder at the top of the steep graded slope. In our scramble through the woods, we'd moved closer to the road than I'd thought.

Oblivious to the noise he was making, James growled as his shirt got caught on a dead tree branch, ripping part of it. His eyes scanned the diverging deer paths in front of him, looking for any sign of April or the girls. As he crashed toward me, I could see that he was clutching something in his hand. It was the multitool from the survival kit: half ax blade, half hammer.

There was no more pretense. The jig was up. There was no trace of the collected, methodical planning in this person moving toward me. His hair, sweaty against his forehead, was matted and wild. His eyes were hard and full of rage. There were no more games to be played or time to bide. April had betrayed him. She'd run away before he was ready to finish her off. And he was going to kill all three of them as soon as he found them.

I didn't know what he was thinking at this moment. I didn't want to. But I could feel the desperation and rage coming off of him in thick waves through the air between us as he passed me, whipping his head from side to side and scrutinizing the terrain.

That desperation was the only comfort I could find. He'd been up and down this dirt road in that damn minivan all these hours without success. Maybe, just maybe, he'd turn around and drive a little farther when he didn't find them near the road.

But he barreled forward, letting out another grunt of rage. I followed him, powerless as ever to do anything to stop him if he found them.

# 46. SKYE

## CASCADE, IDAHO

At first, I stayed hidden with April and the girls, terror squeezing me like a tube of toothpaste as I heard him get closer. I knew he couldn't see me, but part of me was certain that if I poked my head up over the fallen log, I'd see those dark eyes lock with mine.

Meghan didn't seem to share my irrational fears. She stood where she was next to us, arms wrapped around herself like a desperate hug as if trying to hold herself together.

April had been right to tell the girls a bear was chasing us. Because that's exactly what he sounded like, thumping his way down the deer paths, cracking branches and making that angry, awful noise in his throat. He sounded just like an animal: an animal hell-bent on tearing someone apart.

The girls stayed completely still and silent, the only movement the quaking of their little bodies and the heaving of their chests.

Kimmie had her face turned toward the dirt, her body tucked most of the way under April's arms. Emma was huddled at the edge, her blue Elsa shirt clutched tight in April's grasp as her chest rose and fell in fast, shaky gasps.

He drifted a little farther, then a little closer. He was sweeping the area.

When he stopped, a stone's throw away, I finally couldn't help myself. I looked in the direction Meghan was facing, eyes wide, and saw him standing just like I'd feared, staring back at us.

He was breathing hard, his mouth open in a gaping scowl as he caught his breath and looked down the deer path that forked in front of him. Did he see us? Did he hear the girls? It might not matter. Because if he went any farther in this direction, he would walk right past us. And he would see them.

In his right hand, he held the multitool, gripped tight. His gaze traveled down the narrow paths in front of him, and I tried to see what he saw.

There were no footprints in that direction. No disturbed ground. We'd come from the other side of the path. I was almost positive he couldn't see any sign of us. Not yet.

He made a noise low in his throat and took a step forward.

Emma let out the barest whimper, and April clutched the Elsa shirt harder, giving it a little shake.

He stopped and listened, scanning again.

That's when Meghan leapt forward.

At first I thought she was going to attack him, like Brecia had the night before after he dug the graves. But then she was next to his ear.

"They couldn't have made it this far. They're way, way back. You went too far," she screamed at him, matching the wildness I could see in his eyes.

He continued staring straight ahead. Emma was quiet. The woods around us were quiet. I willed the birds to start back up, willed a real bear to walk down the path toward all of us. Of course they did not. There was something far more dangerous here.

There was only silence and the sound of his heavy breathing.

I curled back up next to Emma, hoping somehow she felt the invisible buffer on her other side. She didn't make another noise, but I could tell by the way her chest was trembling that she was silently crying.

Kimmie was so still, tucked under April's shoulder, that I could barely see her shallow breaths. I put my mouth close to Emma's ear, whispering assurances I didn't believe.

"The bear won't get you, baby," I told her. *The bear got me.* "Your mama is here, and she's gonna protect you." *Sometimes, nobody can stop the bad thing.* "Just hang on for a little longer, okay? Don't make a sound." *He's coming this way.*

The sound of footfalls on pine needles started again. I braced and tried to get closer to Emma, whispering the same words I half-believed over and over again, beneath the sound of Meghan—and now Brecia, who had joined her—still screaming at him to turn around. Insisting that this part of the woods was empty. Insisting he'd find them if he just turned around and went back the way he'd come.

Then I heard the most glorious noise. "MOTHER-FU—," he screamed in frustration, the word barely intelligible and cutting out as it ripped through him and turned into a howl.

The sound of crashing footsteps moved away from us as he barreled back toward the road and the minivan.

April waited until she heard the distant sound of the engine turning over and the whisper of the tires on the dirt road until she released her grip on the girls and shakily stood up, turning her tear-filled eyes toward her two terrified babies.

"The . . . bear . . . is gone?" Kimmie whimpered.

"It sounded like he was saying words," Emma managed in a tremulous voice, looking at April with the widest hazel eyes I'd ever seen.

April blinked back the tears and grabbed their hands. "What matters is that he went away. And that we're almost safe. You're both so brave. Brave girls," she whispered again as the words caught in her throat. "Can you run with me one more time?"

The two blond heads bobbed.

I looked up at Brecia and Meghan, who were still standing where he'd been just moments earlier—a stone's throw away from where we'd all been crouching beside the big log.

There was a new, steely determination in the air. Meghan wasn't hugging herself anymore. In fact, she looked like she'd just caught fire. From the half-smile on Brecia's face, she could feel it too.

The scales were tipping. They hadn't landed yet. But they were tipping, with a little pressure from invisible hands.

# 47. MEGHAN

## CASCADE, IDAHO

As we approached the turnoff to Highway 55, the sun was just dipping beneath the ridge to the west, sending the valley into a sort of murky, pre-sunset gloom.

April had been carrying Kimmie for the past few minutes. Emma was holding on to the back of April's shirt, stumbling forward on sheer adrenaline. All three of them were ready to crash.

But we'd finally made it. April would flag someone down, who would take pity on the exhausted young mother with two little girls caked in dust and gasping for breath. The police would be called. The girls would be safe. It would be over.

We could all hear the sound of a vehicle approaching from somewhere down the asphalt, its tires zipping on the smooth surface along Highway 55.

As the sound got closer, April set Kimmie next to Emma. "I'll be right back, okay? Just stay here."

Both Emma and Kimmie looked like they might panic. I understood. Being left alone was not an appealing option right now.

April pointed at the shoulder of the road, up a steep rise. "I'll be a few feet away. You can see me. But I need to hurry." Before they could protest, she turned and scrambled up the side of the steep shoulder to peer over the edge.

Brecia and Skye stayed with the girls, whispering comfort. I climbed the crumbling shoulder with April, staring down the road in the deepening shadows.

As the vehicle came around the bend, April squinted hard.

I felt my heart sink as the nebulous shape moved toward us. With its headlights on, it was going to be difficult to tell what kind of vehicle it was until it was right next to the shoulder of the road. Was it an SUV? A truck? A minivan?

There was no way to know for certain.

Brecia, Skye, and I had popped the minivan's headlights and tail lights back in the garage. But that had been in the daytime. No one had even noticed, as far as I could tell. And no one had driven the minivan since arriving at the cabin.

It was too much to hope that James would drive off the edge of the road in the dark. And given the Carsons' propensity for emergency preparedness, they probably had spare bulbs somewhere in the van itself.

For all any of us knew, any set of headlights might be him. And if it *was* the minivan—and James—he would see April before she had time to dart back out of sight.

So she stayed hidden, closing her eyes as a spray of dust and small pebbles trickled down the shoulder embankment and onto her hair.

The only real option was to keep moving.

The girls didn't ask questions as April scooted back down the embankment and took their hands. She began leading them along the bottom of the embankment, moving onto the road itself for an easier path when the steep rise leveled out and there were no tires to be heard or headlights to be seen.

In some ways, the cover of darkness was comforting. Unless we got caught in the glare of someone's headlights, April and the girls were now invisible. But as another set of tires whirred closer and April pulled the girls back into the meager cover of the narrow shoulder ledge, pressing everyone into the sparse brush, I heard both Kimmie and Emma start to cry in earnest.

"Are we always going to be lost?" Emma hiccupped. "Are we going to have to sleep in the woods?"

"That was scratchy. Where is the bear?" Kimmie sobbed as she swiped at her face, which was now lightly crisscrossed with a patch of angry welts from the brush. Her words dissolved into little shrieks as a branch snapped somewhere out of sight in the darkness of the trees.

April picked her up and stumbled forward without responding as Emma latched back onto her shirt, nearly toppling both April and Kimmie as she tripped over a rock.

I really wasn't sure how long April could keep going like this. There was no clear end in sight. She was still in the crosshairs of a predator. And she was still the sole protector of two little girls on the brink of total meltdown. It was agony to even watch.

Somehow, our posse trudged onward, excruciatingly slowly along the crumbling, narrow shoulder of the road that dipped and fell, weaving through the towering pines overhead. We moved forward in silence broken only by the sound of April and Emma's softly crunching footsteps, the whir of the occasional approaching vehicle, the snapping of branches in the darkness, and the whispers of encouragement from Skye, me, or Brecia when Kimmie or Emma started to whimper again.

I thought about the stories I'd heard about mothers lifting cars off their babies or fighting off a pack of wolves on the Oregon Trail. I'd always sort of thought they were tall tales or at least uncommon. But now I thought that maybe it was just the wolf pack at your door or the car on top of your child that was the rare thing. Maybe this strength, this superhuman power was always there, latent. I thought about my own mom, and how I would show her this moment someday when we found each other again. How I'd tell her that I knew she'd carry me this impossible distance too.

It must have been an hour before Brecia suddenly said, "Look! Do you see that?"

I looked down the stretch of road that had straightened out into a long runway. The shoulder had widened, flanked by tall grasses in a sort of meadow. In the distance, beyond the pines that bookended the narrow highway, the horizon was faintly glowing.

"I think that's Cascade," Skye said, scanning the meadow and the treeline ahead. "Those aren't headlights. And the sun hasn't been down for that long. Those are city lights."

April saw them too, her grim expression suddenly melting just a little into relief. She picked up the pace, letting go of Kimmie with one hand to squeeze Emma's shoulder. "Babies, we're almost there. Do you see those lights in the distance? We're going to be safe soon. We're so close. Just stay with me, okay? Just for a little longer."

# 48. BRECIA

## CASCADE, IDAHO

The little lodgepole building on the outskirts of Cascade—The Big Cat Mountain Lodge—was lit up in neon, advertising "The Best Prime Rib in Idaho" on its glowing letterboard. Beyond it, through the thick pines, there were more speckled lights promising civilization farther down the highway. But the rustic bar and grill blazing with light and surrounded by a few vehicles was the closest by a longshot.

The closer we got, the more April scrutinized each shadow and shape in the darkness. As we approached the trees at the edge of the dirt parking lot, she stood for a few minutes squinting through the night at each of the ten or so vehicles in the parking lot for the shape of the minivan.

We were so close. But if he had any suspicion that she'd somehow made it into town, this was the place she'd end up.

Skye moved ahead into the parking lot to verify what all of us tentatively saw: The minivan was nowhere in sight, and a phone and help were mere steps away.

Kimmie perked up and looked over her shoulder at the bright lights and sound of music coming from the doorway to the Big Cat Lodge. "We made it?" she asked in a small voice.

"We made it," April said in a shaky voice, still not moving from where she stood in the shadows at the edge of the parking lot.

"I really don't think he's here," Skye called from the small collection of vehicles in the parking lot. "She actually made it." The relief in the air felt like helium, lifting all of us as we flanked April and the girls and hurried inside.

The exhilaration I felt as she grasped the door and slipped into the orange glow of the bar with the girls was headier and richer and somehow deeper than almost anything I could remember feeling in my life.

I fully expected the porch lights on the outside of the building to pop. Instead, they blazed brighter with a sudden surge that illuminated the entire parking lot.

I looked at Skye and Meghan in pure bliss.

There was no question they'd made it. And there was no question, in my mind at least, that in some small way we'd tipped the scales to get them here.

There was no changing the past or righting the violence that had led to this dark night. April and the girls didn't have any inkling we were even here. But just knowing that they wouldn't be able to see any of us tonight was the happiest I'd felt for as long as I could remember. I imagined that, decades from now, maybe we'd all meet. But only after they lived long lives far away from the monster that had connected all of us.

Caught up in my reverie, I didn't even notice that April had stopped in her tracks, just inside the doorway.

Because just a few yards away, sitting at the bar, was James.

# 49. SKYE

## CASCADE, IDAHO

He was parked right at the end of the bar, his body facing toward the door. For the moment, his face was turned in a scowl toward the bartender, who had been about to clear his empty beer glass from the bar in front of him.

I'd imagined him out there searching in the darkness. Instead, he'd come here, and he'd been waiting for exactly this moment.

He'd done his best to alter his appearance on short notice. He was wearing a giant, puffy coat that made him look much larger than he actually was. His wet-looking hair was raked backward, slick against his scalp. And he was wearing a pair of April's glasses, which she left in the car for driving. I hoped like hell that they hurt his eyes. He looked like an old-timey shady car salesman. It would have been hilarious if it wasn't terrifying.

If April hadn't noticed him at the exact moment she did—and scooped up both Kimmie and Emma to dart around the corner and inside the restaurant—he would have seen her. It couldn't have been more than a couple of seconds' worth of argument with the bartender, who rolled his eyes and left the empty glass where it was on the counter.

I stayed where I was and watched his eyes lock on the swinging door, then drift toward the restaurant.

"He's coming!" I screamed at Brecia and Meghan, who had followed April and the girls.

But by the time he strode around the corner to poke his head into the restaurant—April and the girls had disappeared into the bathroom.

He sat back down at the bar as I glowered at him, training his eyes on the door again, waiting.

We were trapped. Again. I wasn't sure what he was prepared to do in this public setting if he caught sight of her. Did he have a weapon with him, tucked inside that big-ass coat? Would he pull April and the girls out the door and into the night, playing the "crazy wife" card? He'd been backed into a corner so far that he'd been willing to take the risk in leaving the cabin. He wasn't going to leave without them, no matter what it took.

I knew what he was capable of. But nobody else in the sleepy bar and grill did. Sure, he might attract some attention and concern. He might have to turn on the charm to excuse the domestic kerfuffle. Would anyone see through it? Would anyone try to stop him?

I wanted to believe that the young couple at the bar would call the police. That the gruff bartender with salt-and-pepper whiskers would tackle him to the ground the moment he grabbed April's arm. Would the camo-clad hunters gathered around the table in back reach for the backpack on the floor that—just maybe—contained some type of weapon?

I already knew it wouldn't happen like that. The girls were afraid of a bear—not their dad. As soon as they saw him, they would rush to him in relief, throwing their little arms around his waist and cowering away from April as she screamed for them to stop. I could already imagine the customers' anxious looks of concern fading as James disappeared out the door with all three of them into the parking lot, apologizing for April's seemingly insane behavior while the girls clung to him in fear and April thrashed. The bartender, and the young couple and the hunters would exchange wary looks that said "What the hell was that?" and then hesitantly turn back to their beer or their burger. Later, when they were interviewed for the news, they'd say, "I knew something was off about him." For now though, they would give him the benefit of the doubt. The burden of proof was high to get involved with a stranger's business. I probably wouldn't have done anything different if I were still alive.

# 50. MEGHAN

## CASCADE, IDAHO

April locked the deadbolt to the entire bathroom then pulled the girls into the large disability stall at the far end of the room. The dull exhaustion was gone, replaced with a frantic, wild-eyed desperation.

The girls were looking at her in confusion. To them, this day had been one nonsensical, grueling tour de force that had ended in being rushed into the bathroom. "Mommy, why are we all in here together?" Kimmie started to ask, looking around the dingy stall in bewilderment. She looked like she was about to burst into tears again. Her red cheeks were covered in streaky brown trails. "I need a drink of water. I'm hungry."

April's whole body shook as she set both girls down on the dirty floor. Emma didn't say anything. She looked stunned that she'd been carried as much as anything. I still wasn't totally sure how old she was—maybe seven?—but I could imagine that she hadn't been picked up like that in quite some time.

Skye slipped through the crack in the bathroom door, scattering underneath the hinge. "I'm positive he didn't see them. He's just sitting there, watching the door."

April reached down to smooth Kimmie's hair, mumbling something about everyone needing to use the bathroom first. Kimmie and Emma exchanged a look but obediently moved to the toilet while April walked out of the stall and closed the door behind her, eyes roaming over the bathroom walls as if there might be a back exit in here that she somehow hadn't noticed on the way in.

As the sound of tinkling filled the silence in the bathroom, April moved to the sink and stared at her own reflection in the mirror.

When someone knocked on the door a few seconds later, she winced and shook her head, tears pooling in the corners of her eyes. It was a woman's voice. "Everything okay in there?"

April hesitated, her eyes still darting wildly across the mirrors and around the room. "Um, hold on, okay? One sec."

There was a cork board near the mirrors, covered in advertisements for a local fireworks show, dog walking, boat rentals, ATV sales, babysitters. The usual small-town debris. Some of it was water stained, as if it had been used to dry somebody's hands in a pinch when the paper towels ran out.

"Why doesn't she just let them in? Ask them to call the police?" Brecia asked in frustration.

Skye shook her head. "I don't think it's that simple. What if he walks back here and sees that lady calling the police and standing in the bathroom door? He's not stupid."

Brecia considered this as April stepped to the side of the mirror and scrutinized the cork board up close. The sound of tinkling was still steady in the background. "Okay, but if she keeps the door locked, it's going to cause a scene when that lady goes back? Can't she just pull her in here and then lock the door? She'll have a phone, right?"

I frowned. "What if she screams? She doesn't know anything. I'd scream if somebody yanked me into a bathroom and locked the door. He'll hear."

As we argued, I watched as the panic in April's eyes turned steely. She looked away from the corkboard, and quickly strode to the bathroom door, unlocking it and then opening it just a crack to reveal an older woman on the other side.

I studied the spot on the corkboard where April had been looking and gasped. Brecia and Skye saw the water-stained paper sign at the same time I did.

*On a date that isn't going well? Ask for Andrea at the bar. We'll make sure you get home safe.*

I could feel Skye and Brecia's eyes on me. They knew where I'd seen this sign before, because I had shown them the memory of that night at Gracie's.

The fluorescent bulb in the bathroom flickered as April smiled tremulously and beckoned to the woman, her eyes darting around the strip of bar that the doorway revealed.

I looked at the woman hesitating outside the door. She appeared to be in her mid-forties. Her box-red hair was swept up in a messy ponytail, and she was wearing an oversized black Idaho State University sweatshirt with gray sweatpants. She peered over to study April—who had backed behind the door, mostly out of sight.

April glanced to her right as the big bathroom stall swung open and Kimmie and Emma emerged. "One sec, babies." She turned back to the woman. "Please, can you help me? It's really important. Just tell the bartender that Andrea is needed in the bathroom. Please say just that. Nothing else, okay? You don't have to do anything else." April's eyes moved back and forth across the woman's face, waiting for her to react. Waiting for the puzzled look on her face to harden into skepticism. Waiting for her to slowly back away and loudly tell a waiter that there was a crazy woman in the bathroom.

The woman in the Idaho State sweatshirt looked between Kimmie and Emma, who looked like they'd just rolled down the mountain. And basically, they had. April looked wild and crazy too. The whole situation screamed that something was very wrong. And I assumed the lady had to use the bathroom on top of parsing out what was going on here. She slowly nodded and backed away. "Okay, hon. Hang on."

"Thank you," April whispered, then shut and re-locked the door.

\* \* \*

It was only a minute or two before we heard a soft knock on the door.

Even though April had been listening at the hinge, waiting for it, she still tensed, her eyes moving to the door handle. Kimmie and Emma had stopped asking questions and were scooping handfuls of water out of the bathroom sink into their mouths.

It was a young woman's voice. "Andrea? Are you there?"

As she said the words and April cracked open the door to let her in, I looked at Skye and Brecia in triumph. If I could have cried, I definitely would have.

The waitress couldn't have been more than eighteen years old. About the same age as Skye. But while April whispered the critical parts of her story, trying to keep Kimmie and Emma from hearing, she listened with a seriousness and knowing that told me she'd seen some things too.

The waitress squeezed April's arm reassuringly and told her to re-lock the bathroom door. Then she disappeared back into the restaurant.

Brecia, Skye, and I followed her. She snuck a peek at James, who was still parked near the front of the restaurant, staring at the door and sipping a glass of water. He stretched impatiently and briefly made eye contact with the waitress.

She didn't let her eyes linger on him or stop walking. Instead, she walked to the back of the restaurant, opened a cabinet to reveal her purse and cell phone, and called the police.

* * *

When the red-and-blue flashing lights appeared through the windows of the bar and grill, James stayed composed. He didn't stand up. He didn't crane his neck to look at the police officers as they walked through the dark parking lot and through the front door of the restaurant.

Even when he saw that they were walking toward him, he didn't react. I guess maybe he still thought there was a chance they hadn't come for him. That they were here for someone else. After all, chances were slim that someone in this podunk town had recognized him, or had seen the minivan, wherever he'd stashed it.

He had no idea that April had slipped by him. And the look on his face when a lanky officer with a full beard ordered him to stand and put his hands above his head was the best thing I'd ever seen.

His eyes widened in shock and then rage as he started spitting out bullshit about how he was waiting for his wife. Why was he being harassed? What was going on?

"James Carson, you are under arrest for the murder of Meghan Campbell," the officer told him. "You have the right to remain silent. Anything you say can and will be used against you in a court of law. You have the right to an attorney …"

I felt Brecia and Skye slide next to me, wrapping their arms through mine as he was perp-walked to the door. The decorative string of Edison lights above the bar glowed brighter. The bar, which had moments earlier been filled with a low rumble of voices and clatter, had suddenly gone still enough that the rustle of the officers and their footsteps across the wood floor were the only sounds for a few seconds. The hunters smirked at him in pity and amusement. The young couple at the bar stared at him in horror. The waitress, who had called the police, watched in grim satisfaction from the back of the restaurant near the kitchen.

James clamped his mouth shut, whipping his head around as the officers led him outside, searching the night in vain for April, who was still safely locked in the bathroom.

I felt something in me unclench, as if I'd been holding my breath for a very, very long time. I didn't feel like jumping up and down or screaming for joy. It wasn't that kind of happy. The only way I can describe it is the way I felt when I told Bubbie goodbye at her bedside when she died. Relieved that I'd made it in time. Grateful I was in that room at that moment with people I loved. And devastated about nearly everything else.

# 51. BRECIA

## CASCADE, IDAHO

I watched as Emma helped Kimmie squirt a line of ketchup and mustard onto her hot dog at the empty bar. Impossibly, both girls were smiling again. They still didn't know anything about their dad. Still didn't know that he was the real monster they'd been running from all day, who had forced them through the forest and night and into a dirty bathroom stall, just to escape becoming victims to the same violence he'd been committing right under their noses for their entire lives.

Someday April would have to tell them. There was no getting around it. But I suspected I wouldn't be there for that conversation. And as I looked at Kimmie and Emma's little-girl faces and downy hair, I was glad. I didn't want to see their hearts shatter. It was difficult enough to see April, in the staff room, as she sat with the police, her eyes red and her whole body shaking.

The police were taking her initial statement in the staff room of the bar and grill, while they waited for Detective Domanska, who was driving from Boise, to arrive on the scene. The statewide manhunt was over, and James was being booked into the county jail.

They told April they'd gotten a search warrant for her and James's entire house, including computer, social media accounts, and his phone records. The puzzle pieces were coming together. If they hadn't already, they would find MatchStrike.com. Which meant that, if they dug deep enough through the aliases and ghost accounts, they would find my name in his inbox too.

I could tell that the officers questioning April were hoping to learn just how much she knew. They wondered, like I had in the beginning, whether she was naive. Or stupid, Or both. Whether, in the worst-case scenario, she might have even been an accomplice. But April just cried, apologizing for what she knew too late. Apologizing for what she'd suspected but denied, even to herself. She told the officers about Nina and the text messages she'd gotten in Utah. She admitted to looking up Meghan's name after Domanska called. She cried harder when Domanska asked about Skye.

As more officers arrived and the waitstaff was questioned and released, we learned that the mysterious Marjorie had been located in Caldwell, Idaho, where she had been arrested for helping James elude authorities.

As April fumbled through the sequence of events that had led to the cabin escape, she told police that Marjorie was James's step-mother. James's mother had died when he was six, and his father had remarried Marjorie the same year. They'd divorced by the time James was ten. He'd hinted at but never directly admitted that the constellation of faint scars on his arms, back, and legs—anywhere a t-shirt or shorts would hide—came from her.

Marjorie had tried calling the house in the early years of their marriage, asking to meet April and then the girls. But James had made it clear that he had no desire to see her again. Until he called about the cabin.

When Domanska arrived in Cascade, she drove April and the girls—and me and Skye and Meghan—to a nearby motel for the night. It was nearly eleven at night, by that point. April wasn't under arrest. And the girls were falling asleep at the bar.

When they got to the little log-cabin motel, Domanska led a sleepy Emma by the hand while April carried Kimmie in her arms. Skye and I stayed as April climbed into the king bed next to the girls, not bothering to undress. Meghan followed Domanska down the hall to her room.

"She won't leave without saying goodbye, will she?" Skye asked me quietly as April turned off the bedside lamp, blanketing the room in velvety darkness. The sadness in her voice settled over me, cold and heavy, like fog.

I knew that of the three of us, Skye was the least interested in moving on. She wasn't sure what was waiting for her or how to get there. Not like Meghan, with her grandmother. And even though I hadn't yet allowed myself to drift in the same way, I was ready. Ready to find my Aunt Nelly. To tell her how much she'd meant to me when I was a little girl, and to learn who she was on a deeper level than macaroni necklaces and playdates. The idea of finding her again filled me with a warm glow. I was ready to move toward that light.

"She'll be back," I assured Skye, my own relief and hope filtering through the dewy mist of her sadness like sunlight.

\* \* \*

When Meghan slipped into the dark room an hour later, she came bearing case developments from the past week. Ken—Skye's manager at the Daily Grind—had picked James out of a photo lineup, as the one who had sometimes flirted with her at the counter.

But the video that showed James's license plate in the parking lot didn't show Skye getting into his car. And the Froyo shop's security footage that did show her getting into a vehicle didn't show James's face. When Domanska called Kittleson—who was in bed back in Boise—he made it clear that unless there was some evidence beyond the circumstantial evidence they already had—to connect him to Skye's murder, the DA was not planning to move forward with charges at this time. The car had been clean. They already had him for Meghan's murder in Utah. And they'd learned that he met Meghan—and plenty of other women—on a site called Match-Strike.com.

When Meghan told me that Domanska had said my name—the *Brecia Collier* cold case—I felt a shiver of electricity run through me. A detective from Colorado was on his way to Idaho. My parents and sister would finally learn what had happened to me. Maybe other women he'd crossed paths with through the app would come forward. Nicole. Elle. They'd find answers too.

I knew it wasn't over, exactly. For so many people, the heartache and the horror were just ramping up; however, I knew that my role in this story was finally over. And I was ready to move forward without James Carson.

Then I felt Skye next to me, her sadness curdling into despair.

In an instant, the relief I'd felt curdled too.

The answers her family needed seemed to be right there for the taking. They knew who had killed their baby. But the way things were headed, Skye's name wouldn't be heard in his trial. They wouldn't find her name on MatchStrike.com. Her case would go cold.

I pictured Skye's mother—the one she had shown us in her memories. The lithe, dark-haired woman with the same curls and golden-brown skin. I imagined her watching the news coverage of the grieving families connected to the MatchStrike case. Reading the details in article after article as lawyers battled to put him behind bars for two murders, not three. Knowing her daughter had been allowed to slip through the cracks because it was "too difficult to prove," despite the seemingly smoking gun.

Skye's despair hardened into resignation as she turned away to look at April, who was finally breathing softly and deeply in sleep. "It's okay. I knew this might happen." She closed her eyes and added in a low voice, "I still mattered."

Meghan frowned. "You still do." She looked thoughtful, turning her face toward the slivers of moonlight at the corners of the motel blinds. "Maybe there's something they missed. Maybe they'll still be able to charge him for what he did to you."

Skye snorted. "Kittleson probably missed a shitload. He was ready to move on before they even found me."

Meghan scooted next to her, reaching out her hands for both Skye and me. "Then let's look together to see what he missed."

\* \* \*

We spent the rest of the night sifting through Skye's memories.

We watched every painful detail of "James" flirting with her in the Daily Grind.

Every excruciating moment as shy, hesitant Skye got into his car in the parking lot after work that day.

Every unspeakable moment that came afterward.

We could only see what she saw, remember what she remembered, of course.

But as we watched Skye's memory from the coffee shop, the last time he'd come in, I suddenly yelped.

The disposable coffee cup he was holding in his hands. The one with the little smiley face and the eyelashes and the word "James" and "hot chocolate" in loopy letters.

I had seen it before in my own memories, at his house.

He'd shoved it into the desk drawer.

I let go of Skye and Meghan, frantic to tell them. "Skye, was he holding a coffee cup in any of the security footage?"

Skye shook her head. "I don't know. I haven't seen all of it. Just the parts my mom watched over and over. I know he's on camera, though, from when he was in the coffee shop that morning."

I grabbed her hand and showed her the memory of the coffee cup in his desk drawer. There was no way to know whether it was still there or not. Even if it was, would the detectives executing the search warrant know what they were looking at?

"We have to tell Domanska," Meghan insisted, already moving toward the motel door. "She'll listen."

# 52. SKYE

## KUNA, IDAHO

I just knew Domanska wouldn't find the coffee cup where Brecia remembered.

Who knew if it was still there, anyway? I couldn't imagine him keeping something like that lying around.

While we whispered through the detective's dreams that night, I prepared myself to be disappointed.

My murder would remain unsolved. Lots of murders did. I stayed dead either way, of course. So what did it matter?

But it was harder to lie to yourself without the distractions I'd had while I was alive. No phone. No TV. Just my own thoughts, and the prickles of disappointment that crawled across my body as I stared at the detective—who had fought so hard for Meghan—while she slept.

"She won't find it," I told Meghan and Brecia matter-of-factly.

They didn't correct me. But they didn't stop whispering, either.

I knew she wouldn't find it.

Right up until the moment she did.

\* \* \*

It wasn't tucked into the desk drawer anymore. In fact, it was at the bottom of the recycling bin in the garage, hidden underneath Amazon boxes and food packaging, set to be picked up earlier that week—if he hadn't taken April and the girls and run.

Domanska found it on the Daily Grind security footage—a still frame of James, holding the cup as he walked outside on the morning he'd murdered me—before she found the cup itself.

From the way she lingered on the still frame, zooming in until the little smiley face I'd drawn on the cup, right down to the eyelashes, was visible, I knew she'd listened.

My mom cried when she learned that Detective Andrews, who would be replacing Detective Kittleson on all cases for the foreseeable future, told her that my murder would be added to the charges against the "MatchStrike Killer."

All of us—Brecia, Meghan, and I—were there when he told her. We'd been staying with my mom instead of with April or Domanska.

I hoped the best for April and the girls, but I didn't feel quite the same way about them as Brecia did. I was glad we'd helped her, of course. But I didn't want to see her horror or her tears as she learned the details of what her husband had done.

I didn't blame her for what he'd done; however, I was pretty sure I'd still be alive if she'd looked at her husband just a little bit harder, instead of looking away.

\* \* \*

We visited James, who was being held without bond on three murder charges, in jail.

It was my idea.

I wanted to say a proper goodbye. All of us did.

He looked truly pathetic. His beard had already begun its descent into a nasty bird's nest, and he was wearing a dirty orange jumpsuit that was too short at the ankles.

Confined to a tiny cell with a rangy giant of a man coming down off meth, while awaiting a possible death sentence, he was finally as fearful and powerless as he deserved to be.

We spent a full three days with him.

Each time he fell asleep, we drew close and composed our magnum opus of nightmares.

April, telling the police everything she knew. The steel in her eyes when she told a reporter that the death penalty did not seem excessive.

Women, contacting the news in Idaho and Utah and Colorado to say that they, too, had brushed paths with him.

Elle's eyes flashing as she talked about what he'd done to her and how disgusting he actually was.

Nicole's relieved, mirthless laughter as she shared the texts she'd sent to a friend to get out of her date, leaving him alone in the restaurant with the bill.

Marjorie, selling her side of the story to a tabloid. "My Step-Son the Serial Killer."

His coworkers from Colorado and Utah and Idaho telling the press that he wasn't nearly as smart as he pretended to be at work.

The nightmares had exactly the desired effect.

He awoke screaming and panting after a few minutes every time, babbling about "bitches" and "lies."

He started trying to stay awake, just to avoid the nightmares he knew were waiting for him anytime he drifted off. It made him increasingly touchy, mean, and delirious as the days wore on.

His cellmate, the meth head, didn't appreciate any of this.

On day three, at two in the morning, Meth Head had finally had enough. As James awoke with a pathetic howl, he threw off his bedding on the lower bunk and hauled James off the top bunk in one swift motion.

James hit the floor with a sick thud and scrambled to the corner of the cell, darting his eyes around and trying to orient himself to what was happening. He favored his right arm, which hung at an odd angle.

Meth Head advanced.

James screamed for help.

The lights in the jail stayed off.

As his frantic screams echoed through the cell block, the three of us walked down the hallway and into the moonlight beyond the barbed wire and bars. We didn't look back. He'd taken enough from us in life—and in death, too.

There was no pleasure to be found in whatever happened next. Only justice.

\* \* \*

We stayed with my mom for a week after that, soaking in the sunlight of the little kitchen and the home that, unlike the police station or the cabin, felt like a safe haven.

I didn't linger on goodbyes. And neither Meghan nor Brecia talked about making their way back to Colorado and Utah to see their parents one more time. Knowing there would be reunions with our loved ones in the future made those final farewells feel less dire.

The three of us spent those last moments searching my memories for a link. Looking for someone who would welcome me into the matrix that held my grandparents and great grandparents and everyone who had come before them.

We finally found it in El Salvador. I'd only been there once—when I was just a baby. We'd visited my mom's sister and her two daughters, Rocio and Erica. Both were close to my age—and still very much alive. But on that short trip, we'd met dozens of others, some friends and some relatives. As I replayed the memories from that trip to San Salvador for Brecia and Meghan, I saw introductions to second-cousins and half-brothers and one great aunt.

I felt silly as I called out to the people in my memories as they greeted my mom with big hugs and reached for my rosy cheeks. What was I supposed to say? "Hello, are you dead too?"

The memories stayed the same until my chubby one-year-old self was hoisted into the arms of my great aunt—Marcia.

"Can *you* hear me?" I asked her softly as I watched my baby hands grab at her graying hair.

As I said the words, I instantly felt the memory change. Meghan and Brecia suddenly faded away, and I knew that Marcia was looking right at *me* when her eyes opened wide in surprise and she said my name. Not Skye—the anglo-sounding name I'd insisted on when I

got to middle school—but my birth name: Estela. *Stars in the sky.*
"Ah, mija, Estelita. ¿Cómo puede ser?"

"Go," I heard distantly from the edges of the memory. And for just a moment I lingered in the feeling of being loved from so many different places in time.

I imagined Meghan, finally wrapping herself into the memory of her grandmother like a warm blanket.

I thought of Brecia and her Aunt Nelly.

Then I let myself be folded into the memory, into the arms that were waiting for me.

# NOTE FROM THE AUTHOR

If you enjoyed this book, a positive review would mean the world to me. Like other small-press authors, I rely heavily on word-of-mouth recommendations to reach new readers.

I can promise you that I read every single review. Because each one is a new window into this story. And because if you loved this book, *you're* the one I wrote it for—which is why I'm placing this note *before* the acknowledgments.

Thank you for reading!

\* \* \*

**One last thing:** If you want to know what happened to April, scoot over to my Instagram @noelleihliauthor. You'll find a link to a free short story in my highlights called *The River.*

# ACKNOWLEDGMENTS

My sincere gratitude to everyone who gave their time, talents, and support to this book.

Thank you to Brett Stanfill. Your encouragement, enthusiasm, and feedback have been such gifts.

Thank you to Bryan and Jeanne Allen for your friendship, your beautiful brains, and your support with this project. It's better because of you.

Thank you to Stephanie Nelson. I'm so grateful for your generosity and insights. You're a true kindred spirit.

Thank you to my editor, Patti Geesey: You're a true gem, and I deeply appreciate your care with this book.

Last but not least, thank you to Nate for being my first reader, my home, and my best friend.

# ABOUT THE AUTHOR

Noelle's two great passions are murder and horses (separately, never together).

Noelle is a boy-mom to Luke and Max, and a cat-mom to Michelle. When she's willing to wear pants (which is less often than she aspires to wear them), she can be found in mom jeans. Her husband Nate is the best person she knows.

*Read on for a thrilling excerpt
from Noelle W. Ihli's novel* Run on Red

"Still recovering from this heart-pounding read.
Keep your smartwatch on, because your pulse will be racing."

- Sara Ennis, author of *The Dollhouse*

# RUN ON RED

A THRILLER

# NOELLE W. IHLI

BESTSELLING AUTHOR OF *ASK FOR ANDREA*

# 1

*AUGUST, 2006*

"They're still tailgating us," I murmured, squinting into the lone pair of headlights shining through the back windshield. The sequins on my halter top caught on the lap belt, snicking like ticker tape as I shifted in the passenger seat.

"Maybe it's the Green River Killer," Laura said evenly, keeping her eyes on the road.

I snorted but kept watching as the headlights crept closer. "They caught the Green River Killer. I thought you read that blog I sent."

"It was twenty pages long. Anyway, why do I need a crime blog when I have Olivia Heath in my car?" she asked. As she slowed down to take the next hairpin turn, the watery yellow headlights behind us turned a pale orange where they mingled with our brake lights.

I ignored her and kept staring at the headlights that had been tailgating us relentlessly for miles on the dark rural highway.

*Everything is fine,* I chided myself. There were "No Passing" signs posted every other switchback on the narrow road, and our ancient Volvo was going ten miles under the speed limit as we chugged uphill. Of course they were tailgating us.

When I blinked, two mirror-image red spots flashed behind my eyelids. It was impossible to see the drivers—and I was getting carsick. I glared into the headlights a little longer and committed the license plate to memory: 2C GR275.

"Liv? Earth to Liv. They're probably late to the bonfire. Same as us." Laura was the Scully to my Mulder: ever the optimist, ever reasonable. Ever the one who talked me down from my imaginary ledges. But the question always tapped at the back of my mind: What if there really *was* a ledge?

"The license plate *does* say GR," I grumbled, but turned around, smoothing down my wonky sequins and drawing in a slow breath to calm my sloshing stomach.

"GR?" Laura prodded, glancing at me as we came out of the curve.

"Green River," I clarified with an exaggerated sigh. "Or Gary Ridgway, same guy. Go easy on the turns." I rested one hand out the uneven window ledge, so the cool night air hit my face in a slap that smelled like sage.

The Volvo's passenger-side window had collapsed inside the doorframe a few weeks earlier. Laura's sister Tish had talked about taping up a sheet of plastic in the hole, but since the car didn't have air conditioning, the window just stayed open. I rubbed at a smattering of goosebumps on my bare arms. I should have brought a jacket. The hills were at least twenty degrees cooler than the city, but I'd been too rushed—and too sweaty—after work to care.

The bonfire at the reservoir had started more than an hour ago, and as far as I could tell we were the only car on the road—aside from the tailgaters. Laura had waited until my shift ended at the Pie Hole to make the tedious, winding drive through the hills.

The interior of the Volvo grew brighter as the headlights edged closer. Laura glanced in the rearview mirror. When I craned my neck to do the same, she sent me a warning glare. "Stay facing forward. The only thing you need to worry about is not getting barf on Tish's car." She flicked the fuzzy dice hanging from the mirror. "I can't believe she bailed on us again tonight."

"I'm fine," I insisted, even as my stomach lurched dangerously. I inhaled slowly through my nose to stave off the nausea. "But—"

"Breathe, Liv," she soothed. "They just want to pass us. I'll find somewhere to pull over."

"There's nowhere to pull over," I mumbled, wishing I'd gone to the library with Tish instead of "putting myself out there" tonight. "And this is definitely a no-passing zone." The isolated two-lane rural highway made me nervous, even in the daytime.

"Look, right there." Laura signaled and angled the Volvo toward a shallow gravel pullout carved into the hillside to our right.

The headlights stayed behind us, moving toward the same shoulder at a crawl.

"Why aren't they passing?" I demanded, even while I scolded myself for overreacting. I didn't trust my anxious brain to correctly identify a real threat. It had steered me wrong way too many times.

As soon as the words left my lips, a vehicle with one headlight out—only the second car we'd seen since leaving city limits—whipped into view. It passed us from behind, going way too fast and nearly clipping the driver's side mirror of the Volvo. Once its brake lights disappeared around the next bend, the tailgaters eased back onto the road and zipped past us as well.

Within a few seconds, the hills were dark and quiet again, except for the Volvo's idling mutter.

"See? They were just letting that idiot pass," Laura insisted triumphantly, flashing me a grin before hitting the gas and easing back onto the road. "No serial killers."

When I didn't respond, her eyes flicked toward me. "Have you heard anything from Tish?"

Shaking off the useless adrenaline rush, I sighed and reached down the front of my high-waisted denim cut-offs to open the slim traveler's pouch where I'd tucked my cell phone. Laura snickered at the sound of the zipper.

I ignored her and flipped open the phone. "You know she hasn't texted. You just wanted to see me open the magic fanny pack." I snapped the elastic of the traveler's pouch, tucked just beneath the top button of my shorts, for emphasis. "My pockets can hold half a Saltine, at most. Where the hell am I supposed to put my cell phone when I go out?"

"And your rape whistle, and your pepper spray," Laura chirped.

I rolled my eyes and laughed. "You really should read the blog."

My phone screen showed one service bar. I didn't have any new messages, but I took the opportunity to text Tish the car's license plate: 2C GR275. *Just in case.*

She wouldn't see it until she got home from the library later tonight. And even then, she wouldn't think anything of the text unless the apartment was still empty in the morning. Tish—like Laura—had come to expect the occasional license plate number—or blurry photo of some rando at the gas station who looked like a police sketch I'd seen on Twitter.

Laura shifted in the driver's seat to face me. "You know, we can turn around if you want," she offered gently, the bright white of her teeth slowly disappearing with her smile. "If you're not feeling up for the bonfire—"

"I'm good," I insisted more gruffly than I intended, avoiding her eyes. I could deal with jokes about my red-alert texts and travel pouch and rape whistle. But any hint of sympathy for the underbelly of my social anxiety … not so much.

I zipped my cell phone back into the slim travel pouch, refusing to imagine the last bar of cell service flickering out as we drove deeper into the hills. Then I reached over and turned the volume knob on the ancient boombox propped between us, where the glove box in the old Volvo used to live. It was an indestructible monstrosity, like the Volvo itself. I absolutely loved it.

"I did not wear scratchy sequins to turn around and go home," I sang off-key over Britney Spears. Laura had spent hours making this party mix, first downloading the songs, then burning them to a CD, then recording the CD onto a tape that would play in the ridiculous boombox.

Laura's smile brightened. "Atta girl."

# 2

The music pumping through the old boombox lasted until we approached the final turnoff onto the long dirt road that led to the reservoir.

The tape turned over with a loud click right as the Volvo clunked over a shallow pothole. When Britney's voice reemerged, it was slow and distorted, like the song had been dunked in syrup.

"Brit? Stay with us," Laura coaxed as the song subsided to a tinny whine. The boombox made a sudden, harsh buzzing noise, coughed out a burst of static, then went completely silent.

"I guess not." She laughed and wiggled the volume knob one more time.

I smiled and rested my arm on the edge of the open window, dipping my hand down, then up, then down in the breeze. *The bonfire will be fun,* I reassured myself. *You always have fun once you get there. Just stay with Laura.*

The nervous fizz deep in my stomach remained wary. I leaned out the open window a little and followed the smoky trail of the Milky Way until it disappeared behind the hillside looming to our right. The sounds of night creatures worrying among themselves took center stage in the quiet night as the Volvo slowly chugged up the incline.

A muted scratching coming from the dash suddenly broke through the geriatric drone of the engine. The seatbelt caught as I shifted in my seat, leaving a drooping curl of fabric across my chest.

There it was again: a soft skittering. "Do you hear that? I swear there's something inside the dash."

Laura let go of the wheel with one hand to rap on the plastic of the dash. The sound stopped. "I think there might be something living in that hole, gnawing on the wires," she said, then shrugged as if she'd just made a comment about the weather. "Sometimes I hear that same scurrying sound while I drive. Tish said she does too. It's probably a mouse."

I looked at her in disbelief. "If I see a damn *mouse* come out of your dashboard, I am hurling myself out of the Volvo." I shuddered. "I still can't believe Tish spent money on this thing. It's amazing that it runs."

Laura shrugged again, unfazed. "She got it cheap from Tony's friend. It was like, five hundred bucks." Then she added, "The guy actually said he'd give it to her for two hundred if she threw in a blow job."

"Okay, pull the car over." I mimed gagging and grabbed the door handle.

"Olivia!" Laura shrieked and hit the brakes.

I laughed. "I'm kidding. Mostly. He actually *said* that to Tish?"

She rolled her eyes dramatically. "Yep."

"While Tish and Tony were together?"

"Uh huh."

"Gross." I sat forward in my seat, studying the sloping hills looming in the distance. If I remembered right, we were about twenty minutes away from the reservoir once we turned onto this dirt road.

"How is Tish doing, anyway?" I asked after a minute. "If I didn't see her cereal bowl in the sink, I wouldn't even know she'd been sleeping at the apartment lately."

Laura sighed. "She's okay—I think? I've hardly seen her lately either. Ever since the breakup, she's been weird."

I nodded, still half-listening for the mouse scurrying around in the dash, but Tish's drama was a welcome distraction. Tish and I were friends—but we'd never been especially close. Not like me and Laura, who had been inseparable since the seventh grade. "I thought she was definitely coming tonight," I pressed. "She even RSVPed on Facebook. Why did she stay home?"

Laura slowed the car down to skirt another pothole in the dirt road. "No idea. She texted a few minutes before you got home from work, saying she was staying at the library late." She shrugged again. "I think she just doesn't want to risk running into Tony at the bonfire."

I nodded slowly. "Do you think he'll be there? It's not really a Delta vibe."

"A Delta vibe?" Laura giggled. "You mean like, an AXE Body Spray commercial?"

I burst out laughing. "Pretty much."

Laura raised her eyebrow and smiled. "Are *you* hoping Tony will be there?"

Heat rose in my cheeks. "No way. Tish was *engaged* to him, dummy."

I'd seen plenty of photos of Tish's boyfriend—briefly fiancé—on Facebook, but I'd only really met him a couple of times. Once across the room at a party, and once on the apartment couch in passing. We didn't actually know each other. Not really.

I pictured the smiling, sun-kissed boy I'd seen on Tish's Facebook profile, wearing a Band of Horses T-shirt. He was incredibly good-looking.

Laura sighed and brushed her bangs away from her face. "It's true. He's ruined for all of us now."

"I'm surprised Tish ..." I trailed off, not totally sure how to finish that sentence. Both Laura and I had been surprised when Tish started dating Tony last year. He was what my dad would call a "big man on campus." Handsome, charming, and one of the chosen ones who had been accepted into the Delta fraternity freshman year. As much as I loved Tish, it was impossible to deny that she was Tony's polar opposite: quiet, shy, and maybe a little boring if I was being mean. Basically, she was like me. Laura had always been the designated social butterfly of our little cadre.

Laura giggled. "Hey, at least you've got *Ziggy*."

I snickered, but my stomach tightened at the mention of his name. "Stop it. We aren't discussing him tonight."

"Ziggy," which I now knew was short for "Zachariah," was the supremely awkward humanities TA who stared at me during class. Laura and I had found his Facebook profile one night and learned, to our horror and delight, that he was a member of the Pen and Quill Society: a LARPing group on campus. Ziggy was a "mage": which Laura and I had to Google. It meant he was some kind of magician.

Last week, in an effort to "put myself out there," I'd made the horrifying mistake of accepting a date with a cute guy I'd met on MySpace. His profile photo bore almost zero resemblance to the tall, painfully quiet, acne-covered senior who wrote things like "me likey" and "bomb diggity" on the margins of my papers. I didn't realize it was Ziggy until we met up for happy hour at SpaceBar that night. Things went from bad to worse when I learned he had recognized *me* from my profile photo. I'd made an excuse about a family emergency and booked it out of the bar, vowing to delete my profile the second I got back to the apartment to lick my wounds.

"Did you hear back from your professor?" Laura prodded.

I nodded slowly. Laura had convinced me to email my humanities professor about what had happened, but I still felt weird about the whole thing. "Yeah, forgot to tell you. He wrote back yesterday with a long apology about how this happened earlier in the semester to someone else. Long story short, Ziggy's not the humanities TA anymore."

Laura shot me an impressed look and took a turn in the road a little too fast. "Nice job, killer. What a creep."

I held my breath as our wheels edged toward the thin shoulder that petered off into the darkness beyond our headlights. I tugged on my seatbelt again, hoping it had been engineered to outlast the rest of the car despite its obvious fatigue. "I haven't been up to Coffee Creek in forever. How much farther is it to the reservoir?"

"Coffin Creek," Laura corrected me sternly.

I rolled my eyes. "I hate that name. Do we have to call it that? There's no coffin. Just muddy water and beer cans."

"Because it's fun. And because the freshman who went missing is buried there." She shrugged, then flashed me a wicked grin.

I sighed. "Her name is Ava Robles. And if they knew where she was buried, she wouldn't be missing, would she? If you had read *that* blog post, you'd know they never found her body."

Incoming freshman Ava Robles had gone missing near Coffin Creek three years earlier. The same year Laura and I had started at University of Idaho. I hadn't known her. Neither had Laura. We weren't on the guest list for that particular party.

Ava had been one of the few freshmen who attended the exclusive sorority party that night, at the end of Rush week. Her story had been firmly embedded in campus lore almost as soon as the news broke that she had gone missing. For weeks at the start of the semester, cops stalked sorority and frat houses to interview anyone who had attended the huge toga party.

When rumors—and a few bloggers—started to spread that her body had been dumped in Coffin Creek, the detectives even sent divers to troll the murky waters. They'd found absolutely nothing. From the blog I'd read, the police believed that the rumors might have been intentionally started as a way to throw off the investigation. It worked. And the rumors—as well as the unfortunate nickname—stuck like glue around campus ever since.

The only things they'd ever found of Ava's were her purse and phone, tossed into the sagebrush at the edge of the reservoir. They'd trolled it too, with zero success. All anyone really knew was that Ava had been at that party one minute—and the next she hadn't.

There were no traces of blood. No signs of a struggle. No witnesses who had noticed anything strange.

Everyone assumed she was dead. There was even some speculation that maybe she'd been pulled into the hills by a cougar. It wasn't likely, but it wasn't impossible. Despite the university nearby, this part of Idaho was mostly wild. The hills went on for miles and miles in all directions with sportsman's access.

I shivered. Thinking about Ava Robles was not helping my state of mind. "How much longer until we get there?" I asked.

Laura shrugged. "We'll be there in fifteen minutes, give or take. Is your stomach feeling better?"

"All good," I insisted, not counting the anxious bubbles. "But I'm freezing." I rubbed my arms, wishing again that I had brought my jacket. The last bonfire we'd attended—stoked by overeager freshmen— had burned so hot that somebody's bumper had melted by the end of the night.

"Me too, but this top looks like an old paper bag if I cover up my arms." She gestured to the high-neck cotton blouse that looked nothing like a paper bag. "I never learn. See if you can get the heater to work. Tish swore it did."

I turned my attention to the large knob next to the radio dial, cranking it all the way to the red side. It made a clicking noise, followed by a soft *pop*. "That's a no. It might be time to take the Volvo to a farm." I patted the window frame. "We love you, but you're falling apart."

Giving up on the heater, I settled against the bucket seat, reaching up to touch my hair. I'd cut it from waist-length to a trendy lob with bangs a few days earlier, and my head still felt weirdly untethered without the extra weight.

I shifted slightly to study Laura's long hair in my peripheral vision. It hung down her back and was such a pale white-blond that it seemed to glow against the gray seat. The summer before sixth grade, we'd both tried highlighting our hair with a combination of Sun-In and peroxide. Laura's hair had turned an ethereal white. My dark brown hair had turned Sunny-Delight orange in splotches I hadn't fully eradicated until eighth grade. I made a face and asked, "Was it a mistake to cut my hair?"

She smiled and tapped on the brakes as a deer's eyes glowed white near the side of the road before it bounded into the night. "Stop it right now. I keep telling you, it's gorgeous. And it makes your eyes look huge." She reached up to grab a hunk of her blond hair. "Mine feels like straw lately—how do you get yours so shiny?"

I flipped my short hair dramatically. "Thanks. It's probably from the Pie Hole. All that oil in the air—it's like pizza-scented deep conditioner."

Laura sighed loudly. "Another reason I should've taken summer semester off to get a job. I can't get over the idea that physical education is an *actual* college requirement. Are we not adults now? How am I being forced into running?"

I wound my cold hands into the soft underside of the halter top, keeping my gaze on the shoulder of the road to watch for more pairs of ghostly eyes. "Are you sure we took the right turnoff?"

I glanced at the Volvo's dash clock out of habit, even though I knew it would read 3:03 no matter how long we drove. This far into the hills, it felt like we'd been swallowed up by the night itself.

I didn't hear her response. As the dirt road crested a rise, we passed a skinny ATV trail ducking into the hills. A dark, hulking shape sat angled in the weeds like a black hole in the pale, dry grass.

A truck.

*Everything is fine,* I told myself firmly, channeling my inner Laura.

The moment we drove past, the truck's high beams blinked on, blazing into our rearview mirror as it roared to life and pulled behind us.

# 3

"It's the same car," I mumbled in disbelief.

"What? How can you tell?" Laura asked distractedly, navigating a pothole.

I squinted through the back windshield into the blinding headlights. "Same license plate: 2C GR275. I texted it to Tish earlier."

Laura shot me a look. "Liv, everything is okay. Even if it is the same car, it's fine. If they took this turnoff, they're definitely on their way to the bonfire. Maybe it's a couple that decided to mess around on the side of the road for a while." She grinned then cranked down the driver's side window, signaling for the other vehicle to pass us.

I stared at her in bewilderment as she calmly motioned out the window.

When the headlights in the rearview mirror didn't disappear after a few seconds, Laura slowed the Volvo to a crawl and motioned more dramatically, her pale skin illuminated in the foggy beams. "Go around, dumbass," she said in a soft singsong.

I quietly unzipped the travel pouch beneath my shorts and pulled out the flip phone with shaking hands. No service, as expected. And the battery had dipped to just five percent. Berating myself for not turning off roaming sooner, I quickly navigated to Settings then snapped the phone shut.

"Dick," Laura mumbled, her lips turned down in a frown. Her purple lipstick looked black in the darkness. "Why don't they turn off their brights, at least? They're blinding me. I'm going to find somewhere to pull over all the way. The road is super narrow here."

She hit the gas and brought the Volvo slowly back up to speed.

The other vehicle accelerated behind us.

"They could back off our ass a little," Laura grumbled, hunching in her seat so the glare of the headlights didn't hit her directly. "The good news is that if we get rear-ended, Tish's car won't be the one going in for repairs. It's probably been totaled for the past ten years."

The truck began flashing its brights on and off in rapid succession as if transmitting a message in Morse code.

"Give me a hot second," Laura exclaimed, tapping on the brakes as the road curved and emptied into another steep straightaway. The Volvo decelerated quickly, laboriously crawling up the incline.

"There should be—" I began as the other vehicle abruptly swerved left and pulled up alongside us on the narrow straightaway. It was so close to us that if Laura reached her hand out the window, she could have touched the passenger's side mirror.

"Who is it?" she asked, keeping her eyes glued to the road as we approached the next curve. "They're going to get plastered if they stay in the left lane and someone comes around that bend," she added lightly, as if that might be a favorable outcome.

I didn't answer right away as I stared into the darkness beyond Laura's open window. I had been secretly hoping to see someone we knew. Or at the very least, a car packed with random frat boys, their teeth flashing white as they laughed at our wide eyes. But as the truck came even with the Volvo for a brief moment, I could see the silhouettes of two men inside, facing forward. Each wore a dark-colored hoodie pulled up over his head, concealing all but the barest outline of his profile. Neither one turned to look at me.

I felt like I'd just been dunked in ice water, even though the cell phone in my hand was slippery with sweat. *This is bad,* my gut screamed. *Are you sure?* my brain fired back.

"Who is it?" Laura asked again as both vehicles crawled along in tandem. A hot trickle of adrenaline chipped away at the ice in my veins. "Do we know them or something? Maybe they recognize the Volvo. It's hard to miss."

"We don't know them," I whispered, clutching the seatbelt across my chest. Both men were still facing forward. Neither had even glanced in our direction. "Should ... I call the police?" I asked shakily, hoping Laura would reassure me that the answer was *no.* That there was some reasonable and innocuous reason these men were toying with us. For all the times I'd repeated the catchphrases from my favorite bloggers—"Be vigilant, stay alive," "Screw politeness," "Stay safe, get weird," I knew deep down I'd only call 9-1-1 if I was actually in the process of being murdered.

I moved one finger to hover over the Emergency Call button, glancing between the glowing red text and the headlights. Still no service.

"I—I don't know. What do they look like?" Laura demanded. For the first time, she sounded rattled.

The truck stayed alongside us a moment longer. Then it roared ahead violently, the smell of dust and rubber filling the air as it darted past the Volvo, moved into our lane and disappeared around the approaching bend with mere inches to spare.

I shook my head, already second-guessing what I'd seen. "I—I couldn't tell very much, but I really think we should turn around. There's two guys. Neither one of them would look at me, and they were both wearing hoodies pulled all the way up over their—"

Laura gasped as we took the curve.

Red brake lights blazed just a few yards away.

9 798987 845509